THE
WYCLIFFE
OMNIBUS

THE WYCLIFFE OMNIBUS

Wycliffe and the Winsor Blue
Wycliffe and the Four Jacks
Wycliffe and the Quiet Virgin

W. J. BURLEY

VICTOR GOLLANCZ
LONDON

Wycliffe and the Winsor Blue first published in Great Britain 1987
by Victor Gollancz Ltd, © W. J. Burley 1987
Wycliffe and the Four Jacks first published in Great Britain 1985
by Victor Gollancz Ltd, © W. J. Burley 1985
Wycliffe and the Quiet Virgin first published in Great Britain 1986
by Victor Gollancz Ltd, © W. J. Burley 1986

The Wycliffe Omnibus published in Great Britain 1996
by Victor Gollancz
An imprint of the Cassell Group
Wellington House, 125 Strand, London WC2R 0BB

© W. J. Burley 1996

A catalogue record for this book is
available from the British Library

ISBN 0 575 06249 5

Printed in Finland by Werner Söderström Oy

96 97 98 99   10 9 8 7 6 5 4 3 2 1

Contents

THE
WYCLIFFE
OMNIBUS

WYCLIFFE
AND THE WINSOR BLUE

To my wife:
critic and collaborator

People who know the town of Falmouth may be irritated by inaccuracies in the topography. These are deliberate in order to avoid any risk that a real person might be identified with one of the characters in this book — all of whom are imaginary.

W.J.B.

Chapter One

EDWIN GARLAND FELT uneasy, a vague shapeless unease for which he could find no immediate cause.

'You haven't taken any ham, father.'

'What?'

Beryl lifted a slice of ham on to his plate. 'Are you feeling all right, father?'

'Of course I'm feeling all right! Why shouldn't I?' In fact, he was feeling quite queer.

His son, Francis, was munching away, his protuberant eyes fixed on his father in an unwavering stare.

Beryl was beginning to look like an old woman; her hair was lank and grey, and there were fine wrinkles about her mouth. . . . And that nose which seemed to sharpen with the years made her look predatory. . . . How old was she? Fifty-five? About that. . . . Nine years older than Francis. . . . That gap. . . . Why was she always so damned miserable? Of course she was drinking on the sly, her and her precious friend. . . .

He really was feeling strange, curiously detached, but he struggled to hold on. His thoughts seemed to wander out of control. . . . They were watching him. Concentrate on something! He looked at his wife's portrait which hung on the wall opposite where he sat. Gifford Tate had painted it a few weeks before she died. A fair painting; free in style but at the same time a good likeness. Gifford had gone overboard a bit in the blues though. . . . For some reason this thought made Edwin chuckle to himself.

Francis's owl-like countenance obtruded again. Francis was too fat, his face was podgy and he had a paunch. Soft! Too much food, too little exercise. Greedy from childhood. . . . Hard to credit that he had once fathered a daughter — and a beautiful

13

girl she had turned out to be — like her granny. . . . Funny thing, heredity; hit and miss. Anna was twenty now, living with her mother and some randy young rooster who knew when he was well off.

His thoughts returned to his wife's portrait. The Dresden China look. 'Refinement and fragility' Gifford had said. He was right: Judith had been . . . Judith had been exquisite — that was the word. And a bitch, but that was another story.

What was the matter with him? He was confused; and that was another word, an unpleasant one in the ears of a man of seventy-five. Mealy mouthed jargon for senile. Better eat some of this bloody ham or they would think. . . . He pushed it around with his fork. Soggy! How did they make the stuff hold all that water? An offence to water milk so why not ham?

Back to Beryl and Francis. What a pair! They were Judith's children, so why were they so damned unprepossessing? And they had mean, scheming little minds. He had supported them all their lives and what had they ever done for him except wait for him to die? Watching, like vultures. . . . Well, they wouldn't have long to wait, now, but they had a surprise or two to come.

He caught sight of Beryl's head in profile. Her mother's daughter, but Beryl *exquisite*! He wanted to laugh. What the hell was wrong with him? Time to pull himself together.

Safer to look out of the window, concentrate on the view; that had never let him down. The living-room was at the back of the house, overlooking the harbour, and from where he sat at table he could see right across Carrick Roads to St Just-in-Roseland. Sunlight glittered on the water and the colours . . . the colours were not bright, but the light shattered in reflection, was brilliant. How often had he struggled to make that distinction on canvas? Painting light: that was what it was all about. The Impressionists had tried, God knows! but even they . . .

'I think I shall go down to the studio.'

Beryl said: 'But you've eaten hardly anything, father! Really — '

'I've had enough.' And he added under his breath: 'More than enough!' without being quite sure what he meant.

'Shall I bring your coffee down to you?'

'No.'

'You haven't had your tablets . . .'

'For Christ's sake!'

He went down the stairs, holding tight to the bannisters and swaying slightly. He felt giddy.

He had been born and lived all his life over the shop: E. Garland and Son, Artists' Suppliers and Printers. In the little hall at the bottom of the stairs one door opened into a side passage leading to the street; the other, to the back of the shop through which he had to pass to reach his studio. The shop was closed for the lunch hour. He shuffled past well ordered, dusted shelves and racks, and past the little office where his father had sat and schemed for most of his life. The place was peopled with ghosts and soon he would be one of them. He fumbled with a key from his pocket then opened a door into another world.

Like the living-room upstairs his studio looked out on the harbour. It was more like a workshop than a studio — a painter's workshop. There was a sturdy bench, with an orderly arrangement of tools, where he made stretchers and frames. There was an earthenware sink, a table, a couple of easels, a painter's trolley, a chest of shallow drawers. Empty frames and canvases were stacked against the walls. . . . And almost every object in the room seemed to be spattered with multi-coloured splashes of paint; while the windows were covered with grime and festooned with cob-webs. A scruffy orderliness. That was how he liked it.

When Gifford Tate was alive and used to visit him, Tate had croaked through his beard: 'Why the hell don't you get yourself a decent studio, Eddie? God knows you can afford it! At least get somebody to clean the bloody windows!' And Garland had answered: 'I like it as it is, and as for the windows, that muck is a natural filter for the light and if any interfering bastard ever cleaned 'em I'd twist his credentials off.'

Entering his studio always gave his spirit a lift; it did so now.

He fetched a tobacco pouch out of his pocket and a packet of cigarette papers. With a lifetime of practice behind him he rolled a passable cigarette in his fingers and lit it.

There was a painting on one of the easels and the trolley with his brushes, tubes of paint, and palette was beside it. He pulled up a high stool and stood, his bottom propped on the stool, which he used like a shooting stick, his painting posture for these latter days. The painting seemed complete: another harbour scene. He studied it with growing distaste. 'That water . . . as exciting as a sludge pit in a sewage works.'

He closed his eyes and tried with all the concentration of which he was capable to see with his mind exactly what it was that he had wanted to paint. Slowly the scene seemed to materialise once more out of his imagination: the mist, the swathe of sunlit water; the water like shot silk in the shelter of the boats; ripples elsewhere, tiny vibrant glittering crests. . . . Points of pure light . . . so brilliant that they hurt the eyes. . . .

God! How they hurt the eyes! But for once he believed that he was seeing as he had striven all his life to see . . . Diamond points . . . blinding! They seemed to sear into his brain. He groped vaguely with his right hand as though reaching for a brush and as he did so he experienced an intolerable contraction in his chest, a paralysing pain, and with a cry of anguish he fell, taking the stool with him.

His niece, Cathy Carne, found him when she came back to open the shop after lunch. She was surprised to see the studio door open, he always closed the door when he was working and kept it locked when he wasn't there. Then she saw him, his heavy body lying mounded over the stool which had fallen with him. His jaw sagged and his eyes stared.

Her first reaction was incredulity. The old man had been with her in the shop that morning, the same as ever, gossiping about the business, about the vagaries of their customers, the oddities of town councillors and the perverseness of families — all with a humour that was wickedly spiced. Of course he had been warned; the family had been warned, but . . .

She felt empty inside.

She went upstairs. On the landing she could hear voices coming from the living-room and she pushed open the door. Beryl was clearing the table; Francis, with his hands in his pockets, was staring out of the window. There was an atmosphere, as always when the two of them were left alone together.

Beryl looked at her: 'What's wrong?'

'It's uncle; he's collapsed in the studio.' She added after a pause: 'He's dead.'

Without a word Francis turned away from the window and pushed past her. They heard his heavy footsteps descending the stairs.

Cathy picked up the telephone which stood on a side table. 'I'd better telephone Alan.'

She dialled a number and spoke to the receptionist. 'I'm speaking for Mr Garland at the art shop. Is Dr Tate there?' A pause and when she spoke again her manner was familiar: 'Oh, Alan — Cathy here. I'm afraid it's bad news. . . . Yes, Uncle . . . he collapsed on the floor in the studio. . . . I'm afraid so. . . . If you will. . . . Yes, come to the side door.'

She replaced the receiver and turned to Beryl. 'He'll be here in a few minutes.'

Beryl was standing motionless in the middle of the room, her hand on her heart. 'I knew something was going to happen; I could *feel* it! And he brought it on himself.'

Cathy said: 'We'd better go down.'

They went downstairs; Francis was standing in the doorway of the studio. 'Well, he's dead all right.'

'I telephoned the surgery.'

'Good!'

Cathy was looking past him into the studio. 'Can't we move him?'

'Better not.'

Beryl said: 'I've told him and told him but he took no notice. . . . He wouldn't even take the tablets Alan gave him. He brought it on himself.'

And then it occurred to Cathy that although the old man was lying exactly as she had seen him, something had changed. Surely, there was a different picture on the easel? Odd! She was on the point of saying something but changed her mind. After all, what difference could it make? If Francis was up to something it was nothing to do with her.

Francis, hands thrust deep into his trouser pockets, said: 'I thought he seemed a bit queer at lunch but I didn't expect it to come to this. . . .'

They stood, silent and waiting, until the side door opened and Alan Tate came in. He was slight of build, very dark, with a sallow complexion, and meticulously dressed in a dark grey suit with a silk tie. Son of Gifford Tate, the painter, he had been the Garlands' doctor since, at his father's death, he had returned to Falmouth and set up practice in the family house.

Subdued greetings, then he went about his business. A brief examination, his movements rapid and sure. He spoke in staccato phrases: 'His heart gave out, that's what it amounts to. Bound to happen sooner or later. . . . Give me a hand, Francis — get the stool out from under him; straighten him up a little.' Although first names were being used his attitude and manner were strictly professional.

Beryl said: 'We can't leave him here, he'll have to be taken upstairs.'

Tate looked up at her, his brown eyes enlarged by the lenses of his spectacles. 'He's a big man, Beryl; too much for Francis and me. The undertakers will do it and it will be more decent that way.'

Francis said: 'You'll come upstairs, Alan?'

Tate glanced at his watch. 'I can spare a few minutes.'

Cathy Carne said: 'Shouldn't we tell Uncle Thomas and Mark?'

Blank looks from Beryl and Francis.

'After all, Thomas is his brother.'

Beryl said: 'They'll hear soon enough.'

Cathy gave up. 'Do you want me to shut the shop?'

'The shop?' Francis turned his bulging eyes on her: 'What would be the point of that?'

Cathy stayed in the shop while the others went upstairs. Ten minutes later Tate came down alone. Cathy was in the little office and he came to stand in the doorway. 'They are both quite composed. I doubt if there will be any problem with delayed shock.' Cynical. 'You found him, I gather?'

'Yes.'

'A shock for you. They've been in touch with the undertaker and when I left they were arguing about the funeral.'

'When shall I see you again?'

Tate hesitated. 'I'll telephone.' And added, seemingly in explanation: 'Marcella is very depressed. I'm concerned about her.'

Cathy was feeling the heat; little beads of perspiration formed between her shoulder blades and breasts. She had worn a full-length coat because it was all she had that was decently subfusc; now she wished that she had been less conformist.

She was staring at the coffin, the wooden box with fancy trimmings which held the mortal remains of Edwin Garland, her uncle and employer. She wondered what his comment would have been had he been in a position to make one.

'Man that is born of woman hath but a short time to live and is full of misery. . . .'

They weren't talking about Edwin Garland; Edwin had enjoyed life in his own way.

There were more wreaths than she would have expected and the flowers were already wilting in the merciless sun. She wondered who had sent them all.

Francis, as chief mourner, stood next to the vicar; his paunchiness exaggerated by an old, dark suit that was too small for him. She wondered about the bruise on his cheek: she had noticed it the evening before when he came back from his Tuesday round. 'I walked into a door.' Somebody had hit him. Interesting!

With glazed eyes he was staring into the middle distance. Day-dreaming of life after the shop? More than likely. It wouldn't be long before he closed a deal with one or other of the chain stores who had shown an interest in the site. Then there was the printing works . . . Francis had never shown any real interest in either side of the business and, as far as the shop was concerned, this had meant that Cathy had been free to go her own way under the old man's eye.

Beryl would have to move out, but she would go to live with her friend; two old-maids together. It was what they both wanted and with her share of her father's money Beryl would be well able to provide for both of them in style.

'And that leaves me. . . . At thirty-six.'

She had had a letter from Edwin's solicitor asking her to come to his office the following day. It must mean that she had been mentioned in the will. A picture, probably; she had always admired his work, perhaps a little money to go with it; that would be welcome.

'. . . deliver us not into the bitter pains of eternal death.'

Yes, well, it might not be as bad as that.

It was Wednesday afternoon. In the tradition of the street Edwin was being buried on early closing day so that other traders could attend. But the custom had lost its meaning because there were so few private traders left, and company managers are faceless men, here today and gone tomorrow. All the same, there was a good crowd, the more surprising because Francis had not bothered to organise anything properly.

It was one of the hottest days of the year and the new part of the cemetery was without trees. Most people were out enjoying themselves and she could hear children on the beach which was not far away.

Francis's illegitimate daughter, Anna, was there with her boyfriend. They stood a little way back from the others as though unsure of their right to be there at all, and they were in bizarre contrast to the rest of the mourners. The girl's fair hair was scraped back and held with a slide; she wore a grey shirt, open half-way down the front, and bleached jeans. Her boy-friend had his hair down to his shoulders and wore a bandeau. His sweat-shirt carried the slogan: 'No! to Trident!', and his jeans seemed about to fall apart. Both of them were so beautifully and evenly brown that clothes seemed superfluous.

Cathy looked at them with a mixture of envy and doubt. At their age she had already spent four years working in her uncle's shop. But what would they be doing at thirty-six?

Also standing well back from the grave, Mike Treloar, the printing works foreman, supported himself on a stick. As a boy he had been crippled by polio.

Cathy was almost opposite Alan Tate and he was watching

her, or seemed to be. It was hard to tell because of the sun glinting on his glasses. Looked at objectively there was nothing special about him: a smallish man, slight of build, dark-brown hair *en brosse*, spectacles with thick lenses and a broad, carefully trimmed moustache. Everything about him was meticulous, as though the parts had been made and assembled with scrupulous care. Cathy sometimes wondered why women found him so attractive, why she herself did.

He was with Marcella, his father's second wife and widow. In her late thirties, she was two or three years younger than her step-son. Once she had been attractive, with a good figure: now she was painfully thin and her sharp features gave her a pinched look. She did nothing to improve her appearance; her flaxen hair was cut short so that it fitted her head like a helmet and accentuated the angularity of her features.

Cathy was surprised how ill she looked, there was an area of paleness about her eyes, and her nose was pinched and reddened about the nostrils; perhaps a summer cold, though Alan had said she was depressed.

'Forasmuch as it hath pleased Almighty God of his great mercy . . .'

When the service was over there was the ritual of shaking hands with the vicar. Francis spoke with his daughter and the boy. Beryl chatted with one or two of the bystanders then lingered to look at the cards on the wreaths and this annoyed Francis.

'Come *on*, Beryl! The undertaker will give you a list.'

Francis had not hired cars and Cathy joined him and Beryl in his ten-year-old saloon. As they drove away from the cemetery she spotted the clapped-out van belonging to Anna's boyfriend parked some distance from the gates, a large CND symbol painted on its side.

Beryl sat in the back of the car, her large black handbag with brass fittings balanced on her knees. She delved into the bag and came up with a packet of pastilles which she began to suck, filling the car with a sickly sweet smell.

She said: 'The Tates were there and they sent a big wreath; we ought to have invited them back with us.'

Francis did not answer.

Beryl went on: 'I saw you talking to Anna and that boy. Very friendly all of a sudden.' It was an accusation.

'Why not? She's my daughter, isn't she?'

Conversation between brother and sister was conducted at a level of mutual aggression which stopped just short of exploding into a row. An exercise in brinkmanship.

'What did she say?'

'Not a lot.'

'Did she ask you where you got your bruises from?'

At first it seemed that Francis was going to leave it at that, the ball in his court, but in fact he was trying to decide which would annoy her most: being kept in the dark about his conversation with Anna or knowing the truth. He decided to speak: 'She said she'd had a letter from the lawyer.'

Beryl was roused. 'Why should Shrimpton write to her?'

'I suppose father has left her something; he had a soft spot for Anna, he said she looked like mother.'

Beryl made an angry movement. 'I only hope he's had more sense than to leave her money! She may look like mother, but mother would have turned in her grave if she could have seen that girl today!'

Cathy said: 'I had a letter from Shrimpton, myself. It simply asked me to come to his office tomorrow afternoon at half-past two.'

Beryl was dismissive. 'Yes, dear, that was to be expected. He was bound to remember you with a little legacy. This is quite different! Quite different!'

To further annoy his sister, Francis said: 'Anna is his granddaughter after all.' But the exchange had sown a tiny seed of doubt in his own mind . . .

Francis parked the car and they walked along the street to the shop. When they were in the little hall at the foot of the stairs Francis said: 'Is father's studio locked, Cathy?'

'I don't think so, but the key is in the door.'

'Then lock it and bring the key up with you.'

Beryl said: 'What's this about?'

He turned his sullen gaze on her but did not answer.

Upstairs, Beryl's friend had made coffee and sandwiches for them.

Francis stood by the window. 'There's a mist coming in.'

Beryl's friend said: 'Yes, but they said on the radio that it would be fine again tomorrow.'

Francis sat at his desk making entries on index cards. He wrote in a small, neat, but cramped hand, pausing now and then to refer to one or other of the books and papers spread on his desk. On a two-deck trolley to his right a V.D.U. stood above a computer keyboard. The screen displayed columns of figures against groups of code letters and from time to time Francis referred to these, scrolling the display on or back.

The room in which he worked had been his bedroom since infancy, though now the only evidence of its primary purpose was a narrow divan bed. One wall was wholly taken up with books while the other walls were hung with home-produced charts in which numbers and symbols formed elaborate geometrical patterns. There was a bank of card-index drawers and a multi-drawer filing cabinet.

Francis seemed wholly absorbed, yet once or twice he sat back in his chair and told himself: 'My father is dead!' It was as though he could not be convinced; as though he could hardly accept the fact that his father was no longer there, the final arbiter of all that happened in the business and in their domestic lives. He was like a goldfish, suddenly tipped out of its bowl into a pond, conditioned to continue swimming in circles. Yet his father's death should not have come as a surprise. Six months ago Alan Tate had said: 'His heart is by no means strong and his blood pressure being what it is. . . . If only he would discipline himself to regular medication and give up smoking . . .' Of course Francis had thought about it as something that was inevitable, and he had plans, but they had never seemed very real and he had looked on them as castles in the air. Now . . .

His desk was placed near the window, overlooking the narrow canyon of the street. At this time of night the street was quiet: the occasional car, and now and then a group of rowdy youths asserting their masculinity like stags in rut. Although it was dark outside he had not drawn the curtains. Silvery streaks of rain appeared out of the darkness and trickled down the shining panes. A wall clock ticked loudly: a few minutes to nine. Mitch, his black and white terrier, was asleep in a wicker basket on the floor. Beryl and her friend were in the living-room, across the passage.

At a quarter past nine there was a tap at the door; Beryl came in and stood waiting for his attention. She wore a long raincoat which drooped from her thin shoulders and she carried a small overnight bag. Her pale face was blotched and her lips were moist. When he turned towards her she said: 'I'm not staying in the house tonight, Francis, I'm too upset. I'm going back with Celia but I shall be here in time to get your breakfast in the morning.'

He merely stared at her with his bulging eyes and she went on: 'There are biscuits in the tin by the cooker and there is plenty of milk if you want to make yourself a hot drink.'

In a flat voice, the more insulting by its indifference, he said: 'You don't have to bother about me. Move in with Celia whenever you want.' And he turned back to his desk.

She would have liked to make some cutting rejoinder but none came to mind so she went out, closing the door behind her.

At ten o'clock he switched off his computer and put away his books. Mitch skipped out of his basket, tail wagging, and they went downstairs together. In the little hall, Francis put on a waterproof coat and cap and they went out by the back door.

The shops on the Garlands' side of the street backed on the water and only a narrow paved walk separated them from the harbour. At ten o'clock each evening, except in the very worst weather, Francis and his dog took their walk along the waterfront as far as the yacht marina and returned by the street.

It was dark for an August night. The lights at the docks twinkled mistily, and some of the larger craft at moorings carried lights, but for the most part the harbour was a broad plain of darkness. It was of no consequence; Garland knew every step of the way and Mitch trotted ahead, pursuing an erratic course as he nosed out the rich odours brought to him on the moist air.

For Francis this nightly constitutional had its place in a larger fantasy. He liked to imagine himself an academic, working after dinner in one of those elegant book-lined rooms of an Oxford college. As the clocks chimed and struck all over the city he would stroll down the Broad, along St Giles and round by the Parks. . . . Nature, he thought, had intended him for scholarship yet here he was at forty-six, still a small-town tradesman.

Well that at any rate would change.

'My father is dead!' Well, he couldn't be expected to shed any tears.

There had been offers for the shop which his father had consistently turned down. Offers for the site, not the business. One, a very good one from a firm of chain-store chemists, was still open. In a few months he could leave those rooms over the shop and the shop itself for ever. Of course Cathy Carne was being difficult, already there had been an outburst over something he had said. The old man had spoiled her and it was high time that she faced facts.

Then there was the printing works: it had kept pace with the changing times and if it was put on the market there would be plenty of interest. Then he would be free! As far back as he could remember, those phrases 'the shop' and 'the works' had been spoken by his parents with a certain solemnity, as some speak of 'the church' or 'the monarchy'. Well, all that was over.

Their walk along the wharf was interrupted by a car-park where a scattering of vehicles gleamed in the jaundiced light of a sodium lamp. To his surprise he recognised the battered old van which belonged to Anna's boyfriend and he wondered what it was doing there. Then he saw the glowing tip of someone's cigarette behind the windshield. He continued his walk and thought no more about the van.

'My father is dead!'

In a year the shop would be no more, lorries would carry away the rubble to which it had been reduced, leaving a gap to be filled by yet another chain store. Would he then feel a certain sadness? He thought not: at this moment the prospect afforded him a satisfaction that was almost spiteful in its intensity.

25

Sentiment and nostalgia are for pleasant memories.

A white yacht carrying navigation lights glided in ghostly silence through the seeming maze of moored craft, putting out to sea. He stopped to watch her until she disappeared in the darkness. The tide was lapping the harbour wall within a yard of his feet.

He would have enough money to live comfortably and he would never be bored. For many years his studies had absorbed every moment of his spare time, now they would be his full-time occupation. He would be able to visit libraries, museums and institutions all over Britain and make contact with other numerologists. Even abroad. . . . He was resolved to meet every possible criticism in advance and, eventually, his conclusions would be presented to the world in a scholarly book.

And if in this new life he was to be alone . . . well, he had been alone for most of his life. In his twenties he had taken up with a girl called Freda and got her pregnant. She had given birth to a daughter but Freda had been no more anxious to marry than he had. Since then she had married someone else and been widowed, but she still lived in the district with their daughter, Anna. He saw Anna occasionally but he had not seen Freda for years though he had to admit that he might not have recognised her had he passed her in the street.

Recently he had formed another attachment, one which he valued more. But there was a price to be paid in this relationship and he wasn't sure. . . . He couldn't stand scenes; violence of any sort appalled him . . .

Involuntarily he raised his hand to his face.

They were approaching a point where the wharf walk was bridged over by scaffolding erected to repair the back wall of Benson's furniture shop. Warning lights on the steel supports blinked feebly through the mist.

Mitch growled, then yelped.

'Quiet, boy!'

He had no sense of foreboding, no intimation of danger; on the contrary he felt light hearted, even light headed as vistas of freedom seemed to open ahead of him. Mitch scampered under the scaffolding and Garland followed. The lowest tier of planks cleared his head by at least a foot.

As he emerged at the other end he was aware of a frightful, blinding, stunning pain in his head, and then nothing.

Chapter Two

CHIEF SUPERINTENDENT WYCLIFFE's driver pulled into the car park, which had been closed to the public, and joined a line of police vehicles. A uniformed man, there to ward off sightseers, saluted.

On his way down to take part in an official inspection, Wycliffe had monitored reports on his car radio and so arrived at the scene of crime before his headquarters had got a team together. The Deputy Chief Constable, in his parade uniform, would have to manage the inspection without the assistance of his head of C.I.D.

Falmouth: a town he liked. J.B. Priestley once said that it could never quite make up its mind whether it was a port or a resort, but that very ambivalence had saved it from the worst pitfalls of both. The harbour looked mysterious: the sun had broken through but mist still lay over the docks. Massive superstructures; squat, tapering funnels; slender masts, and the jibs of cranes, merged in a ghostly silhouette. Elsewhere in the harbour the moored yachts, the power boats, launches and dinghies, regimented by the tide, matched colourful reflections in the water.

Wycliffe was reminded of a busman's holiday he had spent, not so long ago, across at St Mawes.

Appraised by bush telegraph or E.S.P. of his advent, Divisional Chief Inspector Reed hurried along the wharf to greet him.

'A nasty business, sir. Very nasty!'

A shaking of hands and a brief excursion into reminiscence. 'This way. . . . He's just beyond that scaffolding. . . . The surgeon has been and gone, he reckons death probably took place early in the night; the coroner has been informed, and the scenes-of-crime chaps are on the job . . .'

They walked together along the wharf; the two men, in striking contrast. Reed was built on an over-generous scale, bull-necked and bulging in his grey pinstripe; Wycliffe, slight of build, and rather pale, was more likely to be taken for an academic than a policeman; hard to believe that he had served a tough apprenticeship on the beat in a Midland city.

The scenes-of-crime van was parked as near the site as it could get, planks had been laid on the ground approaching and under the scaffolding to preserve whatever evidence there might be, and the area where the body was had been screened off. The scenes-of-crime officers had photographed the dead man and the ground for some distance around. Footprints, found in soft mud under the scaffolding, had been photographed and casts made though there was little doubt that they belonged to the victim, not the killer. There were dog prints too. The whole area was littered with fragments of mortar which had been chipped out of the wall by workmen getting it ready for re-pointing.

Behind the screen Wycliffe looked down at the dead man: middle or late forties, probably above average height, bony, but with a tendency to corpulence — sedentary: the disease of modern man. He wore a fawn waterproof, cord trousers, and good quality brown shoes. The left side of his face, in the region of the jaw articulation, looked at first sight as though it had been smashed by a blow, but Wycliffe recognised it as the wound of exit of a bullet which had probably ricochetted inside the skull. Bending down, he looked for and found the wound of entry, a small round hole in the top of the head towards the back. The thin, fair hair had been singed and stained around the wound.

The undamaged part of the face had a puffy softness, an appearance of immaturity, accentuated by a fair moustache of wispy growth. There was an area of bruising below the right eye but, although it was recent, Wycliffe felt sure that it had been inflicted some time before death — probably the day before.

Reed, standing behind him, said: 'A fight?'

'Perhaps, at least several hours before he was killed.'

Murder, that much was evident but the motive was not. They had found the man's wallet in the pocket of his jacket with forty pounds in notes, a credit card, and a driving licence in the name of Francis Garland.

Wycliffe brooded. In the ensuing hours and days he would get to know Francis Garland perhaps better than he knew many of his colleagues and acquaintances. His data would come from relatives and friends, from those not so friendly; from the man's habits, likes and dislikes, his loves and his hates. In the end, if this crime turned out to be something more than an abortive mugging, he would have a portrait of the victim and through that portrait some indication of why he had become one.

Reed volunteered background: 'The Garlands have a shop in the main street, a couple of hundred yards from here: artists' materials, pictures, that sort of thing; they're printers too — they have their works farther along the waterfront, just beyond Customs Quay. You can see it from here — that concrete building. Anyway, this chap lived with his father and sister in the rooms over the shop — until Saturday.'

'What happened on Saturday?'

'His father died of a stroke. A bit of a coincidence, don't you think?'

'Has anyone broken the news to the sister?'

'I've sent Pritchard; he's good on bereavements. Ought to have been an undertaker.'

'So Garland was unmarried?'

'Yes, but according to the local sergeant, there's an illegitimate daughter around somewhere.'

The first bits of the jig-saw. From now on he would be looking for some sort of pattern. He would spend a great deal of time trying to fit in fresh pieces only to find that most of them didn't belong to his picture. Criminal investigation is a sad story of false trails and dead ends.

'Was he a queer?'

'Not as far as we know, but it's possible.'

The church clock doled out ten strokes on its tinny bell. Looking down at the dead man Wycliffe felt guilty because he was experiencing a sense of mild elation. He loathed the sterile ritual of inspections, and this poor devil in his untimely end had saved him from that. He slipped easily into the routine of a murder inquiry.

'Garland's sister must have realised that her brother didn't come home last night.'

'You would think so.'

'Who found him?'

'The builder's men coming to work on this wall. They had the sense not to plough in and now they're laying off until they hear from us.' Reed removed his fisherman's hat, uncovering a bald crown and a fringe of auburn hair. With a large pocket handkerchief he wiped the perspiration from his forehead; it was getting hot.

There was blood on the ground from the exit wound which had not been entirely washed away by the overnight rain. The man must have been shot from above at close range as he emerged from under the scaffolding. Wycliffe looked up at the first tier of planks; the shot must have been fired from up there. If the attack went wrong the assailant stood a good chance of not being identified and if it was apparently successful it would be safe to come down and make sure.

He called to Fox, the sergeant in charge of scene of crime. Fox looked like Bertie Wooster and, for some reason, was known as Brenda to his colleagues. He was good at his job, though not as good as he thought he was, and his smugness irritated Wycliffe.

'Take a look up there where the killer must have stood or knelt.'

Fox assumed a judicial air. 'I thought it better to concentrate on the ground — '

'Just do as I ask, Fox. Now, please.'

There was no point in staying at the scene. Fox and the others would do all that was necessary and a good deal that wasn't, working by the book.

He reassured Reed about local assistance. 'I know you must have a full load so I'll try not to be greedy. I'm going to talk to somebody at the shop — the sister if possible.'

He walked back along the wharf to the car park. On an R.T.

link from his car he spoke to his deputy, John Scales, at headquarters. 'Who've you got for me, John?'

The composition of a team depends on who happens to be doing what at the time. Apart from Detective Inspector Kersey, Wycliffe's usual number one, Scales had sent Sergeants Shaw and Lane. Shaw was a good organiser and internal collator, well versed in computer mystique. Lucy Lane enjoyed the distinction of having convinced Wycliffe that a woman could more than hold her own in the serious crimes squad and not only in rape cases. The three of them, with four detective constables, would set the ball rolling.

Wycliffe left his car on the park and climbed the slope to the street.

Falmouth's main shopping street runs narrowly and crook- edly along the waterfront with shops on both sides but with occasional tantalising glimpses of the harbour. The street is in three parts: Market Street, because there was once a market; Church Street, because of the Church of King Charles the Martyr, built at the Restoration; and Arwenack Street, because it leads eventually to Arwenack House, all that is left of the home of the Killigrews, a mixed bag of soldiers, dramatists, pirates and entrepreneurs, who founded the town and built the church.

As is usual until mid-morning, the street was jammed with vans and lorries unloading, taking up pavement as well as road, so that shoppers had to plot a course through a maze of obstacles. Tourists navigated with resigned expressions: this was Holiday and at least you could understand the lingo.

It was sixteen years since Wycliffe's last case in the town and he was recapturing the atmosphere of the place. For centuries merchant seamen from all over the world have mingled with the local population and now, in addition, for three months every year, holiday-makers flood in like the tide. Yet the substratum of true locals remains, a distinct, identifiable breed, preserving the town's unique parochialism and delighting in the frustra- tion of imported bureaucrats.

Byron, who had no good word to say of the town itself, spoke highly of its inhabitants: '. . . both female and male, at least the young ones, are remarkably handsome, and how the devil they came to be so is a wonder.'

'E. Garland and Son: Artists' Suppliers and Printers': gilt letters on a green ground; a discreet double frontage between a supermarket and a bank. One window displayed easels, folding stools, palettes, stretched canvases, and various shoulder-bags for transporting all the impedimenta of the would-be *plein air* painter; in the other window there were paintings of varied merit and price. There was a framed notice which read: 'Orders taken for printing of all kinds; commercial and private. Estimates on request without obligation.'

Wycliffe decided to avoid the shop for the moment; the family lived in the rooms above so there was probably a separate entrance. He found it in a stone-flagged side passage, a door bearing a small brass plate: 'Garland'. He rang the bell and it was answered by a youngish woman wearing a blue overall.

'Miss Garland?'

'No, what do you want?'

Wycliffe would have been surprised if she had said yes.

He introduced himself and she responded with engaging candour: 'Cathy Carne — I work in the shop. A policeman came earlier to break the news to Miss Garland.'

The woman was slim, dark, and well made, with an air of reserve that made one take her seriously. Dark blue eyes and black lashes: a felicitous dip from the genetic bran tub.

'It must have been a shock to Miss Garland, coming so soon after her father's death.'

'It was. I suppose you want to speak to her? She has a friend with her just now.'

On the spur of the moment he said: 'I would like to talk to you first.'

'If you wish.'

A door from the hall opened into the back of the shop. 'Through here.' She took him into a small office with a window overlooking the harbour. Desk, typewriter, telephone, safe, filing cabinet — all very modern and giving an impression of crisp business-like efficiency.

'Do sit down.'

33

She picked up a cigarette pack from the desk. 'Smoke? . . . No? Do you mind if I do?' She lit a cigarette and inhaled with sensual enjoyment.

'Do you mind telling me your position here, Miss Carne?' She was clearly more than a shop assistant.

A ghost of a smile. 'I sometimes wonder. I suppose you could say that I'm a kind of manageress. Anyway I've been here twenty years — since I left school, and Edwin Garland was my uncle by marriage.'

'Do you live above the shop?'

'I do not!' Emphatic.

'When you arrived this morning did you see Miss Garland at once?'

'She was waiting for me. She said it looked as though Francis hadn't been home all night and she was worried.'

'Had she been worried all night?'

'She wasn't here. She spent the night at a friend's house — the one who is with her now. When she returned home this morning she found Francis's dog, Mitch, whimpering outside the back door. Francis always takes him for a walk last thing before going to bed. It was while we were deciding what to do that your policeman turned up with the news.'

She was calm, self-possessed, incisive, and not obviously distressed.

A young girl, also wearing a blue overall, came into the office. After a brief apology she said: 'Is it all right to allow credit for this, Miss Carne?' She held out a bill form.

'Yes, that will be all right, Alice, but get Mrs Wilson to sign the bill and make sure the signature comes through on the carbon.'

Wycliffe said: 'Could anyone who knew your cousin's habits rely on him taking the same walk at approximately the same time each night?'

'Short of an earthquake or a deluge.'

'Do you know of any reason why he might have been killed?'

She shook her head. 'No. Francis wasn't the sort to make friends and influence people but I can't believe that anybody would want to murder him.'

34

'Somebody already has,' Wycliffe said. 'I'm told that there is a daughter?'

'It didn't take you long to find that out. Anna is twenty.'

'She lives with her mother?'

'And her boyfriend. By the way, somebody should tell her. After all he was her father.'

'Did he keep in touch with her?'

She trickled out a spiral of smoke and watched it rise. 'She kept in touch with him — at intervals.'

'Filial affection?'

She laughed outright. 'I'm in no position to say. My guess would be an upsurge of sentiment whenever the money was getting tight. But then, I'm a cynic.'

'They live near here?'

'In Flushing, just across the water. Shortly after Anna was born her mother married, and a year or so ago her husband died leaving her the house and a little money. The boyfriend moved in at the beginning of the summer; he gets by doing casual work on the farms.' She was watching him through the cigarette smoke to judge the effect she was producing.

A capable woman, nobody's fool; but was she adopting a deliberate pose? And if so, for what purpose?

'Does Anna have a job?'

'She's on the check-out in one of the supermarkets but I think she's on holiday this week.'

'Any other relatives?'

She smiled. 'Yes, but not acknowledged. Edwin's younger brother Thomas and his son, Mark. Mark is about my age and also unmarried.'

'Local?'

'Oh, yes. The two of them live in a house near the docks. Thomas is a retired schoolteacher and Mark is a chiropractor — some sort of osteopath.'

'You said they weren't acknowledged; what's wrong with them from the Edwin Garlands' point of view?'

'Thirty years ago Thomas contested his father's will, he lost but his action split the family; I don't think there's been any contact since.'

'Thomas didn't go to his brother's funeral?'

'No, but I saw Mark lurking in the background as though he didn't want to be seen. He's an odd fish.'

Wycliffe changed the subject. 'You don't seem very distressed by your cousin's death.'

She considered this. 'I suppose not. Of course I'm very sorry but our relationship has never been close. I worked for his father — my uncle, not for Francis.'

'But surely Francis was involved?'

She tapped ash from her cigarette. 'With the printing and outside sales. Two days a week — Mondays and Tuesdays — he went out with the van delivering orders to customers and taking new ones for both the printing and the art sides. The rest of the week he was at the printing works. He didn't interfere here, Uncle saw to that, so I've had a free hand in the shop and although I say it myself I've made a go of it.'

She made an irritable movement. 'There's no point in mincing words, Francis has never been interested in the business and he's never pulled his weight. Although he was supposed to be in charge of the printing works it was the foreman, Mike Treloar, who ran it with Uncle keeping an eye on things and deciding policy. Francis's one idea, if he'd lived, would have been to sell out. The printing works is a good investment for anybody's money and this site is a key one in the street. Uncle had several offers but he turned them all down.'

'When we found Francis his face was marked by fairly recent bruising. Do you know how and when it happened?'

'No, I saw the bruise when he came back to the shop on Tuesday evening and I asked him what he'd done to himself. He just growled something about having walked into a door.'

Wycliffe was trying to make up his mind about Cathy Carne. A good business woman, intelligent, unmarried. . . . But there was nothing of the old maid about her. Her figure, her posture, her attitude to him as a man, all suggested sexual awareness but she had a waspish tongue.

'You live near here?'

'A flat over the printing works. The foreman used to live

36

there until he got married and needed a bigger place, then Uncle let me have it.'

'You live alone?'

A thin smile. 'Of course.'

'From your flat I suppose you can see the back of Benson's where Francis was killed.'

'If I look out of the right window.'

'Did you look out of the right window last night?'

'I didn't see Francis or anything happening to him if that's what you're getting at. In any case it was dark well before ten.'

'You didn't come to work by way of the wharf walk this morning?'

'I never do.'

'Isn't it the quickest way?'

'Marginally, perhaps, but I always come by the street and pick up Uncle's paper from the newsagent on my way.' She pointed to *The Times*, still neatly folded on her desk, and smiled: 'I still do it — force of habit, I suppose.' She crushed out the dog-end of her cigarette and turned towards him, perfectly composed.

'If the business had been shut down and the premises sold, what would have happened to you?'

She grimaced. 'It's not a question of what would have happened if, it's what *will* happen. I shall be out of a job and out of a home. Beryl won't keep the shop on. I suppose I shall get something in the way of redundancy pay but it won't amount to much.'

Wycliffe changed the subject. 'Your uncle died of a stroke?'

'Actually it was coronary thrombosis; he collapsed in his studio.'

'Studio?'

'My uncle used to paint, his studio is next door to this.'

'And he died there?'

'I found him when I came back from lunch. It looked as though he had collapsed while painting.' For the first time she showed emotion.

'Had he been ill?'

'He had high blood pressure and he suffered from angina. It

37

was made worse because he wouldn't do what the doctor told him. He was obstinate.'

'You were fond of him?'

She nodded.

'Presumably the doctor was satisfied that he died as a result of his illness?'

She looked at him oddly. 'Of course! The doctor issued a certificate which gave coronary thrombosis as the cause of death.'

'I'm sorry, but one has to ask these questions. Anyway, thank you for your help. Just one more thing: I would like a list of customers regularly visited by your cousin. Could you have it ready by this afternoon?'

She looked surprised but she agreed.

'Thank you. Now, perhaps, you will ask Miss Garland if she will see me.'

Miss Garland would.

The stairs and landing, lit by a murky skylight, were rarely cleaned, in sharp contrast with the office and shop. Beryl Garland was waiting for him on the landing, a lean, bony woman with uncared-for greying hair, a pallid complexion blotched with an unnatural pink, and restless suspicious eyes.

'Come into the living-room.'

The living-room had once been almost elegant: high, with a deep frieze, plaster cornice, and an elaborate ceiling rose, reminders of a time when even prosperous merchants lived over their shops. The window faced north across the harbour and the water, sparkling in the sunshine, made the room itself seem dark. The furniture was genteely shabby and not very clean. A black and white rough-haired terrier was asleep on the hearth rug.

'My friend, Miss Bond, Superintendent.'

Miss Bond, who was standing when he entered the room, was the perfect complement to Beryl, plump instead of lean, dainty instead of gaunt, amiable instead of forbidding.

'We've known each other most of our lives and we were at school together, so we've no secrets.'

It dawned on Wycliffe that the room was smelling strongly of whisky, and that Miss Bond had probably hidden bottle and glasses while he was being received on the landing.

He was directed to a leather armchair by the empty fireplace while the two women seated themselves on dining chairs at the table. Their movements were deliberate and careful and Wycliffe had the impression of figures in slow motion, indeed of a whole existence that proceeded at a slower pace, muted, subdued, and infinitely depressing.

He expressed sympathy and it was received with complacency. 'My two closest relatives inside four days. Father died on Saturday of a coronary. Of course he's not been well for some time and he didn't take care of himself.' She lowered her voice. 'Blood pressure.' After a pause she went on: 'And angina; he was a difficult man! Wasn't he, Celia?'

Miss Bond shifted her position slightly and smiled but did not reply.

'I've given my life to looking after my father and my brother. I was thirty when mother died. . . . Nobody can say I haven't done my duty.'

He led her to speak of her brother: 'I understand there is a daughter.'

'Ah! So they've told you that already. Francis was a young man when that happened and I can't see what it's got to do with this.'

'I believe the girl lives locally and that she has kept in touch with her father.'

'For what she could get! She and that boy were at the funeral yesterday. You never saw anything like it — the way they were dressed; and their hair! A disgrace! wasn't it, Celia?'

Miss Bond said: 'You know I wasn't there, dear.'

'No, well it was. . . . At a funeral — it was an insult!'

For Beryl Garland the whole of reality was contained within the narrow horizons of her direct experience and her judgements were absolute.

'When was the last time you saw your brother, Miss Garland?'

'Yesterday evening at about nine o'clock. He was working in his room and I went in to tell him that I was going to spend the night with Miss Bond — I was upset, you understand. I came back at about eight this morning in time to get his breakfast and found the dog outside the back door, whining.'

'Has your brother seemed worried or nervous lately? Have you noticed any change in him?'

She shook her head with decision. 'No.'

'And last night when you spoke to him he was just as usual?'

'Just as usual, Superintendent.' She placed a bony hand firmly on the table top and fixed Wycliffe with her grey eyes. 'Francis was killed by hooligans. There's been a lot of that sort of thing in the town lately, and the police . . .' She decided not to finish that sentence.

Wycliffe said: 'But nothing was taken; his wallet, his money, his keys — '

She cut him short. 'Because the dog would have started to bark and that frightened the ruffians off. That's what happened.' She turned to her friend. 'Miss Bond agrees with me, don't you Celia?'

Miss Bond nodded. 'It's true that there have been several unpleasant incidents, mostly with young drunks.'

It was odd; Beryl's determination to convince him that her brother had been the victim of a random attack.

He was learning something of the dead man's background, admittedly from a biased witness, but any policeman knows that all witnesses are biased in some degree. He wanted to get the feel of the place, to find out what it was like to be Francis Garland, living with his father and sister in these rooms over the shop.

Beryl caught him looking at a painting hanging above the mantelpiece, a portrait of a middle-aged woman of exceptional beauty. 'My mother, just before she died at the age of fifty.' After a pause, she added in a church whisper: 'It was a growth — very quick.' She went on: 'Gifford Tate painted that. He was a great friend of my father's. Before Gifford had his stroke they used to go painting together all over the place. He's famous now, his pictures fetch thousands.'

Beryl having said her piece, silence took possession of the room; the two women sat, staring in front of them, scarcely moving a muscle. A trapped fly buzzed intermittently against the window panes and on the other side of the window the life of the harbour went on its unhurried way. The sounds from the street were muted.

Wycliffe, in the big black leather armchair by the empty grate, wondered if he was sitting in the old man's chair. Had Edwin spent idle hours in this room while his daughter made a great parade of doing the housework and kept up a running vituperative commentary on the last person or event to incur her displeasure? Or had he got the old man all wrong? He realised that he knew even less about the father than the son. He realised too that he needed to know about both. Father and son had died within a few days of each other . . .

Beryl broke the silence. 'I have to see father's lawyer this afternoon about the will. Of course Francis should have been there as well.' She looked down at her hands, resting on the table. 'I don't think Francis ever made a will so I suppose his share will come to me.' She shifted uneasily on her chair then, with a quick glance at Wycliffe: 'Is that right?'

'You will have to ask the solicitor about that, Miss Garland.'

'But you're a policeman; you must have some idea of the law. Celia thinks they'll say his illegitimate daughter is next-of-kin. That would be wicked! I mean, she's never done a hand's turn for her father or her grandfather — '

Miss Bond intervened. 'I really don't think the superintendent can help you, dear. You'll have to wait until you see Mr Shrimpton.'

Wycliffe said: 'Is he your father's solicitor?'

'Arthur Shrimpton, yes. The Shrimptons have looked after our affairs ever since my great grandfather started the business in 1900. In those days they lived next door but now they've only got their offices there. Over the bank.'

'Mr Shrimpton also acted for your brother?'

She looked at him in mild surprise at the question. 'Of course!'

Wycliffe said: 'I should like to see your brother's room, Miss Garland.'

'His room? What for?'

'In the circumstances the police need to know everything possible about your brother. It is one of the ways in which we can hope to find out why he was killed.'

'I've told you why he was killed.'

Wycliffe's bland stare decided the issue. She got up from her chair. 'You'd better come with me.'

He followed her across the landing where she opened one of three doors. 'There you are!' Despite her pique about his refusal to discuss the will, she took a certain pride in showing him her brother's room. 'All these books . . . and a computer. Francis spent a lot of time in here studying. All about numbers.'

'Was he a mathematician?'

'Oh, no. He worked on numbers because he thought they controlled people's lives. More like astrology I think it was.'

Wycliffe walked over to the bookshelves. The books fell into two roughly equal groups: occult studies and lives of famous and infamous men and women through history. The occult section was dominated by works on numerology. He glanced over the titles: Gibson's *Science of Numerology*, Cheiro's *Book of Numbers*, Driver's *Sacred Numbers and Round Figures*, and perhaps 40 others. A good collection of scholarly nonsense.

He turned to the desk where there were several index cards in a little pile. Beryl was watching him with suspicious eyes. The cards were all concerned with Frederick the Great; the first, a sort of curriculum vitae, the others dealing with aspects of his character and the principal events in his life. Each entry was marked with a series of numbers. A nest of metal drawers contained several hundreds of such cards in which the lives of other distinguished men and women had been similarly dissected.

She asked: 'Do you understand it?'

'No.'

Beryl was smug. 'I didn't think you would.'

Wycliffe said: 'Did your brother go out much, apart from the travelling he did for the firm?'

'He took the dog for a walk every night.'

'Apart from that.'

'Apart from that he went out every Sunday after breakfast and he usually came back late. I've no idea where he went.'

'Presumably he had friends?'

'If he did he didn't tell me about them.'

'Didn't people come to see him, or telephone?'

'He sometimes had telephone calls but who from or what about I don't know. I don't listen at doors.' She added after a moment: 'I do know he wasn't liked; even as a boy he had no friends.' She said this with relish.

'Do you know if he had any contact with his relatives?'

She turned on him: 'Relatives?'

'I understand that you have an uncle and a cousin who live near the docks.'

'We don't acknowledge them!' Her contempt was regal. 'I'm sure he never went near them.'

'Just one more question: did your father or your brother own a gun of any sort?'

'A gun? Certainly not!'

'To your knowledge there has never been a gun in this house?'

'Never!'

He moved towards the door. 'I'm afraid we shall have to keep this room locked for a day or two.'

'*Locked*?'

'Until we've had a chance to go through his papers. It's quite usual; we shall try to cause as little trouble as possible.'

'It seems to me that it is we who are being treated like criminals but I don't suppose I have any choice.'

A final glance round the room, the books, the charts, the computer, the filing system . . . He had the impression of something out of key — not exactly false, but contrived. As though the setting was more important than the work.

He locked the door and slipped the key into his pocket. 'I assure you that we will add to your distress as little as possible, but we shall be here from time to time and you will also be asked to make a formal statement.' Impossible not to be pompous with this damned woman!

She looked at him with silent aggression and he left it at that.

There were many questions he wanted to ask her but he needed ammunition.

She stood on the landing, watching him as he went down the stairs and out by the side door. He wondered if he would find anyone to grieve for either father or son.

As he passed the bank next door he noticed that it too had a side passage, but this one was decked out with tiles and had painted walls. A brass plate on the door, worn but shining, read: 'Shrimpton and Nicholls: Solicitors and Commissioners for Oaths.'

The street was slightly less congested, the time for unloading had passed and the lorries were gone. People ambled along, indulging in the local pastime of frustrating car drivers who had the temerity to attempt a breakthrough. Cars, of course, could and should have been excluded but that would have spoiled the fun.

Wycliffe had other preoccupations. A man of seventy-five dies of a heart condition and inside four days his son is shot dead. An actuary, assuming no causal connection, might calculate the odds against such a coincidence. Wycliffe thought they would be pretty high, so probability favoured a link. The most obvious one would be the will, but murder by advantaged legatees is a risky business. *Cui bono*? has a too obvious answer. All the same . . .

On the wharf activity was dying down. The body had been removed to the mortuary where Dr Franks would carry out the post mortem. A batch of film had gone for processing along with footprint casts and soil samples believed to be contaminated with blood or other tissue. Fox had found a bullet bedded in the ground and a cartridge case to go with it. It seemed that Francis had been shot with a self-loading pistol, a .32. They would know more when they had the report from Ballistics.

Now, one man was examining the steel tubes and struts of the scaffolding, dusting the surfaces with aluminium powder and squinting at the result through a lens; another was on his knees scrutinising the staging planks in case some fibres from the killer's clothing had become caught in the rough grain of the wood. Real Sherlock Holmes stuff! In reality, slow, monotonous, painstaking work which would almost certainly prove unrewarding.

'Check the register for licensed hand-guns of medium calibre.'

The headquarters team had arrived. Detective Inspector Kersey got out of one of the cars and came towards him. 'We're all here, sir. Lucy Lane is at the local nick taking over the paper work. Shaw is negotiating for that hen house over there.' Kersey pointed to a large portable building adjacent to the car-park. 'It seems a firm of accountants hired it as temporary accommodation while their offices were being refurbished and it's due to be removed. It would suit us better than one of our own mobile sardine cans.'

Kersey and Wycliffe had worked together for several years and their temperaments complemented each other. To Wycliffe's austere, almost puritanical approach, Kersey opposed an earthy realism and both were sufficiently tolerant to make the combination work.

'So, where do we go from here?'

'I'm going to take a look at the Garland printing works but I'll pick you up here in about half-an-hour and we'll go to lunch.'

Wycliffe had to make his way past a small crowd of would-be sightseers held well back by a uniformed policeman. A few yards off-shore several small craft provided others with vantage points but, as a spectacle, a scene of crime study ranks about level with a hole in the ground.

The printing works was a fairly modern concrete building with all the external charm of an army blockhouse, but the receptionist in the outer office was briskly efficient.

'I'll see if Mr Treloar is free.'

A brief exchange on the house telephone, a short delay, then Treloar joined them. A middle aged man in a grey overall, bald, very thin, with a conspicuous adam's apple; he walked with a limp. His manner was that of a man resigned to repeated interruptions: 'I suppose this is about Mr Francis; you'd better come into the office.'

The foreman's office was partitioned off from the shop floor

45

and from it one could see the men at work on the machines — five or six of them — but part of the floor was screened off by large canvas sheets suspended from the roof trusses.

Treloar waved a despairing hand. 'It's chaos! We're having new photo typesetting equipment put in. . . . A fine time for all this!'

His table was set out with batches of proof sheets clipped together, the ashtray was full of stubs, and there was a cup half full of coffee which looked as though it had gone cold hours before.

He drew up a chair for Wycliffe and sat down himself. 'I don't understand economics, Superintendent: why is it that in a country with three million on the dole some of us don't have time to breathe? Something wrong somewhere! Now, sir, how can I help you?'

Wycliffe said: 'Obviously you've heard about Francis Garland — how did you hear, by the way?'

'Cathy Carne rang me — sometime after nine.'

'The news came as a shock?'

Treloar brought out a packet of cigarettes, offered them to Wycliffe, then lit up himself. 'Not a shock exactly; a surprise, certainly.'

Obviously a man who chose his words with care.

'As far as you know did he have any enemies?'

'As far as I know he didn't have enemies or friends either, but I didn't know him very well.'

'You worked with him.'

A slow smile. 'You could say that. He spent three days a week here, more or less. I don't want to speak ill of the dead but as far as the work is concerned I have to say that he won't be missed.'

'What exactly did he do?'

'He saw commercial reps and talked to customers but he always called me in before he put in an order or gave an estimate.'

'So he knew his limitations.'

Treloar trickled smoke from between his lips. 'His father pointed them out to him often enough and he knew that things would drop on him from a great height if he put a foot wrong.'

'Edwin took an active part in the management here?'

A steady look from the grey eyes. 'He was the brains. I ran the place day to day, he decided policy. As long as you remembered that, everything was fine.'

'He came here often?'

'Every morning at half-past ten he would walk in through that door. He'd spend half-an-hour with me and another going round the machines, talking to the men. Apart from that he would be in touch by telephone.'

'You liked him?'

Hesitation. 'I admired him; he was a clever man and he was as good as his word. As to liking, I always had the feeling — I can't quite express it — the feeling that in his eyes I was all right — useful in fact, but that I didn't matter in myself. He had a way of looking at people as though they amused him, just like you might look at the antics of white mice in a cage. Sounds ridiculous, doesn't it?'

'Not to me.'

Treloar smoked for a while in silence, then he said: 'I suppose that was the man's nature but I've wondered sometimes whether it was why Francis turned out so bloody useless . . . if he was made to feel like that from childhood — insignificant, a bit of a joke.'

'What will happen now? Are you worried?'

Treloar pouted. 'Beryl will sell. As to being worried —- no. I'm good at my job and anybody who wants to run this place would have to recognise the fact. Not that I welcome change; I was very satisfied as things were but it was obvious they wouldn't go on indefinitely.'

They chatted for a few minutes but Treloar had nothing more to say. One of his men was waiting to see him, there was a telephone call, a customer was asking for him, and the receptionist was getting agitated.

Wycliffe said: 'Just one more thing then I'll leave you to it. I understand Cathy Carne lives above this?'

'She has a flat up there but most of that floor is a store-room.'

'Surely she doesn't have to come through this lot to go to her flat?'

47

'Hardly! The flat is self-contained and there's an outside staircase on the other side of the building.'

Wycliffe thanked him and left. Outside he walked round the building. In the end facing the harbour steel doors stood open and he could see men at work inside, installing the new machines. The entrance to Cathy Carne's flat was around the corner — a wooden staircase, well maintained, with a canopied landing at the top. He climbed the stairs but could see nothing through the hammered glass panels of the front door. The flat was at the quay end of the premises and from its windows there would be splendid views of the harbour, the waterfront, and the docks. It seemed that Cathy had a lot to lose through her uncle's death.

Brooding, Wycliffe walked back along the wharf to join Kersey in search of lunch.

Cathy Carne stood in the middle of the shop. It was a quiet time and Alice was re-stocking the shelves. Cathy stared into vacancy, seeing nothing. She was trying to grasp the radically changed situation with which she must come to terms. Edwin dead, Francis dead, and in such a short space of time. Four days ago in a similar quiet period she had been gossiping with her uncle, listening to his barbed comments on affairs, on the art world, and on his family. Now she was perplexed and afraid; perplexed because she did not understand what had happened, and afraid of what it might mean if she did.

She realised with a slight shock that she was staring straight at a man who was looking in through the shop window, staring back. It was Mark Garland of the excluded Garlands. She lifted a hand in acknowledgement, and this was all the encouragement he needed to come in.

Mark Garland was slight of build, very fair, good looking in a feminine way. He wore spectacles with thin gold rims which seemed to stress his femininity. Cathy had the impression that he was struggling to control extreme nervousness and his approach was absurdly tentative.

'I wondered whether to risk coming in or not. I didn't know what sort of reception I should get.'

Cathy was brusquely reassuring. 'There's no quarrel between us. Why should there be?'

'No, of course not! It's all very distressing. I'm very upset about Francis . . . more upset than I can say.'

Cathy waited for him to enlarge. He intrigued her, he was such a rabbit, yet Edwin had told her that he was subject to outbursts of violent temper.

'I wonder if you think I could have a word with Beryl? I would very much like to.' Another weak little smile. 'We haven't spoken since I was a child, Beryl and I. Absurd, isn't it?'

'There's no harm in trying; she won't eat you.'

'No . . . How should I go about it?'

'I'll call her if you like — or would you rather go up?'

He hesitated, looking round the shop as though it might help him to a decision. 'No, I'd rather you called her if you don't mind.'

Cathy went into the little hall and called up the stairs.

Beryl's voice answered. 'What is it?'

'Mark Garland is here and he would like a word with you.'

'Well, I don't want a word with him. Nothing has changed; he needn't think it has; I don't want to hear or see anything of him or his father — ever. You can tell him that!' A door slammed upstairs.

Cathy returned to the shop. 'You heard? Sorry!'

He nodded, resigned. 'It's a pity . . . I was hoping to explain . . .' He went out of the shop, head bent, shoulders drooping.

Miss Bond had gone out to buy something simple for their lunch. 'A few sandwiches from Marks and Spencer, dear — but nothing with salmon. You know I daren't touch salmon.'

Beryl was restless and apprehensive, trying hard to find firm ground, and Mark Garland turning up like that had upset her. The gall of these people! Her feeling of insecurity had started some time before her father's death with a suspicion, soon amounting to certainty, that something was going on behind her back. It was mainly due to a subtle change in Francis. She had denied anything of the kind to the police but it was real enough. She knew him and his little moods so well: he had become more aggressive, more overtly secretive — and smug. When he was young he would say: 'I know something you don't!' Not so blatant now, but it meant the same.

And there was his behaviour since their father's death: odd little things she had scarcely noticed at the time but now they began to acquire significance in her mind. She glanced at the clock: five minutes to one. Soon Cathy Carne would be shutting shop to go to lunch. Beryl went downstairs and into the shop. Cathy was in the office.

'Anything I can do, Beryl?'

'No, I just wanted the key to father's studio.'

'But I haven't got it. If you remember, yesterday afternoon, after the funeral, Francis asked me to lock the studio and bring him the key. I did, and he put it on his ring.'

'Isn't there a spare?'

'Not as far as I know. Uncle always kept the studio locked and carried the key about with him.'

To this point Beryl's manner had been almost peremptory, now she became more relaxed and confiding. 'There's something I want to ask you, Cathy. When you came upstairs to say father had collapsed, didn't you think it was very odd, the way Francis rushed down without a word?'

Cathy was cautious. 'No, it didn't strike me like that. I thought he wanted to see if he could help his father, but it was too late.'

Beryl persisted. 'And when we came down together, after you'd phoned Alan. . . . You remember?'

There was a brief pause before Cathy replied. 'Yes, I remember. What about it?'

'You looked very puzzled about something. I saw you staring at Francis; I couldn't make it out.'

Cathy was dismissive. 'I don't know how I looked but I was shocked. We all were.'

Beryl lingered, her grey eyes fixed on Cathy for some time, then she said: 'I see. Well, you'll be wanting to go to your lunch. You'll be at Shrimpton's this afternoon?'

'Yes.'

'I suppose Alice is capable of looking after the shop?'

The first time Beryl had shown the slightest concern for the business. A straw in the wind?

Anna was in the kitchen preparing vegetables, and from where she stood at the sink she could look across the water to Falmouth, a few hundred yards away: the Greenbank Hotel, the Royal Yacht Club, the new flats on the Packet Quays, then the backs of High Street and the pier. The narrow strip of water between was dotted with small craft of every description, all facing upstream. The sun shone and everywhere there was stillness. Life seemed suspended and she had a disquieting sense of being quite alone. She switched on the radio to recover normality.

Her grandfather's death had affected her more than she would have thought possible. She had heard the news with regret, with sadness, but hardly with grief. After all, old men die. A month ago he had come to see her and now she understood for the first time that what he had said to her then would change her life. At the funeral (she had never been to a funeral before) it had come to her quite suddenly that something was ending in herself, that she was being challenged to take hold of her life, to make decisions, and she had quarrelled with Terry because of it.

The front door opened then slammed. Her mother had been to Falmouth shopping. She was back early. She burst into the kitchen, two shopping bags in one hand and one in the other.

'You're early.'

Freda dropped her bags and slumped on a chair. She was flushed and breathing hard. 'I got the first ferry I could after I heard. . . . Shut that damn thing off, Anna!'

Anna switched off the radio.

In the silence she could hear her mother wheezing as she breathed. Freda was grossly overweight. An elaborately floral dress exposed great volumes of lobster-coloured flesh.

'What did you hear?' Anna was accustomed to her mother's histrionics.

'It's about your father.'

'What about him?'

'He's dead, Anna — murdered.'

Anna stood motionless, potato in one hand, knife in the other. There was nothing she could say, nothing she could think because she felt nothing. Only in her mind's eye she saw the image of her father, rather big, fleshy, with bulging expressionless eyes.

'The police are all over the place. I thought they might have got here before I did.'

Anna said nothing.

'He was shot last night when he was taking the dog for a walk.'

'Shot? On the wharf?'

'Yes.'

'Do they know who did it?'

'How should I know?'

Anna picked up the saucepan into which she had been putting potatoes and transferred it to the stove. Her mother watched her.

'In some ways you're just like your father, Anna. You never *feel* anything. You're cold inside!' Freda started to unpack her shopping. At one of the cupboards, with her back to the room she said: 'Terry didn't come home last night.'

Anna said nothing.

'Have you seen him this morning?'

'No.'

'What happened?'

'We had a row.'

'What about?'

'Nothing — everything. I was fed up.'

'Where would he sleep?'

'In the van, I suppose. He's done it often enough before.'

She was thinking of the periodic visits she had made to her father; they were all the same; their conversations could have been scripted:

'How is your mother?'

'All right.'

'And you?'

'I'm all right.'

'Good!' Then when the silence became uncomfortable he would reach into his pocket for his wallet. 'There, now! Buy yourself something.' He thought it was what she had come for. Perhaps he was right. . . . Yet there must have been something more. Now he was dead.

Anna started to slice up runner beans. Freda said: 'You'll still go to the lawyer's this afternoon?'

'I suppose so.'

'Your grandfather thought a lot of you. He remembered you every Christmas and birthday. . . . He must have left you something and you might as well know what.'

There was a knock at the front door. Freda said: 'There they are! The police.'

Chapter Three

WYCLIFFE WAS WATCHING two men in a rowing boat. One rowed while the other held a rope over the stern. They would row about fifty yards in one direction, then turn round and row back, seemingly over the same ground. What were they doing? Were they trawling for something? A lost moorings, perhaps? That was the trouble with harbour-watching, there were so many inexplicable activities carried on at a stately pace and with the deliberation of a choreographed performance.

The team had acquired the use of the large Portakabin recently occupied by a firm of accountants while their offices were being refurbished. Although all fittings and furniture had been removed it was Ritzy accommodation compared to a mobile incident van or the decayed huts and barn-like halls to which they were accustomed. There was even a screened-off cubicle which could be used as an interview room. More to the point, it was next door to the car-park and overlooked the harbour within two hundred yards of the Garlands' shop. A pantechnicon from central stores had delivered the official ration of battered furniture and a communications unit with office equipment, stationery and the basic materials for preparing police tea. A large-scale map was pinned to one wall and there was a blackboard for briefings.

By mid-afternoon they were in business.

Uniformed men and Wycliffe's detective constables were questioning the very few people who actually lived in the street. Publicans whose premises backed on the harbour were interviewed and, over local radio, people were being asked to come forward if they had been in the neighbourhood the night before, especially those who had used the car-park. It was quite possible that the killer had come and gone by car. On the assumption that he or she might not have carried the murder

54

weapon away Wycliffe had ordered a search of the foreshore, and a police frogman was floundering about in the shallow off-shore waters like a porpoise on the point of stranding.

'The dead man spent two days a week travelling for the firm, taking orders and delivering goods. I will let you have a list of his customers and I want them contacted, in the first instance by telephone. Find out when he last called and try to get an impression of what they thought of him. Get them to talk, and if there is a hint of anything unusual report to me.' Kersey, briefing his troops.

'We also want to know exactly how Garland spent his time from Saturday afternoon when his father died to last night when somebody shot him on the wharf. I shall draw up a timetable, hour by hour, and allowing for the fact that he must have slept, I expect to see the spaces filled in.

'The shot that killed Garland was fired at a few minutes past ten. Most of the people who were in the street at that time would have been in one or other of the pubs, but don't forget that the harbour is full of craft of all sorts and there are sure to have been people aboard some of them.'

Wycliffe dealt with the media. Interest was minimal; the fatal shooting of a small-town shopkeeper wouldn't make much of a splash, the ripples would scarcely extend to the National dailies.

Wycliffe's table was placed against the row of windows at one end of the temporary building. He had the pathologist's preliminary report which had been dictated over the telephone. 'A single wound of entry situated in the right parietal bone just anterior to the lambdoid suture and close to the saggital suture. The nature of the wound suggests a bullet of medium calibre fired at close range, under 60 centimetres. The bullet traversed the skull and was deflected in its passage to emerge on the left side, shattering bones in the area of articulation of the lower jaw.

'This would be consistent with the victim having been shot from above and slightly behind. Death must have been instantaneous.

'The facial bruising was caused 24–36 hours before death

and is typical of injury brought about by a blow from a human fist.'

Already officers were returning from enquiries with completed interview-forms and Lucy Lane was going through them as they came in. Kersey was briefing himself from the paperwork so far.

Detective Sergeant Lucy Lane was still well under thirty. A good school record; university. Then what? Something constructive — working with people. But having no wish, as Virginia Woolf put it, 'to dabble her fingers self-approvingly in the stuff of other souls' and believing in the stick and carrot philosophy of human conduct, she joined the police. Oddly, her outlook was more authoritarian than her chief's. After thirty years in the force Wycliffe still held fast to a lingering hope that man may yet prove perfectable; woman too. Lucy, probably influenced by her parson father, was more inclined to a belief in original sin.

'Look at this, sir.' She passed over two reports with items marked in red.

The first concerned the landlord's wife at the Packet Inn. At about ten-fifteen the previous evening she had heard a 'crack' followed by a dog barking — yapping, she said. It had gone on for some time, she couldn't say how long. She was busy serving and really didn't think about it much.

The other report was from the DC who had called on Garland's daughter, Anna, and her mother. They had already heard the news and seemed to take it calmly. The officer had not seen the girl's boyfriend and was told that they did not know where he was.

'So?' Wycliffe returned the sheets.

'Just that Sergeant Shaw checked with Records. This young man, Terrence John Gill, has a conviction. Two years ago he was convicted of causing a breach of the peace at St Mawgan airfield during a CND demo.'

'What happened in court?'

'He was bound over.'

'I don't suppose that makes him a potential killer but we need to find him. Put somebody on to it.'

He thought of Beryl and the need to come to grips with the Garland set-up as it had been before the old man's death. Beryl needed firm handling but losing father and brother inside four days must mean something more than the prospect of a secure income. Lucy Lane with her stick and carrot philosophy might be the best one to deal with her.

'I want you to talk to Beryl Garland. We want background. We also want her formal statement. Take a DC with you and get started on turning over Francis's room. On second thoughts, take Shaw and see what he can make of that computer thing.'

Wycliffe had little patience with and no interest in technological gadgetry. He believed that the human capacity for moral, social, and political adaptation had been stretched to its limit in the first century of the Industrial Revolution and fatally outstripped since.

'Will we be looking for anything in particular, sir?'

'Use your imagination. Whatever Beryl believes or pretends to believe about her brother being mugged, he was in fact deliberately murdered by someone lying in wait for him on the scaffolding. There must have been an involvement in something sufficiently profitable or menacing or both to lead somebody to murder. I've got an appointment with Shrimpton, the lawyer, at four and I shall look in at the shop afterwards.'

He arrived on time for his appointment and he was not kept waiting; the receptionist introduced him at once.

Shrimpton was in the mid-forties, overweight, and slightly larger than life, a sociable type. His skin was bronzed, his thinning hair was bleached by sun and sea, and Wycliffe felt sure that he spent as little time as possible away from boats, the sea, and the club bar. Of course his office overlooked the harbour and was hung with enlarged photographs of yachts and of sailing occasions.

'Smoke? . . . I will if you don't mind.' He lit a small cigar. 'I know why you're here and I might tell you I've had one hell of an afternoon.' He blew out a cloud of smoke. 'I suppose you know our Beryl?'

'I've spoken to her briefly.'

'Then you know her. Edwin was a crafty old so-and-so and he didn't like his children very much — not that I blame him — so I thought I'd better get the beneficiaries together and explain. We had a date for this afternoon but when I heard about Francis it seemed the decent thing to postpone the arrangement. I rang Beryl with condolences and the suggestion that we should meet later in the week. Not on your life! You'd think I was proposing to give away her share to a cats' home. So we went ahead as planned: Beryl, Cathy Carne — you've met Cathy? Great girl! Anna — Francis's side-kick — Alan Tate and Mike Treloar, the foreman at the printing works. Of course Francis should have been with us.'

Wycliffe said: 'Alan Tate?'

'Gifford Tate's son. Gifford and old Edwin were life-long buddies. Alan is a doctor and he lives with his stepmother in the family house — up the hill towards Wood Lane.'

'And Alan Tate is a beneficiary under the will?'

'In a small way.' He broke off, staring out of the window. 'See that?'

A heavily built boat, painted slate-blue, cutter rigged, was gliding downstream. 'That's one of the Falmouth Quay Punts. She's at least eighty years old, of course she's been restored. Before the days of radio, boats like her would race down-channel as far as the Lizard to get first contact for the ship-to-shore trade from vessels making port. Wonderful craft! I envy old Podgy Hicks that boat.

'But perhaps you're not addicted.' Reluctantly he brought his attention back to business. 'Yes, well, Edwin's testament.' He glanced at the document in front of him. 'The will was made about a year ago and this is what it amounts to: "The shop premises and stock and all assets pertaining to the business together with the contents of my studio excepting only my tube of Winsor blue to my niece and dear friend Cathy Carne".'

Shrimpton looked up. 'You can imagine how that ruffled Beryl's feathers! For a moment I thought she was going the same way as her father. Then, £10,000 to Anna, £5,000 to

Mike Treloar, and £1,000 to Alan Tate — "the son of my friend Gifford Tate together with my tube of Winsor blue" —'

'What's all this about Winsor blue? It sounds like a butterfly.'

Shrimpton grinned. 'One of the old man's little jokes. Typical! As I said, Gifford Tate and he were buddies, and it was some argument they had about colours. Winsor blue is a colour used by painters. Of course old man Tate died years ago.

'There's another legacy of £1,000, this time to his friend Martin Burger, "more than enough for that new pair of spectacles which I hope may improve his judgement and help him to see the obvious." Burger wasn't here this afternoon; he's a bit doddery on his legs and doesn't get about much.

'Anyway, the printing works and the business associated with it together with the residue of the estate after discharge of all debts and liabilities are left jointly to Beryl and Francis. That's it.'

'Is the residue going to amount to much?'

'I wouldn't mind it coming my way. Edwin owned the freehold of another property in the street, let on a fat lease, there is more property on the sea-front, and a nice carefully nurtured portfolio of equities. The Garlands have been in this game for eighty years — accumulating, not spending. Edwin liked to pretend that the art business and the printing were his livelihood, in fact they probably represent less than half his assets.'

'Isn't it a bit odd to leave property to joint heirs with no conditions laid down for its distribution?'

Shrimpton nodded. 'I tried to persuade him out of it but he wouldn't budge. A recipe for in-fighting that's what it is, and that's what the old devil intended, although he wouldn't admit it. I think he saw himself, sitting up there, watching the fun. Of course now it's going to be a damn sight funnier than even he imagined.'

'How come? With Francis out of the way — '

Shrimpton tapped ash off his cigar. 'With Francis out of the way Beryl will have to come to terms with his heir and to the best of my belief Francis never made a will. He meant to. He was in this office a fortnight ago saying that it was about time as his father was getting on and one never knew, et cetera et cetera. . . . He promised to bring me a few notes from which I could prepare a draft but he never did.'

'So?'

'You know the answer to that, and so does Beryl now, though I wrapped it up a bit to save her having a fit on the spot. Young Anna is going to be very well heeled but she will have to come to some arrangement with Beryl and Beryl would prefer, much, to deal with the devil himself. If the old man really is up there watching he's in for some good laughs.'

'What was Anna's reaction?'

Shrimpton grimaced. 'Hard to tell. I half thought the implications of Francis's death hadn't got through to her, but that girl doesn't give much away.'

'How did Cathy Carne receive her bit of glad news? Do you think it was a complete surprise?'

Shrimpton was emphatic. 'I'm certain! I've never seen anyone so astonished unless it was dear Beryl. I can't imagine what Francis's reaction would have been. I can't help being thankful I didn't have to cope with it. Incidentally, the old man wrote Cathy a letter which I was charged to pass over unopened. And one other thing you should know for the record: Jimmy Rowe, the old man's accountant, and I are joint executors, God help us!'

Wycliffe was grateful and said so. 'Now I'm going to ask you to be indiscreet. If Francis had made a will have you any idea how it would have gone?'

Shrimpton threw away the stub of his cigar. 'You are asking me to be clairvoyant as well as indiscreet. Francis told me nothing of his intentions so I can only guess.'

'And?'

A broad grin. 'You know nothing of any woman in his life?'

'Nothing. Was there one?'

'I'm not sure, but from things he let drop from time to time I think there probably was. Once or twice lately he's mentioned the possibility that he might "change his way of life" which could mean that he intended to get married, but with Francis it could equally mean that he was thinking of taking up golf or ludo.'

'I gather you were not fond of him.'

'I was not. I went to school with Francis and he was always odd man out. He wasn't very bright and he was more than a bit of a bore with it.' ·

'A couple of adjectives to describe him?'

Shrimpton laughed outright. 'You're a bloody old copper, I must say! Well, it can't do him any harm where he's gone. Two adjectives . . . devious is one, he was certainly that; and I'm afraid the other would have to be spiteful. You can add secretive for good measure though he hadn't much to be secretive about.'

'Somebody killed him.'

'Yes, and I must admit that surprises me. Francis could have been involved in something a bit shady but nothing that would have brought him within range of any violence. He was a timid soul.'

'One more question, then I won't bother you any more. Can you tell me about the Garland relatives — Thomas's side of the family?'

'Not a lot. Thomas was a younger son and it seems he had no interest in the business; he went to university and became a teacher. At some stage he came back to Cornwall and taught. His son, Mark, trained as an osteopath or something and set up in practice here. Thomas's wife died and he and Mark continue to live in the family house down by the railway station.

'The trouble began when grandfather Garland died about thirty years ago — in my father's time — and left almost everything to Edwin. Thomas felt hard done by, contested the will, and lost. I don't think the two sides of the family have had anything to do with each other since.'

They parted on the best of terms. Shrimpton came with him to the top of the stairs. 'If you fancy a bit of sailing while you're here you know where to come.'

Wycliffe was anxious to talk to Cathy Carne again. Since his meeting with her that morning she had learned that she would become the owner of the business and premises. If the news was really unexpected she would be off balance and it is at such times that people are most likely to speak the truth.

As he entered the shop the young girl assistant came forward; she recognised him at once. 'Miss Carne is in the office.'

He went through and tapped on the office door.

A listless 'Come in!'

He found her sitting at the desk which was quite clear. 'Oh, it's you. I let your inspector have the list of Francis's customers you asked for.' She drummed on the desk with her fingers. 'I suppose you've heard?'

'I've just left Shrimpton. Was it totally unexpected?'

She turned on him irritably. 'Of course it was unexpected! What the hell do you think? I'd hoped for a little money, at the very most, a thousand. I can't take it in. I should be over the moon; instead . . .'

'What about Beryl?'

She reached for her cigarettes. 'Yes. What about Beryl? You may well ask. She's moving in with Celia Bond at the end of the month — or so she says. I told her she's welcome to stay up there just as long as she wants and what she said wouldn't bear repeating. I feel guilty, though God knows why I should. I've put more into this place than she and her brother together; a damn sight more!' She lit a cigarette and smoked in short, angry puffs.

Wycliffe sat down without being invited. 'My people are upstairs talking to Beryl and going through Francis's room, looking for anything which might explain why he was murdered. In my own mind I can't separate his death from his father's.'

She looked at him sharply. 'You're not suggesting — '

'That your uncle was murdered? No, merely that there is some sort of connection. He died in his studio; did he spend much time there?'

'A great deal.'

'Doing what?'

'Well, for one thing he did all our framing and there's quite a lot of that, but he painted too.'

'Did he sell his pictures?'

'Oh, yes. A number were sold through the shop though he would never have them put on display; others went to shops and commercial galleries in this part of the world. Of course he never made a name for himself, like Gifford Tate, though Tate himself reckoned uncle was the better painter. They were great friends — there were three of them: Uncle, Gifford Tate, and Papa Burger — I don't know why 'papa' but they always called him that. He had money and was always a bit of a dilettante. They used to go off painting together at week-ends, often in Burger's boat, and they spent quite long holidays abroad. Of course Tate died seven or eight years ago. In his will he appointed Uncle Edwin as his art executor.

'Incidentally there's an exhibition of Tate's work starting in the town next week. After that it goes on tour: Plymouth, Cardiff, London, Newcastle and Glasgow. A big affair. Uncle was really responsible for getting it organised — sponsorship and so forth. He was really looking forward to that exhibition.'

'And Burger?'

'Oh, Papa is still living up at Wood Lane. Didn't Shrimpton tell you, Uncle left him £1,000 to buy a pair of spectacles? A joke, of course. He's lost the use of his legs and doesn't get about much but Uncle went to see him two or three times a week.'

'What do you know about Winsor blue?'

She laughed, the tension suddenly released, and it occurred to Wycliffe that she was very attractive when she laughed. 'It's another joke they had, like Papa Burger and the spectacles. Winsor blue is a trade name for an artists' colour which was first marketed sometime in the thirties. Gifford Tate started to use it as soon as it came out, he reckoned it brought him luck. Uncle used to tease him about it and it became a standing joke.'

'So leaving Alan Tate a tube of Winsor blue — '

'I suppose it was a way of wishing him luck.'

'Alan Tate is a doctor?'

'That's right. He was Uncle's doctor. Mine too, for that matter.'

'Did he issue the death certificate?'

'Of course!'

Wycliffe was impressed by her seemingly transparent honesty and by her spontaneity that had something refreshingly youthful about it. He could understand Edwin entrusting her with his business.

'I believe your uncle left a letter for you.'

'Yes.' The shutters came down.

'You've read it?'

'Yes; and destroyed it as he asked me to do.'

'You were in a hurry.'

'I did what I was asked to do.'

'Are you prepared to tell me what was in it?'

She hesitated. 'It gave me some advice about dealing with problems which might arise.'

'With the family?'

'Yes, and that is all I am prepared to say.'

'Just one more thing: what exactly was Francis doing with his books, his filing system and his computer?'

'I suppose the short answer would be, conning himself. In a burst of confidence one day he told me that he was working out a new system of numerology, developed from a study of people whose lives have been well documented. His father used to say that he was so desperately anxious to amount to something that he chose a subject about which critical people knew nothing and cared less.'

'Sounds a bit harsh.'

'Uncle didn't suffer fools gladly.'

Wycliffe stood up. 'Thanks for your help. I want a word with my people upstairs.'

As he was leaving the office he stopped by another door. 'The studio?'

'Yes, I'm afraid it's locked and Francis had the key.'

'It doesn't matter. I expect we shall come across it.'

He went upstairs. After the crisp freshness of the shop, the flat had a musty stale smell. Edwin must have been struck by the contrast each time he climbed the stairs.

Lucy Lane and Shaw were at work in Francis's room which overlooked the street. The shops were closing and there was that burst of activity before things settled down to the evening

64

calm. Lucy Lane was sitting at the desk, turning the pages of a loose-leaf manuscript file. She looked like a schoolgirl doing her homework. By contrast, Shaw, communing with the computer and making a new friend, looked like one of those whiz-kids who, from their glass and concrete towers, manipulate the world's money markets. It sometimes came as a slight shock to Wycliffe to have this paragon of the modern virtues working under his direction.

He said: 'Anything for me?'

Lucy Lane answered: 'He was writing a book on numerology. To me it's all gobbledegook, but here's the title.'

She held out the first page of the manuscript file for him to read. It was written in a careful script, meticulously spaced: 'A New System of Numerology by Francis Garland.' And there followed a paragraph in smaller script: 'Derived by the inductive method from studies of the lives of famous and infamous men and women, past and present, and including a new Universal Alphabet which disposes of the conflict between the "Hebrew" and the "Modern" systems.'

Wycliffe said: 'You need a dedication to a Noble Lord to go with that.'

Lucy Lane laughed. 'Quarto, with fine portrait vignette on title. Bound in contemporary calf. . . .' She closed the file and put it aside. 'He also kept a diary of sorts though most of the entries don't tell you much. She picked up a hard-covered exercise book. 'It looks as though he had a woman friend; he refers to her as 'M'. She's mentioned frequently but he never gives any clue as to who she is or the nature of their relationship.'

Wycliffe said: 'The lawyer thought there was a woman but he had no idea who she might be. We must try to find out. Anything else?'

'There's an earlier entry about his father.' She turned back through the pages. 'It's dated July 15th — just over a year ago — and he writes: "Today father told me something about himself which I can scarcely believe. It's incredible to think that it's been going on all these years! And when I asked him what would happen if it got known he just smiled and said I could talk if I wanted to. But why tell me? And why now?"'

'Dramatic! What do you make of it?'

Lucy Lane sucked the top of her ball-point. Meditative. 'A man of seventy-five, a widower, well off — what secrets would a man like that be likely to have? I mean, what would make him vulnerable? Unless he was keen on little boys or little girls. . . .'

'Talk to Beryl. She probably won't tell you anything but you may be able to judge whether she knows anything, and if she does, the sort of area we are in.'

He turned to Shaw who had not ceased his manipulations of the keyboard. 'And the oracle?'

Shaw said: 'It's difficult to work out his programme but it seems that he analysed his subjects and classified their attributes, their doings, and the major events in their lives by coded numbers. He used the computer to establish correlations. That's about as far as I've got.'

'Don't spend too much time on it unless it seems to have more relevance to the case. Any correspondence?'

Lucy Lane said: 'There's a drawer full of letters all jumbled together; we haven't got round to them yet.'

He decided to leave them to it, and as he came out on the landing he almost collided with Beryl who must have been eavesdropping. She was flushed, her eyes were moist and her hair was wild.

She attacked at once: 'I suppose she's told you that this is no longer my home so you think you can come and go as you please. Well, I shall move out when it suits me but I want you to know that the *contents* of these rooms are mine and I shall fight for them in Court if need be.'

Wycliffe felt sorry for her; self-centred and cantankerous as she was, she had suffered some shocks. 'I merely wanted a word with my people who are working on your brother's papers.'

Beryl made a derisive sound. 'That girl of yours asked me for a statement and I gave her one — more than she bargained for, and I made her take it all down.'

'I would like to ask you one or two more questions if I may.'

She was about to refuse but thought better of it. 'You'd better come in here.'

He followed her into the living-room but she did not ask him to sit down. 'Well?'

'In your brother's papers there is mention of something your father told him about a year ago which greatly surprised and puzzled him. From the context it is clear that the secret, whatever it was, was of long standing.'

He saw the change in her expression; antagonism replaced by . . . by fear? Was that too strong? At any rate she cut him short: 'Are you saying that my father had a shameful secret of some sort?'

'No, I am not; merely that there was something he had previously kept to himself which he confided to your brother. I am wondering if you have any idea of what it could be?'

Beryl was staring at him, her lips were trembling and it was clear that she was deeply disturbed. In the end she said. 'This is all nonsense! Wicked nonsense! Francis was a fool!'

'So you know of nothing which your father might have confided to Francis which would greatly disturb him?'

'Of course I know of nothing! Francis was always stirring, trying to score off people. . . .' She broke off, on the verge of tears.

Impossible to judge whether she knew or did not know whatever it was that Francis had been told, and there was nothing to be gained by turning the screw too hard.

'Have you noticed any change in your brother recently — say in the past few months? Any change in his relations with his father?'

'I've noticed nothing and I certainly would have if there was anything to notice!'

Back in the street workmen were stretching a banner between the shops above the traffic: 'The Gifford Tate Exhibition of Paintings; Open 11th–22nd August. Admission Free.'

Wycliffe felt that he was getting to know the people who had been closest to the dead man. Eight hours ago he had never heard of any of them, now he was thinking of them by their first names: Francis, Edwin, Beryl, Anna, Cathy. . . . And he was able to fit a face and provisionally a temperament to four of them. Francis Garland was the victim and therefore the central figure in the case. Always start with the victim and try to trace around him the web of relationships in which he was involved. That was how he worked, but in this case he could not free himself of the notion that although Francis was the victim he might not be the central figure. His father seemed a more promising candidate for that role and he had died a natural death. Did that mean that the murder was . . . was peripheral?

He promised himself that he would devote at least as much attention to the father as to the son.

Chapter Four

'WHAT DO YOU want me for?'
  'Where did you sleep last night?'
  'In my van.'
  'On this car-park?'
  'Yes.'
  'Do you usually spend your nights in the back of your van?'
  'No. I live with my girlfriend and her mother in Flushing.'
  'So why weren't you there last night?'
  'We had a row.'
  'What about?'
  'God knows! What are rows usually about?'
  'Money in my experience.'
Once it was known that Terry Gill was wanted for questioning, a young constable who knew him, all bright eyed and bushy tailed, pointed out that his van had been in the car-park all day within fifty yards of the Incident Room.
  'I know him, sir. We keep an eye on him.'
So all they had needed to do was wait and, at five o'clock, the wanted man had turned up. Now he was being interrogated by Kersey in the make-shift interview room.
  'Where have you been all day?'
  'In Redruth to see an old mate of mine.'
  'How did you get there without the van?'
  'By bus. My dynamo has been dodgy and it finally packed up. I was short of a few quid to do anything about it so my mate lent me the money, we went to a scrap yard, picked up a spare and he delivered me back here in his motor, then your chaps picked me up.'
  'What time did you leave here this morning?'
  'Early. Sevenish. I couldn't sleep so I thought I might as well get going.'

For all his long hair, bandeau and earrings which made him look like a weedy Viking, Terry Gill was a very ordinary young man, and pathetic; pathetic because he so obviously wanted to amount to something and had no idea what. Kersey would have written him off as harmless had it not been for his extreme wariness. Each question seemed to come as a relief, as though he had expected something more dangerous.

'So last night at, say, ten o'clock, where were you?'

'In my van, I expect. I'm not very good on time.'

At that point Wycliffe joined them. Kersey looked up. 'This is Terry Gill, sir, Anna's boyfriend. He's telling us how he spent last night here, on the car-park, in his van.'

'So if you were in your van you couldn't have been two hundred yards away on the scaffolding behind Benson's furniture shop?'

This was the bull's eye. The boy looked from one to the other of them and it was a moment or two before he could find his voice, then: 'I don't know what you mean.'

'What are you so frightened of?'

'I'm not frightened.'

'You could have fooled me.' Kersey leaned forward across the table, his rubbery features close to the boy. 'Look, sonny, it sticks out a mile that you want to get something off your chest but you're scared to hell what will happen to you if you do. All I can say is the longer you mess me about the worse it will get. Now let's be serious. Take it a step at a time. When did you last see your girlfriend's father?'

'At the old man's funeral yesterday. He came and spoke to us — to Anna and me.'

'What did he say?'

'He was very friendly and nice; he wanted to know if Anna had been asked to come to the lawyer's about her grandfather's will.' Terry was recovering his voice if not his composure.

'And had she?'

'Yes.'

'So she had expectations.'

'Of something, I suppose.'

'Is that what you quarrelled about?'

'I don't think so. She was very queer after the funeral. I couldn't make her out.'

Wycliffe said: 'Anna's share in her grandfather's will was £10,000.'

The boy looked amazed. 'That's money! I don't think she was expecting anything like that.'

'But now she will get a lot more than that.'

'More?'

'From her father. It seems he didn't make a will and if that is the case Anna will get his share.'

'But her father isn't dead.' The words were spoken mechanically as though by a bad actor.

Kersey cut in. 'But he is, you know. Somebody shot him by the scaffolding behind Benson's just after ten last night.' Kersey's face split into a grin that would have intimidated a gorilla. 'So that brings us back to where we started.'

'You mean he was murdered?' Weakly.

'I mean he was murdered. As if you didn't know!'

'You don't think I . . . I mean, if I'd had anything to do with it do you think I'd have left my van here and come back — '

Kersey cut him short. 'Killers are usually stupid but some people might think it was a clever move to do just that. Did you know that Garland took his dog for a walk along the wharf every night?'

'No — yes.'

'We takes our choice. And you ask us to believe that out of a dozen car-parks and hundreds of side streets you could have chosen you picked this place by chance? Try telling that to your lawyer.'

'My God, I didn't kill him!'

'No? So what did you do?'

The boy paused and seemed to be gathering his wits. 'I admit I wanted to speak to him.'

'What about?'

He hesitated. 'We had that row — Anna and me. She said there was no future for us; me with no proper job and no prospects.'

'Well?'

71

'There's a cottage with three acres going on the Helston road. I know about market gardening and I could make a go of that. Vegetables for the health shop market, organically grown — that sort of thing.' He looked dubiously at Kersey as though he feared the very idea might provoke him to violence.

'And you thought your girl's father might put up the money?'

'As a loan — an investment.'

'Why not go and see him in the proper way instead of lurking around by night?'

He shook his head. 'I couldn't face Anna's aunt Beryl; she hates me — or Cathy Carne either, for that matter.'

'So what happened?'

'I saw him as he was crossing the car-park with his dog.' He was silent for a while and they could hear someone on the telephone in the main room.

Kersey prompted: 'And?'

'I followed him some way behind.'

'How far?'

'To just past Spargo's; I couldn't raise the nerve to catch him up and speak to him. All of a sudden it seemed to be the wrong time and the wrong way to go about it, what with it being the day of the old man's funeral and everything. . . . I decided after all it would be better to go and see him in the shop like you said — '

'If you got as far as Spargo's you must have seen him go under the scaffolding.'

'No, I didn't. I was some way behind, it was misty, and when I got there I couldn't see him. Then, all of a sudden, there was a sort of bang and the dog started yelping and I thought he must have fallen or something and that he might be hurt. I started running and when I reached this end of the scaffolding I saw a woman bending over something on the ground at the other end. I think she must have heard me because she ran off like the clappers towards the quay.'

'You said a woman.'

'I thought it was a woman at the time. Of course I could be wrong I suppose.'

'Wearing a skirt or trousers?'

72

'Oh, not a skirt — jeans I thought.'

'Thin or fat?'

'Not fat, definitely.'

'Short or tall?'

Time to ponder, then: 'Medium height, perhaps on the tall side for a woman.'

'Was he or she carrying anything?'

'Not that I could see.'

The questions were pressed but they could get nothing more definite: 'It looked like a woman.'

'Go on.'

He drew a deep breath. 'I went to look and though it was pretty dark I could see enough. It made me want to throw up. I wanted to get out. I went back to the van and the bloody thing wouldn't start so I waited there till morning when I could catch a bus and . . . and, well, just get out.'

At last he was packed off to sub-division: held for questioning.

Wycliffe said: 'Before we have to turn him loose — which we shall, get Lucy Lane over to Flushing to talk to the girl.'

Wycliffe drove the sixty miles home to another estuary while his team was given lodgings in the town.

The Wycliffes lived in The Watch House, a former coast-guard property overlooking the narrows on the Cornish side. They had a half-acre of garden, which Helen had planned and sedulously cultivated with shrubs and trees, and a plot for vegetables and fruit. Only a little-used footpath separated their garden from the shore.

He pulled into his drive as the church clock at St Juliot was striking eight; a perfect summer evening with the waters of the estuary a mirror to the sky. Helen was in the kitchen preparing a sweet savour as an offering to her lord.

'How did the inspection go?'

'It didn't. I'm on a case.'

'I know; I heard on the radio. You can pour me a sherry.'

'What are we eating?'

'I intended a salad but I thought you might have missed out

73

on lunch so we've got grilled lamb chops with minted potatoes and glazed carrots.'

'Smells nice.'

They sipped their sherry while Helen prepared a fresh fruit salad.

Wycliffe said: 'What do you know about Gifford Tate?'

'The painter? I know that he's dead, that he lived somewhere in West Cornwall, that his pictures are making high prices and that I wish we could afford one. I've got a catalogue of an exhibition of his somewhere and I'll look it out if you're interested. Come to think of it, I remember reading something recently about a new exhibition of his, going on tour. How's that?'

'All right for a start. Now try Edwin Garland.'

Helen frowned and pushed back the hair from her forehead, a habit she had when thinking. 'I've heard the name. Was he a painter too?'

'Was is the operative word: he died last Saturday.'

'Not murdered?'

'No, that distinction was reserved for his son. It seems that Garland and Tate were buddies in their day.'

'I'll see what I can find after we've eaten.'

The french windows of the living-room stood open while they ate and by the time they reached the coffee stage darkness had closed over the hills across the water.

'I'll get that catalogue.'

Helen was not long gone: she had a filing system which covered the composers and the painters she enjoyed. 'Here we are: a retrospective at the Hayward in 1976.'

The catalogue was a glossy production with several illustrations in colour and black-and-white. Wycliffe turned the pages. There was the usual synoptic paragraph or two: 'Born Egham 1907; studied at the Slade Schools. . . . Moved to Cornwall in 1927 and came to the notice of Stanhope Forbes. . . . Painted a great deal in the environs of Falmouth but also in Brittany, the Loire valley, and the Greek islands. . . . Although early in his career he was regarded as a protégé of Forbes he was largely uninfluenced by the so-called 'new realism' of the Newlyn school. . . . Like Alfred Sisley, whom he greatly admired, Tate was a painter of nature, and his work, though late, was in the main stream of Impressionist tradition.

'Despite a disabling stroke in 1970 he continued painting and, surprisingly, his work acquired an increased vigour; he adopted a more varied palette and made use of more vivid colours. It has been said that in recent years his allegiance shifted from Sisley to Monet!'

'Interesting! Tate died the following year — 1977.'

Helen smiled. 'I've heard it said that retrospectives are bad for the health.'

She handed him a Lyle's Price Guide, open at the right page: 'It's three years out of date but look at the prices.'

There were three Gifford Tates recorded as auctioned during the year: 'The Swanpool at Falmouth — signed and dated 1938 . . . oil on canvas . . . £17,550; The Loire at Amboise . . . 1963 . . . £12,610; Helford Village, near Falmouth . . . 1973 . . . £21,200 . . .'

Wycliffe closed the book. 'I see what you mean.'

'But what's it got to do with your case?'

'Good question. It's an odd business and it seems to be mixed up with Edwin Garland's will. He left his art shop and studio to his niece with the exception of his tube of Winsor blue and he left his tube of Winsor blue with £1,000 to the son of Gifford Tate. Another £1,000 goes to his friend, Burger to buy himself a pair of spectacles.'

'Sounds like Lewis Carroll.'

'Yes, the old man had a wry sense of humour though on the face of it the other provisions in his will are probably more important. The residue — a substantial chunk, was left jointly to his two offspring, Beryl and Francis. Now, with Francis dead, apparently intestate, his share goes to his illegitimate daughter, a twenty-year-old. She and her mother and, possibly, her boyfriend, are the only ones who obviously benefit from Francis Garland's death. The trouble is, I don't believe it's that simple.'

Wycliffe lazed in his chair, while Helen lost herself in the zany twilight world of Iris Murdoch. His mind drifted over the people whom he had heard about for the first time that morning, groping for some sort of perspective. He was intrigued by the trio: Gifford Tate, Edwin Garland and Papa Burger, their painting holidays and their week-ends in Burger's boat. Their expeditions recalled the all-male cultural sprees which were a commonplace before the first war. . . . In fact the whole case seemed somehow dated. The Garlands, and their shop with the rooms over, were out of period, relics of a time when the business and management of the town had been in the hands of a few prosperous traders. Wills were of immense significance and the contingent squabbles sometimes spilled over into acts of family treachery and even violence . . .

He tried to visualise the Garland household: Edwin, widower, intelligent, shrewd, inclined to be malicious, discreetly affluent. . . . Despite his chosen role as a small-town shopkeeper he seemed to have been accepted on equal terms by talented cosmopolitans. . . . He had married a beautiful wife.

His son, Francis: goggle-eyed, unprepossessing, in love only with himself and his notion of some sort of scholarly distinction. A youthful affair gave him a daughter, apparently without encumbrance. On two days a week he peddled art and printing materials around the county and, for the rest, he was nominally in charge of his father's printing works. Finally, according to the lawyer, it's likely that he was having a covert affair with a woman.

And Beryl . . . Beryl, with her tunnel vision in all matters of opinion and morality, played out her role of self-sacrificing daughter and sister to the men of the house. Beryl had a friend, and both were partial to little nips of whisky . . .

Downstairs in the shop, Cathy Carne, the niece, competent and a realist. She knew that her uncle's death would radically change her position but did she, as she said, believe that the change would be for the worse?

In all that, was there any motive for murder? Of the old man, perhaps, but it was the son who had been shot.

Wycliffe shifted irritably in his chair. 'Let's go to bed.'

Helen put down her book. 'A night-cap? Or would you prefer cocoa?'

Chapter Five

NEXT MORNING WYCLIFFE spent three hours at headquarters dealing with administrative routine: departmental reports, inter-departmental memoranda, overtime schedules, and duty rosters. Diane, his personal assistant, hovered ready to guide, caution and instruct. Then he spent half-an-hour with the Chief discussing the case. His lordship was moved to reflection.

'It looks like being another of your museum pieces, Charles. When you and I joined the force the majority of homicides were like that — family affairs, or at least concerned with intimate human relationships: legacies, jealousies, frustrated passions — always with a powerful personal element. What the papers called "human dramas". Now killings are more often than not anonymous, motiveless in the sense that there is no relational link between the killer and his victim. A man is murdered because he is a policeman, a security guard, a cashier, a black man, a white man, an Arab or a Jew. At the extreme, his death may be entirely incidental to some criminal lunatic making a political point, or just blind violence like the Belgian supermarket killings. Against that sort of background the old-style domestic homicide seems almost cosy.'

Wycliffe, anxious to get away, kept comment to a minimum.

The Chief sighed. 'It's part of the pattern, Charles; society disintegrates before our eyes and we are expected to paper over the cracks.'

It was mid-day before Wycliffe made his escape. He had his week-end bag in the car and, short of an emergency, it would be several days before he was home again. He lunched at a pub on the way down and arrived at the Incident Room shortly before two. Kersey and Lucy Lane were head to head over the reports. He felt that he had been a long time away.

Kersey said: 'We've no grounds for continuing to hold Terry Gill. I've got his statement and they're letting him go.'

Wycliffe turned to Lucy Lane. 'Anything from you? How did you get on with Anna? — and, by the way, what surname did she take?'

'Her mother's maiden name — Brooks; she's Anna Brooks. I got next to nothing from her, sir. Astonishment at her legacies — genuine, I'd say, though I couldn't be sure; she's a deep one. Intelligent. I must admit I liked her; she won't squander her grandfather's money, that's for sure. It seems she saw her father five or six times a year and her grandfather less often than that, though the old man used to send her substantial cash presents at Christmas and on her birthday.'

'And her mother?'

Lucy smiled. 'Fat, lives on junk foods, strong tea and gossip; short on conventional morality, I'd guess, but not a bad sort. The kind of woman I wouldn't mind having around if I was in trouble though she might be a bit of a trial at other times. She'd spread my business all round the neighbourhood but she'd lend a hand without grudging it.' Lucy was apologetic: 'I know it doesn't get us anywhere and it's subjective, but I can only say what impression I got.'

'Any mention of the boy?'

'They didn't know we'd picked him up and I didn't tell them. Anna was tight lipped about him but mother said: "Terry is a good lad at heart. He'll be back."'

'Fair enough. The women in this case are suspects in their own right, especially if we take notice of that boy, though from what you say I can't see Anna's mother hauling herself up on the scaffolding behind Benson's, or making a run for it when the boy turned up.'

The timetable of Francis's movements after his father's death was still full of gaps but that was to be expected. Edwin Garland had been found dead by his niece at two o'clock on the Saturday. Francis spent Saturday afternoon 'making arrangements' with the undertaker. On Saturday evening he had worked in his room. Sunday was blank. On Monday morning he registered the death and spent some time with Shrimpton —

the lawyer — his father's accountant, and the bank manager. In the afternoon he visited various people who had been on friendly terms with the dead man. He had used his car for these visits. On his return he wrote several letters rather hurriedly because he was anxious to catch the post. On Tuesday he seemed to resume his normal routine of business calls and brought in two or three orders. On Wednesday morning he called on Dr Tate and he had the funeral in the afternoon.

At two o'clock Wycliffe collected the dead man's keys from the duty officer and set out along the wharf. Approach from the rear. The wharf walk had remained closed to the public in case the lab boys wanted a second bite at the cherry. The weather was changing: blue-black clouds were building in the south-east and, as Wycliffe arrived at the back of the Garlands' shop, they obscured the sun. At the same time a wind blew briefly across the harbour, rippling the water and putting the gulls to squawking flight.

It was the first time he had taken a real look at the premises from the back. The building was of a slatey stone, pointed and well maintained; two floors and a couple of attics. The ground floor windows were low enough to look in and he could see into the little office, which was empty. The other windows must belong to the studio but the lower panes were dirty on the inside so that it was difficult to see anything. All the ground floor windows were fitted with iron bars, a sufficient deterrent for the average break-and-enter boys.

He tried the door of the side passage and, to his surprise, found it unlocked. He went right through the passage to the street and entered the shop like a customer. Cathy Carne and her assistant were both serving and he had to wait. Cathy was pale and drawn and she looked tired — not, he thought, like a woman who, expecting the sack, had found herself owning the business. When she was free she took him into the office and sank into a chair as though exhausted.

Wycliffe held out Francis's keys. 'Is the studio key amongst these?'

79

She examined the bunch and picked out a key. 'That's it, I think.'

A five-lever Chubb. The old man had believed in security, inside as well as out.

As he was about to leave the little office he turned back. 'Do you know if Francis had a woman friend?'

'I shouldn't think so.'

'There's Anna.'

'Proving that he's capable? I'd say it was interest he lacked.'

Evidently Francis had never made advances to his cousin.

A new thought occurred to Wycliffe. 'Tuesday was the day he went off in the van and came back with a bruised face; presumably you've got a record of the people he called on that day? Of course it's possible that he made other calls not in the line of business.'

'I wouldn't know about that but I can tell you the business calls he made.' From a drawer of her desk she brought out a number of pink slips clipped together and she separated the top three. 'These were his only calls — all deliveries promised for that day.'

Wycliffe looked the slips over. 'Do you know these people?'

'Only as customers. Bestway Arts and Crafts is a small business in Hayle, dealing mainly in craft stuff; they carry a stock of art materials as a sideline. It's run by a chap called Ferris. . . . The Archway Studio is just outside St Ives and belongs to a woman painter called Eileen Rich. All I know about her is that she's twice a widow. . . . Ah, I'd forgotten about this one: Kevin Brand, there could be a connection there. I've got a feeling he used to live in Falmouth. He has a place out on the downs between St Ives and Penzance, a school of occult studies, would you believe? He runs day classes and in the summer he takes residential students. We print his prospectus. It's possible that Francis found a kindred spirit there.'

Wycliffe made a note of the names. 'Now I'm going to take a look over the studio and I think you should be with me.'

'If you like.'

Having looked at the studio from the outside he was prepared for squalor, but a basic orderliness surprised him. It seemed to be a combination of workshop and studio. There were two easels, and the one near the door had a picture on it, a striking painting of the Falmouth waterfront. It was painted in blocks of flat colour, cleverly apposed, with more regard for pattern than form. Wycliffe was reminded of a stained glass window.

'Is this your uncle's work?'

She was examining a few canvases stacked against the wall but she looked up at his question. 'Yes.'

'Is this where you found him?'

She came over. 'Yes, he had a habit of propping himself on that stool in front of a picture and it must have gone over with him. When I found him his body was sprawled over the stool.'

'And this picture was on the easel then?'

'Yes.'

'Had he been working on it? It seems finished.'

'He may not have been working on it; more likely he was deciding how to frame it.'

Wycliffe looked at the painter's trolley drawn up by the easel. Tubes of colour laid out tidily; there were containers for oil and turps, and two jars containing brushes.

He glanced at the tubes. 'No Winsor blue?'

'No.' But she did not smile.

'And no palette.'

'What? He wouldn't have needed one if he wasn't painting, would he?' She went back to her stacked canvases.

'May I look?'

There were twelve or fifteen finished pictures, all painted in the same manner as the one on the easel, patterns of glowing colour, but the subjects ranged from harbour and river scenes to landscapes with figures.

'So this was your uncle's style?'

'Yes. It was the style he seemed to prefer though he didn't always stick to it. He was attracted to Gauguin and the Pont Aven group.'

'In contrast with Gifford Tate.'

'Yes, Tate saw himself as an Impressionist.'

'And Burger?'

81

'Burger wasn't in the same class as the other two, he didn't pretend to be.'

'But he must have been keen.'

'Yes, he's very knowledgeable about painting and painters but not much of a painter himself.'

Her answers were terse, her manner preoccupied, and she was restless. She moved to another part of the studio and started to turn over a number of stretched canvases, all of them blank.

'What are you looking for?'

'I'm not looking for anything.' She realised that more was called for and went on: 'I'm curious because I've never had a chance to look round here before.'

'Not when your uncle was alive?'

'No, he kept the studio locked except when he was working, then he hated to be disturbed.'

Dark clouds now covered the sky and what could be seen of the harbour was a study in greys, slate blues and silver. It was starting to rain, fat drops slid viscously down the window panes. Cathy switched on the studio lights, further exposing its tattiness but adding to its intimacy.

Wycliffe had found Edwin's books stacked on two tiers of rough shelving. All of them were the worse (or better) for much use. No glossy volumes of coloured reproductions; most were concerned with the history and philosophy of art — Tolstoy's *What is Art?* Collingwood, Roger Fry, Greenberg, Arason, Rewald . . . not forgetting Fischer with the Gospel according to the Comrades. There were studio manuals —— one with a fly-leaf inscription: 'To Eddie from Gifford. Christmas 1936' —— and five or six sketchbooks with pencil and watercolour sketches. If, in his paintings, Garland had sacrificed form to colour and design, it was not because he couldn't draw.

Cathy was continuing her inspection as though she would make an inventory.

Wycliffe said: 'It's all yours now.'

'Yes, I suppose so.'

'Is it possible that there was some secret in your uncle's life which he confided to Francis and which Francis tried to use to his advantage?'

He wondered why portmanteau questions always turned out so damned pompous.

Cathy Carne was derisive: 'You mean did uncle have a secret, which Francis could use to blackmail somebody else? A bit unlikely, wouldn't you say? In any case if he had a secret, Francis is the last person he would have told.'

'Yet we have evidence that your uncle did tell Francis something about himself which Francis found it hard to believe.'

She became obstinate. 'In that case I've no idea what it could be. It all sounds very improbable.'

He was moving about the studio with an apparent aimlessness looking at whatever caught his eye. He examined the rack of mouldings used for making frames and seemed interested in the machine for mitreing the angles. There was a small knee-hole desk and he went through the drawers but found nothing more than discarded pens, broken pencils, old catalogues, a quantity of scrap paper, and an assortment of pins and clips.

From time to time Cathy Carne looked across at him with obvious unease. No doubt she was wondering what it was he expected to find. He wondered himself. What was he doing, prowling about the old man's studio like a nosey neighbour? Either the place was worth searching or it wasn't. Turn it over to a couple of men to take the place apart, or leave it alone. 'You lack a professional attitude, my boy!' He'd been told that often enough in the old days. Time to behave like a policeman.

'We have a witness to the killing.'

She turned abruptly.'A witness? You mean somebody saw Francis killed?' Unbelieving.

'From a distance, yes. The witness is under the strong impression that Francis was attacked by a woman.'

'A woman? . . .' She seemed about to add something but did not.

'Where were you on Wednesday night?'

She made an angry movement but controlled herself. 'I suppose you have to ask that. I was at home all the evening.'

'Alone?'

A momentary hesitation, then: 'Yes.'

'It would be sensible to tell me the truth.'

'I've told you. I was alone.' She turned away.

'Your flat is within two hundred yards of the spot where Francis was killed. You can see the place from at least one of your windows.'

'I've told you; I knew nothing about what had happened until I was at work next morning and one of your policemen came with the news.'

'What did your uncle say in his letter to you?'

'I've told you.'

'No. Your answer was an evasion.'

'I told you that the letter gave me advice on how to deal with the family and that is all.'

'I'll leave it at that for the moment but I may have to ask you that question again. Anyway, I've finished here for the present.'

'Do I get the key of the studio now?'

'Not yet.'

Wycliffe opened the door, waited for her to switch out the lights and pass through, then he locked the door and pocketed the keys. Cathy went into the shop and Wycliffe let himself out into the little hall from which stairs led up to the flat. He happened to glance up and saw Beryl on the landing. She beckoned to him mysteriously and he went up to her.

She spoke in a low voice: 'I heard you down there with her.' It was an accusation but delivered without punch. She seemed subdued, almost amiable. 'I want to talk to you. In here . . .'

She took him into the living-room and made him sit in the black leather armchair. He thought she might be on the point of offering him a nip of whisky but she did not go that far. She remained standing, evidently not very sure how to begin.

Outside a massive pall of cloud hung low over the harbour.

At last she began: 'I've come to see things differently since I've had time to think over what was in the will. I didn't understand at first. When they were lowering my father's coffin into his grave I thought to myself "It's all over!" I should have known better; he'd worked it all out, planned it move by move, just like when he was playing chess.'

'What had he planned?'

'How he could cause the maximum unpleasantness to those he left behind — mainly to me. Nobody, of course, will believe it: "He was such a *nice* man — a bit sarcastic at times but only in a playful sort of way." That's what people said about him. Even my friend, Celia Bond, says I'm imagining things, that I'm suffering from delayed shock or some such nonsense. We had words about it and I told her to go! Of course Celia was an only child — and spoilt; she can't believe that a father would get pleasure by humiliating his children. She's no idea!'

It was astonishing. Beryl was perfectly composed; she was no longer flushed and her hair was tidy; she even had a small smile on her lips. She had found an explanation of events which satisfied her, an explanation which in a curious way brought her contentment. She was being persecuted and it was part of a carefully laid plan. She was no longer the victim of chance, of a malign fate. Someone had hated her enough to. . . . She could live with that, and fight back.

Suddenly the rain came, bursting out of the sky, beating against the window panes, and lashing the surface of the harbour into misty spray.

'Why should your father want to humiliate you?'

'He's done it all my life, it's nothing new. I was not the daughter he wanted. A girl child should be soft and pretty and loving; she should learn to titillate and flatter her father. . . . Of course I failed on all counts and so I was ignored most of the time — passed over. "Beryl!" . . . I can hear him saying it now as only he could, turning my name into an insult.'

'Did Francis suffer too?'

'It wasn't the same. Francis was a boy.'

'How does your father continue to humiliate you now that he is dead?'

She looked at him. 'You ask that after hearing the details of his will? I'm turned out of the house where I was born whether I want to go or no, the house and the business are handed over to . . . to that woman, and I have to share what is left in a *joint* legacy with Francis!'

She broke off as though to allow this to sink in then went on: 'Father knew perfectly well that my brother and I didn't agree, that we would part as soon as possible, so he made sure that we would be tied together in all the wrangling that would go on because of the joint legacy.' She made a vigorous gesture. 'It was his idea of a good joke!'

The lawyer had said of the will: 'A recipe for in-fighting . . . I think he saw himself sitting up there, watching the fun.'

Wycliffe said, quietly: 'There will be no wrangling with Francis now.'

She took him up at once. 'No! I shall have to deal with that girl, but now I understand . . .'

'You can't blame that on your father.'

She looked at him oddly. 'You think not? Who killed Francis and *why* was he killed? I know what I said. That was when I wanted to keep whatever scandal there was, in the family. Now things have changed. When you find out why Francis was killed you'll also find that my father had a hand in it.'

She lowered her voice: 'There are still secrets. Francis knew something — he was smug enough about it. Cathy Carne had a letter handed to her by the lawyer. They are things we know about; God knows what else there is!'

'Are you saying that you feel threatened?'

She pursed her lips. 'I can take care of myself. But I shan't let him continue to ruin my life. That's what he wanted but he won't get away with it. Now that I understand I shall come to terms. You'll see! I'm not the fool he took me for!'

'Just one question: if you had inherited the shop and premises would you have kept it going?'

'Yes, there have been Garlands running that business for nearly ninety years, but it would have been run my way.'

'With or without Cathy Carne?'

A wrinkling of the nose. 'That would have been up to her.'

'But I understood that you intended to live with your friend after your father died.'

'That was because I assumed that the business would go to Francis and then I would have had no say in it.'

Back in the street the rain had eased but there was more to come. On his way back to the Incident Room Wycliffe had to weave a way through milling crowds who had deserted the beaches and taken to window shopping.

He was intrigued by the three old men: Edwin Garland, Gifford Tate and Papa Burger. A friendship, begun in their twenties, had been sustained throughout their lives. Week-ends and holidays were spent together, presumably to the neglect of their families; they had their private jokes, their shared experiences, and above all their obsession with art.

It sounded harmless, even pleasant. Did he have any reason to link their activities with the murder of Garland's son? To begin with, only the coincidence of the deaths of father and son within four days of each other; beyond that his notion of a connection had been no more than a hunch, and he had been in the business too long to back his hunches far ahead of evidence. But now, here was Beryl vigorously maintaining that her father had 'worked it all out — planned it move by move'. She was even ready to see her father's hand in the murder of his son. On the face of it, an absurdity, but was there an element of sense in what she had said?

The lawyer, the printing works foreman, and Beryl had each of them offered facets of the old man's character which suggested not only a cynical vein of humour and a streak of malice but a disdainful attitude to at least some of those closest to him.

There was a strong case for finding out more about Edwin and there were two sources so far untapped: Papa Burger and Edwin's brother Thomas.

The lights were on in the Incident Room. Another rain squall blotted out the harbour and water cascaded down the window panes. Now and then lightning flickered through the gloom, the lights dimmed, and thunder rattled every loose panel and plank in the building. Lucy Lane was typing a report.

'I've just come back from the Thomas Garlands' place, sir.'

'Let's hear it.'

'A modest house with a small garden where the grass looks as though it has been cut with nail-scissors and weeded with a forceps; a dolls' house, with nothing out of place, everything polished and dusted.'

87

Lucy Lane always set the scene and he liked that.

'We talked in the living-room which merges into a conservatory choked with potted plants like a burgeoning rain forest. Thomas is five or six years younger than his brother, knocking seventy; he's tall, lean and a bit owlish. He's not very talkative except on the subject of his plants. He used to teach English in a comprehensive school and he probably had a rough time of it.

'I was daft enough to say his plants looked healthy and I got the Ancient Mariner treatment; a squirt-by-puff account of how he managed it. Luckily, after a while, I noticed a framed photograph of a young man on the sideboard and diverted the flow by asking if it was of his son — '

She broke off as a blue lightning flash coincided with an ear-shattering thunder clap and released a fresh torrent of rain. For a moment or two they watched the rain bouncing off the waters of the harbour.

'It was a photograph of Mark and I heard how he'd qualified as a chiropractor and set up in Falmouth where it's uphill work. Then we got round to Edwin's death and Francis's murder. He seemed genuinely distressed but quite useless. He said his lawyer had persuaded him to contest his father's will and that he'd regretted it ever since. He would have liked to have gone to his brother's funeral but he thought it would only have made matters worse. As to Francis, well, it was inconceivable that such a thing could happen. Let's hope his son can be more helpful.'

'You haven't seen him?'

'No, I spoke to him on the phone. I thought it better to tackle him outside of business hours. I told him I would call at the house this evening but he said he'd prefer to come here. He's coming when he finishes work at about six.'

Wycliffe turned up the reports of telephone enquiries made among Francis's customers to find Kevin Brand of The School of Occult Studies, Carn Kellow, near Penzance. Brand had said, 'Mr Garland came here early on Tuesday afternoon; he delivered some printing work I had ordered and we had a brief conversation. He told me that his father had died over the weekend. . . . Yes, I knew him when I lived in Falmouth five or six years ago . . .'

Worth following up.

Kersey came in and Wycliffe put him in the picture.

'You want me to see this guy, sir?'

'Find out what you can about him first. The local nicks at Penzance and St Ives must have some idea what goes on in a set-up like that on their doorsteps.' He turned to Lucy Lane: 'I'm leaving Mark Garland to you. For the next hour or thereabouts I shall be at the Burgers' house in Wood Lane.'

'They called me Papa because I was the eldest, three years older than Gifford, six years older than Eddie.' Then, wryly: 'There may have been another reason; even as a young man I was a staid sort of chap and they were a bit wild at times. I suppose I was inclined to lay down the law.' The old man laughed. 'I first met Eddie Garland at Lamorna, in 1931, I think it was, when we were both in an outdoor painting group with Birch. I've never been more than a dabbler but I've always had an eye for a painter and I saw at once that he was one. It turned out that we both lived in Falmouth. I was already friendly with Tate, and Eddie knew him through the shop, so we soon made a threesome and we kept together for nearly fifty years.'

Burger was very thin and very tall; he sat back in his armchair, his bony frame draped rather than clothed by a grey light-weight suit. He had kept a sufficiency of silvery hair, his aristocratic face was deeply lined and his yellowed teeth projected slightly under a clipped moustache. His voice was high pitched and from time to time he emphasised his points by restrained movements of his hands. Near his chair was a walking frame.

'My legs have let me down.'

But despite his disability his eyes had a twinkle and Wycliffe felt that he was in the presence of a truly contented man.

Wycliffe said: 'In 1931, as I work it out, Garland would have been twenty-one and already a husband and father.'

A wary look. 'Yes, that is so.'

'I've seen Gifford Tate's portrait of Garland's wife; she must have been a very lovely girl.'

'Oh, she was. Judy was beautiful.'

Mrs Burger, a little dumpling of a woman in linen trousers and a smock, like a Chinese peasant, was listening and smiling. 'Oh, don't be so stodgy, Martin! Mr Wycliffe will hear it all from someone else if you don't tell him.'

Burger deftly arranged the creases in his trousers. 'Ah! I have my brief! Well, Judy was an assistant in the shop and the two young people, both about nineteen, were drawn together. Judy became pregnant and, against his father's wishes, Edwin married her. The child, Beryl, was born and everybody seemed content except that gossip insisted the child was not Edwin's.'

Mrs Burger interrupted: 'With good reason! The girl had been seeing a lot of another young man, an estate agent called Jose, and that association continued after the marriage — long after! Long enough to explain Francis also.'

Burger spread his hands. 'My dear Penny, you have no reason to suggest any such thing — '

'Anyone who knew Jose and looks at Francis doesn't need a reason.'

Wycliffe said: 'Doesn't this imply either remarkable tolerance or remarkable ignorance on Garland's part?'

Burger did a tactical throat clearing but his wife had no qualms. 'Of course it does! But nobody has ever been able to decide which. I doubt if anyone ever dared broach the subject to Edwin and sometimes I think he simply believed what he wanted to believe, that the two were his.'

'Because he was so deeply in love with his wife?'

Burger sighed. 'My goodness, we are getting into deep water!' He glanced up at the mantel clock, then across at Mrs Burger. 'Do you think, perhaps, a cup of tea, dear? It's about our usual time.'

Mrs Burger left them alone and Burger looked at Wycliffe with a small self-conscious smile.

It was raining hard now, beating on the window panes, and the room was in semi-darkness. A pleasantly neutral room: dove grey walls, a Persian square on the floor, grey velvet curtains and white woodwork. But on the walls Edwin

Garland's pictures glowed with dramatic intensity and a curious effect of translucence.

'You obviously admire Garland's painting.'

'Oh, I do! I think Garland was a truly notable painter, and very versatile. He chose to paint in this particular style but his earlier work was quite different.'

Wycliffe teased. 'All this despite your legacy?'

A dry chuckle. 'Edwin was always a joker but the point was that he seemed to undervalue his own work and to think less of my judgement because I did not. I often told him — and so did Tate — that he did himself less than justice by being content to stand in Tate's shadow. Gifford painted excellent pictures, very pleasant pictures — he was a painter of nature, but that, in my opinion, is not of itself art; I agree with Gauguin's cautionary advice to a young novice: "Don't copy nature too much. Art is an abstraction."'

'You have none of Tate's pictures?'

'Oh, yes. I have two, but not in this room. The works of the two painters don't make good stable mates. In any case my Tates are on loan to the exhibition — you know about the exhibition, I suppose?'

'Yes, indeed.'

'A big thing; Edwin was largely responsible for getting it off the ground. He put me on the committee and now they've persuaded me to open the thing.'

'Garland seems to have been a very modest man.'

Burger put the tips of his fingers together and considered what he would say. 'Modest? Modest in the sense that he never proclaimed his talents — and they were real and varied: he was, I have heard, a very good businessman, and I know him to have been a first rate chess player and a notable painter.' Burger shifted his position and looked at Wycliffe with a gentle smile. 'But people who know their true worth often do not feel the need to go about asserting it. I do not think that Edwin set any great value on other people's opinions.'

'What do you know about Winsor blue? I understand that it was the subject of another of Garland's jokes.'

The old man nodded. 'Yes, it was, but it was something

between Gifford and Edwin. I was never in on the joke, whatever it was. All I can tell you is that Winsor blue is one of the trade names for an intense blue pigment, copper phthalocyanine, which came into the palette sometime in the thirties. It was favoured by many painters as a substitute for prussian blue. Gifford dated his success from the time he started to use it; he signed his pictures with Winsor blue and a dab of the pure colour occurs somewhere in them, a sort of trademark.' Burger spread his hands. 'Painters are as superstitious as fishermen. By the same token, Edwin told me that Gifford stopped using it after his stroke.'

From somewhere in the house came the rattle of teacups on a tray. Burger leaned forward quickly and, lowering his voice, said: 'Returning to our earlier subject, Garland half believed himself to be impotent — he probably was, but he was obsessed by that damned girl he married and although she was good to look at, that was all — she was an immoral woman! Ah! That looks very nice, my dear! . . . Could you place that little table, Mr Wycliffe? . . . These legs of mine!'

'Lemon or milk, Mr Wycliffe?'

They drank a highly aromatic China tea and ate little biscuits made with rice flour and honey, spiced with cinnamon.

Wycliffe said: 'Gifford Tate's pictures are fetching high prices. I thought any well-known painter's work tended to slump in market value for several years after his death.'

Burger sipped his tea and patted his moustache. 'Yes, but that isn't a law of nature, Mr Wycliffe; it is sometimes the result of manipulation. It gives interested parties a chance to buy in cheaply. Then, in a few years, one or two judiciously placed magazine articles, the odd programme on TV, an opportune book, and the painter is resurrected with all his best work in the right hands.'

'But Tate's pictures seem to have avoided the doldrums; his prices have much more than kept pace with inflation.'

'Because Edwin, as Gifford's art executor, was very astute and Marcella has much to thank him for. Gifford left most of his money, and the income from his pictures, to Marcella while the house went to Alan.'

'Let me see; Alan is Tate's son — the doctor.'

'Yes, the doctor — a very good one, too. Alan has compassion and that's all too rare in his profession.'

'And Marcella?'

'Marcella is Gifford Tate's wife.'

Mrs Burger amended: 'She is Gifford's *second* wife. His first left him while Alan was still at school. Gifford was sixty-one when he married Marcella, then twenty-two. So she is about the same age as her stepson. People who don't know take them for man and wife.'

Burger smiled: 'But there will be very few who do not know if it is left to you, dear. Anyway! Tate left a number of finished canvases which had never been shown and Edwin decided to release them at the rate of one a year through Ismay Gorton's, the London gallery which handles his work. It has become a minor occasion in the art world. Each year since Tate died the "new Tate" has been unveiled with champagne and gourmet titbits for those privileged to receive tickets for the preview. I attended the first two or three, before my legs started to trouble me.'

'And these unveilings have been going on for eight years? Are there more to come?'

Burger held up a thin hand. 'I'm not sure, but Edwin told me once that there was less than a dozen pictures altogether. Meanwhile, of course, there is this touring exhibition. Will you be going to see it, by the way?'

'I shall try to.'

Burger looked at him with an odd expression: 'I think you should come to a personal preview on Sunday afternoon when I shall be there making sure everything is ready for Monday.'

Wycliffe drove back to the Incident Room with rain lashing against his windscreen. From the fading elegance of tree-lined Wood Lane to the Wharf car park is no more than 500 yards for a purposeful crow, but for a motorist on the one-way system it is the better part of a mile.

So Edwin Garland had almost certainly been incapable of fathering a child. If that was the discovery Francis had made

93

and mentioned in his diary it might have caused him distress but it was hard to see it as providing a motive for his murder.

From his visit to the Burgers, Wycliffe had learned something about art, more about the art trade, and a good deal about Edwin Garland, but he wondered whether it had brought him any closer to establishing a motive for the murder of Francis.

Kersey, kite flying, with a wary eye on Wycliffe, expressed the same doubt. 'This guy was shot at night, on a deserted bit of the wharf. I'm not saying it was a mugging, muggers don't use guns, not on our patch they don't — yet. The chances are we shall turn up some perfectly simple motive. I don't see why we have to drag in father and father's pals with all this art business. Of course I'm only an ignorant peasant and I don't understand these things.'

Lucy Lane rose to the bait and, if she felt out-ranked, she didn't show it.

'I don't see where that argument leads. Garland was murdered because he was Garland, or it was a motiveless killing, or it was a mistake. The fact remains that he was murdered on the night after his father's funeral and if the two are unconnected we are back in the funny coincidences department. That's why father comes into the picture, art or no art.'

Kersey grinned. 'There now, see what it is to have the logic! All I'm saying is that we don't have to go groping about in corners looking for motive, there's plenty of it lying about. His daughter Anna might well have expected to benefit from his death. Her boyfriend likewise, though indirectly. Then there's Cathy Carne. According to her she was convinced that Francis would inherit and dispose of the business, but she might have thought she could do a deal with Beryl. In fact it's not impossible they had an arrangement. Although I can't see Beryl clambering over scaffolding with a .32 tucked in her pants, she'd be quite capable of doing it by proxy. Until she knew what was in the old man's will she and Cathy seem to have been matey enough. Last, but not least, there's the shadowy woman referred to in his diary.'

Wycliffe said: 'Coming down to earth, have you found out anything about Brand?'

94

'Nothing about the local connection yet but I've had a word with the boys at Penzance. Seems he bought a small-holding on the moor a few years back and set up these classes. I gather there are plenty of crackpots who go in for that sort of thing. It's probably harmless, even pleasantly nutty, and Brand makes a living out of them but there's another side to his business: the school attracts more than its share of gays, especially for the residential courses in the summer.'

'You're looking into the local angle?'

'Curnow's handling that, sir.'

Less than 36 hours after the discovery of the body, facts were coming in at a fair rate, though it was still not possible to decide which were relevant and which not. DS Shaw's computer, over in the corner, blank-faced and brooding, was being well fed on a mixed diet.

Chapter Six

WYCLIFFE WAS BOOKED in at a hotel on the waterfront, up river from the wharf and facing the village of Flushing across a narrow stretch of water. For a century or more, in the age of sail, the hotel had been associated with the Packet Service, when Falmouth was the port through which overseas mail and important travellers entered and left the country. Now, with its near neighbour the yacht club, it caters for nautical types of the amateur sort who enjoy messing about in boats. Appropriately the dining room seems to rise almost directly out of the water.

Wycliffe shared a table with a merchant captain whose ship was in dock, a quiet spoken man on the verge of retirement. He had a cottage in the Cotswolds waiting for him and his wife to move in.

'What will you do — in retirement, I mean?'

The Captain laughed. 'Grow roses and keep hens — isn't that the recipe for retired seamen? No; I shall be satisfied just to stop worrying about schedules, cargoes, bunkering, crews, port dues and God knows what else. I'll get by.'

They ate chicken with tarragon, followed by fresh peaches with cream, and split a bottle of Chablis between them.

The case, reported in local newspapers and on the radio, was being talked about, and Wycliffe was aware of other diners watching him. Perhaps generations of detective story writers, from Wilkie Collins down, are responsible for the romantic image of criminal investigation, so that even for a modern hard-bitten public the initials C.I.D. retain a certain mystique.

'You're a celebrity,' the Captain said.

During the meal the rain stopped and the clouds cleared magically, giving way to one of those serenely peaceful summer evenings when harbour and estuary seem embalmed in golden light and one feels that the whole world is waiting.

Wycliffe decided on a walk and his walk took him along Green Bank and down the High Street, where crumbling houses and shops were being rejuvenated or demolished, into the main street.

The Captain had set him thinking about retirement. What would he do when his turn came? Living in a cottage in the Cotswolds or anywhere else isn't an occupation. In any case he was already living where he intended to retire. 'Prepare in advance, cultivate an interest — find a hobby,' the pundits said. Well, he had plenty of interests but none sufficiently systematic to qualify as a hobby. He was not a collector; he did not watch birds, badgers or insects; photography bored him; he was not very good with his hands and the do-it-yourself world of planers, drills, jig-saws, band-saws and sanders had no appeal; he enjoyed gardens, but gardening was a chore. Perhaps he would end up like Emperor Francis of Austria — making toffee.

As though his feet were programmed he found himself at the Incident Room. DC Dixon put out his cigarette and tried to look busy.

'Just one report, sir. A Mrs Richards of Clarence Villa, almost opposite where the Tates live, says she saw Francis Garland on Wednesday morning. He drove up, got out of his car and went in — '

'We know that.'

'Yes, sir, it's in the reports, but she said he was carrying a fairly large flat package — like a picture. She didn't attach any importance to it at the time and it was only when she heard we were interested in anyone who had seen Garland between Saturday and Wednesday that she thought it worth mentioning.'

If nothing else it was a cue for a visit to the Tates.

Wycliffe said: 'You come from this part of the world, don't you?'

'I was born here, sir; my parents and married sisters still live here.'

'Do you know anything about Dr Tate? I mean, is he a popular doctor?'

'Very! It's difficult to get on his list. My mother and sisters swear by him. The funny thing is, he's not very chatty or friendly; people say he's a very shy man.'

'Any gossip?'

'Only that he's living with his stepmother who's younger than he is. People talk but there's probably nothing in it.'

Lucy Lane was at her table, typing serenely: straight back, elbows to sides, using the ten digits God had given her. The only member of the squad who could; the others hammered or pecked with two fingers, swore picturesquely, and reached for the erasing fluid. Wycliffe remembered Mark Garland.

'How did you get on?'

She swivelled on her chair to face him. 'I don't think I did, sir. He's a different proposition from his father. I got the impression that chiropractice — which turns out to be spinal manipulation — isn't a money spinner in this part of the world. Either for that reason or another he's got a monumental chip on his shoulder. He reminded me of the tight-lipped heroes in war films — the name and number ploy; more you will not get even if you carve strips off me. I tried to persuade him that he wasn't threatened, wasn't accused, wasn't even suspected of anything, but he wouldn't have it. He said: "If you think I killed my cousin it is up to you to prove it. I've no alibi. I was out running on Wednesday night at ten o'clock; I am most nights at that time."'

'You say he was out running?'

'He's a keep-fit buff.'

Wycliffe sighed.

'I asked him about his attitude to his cousin and he said he didn't have an attitude but that he was very upset.' Lucy swept her hair away from her face with both hands. 'He was certainly upset about something. I know it sounds thin, sir, but I spent a long time getting no further than that and I don't think we shall do better until we have an angle — some sort of leverage.'

'Not to worry. Something will turn up. Meanwhile we shall keep an eye on him. I'm on my way to talk to Dr Tate.'

'Do you want me with you, sir?'

Wycliffe hesitated but decided not. He located Tate's house

on the wall map. It was at the southern end of 'the terraces' one of the older residential areas of the town, and not far from the Burgers'.

He had the choice of half-a-dozen alleys which led off the main street and climbed to the terraces. The alleys were steep and there were steps at intervals but there was a sense of achievement in reaching the top. His choice had more than its share of steps and when he eventually arrived on a pleasant terrace overlooking the harbour, a pounding in his chest reminded him once more that he was middle-aged. But the Tates' house was only a couple of hundred yards away.

Tregarthen — the house in a garden, Wycliffe's Cornish stretched that far — stood, aloof from the terraced houses, surrounded by a stone wall topped by shrubs. Three or four pine trees created a sombre atmosphere in the evening sun. There were green-painted double gates and a wicket for pedestrians. A brass plate on the wicket: Dr Alan Tate MB, B.Ch., FRCP. A fellowship! What was he doing, slumming it as a GP? Wycliffe passed through into a large, well kept garden — too well kept for his taste: shrubs pruned, grass like a bowling green, edges trimmed. Why not do the whole thing in plastic? The gravelled drive split into two; one branch led to the front door, the other to the back of the house and, according to a finger post, to waiting room and surgery.

A newish Volvo was parked near the house, the off-side front had been damaged and the lamp-housing smashed.

The house itself was 1914 or a bit earlier, steeply pitched slate roofs and high chimneys: bijou Lutyens for the leaner purse. Wycliffe pressed a bell push in a door with stained glass panels. A dog yapped frantically somewhere inside and was subdued. A woman's voice, strident. Footsteps, then the door opened: a man, fortyish, glasses, slim, dark, meticulously groomed; tailored slacks, a silk shirt open at the neck and patent leather house shoes.

'Yes?' Distant.

'Dr Tate?' Wycliffe introduced himself.

Attention focused: 'Ah, yes, I suppose you've come about Garland. You'd better come in.'

A tiled hall with a large oak chest and a long-case clock. Hesitation about which room would be appropriate, then a decision. 'I've been working in my surgery, perhaps we could talk there.'

Tate spoke slowly and precisely as though each word was carefully selected, examined and polished before being released.

Wycliffe followed him down a carpeted passage to a door at the end, a small room overlooking a regimented back garden with a substantial Swiss-type chalet in the middle of the lawn. Gifford Tate's studio? The surgery was equipped with the usual furniture but out of the best catalogue: desk and swivel chair for the doctor, a couple of hygienic-looking chairs for patient and friend, drugs and instrument cabinet, couch, wash basin, and glass-fronted bookcase. Parquet flooring. No dust, no smears on the polished woodwork; a faint and rather pleasing odour of antiseptic.

'Please sit down.'

Wycliffe was half expecting to be asked: 'What exactly is the trouble?' but Tate did not speak; he waited, apparently relaxed, his thin, pale hands resting on the desk in front of him.

'You attended Edwin Garland in his last illness and you were called in at his death. According to your certificate coronary thrombosis was the immediate cause of death.' Wycliffe could not have explained why he had adopted this abrupt, almost challenging approach; the doctor made him feel uneasy.

Tate still did not speak and Wycliffe was forced to enlarge. 'I'm not questioning your judgement but I have to ask whether in view of what followed you have had any doubts?'

'None whatever. Strictly speaking, Garland died of myocardial infarction resulting from a thrombus in a coronary artery.'

'Did his general condition lead you to expect something of the sort?'

Time to consider. Tate doled out words with seeming reluctance. 'Garland was seventy-five, he suffered from atherosclerosis and there was a history of anginal attacks. I warned him that unless he adhered strictly to the regimen I prescribed he would be at considerable risk.' The doctor brought his hands together and seemed to study them. 'But I fail to understand your interest in all this. Surely it is Francis's death you are investigating?'

Wycliffe was brusque. 'The deaths of father and son within a few days of each other raise questions to which I have to find satisfactory answers. You were a friend of the family, I believe?'

'My father and Edwin Garland were very close friends, so much so that I was brought up to regard Beryl and Francis as cousins.'

'And when you came back here after your father's death, to set up in practice, did you resume a family relationship with the Garlands?'

A brief hesitation. 'No. We remained on first-name terms, they became my patients, but I cannot say that there was any particular relationship between us.'

'You are a beneficiary under Edwin Garland's will, I believe?'

'A thousand pounds.'

'And a tube of Winsor blue.'

A slight gesture of impatience. 'A joke.'

'Not one with much meaning for you, I imagine?'

No response.

Wycliffe was getting nowhere, though Tate was answering his questions without protest and, apparently, without guile. In fact, that was part of the trouble, more often than not it is the protestations and evasions of a witness which tell most about him. But there was more to it than that: Wycliffe had not made contact, he had not found the tender spot which, when probed, yields a reflex rather than a reasoned response. He wondered if a three-cornered exchange might be more enlightening.

'I had intended to talk with Mrs Tate also; I wonder if she would join us?'

A brief frown. 'I'm afraid that isn't possible. Mrs Tate is not at all well and she has gone to bed.'

'I'm sorry! A sudden indisposition?'

A pause while he considered his reply. 'She has been unwell for some time; she is liable to spells of nervous depression. In any case I think I can answer your questions without disturbing her.' He fiddled with the batch of NHS forms in front of him. For the first time he had been nudged slightly off balance.

A difficult man to know; perhaps shy, possibly arrogant. A meticulous man, with a compelling need for orderliness, distancing himself from anything which might threaten the harmonious life he was striving to create. When and how did he unwind? And with whom? It was hard to imagine him having a casual chat with anyone, let alone a more intimate relationship. Of course there was Marcella, but one can usually tell, from the way a man speaks of a woman, if there is an emotional involvement and, despite Mrs Burger, Wycliffe felt reasonably sure that Tate did not seek release in the arms of his stepmother.

He tried again: 'When Edwin Garland collapsed in his studio and you were called in, he was lying close to one of the two easels in the studio — is that correct?'

'The one nearest the door.'

'Was there a painting on that easel?'

'Yes. I feel sure there was.'

'Can you say which painting?'

'No, I had other things on my mind.'

'I have heard that Francis Garland brought a picture here on the morning of the funeral — is that correct?'

A faint smile — the first. 'Our neighbour has been talking, but it is quite true. Francis came to tell us about arrangements for the funeral and he brought with him one of my father's pictures which had been taken to the shop for framing. It was a tradition that Edwin should frame all my father's work but his death made that impossible in this instance so Francis returned the picture.'

Game and set.

But Wycliffe fought back: 'Will the picture be in the exhibition?'

Tate's brown eyes, enlarged by his spectacles, gazed intently at Wycliffe for a moment or two before he replied: 'No. Mrs Tate has a contract with the Ismay Gorton Gallery covering all works that were not exhibited before my father's death. I believe that it is to be shown there in February.'

Something prompted Wycliffe to ask: 'May I see the picture?'

Tate was clearly surprised and irritated by the request but after a moment or two of hesitation he said: 'Very well, if you wish. I'll fetch it.'

Wycliffe was left alone. Dusk was closing in, the garden had acquired a certain mystery in the twilight and the room itself was in near darkness. He wondered why Tate had not joined a group practice like most of his colleagues. Perhaps it was just another instance of a preference for his own company.

Tate returned with the picture. It was of moderate size — about two feet by three. He switched on the light before holding up the picture for Wycliffe's inspection. 'There you are! I am afraid the lighting is not ideal.' Sarcastic.

The village of Flushing, as seen from Falmouth in the early morning, with mist rising from the harbour. A good picture, Wycliffe thought, in the Impressionist style.

'Thank you. When was that painted?'

Tate put the picture down. 'I can't tell you exactly, but sometime after he had his stroke. No doubt it is in the record. I assume that it matters to your investigation?' The doctor was becoming more aggressive.

'I have no idea what matters or does not matter at this stage.'

Tate returned to his swivel chair. 'My father left his pictures to his wife; they are really not my concern. Edwin Garland was his art executor and looked after all the business arrangements.' He looked significantly at the little battery clock on his desk.

Wycliffe said: 'I won't keep you longer than necessary, but I should appreciate your opinion of Francis — the sort of man he was.'

'I am not a psychiatrist.'

'And you consider that only a psychiatrist's opinion would be of value?'

A faint flush on the pale cheeks. 'I did not say that!'

'Francis Garland was your patient; did he often visit you professionally?'

'Very rarely. He seemed to enjoy good health.'

'I gather that he led a lonely life with few friends.'

'I believe that is so.'

'Women?'

A look of distaste. 'I'm afraid I know nothing of his sex life.'

Wycliffe got up from his chair. 'Very well, Dr Tate. I may look for another opportunity to talk to Mrs Tate.'

Concern. 'Is that absolutely necessary?'

Wycliffe did not answer. 'Good night, doctor.'

'I'll see you out.'

Wycliffe, unsettled in his mind, made a broad detour on the way back to his hotel. He walked as far as the beaches and along the deserted sea front. Wavelets swished idly over white sand and the broad plain of the sea stretched away into darkness. To his left, St Anthony lighthouse flashed at intervals, and far away to his right the sky was lit now and then by an arc of light from The Lizard. Nearer to hand Pendennis Castle, built by Henry VIII and gallantly defended by John Arundell against Cromwell's soldiers, brooded over its promontory, floodlit for the tourists.

Wycliffe began to feel at peace with himself and the world. He walked on, crossed the isthmus, and passed the entrance to the docks. There were houses with gardens on his left. He was suddenly aware of running feet behind him. He turned and saw a lithe figure in a track suit pounding the pavement towards him. The figure passed, breathing hard, and a few yards ahead turned in at one of the gates.

Mark Garland concluding his evening run.

When Wycliffe had gone, Tate returned to his surgery and to his records. He had scarcely settled to work when his step-mother came in followed by a sad-eyed little King Charles spaniel who immediately began exploring the corners of the room.

Marcella Tate was very pale and her skin was clear, almost transparent, so that fine bluish veins showed on her forehead and at the temples. She sat in the chair Wycliffe had vacated.

'Well?'

Tate said: 'I wish you wouldn't bring the dog in here, Marcella!'

She was immediately contrite: 'Sorry!' She stooped and scooped up the little dog on to her lap. 'There now, Ricky, darling! . . . What did he want?'

'He knew that Garland had brought a painting here on Sunday morning.'

'And?'

'He wanted to see it and I showed it to him.'

'Is that all?'

'More or less. He asked me what I thought of Francis; whether I knew anything about his sex life.'

'What did you say?'

'That I didn't. What did you expect me to say?'

She was bending over the dog, rubbing her cheek against its head. 'Did he ask to see me?'

'Yes; I told him you were indisposed. He said that he might call on you at some other time.'

She straightened abruptly. 'Call on me? But why?' She was suddenly flushed and she let the dog slide from her lap to the floor. 'Why does he want to see me?'

Tate was staring at her, the lenses of his spectacles glittering in the reflected light. 'It's nothing to get excited about. The police talk to everybody in the hope that by hit and miss they might pick up something. You should have been here with me tonight.'

Her voice rose. 'I couldn't face it, Alan! You know I couldn't! If you — '

He came round to her side of the desk and stood by her chair. 'Don't excite yourself. You are working yourself up again. Go up to bed and I'll bring you a hot drink with something to make you sleep . . .'

The words were gently spoken and the woman pressed her head against his body with a deep sigh. 'I depend on you, Alan. You know that.'

'I know.' But he was not looking down at her, his gaze was remote; he seemed to be looking through the window into the darkness of the garden.

Chapter Seven

WYCLIFFE AWOKE IN his hotel bedroom with a sour taste in his mouth and a leaden feeling in his head due to drinking with the Captain the night before. In a session lasting until one in the morning they had discussed Crime in Society with that lucidity which is only achieved at somewhere above the 100 mg per cent level of blood alcohol and with the comforting knowledge that one doesn't have to drive home. He squirmed as he recalled phrases he had used: 'Speaking as a policeman'. . . . 'After thirty years in the Force'. . . . 'When the State usurps the functions of the family' . . . and consoled himself with the thought that he never pontificated unless he was drunk. Or did he? . . .

It was seven o'clock by his travelling clock, and broad daylight. Because he had not bothered to draw the curtains there was a trembling mosaic of light on the ceiling reflected from the water outside and, by sitting up in bed, he could see out of the window across the harbour to Flushing. The view was almost identical with Gifford Tate's picture which the doctor had shown him — the picture that was to be the next 'new' Tate. The village was lit by a swathe of sunlight which cut through the morning mist. Several of the moored craft were caught in its path, others appeared only as ghostly forms.

He seemed to be up to his eyes in paintings, painters, painting materials, and even painters' jokes. . . . Incidentally, what was so funny about leaving the doctor a tube of Winsor blue? Or Burger £1,000 to buy spectacles? And had it in any case anything to do with Francis Garland being shot through the head? It was easy to be side-tracked by the more exotic elements in a case.

He got out of bed and drank two glasses of water from the tap then he put his head out of the window and sampled the morning air, tangy with the smell of salt water and seaweed. Away to his right the pier, jutting out into the harbour, hid the back of the Garlands' premises from his view, but he could see the scaffolding behind Benson's where Francis had undergone either translation or extinction.

Across the narrow stretch of water in front of him was Flushing Quay where the ferry was moored, ready for its first crossing of the day. A row of cottages backed on the water and in one of them Francis's illegitimate daughter, Anna, lived with her mother and boyfriend. He had not paid enough attention to Anna, he had not even seen the girl, and yet she was the only one to benefit obviously and directly from her father dying when he did. In a few days or weeks Francis would almost certainly have made a will and it was unlikely that Anna would have been the principal, let alone the sole beneficiary. In any case she would have had to wait, probably for many years . . .

He took a shower, shaved, and dressed in a leisurely way. The hotel was coming to life: in the next room a woman was scolding a child; there were sounds of pots and pans being shifted about in the kitchen; eventually, from down the corridor, came a rattling of cups and saucers. Early morning tea. Across the water the ferry cast off and its squat bulk made a bee-line for the pier. The mists were gone: a glorious morning, but according to the forecast it would be short-lived. Rain before evening. The chambermaid brought his tea and he drank it avidly. Saturday: the third day of his inquiry. His shopping list for the day: Anna, Francis's hypothetical mistress, Marcella Tate, and Brand. He went down to breakfast and was relieved to find that the Captain had not yet come down. Kedgeree, toast and marmalade. Good coffee. It cleared his head.

He was in the main street before nine o'clock and many of the shops were not yet open; assistants were waiting in doorways for the boss to arrive with the keys. In the Incident Room DC Curnow was duty officer and Kersey, smoking his third cigarette of the morning, brooded over a stack of reports. Greetings were perfunctory, as between members of a family.

All the windows were wide open and the room was pleasantly cool. A couple of hundred yards away pleasure boats, preparing for trippers, were berthed three abreast against the pier. Small-boat owners were off at moorings indulging themselves, checking gear or tinkering with engines. The sea was bottle green and silky inshore, out of the sun, light blue and slightly rippled further out. Wycliffe sensed that feeling of child-like excitement and anticipation which seems to infect those who find themselves almost anywhere on the fringes of the sea on a fine summer morning.

Not Kersey: he was morose. 'I've never known anything like it: over two hundred interviews with people who were in the street, mostly in the pubs, at some time between nine and eleven on the night and nobody saw or heard a damn thing. Not even the usual nutters who invent something to get themselves noticed. And yesterday Dixon and Potter spent the whole bloody day chatting up shopkeepers and others about the Garlands in general and Francis in particular. Nothing to show for it! The Garlands seem to have merged into the landscape. What gossip there is, is folklore: Edwin being cuckolded by an estate agent, that's still good for a laugh — '

'By the way, is that chap still around?' In order to say something.

'No, he was killed in the war. As I was saying: they dig up that and also Francis's moment of passion when he made himself a father — which must have been more than twenty years ago! If you have to go back that far to find dirt you're wasting your time. Of course they laugh at Beryl and her friend, they think Francis was a bit weird, and the old man had the name for being tight fisted, but there's no stick to beat a dog with in all that.'

Lucy Lane arrived: in a green frock figured in black, dark hair expertly set, a shoulder bag matching her frock; she looked as though she had just stepped out of her BMW runabout for a spot of window shopping. 'Good morning!' She signed the book, put her bag in a drawer, and sat at her table.

Kersey glanced at his watch. 'Nice of you to drop in.'

'I was here until after ten last night, sir.'

Wycliffe said to Kersey: 'No mistress for Francis yet?'

Kersey crushed out the stub of his cigarette. 'No, but we've turned up Brand's track record and that could mean something. When he lived in Falmouth, Brand was an art teacher, but he gave lectures on astrology and cast horoscopes in his spare time. That was probably how he met Francis, at any rate it seems they were buddies. Then, five or six years ago, Brand came into money and set up his place on the moor.'

'Where Francis visits on business. You think Francis was gay?'

Kersey said: 'I've been checking; there's nothing in his diary to say that M was a woman but you can't get M out of Kevin Brand.'

'It could be a pet name, surely?' from Lucy Lane. 'My parents call me Bunny and shorten it to B.'

Kersey looked at her. 'Really? Shameful Secrets of the Manse Revealed.'

Wycliffe said: 'You'd better go and talk to him, but find somebody who knows the area or you'll spend the rest of the day chasing your tail on that moor.'

Wycliffe turned to the reports where the only item of interest was negative: not a single .32 pistol among the licensed hand guns in the register.

He put through a call to Dr Franks, the pathologist.

Franks was on the defensive: 'You've had the gist of my report, Charles. The typing is held up because my secretary has gone sick.'

'It's not your report I'm bothered about. I want some off-the-record background on Dr Alan Tate. He's fortyish, a local GP, but according to his plate he's got a fellowship. He runs a one-man practice and his patients think he's half-way between a saint and a witch doctor.'

'You think he's a quack?'

'No, I don't. All I want is some idea of why he tucks himself away down here in general practice running a one-man show —'

'You want dirt, Charles, so why not say so? I'll see what I can do.'

Wycliffe joined the trippers on the pier and made for the Flushing ferry. He had to wait a quarter of an hour, but six or seven minutes after that he was climbing the weedy steps to the quay on the other side. Although Falmouth was less than half-a-mile away there was a curious feeling of isolation. Apart from three other ferry passengers there was no one to be seen. The quay was stacked with empty fish boxes, there was a platform scales, a yellow dog sleeping in the sun, a small battered truck which looked as though it had found its last resting place, and a notice about rabies. He walked past the war memorial and turned off the quay along a deserted street. The houses, whose front doors opened directly on the street, were a mixed bag, ranging from cottages to substantial dwellings of some distinction, originally built for Packet skippers. Anna and her mother lived in a little detached house which looked as though it had been sliced off from some larger building.

He knocked on the door and got no reply. He stood back and glimpsed a face at an upstair window so he knocked again and after a delay he heard someone coming down the stairs. The door was opened by a fair girl in a dressing gown, her eyes puffy with sleep. Wycliffe introduced himself.

'What time is it?'

'Half-past ten.'

'God! I overslept. You'd better come in.'

In the dark little passage she hesitated outside the door of the front room. 'That room is like a morgue, let's go in the kitchen.'

The kitchen was full of sunshine and faced across the water to Wycliffe's hotel and the Yacht Club.

'Like some coffee?'

'Yes please.'

'Only Nes — nothing fancy.'

'Where's your mother?'

She was filling the kettle at the sink. 'Gone across to Falmouth shopping, I expect.'

'And Terry?'

'Gone to work.'

'So he's back.'

'Oh yes, he's back.' She sounded resigned. She spooned coffee into the cups and added hot water, pushed over the milk jug and a packet of sugar. 'Help yourself. . . . Here's a spoon. . . . You want to talk to me?' She swept back her tousled hair with both hands.

'Yes. I am very sorry about your father.'

She said nothing for a moment, then: 'I didn't know him very well.'

'I hear you're going to inherit quite a lot of money.'

She stirred sugar into her coffee. 'So they tell me.'

'Did you expect anything like it?'

'No, I thought my grandfather would leave me something. He told me he was going to. Of course I didn't know about the other — coming from my father, I mean.'

'When did your grandfather tell you he intended to leave you money?'

'About a month ago. He came over one morning when mother was out and Terry had gone to work — just like now.'

'Tell me about it.'

She looked at him frowning, doubtful, then she made up her mind. 'Okay. It was queer at first. He sat there, where you are, just looking at me, then, very abrupt, he said "Go and brush your hair!" I thought he must have gone a bit ga-ga but there was no harm so I went up to my room and did my hair a bit. When I came down he said: "That's better. Thank you, child!" and he just went on looking at me. In the end he said: "You are very like your grandmother, do you know that?" I said I'd seen her picture. Then he asked me to kiss him on the lips and we kissed. He held me for a minute or two, quite tight, kissing and stroking my hair, then we sat down again.

'He said that his heart was dicky and that he wouldn't last much longer. He asked me a lot of questions about myself — what I wanted to do with my life, that sort of thing. . . . He wanted to know if I minded being illegitimate . . .'

'And do you?'

'I never really think about it. Who cares?'

'What else did he say?'

'That I would have enough money to get started in anything I really wanted to do; that he thought I had enough guts to be a success if I put my mind to it. If I wanted to squander the money in six months or a year, I could do that too, but if I did he would haunt me.'

'Did you tell anyone what your grandfather had told you?'

'No.'

'Not your mother or Terry?'

'Nobody.'

She got up from her chair, went to a cupboard and came back with a crusty roll and a dish of butter. 'Have one?'

'No, thanks.'

Wycliffe tried to recall what his own daughter had been like at twenty, which was not so very long ago. Much less at ease with others or with herself, far less pragmatic; she had wanted to meet the world on her own terms — and still did, though her capacity for acceptance was growing. Acceptance, that was Anna's secret. For Anna the world was the world was the world, and she would come to terms with it.

'Did your grandfather say anything else?'

She bit into her buttered roll scattering crumbs, and shook her head. Only after considerable hesitation did she say: 'Not really.'

'I think he did.'

She frowned, wiping her lips. 'It was odd, a bit weird. As he was going — he was in the passage — he turned round and said: "I don't suppose you know that your father and your Aunt Beryl were both illegitimate. It must run in the family, don't you think?" Then he just went. He didn't even say goodbye.' She looked at Wycliffe solemnly. 'Do you believe it?'

'Why would he lie to you?'

'No reason I can think of, but why tell me?'

Good question but not one Wycliffe was prepared to discuss. He changed the subject.

'You used to visit your father occasionally, I believe?'

'Yes.'

'Why?'

She looked at him quizzically. 'That's a funny question;

because he was my father, I suppose. I mean, it's odd: I used to feel sometimes I wanted to talk to him to see what he was really like but I never did. Every time it would end up with him giving me some money. He thought that was what I came for and, in a way, I suppose he was right. I wish I had talked to him though.'

'When did you last see him?'

'At the funeral, the day before he was killed.'

'You know that Terry saw it happen?'

'From a distance.'

'He thought the killer was a woman.'

'I know.'

'I have to ask you: was it you?'

She made no protest. 'No. Why should I have wanted to kill him? He never did me any harm.'

'Where were you that evening?'

'Home here, with mother.' Arms on the table, she was staring out of the window with unseeing eyes then, abruptly, she turned to face him. 'That is a lie! I was in the van with Terry.'

'He didn't say so.'

A faint smile. 'He was trying to keep me out of it.'

'Did you see your father attacked?'

'No, I'd left by then.'

'You'd better tell me about it.'

With apparent concentration she circled the rim of her coffee cup with the tip of her finger. 'After the funeral we went on the beach and in the evening to a disco. The van was on the Wharf car-park. It was one of those days, I was bloody minded. . . . Anyway, in the disco we began to quarrel and just after nine we packed it in and went back to the van. Of course the damn thing wouldn't start and that was the last straw. I started nagging him about money, about not having a proper job and no guts to get one. . . . You know how it is . . .' She looked up to judge whether this quiet middle-aged policeman was likely to know any such thing. She was quiet for a time and when she spoke again her manner was more confiding.

'It was the money grandfather promised me I was worried about. I'd have been a lot more worried if I'd known how much it was going to be. . . . I mean, Terry isn't mean or greedy or anything like that but he would see it as a sort of bonanza, a jackpot. . . . I wanted him to do something on his own.

'Anyway, he didn't say much but that didn't stop me, and in the end I got out and left him there.'

'Where did you go?'

She pushed the cup and saucer away from her. 'Tommy Webber who lives next door works in the bar at The Packet so I went along there and sat in the bar until closing time then Tommy gave me a lift home on the back of his bike.'

'Did you pass under the scaffolding on your way to The Packet?'

She shivered. 'Yes, I did.'

'Did you hear anything which, looking back, might have been suspicious?'

'Nothing, but I wasn't paying any attention.'

'This story of Terry's about going after your father to ask him for a loan to buy a small-holding — what do you make of that?'

She smiled. 'That's Terry. Of course, he didn't actually do it, did he?'

'Have you any idea of the time you left the car-park?'

'The church clock was striking ten as I came up into the street from Custom House Quay.'

Wycliffe said: 'I want you to put what you have told me into a statement. I would like you to come to the Incident Room on the Wharf later today.'

When Wycliffe returned to the quay the ferry was discharging passengers, a score or more from this trip, among them some obvious visitors, but mainly women returning from shopping in Falmouth. There was a fat woman in a floral dress, pink and perspiring, weighed down by shopping bags, who looked at Wycliffe intently. Remembering Lucy Lane's description, he felt sure that she must be Anna's mother.

But he was still haunted by the scene the girl had conjured up: the old man in that bright little kitchen with its ramshackle fittings and earthenware sink: holding her, kissing her lips and her hair; then sitting at the table, questioning her, promising to leave her some money, and finally, as a parting

114

shot, telling her casually that her father and her aunt had both been illegitimate . . .

Marcella Tate sat on the very edge of her chair clutching her little dog to her thin breast. She looked from Wycliffe to Lucy Lane and back again with apprehension that was close to panic. Although her pallor and her drawn features aged her; Wycliffe had the impression of a little girl caught out in some childish fault.

They were in the big drawing-room of the Tates' house and the afternoon sun shone directly through the tall windows which were tightly shut, making the room uncomfortably warm.

Lucy Lane, trying to make contact, got up and stooped over the dog, stroking its head. 'My uncle used to breed King Charles spaniels. What's his name?' She spoke as she might have done to a nervous child.

'He's called Ricky — after my brother who was killed in a road accident when he was three.' She implanted a quick kiss on the little dog's moist nose.

'He looks in splendid condition. Have you ever thought of showing him?'

The two women talked dogs and Wycliffe listened, looking benign.

The room was as much a library as a drawing-room, with bookshelves occupying all the available wall space to within three feet of the high ceiling. As far as Wycliffe could see, the books were a rather austere collection of poetry, classical fiction, and biography. No pictures, but a small cabinet of porcelain figures. Wycliffe thought they might be Chelsea or Chelsea Derby. Helen would have known.

Only when Marcella had relaxed sufficiently to sit back in her chair and release her tight hold on the dog did he risk intervention: 'We came to talk to you about the Garlands.'

'The Garlands?' Did she lay stress on the plural?

'I'm told that Edwin Garland was a close friend of your late husband.'

A flicker of relief. 'Oh yes, he was; a very dear friend, he spent a lot of time here, especially after Gifford had his stroke . . .'

No one spoke so she felt driven to continue: 'I expect you know that I was Gifford's second wife; I married him when I was only twenty-two and he was sixty-one. People said I did it for his money but that wasn't true. I admired him a great deal . . .'

'How did you meet him?' Lucy Lane, very softly.

'I went to a series of lectures on the history of art which he gave in Exeter where I was in my final year reading English. I got my degree before we married. I don't know why he picked on me; I've never been very attractive. But it wasn't sex that really mattered to either of us; he used to say that I was his insurance and consolation in old age.' Another nervous smile.

Wycliffe thought that Gifford Tate had found himself a girl wife, one who, however unconsciously, was looking for a daddy or, perhaps, a hero rather than a husband. Marcella would never grow up, but was it possible that, along with a childish naivety, she had carried forward into adult life the single-minded ruthlessness of the young?

She went on without prompting: 'Although he was a painter he was a very literary man so we had plenty in common. He was wonderful to talk to. . . . He had read widely and deeply in so many subjects!' She turned to the bookcase: 'Those were his books, but after he had his stroke he couldn't read for any length of time without tiring his eyes and I used to read to him. In that last summer before he died I read him the whole of Proust. . . . It was very hot that year and he liked me to sit naked on a chair in the courtyard garden while I read to him.' She glanced down at herself in disparagement. 'I wasn't like this, then.'

'You must have missed him very much.' Lucy Lane, without apparent irony.

'I did! I mean, he'd given me experiences I could never have hoped for. At first when he died I didn't know what to do with myself, I even thought. . . . Anyway, when Alan suggested that he should set up in practice here it seemed a splendid idea.' Her eyes were glistening with tears.

'Did Edwin continue to visit you?'

'Oh yes. Not as often as when Gifford was alive but quite regularly.'

'When was he here last?'

She frowned, playing absently with the dog's ear. 'It must have been a week last Wednesday. He usually came on Wednesday afternoons because Alan is almost always here then.'

'Did he come to see you both?'

'Oh yes. The three of us would chat about anything and everything for a while then Alan would take him into the surgery so that they could be private.'

'You mean for a consultation about Edwin's health?'

'I suppose so; he was Alan's patient.'

'What about Francis? Was he a regular visitor?'

'Francis never came here.'

'Beryl?'

'Not Beryl either.'

'Had there been some sort of quarrel?'

'No! It was just that we had so little in common. I mean, Francis was a very different man from his father.'

'But Francis was here last Wednesday — the morning of the funeral, wasn't he?'

Her agitation was returning. 'He came to tell us about the arrangements, it wasn't very well organised I'm afraid.' She said this with an air of finality as though the subject was closed.

'And to deliver a picture.'

'Well, yes. He did bring a picture with him: one of Gifford's that Edwin was going to frame for us.'

'The "new Tate" for next year?'

'Yes, but Alan will look after that now. I don't know what I should do without him. I don't think I could go on living.'

'Weren't the pictures left to you?'

'Yes, they were, but Edwin was Gifford's art executor and he looked after all the business. Gifford left me the pictures and some money, and he left Alan the house. I was afraid I would have to move when Alan came back but he wanted someone to keep house for him so it worked out very well.'

'Are there other pictures by your husband which have not yet been exhibited?'

'I don't think so. I'm fairly sure this was the last.'

'I suppose you will be at the exhibition opening on Monday?'

She frowned. 'I don't know. If I feel well enough.'

'When Francis came on Wednesday, how long did he stay?'

'About an hour, I think.'

'You were there the whole time?'

'No, I had some work to do in the kitchen and I left them here.'

'What did you talk about while you were with them?'

'About Edwin and about the funeral. That's what Francis came about. Why are you asking me all these questions?'

She was becoming worked up again and there was an element of aggression in her manner which might soon dissolve into tears.

Wycliffe became more formal. 'Mrs Tate, I have to ask you certain questions — questions which have already been put to others who were acquainted with Francis Garland, as were you and Doctor Tate. Was there any friction during Garland's visit here on Monday afternoon?'

'No! I've told you.'

'Where were you on Wednesday evening?'

Her voice was suddenly very low. 'I was here all the evening.'

'Alone?'

'No, with Alan.'

'Neither of you was out of the house after, say, half-past eight?'

'I told you we were in all the evening.'

She looked so pale that Wycliffe was afraid she might faint. He changed the subject: 'Was the chalet in the garden your husband's studio?'

She reacted with relief. 'Oh, yes. I've kept it just as it was and it's surprising how many people come to see it. Alan says we should charge. . . . He's joking, of course.'

'I would like to see it if I may.'

She looked startled. 'You? Why?'

'Curiosity; interest. I admire your husband's work.'

She looked doubtful. 'I suppose it would be all right. You'd better come with me.' She led the way along the main corridor, past the surgery door. 'The key is in the kitchen; we can go out that way.'

She took the key from a hook by the kitchen door and they followed her out into a paved courtyard that was partly glazed over; there were lounging chairs, potted plants and climbers, and a sizeable lily-pond with a fountain. 'The sun comes round in the afternoon and Gifford used to spend a lot of time here after his stroke. Alan and I sometimes sit out here on fine evenings.'

They crossed the grass to the studio, a substantial timber building in the style of a Swiss chalet, well preserved. Several steps led up to the door which she unlocked. The studio was a single large room open to the rafters. Windows high up in the north wall gave a diffused light. The furnishing was simple, functional and of excellent quality: two mahogany easels, a large adjustable work table, a painter's trolley, benches with shallow drawers, racks for canvases, shelves and cupboards. Two large leather-covered armchairs were placed near a cast-iron stove, and between them there was a low table with a chessboard, the pieces set up ready for play.

'This is just as it always was except that I usually have some of his sketch books, a few of his letters, and his work-book on display, but those things are on loan to the exhibition.'

She was more relaxed, taking pride in her role of showman. 'I feel like Miss Havisham — in *Great Expectations*, you know. Except that we don't have any cobwebs.' A nervous laugh.

'Is this where Edwin Garland and your husband spent their time?'

She smiled. 'Always; both of them smoking like chimneys. I fancy sometimes that I can still smell stale tobacco-smoke in here, the place is impregnated with it. Edwin rolled his own cigarettes, my husband was a pipe man. It did neither of them any good, especially after Gifford had his stroke, but there was nothing anyone could do about it.'

'Did you ever join them here?'

The idea struck her as odd. 'Good gracious, no! Gifford hated to be disturbed when he was in here whether he was with Edwin or alone.'

Wycliffe said: 'How did the stroke affect your husband, Mrs Tate?'

She frowned. 'Well, mentally not at all; physically he suffered partial paralysis down his left side. He was left-handed and so the disability was a severe blow but he used to say, "You don't paint with your hands, you paint with your heart and mind", and he proved that, didn't he?'

A good deal of wall space was taken up with framed photographs, each one labelled with a date and the location. Most were photographs of Gifford Tate and his two friends, the settings varied from the garden of the house to the Loire Valley, and to places in the Mediterranean. Several had been taken on a yacht at sea. Women figured in some of the pictures. Marcella pointed to a rather lean, severe-looking woman with deep-set eyes. 'That's Naomi, Gifford's first wife; they separated when Alan was seventeen; she died not long afterwards.'

She opened one of the cupboards. 'This is where I keep a lot of the material for his biography. These are his sketchbooks.' A numbered series, uniformly bound in fawn linen. 'There are fifty-eight of them, dating from 1922 . . . And on this shelf I keep his letters — letters to him that is. I'm having difficulty in getting hold of letters he wrote *to* people but they are coming in slowly. I take photo-copies . . . I've got his diaries in my room; he kept a diary from the age of thirteen.'

Wycliffe thanked her for showing them the studio. 'Some of what you have told us will have to go into a statement which you will be asked to sign. This is normal procedure and need cause you no concern. You can come back with us now or you can call in at the Incident Room on the Wharf later today if you prefer.'

'I'll come this afternoon.'

Wycliffe saw Lucy Lane look at him in astonishment as he accepted the arrangement.

They were seen off after walking round the house to the front. Marcella clutching her dog, wary but to some extent relieved.

As they reached the street Lucy Lane said: 'You were in no hurry for her statement, sir.'

'What would be the point? She would only say what she has said already.'

'And this afternoon?'

'The difference, if any, will be that she will tell a story which has been revised and edited by Tate.'

'Still further from the truth.'

'Very likely; but in our business lies are often more interesting.'

At the Congress of Vienna they cut a semi-circle from one of the grand dining tables in the Hofburg to accommodate the King of Wurtemberg's belly. Detective Constable Potter would have benefited from a similar facility in the office, but his bulk was the subject of severe official disapproval and there was a parallel concern for his health and fitness. A recent medical board had told him to stop smoking, to cut down on beer, and to eat more healthily (the current euphemism for going on a diet), or else. . . . But after three weeks of this Potter claimed to have lost nothing but his good humour.

'Message from Forensic, sir.' He handed Wycliffe a buff memorandum slip. 'And will you please ring Dr Franks, sir.' Morose; no hint of the chirpy fat man who had brewed more police tea than any three others, in the force, put together.

Wycliffe was moved to sympathise. 'I know how you feel, Potter, but stick at it. I gave up my pipe last Christmas.' Smug.

Potter smiled a wan smile. 'And, with respect, sir, for the first month we all knew about it.'

'Really? Was it as bad as that?' Chastened, Wycliffe turned to his memo: 'Bullet and cartridge case submitted August 7th: Preliminary examination suggests that these belong to the same round and that the bullet was fired from a self-loading pistol of 7.65mm calibre (.32 auto. in Britain and US), probably the Mauser H.Sc. Further details later. Best — Haines.'

Haines was a friend in the right place, ready to cut a few corners and pass on information while it was still worth having.

'Call for you, sir — Dr Franks.'

'Wycliffe here.'

'Oh, Charles! A disappointment I'm afraid. Tate's reputation is impeccable, at least professionally. Trained at Kings, first class track record and his fellowship at twenty-nine. A year or two later he took up a consultancy somewhere in the Home

Counties. All systems go, then his father died and he threw in his hand to set up as a GP in Falmouth.'

'Any idea of the reason?'

'A quirk of temperament apparently. Didn't like hospital work — couldn't stand colleagues — any colleagues; he's a loner. I suppose it could be that he just wants to crow in his own back yard. I don't know.'

'Anything else?'

'What more do you want? If you mean his private life he hardly seems to have had one. Dedicated or something I expect.'

Chapter Eight

'BRAND BOUGHT THIS small-holding: house, outbuildings and a bit of land, way out on the moor. He's done a conversion job in ye-olde-worlde style, cart wheels in the yard, bare beams and brick floors, magic symbols all over the place. He runs day classes all the year round and study holidays for resident students in the summer. There are classes in astrology, the tarot, numerology, ritual magic and God knows what else.

'The attraction of the place is that it lies spot-on a ley line — an imaginary line linking a few hunks of granite scattered across the landscape, supposed to have been put there by our ancestors for their spiritual gigs. One of the features of the course is surveying, they tramp over the moor with a theodolite, a staff, surveying poles, and packed lunch, looking for other ley lines. They also go about with a galvanometer and a Geiger counter to measure 'sources of power'. There's a little white-washed room on the campus with a dirty great lump of granite in the middle. When they feel drained of spiritual energy the students go there and lie on the floor, their bare feet against the granite, to re-charge their batteries.'

'Sounds harmless.'

'I suppose so but the whole set-up is as camp as a field full of tents. Brand only advertises in the gay mags and, to judge from those present, that's where he gets his clients. "Most of my students come on personal recommendation." I'll bet they do.'

Three o'clock in the afternoon and the weathermen had got it wrong, the sun still shone and the sky was blue. Kersey reported on his visit to Brand.

'What sort of man is he?'

Kersey lit a cigarette. 'I know gays don't wear ID tags — "no distinguishing physical characteristics" the shrinks say, but you'd spot Brand as a card-carrying queen a mile off. Slight, fair, silk shirt, tight pants, and he walks as though he wants to wee-wee. He's friendly, but wary — very.'

'Where does Francis come in?'

'He attends classes every Sunday. Brand told me that they'd been friendly from way back and when I leaned on him a bit he admitted that they'd had a thing going but it had been broken off two or three years ago.'

'Why?'

Kersey looked like a lion with a tasty Christian in view. 'Our Frankie had found a new friend; guess who?'

Wycliffe growled, 'Get on with it!'

'His cousin, Mark. Mark turned up at these Sunday classes and despite family differences they soon realised that there was a communion of souls. Mark now spends Sundays and Tuesdays there. I don't know what the financial arrangements are but he has a double role, he attends the classes but he also does spinal manipulation and massage for those of Brand's clients who need it or say they do.'

'You didn't leave it there.' Wycliffe, being patient.

'No, Brand was persuaded to unburden himself. When Frankie arrived on Tuesday afternoon with his printing order, he got hold of Mark and they went off on their own. Frankie arrived back by himself about an hour later and drove off without a word to anybody. When Mark turned up he was red-eyed and in a foul temper. "I thought they must have had a quarrel," Brand said, and I had the impression he wasn't heartbroken about it.'

'We must have a word with Mark Garland.'

'Here, at his home, or in his office?'

'I don't want to upset Thomas unnecessarily; let's see him in his office or whatever he calls it.'

'Mark Garland, Chiropractor', painted on the glass door of a small shop. Both door and window were curtained so that it was not possible to see inside. There was a bell-push with the instruction: 'Please ring and wait'. They rang and waited, and after a full minute the door was opened by a man in his thirties, fair, clean shaven, medium height, and slim. He wore a white coat, and glasses which seemed disproportionately large. Wycliffe had to revise a notion based on slender evidence that all osteopaths and chiropractors have the physique of rugby players.

'Have you an appointment?'

Wycliffe showed his warrant card.

'Oh, you'll have to wait. I have a patient with me.' His manner was nervously belligerent.

They were put into a little room, no more than a cubicle, where there were two kitchen-chairs and a table with a few magazines. The partitions were thin and they could hear Garland giving instructions to his patient to make certain movements and assume certain postures. It was soon over, the patient was shown out after making a further appointment, and they were admitted.

The consulting room was as sparsely furnished as the waiting cubicle: two chairs, a desk and a telephone, in addition to the essential couch. Wycliffe and Kersey were given the two chairs while Mark Garland perched on the edge of the couch.

A one-man show, not even a receptionist.

Garland opened with a protest. 'I told your sergeant that I know nothing of my cousin's death. I am distressed enough about it without having you people coming here, interrupting my work.'

Wycliffe was looking round the room. On the walls there was a certificate from a professional institution, an advertisement calendar, and a framed photograph of the harbour. It seemed that he had not heard Garland's little speech but his gaze came round eventually.

He said: 'Let us be clear about your position, Mr Garland. I am investigating a murder. You will be asked certain questions and your answers or failure to answer will decide whether or not you go with us to a police station for further interrogation. Now, what is it to be?'

Garland took off his spectacles and cleaned the lenses with his handkerchief. 'I'll listen to your questions before I decide.'

'No, I shall decide on the basis of your answer to one question: I want to know the circumstances in which your cousin received bruises to his face on the day before he was murdered.'

'I've told you I know nothing about Francis's death.'

Wycliffe leaned forward in his chair. 'And I've told you the options, Mr Garland. We know that you quarrelled with your cousin at Brand's place; he returned from the encounter with his face severely bruised. The following evening he was shot dead while walking his dog along the wharf here. We have reasonable grounds for detaining you on suspicion unless you can satisfy us that you had no part in the shooting.'

Garland was shaken and he was still making up his mind how to react when the doorbell rang. He looked doubtfully at Wycliffe: 'My next patient.'

Kersey said: 'Your notice tells them to ring and wait. This one has rung, now he can wait.'

'It's a woman. Shall I ask her to make another appointment?'

'That's up to you.'

Garland went to the door and they heard a brief exchange. When he came back he had decided to co-operate. 'Ask me what you want to know.' He perched on the edge of the couch once more and Wycliffe realised that he was trembling.

'Why did you attack your cousin?'

'We had a row.'

'You had a homosexual relationship?'

'That's not illegal.'

'No, it's a matter of fact.'

'All right, we had a homosexual relationship and it was understood between us that as soon as it was possible we would go away together and start afresh.' He could not keep still and his eyes reddened as though at any moment he might burst into tears.

'What would have made your plans possible?'

'It was understood that we would go when his father died and the will was settled. Then, when his father did die. . . . Within three days . . .' He broke off, unable to continue.

'Take your time.'

He made an effort. 'Three days after his father died, when it seemed everything would begin to come right for us, that he would be able to leave that business and I would get out of here . . .' He looked round the bleak little room in despair. 'He chose that moment to accuse me of having someone else.' He pressed a handkerchief to his eyes, sobbed, and blew his nose.

'He was jealous?'

'Yes, it was so unreasonable! To threaten everything because of wicked gossip.'

'Gossip about you and . . . ?'

A sidelong look. 'About me and Kevin Brand. Because I gave Kevin massage — I mean, that's one of the reasons I go there.'

'So you attacked your cousin.'

'Yes, I attacked him, if that's what you like to call it! I lost my temper. If it had been a man and woman relationship you would think that was understandable but we aren't expected to have feelings; if we do they're a joke.'

Wycliffe said: 'I'm only interested in what happened at Brand's place on the Tuesday because of what followed.'

Garland shook his head. 'I didn't kill him. I couldn't!'

'So where were you on Wednesday evening?'

'I told you: I went for my usual run. I left home at half-past nine and I got back about half-past ten.'

'Where did you run?'

He made a vague gesture. 'The usual: Swanpool, across to Gyllingvase, along the seafront, around Castle Drive and home.'

'Not through the main street?'

'No.'

'Do you own a gun, Mr Garland?'

'Of course not!'

'Have you ever fired one?'

'Only a .22 sporting rifle when I was at college.'

Wycliffe said: 'I want you to come back to the Incident Room with me where you will be asked to make a full statement.'

'Am I under arrest?'

'No, you are helping us with our enquiries.'

More fodder for the computer if nothing else. A modern investigating officer secures his rear with computer print-out. And more enquiries to be made: anyone walking or driving along the following route between nine-thirty and ten-thirty last Wednesday evening. . . . A man in a track suit, running . . .

"I thought it was a woman." The only first-hand evidence they had and that depended on the observation of a not very bright young man, on a dark misty night, at a distance of a hundred yards.

Wycliffe reviewed possible candidates: among them the women, Cathy Carne, Marcella Tate, and Anna Brooks — any one of them would have been physically capable of committing the crime and sprinting away afterwards. And which of the men might have been mistaken for a woman? As the witness concerned, Terry Gill, had to be omitted (though he remained a suspect); that left Alan Tate and Mark Garland, both of whom were of medium height, slight of build and certainly capable of the agility required.

A reconstruction? Would seeing a re-run of the incident, as he had recounted it, help Terry Gill to a firmer conclusion? Wycliffe thought not. In his experience reconstructions were little more than public relations exercises.

Marcella Tate came to the Incident Room and made her statement which added nothing to the sum of their knowledge.

Wycliffe was late for his after-dinner walk, delayed by the Captain, but he was anxious to establish an element of routine. Without a pattern, some repetitive rhythm in his days, he felt lost.

He walked down the High Street and along the Wharf with the intention of retracing Francis's footsteps on the night of the murder. The time was about right but conditions were quite different: instead of misty rain the evening was clear, the air was balmy with that silky feel, and the waters of the harbour gleamed in the darkness. He passed the barred windows of Edwin's studio; the only light in the building came from an upstairs room, the living-room, where Beryl was almost certainly sitting and brooding alone.

He imagined Francis coming out, and the dog scampering ahead through the mist. Less than 200 yards away was the car-park. When he reached it there was a sprinkling of cars but no decrepit old van with a CND symbol on its side. Had Francis seen and recognised the van? Had there, despite Terry Gill's denials, been an encounter? He passed the lighted windows of the Incident Room and continued on towards Benson's. The lights on the scaffolding shone, unwinking in the still air.

It was the first day the wharf walk had been re-opened to the public and the first night without a PC on guard at the scene of crime. Saturday night; the pubs in the street would be doing good business but it was very quiet, only a faint hiss of escaping steam coming from the docks. He reached Benson's and passed under the scaffold. Old mortar, chipped from the wall, still crunched underfoot. At this point Francis must have had about 20 seconds to live, a few more steps and he would have reached the other end which, for him, was the threshold of death.

Wycliffe always forced himself to envisage every detail of a murder so that he would never become reconciled to the enormity of the crime. Murder appalled him because it took everything from the victim with no possibility of restitution, it blotted out memories of a past and hopes for a future. It was the supreme arrogance of the killer which dismayed him. He could not imagine the stunted, blinkered, and self-regarding mind that could contemplate the killing of another human being.

He stood for a moment or two at the spot where Francis's body had been found. The first stage of the scaffolding was little more than a foot above his head. The killer must have been kneeling there, pistol at the ready, and as Francis emerged he or she had fired at a range of a few inches.

He shuddered involuntarily and walked on towards the printing works.

He could see the rectangular outline of the building and, at the top, at the harbour end, a lighted window open to the night. He had not, so far, met Cathy Carne on her home ground and now was his chance. A moment or two later he was ringing her door bell.

There was a light behind the hammered glass and he could hear Cathy Carne's voice, speaking on the telephone. He could not distinguish her words but she sounded harassed and tense. The bell probably cut short her conversation for almost at once he heard the telephone replaced and she called out: 'Who is that?'

'Superintendent Wycliffe.'

She opened the door; she was wearing a dressing gown. She looked flushed and vaguely dishevelled. 'I'm sorry, but one has to be careful about opening the door at night.'

'Of course!' He apologised for disturbing her.

'It doesn't matter; come in. I was on the telephone.'

He followed her into the living-room. It was snug: a sofa, tub chairs, television, record player, and shelves full of books on either side of the chimney breast. Over the mantelpiece an Edwin Garland landscape with figures. On a low table there was a tray with a bottle of whisky and two used glasses. She whisked the tray off the table and took it away. When she returned she felt the need to explain.

'Saturday is usually hectic in the shop and I'm ready for bed and a book by ten o'clock but tonight I felt the need of a nightcap. 'Do sit down!'

She sat herself on the sofa and pulled the dressing gown around her legs. She was watching him closely and she was talking too much. Something had upset her and he doubted if it was his arrival.

'I didn't ask you; would you like a drink?'

'No, thanks.'

She reached for her cigarettes and lit one. 'Now, what's all this about?' Working hard at trying to sound normal.

'How well do you know Mark Garland?'

'Mark?' She seemed surprised and perhaps relieved. 'Hardly at all. Odd you should ask, though, because he was in the shop last Thursday, wanting to talk to Beryl. It was the first time I've spoken to him in years.'

'Thursday was the day after your uncle's funeral, the day Francis's body was found.'

'Yes.' She was cautious.

'I thought there was no contact between the two sides of the family.'

'There wasn't — isn't; Beryl wouldn't see him.'

'Have you any idea why he came?'

She made a vague gesture. 'No; he seemed upset, edgy. He said he wanted to explain something to Beryl but I've no idea what. When Beryl wouldn't talk to him he went away more upset than ever.'

Wycliffe was taking in details of the room. Self-contained was the phrase that occurred to him; everything was there to hand. The same phrase described the woman who had made it. Not that Cathy Carne˙ was a loner, she wanted — needed human contacts, but she would have them only on her own terms. They must arrive on the doorstep, like the milk.

'Presumably you have friends — outside of business?'

Her eyes narrowed against the smoke from her cigarette. 'Naturally.'

'Did Francis or Beryl ever visit you here?'

'Never.'

'Edwin?'

'No.'

'The Tates?'

She frowned. 'What is all this?'

'A simple question. If you would prefer not to answer it . . .'

'It's not that. As a matter of fact the Tates are friends; after all I've known them for years.'

'They come here?'

She crushed out her cigarette. 'Dr Tate comes here some-times. To be honest he's a fairly regular visitor; he's a lonely man and we have things in common.'

'Something wrong with that? Why be coy about it?'

She wore a watch with an expanding gold bracelet and she fingered it, easing the bracelet away from her wrist and examining the pattern of indentations it left on her skin. 'It's silly really, but Alan is a doctor and vulnerable to gossip, he's also a very private man.'

'Perhaps Marcella wouldn't like it.'

'What are you suggesting?'

'Only that I have an impression that she depends a great deal on the doctor.'

'She does, but there's nothing . . . there's no attachment. That is malicious gossip.' On her metal.

'Was Dr Tate here the night Francis was killed?'

'What are you getting at?'

131

'Again, a simple question.'

She hesitated, then: 'Yes, he was here.'

'When did he come and when did he leave?'

'He came at about seven. I had invited him for a meal, and he left around midnight.'

Wycliffe stood up and went to the window, parted the curtains, and looked out. 'I can see the back of Benson's quite clearly. It's not far, is it? There was a shot and the dog barked, but you heard nothing?'

'Not to notice. Here, by the harbour, there are all sorts of sounds from the docks and the ships, one gets to ignore them.'

He stood, looking down at her, 'And neither of you left the flat between say eight and eleven?'

'Neither of us.'

'Good! Just one more thing. The letter your uncle left you; you say you destroyed it?'

'We come back to that!'

'And we shall continue to come back to it until you tell me what was in it.'

'I've already told you.'

'You've told me nothing which would have been worth Edwin Garland taking the trouble to put into a letter and leave it with his lawyer. It's a serious matter to mislead the police in a murder investigation. Take legal advice if you want to, but I intend to know what it was that your uncle confided to you.'

There was silence during which they could hear singing coming from the street. The clock on the mantelpiece chimed and struck eleven.

Wycliffe said: 'Have you thought that you may yourself be in danger?'

'In danger? Me?' Unconvincingly dismissive. 'I don't know what you mean.'

'Your uncle, for his own reasons, confided something to Francis and Francis is dead. Perhaps it is dangerous to have information and keep it to yourself.'

She looked incredulous. 'That is nonsense!'

'Think it over. I'll say good night and I apologise for disturbing you so late.'

She came with him to the door, uneasy, perhaps scared. She watched him go down the steps. He waited until she had closed the door then went back up, making as little noise as possible. The hall light was still on and he put his ear to the letter box; he could hear her voice on the telephone but could not distinguish her words.

Two women seemed anxious to provide Tate with an alibi, or to use him as an alibi for themselves.

He walked back along the wharf.

Wycliffe spent a restless night. Although his curtains were drawn, moonlight flooded his room and each time he awoke from an uneasy sleep he thought that it was morning. Waking or sleeping his mind fretted away at the case, images drifted in and out of his consciousness, words and phrases came to mind in a confusing jumble but once, in a doze, it seemed that Beryl was actually speaking to him in her clear, cracked voice: 'He worked it all out, planned it move by move . . .'

Beryl's words had impressed him at the time because they summed up his own vague feeling that what had happened and what was happening might be consequences of the old man's cynical, even malicious contrivings. Obviously Edwin had not murdered Francis but he had created a situation in which violence was more likely.

The main provisions of the will were devisive and certain to breed strife, but they provided no motive for Francis's murder. How often had Wycliffe told himself that the only obvious beneficiary from Francis's death was his daughter? But could she have known that her father had not made a will? In any case he could not believe . . . but that was not evidential.

Aside from gain the commoner motives for murder are anger, jealousy, lust and fear. The first three, in combination, or any one of them, pointed to Mark Garland. As to fear, who would have reason to fear Francis? Surely he presented no physical threat to anyone, but it was possible that he had knowledge that was threatening. His father had confided in him and Francis himself had been surprised, not only by the nature of the confidence but also by the fact that it had been made to him.

133

'Something about himself. . . . Incredible to think that it has been going on all these years. . . . He said I could talk if I wanted to . . .'

Cathy Carne had also been told something in her damned letter.

But there were other provisions of the will, dismissed as harmless jokes, but were they? A tube of Winsor blue for Alan Tate, spectacles for Burger . . . 'which I hope may improve his judgement and help him to see the obvious.' To see the obvious — Wycliffe wished that spectacles might do that for him. What was obvious? The relative merits of Tate's and Edwin's paintings? That was Burger's explanation but the truth might not be so innocent.

A tube of Winsor blue for Alan Tate — a way of wishing him luck, Cathy Carne had said.

Wycliffe resigned himself to lying awake for the rest of the night but, in fact, he fell asleep and knew nothing more until he was awakened to broad daylight and seagulls squawking outside his window.

Chapter Nine

SUNDAY MORNING. WYCLIFFE pretended to believe that there was something special about Sunday mornings, a quality in the air which he would be able to recognise however far adrift he might be from any routine or calendar. Certainly everything moved at a slower pace: the day took longer to get going; even the hotel breakfast was later than on other days; but he was on his way to the Incident Room by nine o'clock.

A newspaper seller was setting up his stand at the entrance to the pier but otherwise the street was deserted; shop blinds were drawn and a capricious breeze chased after Saturday night's litter.

Lucy Lane was already on duty, as fresh as the morning. 'There's been a call from Mark Garland's father to the local nick. Knowing our interest they passed him on and I spoke to him. Mark didn't come home last night and he's worried. At a little after eight Mark told his father he was going out; he went, and the old man hasn't seen him since.'

'He didn't say where he was going or when he could expect him back?'

'No, but that's not unusual; the most he ever says is "Don't wait up for me", though he's rarely late home.'

'Did he take anything with him?'

'Apparently not, just the clothes he was wearing.'

'We'd better talk to Thomas.'

They walked along the wharf and at the Custom House Quay they climbed the slope to the main street past the King's Pipe, a free-standing fireplace and a chimney where, in less sophisticated times, revenue men had burned smuggled tobacco. On their right, shops gave way to large houses and on their left, to the harbour. Unhampered by buildings the breeze decided that it was a south easterly and they could see white water off Trefusis Point, a warning to small craft not to venture outside.

A row of terraced houses as they approached the docks, then one standing alone, red brick — incongruous amid all the stone and stucco.

'This is it, sir.'

Thomas opened the front door before they could ring. 'Do come in! I'm rather worried. He's never done anything like this before. I didn't realise he wasn't in until this morning. . . . He wasn't home when I went to bed but that's nothing out of the ordinary because I go to bed early. There's nothing much to stay up for.'

He led the way into the living-room. 'Mark doesn't tell me anything — he never has, so when something like this happens I don't know what to do. I telephoned the police because I wondered if there could have been an accident.'

On a tablecloth, folded over part of the dining table, there was a teapot, milk jug, and a cup and saucer. Sunlight filtered through the greenery in the conservatory making a dappled pattern on the floor. A tabby cat followed in Thomas's footsteps eyeing the visitors. On the wall among a number of framed photographs there was one of a youthful Thomas in cap and gown.

'I gather that your son went out at about eight last evening and you've no idea where?'

'No idea! he doesn't go out in the evenings, much, except for his running. He was on the telephone to somebody — I don't know who — I heard him say, "I'm rather worried, I would like to come and see you", and a little later he came in here, all dressed up, to say that he was going out.'

'Dressed up?'

'He was wearing a suit that he keeps for rather special occasions.'

'Did he take his car?'

'His car is in the garage.'

Suddenly Thomas remembered his manners and found seats for them but remained standing himself.

'Does he go out a lot?'

'Apart from his work he's usually out most of the day on Sundays and Tuesdays. He doesn't have patients those days, you see.'

'Do you know where he spends his time then?'

'I know that he attends classes with a Mr Brand who runs a sort of school for what they call occult studies.' A diffident gesture. 'Not something that appeals to me, but he has always shown an interest in that sort of thing.'

Wycliffe had to probe: 'Do you know that he was a close friend of Francis Garland?'

He had not known and at first he was unbelieving, but when his protests had died away he looked at Wycliffe with fresh concern. 'Are you telling me that Mark not coming home has something to do with his cousin?'

It was Lucy Lane who answered. 'We don't know, Mr Garland, but we do know that there was an intimate relationship between Mark and Francis which reached some sort of crisis last Tuesday. This happened at Brand's place, there was a scuffle and Francis came away with his face badly bruised.'

It was painful. The thirty-odd years which Thomas had spent as a schoolteacher in a comprehensive school must have been perpetual torment. Shy, vulnerable, his blue eyes looked out on a world which seemed inexplicable and hostile.

He sat down by the table; the cat leapt on his lap and he stroked it absently. 'You are saying that Mark is a homosexual. Who told you all this?' He spoke sharply but he seemed less surprised than they might have expected.

Wycliffe said: 'Your son, in a statement he made early yesterday evening.'

'You've been questioning him?'

'He was at the Incident Room helping us with our enquiries into his cousin's death.'

'You're not saying that you suspected him of . . . of killing Francis?'

'No more than others.'

'And now?'

'We must find him first.'

'You're treating him as a fugitive! You think he's run away.'

Wycliffe said: 'We simply don't know what has happened. Did he seem upset or agitated when he came home yesterday evening?'

'He was just as usual, he never says much. I asked him why he was late for his meal and he said that he'd had an extra patient.'

'I gather that he took nothing with him; no suitcase — nothing. Are you quite sure of that?'

'I'm quite sure. By chance I saw him walking down the drive to the gate and he was carrying nothing.'

He was staring at his cup, turning it round and round with his fingers. 'My brother, my nephew, and now . . .'

'We don't know that anything has happened to your son, Mr Garland. As a matter of routine I would like one of us to take a look at his room. You can be there, of course.'

Thomas hesitated then he looked at Lucy Lane: 'I would rather go up with her.'

Wycliffe waited in the living-room but they were not long gone. When they came down again Thomas had tears in his eyes. Lucy Lane said: 'The moment we have any news we'll be in touch.'

The old man stood in the doorway, holding his cat, while they walked the short distance to the gate.

Lucy Lane said: 'He's got a friend who will be coming in later. I feel very sorry for him. Sometimes the idea of being a parent scares me stiff, it's like offering yourself for vivisection.'

'You saw his room. What was it like?'

'Very ordinary; everything neat and tidy; not much of anything and nothing remarkable except a drawer full of soft porn gay magazines, and a collection of books on occult subjects. What did you expect?'

'Thomas knew about the magazines?'

'Of course. That was why he wanted me instead of you to go up with him. Do we put Mark on the telex?'

'Yes, we've got to find him, and the sooner the better; he's not just a missing man, he's a missing suspect.'

'Anything else?'

'We get Mr Kersey to have another heart to heart with Brand.'

'The telephone call — do you think he was keeping an appointment?'

'It looks like it and we have to find out who with.'

As they walked back through the street the church bells were ringing for morning service.

Mark Garland's description was circulated and enquiries put in hand at the railway station, and among bus drivers, taximen and hire-car firms. In their lunch-time bulletin the local radio would ask whoever spoke on the telephone to Mark Garland on Saturday evening and anyone who saw him after eight o'clock, to contact the police.

Wycliffe and Kersey brooded, watching the racing yachts with their multi-coloured sails performing a lively ballet in the fresh breeze.

'Lucy Lane talked to him on Friday evening, here; I saw him with you in his consulting room yesterday and we brought him back here to make his statement. A couple of hours later, after a phone call, he walks out of his home, taking nothing with him, and disappears.'

Kersey rubbed his chin, always bristly however often he shaved. 'Do you think he's done away with himself?'

'Putting on his best suit for the occasion?'

Kersey nodded. 'That's a point. But where does it all leave us?'

'Still searching for a missing man.'

Kersey pitched the stub of his cigarette through the open window.

'Assuming his innocence, his disappearance would be convenient for whoever did shoot our Frankie.'

'The same thought occurred to me.'

At eleven o'clock there was a telephone call for Wycliffe. 'Dr Tate speaking. I've just heard that Mark Garland is missing and I think I should tell you that he was here with me yesterday evening.'

'Was he visiting you as a patient?'

'Yes, although I have no Saturday surgery —'

Wycliffe cut him short. 'It will be best that we meet and talk. I'll be at your house in a few minutes.'

'But —'

'If you please, Dr Tate, in a few minutes.'

'All right.' A grudging concession to the inevitable. 'But please come round the back to my surgery. I don't want Mrs Tate disturbed.'

Wycliffe said to Kersey: 'I want you to meet this man.'

They drove to Tregarthen, walked up the drive under the pine trees, and round the back of the house to a door marked 'Waiting Room. Please Enter'. Before they could do so the door was opened by Tate in person and they were ushered through the empty waiting room into his surgery.

'Please sit down.' The doctor was wasting no time.

Wycliffe introduced Kersey, and Tate looked at him with a certain wariness. 'I find myself in a rather invidious position . . .'

Tate was meticulously turned out, perfectly shaved, his hair had been recently trimmed, his pale hands were manicured and the cuffs of his shirt just showed below the sleeves of his jacket. On the desk in front of him was a medical records envelope labelled Mark Garland.

'As you know, Mark Garland is a chiropractor and though I do not subscribe to the principles of chiropractic I recognise the value of skilled manipulation in certain cases. Garland is a natural and I have referred a number of my patients to him with good results.'

'So you had a professional relationship with the missing man. How did you hear that he is missing? It is not public knowledge.'

Tate was not pleased at this brusque approach but he explained: 'Garland left his wallet behind, it must have slipped out of his jacket when he took it off for me to examine him. At any rate I found it on the floor this morning; I telephoned to tell him and spoke to his father. Of course he told me that his son was missing and that you had already started an investigation.'

'What happened yesterday evening?'

140

A pause, then: 'He telephoned concerning a patient I had asked him to see and he took the opportunity to tell me that he was worried about his own health. After running the previous night he was experiencing certain symptoms which, he thought, might indicate heart disease. It sounded unlikely but he was clearly in an anxious state of mind so I suggested that he should come and see me right away.' Tate paused and sat back in his chair. 'He was here within fifteen minutes.'

The sun had not yet reached the back of the house so that the garden was in shadow and the room itself in a gloomy half light. No sound came from outside and Wycliffe felt that the world had been consciously excluded, that he and Kersey certainly, and even the patients who regularly gathered behind the padded door, were intruders. They might be inevitable, even necessary, but they were not welcome.

Tate was looking at Wycliffe as though he expected a question but when none came he continued: 'I examined him and decided that whatever his symptoms they were almost certainly mental rather than physical in origin. I told him as much and he admitted that he was under considerable stress. Among other things he said that he found difficulty in sleeping. I prescribed nitrazepam, to be taken for a few nights on going to bed, and told him to see me again in a week.'

Tate spread his hands. 'And that was all. He left here reassured, at least in regard to his physical well-being. I must say that it was a considerable shock to learn that he seems to be missing.'

Wycliffe said: 'What time did he leave?'

Tate considered. 'He was here for about forty-five minutes. He must have left at nine o'clock.'

Kersey said: 'Did he tell you what was worrying him?'

So far the doctor had spoken directly to Wycliffe, but from time to time he had cast uneasy glances in Kersey's direction. Certainly Kersey's presence seemed to disturb him but, after only a brief hesitation, he answered the question: 'Not in so many words.'

'But you have some idea of what it was?'

Tate looked at him blankly and said nothing.

141

Wycliffe intervened: 'I'm sure you understand, Dr Tate, that the confidentiality of the consulting room has no protection in law.'

Somewhere in the house a clock chimed and struck twelve.

Tate sat back in his chair as though making up his mind about something then he said: 'I am reluctant to discuss what a patient tells me in confidence but I suppose I have no choice. Garland was worried about being interrogated by the police in connection with his cousin's murder. He told me of the incident in which Francis got a bruised face and of what led up to it. All this, of course, you already know so I am really betraying no confidences.'

Wycliffe chose his words with care. 'You say that he was worried because we questioned him; would you say that his concern went deeper than that?'

Tate made a vigorous gesture of rejection. 'I know what you have in mind but I refuse to be drawn along that line. You are no longer asking me for facts but for speculation. All I can say is that he was deeply disturbed.'

Kersey tried another approach: 'As an experienced medical man and knowing your patient well, would you be surprised if it was found that he had taken his own life?'

Tate pushed away the folder containing Garland's medical records as though symbolically dissociating himself from the question. 'Really, you put me in an impossible position! If I had thought that there was any such risk when he was here last evening I would have taken precautions.'

'But on reflection?'

Tate placed the tips of his fingers together and regarded them. 'On reflection, I will say that I wish I had taken his mental condition more seriously. But that doesn't mean that I think he killed himself.' He got up from his chair. 'Now, Mr Wycliffe, if you will excuse me, I have some work I want to do before lunch.'

Wycliffe remained seated. 'I have some further questions for you, Dr Tate. Do you have any idea where Garland might have gone when he left you?'

Tate frowned. 'I assumed that he would have gone home.

Where else? You must understand, Mr Wycliffe, that my only connection with him is by way of an occasional professional encounter. I know nothing of his private life. Your next question?'

'Did Mrs Tate have any contact with him while he was here?'

'Mrs Tate? Certainly not! It was not a social visit.'

Wycliffe stood up and so did Kersey. 'Thank you, Dr Tate; that is all for the moment.'

Tate was distant. 'I hope that Garland turns up safe and well, but there is nothing more that I can tell you.'

They were escorted out, not through the waiting room, but through the house and out by the front door.

As they walked down the drive they saw Marcella crossing the lawn with her dog. She walked with jerky self-conscious strides and made a point of not seeing them.

Wycliffe closed the wicket gate with a sigh. 'Claustrophobic, wasn't it? What did you make of him?'

Kersey took a deep breath. 'He didn't need much persuasion to overcome his professional scruples. I had the impression that he wanted to tell at least as much as he did tell, and at one point he seemed to be hinting that Mark might well have killed his cousin.'

They were in the car before he spoke again: 'It seems to me that when we know what happened to Mark Garland we shall be in business. Either he is a killer on the run, who may have done away with himself, or he's another victim.'

Wycliffe fastened his seat belt. 'Finding out which is our biggest problem.'

Kersey was driving. Wycliffe never took the wheel if he could avoid it. As they turned away from the terraces, downhill towards the town centre, Kersey said: 'If Mark Garland wasn't the killer then we are up against motive. Somebody killed Francis and presumably they had a reason. At any rate, he's dead.'

Back in the Incident Room Wycliffe slumped into a chair. The duty officer handed him a memo slip. 'Telephone message, sir.'

The message read: 'Expecting to see you at your personal preview this afternoon at 3.00. Burger.'

143

Kersey said: 'I get the impression that we are being taken for a nice smooth ride but unless something breaks I don't see what we can do about it. On Tuesday afternoon Mark Garland had a set-to with Francis who had bruises to show for it. Jealousy among gays can be every bit as vicious as among heteros and on Wednesday night Francis is deliberately murdered by someone lying in wait for him on the wharf. Mark is questioned a couple of times and fails to give a satisfactory account of himself but there is nothing on which to hold him, then he disappears. If he is never found there is a nice tidy case; no more police time wasted, no trial, no burned fingers, and public money saved. Nobody to complain but the lawyers, and who loses sleep over them?'

Wycliffe shook his head. 'Nobody is going to sweep this one under the carpet.'

'So what do we do?'

'At the moment what can we do, except the obvious? — enquiries in the neighbourhood of the Tate house: anybody who saw Garland arrive, anybody who saw him leave, and anything else they can pick up.'

At three o'clock Wycliffe arrived at the Gifford Tate exhibition. He was admitted by an earnest-looking young man with large spectacles and a lisp. Burger, athletically ambulant in a wheel chair, was cordial. A severe looking matron, with a plummy voice and tinted hair, was unpacking catalogues. A young woman was checking the labels on the pictures against the numbers and descriptions in the catalogue.

'You see! My helpers do all the work while I potter. He picked up one of the catalogues in the glossy, illustrated edition, 'Have this with the compliments of the committee. The pictures are distributed over two rooms; start in this one and follow through chronologically.'

The first room housed examples of Tate's work from his student days to 1970, the year when he suffered his first stroke. The great majority of the forty-odd pictures were landscapes: river scenes, woodland glades, farmsteads, châteaux on the Loire, peasant villages in Greece, olive groves and beached fishing boats.

Wycliffe was not very knowledgeable about paintings or painters but the Impressionists had seemed to give him a glimpse of a world before the Kaiser's war, of life on the other side of the Great Divide. Tate had certainly painted in the style of the Impressionists, but after his first tour of the room Wycliffe felt disappointed, without knowing why. Perhaps it was too large a dose of the same medicine, but many of the pictures struck him as sentimental and indulgently nostalgic.

Could it be that the Impressionists painted their world as they saw it while here was an imitator? He thought that over. At least it was something moderately sensible to say to Burger.

Before he could go on to the second room Burger came bowling swiftly over the polished floor. 'Well?'

The old man listened to his diagnosis with interest and some amusement. 'Poor old Gifford! "Sentimental and self-indulgent". Well, there are critics who would agree with you, but now have a look at the other room and see if you revise your opinion.'

There were fewer pictures in the second room: less than twenty, and Wycliffe was immediately struck by their greater vigour; the colours were stronger, on the whole, and there was greater contrast. Nature was still the dominant theme but these were pictures of the contemporary world seen through the eyes and with the mind of a man who happened to employ Impressionist techniques.

Burger gave him little time to consider his judgement before joining him again, and he felt like a schoolboy being tested on his homework.

Burger said: 'These strike you as very different?'

Wycliffe ventured: 'They seem to represent a change of attitude.'

'Yes. With very little change in technique; remarkable, isn't it?' Burger's grey eyes were watching him. 'Angela Bice, the art critic who did the blurb for the catalogue, puts it down to his stroke which she regards as a "seminal event in his life". Art critics talk like that. She sees it as "the first real set-back in his career and therefore a challenge".' Burger smiled. 'It's true that Gifford enjoyed a pretty smooth run until then; his father left him well off, he had good health, his pictures sold, and women found him attractive. What more could a man want?

'Then, almost from one moment to the next, he's paralysed down one side. . . . He took it badly at first, and no wonder!'

'But he rose to the challenge,' Wycliffe said, in order to say something.

'And rather magnificently, don't you think?'

Burger was up to mischief, that much was clear, but Wycliffe could not fathom what particular mischief.

He went on: 'I've spent a lot of time here while they've been setting this up.' A broad gesture, taking in the whole display. 'Although I was on intimate terms with Gifford for fifty years I've never before seen the whole range of his work gathered together in one place. It's been an interesting and instructive experience to see his pictures chronologically arranged.' He looked up at Wycliffe with another of his enigmatic little smiles. 'Death and rebirth at sixty-three! I hadn't realised until now what a dramatic metamorphosis it had been. Perhaps that was why Edwin was so anxious that I should buy new spectacles.'

Wycliffe, floundering, said: 'I gather from Cathy Carne that Edwin was very much looking forward to this exhibition.'

'I'm not surprised. I don't doubt that he expected to enjoy himself enormously, though what the outcome would have been — what the outcome will be — I don't know. Incidentally, in case it interests you, both my Tates belong to his later period. The first was painted soon after his stroke, and he very generously presented it to me, perhaps a sort of celebration of his invigorated talent.'

Wycliffe was well aware that the old man, in his oblique fashion, had been telling him something of importance; he realised, too, that direct questions would get him nowhere. He needed time to think, time at least to work out the right approach.

Almost in self-defence, he moved on to firmer, factual ground. 'There is one question I want to ask you — not about pictures: did you, or Garland, or Tate, to your knowledge, ever own a hand gun?'

A deep frown. Burger was conscious of the change of roles, he was being interrogated. He answered after a moment's thought: 'I never did, and I'm reasonably sure that Edwin didn't either.'

'And Tate?'

Burger hesitated again. 'Well, I do know that he bought a gun during our last Mediterranean trip. Our idea was to sail round Sardinia, and with all the tales of bandits one heard he thought it as well that we should have some means of defending ourselves.'

'When was that?'

'In '69, the year before he had his stroke.'

'You went in your own boat?'

'Good heavens, no! We crossed from Genoa on the regular service and hired a boat with a Sard crew-man in Asinara. It was in Genoa that Gifford bought his pistol — an automatic of some sort, I think.'

Chapter Ten

IT WAS FIVE o'clock, the wind had dropped, the sun was hot and
the street was almost empty. The holiday-makers were getting
what the brochures had promised. It was Sunday afternoon
and Wycliffe felt the need to walk in the sunshine, to ventilate
his lungs and his mind. Through the street, he went past the
Thomas Garland house and the docks and across the narrow
neck of land still marked by Cromwell's earthworks, thrown up
when his men besieged the castle. Wycliffe arrived at the sea-
front and the beaches. His mind was occupied by seemingly
casual recollections of things people had said, things he had
been told. He could always more easily recall the spoken than
the written word. Phrases and sentences seemed to drift to the
surface of his mind and he played with them, linking, rearranging, and eventually discarding those which seemed not to fit.
This was the mind game which he sometimes called musical
chairs.

He walked along the sea-front and stopped to lean on the rail
where he could see the beach. The Falmouth beaches are small
and rather steep compared with the great stretches of flat sand
on the northern coast. Swimming is good, surfing almost non-
existent. There is a family picnic atmosphere quite unlike the
narcissistic-maximum-exposure sun cult of the other coast.
Pleasantly nostalgic.

Wycliffe had started by thinking about the fringe provisions
of Edwin's will:

£1,000 to Alan Tate — 'the son of my friend Gifford Tate
together with my tube of Winsor blue.'

£1,000 to Martin Burger ' . . . for that new pair of spectacles
which I hope may improve his judgement and help him to see
the obvious.'

'Winsor blue is the trade name for an artists' colour . . .

148

Gifford Tate started to use it as soon as it came out, he said it brought him luck. Uncle used to tease him about it . . .'

' . . . the old man wrote Cathy a letter which I was charged to pass over unopened.'

'I hadn't realised until now what a dramatic metamorphosis it had been. Perhaps that was why Edwin was so anxious that I should buy new spectacles.'

'Uncle was really looking forward to that exhibition.'

'I don't doubt that he expected to enjoy himself enormously though what the outcome would have been — what the outcome will be — I don't know.'

Wycliffe sighed and continued his walk along the sea-front. Well, it might have been obvious but Burger himself had only recently tumbled to it and the old fox hadn't come out in the open even now. Only hints, with the implied invitation to make what he could of them.

He completed the circuit, arrived back in the main street, and made for the Incident Room. DC Curnow, the blond giant, was duty officer. Curnow had two obsessions, rugby and self-education. Rumour had it that he was working his way through the Encyclopaedia Britannica and that he had reached E.

Wycliffe put through a call to the Burger house and spoke to Mrs Burger: 'I wonder if it is possible to speak to your husband?'

Burger must have been close by for almost at once his suave, cultured voice came over the line. 'Mr Wycliffe?'

Wycliffe thanked him for the preview. 'I think that I have now understood your remarks but I shall be grateful if you will enlarge on them a little? If I might come and see you at some convenient time . . . ?'

Burger was polite, dry and evasive. 'If you are seeking an opinion on a series of pictures you should call in an expert. I am by no means an authority and my opinion would carry no weight.'

'I was hoping for confirmation of what I understand you to have said.'

A pause. 'I think you have understood me quite correctly but I am afraid that you must look elsewhere for verification.'

There was nothing for it but to thank the old man and leave it there. He had scarcely expected an open acknowledgement, let alone co-operation. All the same it was a set-back. Experts would take for ever and it is their function to disagree. In the meantime . . .

Cathy Carne was certainly not an expert but he suspected her of having knowledge of more practical value. He turned to Curnow: 'I shall be back in an hour if not before.'

He walked along the wharf to the printing works. Church bells were ringing for Evensong. Although sunset was still hours away an evening calm was settling over the harbour and town. On the south coast there is a serenity and a solemnity about fine summer evenings which can be vaguely depressing. It reminded Wycliffe of Heber's hymn about Saints casting down their golden crowns around a glassy sea.

Cathy Carne had lost something of that air of smooth competence which had impressed him at their first meeting. She looked tired and careworn and she was by no means pleased to see him though she did her best to conceal it. The flat, too, was showing signs of unusual neglect: the bedroom door stood open revealing an unmade bed. In the living-room the pages of a Sunday newspaper were scattered over the floor and there were crumbs on the carpet. On a low table there was a tray with a mug of tea and two or three roughly cut sandwiches on a plate.

'I was having tea. Can I offer you something?'

Wycliffe refused.

'You won't mind if I carry on?' She did it to keep in countenance.

'I suppose you have heard that Mark Garland is missing?'

'*Missing*?'

'It was on the local news at lunchtime; in any case, I thought Dr Tate might have told you.'

'I didn't listen to local radio at lunchtime and although Dr Tate is a friend we don't live in each other's pockets.' Snappish.

'So he hasn't told you either that Mark was having a homosexual affair with Francis?'

She paused with one of the sandwiches half-way to her lips. 'Mark and Francis? I can't believe it!'

'They met regularly at Brand's place. Last Tuesday they had a jealous quarrel; that was how Francis came by his bruised face.'

She gave up any pretence of continuing with her tea; she put the sandwich back on her plate, pulled down the hem of her skirt, and seemed to brace herself.

Wycliffe could not make up his mind. Was she really hearing all this for the first time?

The dark blue eyes studied him with disturbing intensity. 'You think Mark killed him; is that it?'

'That is one possibility, but there is another: that Mark too has been murdered.'

Her response was instant. 'I can't believe that! Why should anyone want to kill Mark?'

'Perhaps for the same reason that Francis was murdered — because he knew something which threatened the killer. I've warned you already that you may be running that kind of risk yourself.'

She turned on him angrily. 'And I have told you that I don't know what you are talking about!'

In almost convulsive movements she crossed her legs and clasped her hands about her knees. 'You don't give up, do you? As it happens I've made up my mind to tell you what was in Uncle's letter because I realise that I shall have no peace until I do.'

'Go on.'

'I didn't want to — not because it effects me but because it concerns Beryl and Francis.'

Wycliffe wondered at this sudden consideration for her cousins.

'Uncle thought that I might have misgivings about accepting a substantial share of his property and depriving them of what they might look upon as theirs by right.'

'So?'

'He told me in his letter that neither Beryl nor Francis were his children, both were illegitimate; their true father was a man called Jose, an estate agent.' She reached for her cigarettes. 'Does that satisfy you?'

'No. It's a good try but that affair between Edwin's wife and the estate agent has entered into folklore; Edwin must have known that it was common knowledge and he also knew you too well to suppose that you would be unduly troubled about your cousins' feelings anyway.'

She lit her cigarette with a concentrated effort at composure. 'Be as unpleasant as you like but I've told you what there is to tell.'

'All right, leave it for the moment. Let's talk about paintings: you won't have had a chance to see the Tate exhibition yet but — '

'I have seen it; Papa Burger invited me to a sneak preview this morning.'

'Then you must have noticed the differences between the paintings in the two rooms. I'm not knowledgeable about painting but one could hardly miss them.'

She made a gesture of impatience. 'Of course there are differences. What do you expect when a man resumes painting after a severe stroke? He's not going to take up his brush just where he left off.'

Wycliffe leaned forward in his chair. 'Let's stop playing games. You've known since last Thursday, when you read your uncle's letter, that Tate never painted a single picture after his stroke. All the subsequent work attributed to him was painted by your uncle.'

She was silent for a moment or two, watching him through the haze of her cigarette smoke, then she made up her mind. When she spoke she seemed to be mentally ticking off her points, and her manner was contemptuous. 'Gifford Tate's pictures have been studied and written about by experts, there are several of his earlier and later works in national collections, here and abroad; all his pictures are handled by a prestigious London gallery and many have been bought by notable connoisseurs. Don't you think it surprising that no one has noticed a fraud?'

Wycliffe sounded bored. 'I've nothing to say about art experts and you have no need of their opinions as far as Tate's work is concerned; you know the facts, and you have the word of the man who painted about a third of the pictures in that exhibition. I doubt whether his letter to you came as a complete surprise but that doesn't matter.'

'You are saying that Tate allowed my uncle to use his name and imitate his work over a period of several years — why?'

'Well, there was a very substantial income from the pictures, but I hardly think that carried a great deal of weight. From what you and others have told me about your uncle and Gifford Tate, my guess would be that it all started as a joke — a bit of fun, possibly to cheer up Tate. The first forgery — if we are to call it that — was presented to Papa Burger as a test, and the fact that it was accepted by him as the work of a re-invigorated Tate was irresistible to the jokers. If Burger was taken in it was altogether too tempting to try it on the art world at large. It seems they lapped it up, and still do. In the words of the catalogue poor old Tate's stroke was "a seminal event" in the development of his talent. Heady stuff!'

The sun had come round to shine through the westward facing window and the golden light seemed to emphasise the dust on the furniture and the fluff on the carpet in a room that was usually immaculate.

Cathy Carne sat back in her chair as though dissociating herself from all that had been said. 'If that's what you want to believe then I can't stop you but I don't know where you are going to find the evidence or why you should want it.'

Wycliffe said: 'I don't think evidence will be difficult to come by and I shall search for it because this fraud, and his knowledge of it, was responsible for Francis's death.'

She was engaged in stubbing out her cigarette and he could not judge her reaction.

'The original hoax, dreamed up by Edwin and Tate, was so successful that they found themselves riding a tiger — not, I suspect, that they were all that anxious to get off. The whole thing appealed to their rather malicious sense of humour and it was also very profitable.'

Cathy Carne maintained a slightly amused, contemptuous attitude. 'So why was Edwin so anxious to tell me about it when he died?'

'The answer could be that a hoax loses its point if nobody realises that it is one, but I think there was more to it than that. Edwin left it until his death to confide in you, but he had told Francis a year before.'

She could no longer sit still; she got up and walked over to the window. 'As I've already told you, Francis was the very last person he would confide in about anything.'

Wycliffe went on as though she had not spoken. 'Your uncle had a low opinion of most of the people around him and he seemed to take pleasure in the prospect of frustrating them. Think of his will in which he left the residue of his estate jointly to Beryl and Francis.'

Without turning round she said: 'I agree with you there, but — '

'The way he went about exposing the picture hoax was another example. Francis was briefed first. For a year he had the satisfaction of watching Francis, primed, ready to burst, but unable to speak without risking his expectations under the will. But if, for any reason, Francis failed to speak when Edwin was dead, you had your letter and Papa Burger and Alan Tate, their enigmatic bequests. Who would do what? Another stir of the pudding. But, of course, he wouldn't be there to see.

'As his health deteriorated one has the impression that he became more determined to get as much entertainment as possible out of the situation, to sail nearer the wind, and so we have this exhibition which he didn't live to see. Imagine him if he had, watching the reactions as this severely chronological arrangement of pictures made its impact in moving round the country. It would be seen and reviewed by the Mandarins of the art establishment. Surely somebody would have the insight — and the guts — to blow the whistle? No wonder he was looking forward to it!'

She turned away from the window with a sigh. 'I'm not going to argue with you.'

Wycliffe got up from his chair. 'No, but just think of your position: by your refusal to talk you run a serious risk of being regarded as an accessory and, if Mark Garland was murdered, you will have contributed to his death.'

'And how would Mark Garland have come by this great secret?' She was scathing.

'Pillow talk? I believe lovers are notoriously indiscreet in their confidences. What was it that Mark was so anxious to explain to Beryl? Don't you think that when he failed he might reasonably have tried elsewhere?'

She was very pale but she said nothing. She saw him to the door and stood at the top of the steps as he went down. When she closed the door did she go straight to the telephone? Tonight he was not quite so sure. He was taking a risk, but he had to get the case moving somehow or risk worse to come.

DC Curnow handed him a polythene envelope containing a sheet of mauve writing paper. 'Pushed through the letter-box earlier this evening, sir. Just folded across, no envelope; anonymous, of course.'

Written in a round, schoolgirlish hand, the message read: 'Thelma George says she heard a shot when she passed the Tates house Saturday evening. She works in Paynes coffee shop.'

Explicit, and more literate than most, but every major case draws the fire of practical jokers and nutters. All the same . . .

Curnow went on: 'I contacted DS Lane, sir, and she traced the girl George through the owner of the coffee shop. She's gone to talk to her. She shouldn't be long.'

She wasn't. In ten minutes Lucy Lane arrived back with the girl: a fair, skinny seventeen-year old, packaged in the inevitable jeans and T-shirt. She was nervous and resentful. 'You think you got friends and this is what they do to you.' She examined the anonymous note with distaste. 'That's Sharon James, I'd know her writing anywhere. I never wanted to get mixed up with the police.'

Wycliffe was gentle. 'But you *were* outside the Tates' house sometime on Saturday evening?'

The girl looked at Lucy Lane. 'I told her.'

'At about what time were you there?'

'About half-past eight; I was on my way to a friend's place.'

'And you heard a shot?'

'I never said it was a shot; I said I thought it sounded like a shot but I don't really know what a shot sounds like, do I? It was a sort of crack, not very loud. Anyway, who'd be firing off a gun in a place like that? I didn't think any more about it.'

'But you must have mentioned it to someone.'

'Well, yes. I was out with the usual crowd this afternoon and one of the girls whose mother works at the Tates said the police had been there about that man Garland who's missing and I just said what I heard — just for the sake of something to say.'

'I'm glad you did. Now I would like you to go with Miss Lane and let her write down an account of what happened on Saturday evening for you to sign.'

'Can I go then?'

'Of course! Miss Lane will take you home.'

Lucy Lane shepherded her into the little interview room.

A shot at 8.30 on Saturday evening at the Tates' place! It was almost unbelievable but the girl, a reluctant witness — often the best, had heard something, and the time was significant. At any rate he couldn't ignore it. He contacted sub-division and arranged for the Tate house to be kept under surveillance until further notice. No need for concealment. It would do the doctor no harm to find a police car outside his gates.

PC Dart in his Panda Car had taken up his position outside the gates of Tregarthen at 22.00 and it was now 02.15; nearly four hours of his shift to go. He was unaccustomed to the deadly monotony of surveillance. This was the third time he had been out of his car, walking up and down to stretch his legs and keep awake. A quiet, warm, moonlit night, no one about. The great pines in the garden of Tregarthen rose out of the shadows and towered against the sky. A motor cycle engine, muted by distance, roared briefly then faded. The whole town seemed asleep. He was standing by the drive gates when he heard a scream, followed by another, abruptly cut short. He could see twinkling lights from the direction of the house which had not been there before.

On his personal radio he called his station and reported, then he entered the grounds through the wicket gate and sprinted up the drive. There were lights in the house, upstairs and down. He reached the front door, put his finger on the bell, and kept it there. Three years in the force had not cured him of butterflies in the stomach when faced with a possible emergency. Apart from anything else he dreaded making a fool of himself.

He could hear a man's voice, measured, reassuring. A light went on in the hall and the door was opened by Dr Tate himself; he was fully dressed. Mrs Tate, in her nightdress with a dressing gown over her shoulders, was standing behind him. She looked desperately pale, but more or less composed. Tate said: 'I know you, don't I? PC Dart, isn't it?'

'Yes, sir; I heard screams.'

'Yes, I'm afraid you must have done. Mrs Tate had a distressing nightmare and, as you can see, she is still very upset. I'm going to get her a hot drink then, back to bed . . . Good night, and thank you for coming to our rescue.'

'Good night, sir . . . Madam.'

In other parts of the town PC Dart would have had no hesitation in logging a 'domestic' — a family row.

Chapter Eleven

WYCLIFFE, AFTER AN early breakfast, was at the Incident Room by eight o'clock but Kersey was ahead of him.

'I hear the Tates had a disturbed night, sir. Marcella is supposed to have had a nightmare.'

Wycliffe glanced through the report which had come through from the local station.

Kersey said: 'Do you believe it?'

'I'm reaching a point where I'm prepared to believe anything. You've heard about the girl who thinks she heard a shot?'

'Yes. Seems a bit unlikely, don't you think? I can't see Tate using a gun in his own house; too risky. It's not all that isolated and he's not stupid.'

'Nobody noticed Marcella's screams last night or, if they did, they didn't do anything about it. In any case people instinctively explain away something as unlikely as the sound of a shot, especially in that sort of neighbourhood. Anyway it's given us a lever with Tate; he's got a Panda car sitting outside his gate. Let him try living with that for a bit.'

Kersey selected a bent cigarette from a crushed pack and straightened it with loving care. He said: 'You think the solution lies in that direction?'

'Things seem to point that way. Any one of several people might have killed Francis but, if Mark Garland was murdered, what we know so far suggests that he died on Saturday evening in the Tate house.'

'Because somebody saw him go in and nobody saw him come out?'

'There is also the girl's story of a possible shot at the critical time — 8.30 — and she sounded like a credible witness. But look at the alternative, that Mark Garland was the culprit, not another victim. If he intended to do a bunk would he put on his best suit, leave his car in the garage, and pay a call on his doctor without even a weekend bag?'

'Isn't it possible that he committed suicide?'

'You think that would make the suit and the doctor more plausible?'

Kersey's face, mobile as a clown's, expressed grudging acceptance. 'I must admit, put like that, it sounds better than I'd thought, but I would have expected something more subtle from the doctor. And what about motive?'

Wycliffe retailed the picture saga and Kersey listened with close attention but at the end he was still dubious. 'You are suggesting that Tate killed twice — for what? To cover up the fact that his father and Edwin Garland had bamboozled the art world for years. Is that it, sir?'

Wycliffe shook his head. 'That's not exactly what I had in mind. Anyway, I'm going to tackle Tate this morning and I want you to lay on a search of his premises this afternoon — I'll fix it with Tate without a warrant if possible. If Mark Garland was murdered, Tate's problem was or is to get rid of the body where no one will find it.'

'Would it matter if it was found?'

'I think so. Unless Tate faked a convincing suicide, Garland would lose his value as a scapegoat and our investigation would continue; in fact, it would be reinforced.'

Kersey said: 'It's not easy to hide a body unless you can drop it overboard in deep water with a hefty sinker.'

'That's the point; and it's unlikely that Tate managed that or anything like it on Saturday night. It would be asking for trouble to risk trying by day, and we've had his place under surveillance since yesterday evening.'

Kersey exhaled a cloud of grey smoke and coughed. 'You think the body may still be on the premises?'

'If there is a body — I think it's possible.'

'So you want a search team for this afternoon. You think Tate will consent?'

'It will be interesting to find out. If not, we get a warrant.'

Another beautiful day, still with that morning freshness but with the promise of heat: Wycliffe upheld the dignity of the Force in a light-weight grey suit, with collar and tie, and knew that he would regret it later. A trickle of people made their way to the beaches, lobster-coloured parents and trailing children. He drove up to the terraces and parked near a Panda car outside the Tates'.

'PC Gregory, sir. PC Dart was relieved at six.'

'Anything happening?'

'Nothing much, sir. At 07.30 the woman who works here arrived. At 08.00 Dr Tate came out and asked me what I was doing here. I told him I was on duty and he went in again. At 08.40 a young chap in overalls drove up in a junior Volvo. He opened the big gate and was about to drive in. I asked him what was going on and he said he was from Barton's Garage. He'd come to collect Dr Tate's car for repair and he was going to leave the other as a temporary replacement. A few minutes later he came out driving the doctor's big Volvo and I saw that the off-side bumper was sagging a bit, the headlamp was smashed and the bodywork damaged.'

'I know, I saw it earlier.'

'Since then, nothing except that the receptionist turned up for work at 08.50.'

Wycliffe walked up the drive to the front door and rang the bell. It was answered by a thin, grey-haired woman wearing an overall. He said: 'Chief Superintendent Wycliffe.'

She looked at him with unconcealed antagonism. 'I know who you are. I must say, you choose your time. The doctor has his surgery and there's a waiting-room full of patients. It's none of my business but I should think the police had something better to do than come pestering people like the doctor.'

Obviously a disciple.

'Who are you?'

'Me? I'm Mrs Irons. I come in daily to help out — except Sundays that is.'

Wycliffe said: 'Will you ask Mrs Tate if she will see me?'

She gave him a dubious look, unsure how safe it was to trifle with a chief superintendent. 'She's not well; she shouldn't be worried.'

'Ask her.'

He waited in the black-and-white tiled hall, listening to the grandfather clock as it grudgingly doled out the seconds. A couple of minutes went by before Mrs Irons came back.

'All right. She'll see you in her room. You'd better come with me.'

Marcella's room was between the drawing-room and the dining-room and it had a french window opening to the garden at the side of the house. Marcella, wearing a shabby, green housecoat, was sitting at a knee-hole desk with an exercise book open in front of her. Her little dog was asleep in a basket at her feet. She got up to greet him.

Wycliffe said: 'I'm sorry to intrude; I gather you had a disturbed night.'

A self-conscious laugh. 'I had a nightmare. Absurd really! I dreamt that I was being suffocated and I was terrified. I haven't had anything like it since I was a young girl and I feel really silly.'

Her voice was unnaturally loud and her manner was tense — brittle.

'Do sit down.' She pointed to a chair and sat down herself.

'It must have given Dr Tate a fright.'

'Yes, it did. Luckily he hadn't gone to bed; he was working in his surgery. Paper work; you wouldn't believe! He really needs more help. At least one night a week he's up until the small hours.'

He was shocked by the change in her appearance. In her shapeless and worn housecoat which hung about her in folds, with her haggard features and untended hair, she looked like a severely harassed housewife cultivating an addiction to Valium. But she was more ready to talk than she had been during his last visit; perhaps too ready.

'Will you tell me what happened on Saturday evening?'

She frowned, obviously simulating an effort of memory. 'Saturday evening was when Mark Garland came. I was out, taking Ricky for a walk. I went out soon after eight; I prefer it when there are not too many people about, don't you?'

'Where did you go?'

'Oh, the usual — across the sea-front. It was a lovely evening and we sat, Ricky and I, in one of the shelters for a while.'

'When did you get back?'

'After nine.'

'Was Mark Garland here then?'

'Oh, no; he'd gone. Alan told me what he'd come about but I've forgotten.'

She was well briefed.

'Did you meet anyone you knew while you were out?'

'I don't think so. I talked to a lady in the shelter but she was a visitor, staying in one of the sea-front hotels I think.'

The room was sparsely furnished: the desk, bookshelves, and two or three unmatched chairs. A couple of pictures and a few photographs impressed some individuality on the room which was otherwise tasteless and institutional. But Marcella's pictures were Tates: head and shoulders portraits; one of her, younger and plumper; the other, obviously a self-portrait, of a gentleman with a spade beard and an elaborately cultivated moustache. Looking at the man it was easy to see where Alan Tate had got his large, doggy-brown eyes.

She saw his interest. 'Gifford did them especially for me; he didn't usually do portraits and I wouldn't part with them whatever happened!'

'Of course not.'

She was staring up at the portrait of her husband with a reflective air. She said: 'I know people don't believe it but I loved Gifford, really loved him, and we only had two years together before his stroke.'

'That was very sad.'

She looked quickly at him and away again, bird like. It was odd; her naivety seemed blended with a shrewd concern about the impression she made.

'And yet his stroke made no real difference. In a way it was better for me because he needed me and I had him more to myself. . . . You see, he'd done everything for me, everything!' She spoke haltingly and in a low voice that was almost reverential.

'I mean, I was brought up by my mother in a council flat on social security. I never knew my father. I was very lucky to go to university but it was only like a continuation of school — I couldn't mix much because I never had any spending money.' Another fleeting glance to see the effect of her words.

'It was only after I met Gifford that I realised what real life could be like.' She picked up the exercise book from her desk. 'I told you I was writing his biography, didn't I? This is one of his diaries. There's a bit in here about the first time we met; he took the trouble to mention it in his diary. I'll read it to you.' She found the page and read a passage which she obviously knew by heart: '"After the lecture a sweetly plain little mouse with flaxen hair came up to me and asked questions in the most earnest fashion possible. She said her name was Marcella! What pretentious names parents give their children nowadays!"' She blushed shyly and closed the book. 'He got to like my name later.

'I'm going to call the biography "Renewal" because I remember him saying once: "Who could possibly want eternal life? I should be bored to distraction! Eternal renewal — well, that's a different matter. I think I might settle for that." And in a way he experienced a renewal, didn't he?' Once more she looked Wycliffe in the eyes.

'You've no idea what it all means to me!' She was on the verge of tears. 'Almost everything in this house is as it was when he was alive; the studio and his bedroom are exactly as they were. . . . Sometimes in the evenings, when I am in the house alone, I can believe that *nothing* has changed. I feel that he is *here*, that I have really found a way — '

There was a knock at the door, it was opened, and Tate's receptionist came in, blonde, white coated, and peremptory: 'Excuse me. The doctor will see you now, Mr Wycliffe.'

Wycliffe said: 'I'll be along in a few minutes.'

Marcella immediately became agitated. 'No! No! You must go now. You must! You must!' In her excitement she stood up and almost shooed him from the room.

In the corridor Wycliffe said: 'Has the doctor finished with his patients early?'

'No, he's seeing you between patients and I hope you won't keep him long; he's very busy and grossly overworked.'

Another disciple.

Tate was sitting at his desk with a selection of patients' records in front of him. He was distant but civil. He indicated a chair with a gesture.

'I suppose your visit concerns Mrs Tate's distressing experience last night though why that should interest the police I don't know.'

It was clear that he was under stress; his movements were restrained and precise, his words as carefully chosen as ever, but he looked very tired and even his spectacles failed to hide a darkening about the eyes.

Wycliffe said: 'I am here about Mark Garland's disappearance. I don't think you need me to explain your position, Doctor, but I have an obligation to do so. Mark Garland was seen arriving here, as you yourself said he did, at about eight o'clock on Sunday evening. Despite widespread enquiries we have been unable to find anyone who has seen him since. In the circumstances it is natural that we should begin our enquiry into his disappearance where he was last seen.'

Tate was looking at him with attention but with no hint of concern. 'So what do you propose to do?'

An observer might have thought that they were discussing some academic problem of no great moment to either of them.

'There is another fact to be taken into account: a passer-by, at about eight-thirty on Sunday evening, says she heard a sound like a shot which seemed to come from this house.'

'A shot?' Incredulous.

'Yes, and that information taken with the fact that on present evidence Garland was last seen in this house, makes a search of your premises inevitable. If I apply to the magistrate for a warrant I have no doubt that it would be granted but I would much prefer to conduct a search with your consent.'

Tate smiled. 'I don't doubt it. If I agree, the police have nothing whatever to lose; if I do not agree and you are successful in obtaining a warrant but find nothing incriminatory, the police will look foolish and, with other things taken into account, it might appear that I am being unduly harassed.'

'The decision is yours.'

Tate studied his finger-nails for a moment or two, then he said: 'I am inclined to agree to your search. You are pestering me with your visits, you have a police vehicle apparently on permanent station outside my gate, and you are encouraging my neighbours to spy on me. If a search of my house will put a stop to these intrusions it might be an acceptable price to pay.'

'The search would have to be thorough and unhampered.'

'But I have nothing to hide.'

'You may wish to consult your lawyer.'

'I know my own mind, Mr Wycliffe.' Tate was gathering up certain of his patients' records into a neat pile; when he had done so, he slipped an elastic band around them. 'When will your search begin?'

'At two o'clock this afternoon. I will see that it is carried out with as little disturbance as possible. There's another matter: now that there is a suspicion of foul play in connection with Mark Garland's disappearance I have to ask you and Mrs Tate to put your accounts of what happened on Saturday evening into writing.'

'But Mrs Tate wasn't here, I've told you.'

'Then she can say so in writing. But we will leave it until this afternoon.'

Tate barely controlled his annoyance. 'I think you should tell me, Chief Superintendent, what possible reason I could have for wanting Mark Garland dead. Surely to qualify as a major suspect one has to satisfy criteria based on means, opportunity — and motive.'

It was Wycliffe's turn to consider his words. 'All I can say is that if Mark Garland was murdered it was because he knew why Francis Garland died and who had an interest in his death.'

'And that implicates me?'

Wycliffe returned his stare. 'Only you know the answer to that with certainty, Dr Tate. Just one more request: I would like to take another look around your father's studio while I am here.'

The doctor did not answer at once, his hands clenched but immediately relaxed again. 'If you wish. Miss Ward, my receptionist, will give you the key.'

Miss Ward met him in the passage. 'You will have to come through the kitchen.'

She gave him the key and let him out into the courtyard. 'Lock the door when you've finished and put the key in the kitchen.'

The sun had not yet come round to the back of the house and it was deliciously cool under the green glass roof. Presumably it was here that Gifford Tate had relaxed during his last summer, that blazing summer of '76, while his young wife sat naked in one of the cushioned chairs, reading from the pages of Proust's *Remembrance of Things Past*. Refined titillation for the elderly and the impotent; a scene from a Grecian vase: Satyr with Maiden.

Wycliffe wanted to look at the studio again in the light of what he had learned from Burger. It was the place where Tate had spent most of his time after his stroke, much of it in company with Edwin Garland.

There were too many strands. Changing the metaphor, he felt like a juggler trying to keep too many balls in the air at once.

As he passed the window of the waiting-room all the chairs seemed to be occupied and he suspected that Tate had been concerned to cut short his conversation with Marcella.

He crossed the grass to the studio, climbed the steps and unlocked the door. The substantial timber building was cool in the heat and the north-facing windows excluded the glare of the sun so that the big room seemed dimly lit in contrast with outside. He had seen it all before, but now he was seeing it with new eyes: the pot-bellied iron stove, the coal bucket, the deep, leather armchairs drawn up on either side, and the chess-board between.

Gifford and Edwin. He could imagine them on a winter's afternoon in front of a glowing stove: Gifford, in the early stages of convalescence, and depressed; Edwin, trying to kindle a spark. They would be smoking, both of them against doctor's orders; Gifford, his pipe, Edwin, his homemade cigarettes. There were paper spills in a pot by the stove. From the time of

166

Gifford's stroke it seemed they had seen less of Burger and so, perhaps, they were drawn closer together.

No doubt it began with idle talk. 'Wouldn't it be a laugh if . . . ?'

And later: 'Why not try it?'

A heartening chuckle from Gifford. 'Make a present of it to Papa and see what he makes of it.'

Schoolboys planning mischief.

Wycliffe brought himself back to the here and now. In the afternoon he would have the house and grounds searched, now was his chance to take a look around the studio. Not that he would find anything; Tate had been unconcerned about leaving him alone there. Mechanically, he went through the cupboards and drawers but he made only one discovery: a cupboard full of bottles and glasses: sherry, port, whisky, vodka, gin. . . . The tuck box.

There was nowhere in the studio where a body might have been hidden; he even examined the floorboards and satisfied himself that they had not been lifted since the place was built.

With a certain reluctance, he locked the door and crossed the grass to return the key. The numbers in the waiting-room seemed hardly to have changed.

He had no doubt that Mark Garland was dead, that he had been shot, and that the shooting had taken place in or around this house. The pistol could easily be disposed of or hidden, and it might remain hidden despite his intended search. The body was a different matter. Tate was a clever man but he was not a magician, yet he seemed undisturbed at the prospect of a search.

Wycliffe entered the courtyard under a Moorish arch. It was certainly a very pleasant retreat, cool in the heat and sheltered from most winds. The sun was coming round. The gentle splash of the fountain was soothing and the falling water droplets glistened in the sunlight, sometimes with rainbow effects. There was a waterlily with white flowers and beneath its heart-shaped leaves orange and red fish lurked, half-hidden.

Mrs Irons, the daily woman, was in the kitchen and he handed her the key.

'Do you want to see anybody?'

'No, thank you, I'll go out around the back.'

'Suit yourself.'

As he turned back to the courtyard it occurred to him that the paving slabs immediately around the pool had been very recently cleaned; they were free of the dark lichen which 'ages' concrete or stone paving slabs and was present on all the others. Most people encourage it. His wife, Helen offered libations of stale yoghurt to promote its growth, others preferred the pristine rawness of the builders' yard, but only the slabs near the pool had been scrubbed.

Marcella had said: 'Alan and I sometimes sit out here on warm summer evenings.'

Sunday evening had been warm and sunny. What could be more natural than that Garland should have been taken there instead of to the surgery or the drawing-room? A shooting indoors is likely to leave traces which are difficult or impossible to remove or disguise. How much simpler. . . . And the paving slabs had been scrubbed. There was an independent witness to Garland's arrival but only Tate's word for what had happened afterwards and, according to him, he had been in the house alone.

Wycliffe looked about him with new interest. His eye was caught by something glistening on the very edge of the pool nearest to him. He stooped to see what it was and found a small groove in one of the slabs. Tiny quartz crystals in the concrete, freshly exposed, were catching the light. . . . Was he letting his imagination run away with him? He went back under the green glass roof to fetch one of the lounging chairs and saw Marcella watching him through the kitchen window. Let her watch.

He placed the chair fairly close to the pool and stood behind it. The head and neck of anyone sitting in the chair would come above the back of the chair and, as far as he could tell, a bullet fired from about that position might graze the edge of the pool before entering the water. . . . He put the chair back where he had found it. This was work for the experts.

He walked round the house to the drive and down towards the gate. The resinous scent of the pines, distilled by the heat, filled the air. From the drive there were tantalising glimpses of the harbour and of Trefusis fields beyond. The Tates lived in a very pleasant house in a large secluded garden; they were in good health, they were still short of middle age, and yet. . . . He wasn't sure what it was he was trying to express, unless it was a sense of incongruity between these people, this setting, and violent crime.

Alan Tate seemed to value a calm orderliness in the pattern of his days. When his father died and left him the house he had given up a fairly prestigious consultancy to move back home and set up as a GP in a small town. He had kept his contacts to a minimum; he had accepted his father's young wife as house-keeper and left her free to fantasise over his father, the elderly Prince Charming who, she claimed, had awakened her to life.

For eight years it had seemed to work, until that Wednesday morning, the day of the funeral, when Francis had arrived with a picture under his arm. Had the story which Francis had to tell come as such a devastating shock that murder seemed the only way out?

Wycliffe found himself outside the Tate's gate, standing by his car, conscious of the curious gaze of PC Gregory. He was preoccupied and decided to walk, so he left his car where it was.

Walking downhill, or down steps from the terraces, it is difficult to avoid reaching the main street, so he did not plot a course and, half-way down, after a flight of steps, he arrived in a quiet cul-de-sac, a row of colour-washed little houses opposite a disused burial ground and a yard at the end with a sign on the double gate: Barton's Garage. Car-body Repair Depot. Presumably where Tate's car was under repair. A steep slope and another flight of steps and he was in the main street.

'Fox, Curnow, Dixon and Lucy Lane, that makes four; five with you. Lucy will probably have to cope with Marcella as an extra.'

Wycliffe, Kersey and Lucy Lane in planning session. Kersey was not altogether happy. 'I take it the team will be searching for a .32 automatic and/or Mark Garland's body. Do you think they stand any chance of finding either?'

'They will also be looking for evidence that a shooting did take place on the premises and that could be a better bet.'

It was very hot in the Incident Room, all the windows were open but there was not enough movement of the air to stir the papers on the tables. The sky was blue and so were the waters of the harbour; there was an all-pervading stillness. If there was any sailing it must be going on out in the bay where they might just catch the whisper of a wind.

Kersey lit a cigarette and stared out of the window. 'Tate must have got rid of the body if there is one or he would have tried to stall the search.'

Wycliffe said: 'Has anyone found a decent place for a light lunch?'

Lucy Lane volunteered: 'If you're willing to trust my judgement, sir.'

'Implicitly.'

'It's called Twining's and it's just around the corner from here.'

She took them to a place not far from the car-park where they had a seat by a window overlooking the harbour. *Ratatouille au gratin* and a bottle of hock. They were disputing whether a light lunch could be stretched to include a dessert when Wycliffe was called to the telephone. It was Potter at the Incident Room.

'I heard you say where you were going for lunch, sir. You're wanted at the Tates' house urgently. Dr Tate has been found in his surgery, shot through the head, he's dead. PC Gregory reported on the telephone from the house just before one o'clock.'

Chapter Twelve

WYCLIFFE STOOD LOOKING down at the doctor's body which
had slumped on its left side between the chair and the desk, the
head towards the window, resting on the carpet which was
stained with blood. There was a smallish hole in the right side of
his head just above and in front of the ear pinna. His right arm
rested limply behind his thigh as though it had slipped into that
position as he collapsed. Wycliffe could see the pistol under the
desk and slightly in front of the body. The swivel chair was
farther from the desk than it would have been in use, probably
pushed back as the body slumped sideways.

On the face of it, suicide.

The spectacles, their thick lenses apparently undamaged,
were lying at a little distance from the dead man's face, the dark
brown eyes were open and staring.

'A compassionate man,' Burger had said.

The little clock on the desk, flicking the seconds away,
registered 29 minutes past one. Less than three hours earlier he,
Wycliffe, had been sitting in the patients' chair on the other side
of the desk. The bundle of medical records about which the
doctor had slipped an elastic band was still there. Wycliffe
shuddered in a brief spasm of revulsion against himself and his
job; for an instant he was overwhelmed by guilt. He had not
caused this man's death but if he had foreseen it, as he might
have done. . . . Then professionalism came to his rescue: no
sign of a note.

Kersey had taken over the dining-room where there was a
telephone, and Wycliffe joined him there. PC Gregory was
making his report; a lean, dark man in his thirties with enough
experience not to be flustered.

'At 12.45 I heard what I took to be a shot though, I must
admit, if it hadn't been for all that went before, I might not have

thought so. I reported in on my radio then I ran up the drive to the house. I tried the door but it was secured. I rang the bell but didn't wait for an answer. I went round to the back; the waiting-room door was locked so I found my way through the courtyard to the kitchen. That door wasn't locked but it was on a chain and I couldn't get in. In the end I smashed the glass of the kitchen window and climbed in over the sink.

'I couldn't hear anything at all. I called out but there was no answer. I went through the kitchen and into the passage and found Mrs Tate standing in the doorway of the surgery. She was sort of holding herself with both hands and when she saw me she said: "He shot himself! He shot himself!" and she kept on saying it. She seemed dazed. I could see the doctor behind the desk. I made sure nothing could be done for him then I got Mrs Tate in here and I telephoned. I called the Incident Room at 12.57.'

Kersey said: 'What time was it when you actually got into the house?'

The man shook his head. 'I don't know, sir, but with one thing and another I think it must have been at least five minutes after the shot before I was actually in the house.' He looked uneasily at Wycliffe who was gazing at him heavy-eyed.

Kersey said: 'That's honest anyway. Did Mrs Tate say anything more?'

'Not a word, sir. She seemed completely dazed and she let me guide her around as though she had no will of her own.'

'Any idea where the cleaning woman was in all this?'

'She left at twelve, sir. She lives close by and she goes home from twelve till two to give her husband his lunch.'

'All right, when your relief arrives, go back and write your report.'

The front doorbell rang and Wycliffe said: 'That'll be the police surgeon. Don't forget the coroner's office.' He went to meet the police surgeon, a young, unassuming Scot, sandy haired, with freckles.

'Dr McPherson.' The two men shook hands.

'He's in his surgery.'

McPherson followed him down the passage to the surgery, glanced about him with professional interest at his colleague's furniture and fittings, then bent over the body. A very brief examination with the minimum of disturbance. 'Well, you don't need me to tell you that he's dead or how, or when. It's a sad business; he'll be missed by his patients and by some of us. He was a first rate physician and a good GP. I don't mind admitting he's helped me out more than once. Will you be wanting me for the PM?'

'I think the coroner will nominate Franks.'

A look of surprise. 'For a suicide?'

'There may be wider implications.'

'I see. Well, I won't say I haven't heard talk about police interest but I never imagined . . .'

'Will you see Mrs Tate?'

'Ah, yes, Marcella. Where is she?'

'Upstairs, a woman officer is with her. I gather she's in shock.'

'I can believe it.'

Wycliffe was making a painful effort to come to terms with what he believed to be his own failure. 'A compassionate man, a first-rate physician and a good GP.'

Sergeant Fox, the scenes-of-crime officer, arrived and there was a telephone call from Dr Franks, the pathologist. Wycliffe took the call in the dining-room.

'I've just had your message, Charles. As it happens I'm in Plymouth and my secretary phoned through. I can be with you in about 75 minutes.'

Wycliffe, always mildly irritated by the ebullient doctor, snapped: 'The man is dead, there's no point in maiming somebody else to get here.'

Franks was notorious for fast driving.

'They'll direct you from the Incident Room on the Wharf car-park.'

He could hear a woman's voice raised in the kitchen and found Mrs Irons, the cleaning woman, confronting DC Curnow. She seized on Wycliffe, wide-eyed and trembling: 'He says the doctor is dead!'

173

'I'm afraid that's true.'

'But how? I mean, what's happened? He was all right when I left . . .'

'We don't know exactly what has happened.' He was sorry for her; she seemed deeply distressed.

'Where is Mrs Tate?'

'She's up in her bedroom; a doctor is with her.'

'Then I'm going up.' Challenging.

'Yes, I think that would be a good idea. Just a couple of questions first: When you went to lunch where were the doctor and Mrs Tate?'

Through her tears she said: 'He was in his surgery and she was in the kitchen preparing lunch.'

'Nothing unusual happened?'

'Nothing!'

'Just one more question: Where is Miss Ward, the receptionist?'

'She goes as soon as she's cleared up after morning surgery and she doesn't come back until four.'

In the surgery Fox was photographing the body from all accessible angles, and every aspect of the room. Fox was a very efficient scenes-of-crime officer; his Punch-like nose and receding chin gave him a comical profile and his conceit alienated goodwill, but he worked smoothly, with scarcely a pause, knowing precisely what he was going to do and the order in which he would do it. When he had all his photographs he recovered the pistol with the help of a long-handled forceps which gripped the trigger guard width-wise.

'I understand you don't want the body disturbed until Dr Franks arrives, sir.'

'That's right; get the pistol off to the lab straight away: dabs, and a full ballistics report.'

Fox placed the pistol on a prepared bed of cotton-wool in a cardboard box.

Wycliffe said: 'I want swabs taken from his and her hands for the rhodizinate test. Tell her that the test is routine.'

As he left the surgery Wycliffe met Dr McPherson coming to look for him.

174

'How is she?'

'She'll be all right. An emotional shock takes different people in different ways; her pulse rate is a bit erratic; she keeps feeling her throat, probably an hysterical constriction, and she's a bit vague. There isn't much to worry about, physically speaking, but it would be as well not to leave her alone. Rest and soothing companionship. I wondered about sending along a nurse? Mrs What's-her-name seems a decent soul but it might be better to have a professional. Do you know of any relatives?'

'None. I think she should have a nurse. What about questioning her?'

'Give her a couple of hours. I'll look in again this evening.'

Wycliffe rejoined Kersey in the dining-room.

Kersey had had time to ruminate. 'He couldn't face the prospect of a search, I suppose.' And then, as a new thought struck him, he looked up at Wycliffe. 'You're not blaming yourself?'

Wycliffe did not answer directly. 'I don't think the search had much to do with it. I think he was prepared for that.'

'What then?'

Wycliffe was standing by a french window which opened into the courtyard. 'Come out here.'

Kersey followed him out under the green glass roof. The afternoon sun was shining directly into the paved yard; the stone urns, filled with flowering geraniums and lobelias, looked like floral flags, and two lustrous dragonflies darted over the pool, dodging the water from the fountain.

Kersey said: 'Pretty! Am I supposed to see something?'

'The paving slabs near the pool, they've been scrubbed.'

'So they have!' The two of them had been associated for so long that they had evolved a pattern of almost reflex responses to each other's moods. When Wycliffe seemed more than commonly disturbed, Kersey's reaction was to fence.

Wycliffe pointed to the tiny groove in the edge of one of the slabs. 'What caused that?'

Kersey crouched down and carefully examined the scarred slab. 'A grazing bullet?'

'You think so?'

'I'm no expert but I'd be prepared to bet.'

'So the bullet, if it is one, is probably embedded in the opposite side of the pool. From this angle it would miss the fountain. It means that Garland must have been brought here when he arrived on Saturday evening.'

'Hardly the place for a medical examination.'

'No, but Garland didn't come here about his health, he came to talk about pictures. He struck me as not very bright, a rather weak character but conscientious, hard done by, and with a strain of obstinacy which made him aggressive. My guess is that he knew about the picture hoax, Francis had confided in him, but with Francis dead, the secret was too much for him. He wanted somebody to tell him what to do, so he tried the people directly concerned — first Beryl, then, when she wouldn't see him, the Tates. A preparatory telephone call, his best suit to boost his ego, and he presents himself.'

'You don't think he was trying his hand at blackmail?'

'I don't, but the fact that he knew, was enough to finish him.'

Kersey indulged in one of his grotesque parodies: '"Let's talk in the courtyard, it's lovely out there this evening. . . . Make yourself comfortable. . . . Would you care for a drink? Long and cold? Coffee if you prefer . . ." Then the poor bastard gets it in the neck — literally.'

'It could have been something like that, I suppose.' Wycliffe shivered. 'I hate this place!'

Kersey went back under the glass roof and dragged forward one of the metal chairs with its loose, striped cushions. He placed the chair with care, eyeing the scarred slab. When he sat in the chair his head came well above the cushions.

'I think this is it, sir.'

'I went through the same antics this morning.'

'And he saw you?'

'She did.'

A quick, comprehending glance from Kersey. 'Ah! . . . So where do we go from here?'

'Tell Fox to leave the surgery for the present, that can wait until after Franks has been. Start him off on this and give him what help he needs. I shall be back in. . . . Anyway, you know what to do.'

Kersey looked at him with concern. 'Something wrong, sir?' Kersey was troubled.

'Yes, an unnecessary death.'

Wycliffe left Tregarthen and retraced the route he had taken that morning, down the steps and into the secluded cul-de-sac where Barton's had their car-body repair shops. The front doors of some of the little houses stood open to the sunshine.

A first rate physician and a good GP.

He walked to the end of the street and into Barton's yard which was built up on three sides with sheds of varied structure and size. Just inside the gate there was a little building labelled 'Office' and a young girl typist told him that the foreman was in the stores on the other side of the yard.

'Are you the foreman?'

Thirty-five, dark, wearing greasy overalls and sporting a Mexican moustache. 'That's right.'

Wycliffe showed his warrant card. 'Chief Superintendent Wycliffe. I believe one of your men fetched Dr Tate's car this morning to carry out repairs.'

'Is there something wrong about it?'

'I would like to see the car.'

The foreman, puzzled, and a little worried, led the way to another shed where Tate's car had been stripped of the front over-ride, the near side lamp housing and wing panel.

Wycliffe's manner was unusually curt, almost aggressive. The truth was that he was tense and angry but his anger was directed against himself. An unnecessary death.

'When did Dr Tate have his accident?'

The foreman inspected a job sheet clipped under the screen wiper. 'The 5th, a week ago today. It was nothing much, somebody backed into him on a car-park. The insurance rep inspected the damage at the doctor's place on Friday and authorised the repair. Dr Tate arranged for us to collect the car on the 12th — that's today, and we did.'

'When was that arrangement made?'

177

'He telephoned on Saturday, I took the message myself.' The foreman plucked up courage. 'Don't you think you should talk to Dr Tate about this?'

Wycliffe said: 'The doctor is not able to talk to me. How long were you expecting to keep the car here?'

'We budgeted on four days, allowing for spraying.'

Four days: days when the heat would be on; after that . . . But it would require nerve . . .

He walked round the car to the rear. 'Will you open the boot, please?'

The foreman joined him. 'I can't, sir, I don't have a key.'

'But surely your man must have had the keys to drive it here.'

'The ignition key only. Of course that opens the doors but it doesn't unlock the boot. I suppose the doctor thought we didn't need it — which we don't.'

Wycliffe said: 'May I use your telephone?'

'In the office.'

He had to make his call with the foreman and the typist listening.

It was Kersey who answered.

'I'm speaking from Barton's car-body repair shop in Cross Street. Has Franks arrived? . . . Good! Tell him I'll be in touch before he leaves. I want you to look in the desk for car keys, possibly a spare set; also get Franks to look in Tate's pockets . . . I'll wait while you check.'

For three, four . . . possibly five minutes the little office seemed to exist in limbo. The typist sat at her machine staring out into the sunlit yard while the foreman pretended to be occupied in turning the pages of a trade catalogue. A clock on the wall, advertising a brand of tyres, showed ten minutes to four.

Wycliffe stood by the girl's desk, still as a graven image.

A cross between a saint and a witch doctor.

Kersey came back to the phone.

'Send down what you've got . . . now, at once. I'll be in touch.'

He replaced the telephone. 'I shall be outside.' He walked out into the sunshine and stood by the gates, waiting. It was very quiet, just a murmur of traffic in the main street. One of the high days of summer, with perfect weather, one of those days which would colour the memories of thousands of people in the winter ahead and persuade them to send for next year's brochure. To him it all seemed as remote as another world.

An unnecessary death.

A police car nosed along the street and pulled up by the gates. He was handed a brown envelope. 'From Mr Kersey, sir.'

'Pull into the yard and wait.'

Two sets of keys — different, and an odd one which seemed to match one of the others. With luck . . .

The foreman, without a word, followed him back to the shed where Tate's car was. Wycliffe went to the back of the car and inserted the odd key in the lock of the boot. It fitted. He lifted the lid. The boot was large; it held a heavy-duty polythene bag and through the semi-transparent plastic he could see the form of a man crouched in the posture of an embryo in the womb.

The foreman spoke in a whisper: 'Christ Almighty!'

Back to the little office. The girl looked up at the foreman. 'What's up, Jack?'

The foreman shrugged and said nothing.

Wycliffe picked up the phone. 'Perhaps you will leave me alone in the office for a few minutes?'

The two of them went out without a word and stood in the yard, talking in low tones.

Wycliffe spoke to Kersey, then to Dr Franks; he was on the phone for nearly ten minutes. When he had finished, the girl, looking dazed, went back into her office and the foreman listlessly set about picking up bits of junk around the yard and carrying them to the scrap pile. Wycliffe had another wait in the sunshine.

Fox and Curnow arrived in the scenes-of-crime van, closely followed by Dr Franks in his Porsche. The pathologist, tubby, immaculate, and jaunty as ever, greeted Wycliffe: 'Lovely day, Charles! Too good for work. Where is he?'

Wycliffe, sombre and taciturn, led the way to the shed where Tate's car was housed.

Fox and Curnow set to work placing flood lamps in the rear of the shed where the lighting was poor. Fox, with his conspicuous nose, receding chin, and stalking gait, reminded Wycliffe of some stork-like bird absorbed in the serious business of nest building. Work in the yard had come to a stop and half-a-dozen men in overalls gathered to watch but they kept their distance.

Wycliffe called over to the foreman. 'Can the car be driven?'

'No reason why not.'

When Fox had taken his photographs of the body in situ the car was driven out of its shed; the body, still in its plastic envelope, was lifted out of the boot and laid on the floor in the empty shed so that Franks could make his preliminary examination. Apart from the pathologist only Wycliffe and Fox were in the shed with the body. It was a macabre scene with the three men bending over the encapsulated corpse under the powerful lamps.

Franks said: 'Like a giant embryo in its caul.'

The heavy polythene bag, of the sort used to pack mattresses, had been carefully sealed with a broad strip of adhesive bandage. Franks cut the bag away and exposed the body so that they saw it plainly for the first time.

No doubt about identification; it was Mark Garland. He was fully dressed: grey pinstripe suit, grey socks and shoes, pale blue shirt and matching tie. He had been shot through the base of the skull and the bullet had emerged below the bridge of the nose, shattering a relatively small area of the face. There must have been a quantity of extruded matter for some still adhered to the bag.

Franks was straightening the limbs. 'He's been dead more than 24 hours. I'd say between 36 and 48.'

'Saturday evening at 8.30?'

'I wouldn't argue with that. No more I can do here.'

The mortuary van arrived, the body was placed in a 'shell' and driven off.

Wycliffe turned to Fox: 'When you've finished here get back to Mr Kersey at the house.'

Fox said: 'We've made a start there, sir, lowering the water level of the pond.'

'Good!' Wycliffe was getting used to Fox and beginning to like him. 'Tell Mr Kersey I'll be back in under the hour.'

He left the yard and continued down the steep, narrow alley to the main street. It was quiet, very little traffic, very few people; even the locals must have made for the beaches or the boats. In the art shop Cathy Carne's assistant was perched on a stool by the till, reading. She came over to him at once.

'Miss Carne is upstairs in the flat with Miss Garland and Anna.'

'Something wrong?'

A faint smile. 'I think they're having a kind of meeting.'

Coming to terms? Beryl had said: 'I shan't let him continue to ruin my life. That's what he wanted . . . I shall come to terms in a business-like way.'

Wycliffe went through to the little hall and up the stairs. He could hear someone talking in the living-room — Beryl, being dogmatic: 'We must keep lawyers out of this until we've reached agreement.'

He tapped on the door and it was answered by Beryl.

'Oh, it's you. I've got people with me.'

'I want to talk to Miss Carne.'

Reluctantly she stood back from the door. Cathy Carne was seated on one side of the table and there was a young woman opposite her. There were coffee cups and a plate of biscuits on the table. A social occasion. It took Wycliffe a moment or two to recognise Anna. Anna had taken herself in hand; a stylish hair-cut, a well-fitting cornflower-blue dress, a coral necklace, smart shoes and a handbag. A youthful version of Cathy Carne.

Cathy took his intrusion in her stride. 'Ah, Mr Wycliffe; you want to speak to me? We were talking things over, business-wise.'

Wycliffe looked at her with a leaden stare. 'In your office if you don't mind.'

She stood up. 'I'll be back as soon as I can.'

They went down the stairs and into her office. Despite her effort to appear relaxed she looked at him with apprehension.

'Dr Tate is dead.'

She stiffened; her whole body became tense. 'Alan . . . *Dead?*' She seemed to withdraw into herself like a snail into its shell.

'Shortly before one o'clock he was found dead in his surgery; shot through the head.'

She reached for her cigarettes, her fingers fumbled with the cigarette pack, then with the lighter. Only when she had taken the first draw did she look directly at him.

'His body was slumped between the chair and the desk, the bullet entered his skull just above and slightly in front of the right ear.' He was deliberately, cruelly explicit, and for an instant there was hatred in her eyes.

'The gun was on the floor beside him.'

The little office had become a focus of tension and emotion, isolated from the world.

'He shot himself?' She stumbled over the words.

'There is something else: Mark Garland's body has been found in the boot of Dr Tate's car.'

She was watching him intently and for the first time he detected fear in her eyes. 'Why are you being so brutal to me?'

'Because you have your share in what has happened. You have deliberately withheld information and you have lied. I feel sure that you did not destroy your uncle's letter. Unless I misjudge you, you are not the sort to destroy evidence of any sort.'

She looked at him as though she had been paid an unexpected compliment, then she opened a drawer of her desk, took out a key, unlocked the safe and handed him an envelope. 'You are quite right, I never destroy anything.'

The letter was written on the firm's paper in the old man's powerful script:

Dear Cathy,

There is something I want you to know when I am dead (if you do not know it before). Gifford Tate did not paint any pictures after his stroke; all the work attributed to him since then is mine. It started as a joke we thought up together to have fun with Papa and with the critics who are mostly imbeciles. We were more successful than we thought possible and it was too good not to keep it going. After Gifford died without letting the cat out of the bag (I thought he would have done so in his will), I set up the Ismay-Gorton annual farce in which I play the privileged role of friend and art executor of the lamented painter. You of all people will understand what a hell of a good laugh it is! (*was*, when you read this).

But I begin to want to share the joke while I'm still around to see the red faces, so I'm opening certain lines of communication (arranging leaks). Today I told Francis the whole story. I shall be interested to see how long he can keep it to himself. My guess is that greed will outweigh his yearning for self-importance and that he will hold his tongue until I am gone and he is secure in his inheritance, but we shall see!

I am also trying to get a major touring exhibition of Gifford's(!) work to give the critics a better chance.

If despite all this I still die before the world has heard the joke it will be up to you to tell them about it with the help of one or two cryptic references in my will.

Love from Uncle Ed who now knows all — or nothing!
PS If they want more than the evidence of their eyes, tell them that Gifford always signed his work in Winsor blue and put a blob of it somewhere in the picture. I've never used it in my life. E.

Wycliffe folded the letter and put it back in its envelope. 'Nothing about destroying it there. Quite the contrary.'

She said nothing.

'Did Tate know about this letter?'

'No, there seemed no point in telling him; by the time I received it, the day after Edwin's funeral, Francis was dead.'

'And Francis had been to see the Tates on the morning of the funeral with a picture under his arm to tell them what he knew.'

'I didn't think it was up to me to make it worse for them.'

'Perhaps you were afraid.'

She made an irritable movement. 'All right! Perhaps I was, you kept telling me I had reason to be.'

She was making a great effort at self-control and her reactions were deliberate and slow. With uncharacteristic fussiness she brushed ash from the folds of her skirt as though it were an action of importance. 'You won't believe me, but Alan told me nothing of what happened. Nothing! I've only been able to guess at what's been going on. You say I've had a share in what happened but it's been a nightmare: Alan afraid to speak, and I afraid to hear.'

'And this continued when Mark Garland went missing?'

'Just the same. We exchanged purely factual information — about your visits, what you had to say, Marcella's behaviour, that sort of thing, but nothing which committed either of us to certain knowledge.'

'Yet you knew.'

She lit another cigarette; she was very pale and her hands still trembled.

Wycliffe said: 'One more question: At what time did Tate leave you on Sunday evening — the evening Mark Garland disappeared?'

'He wasn't with me — '

Wycliffe sounded weary. 'That is what he told you to say but now that he is dead, do you still need to lie?'

She shook her head. 'No! I don't need to lie; he left me shortly after nine; he said he was worried about leaving Marcella alone.'

There was a tap at the door; Cathy's assistant was standing in the entrance to the office. 'Is it all right to shut the shop, Miss Carne? It's past closing time.'

Chapter Thirteen

As WYCLIFFE LEFT the shop, pleasure boats were returning from their afternoon trips and people were streaming off the pier. In the past five days three people had died; for two of them he felt no personal responsibility; he could not have anticipated their deaths. The third was a different matter. If only that morning, in the doctor's surgery, he had foreseen the possibility . . .

An unnecessary death.

He entered one of the alleys and climbed the steep slopes as though he could appease his pent-up frustration and guilt in a furious outburst of physical energy. He arrived at the gate of Tregarthen, his heart racing, breathing hard, deeply flushed.

Now there was a uniformed constable stationed outside the gate and a string of police vehicles parked in the drive. A small crowd had collected on the opposite side of the road and people were watching from the windows of the houses. If his arrival caused a ripple of interest he was totally unaware of it.

He walked up the drive and around to the back of the house. Fox and Curnow were in the courtyard, shirt-sleeves rolled up, sweating under the afternoon sun. The fountain had been turned off and they had lowered the level of the water to expose the top three courses of brickwork. Buckets, slimy with green algae, stood in a group.

Fox stooped and pointed to a scar in the lining of the pool where the algae had been scraped away: 'There it is, sir; no doubt about that. I think we'd better lift out the whole brick to make it easier to recover the bullet.'

He came around the pool to join Wycliffe. 'As I see it, sir, Garland was sitting in one of those lounging chairs, leaning forwards — perhaps he was watching the fish; at any rate he was shot in the back of the head and he must have pitched forward on the paving. That would explain why we've found no stained cushions: all the mess was on the paving slabs.'

Wycliffe stared at the pool and said nothing and after a moment or two Fox returned to his work.

Kersey was in the dining-room juggling with sheets of paper. 'The doctor's body has gone off to the mortuary. You know what's happening down at the garage, and you've seen Fox and Curnow out there in the courtyard. Lucy Lane has gone to break the news to Thomas.'

'Marcella?'

'Oh yes, Marcella. She's still upstairs with the cleaning woman — Mrs Irons and our woman PC from the local nick. Dr McPherson's nurse arrived but Marcella sent her packing.'

Kersey lit a cigarette. 'I'm curious about the body in the boot; was it a hunch, a tip off, or what?'

'It was a hunch which seemed so unlikely that I kept quiet about it. Tate made no real protest about the search so he must have felt reasonably safe, but I couldn't see how he'd managed it. Then it occurred to me that his car had been able to leave the premises openly, also that the repair people wouldn't want access to the boot. Taken together . . .'

Wycliffe walked over to the window and stood, looking out. 'Tate foresaw the possibility of a search, and the fact that his car was due to be in the repair shop for a matter of days must have seemed providential. What he did, required nerve but, if it worked, by the time he had his car back, the heat would probably be off and he would have all the time in the world.'

'Ingenious, but I can see why you kept it to yourself.'

For once exchanges between the two men were stilted and strained. They lapsed into silence and, after a moment or two, Wycliffe said: 'I'm going upstairs.'

As he reached the top of the stairs Mrs Irons, flushed and agitated, was coming down the corridor towards him. 'I'm worried about Mrs Tate; she's behaving very queer. She wouldn't take the sedative Dr McPherson left for her and she ordered his nurse out of the house.'

She looked at him with worried eyes, wondering how far she dared confide in this grim-faced policeman. 'I think she must be out of her mind, she's talking wild and saying terrible things about the doctor. I mean, I've known him since he was a schoolboy; he might seem a cold sort of man and a bit off-hand to strangers but he wouldn't hurt a fly! Nobody knows what he's done for people. And the way he's looked after her . . . I mean, it's his house; he didn't have to let her stay on, but far from turning her out, he couldn't do enough for her. It's been more like he was living in her house. And she isn't easy to live with, I can tell you! What with her nerves and going on about Mr Gifford as though he was still alive. . . . Morbid, I call it!'

'Which is her room?'

'I left her in Mr Gifford's room. It's the door facing up the passage. I'm going down to make a pot of tea.'

The door was open. Gifford's bedroom was large; the furnishing, circa 1930 was massively functional. Pyjamas were laid out on the double bed and there was a padded dressing gown thrown across the foot, all in readiness for the Master. A sectional wardrobe occupied most of one wall and all the doors stood open; there were suits, overcoats, and shirts on hangers, trays of underclothes, a rack for ties and a number of small drawers presumably containing accessories. Two sections of the wardrobe were empty.

The WPC came in, anxious and solemn; she spoke in a low voice: 'Mrs Tate is next door, in her own room, sir. I think she's intending to move in here; she's taking all her clothes out of her wardrobe.'

'Has she said anything?'

'Only to Mrs Irons, not to me.'

'Go and have a break; come back in half-an-hour.'

The girl went out and almost at once Marcella came in loaded with an armful of dresses still on their hangers. She dropped them on the bed, then started shaking them out and hanging them one by one in an empty section of the wardrobe.

Wycliffe stood with his back to the window and at first she took no notice of him, apparently absorbed in her work. Then his continuing presence seemed to make her uneasy and from time to time she glanced across at him, her eyes half fearful, half defiant.

Abruptly, in the act of shaking out the creases from one of her

187

dresses, she said: 'I'm moving back in here with Gifford. Of course I slept here before, but when he was ill he said he disturbed my rest so he made me move next door.'

Wycliffe said nothing and after a while she went on: 'You haven't been in this room before, have you?' It seemed that she was trying to divert his attention, perhaps his thoughts. 'Just like the studio, I've kept everything exactly the same here as it was before Gifford was taken ill. . . . Look at all his clothes! He has always been very particular about his clothes. Alan was like him in that way. . . . Always immaculate . . .'

After another silence, during which she went on putting away her dresses, Wycliffe said: 'Why have you been telling Mrs Irons that Alan killed Francis and Mark Garland?' He put the question almost casually.

Abruptly, she sat on the edge of the bed and ran her hands through her hair. 'I really don't want to talk about it any more! I should have thought I'd suffered enough.'

'I want you to tell me what really happened on Saturday night when Mark Garland came and what happened last night when you screamed.'

She looked at him, vaguely. 'Last night?'

'You said you had a nightmare.'

She pressed her hands to her head. 'Did I? I'm so muddled! Alan always told me what to say and now I don't know where I am. I don't know what I said and what I didn't; I don't know what I'm supposed to say.' As she spoke she was watching him through half closed eyes.

'It doesn't matter about what you are supposed or not supposed to say; you know what happened on Saturday night when Mark Garland was here, and you know what happened last night to make you scream.'

She nodded slowly. 'I know about last night!' She repeated with a curious emphasis: 'I know what happened then. I saw Alan with Mark Garland's body.'

'Let's start with the night before — Saturday night, when Mark Garland came. You said that you took your dog for a walk and that it was after nine when you came back. What happened then?'

She frowned and clasped her hands tightly together. 'Well, I just came in and went to bed.'

'Did you see Dr Tate?'

'Of course! He said I looked very tired and he insisted that I go straight up to bed. I did, and he brought me a hot drink in bed.'

'Did he say anything about Mark Garland?'

'Just that he'd been; I think he said something about Mark being ill or thinking he was ill; I can't remember.' She gave him one of her quick, appraising glances.

Wycliffe was silent for a while and, hesitantly, she got off the bed and resumed putting her clothes away. Somewhere in the house a clock chimed the half-hour. Six-thirty.

'Who scrubbed the courtyard?'

She turned to face him. 'Oh, Alan did. I heard him at it early yesterday morning before I was up.'

'Now tell me about last night.'

She sat on the bed again; placed her hands together between her knees and leaned forward. She moistened her lips. 'I suppose I've got to. . . . It was about two o'clock in the morning; I woke up and I could see a faint light coming from the corridor. I always leave my door open a bit for Ricky. I got out of bed and I could see that the light was coming from downstairs. I went to the top of the stairs and called. Alan answered, he said: "It's all right, Marcella; go back to bed." '

She shook her head and in a low voice she went on. 'I didn't go back to bed. I went down the stairs, but before I got to the bottom the light was switched off and I couldn't see a thing. I worked my way along the wall to the switch and when the light came on I was standing. . . . I was almost touching a great plastic bag . . .' She shivered. 'And in the bag there was a body. . . . I could see it. Then I screamed.'

There was a long pause; she shuddered, and said, nodding her head as though she had settled some problem: 'Yes, that was how I knew for certain what he had done.'

Some truth and some lies; her own bewildering blend of fact and fiction, reality and fairy tale. That would be the pattern of her response to all interrogation. Sometimes naive and sometimes cunning, she would rely on those quick bird-like glances to pick her way through the maze.

'Why would Dr Tate want to kill Francis and Mark Garland?'

She stiffened and looked at him, her eyes wide. She raised her voice. 'Why? I don't know! He didn't tell me; he never told me anything . . .'

'And you say you were out on Saturday night when Mark Garland came?'

'I keep telling you I wasn't here! Alan told you.'

The door opened very quietly and Mrs Irons came in with tea things on a tray. She put the tray down on the chest of drawers and stood, waiting. Marcella seemed not to see her.

In a low voice Wycliffe said: 'Mark Garland was shot at half-past eight on Saturday evening.'

She looked her question.

'We have evidence that Dr Tate didn't arrive home until well after nine o'clock.'

Marcella became excited: 'That is a lie! That's what Cathy Carne told you! She's been trying to. . . . She will do anything! Look at the way she wormed her way in to get all she could from Edwin! For years she's been trying to get rid of me so that she could move in here with Alan!' In her frustration she beat on the bedclothes with her clenched fists.

Totally unexpected, Mrs Irons spoke in her rather harsh, masculine voice: 'It's you who is telling the lies. Ever since Mr Gifford died the doctor has looked after you and let you carry on in your own sweet way, as though he didn't exist except to dance attendance on your selfishness. Any ordinary man would have kicked you out in the first six months. Lucky for you the doctor was no ordinary man, but that's neither here nor there now; what I have to say is that I saw the doctor, coming up Quay Hill at a quarter-past nine on Saturday evening. And I'll swear to that in the witness box if I have to.'

Marcella looked across at Mrs Irons, she opened her mouth but no words came; for a long moment she seemed to be frozen, petrified; then she screamed and kept on screaming. She rolled over on the bed, kicking her feet and pummelling the clothes with her fists.

Mrs Irons looked down at her, totally dispassionate. 'Don't worry! That's nothing that a good slap wouldn't cure.'

Wycliffe wondered if Mrs Irons had really seen her doctor that evening but he had no intention of trying to find out.

Wycliffe looked and felt very tired. He was back in the dining-room with Kersey.

Kersey said: 'It didn't occur to me until we were out in the courtyard this afternoon that he was covering for her. Do you think he knew — really knew that she had shot Francis?'

'I doubt if he could have lived in the house without knowing, but he felt bound to protect her. I think that was genuine; I very much doubt if an exposure of the picture fraud would have weighed with him very heavily, certainly not to the extent of compounding a murder. What he didn't know was that it hadn't ended with the shooting on the wharf. If he'd even guessed at the possibility of another killing, then things would have been different. I don't think he would have knowingly set another life at risk.'

'He must have had misgivings about the gun.'

'She would have sworn to him that she'd thrown it in the harbour. She's a convincing liar when she puts her mind to it.'

'Then the poor bastard comes home one night to find a corpse literally on his doorstep and he's committed to something far more hazardous than keeping his mouth shut — and hers.'

Wycliffe was sitting by the window staring out into the courtyard and through the Moorish arch to the garden beyond. The low sun lit up a tiny window in the gable-end of Gifford's studio so that it seemed to blaze like a fire. He said: 'It makes my flesh creep to imagine what it must have been like for Tate in this house during that 40 hours from Saturday night to lunchtime today, with him certain now that she still had the gun. By day there was almost nothing he could do, he could only use the night when they had the house to themselves, to dispose of the body; to reason, to plead — and to search.'

'You think the case against her will stand up?'

'Yes, if it ever comes to court.'

191

'Unfit to plead?'

'That's what the shrinks will say.'

'And what do you think?'

Wycliffe said nothing for a time then: 'The thought of her going into the surgery, hiding the pistol, saying something quite ordinary and, as he looks up from his work. . . . She needed a scapegoat and her need excluded every other consideration. That to me is wickedness. There is no other word.'

There was a long silence then Wycliffe said: 'This case has been about children, about arrested development; Gifford, Edwin and Papa Burger — they didn't grow up either. All three of them needed mothers rather than wives but only Burger was lucky enough to marry one.'

And after another interval he went on: 'Three deaths to preserve this woman's fantasies. I wonder if Edwin, wherever he is, will feel now that his prank got out of hand?'

THE END

WYCLIFFE
AND THE FOUR JACKS

People who know Roseland will recognize the places described, and they may be irritated by inaccuracies in the topography. These are deliberate in order to reduce any risk, through an accidental resemblance, that a real person might be identified with one of the characters in this book—all of whom are imaginary.

W. J. B.

Chapter One

As USUAL CLEEVE was in his library study by nine-thirty. He stood by the window gazing out over his own garden and the clustered rooftops of the village below, across the creek to the headland where a line of pine trees descended with the profile of the promontory in a perfect curve, almost to the fringe of white water and the sea. Grey slate roofs, the glittering surface of the creek, rising green fields, and the arc of the pines against a misty-blue windy sky. Rain in the offing.

Seven or eight years ago, when he first came to live at Roscrowgy, there had been twenty pines, now there were thirteen; gales and old age had taken an erratic toll. It was absurd, but each morning he counted them in a ritual act, not that he needed to, for any fresh gap would have been immediately obvious.

June 16th; on June 16th, 28 years ago . . .

He heard his secretary moving about in the next room; in a few minutes she would bring in his mail and then he would know.

He watched a fly, a large grey fly with a chequered pattern on its abdomen, crawling up the window pane; it reached the top without finding a way out and went back to the bottom again. He watched while the performance was repeated twice more, then he opened the window and let the creature out, to be whisked away on the wind. As a small boy he had often sought to appease a hostile fate by such little acts of grace.

There was a tap at the door and Milli came in with the mail. She had opened and vetted most of it—everything from his publishers and his agent, everything addressed to him as Peter Stride; she was not permitted to open his Cleeve mail.

He did not turn round, determined to be casual, ordinary.

'Good morning, Mr Cleeve.' Milli bright and brittle.

He said, 'Good morning!' with just the right degree of preoccupation.

Milli was small, with black hair and dusky skin; lithe and agile as a monkey; he sometimes thought she might be capable of all 30 classical positions, but not with him; athletic sex was diversion for the young.

'Anything in the post?'

'Nothing I can't deal with.'

'Then take it away. I want to get on with the *Setebos* revision, so Milli—no telephone.' She was already moving to the door having left the Cleeve mail on his desk. Normally he would have added something facetious. 'Tell 'em I'm suffering from premenstrual tension.'

It seemed all right but at the door she looked back and he fancied she had sensed his unease; not that it mattered.

Childlike, he counted to a hundred before he would allow himself to look at the few items of mail on his desk: four buff-coloured envelopes, probably bills; two white ones with typewritten superscriptions and a third, addressed in bold, well-formed capitals. That was it! He held the envelope for a time without opening it. When he did, he drew out a single playing card—the Jack of Diamonds. Along the top margin of the card someone had written: Thursday June 16th and the number four.

He sat at his desk and with a key from his pocket unlocked the bottom left-hand drawer. It was here that he kept his automatic pistol, the current volume of his journal, and certain lists which might be of use to his executors. There was also a cardboard box which had once held a hundred cigarettes. From the box he removed three envelopes similar to the one he had just received. From each of the envelopes he extracted a playing card, three Jacks of Diamonds identical with the fourth he now had, but each carrying a different date and number. He arranged them on his desk, from left to right: Saturday September 4th—1, Tuesday March 8th—2, Friday May 13th—3, and Thursday June 16th—4.

He stared at the cards for some time, then with a grimace

196

gathered them up. He put them back in their envelopes and returned the envelopes to the box and the drawer.

Still seated at his desk he reached for the fat wad of typescript which was *Setebos*, picked up a ball-point and set to work. He had thought the opening chapter good, now it had the impact of a wet sponge, but he perserved, making deletions and insertions, knowing they would come out again in a later revision.

Writers come in all shapes and sizes but Cleeve was a surprise to the few people who penetrated his privacy. They found it hard to accept that David Cleeve, who looked and sometimes spoke like a prosperous farmer, must be reconciled with Peter Stride, the sophisticated creator of the terrifying Manipulators in *Xanadu* and the sadistic Preceptors in *Medicus*. A generous build, an open countenance, a fresh schoolboy complexion and guileless blue eyes—these, with an exuberant moustache, sandy hair and freckles, must surely mean innocence and simplicity of soul.

The room darkened as clouds crept up the sky and the first flurry of raindrops spattered against the window. At eleven o'clock Milli came in with a cup of black coffee and when she had gone he laced it with whisky.

He existed in two worlds; in this comfortable room with his books and the paraphernalia of his work about him; defined, secure and purposeful; and in that other world of more than a quarter of a century ago through which he had prowled like some feral young animal. That world was no longer real, even his memories of it were vague, like the recollections of a dream, yet it acquired fresh substance through those four cards.

He drank his coffee and when it was gone he went to the drinks cupboard again and poured himself a whisky. He took it to the window and stood there, looking out. A vestige of sunlight silvered the edge of the blue-black clouds and miniature white horses reared on the dark water of the creek, sending the sailing dinghies scurrying for shelter like a flock of frightened geese. During the next hour or so he made other visits to the drinks cupboard and between times sat at his desk brooding over the typescript.

Patricia would diagnose one of his Occasionals—her word for episodes which occurred without warning and at longish intervals, but always with the same scenario. He would start drinking in the morning, contrive some sort of scene over lunch, then continue drinking through the afternoon. In the evening he would go to sleep in a small bedroom near his study and stay there until morning.

The buzzer sounded for lunch and he got to his feet; he was not yet drunk, for his step was firm. In the corridor outside his study he paused by the open door of his secretary's office where she was working, oblivious.

'Milli!' A bellow.

She looked up, startled and annoyed.

'Lunch!'

Roscrowgy sprawled across the flank of a hill, two storeys at each end, single-storeyed between, built on split levels and accommodating to vagaries of contour like a Tibetan monastery. Cleeve had his working suite of rooms on the upper floor at one end, while the dining and reception rooms were at the other. He went down an oak staircase and along the length of a broad passage which had occasional steps both up and down; the floors were of polished wood with Afghan rugs, and the white walls were relieved by a series of large uniform pictures of a Graham Sutherland genre. Patricia's taste; it reminded him of a well-endowed nunnery and he was accustomed to refer to the pictures as Stations of the Cross.

'Bloody hell!' An inarticulate protest.

The dining-room continued the monastic theme; oak floor with rugs, white walls, furniture in natural beech. The table was laid for five but the room was empty. He went to the sideboard and poured himself a whisky.

His wife came in silently and he did not see her at once. Cleeve might have been mistaken for a farmer but there was no mistaking Patricia Cleeve for a farmer's wife. She was a Tull of the Oxfordshire Tulls and God had thoughtfully endowed her with features admirably suited to half-tone reproduction in *The Tatler*. Patricia was forty-three, nine years younger than her husband; an English rose, not yet faded; a blonde, with a pink and white complexion, but with large limpid eyes whose steady gaze could unsettle the most hardened conscience.

Cleeve saw his wife and turned away, but not before she had recognized the symptoms.

Carrie Byrne wheeled in a trolley of food; bowls of salad and other vegetables and a platter of sliced chicken-breast. Carrie, a Tull cousin of thirty-eight, occupied an ambivalent position in the household; somewhere between a member of the family and a housekeeper. In colouring, personality and opinions Carrie was neutral, a congenital "don't know". In Cleeve's words, "Clay which had waited too long for the potter".

They took their places at table; Milli joined them with a muttered apology. Patricia said, 'There's chilled fruit juice if anybody wants it.'

Cleeve mumbled unintelligibly. It was a relief to take refuge in the established routine of an Occasional. No one would question it. 'Are we not to have the twins' company at lunch?' Ponderously aggressive.

'I told you. Andrew is at the School of Mines today. Some vacation work he has to do for his course at the university. Christine is changing; she came back wet from the dig.'

Cleeve looked out of the window at the rain sweeping in from the sea. 'What does she want to spend her time up there for? Surely at her age she's got better things to do.'

Nobody spoke. Plates and bowls passed from hand to hand. With an imperious gesture Cleeve refused the salad but speared several large slices of chicken breast with his fork. Seated at the head of the table he munched the chicken with pieces of bread roll, scattering crumbs and eyeing the three women with sullen aggression. The syndrome was complete.

Christine came in; a slim girl of nineteen with her mother's looks and her father's colouring. She wore skin-tight jeans and a denim shirt; the bloom was intact. She sat in her place, glanced at her father, then at her mother—questioning; her mother answered with the faintest shrug.

At the age of three Christine had dubbed her father 'daddy bear', and it had never been improved upon. It spanned the whole repertoire of his moods, from playful, affectionate whimsicality to the aggressive unpredictability of his Occasionals.

They ate in silence; when it seemed that someone might speak the tension rose, only to subside again when nothing happened. It was Patricia who finally took the plunge: 'How is the dig going, Christie?'

Christie responded with self-conscious enthusiasm. 'Oh, very well. Of course, we spent most of this morning in the shed sorting out pottery sherds; there was nothing we could do outside, but Gervaise says that with any luck we should finish excavating the third hut by Tuesday or Wednesday. Of course, it all depends on the weather. . . .'

Christine was a lively, kindly girl with boundless enthusiasm, searching for a cause; the present candidate was archaeology and she had given up her vacation to an Iron-Age dig in Henry's Field, a site adjoining Roscrowgy. The enemy was philistinism in the shape of developers, farmers, tourist boards and planners of every ilk.

Cleeve made a sound which could only be described as a deep growl and turned to Carrie Byrne. 'Did you hear that, Carrie? I don't suppose you've been up to the dig this morning?'

Carrie, realizing that she was to be the focus of today's scene, seemed to shrink into her thin frame like a snail into its shell. She said, 'No, David, I've been doing the shopping.'

'Pity!' He mimicked his daughter's enthusiasm with grotesque cruelty: '"Gervaise says that with any luck we shall finish excavating the third hut by Tuesday or Wednesday." Think of that now, Carrie! Of course it all depends on the weather.' After a pause he said, 'Gervaise . . .! Bloody pouf!'

Christie flushed but she said nothing. Cleeve glared round the table as though challenging a response and when none came he went on: 'Who cares about the sodding huts anyway? Or the squalid little savages who lived in 'em? If it hadn't been for their screwing we wouldn't be here now and the world would be a better place.'

Patricia turned her steady, disquieting gaze on her husband. 'You are being quite disgusting, David.'

'Me?' He feigned surprise. 'Oh, I forgot! We don't screw in the Shires, we "make love" or we "have sex".'

200

Patricia said nothing but she persisted in her gaze until he lowered his eyes. The meal continued in silence; only Milli seemed quite unaffected by the exchanges; she behaved as though the others did not exist.

When there was no more chicken left on the platter Cleeve got to his feet, pushing back his chair so that the legs scraped over the floor.

'Aren't you staying for dessert?'

He glared at his wife and turned away without a word. For an instant he seemed to stagger, but recovered his balance and walked to the door which he left open behind him. They listened to his footsteps down the corridor.

Carrie got up and closed the door. 'David isn't himself today.' Carrie had an unchallenged mastery of the banal. Before sitting down again she went to the kitchen and returned with a bowl of fruit.

They helped themselves except for Christie; she got up from her chair: 'If you will excuse me. . .'

'Aren't you having any, Christie? You mustn't let father upset you like that.'

The girl was near to tears. 'It's so unfair. I mean, it's his land; he gave permission for the dig and he's even paying for it. It doesn't make sense!'

Patricia looked uneasily at Milli, but she was busy dissecting an orange. 'You must know your father's moods by now, darling; he'll be up there as usual tomorrow, telling you all what a good job you're doing.'

'Will he!' Christie went out and her mother watched her go.

'Don't get up again, Carrie; I'll make the coffee.'

While Patricia was in the kitchen the telephone rang; there was a phone in the short passage between kitchen and dining-room and she answered it there.

'Roscrowgy, Mrs Cleeve speaking.'

A man's voice: 'It's me. . . . Is it all right to talk?'

'I suppose so; what is it?' She had lowered her voice, so that she would not be overheard in the dining-room.

'I must talk to you, can you come down?'

'If I must.' She was in no mood for her brother's problems.

'It really is important, Tricia.'

'It usually is; I'll be there in about an hour.'

'Can't you make it sooner? I'm really worried.'

'All right, I'll come as soon as I can.'

'Thanks, darling! I know you think—'

'I'll be there as soon as I can, Geoffrey.' And she replaced the receiver. She finished preparing the coffee tray and carried it into the dining-room. 'Where's Milli?'

Carrie said, 'She's gone back to work; she didn't want any coffee. Was that Geoffrey?'

Patricia nodded. 'He's really upset. Of course, it's money. I'm going down there. If anybody asks, I'm taking Biddy for a run.'

A few minutes later Patricia, followed by her English setter, walked down the drive and through the white gates. The rain had eased to a fine mist blown landward by the wind. The estuary and the bay beyond were a waste of grey waters under a grey sky; only the tower of the little lighthouse, like a stumpy candle, stood out white in the gloom. June in Cornwall; but tomorrow, or the next day, or the next, could be gloriously fine.

Down the steep hill, past expensive villas, hidden in their own grounds, to the fringes of the old village. Mount Zion Chapel, then Mount Zion Steps, leading down to the waterfront and the harbour—really a steep, narrow, cobbled street with steps at intervals to ease the slope. Several of the little granite cottages had been tarted up and three or four had been turned into shops.

Patricia made her way down the Steps among tourists, disconsolate in the rain. They turned to look at her and her dog, an unselfconsciously elegant pair. Near the bottom of the Steps a shop with a bow window exhibited a neat sign, gold-on-green: "Geoffrey Tull, Herbalist and Naturopath."

There was a "closed" sign on the door, but Patricia tapped on the glass and a man in his middle thirties came to open it. Geoffrey was fair and good-looking, a blond moustache glistened in the light. But his features were too soft and he was slightly overweight. He wore a green silk shirt and fawn trousers.

Patricia angrily evaded a kiss. 'Don't be so foolish, Geoffrey!'

He was immediately contrite. 'Sorry, darling! But bless you for coming. I would have phoned before but I wanted to make sure that secretary of David's wasn't listening-in at the other end.'

Patricia snapped. 'You know perfectly well that the house phone is a separate line.'

Inside, the shop was laid out like a small Edwardian pharmacy with gilded glass jars on the shelves and a battery of little polished wooden drawers behind the counter, each labelled with its white-enamelled plaque: *Arctium lappa, Laurus nobilis, Spiraea ulmaria.* . . .

'Come through to the back where we can talk.'

Biddy settled complacently on the doormat.

The back room was a laboratory-cum-kitchen where the herbal decoctions, extracts and tinctures were prepared.

They sat on stools. 'Now, what is this about?'

He put on an absurdly guilty look, like a small boy confessing to naughtiness. 'It's about money, Tricia, dear.'

'So I imagined.'

'But this is worse than anything . . . Connors from the bank rang this morning and asked me to come and see him.'

'Well?'

'He's stopping my cheques unless I can find a guarantor or pay off my overdraft.'

'You must have seen this coming.'

Geoffrey squirmed. 'Actually, Tricia, I didn't. The money has been coming in pretty well lately; business is brisk, and I just didn't do my sums.'

Patricia sighed. 'Will you never learn?' She shifted impatiently on her stool. 'What exactly are you asking me to do? I'm not made of money, Geoffrey: I only have what David gives me and he likes to have some idea where it goes.'

Saturday July 16th

In a rented cottage on the waterfront Wycliffe stood at the window and looked across to that same headland and those same pine trees which Cleeve contemplated ritually each morning. Only the narrow road to the castle and the low sea wall separated the cottage from the water. In the creek, sailing dinghies formed a fixed pattern on the surface of an unrippled sea. A boy in a rowing-boat, oars shipped, trailed a fishing line; children idled in the shallows. There was a raft moored off-shore for swimmers and on it a girl in a bikini stood motionless. It seemed to Wycliffe that the scene had been frozen in an instant of time, as though a ciné-film had suddenly cut to a single frame. Then, into this static world, came a bustling ferry boat, pushing a moustache of white water ahead of blue bows; another cargo of trippers from Falmouth, and more to come. They would spill out on to the quay and spread through the village spending their money in the shops and cafés, helping to sustain the inhabitants through the long close season.

The Wycliffes had arrived that morning for a fortnight's holiday walking in the Roseland peninsula. It was no more than 50 miles from home, and part of his police territory, yet they had never explored the area, never visited the places with those evocative names which sprinkled the map: St Just, St Mawes, St Anthony, St Gerrans, Percuil. . . .

They had lunched at a wine bar a few doors away; crab salad with a carafe of white wine. Since then Helen had made up their bed in the little upstairs room which had a timbered ceiling and a latticed window. It was beginning to feel like a holiday.

Helen was taking off her apron. 'I thought we could look round the village this afternoon—perhaps go over the castle, then tomorrow we could start our real walking. . . .'

They joined the drifting movement of visitors and trippers along the waterfront in the direction of the quay. There were shops and pubs, toytown banks with original opening hours, and some elegant little houses that had metamorphosed from fisherman's cottages. Most of them had their pots of geraniums, begonias or mesembry-anthemums outside.

The beach was a strip of grey shingle. White and pink flesh was exposed there within the limits of decency; there were no deck-chairs, no life-guards (only a leaden soldier could drown there) no radios—in fact, no anything but the rather grubby-looking shingle and the well-mannered sea.

The shops seemed unexciting, at least resistible, but Helen

dawdled and Wycliffe said, 'I'll wait for you by the harbour.'

He rejoined the meandering groups; all ages and both sexes clad in shorts, T-shirts and bikinis, sometimes with startling effect. Alone among them an elderly man made his dignified way, immaculate in a pale-grey suit and a white straw hat; he carried two library books; a relic. To Wycliffe he seemed like a gentle dinosaur loose among baboons.

Arrived at the harbour, Wycliffe lit his pipe and rested his arms on the sea wall to watch three youngsters—two girls and a boy, putting off in a tiny drop-keel sailing boat. Orange lifejackets and blue shorts. He had been brought up on Arthur Ransome long before he had even seen the sea. Did these children lead story-book lives? After 30 years in the police he was still looking for the kinds of people he had read about as a child. The man in the white straw hat, these children. . . .

Helen joined him and they continued their walk but almost at once she was diverted again.

'Look!'

A narrow cobbled street, little more than an alley, rose steeply away from the waterfront, the knobbly spine of the old village. A blue and white enamelled sign read: Mount Zion Steps—and there were steps at intervals to ease the slope and a tubular iron handrail to assist the weary. The granite-fronted houses were stacked against each other like steps themselves; one had a "Police" sign over the front door. There were a few shops, rather twee: a herbalist's with a bow-fronted window, a vegetarian restaurant all varnished pine ('We must eat there sometime'). Further up a shop sold silver brooches and buckles of Celtic design, and next to that was a photographer's which looked as though it had been left behind by the 'twenties.

Helen was attracted by the brooches displayed on simple velvet cushions in the little window of the jewellery shop; they were oddly interspersed with books bearing esoteric titles: *Earth Magic, Leys and Power Centres, The Psi Connection*. . . . There was also a handwritten poster headed, 'The Celtic Society of Roseland' and announcing, 'There is still time to halt the desecration of Henry's Field! Details inside.'

The shop was so small that they had just room to stand between the counter and the door. Jewellery was displayed in the glass-topped counter-case, and on shelves behind the counter were more books of pseudo-science for the lunatic fringe.

A woman came from somewhere at the back: middle forties, big-boned, strong features, with blonde, shoulder-length hair, a striking woman. She wore an emerald-green frock that was almost a gown, a silver torque round her neck and silver bangles on her arms which were bare to the elbows. Theatrical but effective.

Her manner was crisp. 'As you see, the showcase is divided into three: hallmarked silver pieces to authentic Celtic designs on your right; modern enamel-on-copper pieces in the middle; and a selection of similar enamel-on-silver designs to your left.'

She stood, monumentally immobile, an operatic princess awaiting her cue. Helen asked to see a particular tray of the Celtic designs and it was lifted out on to the counter without a word.

Helen pointed to a brooch of intricate pattern, 'I think this one is very beautiful, don't you, Charles?'

The princess volunteered, 'That is late-Irish—the triskele design is based on an eighth-century medallion in the National Museum, Dublin.'

A Siamese cat came from somewhere and leapt on to the counter, examining the customers with green-eyed suspicion. Wycliffe reached out to stroke it.

'I shouldn't touch her! She can be quite aggressive with strangers.'

Helen, concentrating on the brooches, said, 'Do you make these lovely things yourself?'

'I do.'

They bought the brooch and while it was being packed in its box with a certificate of provenance Wycliffe said, 'What's this about Henry's Field?'

The blue eyes sized him up. 'Henry's Field is on the hill above the village. With the Stone Field next to it, it is one of the sacred places of the Celtic people and the ground should never be broken or ploughed. It is situated at the convergence of ley-lines from early Celtic settlement sites over the whole Roseland peninsula and is a centre of power.'

'So, what are they doing with it, building council houses?'

She suspected him of levity and became more severe. 'If you are genuinely interested you should read the Society's leaflet.' She handed over a couple of pages of duplicated typescript, clipped together. 'You will see that after remaining undisturbed for close on two thousand years the site is now being excavated by archaeologists who should know better.'

They escaped. Outside, with her brooch, Helen said, 'It cost a lot of money, Charles.'

'Never mind, call it an unbirthday present.'

At the top of the Steps they were brought face to face with the non-conformist Gothic of Mount Zion Chapel; they had reached the boundary of the old village. Further up the hill, nineteen-twentyish villas peeped out from behind their thickets of laurel and bamboo, escallonia and hebe, and there was a larger building which looked like an hotel. A black-on-yellow AA sign pointed still further up the hill: *To the Excavations.*

Wycliffe said, 'This must be what Boadicea was talking about; shall we take a look?'

The hill was steep and the sun was hot but the climb was short and, looking back, they could see the creek, the Fal estuary, and the bay spread out like a sixteenth-century map, with Henry VIII's two castles facing each other across the narrows, and the lighthouse at the bottom of its grassy promontory, its feet almost in the water. A container ship in ballast, putting out from the harbour, churned up a foamy wake.

They passed an estate with Roscrowgy on the white drive-gate, and immediately beyond there was open land covered with gorse and heather. At a considerable distance from the road they could see, well spread out, a large wooden shed, two bell-tents which looked like army surplus from the Boer war, and a caravan. Another AA sign directed them down a narrow, stony lane and brought them to the shed. Over a large area, where gorse and heather had been cleared, the ground was marked out with surveying poles and ribbons and a number of young people, minimally clad, were working in trenches.

A notice on the shed read: "Henry's Field Iron-Age Site. Visitors

207

welcome. Please report here." Field archaeologists are usually polite, probably because they are territorial intruders.

The wooden hut was part office, part museum and part laboratory, all in a space less than 20 feet square. A pretty, auburn-haired girl was scrubbing something in a sink and a minute or two went by before she became aware of the Wycliffes and came over, wiping her reddened hands on a towel.

'My name is Christine. If you know anything about archaeology please say so; there's no point in me nattering on about things you know already.'

They were shown aerial photographs of the site before excavation began.

'These were taken in winter when the vegetation had died down. You see the outlines of the hut-circles? They seem to be cut off abruptly at the Roscrowgy boundary, that's because the settlement extended into what is now part of the garden of the house. . . . We'll look at the actual dig first, then we'll come back here and you can see some of our finds. . . .'

They followed her out of the hut to where the work was going on and she dutifully kept up the flow of information. 'Henry's Field is most likely a corruption of an old Cornish name for the place, *Henrōs—hen* means old and *rōs* means heath. . .the field bit has been added. This is the hut numbered "one" in the photograph—'

'Mr Wycliffe! A surprise to see you here!' Gervaise Prout, whom Wycliffe had met in connection with security arrangements for a touring exhibition of archaeological goodies from the Far East. A man in his early fifties, with a mass of white curly hair, a long thin face with a healthy outdoor tan and slightly protruding teeth. His voice was high-pitched and there were occasional disconcerting ascents into actual falsetto.

The girl looked disappointed at losing her audience and Prout apologized handsomely: 'I really am sorry, Christie, but Mr Wycliffe and I are already acquainted.'

This disposed of, he turned to Helen and greeted her with nervous cordiality. 'A pleasure, Mrs Wycliffe! I hope you and your husband will allow me to show you round.'

So they were shown round the site by Prout instead of the girl.

'Actually it's a very promising dig. Plenty of "B" pottery as we expected, but I'm fairly sure some of the fragments are from the "A" period which would put us in the same league with Bodrifty. . . .'

They had reached the highest point of the field where they were able to overlook the house and part of the garden next door.

Helen said, 'How extraordinary! It's like a ranch house—who lives there?'

'Don't you know?' Prout seemed surprised. 'That's Roscrowgy—David Cleeve's place. He owns this field and the Stone Field next to it. As a matter of fact he's our patron. He put up most of the money for this dig.'

Wycliffe asked, 'Should we know him?'

Prout laughed. 'Perhaps not as Cleeve but you will have heard of Peter Stride. You must have seen his books in the shops even if you haven't read them. I must confess, I'm no addict.'

But Helen was, with a row of Stride's fat masterpieces on her shelves. She was impressed. 'You mean he lives there? Is he there now?'

Prout seemed pleased to display his intimacy with a celebrity. He glanced at his watch. 'Half-past three. You may see him while you are here. He often takes a stroll round the site at about this time. Incidentally, Christine, the auburn-haired girl who brought you over, is his daughter. Charming girl!'

Wycliffe had read Stride's books and seen three or four of them serialized on TV, though with less enthusiasm than Helen. The man had a remarkable ability to create an atmosphere of brooding dread, a chilling awareness of violence.

Wycliffe said, 'I gather you've had some opposition to your dig.'

A short laugh. 'Madam Laura and her ley-lines! There's an old superstition about this having been an ancient Celtic burial ground for the whole Roseland peninsula, so anyone who disturbs the dead et cetera et cetera. . . . It seems that the tale got a fresh lease of life some years back when the previous owner of Roscrowgy took part of Henry's Field into his garden and was dead within the year. Nobody mentions that the poor man was a cardiac case.' Prout made a dismissive gesture. 'In any case this has never been a burial place nor was it a sacred enclosure. It is an ordinary settlement site which seems to have enjoyed an unusually long period of occupation, making it more interesting than most.'

They completed their tour and Prout led them back to the wooden hut. He pushed open the door and they were confronted by two men in earnest conversation; one was large and pleasant-looking with a luxuriant reddish moustache. There was something expansively Edwardian about him and he carried a polished cherry-wood stick with a silver mount that was almost a staff. The other was very tall, of a skeletal leanness, with a completely bald head; he was terribly disfigured down the left side of his head, face and neck, as if by burns.

Prout, for no obvious reason, was clearly displeased by the encounter, but with contrived affability he performed the intro-ductions—'Mr and Mrs Wycliffe, Mr David Cleeve, of whom you have heard, and Mr Kitson, a neighbour who takes a great interest in our work here.'

A mild surprise for Wycliffe to discover that the amiable-looking one with the reddish moustache was Cleeve.

A shaking of hands and murmured exchanges without meaning. Kitson immediately excused himself and left. Wycliffe noticed that the disablement extended down the whole of the left side of his body, for he limped badly and held the arm on that side at a curious angle.

Cleeve had been formally polite, then his manner changed to sudden interest: 'Wycliffe? Not Superintendent Wycliffe?'

'I'm afraid so.'

Cleeve laughed. 'This is my lucky day! I've always wanted to meet a real live detective. I cut my literary teeth on what the French call *le roman policier* and criminal investigation fascinates me still.'

Hard to believe that this pleasant man, apparently anxious to be agreeable, was the author of a dozen books which were not only money spinners but considered worthy of detailed study and analysis by literary critics and psychologists, so that there was already a considerable literature on the Stride phenomenon.

They chatted easily for a few minutes then Helen said, 'You live in a beautiful place, Mr Cleeve, and you seem to have a delightful garden.'

'Are you interested in gardening—either of you?'

Wycliffe said drily, 'Helen is, and I'm learning.'

Cleeve chuckled. 'I sympathize; it's the same with us. Patricia —my wife—is the gardener but I have to sort of caddy for her and make the right noises.' He broke off abruptly. 'Why don't you come over while you are here and let Patricia take you round? She never misses a chance to show off her garden.'

They displayed a proper reluctance, but allowed themselves to be persuaded. They were shepherded across the field, through a wicket gate into the garden of the house, and along a mossy path through a rhododendron tunnel which brought them to a door at one end of the long, rambling building.

Cleeve pushed open the door and they were in a garden room with a blue-and-white-tiled floor, ornamental white tables and chairs with striped cushions. Almost the whole of one wall was open to a courtyard garden where there was an ornamental pool and a fountain with Berniniesque figures.

'I'll find Patricia—do make yourselves at home. What can I get you to drink?'

They refused drinks.

'Later, perhaps,' Cleeve said.

Helen whispered, 'What a charming man! But not a bit like I expected; he's so *ordinary*.'

Cleeve came back with his wife, a slimly elegant blonde. She wore a cornflower-blue frock which fitted without a crease and made Helen feel uncomfortable in her M & S slacks and blouse. But Patricia Cleeve was cordial in her welcome.

'David is quite right; I love showing off my garden but I get little opportunity. Most of our visitors are only interested in publication schedules, copyrights and royalties. But really a garden is not much fun unless friends come to look at it—don't you agree, Mrs Wycliffe?'

It seemed obvious that the two women would hit it off.

'Shall we start here in the courtyard?'

Cleeve said, 'I'm going to be selfish and cut the garden routine, if I may. I want to show Charles my workshop.'

A fairly smooth operation, but Wycliffe was in no doubt that

211

it was one, and had been from the first moment of their meeting.

Cleeve took him along a corridor, elegant but severe, with disquieting pictures and institutional undertones, up a flight of stairs to a landing with doors opening off. Wycliffe could see into one room, a business-like office where a girl was sorting pages of typescript. Cleeve's own room was next door; large and L-shaped, a combination of office and library with creature comforts catered for, but it was in total contrast with what he had seen of the rest of the house: Edwardian; thick red Wilton on the floor, heavy mahogany bookcases, straight-backed leather armchairs and a huge desk with an inset leather top.

'Sit you down. You'll find my chairs comfortable. If a soldier marches on his stomach a writer writes on his backside, so I've made a study of chairs. You can lounge in one of these or you can sit at a desk—both in comfort; and you can push it around on its castors. I abominate those articulated swivel things which remind me of the dentist's. Darwin wrote his *Origin* sitting in one like this so that gives me a chance.'

He opened a drinks cupboard. 'What will you have? Whisky is my tipple.'

'A small one then—no water.'

Cleeve brought over the drinks; half a tumbler for Wycliffe.

They prepared to engage. Wycliffe said, 'This is good whisky.'

'Whiskey with an "e"—it's Irish. My publisher has a house in Kerry. I've no idea where he got this but, knowing him, I wouldn't be surprised if it was moonshine out of a Kerry bog.' Cleeve was watching Wycliffe, trying to gauge his responses, but Wycliffe was at his most bland, wearing what Helen called his "well-meaning-vicar look".

'Have you read any of my books?' The question came with a disarming grin.

'All of them, I think.'

'And?'

A thoughtful pause. 'I think they are extremely well written and compelling. Does that sound patronizing?'

'If it does, I asked for it. So you don't like my books, but do you take them seriously?'

Wycliffe drank some more whiskey with an "e": it really was very good—smoother than the scotch to which he was accustomed. 'I take them very seriously.'

'But in official jargon you probably feel they tend to corrupt and deprave; is that it?'

'No, it isn't!' Wycliffe was short. 'Your books depress me because you write about a world without hope. God is dead; heaven is empty. I'm simple enough to hope and believe that there must be some chink of light in the darkness somewhere.'

Cleeve laughed. 'I've said already, this is my lucky day. Drink up! The prophet of doom and gloom! One critic called me Bunyan without a pilgrim.' He became serious again and looked at Wycliffe quizzically. 'A non-conformist background? Liberal-cum-Fabian Socialist? Don't be offended; it's no good if we waste time being polite. Have I got it right?'

'Just about.'

A satisfied smile. 'I'm out of the same stable. Totally backslid, I tell myself, but it sticks like shit to the proverbial blanket. It left Arnold Bennett too inhibited to indulge the one vice he really fancied—screwing nubile girls under pink lampshades. I must say it's never got me that way—stopped me, I mean.'

Wycliffe pursued his theme in self-defence. 'Even your "good" characters seem doomed through circumstance to add to the evil in the world—'

Cleeve cut in sharply. 'And that worries you? Don't you think it worries me? But I write about the world as it is—at least as I see it; a world with no sense of guilt because it has lost its sense of sin. After thirty years in the police you must surely go some of the way with that.'

Wycliffe smiled. 'I will admit I sometimes wonder if our generation was the last to be burdened with a sense of guilt. I don't think it follows that people no longer distinguish right from wrong or that the future is wholly black.' He emptied his glass. 'Anyway, now that the courtesies have been exchanged and the ice broken, perhaps you will tell me why I am here.'

213

Cleeve's face was like water which takes on the changing moods of the sky; the blue eyes and the fresh, open countenance could darken in an instant. They did so now.

'I do want something from you; something I'd be very unlikely to get from the nearest cop-shop—advice without strings. Your profession is one of those where it's very difficult to bypass the G.P. and get to the consultant direct.'

'Except by kidnapping the consultant.'

A brief smile. 'The fact is, my life is threatened. I know that sounds dramatic but I'm satisfied that it is the case.'

Wycliffe waited.

'The threats have come through the post—four so far, extending over a period of about nine months.' Cleeve's nervousness showed; he fingered his rather ragged moustache and looked at Wycliffe with obvious anxiety.

'Have you any idea who is threatening you?'

A momentary hesitation. 'None.'

'Is it David Cleeve or Peter Stride who is threatened?'

A quick, appreciative glance. 'Oh, Cleeve. Because of the kind of books I write all sorts of cranks send abusive and threatening letters addressed to Stride. I take no notice of them.'

The casement window was open and voices came from the garden below. Patricia Cleeve's, rather high-pitched but musical; Helen's softer, her words inaudible. Wycliffe felt irritated; they were on holiday and they had come, casually, to look at an archaeological dig, now they seemed trapped in other people's lives. He made an effort.

'So the threats are personal and you take them seriously. In that case I think you must have some idea why you are threatened.'

Cleeve picked up the whisky bottle. 'Let me top you up!' Wycliffe refused and Cleeve replenished his own glass. 'I've told you I don't know who is threatening me.'

'May I see these threats—I suppose they take the form of letters or cards?'

'I destroyed them.'

Wycliffe was patient. 'You say you received the first one about nine months ago; when did you get the last?'

A frown. 'About a month ago. It indicated that time was running out.' He grinned self-consciously. 'Sounds like something out of Agatha Christie, doesn't it? "The end is near."'

'Is that what it said?'

'Of course not, but that is what it amounted to.'

It was obvious he was lying; at least suppressing most of the truth. 'Did these communications have postmarks?'

'Oh yes—all over the place—one was from London, another from Durham and the last was posted in Exeter. I think the third one came from Bristol—something like that anyway.'

Wycliffe took refuge in the official manner and sounded pompous. 'Mr Cleeve, if you want help from the police you will have to be more open with me. Originally you said that you wanted my advice—it's this: whatever the circumstances, if you think you are in danger, you must be completely frank. Without more to go on it isn't possible for me to tie up for your protection men needed elsewhere.'

Cleeve said quietly, 'I am not asking for protection; I don't want it.'

'What, then?'

He leaned forward across the desk and spoke with great seriousness. 'I want to be sure that if anything happens to me—if these threats are carried out—my family will not be plagued by the police. You understand?'

'I'm not sure that I do.'

Cleeve sighed. 'It's not easy to explain; that is why I'm talking to you instead of to some cloth-eared detective sergeant in the nearest nick. If a man in my position is murdered the police will dig into his private life and find God knows what reasons for suspecting his relatives and close associates—money, jealousy, sex. . .I don't have to tell you what the family of a murdered man has to go through if there is any mystery about the crime.' A twisted little smile. 'I don't have to tell you either what may come out when the lid is lifted off that Pandora's box which we call family life.'

'You are saying that if you are murdered the police should look for suspects outside the circle of your family and friends.'

'Exactly! I would rather they didn't look at all, it wouldn't do me any good, but that would be too much to hope for. I've thought of putting this in writing and attaching it to my will or something of the sort, but when you turned up out of the blue it seemed too good a chance to miss.'

He was smiling, a nervous tentative smile. 'I'm trouble enough to my family alive; I don't want to haunt them when I'm dead.'

Wycliffe was brusque. 'There is very little I can say to you, Mr Cleeve. Your obvious course is to allow the police to investigate the threats to your life and prevent them being carried out. If you decide to do this or if you have any more to tell me, you can get in touch at any time. I advise you to think it over.'

Cleeve nodded. 'The official line; I couldn't expect anything else but I've said my say and you will remember it if anything happens.' He got up from his chair. 'Now, let's see how the women are getting on.'

Wycliffe felt uneasy; even guilty, but what more could he do? His irritation increased. Why couldn't he and Helen have a holiday like anybody else?

They ate coq au vin with a green salad and drank a bottle of over-age Beaujolais in a restaurant close to the harbour. The other diners were mostly unisex boating buffs in blue jerseys and carefully bleached jeans with expensive labels on their bottoms. They wore canvas shoes and talked a cryptic jargon incomprehensible to the uninitiated. The meal was second-rate, but for the buffs it was the chance to talk that mattered. Wycliffe seemed preoccupied.

Over coffee Helen said, 'What exactly did David Cleeve say to you? You've been broody ever since we left them.'

Wycliffe looked around at the other diners, babbling away for dear life and none of them listening. It depressed him. A character in one of Cleeve's books had been made to say: 'Once people were individuals; they struggled; at least with the illusion that they might change things; now, unresisting, resigned, they're swept along by a great wave which must soon break.'

For Wycliffe, that was the real trouble with Cleeve's books, they focused the mind with the unrelenting intensity of a burning glass.

He muttered, 'I'll tell you later.'

When they left the restaurant the sunset was glowing red over the castle, and overhead the sky was pale blue-green. The air was silky and people were sitting out at tables in front of the pubs, feeling just a little awed by the vast stillness of it all. The trippers had gone home, there was no traffic, and the waters of the harbour mirrored the moored craft. Herring gulls, nicely spaced on the sea wall, meditated on eternity.

'Well?'

'He thinks his life is in danger.'

'You mean someone wants to kill him?'

'That's what he says. Someone is threatening him; he doesn't know who or why. Of course he's lying.'

'You mean he isn't being threatened?'

'I mean that if he is, he knows where the threats are coming from and why.'

'What are you going to do?'

He snapped, 'What can I do?' Then, quietly, 'Sorry! But unless he is prepared to give me the facts I can't spend police time on him; he doesn't even want it. Did you get any impression of the family from his wife?'

Helen considered; always careful about making judgements of other people, she made a dull gossip. 'She seems a very pleasant woman, fond of her children and interested in what they do.'

'And her husband?'

Longer consideration. 'I had the impression that she looks upon him not so much as a man and a husband, rather as a kind of monument or institution to be preserved.'

'Not much affection between them?'

'I don't know. People can become very attached to monuments and institutions even when they are something of a liability.'

Back at the cottage he lit his pipe and stood in the doorway, watching the dusk take possession of the creek, the hill opposite, the pine trees and the bay. Finally he turned away. 'I'll sleep on it.'

Chapter Two

THEY AGREED TO split up for the morning. Helen would walk along the coast path to St Just then on to Philleigh in time for a snack lunch at the pub and Wycliffe would join her there with the car.

'I want to find out what the local sergeant knows about the Cleeves.'

Sunday, a day like any other; there would be the same tourists, and even more trippers, the same parade along the waterfront, the same sailing and wind-surfing (given some wind) but it would all take a little longer to get started. Sunday is a sluggish day, as though God, unable to preserve His day of rest, has nevertheless applied the brakes.

As Wycliffe climbed Zion Steps to the house which was home and office for the police sergeant, the single bell of the village church called to worshippers with a blatant and monotonous insistence. In the chapel they were already singing. 'There is a land of pure delight. . .' Let's hope so.

Sergeant Pearce answered the door in his shirt sleeves, a grey-headed old warrior with his years of service recorded on his countenance like notches on the stock of a gun.

'Just a courtesy call,' Wycliffe said.

'I heard on the grape-vine that you were with us, sir.'

Wycliffe took him out for a drink and Pearce introduced him to a bar at the back of The Buckingham Arms.

'Non-emmet,' Pearce said. (The word emmet derives from the Old English for ant and is the Cornish vernacular for a summer visitor.)

The Buckingham presents a brash face to the waterfront but keeps a little bar at the back for locals.

Pearce explained: 'The emmet who strays in here soon begins to feel like a pork butcher in a synagogue—unless, of course, he's somebody's guest.'

They drank lukewarm beer, sitting on hard seats, but without space invaders, fruit machines or juke boxes, and with plenty of privacy. The bar had just opened and they were the only customers.

'They'll get busy later.'

Wycliffe mentioned the Cleeves.

'We hardly ever see Cleeve himself but his wife and daughter do a bit of sailing and they're members of the club. Mrs Cleeve seems a nice woman. Then there's a son—the children are twins —he's about quite a lot in the vacations. He's got a rebuilt M.G. which is the envy of all the young blood in the village.'

Pearce got out his tobacco pouch. 'I hear you're a pipe-smoker—try some of this, sir. I grow it and cure it myself but it's not at all bad.'

They filled their pipes and smoked peaceably. Wycliffe found the tobacco pleasant; mild and sweetish to the tongue. Rum and molasses.

'Going back to Mrs Cleeve, she's got a brother in the village, a chap called Tull—Geoffrey Tull—he runs a herbalist's shop further down the Steps; you may have noticed it. He calls himself a naturopath, whatever that is. He seems to have a good business but I fancy he spends faster than he gets and I've heard that his sister has had to bail him out of trouble more than once.'

Wycliffe diverted the flow. 'I gather Cleeve isn't too popular with some people over these excavations.'

Pearce chuckled. 'The Roseland Celtic Society. Chairperson, Mrs Laura Wynn—she's got a shop on the Steps too—jewellery, near the top. She's a strange one. If she was ever married I don't know what happened to her husband but it wouldn't surprise me if she'd eaten him.'

'Is the feeling over the dig very strong?'

Pearce scratched his cheek with the stem of his pipe. 'I doubt if the real Roselanders care a cuss either way, but some of the newcomers want a bit of colour in their lives and they've decided to revive what they call the Celtic tradition.'

'What do they do?'

Pearce was intrigued by Wycliffe's interest but he asked no questions. He took a swallow of beer and wiped his lips. 'Until this excavation lark started, not much that I could see. They have a bonfire on the Stone Field twice a year—Mayday eve and Hallowe'en, and I believe they go up there sometimes at sunrise to dance round in their nightshirts in a yoghurt-induced frenzy, pretending to be druids or something.' Pearce spoke with a vast tolerance of human vagaries bred of a lifetime in the force. 'I got to admit I was never up there to see.'

'And since the excavations started?'

'Ah! Officially I don't know anything about that as nobody made any complaint, but I understand they went up there two or three times in the early stages and pulled up all their markers—that sort of thing. It seems they've stopped that caper now and decided to play it legal; they're getting up a petition and talking about an injunction, though I can't think who'd put up the money for any court case.'

'I don't suppose it bothers Cleeve too much.'

'You wouldn't think so, but about the same time as they began talking about the dig in Henry's Field, Cleeve employed a firm of private inquiry agents to investigate Laura Wynn.'

'How do you know that?'

'A complaint from the lady herself about a strange man asking her questions and talking about her to her neighbours. I made a few enquiries, asked around a bit, and it turned out to be Charlie Cox who used to be a D.C. at sub-division and now works for Sowest Security Services. Over a jar Charlie told me his agency had been briefed by Cleeve.'

'To do what?'

'To find out who the woman was and where she came from—that was all.'

Wycliffe looked at the empty glasses. 'Shall we have another?'

'No, sir; thank you. Not for me; I've had my ration for a morning session.'

'Me too; I'd like to get back to your office and use the telephone.'

In a neat little office, looking out over Zion Steps, where even the rubber stamp knew its place, Wycliffe telephoned his headquarters.

'Who's on duty in C.I.D.?'

'D.S. Watson, sir, but Chief Inspector Scales is in his office as it happens.'

'Good! Put me through, please.'

He talked to his deputy, John Scales. The usual smokescreen of words which takes the place of the sniffing ritual in lower animals, then: 'I want you to set going a few enquiries, John. Have you heard of Peter Stride?'

'Who hasn't? But he's not a favourite of mine at the moment. Jane has an American girl over here doing a Ph.D. thesis on *The Man and his Work.* (Jane Scales was a lecturer at the university.) She can't get near him. Just a note from his secretary: "Mr Stride thanks you for your interest but he does not give interviews, neither does he furnish details of his private life. He prefers to be judged on his published work alone."'

'He may have good reason for that! Anyway, I want you to find out what you can about him through the usual channels. You probably know already that his real name is Cleeve—David Cleeve; he's a little older than me, married to Patricia née Tull—an Oxfordshire family. She's several years younger. They have twin children, boy and girl, aged about nineteen. . . .They've lived here for several years. . . .No, I don't mind if he gets wind of our interest. . . .As far as I know he hasn't done anything except tell me a half-baked yarn about his life being threatened. . . .No, I'm quite prepared to believe he's being threatened but he won't give us enough detail to help him. . . .Yes, it's pretty obvious he's afraid of incriminating himself in some way. . . .'

That and a word to sub-division arranging for the Panda patrols to keep an eye on Roscrowgy, made him feel better. Not that it would do Cleeve any good if someone had decided to stem the flow of contentious masterpieces with a bullet or a loaded sock, but it was all he could do.

He joined Helen at the Philleigh pub for lunch and afterwards they crossed by the chain-ferry to Trelissick and spent the afternoon walking in the gardens and woods. Wycliffe grew nostalgic about life in the great days of houses like Trelissick, until he remembered that he would have been among the forelock-touching minions on the wrong side of the green-baize door.

A pleasant tea in a former barn with the chaffinches more than ready to go shares.

Monday July 18th
Cleeve was following his morning ritual, counting the pine trees. The sun was shining directly into his room and it was already hot. He opened the window and let in the fresh air along with the sounds from outside, the gulls screeching, the shouts of children playing in a garden further down the hill, a helicopter pulsing distantly, somewhere over the bay. For most people it was another summer's day; for him it was Monday July 18th and he was waiting for Milli to bring in the mail.

She came at last, wearing a sleeveless frock with shoulder straps and a plunging neckline, more provocative than if she had been nude. But today he hardly noticed.

The routine 'Good morning!'

Milli said, 'There are a couple of queries from Lester about a TV serialization of *Medicus* you'll have to look at. Apart from that. . .'

'Leave it on the desk with the others.'

On the way out she stopped. 'Are you all right?'

'Why shouldn't I be?'

A shrug of the bare shoulders.

After an all but sleepless night he had been up since first light and from eight o'clock he had felt like a man living on borrowed time, as though the minutes, the seconds, were being doled out to him with miserly reluctance. Once more he seemed to bestride two worlds.

He crossed to his desk; the Cleeve mail was there, five or six envelopes. . .the third was white, addressed in block capitals, postmark Truro. He opened it, the card was there but it was in two pieces; a Jack of Diamonds roughly torn across. In the margin of each half, the date: Monday July 18th and the number 5.

After a while he returned the torn card to its envelope, unlocked the bottom left-hand drawer of his desk and added the envelope to

222

the four others contained in the cigarette box. Automatically he checked the other contents of the drawer: his pistol, three clips of ammunition, the current volume of his journal, and a slim file of documents.

He closed the drawer and locked it. For a while he stared out of the window, watching a squadron of herring-gulls perform breathtaking aerobatics as they mobbed one of their number who carried a coveted morsel of food in its beak. He reached a decision and went out into the corridor, calling to Milli.

'I'm going out.'

'Out? What if Lester phones?'

'Tell him.'

'Tell him what?'

'You'll think of something.'

He collected his stick and let himself out of the house by a little-used side-door, crossed the garden, and passed through the rhododendron tunnel and the wicket gate to Henry's Field. There he followed a path diagonally across the field to the wooden shed. He raised his stick in salute to the students at work on the dig, and came to the shed and the narrow, rutted lane which led in from the road. He continued down the lane and reached an area of woodland, part of what was once a much larger area preserved for shooting. As he entered the trees he felt calmer; there was an atmosphere of claustrophobic seclusion and remoteness which brought to mind the sombre fairy-tale forests of childhood and, paradoxically, made him feel safe.

He came to a house in a clearing, pushed open the slatted gate and walked up the garden path. The garden had run wild, a paradise for butterflies and bees. An old wicker chair with sun-bleached cushions stood by the front door; the door was open and Cleeve could see into the dimly lit interior of the cottage. A table covered with a green chenille cloth, shared between an ancient Remington portable, a pile of books, and a sleeping tabby cat. Peace descended upon him like the holy dove.

'Anybody home?' He tapped on the door with his stick.

A moment, and Kitson's lean figure emerged from the kitchen at the back, stooping to clear the low lintel. In an old cotton shirt and trousers which were too short he looked like a broomstick man.

'Ah! The squire on a tour of inspection of his property.' The voice was soft and the words were accompanied by a smile which, because of his disfigurement, involved only half his face.

Years of mortifying self-consciousness had established a conditioned reflex so that he usually contrived to present his uninjured profile.

'Aren't you going to ask me in?'

Kitson turned back into the house and Cleeve followed him into the front room which was a combination of living- and work-room. Sparsely furnished, with just the table and three or four chairs, the room overflowed with books; there were shelves everywhere. Two small, square windows looked out on the garden wilderness and in each was a jam-jar of wild flowers—foxgloves with flowering shoots of meadowsweet.

Cleeve was tentative. 'I know you don't like day-time visits. . .'

Kitson said, 'You're here now. What about a drink? Elderberry, dandelion or blackberry. . .'

'Christ! I should have brought a bottle.'

'Yes. The squire should never visit empty-handed.' The gentle and whimsical manner seemed to belie his words.

Kitson went into the kitchen and came back with a bottle and glasses. They sat on the hard wood chairs—Windsor strutbacks, and Kitson poured two glasses of slightly viscous purplish wine.

'Elderberry; said to ease the bowels.'

Cleeve said, 'My bowels won't need easing today.'

Kitson sipped from his glass. 'My calendar says Monday July 18th. I can guess why you're here.'

Cleeve nodded. 'You guess right.'

But he felt relaxed here as nowhere else. There was an atmosphere of timeless serenity and for a little while it was possible to believe in Shangri-La and Santa Claus.

Kitson earned a meagre living, translating Russian texts for publishers and others.

Cleeve, self-absorbed, said, 'It's an uncomfortable feeling, Roger—unnerving. I would never have believed it could have affected me so.'

Kitson smiled. 'You're a fraud, Davy! You write as though it needed more courage to live than to die but, come the crunch, and you tremble before the Old Reaper like the rest of us. "Be absolute for death", Davy, then "either death or life shall thereby be the sweeter".'

Cleeve laughed despite himself. 'You always were a Job's comforter, you old devil!'

On that same Monday the Wycliffes crossed to St Anthony and visited Place House, site of an ancient Celtic religious foundation, made holy in the first place, according to local tradition, by earlier visitors of greater distinction, none other than the boy Jesus and his uncle, Joseph of Arimathaea. Later visitors are supposed to have included Henry VIII and his new bride, Ann Boleyn, completing a honeymoon begun at Hampton Court. Now it can look with condescension on other houses whose only boast is "Queen Elizabeth slept here".

Tuesday July 19th
A hot, sticky night; the Wycliffes had tossed and turned in bed, disturbing each other, then at first light they had fallen into a dead sleep and awakened unrefreshed.

They planned to drive to Pendower, to walk the coast-path to Portloe, and return to the car by way of Veryan.

'Have we got the map?'

'It's in the car.'

'The binoculars?'

'They're on the window-seat.'

'We're ready then. . .'

The telephone rang and Wycliffe answered it. Sergeant Pearce.

'Divisional Inspector Knowles's compliments, sir. He'll be over as soon as possible. He's notified headquarters, but as you're here he thought you should be told. . .'

'Told what?'

'There's been a death by violence, sir—here in the village; suspected murder.'

Wycliffe thought of Cleeve and his heart missed a beat. 'Who?'

225

'A young woman found dead on her bed.'

'How did she die?'

Pearce was cagey. 'There's some doubt about that, sir—not straightforward at all. Dr Hodge spoke of poison which, he said, was not self-administered.'

Wycliffe looked out of the little latticed window. The sun was still shining on the water and on the fields beyond; there were still dinghies whistling for a wind, and people continued to pass to and fro along the waterfront, but he was no longer part of it.

'Where is she?'

'Mount Zion Steps; two doors down from my place. The house is in two flats and hers is the lower one.'

'Who found her?'

'The milkman, and he came to my place to telephone for a doctor. It wasn't until Dr Hodge had seen her that there was any thought of foul play.'

'All right; I'll meet you at the house shortly.'

He looked across at Helen; she was standing by the window with her back to him but when she turned round she was already resigned. 'A murder case?'

'It looks like it; too early to say for certain. What will you do?'

'Don't worry. I may drive into Truro if you don't want the car, or I could take the ferry to Falmouth.'

He telephoned John Scales.

'Ah! I'm glad they got hold of you, sir. . .'

It was all arranged. Initially, Scales was sending Detective Sergeants Smith and Lane with three constables. 'I'll get two more D.C.s off to you later in the day, sir.'

Detective Sergeant Lane—Lucy Lane, a recent recruit to his squad. Wycliffe professed freedom from sex prejudice but he recalled Dr Johnson on the subject of women preachers—"like a dog walking on his hinder legs. It is not done well; but you are surprised to find it done at all"—and reserved judgement.

Time would tell.

'What about Franks?' Franks was the pathologist.

'I caught him at the hospital; he's hoping to be with you about midday.'

Wycliffe turned once more to Helen: 'I'll be off then.'

Helen said, 'A floral shirt and light-fawn slacks might raise a few eyebrows, don't you think?'

He had to change.

The little house was half-way up Zion Steps, almost opposite the jewellery shop where Helen had bought her brooch. It was like being suddenly transported backstage from a seat in the stalls.

The sombre granite frontage had been tarted up with bright-blue paint on the woodwork of windows and door. Pearce was waiting for him outside.

'Better go round the back, sir.'

A little way down, there was a passage giving access to a narrow lane running along the backs of all the houses in the block, and the house of the dead girl had a yard from which blue-painted steps gave separate access to the upper flat.

Pearce pointed to a ground-floor sash window, open several inches at the bottom; the curtains were drawn but didn't quite meet. 'She's in there, sir; that's her bedroom.'

'Who is she?'

'Celia Dawe—a girl in her early twenties; a real eye-catcher, the sort men turn to look at in the street—women too, for a different reason.'

'Local?'

'Yes. She was an orphan, brought up by her uncle and two maiden aunts—the Borlases, who keep the photographer's shop further up the steps. She's been away for a few years but she turned up again last season. Jack Polmear, the landlord of The Buckingham Arms, gave her a job and let her have this flat which used to be his mother's until she died a year or two back. There's an old lady in the top flat still—Maggie Treloar—she worked for the Polmears for donkey's years.'

'The girl didn't go back to her relatives?'

Pearce scratched his long nose. 'I don't think it would have worked; she probably left in the first place because she couldn't get on with her uncle and aunts—they're an odd family, great chapel people and probably very strict.'

'Have they been told?'

227

'Dr Hodge went over there. I thought I'd better not leave here more than I had to.'

'This chap Polmear seems to have put himself out for the girl.'

A sly grin. 'Jack's wife divorced him a year or two back but as long as I've known him he's had a succession of girl friends; this one is just the latest in line.'

'Was she a tart?'

Pouted lips. 'I wouldn't say that; I think she looked on a man as security. Incidentally, she's been seen about a lot with young Cleeve since he came home on vacation a few weeks ago.'

'I gather the milkman found her?'

'Yes, it seems they had an arrangement; if she wasn't up and about when he came he was to bang on her bedroom window. He did this morning but got no reply, then he saw her through the gap in the curtains. He realized something was wrong when she didn't wake and tried the back door; it wasn't locked and he went in. . .'

'Have you got his statement?'

'No, when the doctor came he went on with his round but we can pick him up.'

'Is there access to this yard other than through the alley from the Steps?'

'Yes, the back lane continues up into Chapel Street.'

Wycliffe found it hard to realize that he was starting on a murder inquiry. So far these people were not real to him; he still felt detached, as though he were reading about them in a newspaper; he was still on holiday.

'Let's go inside.'

Through a small kitchen which was modern, though none too clean; the remnants of a fish-and-chip take-away on the table; dirty dishes in the sink.

Pearce said, 'Apart from this and the bathroom she only had the two rooms—a little parlour facing out on the Steps and her bedroom overlooking the yard.'

In the passage Pearce pushed open a door and they stood just inside the girl's bedroom. There was a carpet on the floor; a double bed and a dressing table took up most of the space. A television set on a stand was placed at the foot of the bed; the clothes she had been wearing were in a little heap on a tub chair, and there was a floor-to-ceiling cupboard, presumably her wardrobe. White curtains were drawn across the sash-window but they did not meet and the window itself was open a little at the bottom so that the curtains were stirred by a draught. Despite the fresh air, there was a stale smell blended of cosmetics and woman.

Celia Dawe, completely naked, lay on her right side; a grubby sheet and a duvet trailed over the foot of the bed; her shoulder-length blonde hair spread over the pillow. There were no obvious signs of injury or violence but her features were contorted as though in a spasm of pain.

'She was lying on her back,' Pearce said, 'but Dr Hodge shifted her. You see he's marked a small puncture wound in her left buttock.'

A reddish ring, apparently drawn with the girl's own lipstick, surrounded a tiny puncture high up on the left buttock where the hips began to narrow to the waist. The puncture itself was at the centre of a brown spot like a mole.

They were standing by the dressing table which was littered with cosmetic bottles and jars. Pearce pointed to a glass specimen tube lying in the lid of a jar of face cream. In the tube was a little dart-like object which seemed to consist of a fine needle in a brass holder. The needle was stained brown as though by rust.

'Dr Hodge found the dart on the floor by the bed; he reckoned it must've dropped out of the wound and rolled there.'

Wycliffe examined the tube, removed the stopper and sniffed. 'Nicotine!'

'That's what the doctor said, sir.'

There was nothing they could do until the technical people had done their work so they went out into the yard.

'You haven't had a word with the old lady upstairs?'

'No, sir, I haven't had a chance but I'll do it now.'

Wycliffe said, 'Leave it. There's something else I want you to do. We shall need an incident room; I'd prefer a large room or a small hall—somewhere with a bit of space. I hate those caravan things where you're afraid to breathe for fear of upsetting somebody else's cocoa. Any ideas?'

Pearce nodded. 'I'll see what I can do, sir.'

The divisional inspector had left again with his D.C., relieved to be let off so lightly. Wycliffe had said, 'It's too early; I'll let you know if I need more local assistance, it depends on the amount of leg-work. At the moment I want Pearce freed of normal duty and assigned to me. In addition, you can leave me your uniformed man to defend us from snoopers.'

The truth was that he preferred to work with a small team of his own men.

Now he was going up Zion Steps to the photographer's shop. Tourists were plodding up and ambling down in a thin stream, women with sun-reddened skins, paunchy men and bored children. Nobody showed the slightest interest in what might he happening in the little house with the blue paintwork, but that could change once word got round.

A tall, bald-headed figure threaded his way among the tourists; an animated scarecrow, his head and face were terribly scarred on one side; Kitson, carrying a plastic bag, doing his shopping. Mutual recognition and acknowledgement.

It was hot, Wycliffe could feel the damp patches under his arms and he promised himself a cold beer at lunchtime.

W. Borlase and Son, Photographers: faded gilt lettering on a brown fascia; a double-fronted shop with one window devoted to wedding photographs and child studies while the other was filled with historical photographs recording the life of Roseland through more than a century.

Joseph Borlase stood in his shop, a little back from the door, watching the approach of his visitor. He was a soft, fleshy man of about fifty with the unformed features of a plump baby; he wore a fawn linen jacket, a white shirt with a bow tie, and dark trousers. He saw Wycliffe pause for a moment outside, sizing the place up, then the door opened and a bell sounded discreetly. Everything in the shop was both dusty and discreet, the potted palms, the framed photographs on the walls and displayed on easels, the ornately carved screen with velvet curtains which separated the shop from the studio; the place could scarcely have changed in 50 years.

Wycliffe introduced himself. 'I think Dr Hodge broke the news of your niece's death. . .I'm very sorry. . .I understand that you and your sisters are her next of kin—is that correct?'

Borlase was sweating though it was cool in the shop; there were beads of sweat under his eyes and he wiped them away with a silk handkerchief from his breast pocket as though they were tears.

'Celia's parents were killed in an accident when she was three . . .' His voice was soft as melting butter. 'My sisters and I brought her up. . . .My sisters are a good deal older than I. . .it wasn't easy.'

Wycliffe said, 'I don't know what Dr Hodge told you but we suspect that your niece was murdered.'

'Murdered!' A murmured exclamation of horror.

'Did you think she had died a natural death?'

'What?' The blue eyes were troubled. 'Dr Hodge mentioned poison. . .I thought it must have been an accident. Perhaps that she had taken her own life—not murder. . .' His words seemed to hang in the air, breathy and moist.

'Your niece left home several years ago, I believe. Where did she go?'

Joseph rolled his handkerchief into a ball and was kneading it with both hands. 'I don't know, superintendent. . . .After breakfast one morning she went out and never came back. . . .We found that her clothes were missing. . . .She was eighteen. Three days later we had a card with a London postmark. It said that she was well and that she wouldn't be coming home. . . .We heard nothing more until at the beginning of last summer she arrived back in the village.'

'Didn't she offer any explanation of where she had been or why she had come back?'

'She never came near us—we heard she was back from neighbours and then she came to live just a few doors away. She never came to see us.'

'Did you or your sisters go to see her?'

He looked mildly shocked. 'It wasn't our place. . . .After all we'd done for her, to be treated like that!' He wiped his face once more; his pores seemed to ooze moisture.

'So you have had no contact with her since she came back?'

231

'None.'

'For practical purposes, Mr Borlase, I have to ask whether you are willing to act as next-of-kin—there will be formalities, the body will have to be identified, there will be an inquest and arrangements to be made for the funeral.'

A sigh. 'I quite understand. I hope I know my duty.'

Wycliffe looked round the shop with its air of dusty, fossilized gentility. Celia Dawe had lived in the place with this man for fifteen years of her life. 'Is there anything you would like to ask me, Mr Borlase?'

'Ask you? No. . .I don't think so. . . .There is, perhaps, one thing. . .I mean her belongings.'

'What about her belongings, Mr Borlase?'

'I wondered. . .' He hesitated. 'Shall I be able to claim them? I'm sure that my sisters will feel. . .I mean things of family interest. . .'

'If she has left no will I imagine all her property, whatever it is, will come to you and your sisters eventually.'

It was evidently not what he had hoped to hear. The handkerchief was kneaded more vigorously. 'Perhaps I could come over and go through her things. . .I mean, we ought to know exactly what her circumstances were. . .'

Wycliffe was puzzled. He said firmly, 'I'm afraid there can be no question of that until our investigation has gone a good deal further than at present. Of course, there is nothing to stop you getting in touch with your solicitor regarding your rights.'

He shook his head with unaccustomed vigour. 'No! No, we wouldn't want to do that. . .I merely thought. . .The whole business is so very painful.'

Wycliffe decided to leave it there. Borlase came and stood on the step, watching him as he crossed over.

Cleeve was at his desk; he had the typescript of *Setebos* in front of him but it was no more than an excuse, he had scarcely turned a page for the morning. He was not drinking either, he was waiting. Since half-past nine when Milli brought the mail he had seen no one and no one had telephoned. Unless he gave specific instructions it was rare for him to be undisturbed for so long.

The windows were open and from time to time he went over to stand, looking out. Not a cloud in the sky, the sun blazing down, the air shimmering in the heat, and everywhere, silence. A strange silence it seemed to him, even a conspiracy of silence. He dismissed the fanciful notion but without conviction. He looked at the long-case clock which he wound religiously every Saturday morning—ten minutes to eleven. In ten minutes Milli would bring him his coffee. Perhaps then. . .Milli had her own way of gathering news; he suspected her of operating her own K.G.B. in the village.

The night of Monday July 18th. . .last night. An incredible coincidence and an incredible stupidity on his part; he could almost believe that the events of the night had been a dream.

The old clock cleared its throat, as it always did a couple of minutes before striking, and just then there was a tap on the door. Milli came in with the coffee on a little tray.

'Do you really want this? Or is it too hot for coffee?'

'Don't I always have coffee?'

She shrugged. 'As you like. Do you mind if I have a shower? It's sticky in that room.' She squirmed inside her frock and her hard little nipples protruded through the thin material like beansprouts.

She was signalling; he could have her if he wanted, as he had done before, still wet from the shower. He was tempted, but this was not the time.

He said with contrived casualness, 'By all means have a shower if you want one. No calls?'

'No, it's quiet this morning.' She paused, looking at him. 'All right, I won't be long. I'll switch the phone through.'

He could imagine what she would do in the shower. 'Little whore!'

He laced his coffee with whisky. Two or three minutes went by and there was another tap at the door; he thought it was Milli, back on some pretext, but to his astonishment it was Patricia. He couldn't remember the time when she had come to him in this part of the house.

As always, Patricia looked relaxed and cool. 'I hope I'm not disturbing you?' Her calm gaze took in the whole room and he was sure she had not missed the lingering fragrance of whisky.

233

'Of course you're not disturbing me! Sit down. Will you have something? Coffee? A drink?'

It was absurd, he was treating her like a visitor.

She remained standing, aloof. 'I was in the village this morning and I met Nancy Hodge—the doctor's wife.' Patricia was never sure how much he knew of the village. 'Hodge was called out this morning to that little house on Zion Steps which Polmear turned into flats . . .' Her eyes were on him, unwavering. He sat at his desk, gently stroking the ragged ends of his moustache.

'Celia Dawe—Borlase's niece—has been living in the bottom flat and working at The Buckingham. . .The milkman found her this morning, dead on her bed.'

'Dead? What did she die of?' His voice sounded unreal.

'That's the point. Hodge called in the police and now your friend Wycliffe is down there. Nancy hinted that they think the girl was murdered.'

'Murdered? That is ridiculous!'

'Why is it ridiculous?'

He realized that he had been too emphatic. 'Well, who would want to murder the girl?' Feeble.

Patricia did not relax her gaze. 'I'm worried, David.'

'Worried?'

A flicker of annoyance. 'Please don't fence with me! You think if you close your eyes you can't be seen.'

Cleeve spread his large freckled hands on the desk and seemed to study them.

Patricia went on: 'There is Andrew to consider.'

'Andrew?'

'You must know that he has been seeing a lot of that girl since he came home this time. That at least will be common talk in the village.'

Cleeve said nothing. Patricia remained standing; she had gone as far as she was prepared to go.

'You remember that we shall have guests this evening?'

'I hadn't forgotten.'

The headquarters party arrived; they trooped into the back yard of

234

Celia Dawe's flat led by Detective Sergeant Smith—the squad's photographer, fingerprint man and resident Jeremiah. He was trailed by Detective Constable Shaw—the administrative assistant, and two D.C.s carrying gear—like porters in darkest Africa. Smith would take charge at the scene-of-crime; Shaw would look after communications and records.

'We had to park a quarter of a mile away.' Smith, the eternal victim.

Wycliffe said, 'Is D.S. Lane not with you?'

'She's coming in her own car.' This, too, seemed a matter of grievance.

Franks, the pathologist, was not long after the police party. By contrast, Wycliffe had never known the plump little doctor anything but cheerful. He was ruled by two passions, women and fast cars, and age had not withered nor the years contemned.

'Seventy minutes from the hospital, Charles! Not bad over these roads.'

Wycliffe, whose speedometer rarely touched 60, was unimpressed. 'One of these days a bright lad in traffic will stay awake long enough to book you. I only hope it happens before you kill somebody.'

Franks grinned. 'Still the same old Charles! Where is she? It is a she, isn't it?'

Wycliffe led the way into the house. Smith had already taken a number of shots of the room and the body; now he would record each change of position during the pathologist's examination.

Franks looked down at the dead girl. 'She was beautiful, Charles! "The nakedness of woman is the work of God. . . .The lust of the goat is the bounty of God." You wouldn't approve, you old Puritan! But Blake said that—it's poetry. . . .What's the hieroglyph on her bottom in aid of?'

Wycliffe pointed to the specimen tube containing the dart. Franks picked it up and examined it through the glass, then took out the cork and sniffed.

'Nicotine, my God! Fancy stuff, Charles. It's a long time since we've had a decent poisoning—gone out of fashion. Too much bother; needs a bit of nous—planning. Easier to clump somebody over the head.' He held up the little tube. 'Who has a go at this? Me or Forensic?'

As always, Wycliffe reacted to Franks with gloomy disapproval. 'You know better than that. You do your Stas-Otto on the tissues and leave the clever stuff to the whiz-kids at Forensic.' After a moment, he added, 'I suppose there's no harm in you taking a look before passing it on.'

Franks said, 'You'll want to know whether she had a man.'

Wycliffe waited in the yard. The professional callousness of pathologists made him uncomfortable. But things were beginning to move. After a while, Pearce came back wagging his tail like an old spaniel with his master's slippers. He had found a little building once used by the village school, now in planning limbo.

'Where is it?'

'In Chapel Street at the top of the Steps. It belongs to the chapel and they're always glad to make a few pounds by letting it.'

'Good! Put D.C. Shaw in the picture and let him get on with it. I want you here.'

Shaw would arrange for a pantechnicon to bring furniture, office equipment and a communications unit from central stores.

Detective Sergeant Lucy Lane put in her appearance; this would be the first time she had worked directly under Wycliffe. She had applied for a vacancy in Serious Crime Squad from a divisional C.I.D. and, with an ear for his conscience and an eye on the discrimination acts, Wycliffe had agreed to the appointment. Her qualifications were impeccable, beginning with an honours degree in English Literature. She had the vital statistics of a Miss World and at first had been a major distraction in the duty room, with cases of the wandering hand as well as the wandering eye. In the end she had put a stop to it in a single memorable sentence; she said simply, to all within earshot: 'If you want sex in your work you can play with each other or with yourselves, not with me.'

Wycliffe gave her her instructions: 'I want you to brief yourself with the local man, Sergeant Pearce; let him put you in the picture about the place and the case. Then you can start on house-to-house with D.C. Curnow to assist. There's an old lady who lives alone in the flat above this; she might have something to tell us. Obviously we want to know whether anybody saw or heard anything last night—they probably didn't; but we also want gossip. Don't turn your nose up at gossip. More than half the leads in a case like this stem from it.'

The dark eyes were innocent.

'Yes, sir. I remember you making that point in a lecture you gave when I was in training school, way back in '78.'

First blood to the lady.

Franks's preliminary examination did not take long and he rejoined Wycliffe in the yard.

'You can have her shifted, Charles. In my opinion she's been dead between fifteen and twenty hours, which puts it between nine and two last night. The only sign of injury is the puncture wound and what I've seen is consistent with her having died of a quick-action poison injected into her system. Nicotine would fill the bill very well and that dart stinks of the stuff. Of course I'll be able to tell you more when I've done the P.M. and the tests.'

He wiped his bald head with a silk handkerchief. 'God, it's hot! Nicotine—where would he get it? It used to be used by horticulturalists as a pesticide but I don't know if it still is—you and Helen are the gardeners. Vets use it as a vermifuge. . .'

'Surely penetration of the skin by a needle simply dipped in nicotine wouldn't be fatal?'

'No; there must be more to that dart. You're after a man of ideas, Charles, and God knows, there aren't many of them left. Murders these days are merely brutal. The Borgias invited their victims to dine; this chap coaxed his into bed—I like that.'

'She definitely had a man with her?'

'Definitely! I might be able to tell you his blood group from the semen, though much good that will do you at this stage.'

The mortuary van came to the top of the Steps and the girl's body had to be carried up on a stretcher, providing a brief diversion for the sightseers. End of Celia Dawe who left home at eighteen for the big city but came back to her village five years later to work as a barmaid and sleep with her boss. Wycliffe muttered irritably, 'Stupid youngsters! Chasing rainbows!'

237

But now they could get on.

Wycliffe went back to the flat. Smith and his assistant were creating havoc in the bedroom, looking for unconsidered trifles. Smith was good at his particular job because he could be single-minded about little things; no detail would escape him, his problem was to see the broader picture.

Wycliffe poked about in the kitchen. Celia had not been a housekeeping girl. The cupboards were empty except for a few basics—tea, coffee, sugar, a packet or two of breakfast cereal and a few tins. She had probably eaten most of her meals out. In the bathroom, the bath and basin had a soapy rim and the loo cried out for that wonder liquid which kills "all known germs DEAD!". Knickers and bras were draped on a string stretched over the bath.

He went into the front room—the parlour; a dreary little room with a window looking out over the Steps. No sun and little enough light. It was furnished with a dusty three-piece suite, a sideboard, a table. . . .There was a carpet on the floor and framed prints of soulful maidens looked down from the walls. Even on this hot July day it smelled of damp and disuse; it was almost certainly as Polmear's mother had left it. The girl had used the flat only as a place to sleep.

Wycliffe let himself out by the front door and stood for a moment looking up and down the narrow street, taking it all in afresh. Subconsciously he was beginning to see the place through the eyes of a local. Opposite was the shop where Helen had bought her brooch, and he was aware of being watched by the lady with the long blonde hair. She must be wondering what he had to do with the happenings across the road. Next door to the jeweller's was the photographer's and it was in those rooms with the bay windows over the shop that Celia Dawe had spent most of her childhood.

Feeling more at home he strolled down the Steps to the waterfront and the lounge bar of The Buckingham. The pub did a good trade in light lunches; most of the tables in the bar and in the walled courtyard were occupied by people eating crab or prawn salad, cold meats, or grilled fish. He chose the prawns and found a table in a corner by the bar. He wondered where Helen was lunching and felt hard done by at missing his holiday in such ideal weather.

Waitresses in blue nylon overalls flitted between the tables with trays held high. He felt conspicuous in a suit. Behind the bar a middle-aged man, running to fat, kept an eye on it all. He wore a white shirt, a bow tie and black trousers: Polmear, the landlord. His fair hair was thinning but carefully combed to disguise the fact. His eyes rested momentarily on Wycliffe, registered his presence and moved on.

Wycliffe took his time over the meal; drank two glasses of chilled lager and followed this with coffee. By that time customers were dwindling, a bell sounded. 'Last orders for drinks, please.'

The waitresses were beginning to clear the tables; Wycliffe went over to the bar where Polmear was lighting a cigarette.

'Mr Polmear?'

Recognition, not of the man but of his mission. 'You are. . .?'

Wycliffe told him: 'I think you know why I'm here.'

'Yes, it was a shock.'

'I would like to talk to you in private for a few minutes.'

Polmear called through a hatch to another bar. 'Chris! Take over here for a bit. . . .This way.'

Wycliffe followed him into a little office where there was just room for a desk and two chairs; no natural light. 'Will you have something?'

'Not now, thanks.'

Polmear tapped ash from his cigarette into an ashtray advertising lager.

'You've known her a long time?'

'Since she was a kid—three or four years old. Her parents were killed in an accident somewhere up north and she came to live with her aunts and uncle—the Borlases—they're a brother and two sisters.'

'You've taken an interest in her since she came back?'

A shrewd look. 'I gave her a job and found her somewhere to live.'

'Altruism?'

Polmear trickled smoke through his thick lips and watched it rise. 'Not altogether; I did feel sorry for her—she was down on her luck

239

but I also thought she'd make a good barmaid, and she did; she had looks, a pleasant manner, an eye for the till and, when necessary, she knew how to cool it.'

'Couldn't she have gone back to the Borlases?'

A broad grin. 'You must be joking! I mean, she stuck it as long as she could the first time round. The Borlases have to be seen to be believed and he's as kinky as they come, in spite of his chapel-going.'

'So Celia Dawe was simply an employee of yours whom you helped in various ways?' Wycliffe at his most bland.

Polmear grinned. 'You know damn well she was more than that; the whole village knows I spent most nights up there. It suited us both, I'm divorced and Celia had got into the habit of having a man in her bed.'

'Were you there last night?'

He looked shocked. 'My God, I wasn't! I haven't been up there for more than two months.'

'Why not?'

'Because she found somebody else. That was fair enough. She was looking for security and she knew she couldn't expect it from me. She told me she'd taken on somebody else and that was the end of it as far as I was concerned. No hard feelings; I've never gone short.'

'Who was this other man?'

'I don't know—none of my business.'

'But I expect you could make an informed guess.'

He shook his head. 'Straight up, I couldn't. They must have kept it pretty quiet because I never heard a whisper. Now, I suppose, he's done for her. She was an unlucky kid—never got it right.' His manner was relaxed and natural, concerned but not nervous. He was playing with a ball-point, flicking it in and out. 'She liked to play it rough: some women do; I suppose he went too far and strangled her.'

'She wasn't strangled.'

'No?'

'She was poisoned.'

'*Poisoned*!' Polmear was incredulous. 'Then I'm a long way out. . . .If that's the case it sounds like a woman. . . .Are you sure it wasn't an accident?'

'Could her new bedfellow have been young Cleeve?'

Polmear shrugged. 'It started before he came home on vacation. It's true she's been running round with the boy but I guess that was fun, not business.'

'When did you last see her?'

'Last night when we closed.'

'Was she her usual self?'

'She seemed so to me; she was in the other bar and I didn't see a lot of her.'

'One last question. Have you any idea where and how she spent the years she was away?'

Polmear lit another cigarette. 'I know she was in London and that she had several jobs; she had a spell in a strip club then, through her boy friend, she got bit parts in the theatre. By the time she decided to chuck it and come home she was sharing a flat in Bayswater with a girl friend and working in a café in Queensway. . . .Come to think of it, she used to hear from that girl so you may find letters.'

Wycliffe left the pub and joined the crowds on the waterfront. The holiday circus was in full swing, the car park was full, boats peeled off from the quay, laden with their quota of emmets, to "cruise round the creek and view the lighthouse" or "tour the harbour and docks at Falmouth". Laughs, cries, shouts and occasional shrieks came from the shingle beach, now at its greatest low-tide extent. Village, creek, castle and pine trees shimmered in the afternoon heat.

He was beginning to get some sort of picture of the dead girl—of whom he had never heard until that morning. Like thousands of others she had set out with little more than an undiscriminating greed for life. Such a girl might, conceivably, end up being strangled by a lover; it was a credible climax. But this girl had been poisoned—poisoned by someone who had carefully and deliberately planned to murder; someone with a knowledge of poisons and access to one of the most lethal; someone with the ingenuity and skill to prepare a dart which must have functioned as a miniature hypodermic.

Not a crime of passion but of cold, festering hatred.

The man who had slept with her on the night of her death was the most obvious suspect but, in Wycliffe's view, not the only possibility.

He saw the bedroom in the eye of his mind; the bed across the window, with only a couple of feet of space between; the window open at the bottom to the yard, the flimsy curtains scarcely stirring; the night sultry and still. The girl on the bed quite naked.

He sensed that this would be a plodder's case, nothing to be gained by running round in ever diminishing circles to meet the fate of a certain legendary bird, but step by step; stone on stone.

Back to the present. He had been leaning on the sea wall staring at nothing. In his sombre suit he must have looked like an undertaker at a party. A few feet away a woman painter in water colours had set up her easel; her colours were spread out on a little tray and a water-pot dangled from a hook. It needed courage, so nakedly to expose one's talents.

Wycliffe made for Zion Steps. As he passed the herbalist's he was recalling his encounter with Cleeve. Within three days of his arrival in the village on holiday he had been consulted about threats to a man's life and confronted with the murder of a girl. Coincidence? Reason said 'Yes', but instinct, cautiously, 'Perhaps not'. Was young Cleeve's association with the dead girl a significant link? Cleeve had made a deep impression on Wycliffe and though his first reaction was antagonistic he sensed the man's profound disquiet, his self-disgust, and wondered what the cause might be.

At the girl's flat Smith was still in the bedroom, his assistant, D.C. Edwards, had been assigned to the other rooms. The bedroom looked as though the removal men were expected at any moment. The dressing table had been cleared of cosmetics and toiletries and in their place was an array of labelled polythene envelopes, large and small. Smith, wearing his rimless half-glasses, sat on the stripped bed writing in his notebook—always an exercise in copy-book script which magistrates and even judges had commended.

'Anything to tell me?' One had to be careful with Smith, a too-precise question might elicit a long exposition of some side-issue while more vital information waited in the queue.

Smith got up from the bed, removed his glasses, and pointed to his envelopes. 'There's a lot of stuff to go through when I get back.'

'Anything of immediate interest?'

Smith smoothed his lantern jaw. 'She was saving money.' He picked up one of the envelopes. 'Building Society pass-book. In the past year she's paid in four thousand pounds, a hundred or two at a time, and she didn't do that on a barmaid's wages, even allowing for tips.'

'Anything else?'

Smith looked over his collection in the manner of a connoisseur selecting his best pieces. 'A few letters—not many—but one recent, from a girl she seems to have been with in London. That might mean something.' He searched through another envelope and came up with a two-page letter written in a large, round hand and almost devoid of punctuation. 'I've marked the bits which might be interesting.'

Wycliffe skimmed the lines. "It looks as though you was right to go back you seem to have struck it lucky for once. I never heard of him but I wouldnt would I. The boy seems nice even if he is a bit wet but I think you could make trouble that way. . .What about your uncle. Have you seen him again. . .Yes I would like to come down for a week in September if I can get time off then. . ."

The letter was signed "Liz" and there was no address.

I never heard of him but I wouldnt would I. The boy seems nice even if he is a bit wet but I think you could make trouble that way. . .The boy was obviously young Cleeve. Could the other, of whom Liz had never heard, be his father? *You could make trouble that way.* By running father and son in tandem?

Wycliffe shrugged. Perhaps he had Cleeve on the brain.

Polmear had said that Celia had worked at a café in Queensway; if necessary the Met would find the café and from there it should be possible to find Liz.

Smith was scratching his grey cheek with an earpiece of his glasses—one of many idiosyncracies which would have endeared him to a cartoonist. He said, 'I had a visitor this afternoon, sir—the girl's uncle who keeps the photographer's shop. He wanted to help in sorting through her stuff. I told him we could manage. He seemed upset.'

Wycliffe went through to the back yard; he wanted to satisfy himself that it would have been practicable for the killer to enter the yard and approach the open window of the girl's bedroom without any great risk of being seen.

The yard was too small to swing the proverbial cat but it was private, only overlooked by windows belonging to the two flats and, standing close to the bedroom window, one was shielded from view in the upper flat by the projecting landing at the top of the stairs. Wycliffe stood there without being noticed by Smith who was sitting on the bed with his back to the window.

A blue-painted door in a stone wall opened into the back lane. Wycliffe let himself out and walked up the narrow, grass-grown track which had a step or two at intervals, until he joined Chapel Street. He was satisfied that at any time after dark the killer would have been very unlucky to be spotted if he approached the house that way.

Chapter Three

IN THE CHAPEL schoolroom Shaw had worked a transformation; it had already acquired the atmosphere of a duty room in a rather sleazy nick with the traditional amenities: battered furniture, ancient typewriters, buckled filing cabinets, and tin-lids for ashtrays. On the whole it was a convenient arrangement, certainly preferable to those mobile rabbit hutches where it is scarcely safe to sit down without warning. There was even a little cubby hole with a window which would serve as an interview-room. There had been three or four calls from press and radio, routed through sub-division. Shaw had handed out Wycliffe's prepared statement to the effect that a young woman had been found dead in bed in suspicious circumstances, and that the police were investigating the possibility of foul play.

Wycliffe was facing the prospect of coming to terms with the Lane girl and regretting the loss of his old sergeant—now inspector—Kersey. ("You lose your best men in the promotion stakes.")

There she was, sitting at one of the typewriters, looking cool and competent in a butcher-blue frock which seemed right for her colouring. He had to admit that she dressed sensibly; that she had a professional look, crisp and clean as a new banknote, which was more than could be said for some of her male colleagues.

Shaw was duty officer and Sergeant Pearce was helping D.C. Edwards with his share of the scene-of-crime report. Two old-timers got together! Add Pearce's service to Edwards's and you had a lifetime.

Shaw said, 'Cuppa, sir? Tea or Instant?'

The chipped mugs were lined up, plastic spoons at the ready; home from home.

Shaw went on: 'Dr Franks would like you to ring him at this number, sir, and Mr Scales rang to say that Potter and Dixon will be here sometime this evening.'

Wycliffe was put through to Franks.

'How's this for service, Charles?' Franks full of himself as usual. 'Your girl died of nicotine poisoning—no doubt about that. No doubt either that it was injected by that dart which was really a miniature hypodermic, crude but ingenious: a bit of brass tube, sealed at one end and fitted with a hardwood plunger, well greased and pierced with a sawn-off length of hypodermic needle. The nicotine was contained in the tube behind the plunger and as the needle entered the skin it was forced through into the tissues. Not exactly a precision job, but effective. I estimate that it delivered the equivalent of sixty milligrams plus of the pure alkaloid. I expect the boffins at Forensic will set up all sorts of elaborate gadgets to demonstrate how it worked, but you can take it from me the girl died because that thing was jabbed into her backside.

'What puzzles me is why he didn't use an ordinary hypodermic; they're easy enough to come by. I suppose it would be a bit awkward, going to bed with one and biding your time. . .but the more you think of it the more extraordinary it seems that a man should choose that way of murdering his mistress.'

Wycliffe said, 'We are assuming that she was killed by the man who slept with her.'

'Surely that's the most likely?'

'I don't know. What is the external diameter of the brass tube?'

'External? I can't say offhand, but I made a detailed sketch of the thing before passing it on. I'll check.' He was soon back: 'Almost exactly five millimetres—why do you want to know?'

'Just curiosity.'

Franks sighed. 'Well, if it wasn't the guy who was screwing her then your case really is wide open. I wish you joy, Charles.'

As Wycliffe put the phone back on its cradle he muttered to himself, 'Not that wide.' The killer must have had access to nicotine and the knowledge and manual dexterity to contrive a suitable dart for its injection. Added to that, he had, presumably, sufficient acquaintance with Celia Dawe to generate a motive for murder. Really a fairly neat set of crossbearings.

He! Always he! But might not the killer have been a woman? It is a cliché to say that poison is a woman's weapon, but statistically true. And there was something about the sustained rancour suggested by the careful and lengthy preparation which pointed, perhaps, to a feminine cast of mind.

He had been standing in the middle of the room, hands in pockets, brooding; now he turned to Lucy Lane and tried out his thoughts after bringing her up to date.

She met him half-way.

'I agree, it's hardly the way a man would murder his mistress.' She had a way of wrinkling her forehead as she spoke which gave her words an added seriousness. 'All the same, the man who was with her must have been there up to a short time before, if not actually when she died, and you would expect him to come forward.' She hesitated, then went on, 'As to the feminine cast of mind when it comes to nursing a grievance, my brother teaches in a school where three male members of staff haven't addressed a single word to each other in fifteen years.' She grinned. 'But I suppose you would call them "old women" anyway.'

Wycliffe laughed. 'Speaking of old women, have you seen Borlase yet?'

'Borlase and his two sisters. I saw them in the house-to-house routine and I'm just writing up my report. They're a weird trio and I feel sorry for any girl brought up by that lot. Incidentally, the old lady who lives above Celia Dawe's flat says Borlase has been to see his niece several times since she came to live there and that more than once she's heard voices raised as though they were quarrelling.'

No surprise there. He had suspected as much. 'She may have been trying to blackmail her uncle—perhaps succeeding. He was desperately anxious to take possession of what he called "her things" and when I turned him down he had a go at Smith, offering to help with the sorting out. He's obviously scared of what we might find, but in point of fact Smith has almost finished there and we've found nothing that need worry him.'

Wycliffe had perched himself on the edge of her table, now he got out his pipe and started to fill it; a sure sign that he was relaxing his guard. 'Did you get anything from the old lady in the top flat about the girl's night visitor?'

'Nothing. She either couldn't or wouldn't help. She said she went to bed to go to sleep and that was that.'

'Anything else?'

She shuffled through her papers. 'Nothing much. I talked to Laura Wynn, the woman who runs the jewellery shop.'

'Boadicea.'

A polite smile. 'She's certainly a dragon; I didn't get beyond the shop and I had very little to show for a ten minute fencing match. Her attitude was: "Surely, with girls like that, murder is an occupational hazard." She says she saw nothing and knows nothing.'

'What do the neighbours say about Mrs Wynn?'

'What don't they say! They call her "the duchess". It seems she has a habit of casually referring to "my family" as though she belonged to the landed aristocracy. Among her other accomplishments she tells fortunes—not for money, of course! "Just leave a little something for charity." But according to her neighbours, her charity begins at home and stays there.'

Wycliffe said, 'You know she was investigated by a private detective working for Cleeve?'

'Sergeant Pearce told me. I think there might be more to be got out of Mrs Wynn.'

'Then perhaps you should try again.'

A small smile. 'With respect, sir, I think you would inspire greater confidence in the lady.'

A working relationship? Something like it, anyway. A start. He had to admit that he wouldn't have got a more concise or shrewder summing up from any of his men. And she had tolerance, a quality he looked for in all of his staff.

He gave her her instructions: 'I want you to tackle the nicotine angle—people who would have access to nicotine through their work—horticultural, veterinary or agricultural. . .The county advisory services would probably help in identifying trades in which the stuff is used. Then there are others likely to have the knowledge and resources necessary to extract nicotine from tobacco leaves as grown, or as sold for smoking. I don't think it's all that difficult. . . .

'Anyway, you've got enough to be going on with. I think we'll let Borlase simmer for a while and I'll talk to Madam Laura later.'

He left the Incident Room and walked down Zion Steps. It had occurred to him that few people could be in a better position to extract vegetable poisons from their source than a practising herbalist. Of course, it was too obvious; no man in his senses would risk drawing attention to himself so blatantly . . . and yet, enterprising criminals, especially the clever ones, often have a blind spot. In any case, Wycliffe was too old a copper to ignore the obvious.

For the first time he looked at Geoffrey Tull's shop with more than casual attention. A colourful sign showed a bouquet of herbs, apparently well painted, but he was too ignorant to identify them. The bow-fronted window exhibited only a printed card with an ornamental border of which the text read: "Infusions, decoctions, extracts, tinctures and tablets, prepared on the premises from finest ingredients. Consultations by appointment. Geoffrey Tull M.B., B.Ch."

Beyond a low screen at the back of the window he could see into the shop. A large number of little varnished wooden drawers with white-enamelled labels and, above them, shelves with rows of glass bottles carrying gilt labels. It was reminiscent of a shop in a city museum: "Pharmacy—*circa* 1910." The era of Seidlitz powders, castor oil and ipecacuanha wine.

Although it was half-past six the notice on the door read "Open". He entered and a bell buzzed somewhere as he stood on the mat, but there was no response. The shop was elegantly neat, the glass jars gleamed in the dim light and there was an attractive smell of aromatic herbs. The labels on the drawers and bottles read like an index to one of the herbals; a cornucopia of healing.

'Can I help you?'

A voice almost at his elbow. Geoffrey Tull was tall, somewhat overweight, with a carefully trimmed moustache. He had his sister's colouring though his features were plump and soft, the face of a spoilt child.

'My name is Wycliffe—Detective Chief Superintendent Wycliffe.'

'Oh, yes?'

'I am investigating the murder of Celia Dawe.'

'Your sergeant has already spoken to me. I knew the girl, of course, but I can tell you nothing which isn't common knowledge.'

'You have heard how she died?'

'I have heard rumours—no more.'

There was something familiar about Tull; not that Wycliffe had ever seen him before, but he belonged to a type, a type once familiar in seaside hotels in the company of widowed or divorced ladies. Not a crude con-man, rather a professional companion for well-to-do lonely women.

'She died of nicotine poisoning; the nicotine was injected into her body by means of a hypodermic device.'

'I see.'

Getting nowhere, Wycliffe tried another approach. 'You are a registered medical practitioner?'

'I am medically qualified but I practise only as a naturopath. I am not in medical practice.'

An evasion; he had probably been struck off.

'You prepare your own medicines?'

'I prepare most of my herbal prescriptions.'

'So you have a laboratory or dispensary—something of the sort?'

'Something of the sort.'

'Have you any objection to showing me where you work?'

Tull did not reply but he moved aside to allow Wycliffe to pass between two counters to a door at the back of the shop.

'Through here.'

The room, looking out on the back yard, was more like a kitchen than a laboratory.

Tull said, 'Most of my preparation work is in the nature of cookery. As you see, I use slicers, shredders and mincers to deal with leaves, roots and stems. The heating is done on an electric hotplate. . .I suppose one of the main differences is that I use glass utensils exclusively, though most of these are bought at kitchen shops.'

'What about distillation?'

A faint smile. 'Few of my preparations involve distillation but I am equipped.' He opened a cupboard door. 'See for yourself. For distillation I use ordinary chemical glassware—flasks and condensers. I also have apparatus for boiling under reflux in certain extraction processes.'

His manner was casual, teasing. He closed the cupboard door. 'You see, Mr Wycliffe, I have quite enough equipment to extract nicotine from tobacco but I have never had occasion to use it for that purpose.'

Patronizing bastard! Wycliffe was becoming irritated but Tull was no fool, he hadn't put a foot wrong.

'You live alone?'

He received a long cool look before an answer. 'I do.' A brief pause, then: 'I think I've answered all your questions frankly, Mr Wycliffe, so if you will excuse me, I am expecting a patient.'

'Do you have an assistant?'

'I do. She looks after the shop while I am dealing with patients who come for consultations, but she finishes work at five-thirty.'

'Does she have anything to do with the preparation of medicines?'

'Nothing whatever.'

'You receive your patients here?'

'Certainly not! I have a consulting room upstairs.'

'Perhaps you will give me the name and address of your assistant.'

He would have liked to refuse but realized there was no point. 'Sonia Penrose, 4 Veryan Close. I hope. . .'

'Yes?'

Tull shook his head. 'Nothing.'

The shop doorbell sounded and a moment later a woman stood in the doorway of the dispensary.

Tull said, 'Oh, there you are, Mrs Wynn! Do come in, Mr Wycliffe is just leaving.'

The statuesque proprietor of the jewellery shop.

Outside, Wycliffe wondered how much his suspicion of Tull was due to dislike.

The Cleeves and their guests were taking coffee in the paved courtyard by the ornamental pool: Cleeve and Patricia, her brother Geoffrey, the archaeologist Gervaise Prout, and Roger Kitson. Andrew had not put in an appearance at dinner and Christie had excused herself immediately afterwards.

Patricia explained: 'She is very upset about the dead girl.'

Otherwise there had been no mention of Celia Dawe.

Carrie Byrne was in the house supervising two daily women from the village who stayed on to help whenever the Cleeves were entertaining.

The air was warm and sensuously soft; heavy with the scent of dracaena palms in flower. Colours were muted by the dusk, and water trickled musically from an incontinent Cupid, into the pool.

Cleeve had been drinking before, during and since the meal; now he was flushed and his eyes were heavy. He had himself in hand but he was edgy and from time to time his temper showed in barbed sallies. Patricia, by adroitly changing the subject or deliberately misunderstanding her husband's words, had so far avoided unpleasantness.

Prout sat erect in his cane chair, his suit almost white—like tropical 'drill', a pukka sahib. Through dinner they had talked largely of the dig and he had bemoaned his lot as a 'prehistoric' archaeologist with no written records to help in interpreting his finds. 'Think of some of those classical chaps with a library of contemporary literature at their backs!'

Later, by some quirk or, perhaps, by intent, the conversation had turned to herbal medicine and Cleeve had made a couple of snide jokes about his brother-in-law, referring to him as "our resident shaman". Now Kitson, in a threadbare suit, his long body half coiled in his chair, his injured profile turned from his audience, was holding forth on remedies to be found in the great herbals of the Chinese Sung. Kitson was an encyclopaedia of unlikely information and he had that rare gift which can make a railway timetable interesting.

Cleeve said, 'When I was getting together background for *Medicus* I remember being impressed by the number of really virulent poisons which could be extracted from quite common plants.'

Prout, apparently anxious to make himself agreeable, said, 'Yes, it really is remarkable. I've often wondered why we bother so much with legislation about the sale of poisons when anybody with a bit of nous can prepare extremely toxic alkaloids from plants which grow freely in hedgerows and gardens. Isn't that so, Mr Tull?'

Tull had seemed to be absorbed in contemplation of the carp in the pool and he looked up, startled, at being addressed directly. There was an awkward silence while he studied Prout as though trying to decide whether some innuendo had been intended, then he said, 'I am not interested in toxicology.'

Kitson gave a shrill little laugh. 'I think you two are at cross-purposes. Gervaise is amazingly well informed about the migration of Celtic tribes over the face of Europe two thousand years ago but not so well briefed on today's or yesterday's news. I doubt if he has heard that the Dawe girl was poisoned by one of his toxic alkaloids.'

Prout flushed with annoyance but it was Cleeve who demanded in a harsh voice, 'Where in hell did you get that tale, Roger?'

Patricia's voice warned: 'David!'

But Kitson was unperturbed. 'I never reveal my sources.'

Tull said, 'I told him.'

Cleeve turned on Tull. 'You? Is it true?'

Tull, clearly annoyed by Cleeve's manner, contrived to keep his dignity. 'Of course it's true! The superintendent told me that the girl died of nicotine poisoning.'

'And did the superintendent say that she had been murdered?'

'He did.'

Cleeve was frowning and intent. 'Did he say how the stuff was administered?'

'By some hypodermic device.'

'Why should he tell you all this?'

Cleeve's manner was offensive but Tull's calm replies were an effective rebuke. 'I assume it was because he thought I would have the knowledge and resources to extract nicotine from tobacco and might therefore rank as a suspect.'

Cleeve looked like a man who had received a considerable shock but he laughed self-consciously, beginning to feel foolish. 'A suspect. I see! Well, well!' His eyes travelled round the little group. 'Who's going to help me out with this brandy?'

253

*

When Wycliffe got back to the cottage, Helen was in the kitchen, wearing an apron, ready to get to work.

'Ah, you've come! I was afraid you would be late. How do you feel about having a meal here instead of going out?'

'I doubt if I could keep awake in a restaurant.'

'A rough day?'

He yawned. 'It didn't feel much like a holiday. What have you been doing?'

'I went across to Falmouth on the ferry and I've been extravagant. We're having fresh salmon steaks, cooked in white wine. There are a couple of bottles of Muscadet in the fridge. If you feel like sampling it you can pour me some; I shall only need a little for the salmon.'

Just like home; drinking in the kitchen while the food was being prepared.

They had their meal in the front room with its latticed windows open to the waterfront so that the voices of passers-by sounded as though they were in the room. They ate their salmon with small boiled potatoes garnished with parsley and they finished the Muscadet.

Wycliffe began to feel human. 'And for dessert?'

'Peaches. There's clotted cream if you've given up worrying about your cholesterol.'

Coffee, and then a walk. A circuit of the village, returning down the hill by the castle in time to see the estuary and the whole western sky glowing red.

Red sky at night; shepherds' delight. Emmets' too.

Early to bed.

Wednesday July 20th

Wycliffe was a small boy again, back on his parents' farm; the little square window overlooked the farmyard and he could hear the cows' hooves pattering on the cobbles. His mother's voice came from downstairs: 'Charles! Charles! You'll be late for school again!' His mother had been the only member of the family who, like Helen, refused to call him Charlie.

254

It was Helen calling up the stairs. 'It's half-seven, Charles!'

A fine day as promised but, according to the radio, a temporary change on the way, with drizzle and coastal fog in the outlook period.

'I'll make the most of today,' Helen said. 'There's a trip across the bay to Helford.'

It was almost nine before he arrived at the Incident Room in Chapel Street. Two more D.C.s, assigned from headquarters, had arrived—Dixon and Potter, known to intimates as Pole and Pot in reference to Dixon's height and Potter's paunch. Potter was duty officer, and alone. He did not hear Wycliffe come in; only a close encounter detached his feet from the table and his attention from the sports pages of *The Sun*.

'Sorry, sir!' He reached for the log. '08.33 hours: message from Mr David Cleeve of Roscrowgy. He would like to see you as soon as possible; he will call here at your convenience or be available at Roscrowgy at any time to suit you.'

'Very accommodating of him. Where is D.S. Lane?'

'Due on at 10.00 hours, sir, with Edwards, Curnow and Shaw. D.C. Dixon has gone round the back to the loo.'

'A veritable hive of activity.'

'Yes, sir.' After a moment, Potter added brightly, 'Coffee, sir?'

'No.' He sat at his table, sucking the end of his ball-point and brooding on Celia Dawe. The girl had been mercenary; she had slept with men as an investment in security and hoarded her gains. Her upbringing probably accounted for that. Otherwise there was nothing special about her but her looks. Only by being murdered did she stand out from the crowd in false perspective. Who would have cause to hate or fear such a girl enough to plan and contrive her death with such patience and care?

Lucy Lane arrived, wearing green, and cheerful with it. 'Good morning, sir! Another lovely day.'

He preferred the morose taciturnity he was accustomed to from his male colleagues. He answered glumly.

She went to her table, opened her shoulder bag and took out a bulky envelope. 'I think this is what has been worrying the Borlases.'

She emptied the contents of the envelope on to her table. Wycliffe went over. About 20 full-plate photographs; all of girls of different ages either nude or scantily clad; a voyeur's collection. Then he realized that they were photographs of one girl—of Celia Dawe, a record of her growing up from the age of three or four to early maturity. The quality was high and though the studies were intimate they were neither vulgar nor obscene. All the same, they made Wycliffe feel uncomfortable, as though he had stumbled into the very private world of a young girl. He had to admit that in all his years in the police he had never seen anything quite like them.

'How did you get them?'

'Luck, sir. I thought it might be useful to talk to the other girls who worked at The Buckingham, so I looked in there yesterday evening. Well, they couldn't or wouldn't tell me much about her. It was obvious they didn't like her, probably because she slept with the boss. Anyway, as I was leaving, one of the girls asked me what was to happen to Celia's belongings because they needed her locker. In the season they have a staff of five women and three men and each of them has a locker for personal things. Of course I didn't have her keys but Polmear found a duplicate. Her locker contained an overall, a raincoat, an umbrella, a pair of shoes, and these.'

'Good for you! What do you make of them?'

She turned the prints over, puckered brow. 'At least they explain what Borlase was so agitated about. He couldn't afford to have these passed round among his chapel friends.'

'Do you think his sisters know about them?'

It was a silly question and she looked surprised. 'They must have done; this was going on for thirteen or fourteen years. I imagine they were glad to keep his rather mild sexual vagaries in the family. I don't suppose they did anybody any harm.'

'Not the girl?'

'I shouldn't think so. I doubt if he touched her; he's a brooder, not a doer. It would be enough to have her to gloat over; and for her it would be routine. On Thursday night you wash your hair; Friday is bath night; and on Saturday afternoon or whenever, you strip and pose for uncle. She might have thought it a bit odd as she got older but she would be used to it. I doubt if these were among her reasons for leaving home.'

Wycliffe told himself that women in general and this one in particular were full of surprises. He said, 'All the same, it seems likely that she was getting money out of him on the strength of the pictures. In other words, he had a motive.'

The brown eyes looked incredulous. 'For murder? I can't honestly see Borlase as a killer unless one imagines a homicidal rabbit.'

Wycliffe laughed; their relationship was beginning to gel. 'Do you want to follow this through?'

He thought of Borlase's torturing embarrassment at being questioned about his photographs by a girl, and decided he deserved it.

But Sergeant Lane had other ideas. 'In the long run I think there's more to be got out of his sisters and they're more likely to talk to you than to me, sir.'

'I'll think about it. Meanwhile Cleeve wants to see me.'

'About the case?'

'What else? I suppose you know he's Peter Stride, the author?'

'I had heard.' Drily.

'You know his work?'

'I'm an addict; I took him for my special paper in finals.'

'Good! You may have a chance to get to know him better.'

Wycliffe was regretting that he would have to talk to Cleeve before he had news from John Scales of the man's background but, on cue, the telephone rang.

'Mr Scales for you, sir.'

'Well, John?'

'I've got something on Cleeve at last; it doesn't amount to much—nothing you'd think he'd want to conceal unless he really is a very shy bird. No biographical titbits in any of the tomes which list the works and whims of the literary. I got on to him finally by chance, through a chap who works on the *News*. A couple of years back he thought of doing a piece on the man but he came up against the same brick wall as Jane's student. It made him inquisitive and he did some poking around but the game wasn't worth the candle and

257

he packed it in. Anyway, he gave us a start and we were able to carry on where he left off. David Paul Cleeve was born in Bristol, September 5th 1931, son of David Gordon Cleeve, solicitor's clerk, and Elizabeth née Cotterell. Nothing so far on his childhood or education but in either '47 or '48 he joined the staff of the local paper as a trainee journalist. National Service was still in force then but he was exempted on medical grounds—he was an epileptic. He's still remembered on the paper as the reporter who had fits—he had one in a council meeting.

'In 1953 he moved into our territory at Exeter, and set up as a freelance, contributing to newspapers and writing articles for magazines. But by the time he published his first book—*Xanadu* in October 1955—he was living in London. *Medicus* followed in '57, *Magistra* in '59 et cetera et cetera.

'In April 1962 he married Patricia Elizabeth Tull at a register office in Oxford, a successful author, already very well-heeled. They lived in Surrey, then in Dorset, and moved to Cornwall in '74 or '75. Of course by then they'd had their twin children who were at boarding school.'

'Is that the lot?'

'I'm afraid so up to now.'

'A blameless career in fact.'

'It looks that way. Do you want the enquiry kept open, sir?'

Wycliffe hesitated. 'I'm seeing Cleeve later this morning so carry on unless you hear differently.'

They talked for a while about other cases then Scales, with good-humoured cynicism, wished him a happy holiday.

Wycliffe said to Potter: 'Ring Roscrowgy and tell them I'm on my way.'

He decided to walk to give himself time to think.

He left the Incident Room and turned up the hill by the chapel, leaving the tourists' village behind. Larger houses modestly concealed their virtue behind high dry-stone walls topped with escallonia in crimson flower. Only the bees disturbed the stillness and in the dry, fragrant heat it would have been easy to believe that he had the Mediterranean at his back instead of the English Channel. But his mind was on other things.

David Cleeve, Peter Stride. . .Why was he bothering his head about this man? Did he believe that Cleeve had killed the girl? He had no reason to think so, and yet. . .'*I never heard of him but I wouldnt would I. The boy sounds nice even if he is a bit wet but I think you could make trouble that way. . .*' The gospel according to Celia Dawe's friend, Liz. He had asked the Met to contact the girl. But even if Cleeve was sleeping with Celia Dawe was there any reason to link her death with Cleeve's past and the nebulous threats he had been so coy about?

He left the villas behind and came out on the *ros*, or heath, which gives Roseland its name. He walked on past the gates of Roscrowgy until he could see what was happening in Henry's Field. They were there, working like beavers preparing for a flood. Nothing had changed except that there were posters on boards set up in the hedge: 'Stop this desecration of land sacred to the Celtic People!' Followed by small print explaining how to set about doing it; all nice and legal.

Wycliffe retraced his steps and went through the white gates and up the long drive to the house. It brought him to a different entrance from the one Cleeve had taken him to—how long ago? Just four days! He was about to ring the bell when the door was opened by Cleeve himself.

'I happened to see you from the window. . .good of you to come.' Bland good manners which failed to conceal an underlying anxiety.

Wycliffe followed him along a short passage which joined the main corridor, then up the stairs to the study. The little dark girl looked up and saw them as they passed the open door of her office.

'Sit you down. . .whisky?'

'Not just now, thanks.'

A wry smile. 'I suppose not. You won't mind if I do? I shall probably need it.'

Nothing had changed; the sunlit creek, the estuary, the white-sailed yachts weaving their slow patterns on a smooth sea. In the study the smell of polished wood, of leather, of books and whisky. . .

'You wanted to see me?'

'I had to. Of course, it's about this girl—Celia Dawe. All this talk of her being murdered—poisoned.'

'You knew her?'

Cleeve made an impatient movement. 'Let's not beat about the bush! If you haven't heard already you soon will; I've been sleeping with her.'

'You visited her at her flat?'

'A couple of times a week over the past two months.'

'At more or less regular intervals?'

'Usually Monday and Thursday of each week.'

'You are being very frank.'

'I need to be. I was beginning to wonder when I was going to be haled off to the nearest cop-shop—"a man is helping the police with their enquiries". All this nonsense about murder. . .'

'Were you with her on the night of Monday/Tuesday—the night she died?'

Cleeve fingered his moustache, belatedly hesitant at the final fence. 'Yes, I was.'

'Then I should warn you—'

'To hell with that! I want to tell you what happened, then you can tell me what it's all about.' He paused, fiddling with his whisky glass, twisting the crystal tumbler between finger and thumb. 'I was with her when she died and I can see no way in which she could have been murdered.' He broke off and looked at Wycliffe. 'They're talking about nicotine poisoning—injected. Surely that would be quick acting?'

'Very.'

'Then there *is* no way she could have been murdered! I can't understand how all this started. . .I'm putting myself in your hands, I've got to rely on you to believe what I tell you.'

Wycliffe said nothing and Cleeve paused to collect his thoughts. When he spoke again it was in a different vein, he even summoned up a grin.

'I wonder how much you know about women. I suppose most men imagine themselves to be experts but I don't mind admitting they defeat me. . . .You know those boxes of assorted chocolates with a little chart to tell you what's inside the different shapes? I need something like that in dealing with women; it's too late when you've bitten through the chocolate coating. . . .Looking at that girl you'd have thought all that was needed was a match to the blue touch paper but, in fact, she was frigid. She put on a damned good act, but an act it was, and in a dozen subtle ways she let you know it. . . .I always thought she was laughing at me; she was clever, I think she got a kick out of it, but it was tantalizing—humiliating, I suppose. . . .A man likes to think. . .'

He looked at his glass which was empty. 'Are you quite sure you won't?' Wycliffe shook his head and Cleeve pushed his glass aside. 'I suppose I'd better not either. I've had enough already.'

He shifted heavily in his chair. 'I was going to say that on Monday night it seemed different.' He looked boyishly embarrassed. 'I thought I'd made it—you understand? I mean, all the signs, the sort of thing they can't fake—that shuddering spasm. . . .Then she went limp and I must admit, my only thought was, "Got you this time, my girl!"'

Wycliffe found it hard to remember that he was listening to the creator of *Medicus*, and not to any man only haltingly articulate on the subject of his sexual experience. An author without his typewriter is a soldier without his gun.

'She was dead.'

The words hung uncomfortably in the air.

It was hot and getting hotter. Cleeve was red-faced and sweating; he got up and opened a window, letting in the sounds from outside with a breath of air and the smell of freshly cut grass. Someone was mowing the lawns.

He returned to his chair. 'It took me minutes to realize what had happened, and when I did I thought she must have died of heart failure or a blood clot or something of the sort. . . .I did all I could—'

'Except call a doctor.'

He nodded. 'I was a fool, but I couldn't face it, and once I was certain nothing could be done. . .' He hesitated. 'I was right, wasn't I? Nothing could have been done?'

'As it happens, you were right.'

'Then I don't understand all this talk of murder—of poison. She died in my arms—literally, and I was with her for about two hours before that. You see, it's not possible.'

'The girl was killed by a dart made from part of an ordinary hypodermic needle set in a brass tube which held the nicotine. It functioned like a miniature hypodermic syringe. The needle entered the girl's left buttock and the poison was injected into her system. Subsequently—perhaps when you moved away from her, the dart fell out and rolled onto the floor where Dr Hodge found it.'

Cleeve was looking at him in ludicrous astonishment. 'I suppose you know what you are talking about, but I was there—'

Wycliffe cut him short. 'The sash window of the bedroom was open a little at the bottom?'

'Yes, it was; I remember the curtains moving slightly but I don't see—'

'She could have been killed by someone in the yard; someone standing by the window.'

'You mean that someone reached in and plunged that thing into her while we were. . .'

'I think it's more likely that the dart was fired from some sort of air weapon or spring gun.'

Cleeve had lost his high colour and for a moment Wycliffe wondered if he would faint. It was some time before he could speak then he said in a low voice: 'So she really was murdered! Murdered while. . .' It was obvious that he was deeply affected, unable to come to terms with what he had been told. All his 'man-to-man-let's-settle-this-together' attitude had deserted him. He got up from his chair and made a slow circuit of the room, pausing now and then to stare at books on the shelves then, abruptly, he turned to Wycliffe. 'Have you any idea who did it?'

'None.'

'Or why?'

Wycliffe shook his head. 'I can think of no reason why anyone would want to murder Celia Dawe, can you?'

He looked startled. 'Me? Of course not! I've told you, I couldn't understand this talk of murder.'

Wycliffe was impressed by the change in the man. Celia Dawe had died in his arms yet he had been sufficiently detached to gossip, even make little jokes, but now that he understood how she had died he was overcome. Wycliffe thought that he knew the reason for that.

'What time did it happen?'

A moment to consider. 'Between half-past one and two; I can't put it closer than that.' He came back to stand by his chair, looking down at Wycliffe. 'So you believe me—my version of what happened?'

Wycliffe made a small movement with his hands. 'It's too early to say; I can say that, in the light of what I already know, what you have told me is believable.'

Cleeve nodded. 'That's all I can expect. Thanks. What happens now?'

'You will be invited to make a statement. I suggest you come to the Incident Room in Chapel Street this afternoon. One of my officers will be expecting you and you will be asked about the events of Monday night and invited to make a statement in writing. Shall we say at four o'clock?'

'I'll be there.' He seemed to answer mechanically, preoccupied with his thoughts.

Wycliffe went on: 'At the same time I want you to allow your finger-prints to be taken.'

Cleeve looked surprised. 'Finger-prints? I've admitted being in the room with the girl; my prints are probably all over the place.'

'All the same we shall need your prints for comparison purposes.'

A shrug. 'As you wish.'

Wycliffe allowed a silence to drift on. Cleeve resumed his seat and the two men were once more facing each other across his desk. When Wycliffe spoke again his manner was less formal.

'Have you thought any more about our conversation on Saturday?'

'What? Oh, yes, I'm getting a security man to patrol the grounds at night.'

'Have there been any more threats?'

'No—none.'

'Do you feel at greater risk because of what happened to Celia Dawe?'

Cleeve reacted sharply. 'Why do you ask me that? Why should I?'

Wycliffe was matter-of-fact. 'Because since I told you that Celia

Dawe had been murdered and explained how it was done, you have been wondering whether the dart that killed her found its intended target. That is reasonable. After all, it would be a very odd coincidence if, while your life was being threatened, the girl who shared your bed was murdered in an unrelated incident.'

Cleeve's powerful hands were lightly clasped, resting on the desk. A craftsman's hands, stout fingers, square ends. He seemed to be studying his hands and did not raise his eyes. 'Of course the idea occurred to me.'

'And?'

He shook his head. 'I don't know.'

Wycliffe got to his feet. 'You must think about it; but whatever you decide, now that I know you were with the girl, I have to look at the case from a new angle. Unless there is fresh evidence soon, which makes sense of the girl's murder, we shall assume that you were the intended victim; then your reticence about these threats will have greater importance.'

'Is that a warning?'

'Not a warning. I'm pointing out the direction our enquiries will take, and giving you the chance to make your voluntary statement as complete as possible.'

'I see.'

'Once we know the nature of the threats you received and once you have told us something of the reasons behind them, we can provide you with whatever protection is needed.'

Cleeve, too, got to his feet. 'I shall be at the Incident Room at four o'clock. I'll see you out.'

They walked down the long, inhospitable corridor and Cleeve saw him off at the front door. Wycliffe felt depressed. Sometimes it seemed to him that his was a degrading occupation, exposing the nakedness of men, the deceits and evasions of the weak and the pathetic deviance of the wicked; pinning out their sins, like insects in a box, and saying, 'This is what you are!' Not that he would condone crime, but sometimes he yearned for a more inspiring concept of justice, perhaps like the classical Chinese—the restoration of the pattern.

Back to earth: he was convinced now that his hunch had been

correct, that the little dart had been carefully and cunningly contrived to be fired from an airgun or something of the kind. Franks had said that the external diameter of the brass tube was close to five millimetres and that meant it could be fired from a variety of air and spring weapons. Further than that, he was convinced that it had been aimed at Cleeve, not at the girl.

It was twelve-thirty—time for lunch and, on the spur of the moment, he decided to try The Vegetarian.

It was comfortably full and he was asked to share a table with a man of about his own age, a lean man of saturnine countenance. He looked at the menu; the waitress said: 'The sweet-corn-and-cheese-bake is our special today.'

'All right. Are you licensed?'

'No, but you can have fruit-juice, tea or coffee, or various herbal drinks.'

Depressing. 'I'll have coffee later.'

The saturnine man said, 'I've never understood why vegetarian-ism and total abstinence seem to go together.'

'I'll start with the soup.'

'Are you ready for your main course, Dr Hodge?'

Dr Hodge. The eyes of the two men met and Hodge smiled. 'I think it's Chief Superintendent Wycliffe. . .'

They talked about the village.

Hodge said, 'I've been here for twenty years. It's not a village, it's a suburb without any urb to be sub to; a cosmopolitan collection of people with nothing in common but the conviction that they've escaped from something—from what, they're not quite sure. Interesting though. You'll need a side-salad with that bake thing when it comes. There aren't many of the original inhabitants left and those that are don't count any more; no more than mice in the woodwork.'

Wycliffe lowered his voice though there was no need; people were chattering nineteen to the dozen. 'You found the dart.'

The waitress came with the doctor's main course—a three-egg omelette with a brown-bread roll and butter. High cholesterol. 'My wife won't let me have eggs at home; says they're bad for me. Yes, cunning little thing, wasn't it? Somebody spent the whole winter

265

concocting that, brooding on it. They're great brooders hereabouts —nothing else to do in the winter. But why the girl? That's what puzzles me. She was a good-looker but apart from that she was ordinary enough. The trouble was she had old-fashioned ideas—she thought somebody would be fool enough to set her up and keep her for what they could get in bed. It's funny; some of these girls don't seem to realize that sex is off ration now so there's no longer a black market. Leathery!' The doctor was prodding his omelette. 'Cooked too slowly; they're usually better at it here.'

'Do you mind if I ask you a professional question?'

'Why not? Everybody else does.'

'Would you say that epilepsy—*grand mal* epilepsy, where the patient is subject to recurring seizures—is curable?'

Hodge shrugged. 'It depends; every case is different, but for a young person who submits to treatment and behaves sensibly, the prognosis is good.'

'Is there a chance that he might be able to come off drugs and lead a normal life?'

'In many cases—yes.'

'Alcohol?'

A quizzical look. 'Oh, no, I'd strongly advise anybody with a history of epilepsy to lay off the booze.'

'For good?'

'Certainly, he'd be tempting providence otherwise.'

'Thanks.'

They finished their meal.

'If you and your wife are still here on Saturday afternoon, you might care to come sailing. . .'

Back in the Incident Room he briefed D.C. Edwards to take Cleeve's statement. Edwards was slow but nothing got past him and he had the integrity of an elephant. 'Also, get hold of Sergeant Smith and ask him to be here to take Cleeve's prints—I want them checked with C.R.O. immediately.'

At a quarter to four Wycliffe pushed open the door of the photographer's shop, the bell buzzed, but no one came. He went through to the studio at the back, pushing aside the velvet curtains: a camera on a stand various lamps and screens and an assortment of

266

studio props dating from the 'twenties. Carpeted stairs to the floor above.

He could hear the photographer's voice, softly insistent. He stood at the bottom of the stairs and called: 'Is anyone at home?'

An interval, and Borlase came to the top of the stairs, wiping his mouth with a table napkin. Afternoon tea: the photographer's too-solid flesh demanded frequent nourishment. He was anxious, startled.

'Mr Wycliffe!'

'Don't bother to come down; I'll come up.'

Before Borlase could stop him he was at the top of the stairs, on a landing with several doors. Two of the doors at the back were open, one to a gloomy kitchen and the other to a dining-room, furnished in oak which would have been thought handsome 60 years before. Smells of cooking, stale clothing, dust, and dog blended uneasily.

Borlase's sisters had come out on to the landing to see what was happening.

'This is my sister, Helena, Mr Wycliffe.' Tall, gaunt and grey, supporting herself on a stick. 'And this is Posy.' Younger and stouter than Helena, having split a packet of genes with her brother.

'This is Mr Wycliffe, the gentleman from the police.'

Helena rounded on her brother. 'I know who he is; the question is, what does he want?' Her voice was harsh and masculine.

The photographer, embarrassed, said, 'Perhaps you will come into the dining-room, Mr Wycliffe. . .? Will you join us in a cup of tea. . .? Are you sure?'

On the table was a plate of sandwiches, another of sausage rolls and a third of dough buns.

A yellowish dog of dubious provenance, an obscene-looking creature, patchily bald, roused itself from sleep on the hearth-rug and lumbered across to Wycliffe, wagging a truncated tail. Wycliffe took a large envelope from his bag with a police inventory tag stuck to the outside. The photographer brushed crumbs from his shirt front, his gaze riveted on the envelope.

'I think these are what you have been looking for, Mr Borlase.' Wycliffe slid the photographs on to the table top.

Borlase was speechless; he squeezed his napkin into a ball and began to knead furiously.

Helena glared at the photographs, then at Wycliffe, finally at her brother.

'How did he get hold of these?' The voice was menacing.

Wycliffe said, 'You told us lies, Mr Borlase. You said you hadn't been in touch with your niece since her return; in fact, you've been to visit her several times and, on more than one occasion, you quarrelled.'

Borlase shook his head helplessly and little beads of sweat appeared on his forehead and lips. 'It was the photographs, Mr Wycliffe. . .I had to get them back. She took them when she went away and she was threatening me. When a painter paints a nude, it's art, but when a man like me, a photographer. . .' He picked up one of the prints. 'This is work of a very high quality, Mr Wycliffe—any authority would tell you. . . .You have to believe me; there was nothing. . .it was entirely innocent, I assure you. . .' The weak, rather sensuous mouth was trembling.

'Then why did you allow your niece to blackmail you?'

He shuddered. 'Blackmail! Dear God, I assure you—'

Wycliffe's expression was blank. 'An unpleasant word, but still not so unpleasant as murder.'

'Murder!' A whisper; his voice all but let him down completely. 'You can't think that I. . .'

Helena hammered on the floor with her stick and shouted. 'Will you tell me how *he* got them? You said you'd made her give them back!'

It was Posy's turn. With a grim I-told-you-so smile, she said, 'You should never have gone to see her in the first place, Joe! You wouldn't have gone if it had been left to me, but other people know better.'

Helena snapped: 'If people listened to you they would never do anything, not even keep themselves clean.'

They were laying the foundations for a future quarrel in which Joseph's role would be no more than that of a carcass squabbled over by jackals. But there was no time now. Helena concentrated on her brother; her wrinkled lips quivering with frustrated rage:

268

'Five hundred pounds you said you gave her! What happened to the five hundred pounds?'

'She took the money but she wouldn't give me. . .' Words failed him.

Helena shouted and banged her stick on the floor. 'Fool! Fool! Liar!'

And Posy said, 'They really will come to lock you up one of these days if you go on like that, Lena.'

Lena and Posy. A long time ago they must have been young girls, a few years' difference in their ages; Lena, slim and dark; Posy, fair, plump and rosy-cheeked. In fact, there was a hand-coloured enlargement of two such girls over the mantelpiece.

But it was not his sisters who were worrying Borlase at that moment, but the seemingly impassive policeman. He turned to Wycliffe.

'Celia said they were photographs of her, so they were hers, and if I wanted them back I would have to pay for them. Then, when I gave her the money she asked for. . .'

'But why did you want them so badly? Surely you had negatives?'

The photographer raised his hands in helplessness. 'You don't understand, Mr Wycliffe! She threatened to show them round the village! In a place like this I would never live it down; they would say that I. . .that I. . .' His voice broke in a sob and he covered his face with the wretchedly crumpled napkin.

His sisters watched him and Helena said, 'Murder? You can see for yourself. He couldn't step on a cockroach!'

Wycliffe was feeling grim. He gathered up the photographs and replaced them in the envelope. 'These will be retained until the case is over; then you will have them returned to you. It would have saved a lot of trouble, Mr Borlase, if you had told us the truth in the first place.'

Early in his career he had discovered that if one has greater sensitivity than a punch-bag, humiliation recoils. Ashamed of this scene he turned to the window and stood looking out, giving them a chance to recover some semblance of dignity.

From the window he could see down into the yard next door. Laura Wynn was in her workshop, bending over a sink, her golden hair like a crown. The houses on this side of the street had long narrow gardens. The Borlases' was a wilderness but Laura Wynn had put hers in grass and not far from the house there was a little gazebo.

'Keeping an eye on her?' Lena's harsh voice at his elbow. Incredibly, after all that had gone before, her manner was relaxed and conversational. 'You should! She and her cats! She's been there two years and still nobody knows who she is or where she came from. You should ask her what she was doing the night Celia was murdered—prowling round till all hours.'

'You said nothing about that to Sergeant Lane.'

She sniffed. 'Perhaps I forgot.'

'Well, you've remembered now; what did you see, and when?'

'I've told you. It was Monday night. I'm an old woman and I can't sleep. My bedroom is in the front and sometimes I get out of bed and sit in a chair by the window for a bit. I saw her in the street, wearing some dark-coloured dressing-gown sort of thing.'

'What was she doing?'

'She was crossing the street when I saw her.'

The photographer had recovered sufficiently to intervene. 'I think Lena should tell you that Mrs Wynn is often out at night, looking for her cats. She's got four Siamese and they wander away.'

To Wycliffe's surprise Helena did not seem to resent the interruption. She said, 'That's as maybe, but it's funny why she had to go down the alley that leads round to the backs of the houses.'

'You saw her go down the alley?'

'It looked that way to me.'

'You either saw her or you didn't.'

She shrugged. 'It was dark on that side of the street.'

Wycliffe said, 'I shall have to ask you to make a statement about this. It's obviously important to get it right. Are you sure—'

She interrupted. 'I don't trust her. She calls herself Mrs but there's never been any sign of a husband nor talk of one and she came here in the first place because of that man, Cleeve.'

'Because of Cleeve? What makes you say that?'

She looked smug. 'It was obvious. She hadn't been in the place

270

five minutes before he was paying her visits and staying half the night. I thought he'd set her up here.'

'And you no longer think so?'

'If he did, it didn't last long—not more than four or five months; then he stopped going there. It wasn't long after that they started on about digging up Henry's Field and she was all against it—spite!'

She was a thoroughly unpleasant old woman but what she said made some sort of sense.

'I'll send someone to take your statement, Miss Borlase.'

'Suit yourself!'

Borlase came with him to the shop door. 'I hope. . .'

'Yes, Mr Borlase?'

'Nothing, I'm sorry.'

Wycliffe found himself out on the Steps with a sense of relief, wondering why people, families in particular, contrive their own peculiar hells.

He arrived back at the Incident Room as Cleeve was signing his statement. Cleeve in checked shirt and khaki slacks, looking like the lord of the manor who has called on his steward to sign a few boring documents before proceeding to more interesting concerns. Edwards, sitting opposite him across the table, was respectful but firm.

'The declaration at the start, then each page separately, sir, then the declaration at the end.'

Cleeve signed with a flourish and a gold pen, disregarding the miserable little ball-point he had been offered. When the last signature had been given he looked up and saw Wycliffe.

'Oh, it's you, Mr Wycliffe.'

'Good afternoon, Mr Cleeve.'

Very formal, Wycliffe took the statement and turned over the pages, unhurried. When he had finished he said, 'I see you have included nothing fresh in your statement.'

'No, it covers the same ground we discussed this morning—everything relevant as far as I can recollect it.'

Wycliffe nodded. 'There will be two men on duty round the clock—in the grounds close to your house, if you will allow it, otherwise outside.'

'Am I under observation, house-arrest, or what?'

'You are being given police protection.'

'Am I free to come and go as I please?'

'Of course! But I shall be grateful if you will keep my men informed of your movements, for your own safety.'

'I see.'

When Cleeve had gone, Wycliffe talked at length to Lucy Lane.

'Cleeve must know as well as I do that Celia Dawe was killed in an attempt on his life. He must know too that the attempt could only have been made by someone with an intimate knowledge of his movements.'

Lucy Lane thought he seemed preoccupied, unsure of himself. He stood by one of the windows, watching the unexciting life of Chapel Street. Another meal time loomed and the emmets had drained away from the streets as though someone had pulled the plug on them. A grey-haired woman stood in her open doorway, staring at nothing; a dog sniffed along the pavement; a man in a blue jersey went by, carrying three or four mackerel strung together by their gills.

'The attempt on Cleeve's life must have been made by someone intimately acquainted with him and his routine.' Wycliffe repeated the words to himself as though to lend them emphasis. Yet Cleeve's whole point at that first, fortuitous meeting had been that he was being threatened by someone outside the circle of his family and friends. . . .

In any case, there could hardly be many who could claim close acquaintance with the man. Who were the initiates? Patricia and the twins, the brother-in-law Geoffrey Tull, the housekeeper Carrie Byrne, and, according to Helena Borlase, Laura Wynn. Were there others? What were Cleeve's relations with Gervase Prout? With the mutilated Kitson?

Whether or not the attempt on his life had arisen from something in his past, whoever made it must belong to the here and now.

Wycliffe sighed. He had committed men to Cleeve's protection; he had little choice once it became obvious that the man's life really was under immediate threat. With or without Cleeve's co-operation the obligation remained, but whether the protection could be effective was another matter.

Chapter Four

WYCLIFFE WAS STANDING on the edge of a trench; it could have been part of the dig in Henry's Field or it could have been a grave. Lying in the trench was a man, fully dressed. It was Cleeve and he was looking up at Wycliffe with an enigmatic smile. Wycliffe felt giddy and was afraid of falling into the trench; at the same time there was a ringing in his ears. Helen's voice came, peremptory but irrelevant:

'It's the telephone, Charles!'

Consciousness returned. The telephone. It was ringing downstairs; no bedroom extension in the cottage.

'Damn!'

He went down the narrow, break-neck stairs, mumbling to himself. It wasn't completely dark, just light enough to see the time by the wall-clock with the brass pendulum: four forty-five.

It was Pearce. 'I'm ringing from Roscrowgy, sir.' He spoke in a low voice as though concerned not to be overheard. 'There's been a fire on the Henry's Field site, the wooden shed they use as an office and museum has been burned down. The brigade was on the spot before me, and Bert Chinn, the fire officer, says it was burning so fiercely when he arrived that he suspects arson.'

Wycliffe was not pleased to be woken at dawn to be told that the Celtic Society might have had an unscheduled bonfire. He muttered something under his breath.

'Sir?'

'Never mind. What do you want me to do? Arrest the Wynn woman?' Heavily humorous.

But Pearce had saved his real news. 'I knew you wouldn't want to be got out of bed just because Laura Wynn might have got the bit between her teeth, but there may be more to it than that, sir. It looks as though Cleeve is missing.'

'Missing?'

'It seems that way.'

'Either he is or he isn't. What about our chaps who are supposed to be patrolling the place?'

'It was one of them who spotted the fire and phoned the brigade, but it looks as though Cleeve must have given them the slip. When the son went to tell his father about the fire, father was nowhere to be found. Mrs Cleeve is obviously worried but I can't get her to admit that she hasn't a clue where her husband is. I think she's afraid of starting something then having him turn up saying, "What the hell?"'

'All right. You were quite right to phone; I'll be along.'

He went back upstairs and groped for his pants.

'You've got to go out?'

'They think I'm the fire-brigade.'

The weather had changed—only temporarily, according to the forecast—the creek was obliterated by heavy mist, and moisture condensed out of the chill morning air. He seemed to be the only human being out of bed. His car was parked behind the cottage on a little rectangle of beaten earth advertised as 'space for car'—barely space enough to manoeuvre into the narrow lane, so testing his modest driving skills to near their limit. He cursed silently, and the engine was dubious about this early start on a damp morning. Further up the hill the mist became a fine drizzle.

Henry's Field was a dreary prospect; the large wooden shed had collapsed in on itself and was no more than a tangled heap of carbonized timbers, still smoking and steaming. The firemen had decided that the fire was out but they were in the cab of their tender, maintaining a watching brief. No sign of the archaeologists; the flaps of the bell-tents were down and the curtains of the caravan were drawn. Henry's Field was a depressing sight and Wycliffe decided it could hardly have been a health resort for its Iron-Age occupants.

Pearce was waiting. He nodded towards the tents. 'They've gone back to their sleeping bags.'

'What did Gervaise Prout make of it all?'

'Prout isn't here; he went off early yesterday and he isn't expected back until lunchtime today—some university meeting. It seems he took the site records with him to show his mates. Just as well, otherwise they would have gone up in smoke too.'

'So who's in charge?'

'Young fellow called Wrighton; Prout's assistant; all hair and glasses, looks at you like an owl.'

'What does he have to say?'

'That the fire must have been started deliberately; that there's no way the place could have caught fire otherwise. The lighting is electric, powered by a pocket-sized Jap generator in that dog-kennel over there and it's switched off at night.'

'Anything inflammable stored in the hut—petrol? Paraffin?'

'According to Wrighton there was a five-gallon drum containing about two gallons of paraffin. They use it for the generator.'

'And one of our chaps raised the alarm—at what time?'

'He logged it at 02.07.'

Wycliffe shivered; the chill dampness seemed to be seeping into him. Hard to believe that only the day before the site had been sweltering under the sun. He looked at his watch. 'Half-past five. Have the Roscrowgy contingent gone back to bed too?'

'I very much doubt it, sir.'

'Then I'll try talking to them. I want you to find out from the fire officer when this debris can be handled without people getting choked or burned. If necessary, get them to damp it down some more. I would like somebody down from Forensic this afternoon— somebody with experience of arson.'

Pearce seemed surprised. 'You're taking this very seriously, sir.'

'Yes.'

He left Pearce and crossed the field to the wicket gate, he passed through the rhododendron tunnel where water dripped from the foliage and as he emerged from the tunnel one of the uniformed men on duty came towards him.

'P.C. Julian, sir.'

Wycliffe, becoming an expert on the brogues of the two counties, placed him as a Camborne man.

'I spotted the fire, sir. I was doing my rounds behind the house when I saw a glare in the sky somewhere over Henry's Field. It was clear then, the mist came in just before dawn. I reported in on my pocket-set and Control alerted the brigade. I heard them arrive ten or fifteen minutes later.'

'You didn't go over to the site?'

'No, sir. I talked to my mate and we decided our brief was here. I hope we did right?'

'In the circumstances—yes. Did you wake the people in the house?'

'We thought about it, sir, then decided not; but at about half-two or a bit later, young Cleeve turned up; he'd been to some party in Truro and he'd seen the fire on his way home. He was a bit shirty because we hadn't told his father and went off to do it.'

'And?'

Julian shifted uneasily. 'Well, his father wasn't there, sir.'

'When did you last see Mr Cleeve?'

'Neither of us have seen him since we came on at ten, sir. With respect, it's very nearly impossible to keep this place boxed up between the two of us. Altogether, there are five doors—'

Wycliffe said, 'I know; I'm not blaming anyone.'

He walked on towards the house. There were lights in several of the windows, competing with the grey morning. He rang the bell and the door was answered by a youth immediately identifiable as Andrew Cleeve because of his likeness to his sister.

'Mr Cleeve?'

The boy was pale, and hollow-eyed with tiredness. 'You are Mr Wycliffe—I think my mother will be relieved to see you.'

He took Wycliffe's raincoat and led him through a large drawing-room to a small boudoir which opened off it; an hexagonal room, plainly furnished: a dove-grey carpet, a business-like desk and a couple of spoon-back chairs; the whole redeemed and relieved by an Ivon Hitchens flower study over the fireplace and a bowl of pink roses on the window sill; the office of an up-market headmistress. Patricia Cleeve was fully dressed, pale, but apparently composed.

'Mr Wycliffe, I'm so glad you've come; I scarcely know what to do.' She said this in the manner of a lady putting at ease a guest who feels that he has arrived at an awkward moment. 'May I offer you something?' She made sure that he was comfortably seated. 'Thank you, Andrew.'

Wycliffe refused refreshment though he would have given a great deal for a cup of black coffee. 'I expect you are very concerned for your husband.'

She arranged her dress to cover her knees. 'I must admit that I am, and very puzzled.'

'You would have expected him to tell you if he intended to stay out?'

'Of course! We don't share a bedroom because we have different sleeping habits but he usually tells me if he intends to spend the night or any part of it away from home.'

Different sleeping habits. . .the night or any part of it—no beating about the bush; these are the facts; why pretend otherwise?

'You have no idea where he might have gone?'

'No.' She considered carefully before enlarging. 'In the circumstances, I was very surprised to hear that he had gone out.'

She did not say, 'with that girl lying dead', but her meaning was clear.

'Sometimes in the past he would take a stroll round the grounds before settling down for the night but not, I think, recently.'

'Can you tell me when you last saw your husband?'

'At our evening meal which we have at seven-thirty. Afterwards he went back to work as usual.'

'You have been to his room?'

'His bed has not been slept in.'

With caution, Wycliffe said, 'When you were speaking to Sergeant Pearce earlier he had the impression that you were reluctant to admit that you had no idea where your husband was.'

A little smile. 'Was it so obvious? I'm sure you will see that my husband would not have welcomed a hue and cry about nothing.'

'Since then, something has occurred to change your attitude?'

She played with her thin gold wedding-ring, twisting it round and round on her finger. 'Only that some hours have gone by and he still hasn't come home.'

She was superficially calm but underlying nervousness showed in her restless hands. She went on: 'When you were here on Saturday you had a private conversation with David and I'm sure he must have confided in you to some extent.' She added with a shrewd smile, 'Otherwise I hardly think you would be interested in a man who has been missing from his home for only a few hours.'

Wycliffe nodded. 'And by the same token, if he hadn't taken you into his confidence, you would probably be less anxious now.'

She swept back her blonde hair with an impatient movement. 'I assure you, Mr Wycliffe, that David doesn't share his troubles with me; he seems to think that it is his duty to shield me from worry, which of course means that I worry all the more.' Her voice became brittle. 'You are probably in a better position to form an opinion about what danger he may be in than I am.'

'Is he on friendly terms with anyone in the neighbourhood whom he might conceivably have visited last night?'

She considered her reply. 'Leaving aside his affairs with women, about which there can hardly be any secret, there is only one person he is in the habit of visiting, that is Roger Kitson. I think you met Roger, he was with David when you were at the dig on Saturday. Roger has a little cottage in the plantation and David often goes there; they seem to have a lot in common. But he wasn't there last night; Christie and Andrew went over to enquire. We tried to telephone but Roger's phone is out of order. Since then they've been searching the whole area in case there's been an accident of some kind. I gather that Roger has been out too.'

Wycliffe was thinking that the mating game brings together strange partners. This woman, perceptive, forceful, but restrained; probably tantalized by sex though prudish by nature. . .she must have had a hard time with her brilliant, often sombre, always wayward and egocentric husband.

Wycliffe said, 'Forgive me, but I suppose there is no possibility that he was visiting another woman?'

A faint smile. 'I think not.' She added after a moment, 'He would allow a decent interval.'

'Could he have left the area for any reason? Simply cleared out?'

She looked surprised. 'Walking? The cars are in the garage, and as far as I can tell he had only the clothes he stood up in.'

Difficulties easily solved with money but he did not press the point.

He allowed a minute or two to pass before putting his next question and she waited, quite still now.

'Do you think there may be a connection between your husband's absence and the burned-out hut?'

'If there is I can't imagine what it could be.'

Wycliffe thought: That makes two of us. He said: 'Yesterday afternoon he came to the Incident Room and made a statement in connection with Celia Dawe's death. The statement did not incriminate him but it makes him a key witness so he is certain to be called to give evidence at the inquest and at any trial there may be.'

She looked at him, her blue eyes non-committal. 'So?'

'Do you think he would have been very upset at such a prospect?'

'I'm sure that he would. David has an intense dislike of publicity which amounts to a phobia; he even tries to prevent it being generally known that Peter Stride and David Cleeve are one and the same.' She smiled, as at the whims of a child. 'He never gives interviews, never fills up biographical questionnaires, and his photograph doesn't appear on the dust covers of his books.'

Wycliffe thought: Let it go at that for the moment. He dispensed balm with professional skill and it was received by one adept in the art of acknowledging courtesy with grace. . . 'I know that you will do all that is possible, Mr Wycliffe.'

Wycliffe got to his feet; then, as though the thought had just occurred to him, he said, 'Do you know if your husband, as a young man, was subject to epileptic seizures, Mrs Cleeve?'

She too was standing, and she looked at him in astonishment. 'David? What makes you ask that?'

'Was he?'

'If he was, he told me nothing of it and there has never been the slightest suggestion of anything of the kind since our marriage. I would like to know—'

Wycliffe cut her short, gently but firmly. 'We have to think of every possibility.'

Andrew Cleeve was waiting for him in the big drawing-room. 'I'll see Mr Wycliffe out, mother.' The boy clearly doted on his mother and wanted to save her from distress as far as he could.

In the hall he helped Wycliffe on with his raincoat.

Wycliffe said, 'Walk back with me to the site.'

It was obvious that Andrew was waiting for a chance to talk. 'Take a coat or something; it's quite wet out.'

Andrew went to a hall cupboard and came back, struggling into an anorak that was already wet.

Outside, it was the boy who spoke first. 'Do you think that something has happened to father?'

'I don't know what to think; what is your opinion?'

The question took him by surprise. 'I don't know. . .he's been very odd lately. Since I've been home this vacation he's hardly been outside the grounds except. . .It's true he never went out much. Then he's been talking of employing a security johnny to patrol the grounds at night; he says it's because there have been one or two burglaries in the neighbourhood but I can't help feeling he's scared of something. . .'

'Do you get on well with your father?'

He thought about the question or, perhaps, about the answer he would give, then he said, 'No—not really.'

'Rows?'

'Not rows; we just keep out of each other's way.'

'Is this strain something new? Is it connected with Celia Dawe?'

In a dead-pan voice the boy said, 'So you know about that; I suppose you are bound to.'

'I know about your father and Celia and about you and Celia.'

'Yes, and that's what caused the trouble. I don't want to say much now but it's disgusting! He's more than old enough to be her father and, in any case, it's so humiliating for mother.'

'You weren't madly keen on the girl?'

They passed through the wicket gate and were able to walk side by side over the wet grass.

'I liked her; she was good fun but it wasn't serious for either of us. She was a really nice girl who'd had a very rough time and I felt sorry for her. But first Polmear, then my father, treated her like a tart.'

'How did you find out about her and your father?'

'She told me. She was very straight about it; she wouldn't let me take her out until I knew the situation. I thought that was very honest.'

Wycliffe thought that there might be other words to describe it but he said nothing.

'So your father sometimes went out at night if he didn't by day.'

'Yes! Sneaking out of his own house like a delinquent schoolboy!' He was silent for a while and they came to a halt in order not to reach the fire-tender before they had finished their conversation. 'Of course, the rules that apply to ordinary people are not for The Great Writer. I know that sounds harsh, but all that crap makes me sick!'

'There are many people, all over the world, who think your father is a great writer.'

'So what? My tutor at university is internationally known as a geologist but he's an ordinary, pleasant chap; he takes his wife and kids on holiday, he watches telly, and when he gets drunk he does it in company because he's enjoying himself—not alone in his room as an outlet for creative frustration.'

'But don't you think that the emotional demands on a first-rate writer or painter or musician are probably greater than those on your geologist?'

The boy shrugged. 'Possibly; I don't know, and I don't want to know. I prefer to be stupid and to live like other people.'

Wycliffe changed his ground. 'Do I need to tell you that your father didn't kill Celia Dawe?'

The young man seemed to consider this for a while though he made no comment but after a little more time the question came, hesitant and a little fearful, 'Was he with her that night?'

'I'm not going to answer that; I've said more than I should already. Now, you must tell me something. Did Celia say anything to you which might have implied that she was frightened of someone or threatened by them?'

'Never!'

'Did she talk about her uncle?'

'Only about the way she was treated by him and her aunts.'

'Ill-treated?'

'Not exactly that; they were incredibly old-fashioned and she was made to dress and behave as if she was living when they were young. Even after she was sixteen, there was a row if she didn't go to chapel every Sunday, and she had to tell them exactly where she was going before she was allowed to go out of an evening. It was Victorian!'

'I understand you spotted the fire on your way back from Truro at about half-past two this morning.'

'Yes. I'd been to a sort of farewell party to a chap I was at school with; he's off to work in Tunisia. . .I know it sounds a bit heartless with Celia and all that. . .'

'It's natural enough; I shouldn't let that worry you. You didn't see anything unusual along the road—apart from the fire, that is?'

'No, nothing. In fact I don't think I saw a soul—not a thing on the road—from Tregony home.'

Wycliffe thanked the boy and they parted. Andrew turned back towards the house and Wycliffe continued across the field. There was more activity on the site: unisex students in all manner of dress, looking damp and dismal, drifted to and fro between the tents and the screened-off wash-ups and loos. Near the burned-out hut Sergeant Pearce was in conversation with a sturdy, bearded young man with a mass of curly black hair and king-sized spectacles; presumably Prout's assistant.

Pearce turned to Wycliffe. 'Mr Wrighton tells me he knew nothing of the fire until a student came banging on the door of the caravan where he was sleeping. By that time the fire-tender was already entering the field.'

Wrighton looked at Wycliffe, solemn and anxious. 'I must admit to being a very sound sleeper.' He confessed it as a fault.

Wycliffe said, 'I suppose this is a major set-back for your work?'

The young man removed his glasses to wipe them and blinked myopically. 'I shouldn't think so. Ours won't have been the first hut to be burned down on this site; it must have been a fairly common occurrence when the original inhabitants were in possession.'

'But they weren't archaeologists working to a budget.'

A quick smile. 'They weren't insured either. No, most of our artefacts are pretty durable; they wouldn't be here otherwise after so many centuries. I expect most of our finds will turn up again in the debris. Luckily all our instruments are kept in the caravan.'

'And your records?'

The glasses were replaced. 'Ah, there we really had some luck. Dr Prout had the bulk of our records with him and I was working on the current stuff in the caravan last night.'

'I understand that you and Dr Prout live in the caravan, but that he is away.'

'Dr Prout is away and he'll be returning some time this afternoon, but I only sleep in the van when he's away. At other times I'm in the tents with the others.'

'Is he here most nights?'

'Oh, yes, he's never away more than one or two nights a week. Although he only lives at St Germans and could, I suppose, go home every night, he prefers to stay on the site.'

'Tell me how you spent yesterday evening.'

'I was in the caravan writing up our log. I worked until about ten-thirty, then I made myself a hot drink and went to bed and to sleep.'

'Did you see Mr Cleeve at all?'

'No, I didn't; he hardly ever comes here in the evenings.'

'When you went to bed, had the students settled down for the night?'

A tolerant smile. 'No, they certainly had not. On Wednesday evenings there is a disco in the village and they went off in a body. I understand they came back at about half-past eleven but I'm afraid I didn't hear them.'

'How many students do you have on the site?'

He considered. 'Let me think. . .yes, twelve—ten of them, six girls and four boys, are living in the tents; the other two are local and one of them is Christie Cleeve.'

Wycliffe thanked him.

'If there is anything more I can do. . .I'm sure that Dr Prout would want me. . .'

'We may ask you for a written statement later.'

Pearce's owl seemed to Wycliffe more like an earnest, myopic teddy-bear.

Back in his car, Wycliffe put through an RT call to division, asking for additional men. No point in ringing Forensic until the witching hour of nine a.m.

It was still a little short of eight o'clock when he let himself into the cottage. The mist showed no sign of clearing and a very fine rain had spread down from the hill. No sailing today; no trippers; no cruises round the docks or to the lighthouse.

Helen was in the kitchen, in her dressing-gown.

'Coffee?'

Her auburn hair was set off by the blue of her dressing-gown and he thought how young she looked to be the mother of grown-up children. He kissed her on the nape of her neck.

'What was that for?'

They sat on stools in the kitchen, eating toast and drinking coffee.

'What happened? You said something about a fire.'

'The archaeologists' hut has been burned down—almost certainly with malice aforethought. More important, it looks as though Cleeve is missing.'

Helen paused with a piece of toast half-way to her mouth. 'Missing?'

'It seems he went out late last night and he hasn't come back.'

'You've talked to his wife?'

'Yes. She didn't miss him until they were all woken up about the fire. They don't sleep in the same room.'

Helen nodded. 'I thought there was something. Poor woman! With all her breeding she couldn't hide the fact that she had her troubles. It can't be easy living with a man like Cleeve. Since we were there I've thought about them a lot; it's one thing to read the work of a man who is obsessed by the evil in the world but it's quite another to have to live with him.' She grinned. 'I suppose there are worse things than being married to a policeman.'

After a pause she said, 'Do you think there's a connection between the fire and Cleeve's disappearance?'

Wycliffe sighed. 'I wish I knew.'

'Surely in a village of this size, a murder, arson, and a missing man, all in the space of three days, are more likely to be linked than not?'

He nodded. 'You'd certainly think so, but piecing them together is another matter. It reminds me of homework we used to get at school: "Put the following incidents into a story of three hundred words—".'

'Taxis and hire-cars in Roseland itself and the district up to and including Truro and St Austell; you'll need a description of Cleeve and of the clothes he was wearing when he went out. If we haven't found him by late afternoon I shall issue a press release then we can ask for public co-operation—anyone driving along the A 3078 after 20.30 hours last night blah blah. . .'

Lucy Lane was making notes. 'You really think he's cleared out of his own accord?'

'Or he's under the debris of the burnt-out hut, or he's lying injured or dead somewhere in the neighbourhood, or he's been kidnapped by little green men with an Irish accent.'

'Sorry, sir.'

'No, it's me.' Wycliffe sighed. 'After talking to him yesterday I feel I should have kept closer tabs on him. Then there are the watermen.'

'Watermen?'

'Down at the harbour. It's not impossible that he took a boat, his own or somebody else's. We also want to know where everybody was yesterday evening and night. I've asked division for more men.'

'Anything else?'

'Yes. Laura Wynn's Celtic circus. It seems that somebody set fire to the hut and arson is arson whether or not it is connected with Cleeve's disappearance. So: anybody seen loitering in the neighbourhood with a dangerous box of matches. . .'

'But seriously—'

'Seriously, you get from Pearce a list of Laura's dyed-in-the-wool activists and make 'em account for themselves. It will be a waste of time but "no stone unturned" and it might teach 'em a lesson.'

Six constables, including three dog-handlers with their dogs, arrived from Division and were allocated to Sergeant Pearce to work over the fields and lanes, the cliffs and shore lines to the north of

285

Roscrowgy—the area within which Cleeve might conceivably have walked and met with some mishap without being found. Before turning them loose, Wycliffe telephoned Patricia to make sure there had been no news. In telling him there had not she effectively hid whatever feelings she may have had under the veneer of her impeccable manners.

Dr Bell, an old friend at Forensic, telephoned to say that Horton, the fire expert, would be on the scene by three o'clock. He also confirmed that the dart had probably been projected from some sort of air or spring gun: they had found traces of oil on the brass tube probably from the barrel of the weapon and, more significantly, tiny fragments of hard wax adhered to the blank end of the tube, almost certainly a substitute for the flaring of the pellets normally fired from airguns, which stops them sliding down the barrel.

The killer had thought of everything.

Tests were being carried out to determine the effectiveness of the dart when fired from different types of air weapon.

Wycliffe said, 'The killer couldn't have counted on an open window and a naked target. He might have had to wait for his victim to leave, fully dressed. What about the effectiveness of the dart then?'

Bell was definite. 'I think it would have penetrated all but the thickest clothing and remained effective when fired from a modern airgun or pistol.'

For an hour Wycliffe created an atmosphere of unease in the Incident Room, standing about, brooding, drinking cups of Potter's coffee and smoking. He spoke with two reporters who were quite content to be briefed with the details of Celia Dawe's murder; they showed no interest in the fire, and had not yet heard that the country's most controversial and best-selling author was missing from home.

Cleeve missing. Since yesterday's encounter Wycliffe had been convinced that Celia Dawe was the accidental victim of a dart intended for Cleeve. The middle of the night, the lighting poor, the killer nervous, and the two bodies on the bed anything but still; a sudden convulsive movement on their part had probably reprieved the man and condemned the girl. Polmear, landlord of The

Buckingham, had said it: 'She was an unlucky kid—never got it right.' Wycliffe hadn't been a policeman for nearly 30 years without knowing that there were such people—Fate's preferred targets.

But it was Cleeve, missing or not, on whom the investigation must concentrate now.

He said to Potter: 'I'm going to talk to Laura Wynn.'

The mist had thickened; on the Steps visibility was less than 20 yards; a sea mist with the tang of salt. Invisible, a jet-fighter ripped through the air above the mist—in yesterday's weather. In this steep narrow lane between granite cottages it was easy to imagine that the figures looming out of the fog were fishermen returning from sea; in fact they were disgruntled emmets in plastic macs, wondering what there was to do but eat. Now and then the fog-horn on the lighthouse boomed out like some monstrous animal in its last sad hours.

Wycliffe pushed open the door of the jewellery shop and stepped down into the well-like area in front of the counter. A moment or two went by before Laura Wynn appeared; Laura in working rig—blue nylon overall, her hair caught back in a youthful pony-tail, no torque, no bangles. Probably she did not expect customers in such weather and she looked at him without enthusiasm.

'Mr Wycliffe, isn't it?'

'I would like to talk to you, Mrs Wynn, in connection with the murder of Celia Dawe.'

She indicated by the slightest movement that there was nothing stopping him.

'It would be more convenient if we could sit down.'

She seemed on the point of refusing but changed her mind. She went to the door, lowered the catch and changed the sign to closed. 'This way, then.'

Through the door at the back of the shop, along a narrow passage to a room which looked out on the back garden. A pleasant room, white walls, chintz upholstery, shelves on either side of the chimney-breast filled with zany books. The pictures were framed repro-ductions of mediaeval illustrations of the Arthurian legend. She indicated a chair on one side of the empty fireplace and sat herself opposite him.

287

'I've already told your detective that I know nothing of the dead girl or of the people she associated with.'

A woman striving to achieve a serenity which did not come naturally to her; one could imagine her attending yoga classes, and dutifully consuming her fruit and fibre with live yogurt. At least she had achieved a clear eye and an intimidating gaze. Not a woman who had spent much of her life with men.

'You are acquainted with David Cleeve?'

It was obvious that the question came as a surprise. 'Why should—'

Wycliffe was firm. 'Perhaps you will allow me to ask the questions. Of course you don't have to answer them but I hope you will. This is a murder inquiry and I assume you wish to help.'

'All right. As we live in the same village it would be surprising if we were not acquainted.'

'Do you know that he was on intimate terms with the dead girl?'

A hardening of the facial muscles. 'It doesn't surprise me.'

'But did you know?'

A momentary hesitation. 'No, I did not know.'

'You were out on the Steps very late on the night of Monday/Tuesday.'

'So?'

'What were you doing?'

'I was looking for Tripitaka. Although he has been neutered he is very wayward at night.'

'Did you go down the alley which leads to the backs of the houses opposite?'

'A short distance—yes. I called Tripitaka and suddenly he was there at my feet. I picked him up and came back here.' Her manner was detached, objective.

'What time was this?'

'About half-past twelve.'

'Did you meet or see anyone while you were out?'

'No one.'

She was a good-looking woman—splendid was the word; too statu-esque for Wycliffe's taste, but she might well have been a challenge to Cleeve. A modern Hera. Wasn't it Hera who annually renewed

288

her virginity at the Argos spring? Women like Laura never really lost theirs and he suspected that this was true of Patricia too. Psychological virgins.

'David Cleeve is missing.'

'*Missing?*'

'He went out last night and he hasn't come back.'

She looked incredulous. 'You think something has happened to him?'

'That's what I'm trying to find out.'

'But why come to me?'

'The big wooden hut on Henry's Field was burned down during the night. Arson, by the look of it.'

A worried frown. 'You don't think that any of our people would do such a thing?'

'No? It seems they've been pretty active on the site before now.'

'But nothing wilfully destructive!' Anxious, shocked.

He moved in. 'I suspect that you knew Cleeve before you came to live here.'

Hesitation. She was saved from immediate reply by the arrival of one of her tribe of cats, a wicked-looking seal-point. The creature leapt on to her lap, flexed its claws in a way which must have been painful, and settled down, sleek and graceful as a snake.

Laura made up her mind to be co-operative, though her manner was more aggressive. 'I suppose I shall be badgered until I tell you, and I've nothing to hide. When I was at school I lived with my mother in a flat in Exeter. We had been deserted by my father who went off with another woman. David Cleeve and a friend moved into a flat on the same landing.'

'What year was this?'

She reflected. 'It must have been early in the summer of 1953, I remember the city was decorated for the coronation. They were still there when we left in September '54.'

John Scales had established that Cleeve moved from Bristol to Exeter in 1953 and set up as a freelance journalist. Now, here he was pin-pointed in an Exeter flat with a friend. Nice when the wires crossed on target.

'Where was this flat?'

'In Mellor Road—number fourteen. The houses in Mellor Road were four-storey Victorian town houses and most of them had been converted into flats. They're all gone now—replaced by modern flats, half the size and ten times the price.'

'Cleeve would have been about twenty-two at that time?'

'I suppose so, about that.'

'This friend he lived with. . .'

'A young man of about the same age. He was called John—John Larkin. They were journalists of some sort and they were both writing books.' She seemed slightly embarrassed. 'At that time I had visions of becoming a writer and I was impressed.'

'Did you know them well?'

She shook her head. 'No, we just met occasionally on the stairs. I was never in their flat or they in ours. I was only a schoolgirl and my mother didn't like me talking to them; she thought they were a bit odd.'

'I suppose they chatted you up?'

She frowned. 'No, it wasn't like that. We talked about books and they used to tease me about being serious. Anyway, when I was seventeen we moved to London and a bit later I went to the School of Art and Design.' She smiled, a rueful little smile. 'No more writing.'

'Did you see either of them again?'

'No, it wasn't until just after I came to live here—David came into the shop to buy a present for his wife and I recognized him.'

'After nearly thirty years?'

'Why not? People don't change all that much.' She smiled, softened by recollections of youth. 'I got mixed up, though, and called him John.'

'These two, when you knew them in Exeter, how were they living? Lots of friends—parties—girls?'

'No, nothing like that; they lived very quietly. Of course they were out a lot because of their work. They seemed quite well off; one of them had a car and not so many people did then.'

'I suppose your mother remembers them?'

'Mother died before I came to live here.'

'Perhaps you will tell me your maiden name?'

She hesitated, then made up her mind. 'I've never been married. I adopted the "Mrs" to avoid unwelcome attentions.'

'That's understandable. Did Cleeve seem pleased to see you again?'

'He didn't remember me at first.'

'And afterwards?'

She actually coloured. 'I saw him from time to time.'

'Do you know what happened to his friend—John Larkin?'

'No; I asked him, but it seems they lost touch. Not long after we left Exeter David moved to London himself and published his first book—*Xanadu*, the one that made his name. It was strange, I suppose, I actually read all the Peter Stride books without having the least idea that they had been written by him.'

'Can you give me the names of other people who were living in the Mellor Road flats who might remember the two young men?'

He got three names. Progress of a sort; at least a Knight's move.

As he was leaving he asked to see her workshop. She looked doubtful, but led him to a room which had been built onto the kitchen. Not very big but meticulously arranged to make use of every inch. Two benches, one for the metalwork, the other for enamelling. Tiny tools—snips, pliers, various little hammers, some of metal others of hard wood, tweezers and tongs; doll-size anvils and vices; a kiln and another little furnace; bottles labelled with cabalistic signs containing the enamelling colours. . . .No doubt at all that Laura would have found the making of the dart well within her capability.

'Very interesting—thank you.'

Lunch, he thought, at The Buckingham.

The Buckingham was full of people and talk; waitresses dodged between the tables while people queued at the bar for drinks. Wycliffe hovered at the entrance to the lounge bar and was instantly spotted by the all-seeing Polmear. A signal to one of the waitresses and he was piloted to an alcove where there was a table laid for one—presumably for Polmear, when he found time to eat.

'The plaice is very good, sir. Fresh-caught this morning. . . .With a side-salad. . .dressing?. . .And a lager?'

Near the end of the meal Polmear came and sat opposite him, nursing a bottle of brandy. 'To sweeten the coffee.'

Wycliffe said, 'Weather not so good today.'

'I'm not complaining; a couple of days a week like this and the money just rolls in—they've nothing to do but eat and drink; but if the weather stays bad longer than that they think about going home.'

The ethology of the emmet.

'Progress?'

Wycliffe shrugged.

Polmear said, 'I hear they had a fire up at the dig last night.'

'I heard that too.'

Polmear poured brandy into balloon glasses. 'Since you told me about Celia, I've been thinking: it could have been a jealous wife. There are women who can't take that sort of thing. . .'

Whatever Polmear had or hadn't known before, he knew something now.

'Thanks for the brandy.'

Wycliffe strolled along the waterfront; he found the tangy mist invigorating. One of the ferry boats was berthing with hardly anyone aboard. He turned up Zion Steps, loath to get back to the grind. The herbalist had a "Closed" notice in his glass door; the vegetarians were champing away; the jewellery shop and the photographer's had a sealed look. In the Incident Room Dixon had taken over from Potter.

'Coffee, sir?'

'I'm awash already.'

He stood by one of the tall, narrow Gothic windows of the little building, looking out into the grey gloom with a morose unseeing gaze.

In a murder case the rules are clear; you look to the oracles, the Three Wise Monkeys of criminal investigation: Motive, Means and Opportunity, and the greatest of these is Motive. He had asked: Who had a motive for murdering Celia Dawe? And the oracle had remained dumb. Now it seemed the question should have been: Who had a motive for killing Cleeve? But the oracle was no more communicative.

Cleeve had been threatened and there had been an attempt on his life; now he was missing.

Wycliffe brooded on Cleeve. The reporter on the local paper who had "fits"; the freelance in Exeter, sharing a flat with another journalist, John Larkin; the schoolgirl Laura Wynn, living in the same building. Then, London, *Xanadu*, *Medicus*, *Magistra*. . .fame, marriage, the twins, Roseland. . .no more fits.

Patricia had said, 'If he was [an epileptic] he told me nothing about it and there has never been the slightest suggestion of it since our marriage.'

There was another remark playing hide-and-seek on the fringes of his consciousness, a remark someone had made recently. He made an effort of memory—almost always fatal to the trapping of such will-o'-the-wisps—and failed. He thought it might have been something from Laura Wynn but could get no further.

Perhaps it would come back if he stopped trying.

He turned to Potter. 'See if you can get Mr Scales on the telephone.'

Scales would be in his—Wycliffe's—office, sitting in his—Wycliffe's—chair. It was an odd feeling; somehow the job seemed more important when someone else was doing it. When he sat in that chair he felt at everybody's beck and call; when someone else sat there they seemed to acquire a certain eminence. Absurd!

'I've got the address of the Exeter flat, John, but it's been pulled down.'

Scales already had men working on the Exeter angle, so far without success, but with the address and the names of occupants contemporary with the two young men they might do better.

'Has Horton arrived yet, sir?'

'I'm expecting him at any moment.'

'No news of Cleeve?'

'No, the search party is out and as soon as Horton arrives we shall start turning over the debris of the fire. Keep watching this space, John!'

A man had come into the room and was talking to Potter. Wycliffe recognized Horton, a dark, undistinguished little man with whom he had worked before and admired for his self-effacing manner as well as for his professional skill. He did not look like a veteran of the courtroom but he had a reputation among criminal lawyers for never getting ruffled and for never being jockeyed into saying more or less than he intended.

They shook hands. 'Are you coming with me to wherever it is?'

'I'll run you up to the site.'

Henry's Field was a bleak prospect. The drizzle had stopped but the landscape was obliterated by mist, and the fog-horn on the lighthouse punctuated the silence with its eerie blast. They were working on the dig and figures were dimly visible through the mist. It was arranged that the earnest Wrighton would work through the debris of the hut with the police to rescue the second-hand artefacts.

Horton cast a professional eye over the tangled mass of carbonized and charred timbers and seemed mildly surprised.

'This is important?'

'If there is a man underneath.'

'A funeral pyre?'

'Could be.'

Horton turned to the two men who would do the heavy work. 'All right, you can get started. As you work, try to cause a minimum of disturbance and lay the timbers out in order as you remove them.'

Wycliffe walked over to the dig. Christie Cleeve was the first to see him. 'Is there any news?'

'I'm afraid not.'

She looked grey-faced and heavy-eyed. 'Mother says it's better for me to carry on here.'

'I think she's right and I'll make sure you know the moment we hear anything.'

Gervaise Prout's slim figure emerged from the mist, his white hair glistening with moisture. 'Mr Wycliffe! I'm so glad to see you.' He turned to Christie: 'Jane has found something at number five and she's not sure what it is, see if you can help her.'

The girl went off.

Prout said, 'I feel so annoyed with myself for not having been here, but I really had no option. There was a symposium in Exeter at which I had to read a paper.'

'I don't see what you could have done if you were here.'

Prout made a gesture of impatience. 'It's such a blow to our work when it was going so well.'

'Are you thinking of the loss of your hut or the disappearance of your patron?'

He received a quick appraising glance as though Prout suspected him of sarcasm but Wycliffe's bland features gave nothing away.

'I was referring to the loss of the hut.'

'I understood from your assistant that it would be no great setback because you had the bulk of your records with you and the rest were in the caravan.'

A frown. 'Wrighton is an enthusiastic youngster, a good fieldworker in the making, but he has no idea of administration and its problems.' Prout rubbed his bony chin until it shone like a little red apple. 'I was deeply shocked to hear about Cleeve. What does it mean?'

'That he went out last night and didn't come back.'

'You know no more than that?'

'At present, no. We are searching the neighbourhood, so far without result.'

'Do you suspect foul play?'

Wycliffe shrugged. 'Do you? You probably know the man and his circumstances better than I.'

Prout seemed to resent having his question turned back on him. 'I'm naturally very concerned. David is not only our patron here but I may say that he has become a friend. Have you spoken to Kitson?'

'Not yet. You think he might be able to help?' Naïve.

'I don't know. . .' After a pause he went on, 'I certainly have the impression that David and Kitson are very close.'

Wycliffe was casual. 'I suppose that is natural; two very intelligent men, living as neighbours. . .'

Prout would have liked to let it go at that but he was urged on by the desire to seem well informed. 'You may be right but I feel there is more to it than that. . . .Whenever David visits the dig, Kitson is rarely far away and one frequently comes upon the two of them in seemingly intimate conversation. What really strikes me as odd is that David seems to defer to him in a way that he would do to nobody else.'

Wycliffe recalled the curious moment of strain when, on his first visit to the dig, returning to the hut with Prout, they came upon Cleeve and Kitson in earnest discussion.

Prout had talked himself into yielding confidences. 'You may think it petty, but raising funds even for a small project like this is difficult—one has to nurse one's patron, to catch and hold his interest. . . .It is true that we have sufficient money for the present dig but I had interested Cleeve in a more ambitious scheme. . .'

'And Kitson talked him out of it?'

'I'm sure that he did.' Prout had his eyes on the wall of mist which all but hemmed them in. 'Altogether, I feel that Kitson must be a. . .must have very considerable influence on David.'

'Are you suggesting that there might be something sinister in their relationship?'

Prout shied away from that like a frightened colt. 'Not sinister! Of course not! I'm merely saying that for Kitson to have so much influence over David he must know him better than anyone else. I suspect that they have known each other a long time—certainly before Kitson came here to live.'

Wycliffe said, 'Do you know anything of Kitson's background?'

Prout prodded a clump of heather with the toe of his bespoke fell-walkers. 'I met him for the first time when I came here to talk to David about the dig eighteen months ago.'

'But you've been making a few enquiries among your academic friends—quite natural in the circumstances.'

Prout let this pass though he looked uncomfortable. 'I really know very little about him. He doesn't seem to have a formal academic background. I gather that he translates Russian and other Slav languages for anybody who will pay him and he's made something of a reputation as a linguist. I've heard that he undertakes hackwork for scholars in the field of Slavonic studies—manuscript reading, indexing, proof checking—that sort of thing.'

Wycliffe guessed that he had got all that he was likely to get from Prout and he was anxious to move on. 'Thank you for being so helpful. I shall treat what you have told me in confidence.'

The Land Rover which had brought the searchers from Division, parked on the skyline at the highest point in the field, looked grotesquely enlarged by the mist. Sergeant Pearce was in the cab, a map spread in front of him, a flask of coffee on the seat beside him; he was monitoring the search through the personal radios of his men.

'This has worked well, sir. Very few radio blind spots and no blisters on my feet. Unfortunately, no luck either. They've covered the ground we mapped out for them and, in any case, I shall have to call them off for refreshment shortly.'

'Don't send them back until you hear from me.'

'You don't think he can be out there, sir?'

Wycliffe growled something unintelligible. Why did they all ask questions as though he had a crystal ball?

He plodded through the heather and joined Horton by the burned-out ruin. Already a large quantity of charred timber had been laid out on the ground and the site was looking less like a Guy Fawkes bonfire which had been caught in a deluge.

Horton said, 'I think we've found what you are looking for.'

Chapter Five

IT WAS A moment before Wycliffe, peering down through the still considerable tangle of carbonized wood, saw a human foot; a foot burned through to the bones of the toes but, for the rest, still enclosed in the ghostly remnants of a shoe. The leg, dealt with in the same freakish manner by the fire, was visible to the knee, but whatever remained of the body was hidden under more charred timbers.

'Is this what you expected?'

Wycliffe was subdued. 'I think this is the man we are looking for.' He glanced across at the industrious Wrighton, squatting on his haunches, sorting through ashes and rubble with no eyes for anything else. 'Does he know?'

'No.'

'Then find some pretext to send him away. I don't want the news to get around until we are sure. Another thing: It's possible that he died in the same way as the girl—injected with nicotine by a hypodermic dart. Obviously it's vital to find the dart if there is one.'

He went over to the Land Rover and made a number of calls on the RT; to the coroner; to Franks, the pathologist; to the local G.P.; to his headquarters and to the Incident Room.

Another half-hour and the body was completely uncovered. It was Cleeve; no doubt about that. In the whimsical way of fires, objects near the ground had suffered less actual burning than others higher up, probably due to the reduced oxygen supply. Horton said, 'A body takes a lot of burning.'

All the same, Cleeve was no sight for the public gaze and Wycliffe posted Pearce and his men to keep people away until the screens were delivered.

Dr Hodge, the local G.P., came in his battered Metro, bouncing over the rough ground. He got out, slammed the door, and came to stand, looking down at the remains of the dead man. He muttered: 'Is it Cleeve?' Then he turned to Wycliffe, 'If at first you don't succeed, try, try again—is that it?'

'We don't know how he died yet.' Wycliffe was terse.

'No, but we can make a good guess.' Hodge rubbed his dark chin, always a little in need of a shave. 'Well, it makes more sense; I couldn't believe that anybody would take that trouble over a silly girl. Poor little so-and-so! Ah, well!' The doctor sighed. 'I suppose you've notified the coroner?'

Wycliffe made his way across to the dig. He spotted the auburn head in one of the trenches and was immediately seen himself. Christie was like a young doe, alert to the slightest signal. She came to him, frowning, anxious, 'You've heard something?'

'I'm afraid it's bad news.'

'Tell me.'

He told her. The news of her father's death did not come as a great shock, rather a confirmation of something feared; it was the circumstances of his death which distressed her.

She murmured: 'He died in the fire. . .in the fire. . .'

Wycliffe said: 'I'm sure we shall find that your father was already dead when the fire started.' He added after a moment: 'I mean that. Now you must go to your mother.'

She seemed to hesitate and he said: 'Would you like me to break the news first?'

She shook her head. 'No, but I must find Andrew.'

Wycliffe was reminded of his own twin son and daughter, several years older, but still in moments of crisis reaching out to each other. He watched her set out across the field to the wicket gate, deeply puzzled and distressed. In his turn he was being watched curiously by the students working on the dig; they must have realized that there had been some development.

Cleeve was dead and Wycliffe was in no doubt that he had been murdered, though he would have to wait for Franks to provide official confirmation.

Why had he gone out late at night knowing that his life was threatened? Wrighton, who had spent the evening working in the caravan, had not seen him, though his body had been found in the shed.

Lucy Lane arrived and he put her in the picture. 'I want you to be with me when I talk to Mrs Cleeve.'

Just short of the wicket gate they were waylaid by Dr Prout, very subdued. 'I've just this moment heard. . .' And then, 'I suppose it's too early to call on Patricia?'

Wycliffe agreed that it was.

Through the wicket gate and the rhododendron tunnel. The mist was lifting at last and, as is often the case on this coast, there was a prospect of a fine evening after a dismal day. He led the way round to the front door and rang the bell.

The door was opened by a woman Wycliffe had never seen before, a little brown mouse of a woman, probably still on the right side of forty but she would look very little different at sixty. Her features looked pinched and he had the impression that a single harsh word would send her scurrying for cover, or that she might burst into tears.

Wycliffe introduced himself and Lucy Lane. She said, 'I am Mrs Cleeve's cousin; my name is Byrne—Miss Byrne.'

'I suppose you have heard?'

She nodded without speaking, eyes cast down like a nun.

'This is a distressing time for you all. . .I am anxious to find out exactly what happened last night and I hope you will answer a few questions. . .'

Another nod.

'Did you see Mr Cleeve at all?'

'We all had dinner together, as usual.'

'At what time?'

'At seven-thirty.'

She seemed so distressed that he felt heartless in questioning her. 'Can you tell me what happened after dinner?'

She made an obvious effort. 'The same as usual. David had a

strict routine which he followed unless we had guests. He worked in the morning, then he was free until dinner. After dinner he would go back to work until midnight or even one in the morning.'

He saw with surprise that her eyes were glistening with tears.

'You were fond of him.'

She flushed. 'He was his own worst enemy. He was a hard-working man and except at odd times when he'd had too much to drink, a kind man—too kind, sometimes.' She turned her head away.

'Were you surprised to hear that he went out last night?'

She nodded. He was afraid that if he questioned her further she would break down. He said something soothing and asked her to find out if Mrs Cleeve would see them.

'She's expecting you.'

They were taken to the big drawing-room. 'I'll tell her you're here.'

A clock in the passage chimed and struck five. Several minutes went by before Patricia Cleeve came into the room. After being introduced to Lucy Lane she apologized for keeping them waiting, sat herself in one of the armchairs and smoothed her skirt.

'Christie and Andrew have each other; I've left them together.' She was completely controlled but there was tension in every line of her body.

Wycliffe repeated the usual phrases with obvious sincerity and she accepted his sympathy with dignity. Wycliffe thought: These are the forms, and she is the kind of woman to be strengthened and supported by their observance. No hiding away; no hole-in-corner grief, self-indulgent and destructive; there is a ritual for bereavement as for everything else.

'There are questions I shall have to ask you, some of them very personal, but if you would prefer to put it off until tomorrow. . .'

In a deliberate, emphatic tone she said, 'I would prefer, Mr Wycliffe, that you do whatever you think necessary to find out what is behind all this; how David came to die. It is certainly not pleasant to be interrogated but it is much worse to be kept in the dark. . .in the dark about almost everything.'

Wycliffe nodded. 'I understand.'

301

The windows of the drawing-room looked out on a terraced lawn, falling away to a fringe of trees and, beyond the trees, to the creek, the headland and the pines. The mist had vanished magically, like the lifting of a veil, and already a watery sunshine was restoring colour to the scene.

'As you know, your husband's body was found in the ruins of the archaeologists' hut—can you think of any reason why he would have gone there late at night?'

A slight shrug. 'No, I certainly cannot. It's true that he was more interested in the dig than he was willing to admit and I think Gervaise Prout sometimes worked very late but I understand he was away.'

Wycliffe cleared the decks. 'So far, of course, we have no evidence that his death was other than accidental but—'

She cut across his words. 'Please don't feel that you have to spare me, Mr Wycliffe. David was murdered. You know that as well as I do. The horror of publicity he has had ever since I've known him arose from some sort of fear and in recent months that fear has been catching up with him. Although he would never discuss or even admit the existence of anything of the kind, I've no doubt in my mind that he believed his life to be threatened. When I saw how anxious he was to talk to you on Saturday, I hoped that he was going to tell you about it.'

Few women in his experience could have disciplined themselves to speak so objectively of a husband, recently dead.

'Up to a point your husband did confide in me; he told me that he was being threatened but he claimed to have no knowledge of the source of the threats or of any possible reason for them. He was extremely vague as to their nature though he did say that they had arrived through the post—four of them spread over the past nine months. When I asked to see these communications, whatever they were, he said that he had destroyed them.'

Lucy Lane had been sitting bolt upright in her chair, her bag on her lap, her eyes moving from one to the other, taking in every nuance of the exchanges; now she said, 'When someone makes that kind of complaint to the police, Mrs Cleeve, it usually means that he or she is well aware of who is threatening them and why, but

without embarrassment or some incriminating admission they can't
or won't speak out. With no facts it is impossible for the police to act.'
   'Yes, I see that.'
   Wycliffe said, 'And the situation hasn't changed so far as those
threats are concerned; we still need to know more about them,
which means that we must know more about your husband's past.'
   She made a small gesture of helplessness. 'But I know so
little—virtually nothing about his life before our marriage.'
   'And you feel that whatever made him so. . .so wary of publicity
of any kind, must have occurred before you met him?'
   She was emphatic. 'I do! Very early in our marriage I questioned
him about it.' A wry smile. 'Needless to say, I learned nothing
except not to ask such questions in the future.'
   'Did you ever meet any of his relatives?'
   'No, his father and mother were already dead; he was an only
child and, though he admitted to cousins, I don't think he was ever
in touch with them.'
   'When did you first meet?'
   'It was one Christmas, in London—Christmas 1961 it must have
been. We were married the following April.' She smiled. 'It was
hero-worship on my part. I had read his books and I was an eager
disciple. I saw him as a genius.' She glanced across at Lucy Lane as
she said this.
   'Where was he living at that time?'
   'When we met? In a bachelor flat off Gower Street. As far as I
could tell he had few, if any, friends—a loose acquaintance with a
couple of fellows in a neighbouring flat—they, in fact, came to our
wedding, the only ones from his side.'
   'Not his publisher or his agent?'
   She spoke with deliberation. 'You may find this incredible but at
the time of our marriage, David had never met either his publisher
or his agent. All the business was conducted by correspondence.'
   Wycliffe kept the questioning in a low key, allowing intervals of
silence when the three of them sat, each apparently absorbed in
private thoughts.
   'This man, Roger Kitson—is he a recent acquaintance?'
   Another frown. 'I think David has known Roger for some years.

303

Very occasionally David had to go to London to deal with the business side of his work and when he came back from one of those trips he said that he had offered the cottage to someone. That was nearly two years ago, and a month or so later Roger turned up and took possession.'

For a while she sat, looking down at her hands, clasped in her lap, then she raised her eyes and looked straight at Wycliffe. 'You must think it very strange that after more than twenty years of marriage I know so little about my husband but ours was not a conventional marriage. I've already said that I regarded David as a genius; certainly he was no ordinary man and he did not behave like one. He lived much of his life in a sort of limbo between imagination and reality and, as you will know from his books, the world of his imagination could be strange and terrifying.'

Her gaze shifted from Wycliffe to Lucy Lane as though the girl fitted more easily into the pattern of her thoughts. 'Even as a young wife I realized that I could not expect to monopolize any part of such a man—that it would have been inviting disaster to try.

'When we had the children I asked only that he would not allow the assertion of his own personality to blight or smother theirs and, in the main, he kept that bargain.' She made a small gesture with her slim hands. 'Of course, he had many women; there were occasional bouts of drunkenness, he was sometimes thoughtlessly cruel, and always obsessively secretive. . . .But I knew that he couldn't be otherwise; he was the man I married.'

She was looking down at her hands once more. 'I flatter myself that I understood his needs and that I made life easier for him. I saw that as my role. But you will see that I am not in a position to tell you much about him.'

Wycliffe was beginning to feel stifled in this atmosphere of reasonableness and studied calm which seemed to create its own peculiar tension. He admired the woman's self-control but it was unnatural. Oddly, he felt sympathy for Cleeve; such repression would probably have provoked him to either violence or obscenity and either response would have been incomprehensible to Patricia.

'What an extraordinary woman! I never really thought of him

as having a wife, but a woman like that. . .' Lucy Lane in admiration.

They walked along the broad corridor with its disturbing pictures and erratic changes of level and climbed the stairs; Lucy all eyes. As they reached the secretary's office the girl came to the door and Wycliffe introduced himself and Lucy Lane.

Milli looked them over in cool appraisal. 'I know who you are.'

It was the first time Wycliffe had seen the girl at close quarters. 'I suppose you know that Mr Cleeve's body has been found?'

'Mrs Cleeve told me.'

'Did he seem much as usual yesterday? Or was he nervous, edgy—you know the sort of thing?'

She shrugged her thin shoulders. One had the impression that her body was infinitely pliable rather than jointed and, though she was perfectly proportioned, she was very small. She said, 'You were here yesterday, you saw as much of him as I did.'

'But you knew him, you could compare his behaviour with some sort of norm.'

'There was no norm; he was never the same two days together, it depended on how the work was going, whether he had slept the night before—even on the weather.' She added grudgingly, 'But he was upset yesterday. I noticed it when I arrived in the morning, then you came, and he was out most of the afternoon so I didn't see much of him.'

'Do you live in the house?'

'I do not! I live in the village but I have my lunch here.'

'With the family?'

'Of course.'

'How long have you worked here?'

'Nearly five years.'

'We shall be in the library for a while but I would like to see you again afterwards.'

She glanced at her watch. 'I finish work at half-past five and it's already quarter to six.'

'I won't keep you longer than necessary.'

For the third time in six days Wycliffe found himself in Cleeve's library, so much in contrast to the rest of the house.

Lucy Lane exclaimed in astonishment: 'It's Edwardian! I'd always imagined him against a background of white walls, steel-framed abstracts, and Giacometti figures on the bookcases.'

'That sounds more like his wife.'

Looking round the big room he experienced a mild elation and immediately felt guilty. The truth was that he always had a pleasurable sense of anticipation when he was able to look behind the scenes at another man's life. Asexual voyeurism, he called it—the vice which sells autobiographies, published journals and diaries. Wycliffe was one of that army of unassuming people who feel the need to match themselves against the grain of other people's lives; perhaps that was why he had found his vocation in the police.

Cleeve's desk was orderly: a thick wad of typescript in a limp cover, labelled *Setebos*, presumably the next novel in final draft, waiting for the author's finishing touches and seal of approval. But even without them, good or bad, *Setebos* would be 'Peter Stride's last and greatest masterpiece, published posthumously'. And if publication could coincide with a well publicized trial of his killer then the sky would be the limit.

Wycliffe said, 'Why Setebos, I wonder?'

'Setebos was Caliban's creator-god, and in Browning's poem Caliban thought Setebos had created the world for his own amusement.' Lucy Lane, B.A. Hons. (Eng. Lit.). Very prim.

'Ah!'

On the desk there was a crystal pen-tray with coloured ball-points and pencils; a paper-knife with an ivory handle in the form of a lion couchant, a memo pad, and two telephones. . . .On the memo pad were three lines of notes: 'Lester. . .RC WE 9/8. . . Saunders for Medicus???' The notes had been written in green and below them there was an odd little doodle of a man upside down.

'Ask Miss Who-is-it to come in.'

Lucy was looking at the bookshelves; she fetched the girl from the office. Milli came in and looked disapproving when she saw Wycliffe sitting in Cleeve's chair.

'I wonder if you can explain these notes?'

She glanced at the pad. 'I think so. Colin Lester is Mr Cleeve's agent and this is a memo to ring him; RC is Russell Cowdray, his

English publisher. Mr Cleeve was arranging for Cowdray to spend the weekend beginning Friday August 9th here. Saunders for *Medicus*—that refers to dramatizing *Medicus*—one of Mr Cleeve's books—for TV. The company want to use Neville Saunders but Mr Cleeve wasn't sure they'd chosen the right man for the job.'

'And these notes were made yesterday?'

'Oh, yes.'

'Thank you; that is very helpful. But what about the little upside-down man?'

A ghost of a smile. 'That's typical of Mr Cleeve—a doodle.' She looked more carefully at the little drawing. 'I think it's a version of the hanged man in the Tarot pack. He thinks—thought in symbols, he really did. Even people who read his books (the inference being that Wycliffe was unlikely to have done so) don't realize the amount of symbolism there is in his writing.' She waved a hand vaguely. 'You'll find a whole section of the library devoted to books on the subject.' She paused. 'Is that all?'

'For the moment, thank you, but don't go home yet.'

So Milli was something more than an animated doll.

The room would have to be meticulously searched and this was a job for Smith but he wanted to get the feel of it, to glimpse the private world of David Cleeve. It wasn't possible to step into the dead man's shoes but from the things he kept close to him one could, perhaps, guess at the vision he had of himself.

The room was L-shaped and he had never seen the other leg of the L. Here there was a second window, looking out from the back of the house to a wooded area of the estate. As in the rest of the room the walls were lined with mahogany bookcases which reached to within a couple of feet of the high ceiling. There were eighteenth-century library steps with hand rails, and a long, polished table with several of the favoured straight-backed armchairs so that wherever one happened to be there was a convenient place to sit and look up a reference or make a note; there was even another telephone. One whole section of the bookcases was devoted to Cleeve's own works in a babel of languages and a rainbow pattern of jackets. An impressive card index stood next to a sinister electronic device with a blank screen, no doubt scheming a take-over.

There was a door in the end wall of the L. Wycliffe opened it and found himself in a bedroom, very simply furnished; aseptic like a private room in a hospital, but with a double bed. A wall-cupboard turned out to be a well-stocked wardrobe. There was a bathroom and a loo, accessible from the corridor as well as from the bedroom.

Wycliffe, hands in pockets, returned to the library and mooned about, feeling none the wiser. He was thinking of the young man who had started it all, the acquaintance Laura Wynn had made in a block of Exeter flats. He had moved to London and, through his talent as a writer, he had become rich and famous, but after 28 years it seemed that he had still felt menaced because of something which had occurred in those early days.

He rejoined Lucy Lane. 'We must let Smith loose in here, and make a note to get Inspector Royal down. Somebody will have to look into Cleeve's affairs and cope with his lawyers.' Royal was the department's legal and financial expert.

They moved to Milli's office which she shared with two kinds of copier, a word-processor, a duplicator which looked like a space machine and, surprise, surprise, a finger-powered typewriter—no doubt in reserve like an oil-stove against a power cut.

'Is there a safe where Mr Cleeve kept valuables?'

She was filing correspondence and she did not stop in her work. 'If there is I don't know of it; he kept important documents and all his manuscript material at the bank.'

'What other rooms are there on this level?'

'Apart from the library and this office there is a stationery store, a bathroom, loo and bedroom.'

'Do the rest of the family come up here?'

She slammed shut the drawer of the filing cabinet. 'I've never seen Mrs Cleeve on this floor—that's not to say she doesn't come here. The twins used to come up here when they were younger—not now.'

'Does Mr Cleeve sleep up here?'

'I suppose so. I'm not here at night to see.'

'What is your impression of the household; do the Cleeves get on well together?'

She shrugged. 'So-so, like most families, I suppose.'

'You know that Mr Cleeve had other women?'

'It doesn't come as a surprise.'

'You?'

'On occasion.'

'Did Mrs Cleeve resent these relationships?'

'I don't know; I've never asked her.' She glanced at her watch. 'Now, if there's nothing more. . .'

The burned-out hut was now screened from the public gaze and two uniformed policemen, bored to their boots, stood guard. Franks's automobile, looking as though it had escaped from a James Bond film, stood at a sprawling angle to a line of other parked vehicles which included the mortuary van. Wycliffe recognized Smith's Land Rover among them.

The constables, galvanized into efficiency, saluted. Wycliffe passed behind the screens into more or less ordered chaos. Franks saw him and came over.

'Ah, there you are, Charles! I must say you go in for variety: a pretty tart on Tuesday and on Thursday, Britain's up-market answer to the horror comic. He'll be missed, Charles, and not least by those sharks at the Inland Revenue.'

Wycliffe said, 'You haven't shifted him yet.'

'No, there's a little problem of keeping him more or less in one piece. They're getting a plastic sheet under the body now.'

'I hope they're keeping their eyes open.'

'Horton is, and he won't miss much.'

The debris had been almost cleared away and four men in green overalls were bending over what remained of David Cleeve, manipulating the edges of a plastic sheet while Horton crouched, watching every move. Sergeant Smith was packing his photographic gear into two custom-made holdalls of his own design.

The plastic sheeting was patiently edged under the body and folded over to make a secure envelope which was finally lifted clear and carried to the mortuary van. Inspector Knowles had arrived from sub-division and he would accompany the body and attend the post-mortem to maintain continuity of evidence.

End of an author. The rag-bag of contending emotions and

creative energy that was Cleeve had been obliterated, and in its place were the charred remnants of a body in a plastic envelope. Wycliffe, despite his years of experience, was always deeply shocked and angered by murder; he found it difficult to conceive of the arrogance which allowed one man to take all from another, leaving no possibility of restitution. And in this case his emotions were more than ever involved because he had known the dead man; just five days earlier he had been drinking his whisky.

Horton was beginning the detailed examination of the ground where the body had lain and, later, the rest of the debris would be removed and the whole area subjected to minute scrutiny, as thorough as anything undertaken by the archaeologists.

Back in the Incident Room Wycliffe dictated a press release: 'The body of Mr David Cleeve of Roscrowgy in Roseland has been found in the ruins of a burned-out shed used as an office and site-museum by a group of archaeologists excavating in a field near his home. Mr Cleeve went out on Wednesday evening and did not return. During the night, the fire brigade was called to a fire which completely destroyed the wooden shed and Mr Cleeve's body was discovered late on Thursday afternoon when the debris was being removed under the supervision of a forensic expert. The police are investigating the possibility of foul play.'

Wycliffe sighed. 'Once the press realize that David Cleeve is Peter Stride we shall have a hornet's nest about our ears.'

The routine of the case seemed to acquire a life of its own; nourished by large quantities of paper and by an increasing number of people. Every table in the Incident Room was occupied; reports were being typed, duplicated and filed; index cards, recording every item of information collected during the investigation, were lodged in the carousel; lists were prepared and compared. . . .

D.C. Curnow was checking a list of people who, for one reason or another, used or had access to nicotine. As far as he could see, none of them had the remotest connection with the dead girl or with Cleeve. Another list recorded those who might have sufficient skill and apparatus to extract nicotine from tobacco leaves or from tobacco on sale in the shops; these included two teachers of chemistry and a former professor of pharmacology, but here again, there seemed to be no link with the girl or with Cleeve; the single exception was the herbalist, Geoffrey Tull.

Quite a number of people appeared on a third sheet—those likely to have the skill and tools necessary to contrive the dart, but few of these cross-checked with either of the other schedules and, of them all, only Laura Wynn was known to have been acquainted with Cleeve and Celia Dawe.

Wycliffe digested it all and was depressed. Sufficient unto the day—and it had been a long one. 'I'm going home.'

Helen was concerned for him. 'I had no idea when you were coming so I couldn't get anything ready but it won't take long, then early to bed!'

'Can't we go out?'

'Of course, if you really want to.'

Helen had heard good reports of a restaurant at Veryan and, encouraged by the dramatic improvement in the weather, they decided to eat there.

Veryan is a neat little village which somehow manages to escape the worst symptoms of the emmet plague. They had their evening meal in a small restaurant which offered a simple menu, the food well-cooked and presented, the wine sensible, and value for money. A vegetable soup, chicken-in-cider, followed by a delicious apple crumble and the cheese board. Half a bottle of German hock.

Helen said, 'This is definitely holiday eating; we mustn't make a habit of it.'

Wycliffe had been unusually silent; now he said, 'Cleeve is dead. They found him in the ruins of the hut.'

Helen was shocked but she said little, there was no point.

They were silent for a while then Wycliffe said, 'In the mirror—that couple who have just come in. . .'

Laura Wynn with her golden hair. (How long would she contrive to keep it like that?) Another green frock—she must think that green was her colour and certainly she drew attention from all over the room. The hair and the frock were discreetly garnished with jewellery from stock. Her companion was the herbalist, Geoffrey Tull, in a suit of fine grey cord. They were obviously known to the proprietor.

Wycliffe muttered, 'Those two together. . .'

'What about them?'

He made an impatient movement which meant that he didn't want to commit himself to words. 'Shall we have our coffee?'

When they were leaving they had to pass close to the other couple's table. Tull looked sheepish but Laura greeted them with the aplomb of a real duchess.

It was half-past ten when they got back to the cottage and quite dark. He had been up since before five that morning but he was disinclined for bed.

He said: 'I'll be up later.'

He opened the front door, crossed the road, and smoked his pipe leaning on the sea wall. The sea was quiet, just the ripple and swish of wavelets advancing and retreating over the shingle. Navigation lights and street lamps cut paths across the dark water and at 20-second intervals the lighthouse flashed. He counted the seconds through three or four cycles and got it wrong every time. It was then, by one of those subterranean tricks of the mind, that he remembered what it was that Laura Wynn had said, the remark he had tried so hard to recall.

It came as an anticlimax. She had been telling of her first meeting with Cleeve after more than 28 years, when he came into her shop and she had recognized him.

Wycliffe had said, 'After nearly thirty years?'

'Why not? People don't change all that much. . .*I got mixed up though, and called him John.*'

A natural enough mistake; on her own admission she hadn't known the two young men at all well. . . .All the same, taken with the epilepsy. . .

He went back indoors to the telephone and dialled John Scales's home number.

'I hope you are not in bed, John.'

'I should be so lucky! Jane is entertaining some of her departmental colleagues. Did you know that academic shop is even more boring than police shop? That academics have more expensive taste in booze and that they get tipsy quicker?' John sounded a bit tipsy himself.

312

'It's a very long shot, John, but there could be something in it. I want you to get somebody to check registrations of death in the Exeter area between September '54 and, say, June '55. The chap could have died in hospital and that might be a different registration district from his home address.'

'Does this chap we are talking about have a name, sir?'

'Yes: David Paul Cleeve, born September 5th 1931 at Bristol— will that do?'

Scales was impressed. 'So that's the way the cookie crumbles! I'll get somebody on it as soon as the offices open. Anything else?'

'Yes. I don't want Jane to break any professional confidences but I suppose she must know Gervaise Prout. If she does, I'd appreciate her off-the-record summing up.'

Scales chuckled. 'We've been talking about him recently, since he cropped up in this case. Jane knows him, though he isn't employed by the university. He's a freelance with private means. He's a bachelor, with a house near St Germans. It seems he's well thought of academically and he's got a knack for raising funds for his digs. He does some extra-mural work for the university and he's a visiting lecturer at several places. The funny thing is he's a bit of a joke, but nobody knows quite why.'

'Thanks, John. Enjoy the party!'

Wycliffe climbed the narrow, twisted stairs to bed. Helen was propped up, reading a dog-eared copy of *Magistra*.

Chapter Six

A FINE SUNNY day but with a light breeze; enough for the sailing
fraternity and for the wind-surfers, not too much for the beach
loungers. The emmets, convalescing after yesterday's gloom,
agreed with each other: 'We were right not to go to Spain this year
after all.'

Helen had decided on a rather special trip—up the coast to
Portscatho then on to the Gull Rock and the Nare.

'It will be choppy.'

'You know I enjoy it.'

Wycliffe didn't, he was prone to sea-sickness.

At half-past eight he was walking up the Steps to the Incident
Room. Hardly anyone about; cats sprawled elegantly on the sunny
side, performing their morning toilet; the postman was on his
round; Borlase, with bucket and mop, was washing down his shop-
front.

A nervous 'Good morning' from the photographer.

Already the press-release had brought reporters with photographers in tow and there was a group outside the Incident Room.

'Is it murder?. . . Any connection with the girl?. . . Is it true that
he was scared of something?. . . Is that why he was press-shy?'

Wycliffe made his way through. 'I can't tell you anything because
I don't know anything. As soon as I have the result of the post-
mortem I'll talk to you.'

In the Incident Room there was a feeling of being under siege and
it must have been the same at Roscrowgy for there had already been
a report from the man on duty about fending them off.

His table was dotted with little piles of paper neatly arranged.

Horton had left a memo, preliminary to his full report. Wycliffe glanced through the clipped sentences:

'. . . fire almost certainly started in the area where the body was found. The initial intensity of the blaze suggests paraffin or similar . . .A 20-litre drum, screw-top missing, was identified by Prout and his assistant as the drum in which they stored fuel for the generator. . .it was said to have contained less than half that amount. . .Possible that paraffin was poured over the body, then set alight. . .'

Nothing really new, he was waiting for Franks to pronounce. Potter said, 'The chief for you, sir.'

Mr Oldroyd, the big-chief in person. 'You've run into a hornet's nest there, Charles! Sorry about the holiday. . . .The case is bound to draw a lot of attention and there will be plenty of sniping. . . . Have you got all the assistance you need? I know you like to work with a small team. I'll do my best to keep the press off your back. Pity about Cleeve. I can't say I *enjoyed* his books but they were compulsive reading. They seemed to catch the spirit of our time, like Terry Wogan and sliced bread.'

The chief, dispensing moral support.

Another memo on his table informed him that C.R.O. had no record of Cleeve's prints so he had never been convicted of any crime. A criminal record might have explained his fear of publicity and, perhaps, his fate.

Detective Sergeants Smith and Lane were at Roscrowgy with a D.C. to assist. Smith and the D.C. would make a systematic search of Cleeve's suite of rooms while Lucy Lane smoothed their path with the family.

Franks came through at last, and after the usual preliminaries, salted with Franksian cynicism, he said, 'I have had a hell of a job with this chap, Charles, but there's no real doubt; he was killed in the same way as the girl.'

'Have you found the dart?'

'Yes, among the odds and ends that were gathered up with the remains, but God knows where it got him.'

'Have you been able to do any tissue analysis?'

Franks laughed. 'Don't rush me, Charles! I'm fragile this

morning. I've done preliminary tests on liver tissue and on muscle preparations taken from the rump—both show unmistakably the presence of nicotine. I've got other samples and later I may be able to give you some idea of probable concentration but I think you can take it that they poisoned Cleeve before they cooked him.'

That was what he had wanted to hear, if not in those words. It would give the press something and be of some consolation to the family. He translated the pathologist's words for the benefit of the waiting reporters:

'The preliminary indications are that Mr Cleeve was poisoned and that he died before the fire.'

'Poisoned in the same way as the girl?'

'It seems so.'

'Are you saying that he was murdered?'

'This is now a murder inquiry.'

'That makes two.'

'Yes, I had worked that out.'

'Is it true that Stride made a statement to the police in connection with the murder of Celia Dawe?'

(Of course it would be "Stride"; the public for whom these boys were working had never heard of Cleeve.)

'Yes, he did.'

'Was he wanted by the police in connection with that case?'

'No; his statement along with facts already known to us, made it possible to eliminate him as a suspect.'

'Stride has always avoided publicity like the plague; is it possible that something in his past caught up with him?'

A leak, or a shrewd deduction? Wycliffe said, 'I don't know the answer to that. There must be many reasons why a man would want to avoid publicity; I can think of several at this moment.'

They let him go, more or less good-humouredly, but a crowd was gathering and that would take up the time of another uniformed man who could be better employed.

Wycliffe drank Potter coffee and moped about the Incident Room trying to clarify his ideas. The case seemed to split into two—the Exeter end, where Sergeant Mitchell was digging into Cleeve's past and trying to establish a motive; and the Roseland end, where the murders had been committed and the job of the police was to identify the killer. Laura Wynn linked the two locations but was she the only one?

He let himself out into the sunshine; the reporters had gone but they would be back; the emmets had resumed their wanderings in search of God knows what—the Golden Fleece or the Second Coming. He turned up the hill towards Roscrowgy.

What if, after all, it turned out to be a purely local crime—even a family affair? Then what of the threats Cleeve had talked about? Were they real or had he invented them to draw attention to a danger which he saw but dared not name? With Cleeve out of the way Patricia would surely be a wealthy woman in her own right. . . .Was it possible that someone—Tull, for instance. . . ?

He was wool-gathering. Cleeve's whole point had been that, whatever happened, it would have nothing to do with the family. But Celia Dawe and David Cleeve were dead and they hadn't been killed by remote control.

At the top of the hill he turned in through the white gates where there was a policeman on duty; he walked through the garden and into Henry's Field.

Henry's Field was like a painter's palette, with splashes of yellow gorse, a whole spectrum of greens, and some synthetic purples from the heathers. Nature advertising her wares, blatant and shameless. The bees were busy, the students too; plump girls in tight bras and shorts in uneasy alliance with awkward angular youths.

They watched him pass and answered his wave with suspicious reserve. He wondered how Prout was managing without his hut.

He was taking the short-cut to Kitson's cottage; the path led past the ruined hut and joined the lane just beyond it. He continued along the lane and entered the trees—trees that were wind-blasted at first but rose later to the dignity of a high canopy. It was utterly silent. Abruptly he came upon the clearing with the cottage set in a neglected garden surrounded by a decaying fence. Wycliffe thought it might be a good place to live for anyone not bitten by the improvement bug.

Kitson was sitting in an old wicker chair by the front door, reading.

He looked up as Wycliffe pushed open the creaking gate. 'Ah! I expected you yesterday.'

They went into the living-room where a pleasant smell of stew came from the kitchen and one could hear a lid trembling on a saucepan that was simmering too vigorously.

'Excuse me, I must see to my lunch.'

When Kitson returned he sat at the table, one elbow resting on it, the injured side of his face cupped in his hand.

'You know, of course, that Cleeve's body has been found?'

Kitson said, 'I was over there last evening. My telephone has been out of order and it was only repaired this morning.'

'Was it out of order on Wednesday night when Cleeve went missing?'

'I don't know; I only found it out when Christie and Andrew came over in the morning to ask me if I had seen their father.'

'So you didn't telephone him on Wednesday night?'

Kitson's manner became more reserved, cautious. 'No, I did not.'

'Someone or something induced him to go out late at night and to cross Henry's Field in the dark.'

Kitson said nothing and Wycliffe went on: 'What was wrong with your phone?'

'The engineer said the line had broken opposite the hut where the fire was; he seemed to think it might have been something to do with that. The telephone to the hut came off the same pole.'

'When did you last see Cleeve?'

'On Tuesday evening. Periodically Patricia takes pity on her bachelor acquaintances and then she lays on a decent meal for them. She did on Tuesday.'

'Who were the bachelors?'

'Her brother—Geoffrey Tull—Gervaise Prout and myself. Prout, of course, is a bird of passage.'

Kitson had very dark brown eyes of bovine serenity, in sharp contrast both with his pallid skin and his almost bird-like awareness. He avoided looking at a companion directly and spoke, as it were, in profile so that he seemed to be talking to someone else.

'Have you known the Cleeves long?'

A quick glance from the dark-brown eyes before answering. 'I met David in London in '61, I think it was. That was before he married Patricia. He had a flat off Gower Street and he was spending his days at the British Museum reading room, getting together material for *Caliban*—his best book, in my opinion, but the one we hear least about. As it happened I was working in the museum too, but we actually met in a pub. We found that we had interests in common and we've kept loosely in touch ever since.'

He spoke slowly with pauses between each sentence in the manner of a man who is much alone.

The room was long and narrow with low ceiling beams—two of the cottage rooms knocked into one. A paraffin lamp hung from gimbals over the table. The walls were lined with improvised shelving, loaded down with books, and there were books on the table along with a sheaf of manuscript notes and an ancient portable typewriter. Most of the books were in Russian or in some other language which used the Cyrillic alphabet. Furniture was minimal and basic. A tabby cat slept on one of the two window-sills, next to a jam-jar of wild flowers.

'So you've known Cleeve for more than twenty years; when did you come down here to live?'

'I moved in here nearly two years ago. I was fed up with London and I asked David if he knew of some little property I could buy or rent. He offered me this, so I cast off the ball and chain and here I am.'

'Did you see a lot of Cleeve?'

Kitson produced a little machine for rolling cigarettes and charged it with tobacco. He worked mainly with his right hand for his left shared in the injuries to the left side of his body and the fingers seemed to be stiff and poorly co-ordinated.

'He would drop in here three or four times a week, usually in the early afternoon.'

'And the last time?'

'The last time he was here on Monday morning, but that was unusual.'

'He had a particular reason for coming?'

Kitson extracted a passable cigarette from his machine, tapped it down, and lit it. 'Yes, he had a particular reason; he wanted somebody to talk to.'

'Something was worrying him?'

Wycliffe received a sidelong glance. 'I think you know—at least the kind of thing I'm talking about. He told me he had spoken to you.'

'He told me a story about warnings or threats he had received through the post but he refused to give me enough detail to take any action.'

An emphatic nod. 'Exactly! According to him he had been receiving these things for months but he never discussed their nature or the reason for them. All I can say is that he got very agitated when one was due.'

'You mean that he knew when to expect them?'

Another quick glance. 'Didn't he tell you that? Oh, yes, he knew when one would come. Sometimes I wondered if it wasn't all in his imagination or even whether he was sending them himself, but he seemed genuinely scared and now he's dead.'

'He had one of these things on Monday?'

'Yes.' A pause while Kitson re-lit his cigarette which did not seem to draw very well, then he went on: 'Like a lot of highly creative people David lived in a world largely of his own imagining and, to some extent, signals from outside had to be tailored to fit.'

Wycliffe was looking out of the window through tiny panes which gave a chequered view of the sunny wilderness. Everything was still and the silence was so profound that one felt subdued by it—muted. He shifted irritably on his chair. 'But he *is* dead so it seems the threats must have been real enough and if you or I had persuaded him to talk he might be still alive.'

Kitson shook his head. 'I don't deal in "ifs". As I see it, we are born and we die, we have little say in either event so what gives us the idea that we can influence the bit in between, I don't know.'

'Did Cleeve ever speak to you of his life before you met?'

'We never discussed the past; I assumed that like me he preferred to forget what had gone by.'

'When you first knew him was there any question of him being or having been an epileptic?'

320

Kitson's astonishment showed in his face. 'Epileptic? I've never heard anything of the sort. Whatever gave you that idea?'

'Apart from these threats which he discussed with you, did he ask your advice on other aspects of his affairs?'

Pursed lips and a longish pause. 'David needed someone to talk to about himself and about his nightmare view of the world which, I believe, was genuine—and damned uncomfortable to live with. Sometimes it seemed to me that he felt guilty for being human; he would quote papa Nietzsche—"this disease called man" and all that. . . .Once he said—no doubt he thought it up in advance— "We are God's sick joke; automata with a sense of sin." ' Kitson stubbed out his ailing cigarette. 'He was a man possessed by a tormenting spirit and his books were intended as an exorcism, but they didn't work.'

'Do you think he talked to his wife?'

Hesitation. 'That's what he should have done. Patricia would have been a source of strength, but she was a woman and that would have injured Davy's self-esteem. In any case, he was afraid of her.' A short laugh. 'I suppose he needed an ego-boost from a neutral corner and he sometimes came here to get it.'

'Did you influence him in his dealings with Prout?'

A slow smile. 'Poor old Prout is an academic wheeler-dealer like so many of his colleagues these days, scrambling for grants and subsidies; he might as well be selling motor cars or replacement windows but it happens to be archaeology. David had little sales resistance.'

'One more question Mr Kitson, were you here the whole of Wednesday evening and night?'

'I didn't leave the cottage.'

Kitson came with him to the gate; so did the tabby cat, stretching its legs and arching its back after a long sleep.

Wycliffe returned to Henry's Field and by the burned-out hut he stopped to look at the dumpy telephone pole perched on the hedge. A new length of wire marked the repair, while the line which had served the wooden hut was coiled and secured to the pole. He continued on, through the wicket gate and into the grounds of Roscrowgy. He rang the door bell and once again he was admitted by the cousin-housekeeper, more mouse-like than ever. She looked at him as though fearful that he might be the bearer of still more bad news.

'I've come to see my people who are working in the library; I know my way.'

She let him pass without a word and closed the door behind him. He walked along the now familiar corridor and up the stairs.

Milli's door was open and she saw him pass, glancing up from her work. Strange girl! Wycliffe wondered what would happen to her now. Probably Cleeve's literary executors would be glad to use her, in which case her future would be secure for a long time.

The library looked much the same except that Smith and Curnow were standing by the big table examining a heterogeneous collection of objects: their haul so far.

Smith complained, 'There's not much here to tell us about his present, let alone his past. According to the little vixen next door, he kept all his papers including his manuscripts, in a safe deposit.' Smith had met his match in Milli.

Wycliffe pointed to two chargers for an automatic pistol which were among the collection. 'No gun?'

'We haven't found one and he's not a registered holder.' Smith picked up one of the chargers. 'These are Mauser 7.63 mm—what we used to call .30 in the days before we went continental. There are quite a few pistols which might fire them.'

Of course, it was quite likely that Cleeve had provided himself with a gun and that he had taken it with him on his late-night excursion, but no gun had been found.

'You might take a look at these, sir.' Smith handed him a cardboard box which had once held cigarettes. 'That was in the same drawer as the ammo, the only locked drawer in the desk. Take a look inside. . .'

Wycliffe lifted the lid and found several ordinary white envelopes addressed to Cleeve in block capitals. He glanced at the post-marks—Durham, Bristol, Exeter, London and Truro.

Smith said: 'Look in the envelopes, sir. Don't bother about dabs, I've been over them.'

Wycliffe slid out the contents of the envelopes on to the

table—five Jacks of Diamonds. Each card was numbered and dated in one of the margins. One of the cards had been torn in two and was numbered and dated on both halves. All were from mint decks and were identical with each other except that the backs of two were pink while the others were blue.

'What do you make of them, sir?' Smith's questions were usually in the nature of a challenge.

'Not much.'

Wycliffe spread the cards out and arranged them in numerical order—one to five; the dates then read: Saturday September 4th; Tuesday March 8th; Friday May 13th; Thursday June 16th and, finally, Monday July 18th—the card which had been torn in two.

Smith said: 'Celia Dawe was murdered on the night of July 18th.'
'So?'

'I don't know.'

'Neither do I but it's worth remembering.'

Wycliffe stared at the five cards: five Jacks of Diamonds which had seemingly arrived through the post at irregular intervals over the past ten months and been interpreted by Cleeve as threats. There was something melodramatic, something juvenile about it all—the Black Spot updated, yet Cleeve was dead and Celia Dawe had died apparently in a first abortive attempt to kill him.

Smith said: 'What about the intervals between the dates?'

'Work them out and see if they mean anything to us.'

Smith set to work, his glasses on the end of his nose. 'The interval between the first and second dates is one hundred and eighty-five days—near enough for six months; between the second and third, it is sixty-six days—just over nine weeks; between the third and fourth, thirty-four days—five weeks; and between the fourth and fifth, thirty-two days, or just over a month. Means nothing to me, sir.'

'Nor to me.' Wycliffe grinned. 'In *Alice* the jurymen added up the dates given in evidence and reduced their answers to pounds, shillings and pence.'

Smith did not smile. 'That would be before we went metric, I take it, sir.'

Wycliffe wondered, as often before, what went on behind that grey and gloomy façade.

They brooded over the cards then Wycliffe said: 'As it happens, the day of the week and the day of the month in the card dates correspond with the present year, but it surely meant more to Cleeve than simply the day on which they were sent. The intervals must have meant something too.'

Smith was staring at the cards over the tops of his glasses. 'You think these dates refer to events in the past?'

'I think they must do; otherwise what significance could they have? We might make a guess at the year.'

D.C. Curnow, a studious young man with old-fashioned ideas of self-improvement, was browsing through the books on the shelves. Wycliffe called to him: 'There's a whole shelf of *Whitaker's* just on your left, bring over a recent one.'

Wycliffe leafed through the almanack to find the perpetual calendar. 'If his wife is right, Cleeve's fears date from before their marriage in 1962.' His finger moved over the tables. 'Here we are, 1955 is the first year before that in which the days fit the dates; the one before that again is 1949. But in 1949 Cleeve was only seventeen—a bit young to start a feud which lasted through the rest of his life. My bet is that the card dates refer to 1955.'

Smith took off his glasses and polished them with a lens tissue. 'You are saying that the dates on the cards refer to events between September 1954 and July 1955—is that right, sir?'

'I think it's a strong possibility.'

With magnanimity Smith said: 'You may be right at that.' He went on: 'There's something else in the same line.' He handed over a lapel badge in the form of a playing card club. 'This was also in the locked drawer.'

A pretty thing; the trefoil shape was done in black enamel and set in plaited gold wire. In the centre of the badge a gilt 'J' was embedded. A Jack of Clubs?

Wycliffe turned the thing over in his fingers. The whole business was acquiring an Alice-in-Wonderland zaniness. 'I'll give you a receipt for this and the cards.'

He was driven back to the Incident Room. No news from John

324

Scales but Inspector Royal had arrived and Wycliffe put him in touch with Cleeve's solicitors.

Afterwards he walked down the Steps; the parade had thinned because it was lunchtime. The photographer and his sisters would be tucking in to something substantial—something with suet in it; Boadicea would probably be toying with a little steamed fish washed down with fruit juice. And Geoffrey Tull? What was the diet of naturopaths in captivity? To judge from Geoffrey's smooth, slightly oily skin, something rich. Perhaps in terms of food he and Laura Wynn would not see eye to eye, but in the matter of preparing a hypodermic dart charged with nicotine they could be an unbeatable combination.

It occurred to him that Cleeve had moved to the Exeter flat in '53 and that he was still there when the Wynns left in September '54—the most probable date for the event recorded by the first card.

Having made himself diet-conscious by his speculations about food he settled for The Vegetarian and ordered an omelette with salad. Afterwards he walked down to the waterfront and went into a pub he had not visited before. He drank a pint of lager, standing at the bar, while a step away from him a group of reporters were having a liquid lunch, but they were far too busy talking shop to notice him.

Jack of Diamonds. . .Jack of Clubs. . .the sort of aliases young crooks might have fancied; tearaways with romantic notions of crime. A gang? The 'fifties were, after all, the era of the Teddy-boy, boot-lace ties and winkle-picker shoes.

By two o'clock he was back in the Incident Room and at a quarter-past John Scales telephoned.

'You've found the man who died twice, sir.' John in buoyant mood. 'David Paul Cleeve, born September 5th 1931 at Bristol, son of David Gordon Cleeve, solicitor's clerk, died October 12th 1954 in Exeter General Hospital of multiple injuries sustained in a road traffic accident earlier in the day.'

Wycliffe sighed his relief. 'Any details?'

'Some, but this goes back to the days of the old city force. Records stirred themselves and blew the dust off a couple of files. It seems that Cleeve had an epileptic fit in Queen Street during the morning rush-hour. The R.T.A. report says he was struck by a bus as he fell, sustaining injuries from which he subsequently died without recovering consciousness. The body was identified by his flat-mate, John Larkin, and the next-of-kin was given as Elizabeth Cleeve, mother.'

'No question of foul play?'

'No hint of it. I've seen the inquest report. Cleeve's doctor testified that he was subject to epileptic seizures and that he was unreliable in taking his medications so that the seizures were not kept in check as they might have been.'

So John Larkin had become David Cleeve and David Cleeve had become the celebrated Peter Stride, one of the western world's best-selling and most controversial novelists. But why had he taken another man's name?

Scales said, 'This will be a meal ticket for the media when they get hold of it.'

But Wycliffe was not thinking of the media. 'You realize, John, that the stuff we scraped together on Cleeve's background no longer applies. The man who was killed on Wednesday night, who married Patricia Tull, and was responsible for the Stride canon, was John Larkin, and we know virtually nothing about him except that he didn't have a criminal record. We start from there. I imagine Larkin had other than aesthetic reasons for changing his identity and we've got to know what they were. We've only got the Exeter flat as a starting point; I know it's nearly thirty years ago, but there must be people in Exeter who still remember him. Get some men on it, John, and see what you can do.'

The widow took the news with no outward sign of shock or distress and she made no attempt to contest it. She was silent for a while then in a resigned voice, she said, 'If what you say is true, and I have no reason to doubt it, who was the man I married?'

'At the time of Cleeve's death your future husband was calling himself John Larkin and I have no reason to think that was not his real name. The two men, Cleeve and Larkin, were journalists and they shared a flat in Exeter. Laura Wynn, the woman who makes jewellery, lived with her mother in another flat on the same floor.'

A tremor of distaste. 'That is unfortunate! Did this woman know that my husband was. . .that he was impersonating someone else?'

'No, she thought that her memories of the two men had become confused; she had not known them very well.'

'But she recognized him?'

'As one of the two—yes. At the time Cleeve was killed, she and her mother had already left Exeter.'

Another prolonged silence. One of the large casement windows was open and a cool breeze stirred the curtains. Patricia sat very still; obviously she was trying to grasp the implications of what she had heard.

'Was my husband a criminal?'

'He was never convicted of any crime but he must have had some compelling reason for taking on another man's identity.'

'To escape being caught?' Wycliffe did not answer, and after a pause she said, 'Will all this have to come out in the press?'

Cleeve's words came back to him: 'I don't have to tell you what the family of a murdered man has to go through if there is any mystery about the crime.' He felt sorry for the woman but there was no reassurance he could give. 'It must come out; the reason for your husband's change of identity is almost certainly connected with how he came to die.'

'Yes, I'm sorry.'

He changed the subject. 'Do you know if he had a gun?'

'A gun?'

'An automatic pistol; we found ammunition for an automatic in a locked drawer of his desk, but no pistol.'

She shook her head. 'If he had a gun, I knew nothing of it, but there was so much I didn't know.'

'In the same drawer—the only locked drawer—we also found these.' He drew out of his pocket the envelope containing the playing cards and laid the cards out in order on a small table close to her chair. Finally he added the little lapel badge.

'May I?' She picked up one of the cards, then another; when she had examined all five, she put them back on the table and picked up the lapel badge. 'I don't understand—what are these things?'

327

Wycliffe said, 'Each of the cards, as you see, is dated, and the dates run from September 4th to July 18th. Without going into detail, we think those dates refer to the years '54 and '55. There can be no doubt that these were the warnings which he spoke to me about.'

She looked from the cards to Wycliffe. 'They mean nothing whatever to me. It seems all the more strange because he hated card games and I doubt if there is a pack of cards in the house.'

Wycliffe said, 'We shall have to find out what they meant to your husband.'

She nodded. 'I suppose so, but I shall be sorry if what you discover about his past casts a shadow over his memory and over our children.'

He had no more questions and he stood up. She was apologetic. 'I really am sorry not to be more helpful but I know so little. . .'

'If anything occurs to you, however trivial it may seem. . .'

'I will let you know, of course.'

She came with him to the door. He had left his car down the drive by the white gates but instead of making in that direction he walked round the house to the rhododendron tunnel and on through the wicket gate to Henry's Field.

He felt vaguely depressed, for despite the news about Cleeve's true identity he could see no way ahead. He reminded himself that Celia Dawe's body had been found on Tuesday morning, Cleeve had gone missing on the night of Wednesday and it was now Friday afternoon. Not long for the investigation of a double murder, but his case was by no means wide open. It was not what he called a computer exercise. A girl is found raped and strangled in a ditch by the motorway; a householder is stabbed to death in his burgled house—these are computer exercises—crimes without an obvious context. Thousands of scraps of information have to be matched against each other and correlated—or not. Finally, something like an answer may pop up on the screen if you are lucky enough to have fed in the vital facts and clever enough to have pressed the right keys. But this was definitely not such an exercise; there were clearly defined links between the murdered man and a small number of people.

He muttered to himself a list of names: Patricia, Geoffrey Tull, Laura Wynn, Roger Kitson, Gervaise Prout. . . .He might have added Borlase, the photographer, but he had ceased to take him seriously. Then there was a possible unknown who might have sent the card messages through the post but would need to have been on the spot on Monday night when Celia Dawe was murdered and again on Wednesday night when Cleeve died.

As he emerged from the garden on to the heath he was astonished to see men erecting a small marquee close to the dig; two of the girls were conducting parties round the site—probably made up of people more interested in homicide than archaeology; Gervaise Prout was supervising other students who were taking out a fresh trench near one of the excavated huts. Only a large, roped-off area round the site of the fire, and the presence of a bored policeman, remained as evidence of the tragedy. For the archaeologists it was business as usual. The press had been and gone.

Wycliffe followed a newly made path through the heather and was greeted by a lugubrious Prout.

'I suppose we are right to carry on, Mr Wycliffe. Patricia says that we should, though I have little heart for it at the moment.' After a pause he went on: 'We have come across a length of walling linking this hut with another, not yet excavated, and the interesting thing is that the wall seems to have been built from stones brought up from the seashore . . .'

Wycliffe said, 'I see you have a marquee going up.'

Prout sighed. 'Yes, we had to have something if we were to carry on and that will serve as long as we don't have any unseasonable gales.'

They stood for a while, watching the students clearing soil from either side of the newly excavated wall.

Prout said, 'I suppose you have just come from Patricia? I met her briefly yesterday evening in the lane on the way to the cottage. She is a remarkable woman.'

'The cottage?' Wycliffe playing dumb.

'Kitson's place.' Prout stooped to examine the loosened soil by the wall. 'You have something there, Donald. . .Let me see. . .' He came up with a piece of pottery which he rubbed free of soil with his thin fingers. It was part of a largish pot and it included a segment of the rim with an area decorated with a spiral motif. 'Glastonbury ware—rather later than most of our finds, perhaps first century. . . . Go carefully, Donald, there is probably more.' He turned back to Wycliffe. 'What was I saying? Oh, yes—Patricia, a dear lady, so kind and generous. I dare say Kitson arouses her compassion.'

The reporters were back outside the Incident Room, though not in strength. Perhaps his proper course would have been to prepare a statement on the Cleeve/Larkin change of identity and issue it then and there but he decided not to be precipitate.

'No developments I'm afraid. Believe me, we're working on it.'

'The widow won't talk to us.'

'Can you blame her?'

'Is it true that Cleeve's life was threatened?'

'I've told you—no developments. I'll give you a statement when I've got something to say.'

Sunlight streamed in through the tall narrow windows of the old schoolroom and there were splashes of coloured light on his table, due to a bit of stained glass in one of them. He was in a strange mood, suddenly everything had become unreal: the bare schoolroom with its peeling green walls, the battered tables, the scratched filing cabinets, his colleagues bending over their reports. . . .He had known such experiences since childhood when, quite suddenly, everything seemed remarkable, nothing was ordinary any more. His mother would say: 'Why aren't you playing with your toys, Charles?' Later, at school, it was 'Day-dreaming again, Wycliffe!' Now D.S. Lane was watching him and probably thinking, 'Why does he just *sit* there?'

He forced his thoughts back to the case, to his brief catalogue of names: Patricia, Geoffrey Tull, Laura Wynn, Roger Kitson, Gervaise Prout—one of them? Or two of them in collusion? Of the five, three were newcomers: Laura Wynn had lived in the village for just over two years, Kitson for less, and it was only eighteen months since Prout's first visit to talk about the dig. Cleeve's playing cards had started to arrive ten months ago. Laura Wynn and Kitson admitted to an acquaintance with Cleeve going back more than 20 years. Those were the facts.

And those cards; the five Jacks of Diamonds, their dates as enigmatic as the strangely stylized features of the two-headed knaves. Taken along with Cleeve's secrecy about them and the Larkin/Cleeve identity switch, they must surely mean that Larkin had been involved with others in some criminal act. Yet Records had no trace of him, so he had escaped the law. Had his accomplices been so lucky? If not, the threats and his reaction to them might be explained.

But after 28 years?

He brooded while the little splashes of coloured light on his table crept nearer the edge.

Cleeve had employed a firm of Exeter inquiry agents to investigate Laura Wynn; had he thought it worth doing the same for others? Such firms were notoriously cagey but with a little pressure they could usually be induced to co-operate and it was a line worth following. It occurred to him too that whatever had prompted Larkin to adopt his flat-mate's identity must have happened while he was in Exeter. D.S. Mitchell was looking after enquiries at that end but a visit would do no harm and it would be a chance to look in at headquarters. . . .He was talking himself into it. The truth was that he felt the need to look at the case from a different perspective.

He turned abruptly to Lucy Lane: 'I'm going home this evening; I shall be in Exeter tomorrow and I expect to be back either tomorrow evening or early on Sunday morning. I'll keep in touch.'

'Any special instructions, sir?'

'Yes, I want a round-the-clock watch on Kitson. Unobtrusive, so try not to use the foot-putters. I simply want to know his habits, his comings and goings and any visitors he may have.'

'Is he to be followed if he goes out?'

'No, that won't be necessary.'

At a little before five o'clock Wycliffe was on the quay, waiting for Helen to return from her trip.

'There she is now, Mister. That's Billy's boat jest rounding the

331

point. I told 'ee Billy wouldn't be late tonight, 'ee got a fishing trip laid on for six an' no gear aboard yet.'

The tubby little man in a squashed sailor-cap was pointing to a beamy craft, low in the water, making her way up the creek.

'What's it been like today outside—rough?'

'No; sou' east by east, a bit o' breeze. They'd run into some chop going but they've 'ad wind an' tide be'ind 'em coming back. I reckon they'll be coming ashore direc'ly thinking they'm bloody Nelsons.'

'Wasn't he sick at the start of every voyage?'

A fat chuckle. 'So'll some o' they 've bin I reckon.'

Helen came ashore, flushed by sun and wind but there were a few pale faces.

'Had a good day?'

'Marvellous! I wish you could have come.'

'I thought of going home tonight; I want to look in at the office and there are one or two enquiries in Exeter. . . .I shall be back Sunday morning if not before. Do you want to come?'

She hesitated. 'No, I don't think so, we might as well get what we can from the cottage, it seems silly to go home. You'll sleep at the house?'

'Where else?'

'Then I'll ring Nora and ask her to air the bed.'

Nora was a daily woman who had agreed to sleep at the house and look after the cat while they were away.

Chapter Seven

WYCLIFFE ARRIVED HOME in the late evening. The Watch House, an old coastguard station, stood overlooking another estuary, another river. A mile upstream was the little village of St Juliot, and beyond that the naval base and the city sprawled over its creeks and hills like a grey lichen encrusting the landscape. But of this, nothing could be seen from the Watch House, here there was only the channel and the slopes and fields opposite. Now they were visible through a golden haze, the last rays of the setting sun.

'Why do we go away?'

Nora, a pragmatist, said, 'I suppose because you want to. I'll get you something to eat.'

He poured himself a drink and took it out into the garden. A tour of the demesne, taking stock, his every movement monitored by Macavity, green-eyed and stand-offish after days of having only Nora for company. Grass to be cut, weeding and dead-heading to be done, hedges to be trimmed, but no damage—no damage because no gales.

A makeshift supper, then bed.

Saturday

By eight o'clock next morning he was in his office but his personal assistant was already waiting for him. Diane, alias the Snow Queen, alias the Ice Maiden.

'Mr Scales intended to be here but there's been a big robbery somewhere near Buckfast—silver and glass, a connoisseur's job, he said.'

She was blonde and exquisite, made up with resolute restraint, a

333

hint of eye shadow, a touch of lipstick, a whiff of perfume—no more. She could have been of any age between twenty-two and thirty; the record said twenty-eight but she would hardly change for many years to come. 'Beauty in cold storage,' Scales said. With it all she was inexorably efficient.

'Your appointment with Sowest Security is for twelve o'clock, with a Mr Jim Harris. It will take you an hour to drive to Exeter (she always allowed for his sedate driving) which means you must leave by ten forty-five.

'Mr Scales asked me to remind you that D.S. Mitchell is in charge of the enquiries in Exeter and you can contact him at the Central nick there.'

He was fiddling with the things on his desk, the telephones, the clock calendar, the desk diary—putting them back where they *belonged*.

Diane said, 'I was sorry about your holiday; I hope Mrs Wycliffe wasn't too disappointed.'

He spent an hour dealing with the paper work she presented to him and left for Exeter on schedule.

He liked Exeter, it was his idea of the right size for a city and it was still a cathedral and market town not dominated by industry. Despite Hitler, post-war architects and developers, enough of the old town survived to preserve a sense of history. He parked off Fore Street and walked to Langdon Row where Sowest Security had their offices over a building society. He presented himself at the reception desk on the second floor at one minute to twelve. Diane had done it again! A pert brunette with a high and prominent bosom admitted that he had an appointment and he was shown into a rather seedy office where a little man with dark curly hair was feeding papers into a pocket file labelled with the name of a famous firm. Mr Harris had rehearsed the occasion.

'Ah, Mr Wycliffe! I'll be with you in one minute. . . .Do sit down.'

Harris put the file in a drawer and extended a soft hand. 'Always a pleasure to assist the official arm—provided there is no betrayal of a client's confidence, eh?'

'This client is dead.'

Mr Harris had broad, squat features and his wide mouth had been extended in a toothy smile, now it contracted promptly. 'Dear me—'

'Murdered. David Paul Cleeve of Roscrowgy-in-Roseland. He employed you just under a year ago to investigate a lady called Laura Wynn and, more recently, you may have been asked to supply a security guard for his property.'

'Indeed?' Harris spread his hands. 'At any one time, Mr Wycliffe, we have on our books—'

'I'm quite sure, Mr Harris, that you don't run your business by not remembering clients as celebrated as David Cleeve, or by not knowing that the report of his murder was spread over yesterday's papers.'

Harris was unperturbed. 'I don't concern myself with the day-to-day work of my operatives, but I do know that Cleeve was a client, as you say. I also saw the report of his tragic death in the paper yesterday. What, exactly, did you want to know?' The smile was back but less expansive.

'Whether Cleeve employed you to investigate other subjects and, if so, who they were and what you found out.'

A hoarse chuckle. 'It's a good job we don't stand on ceremony round here, Mr Wycliffe. Some of my acquaintances in the business would want an application in triplicate pinned to a court order before they would part with that much.'

'Does that mean that you did have other commissions from Cleeve?'

'One other.' A sly smile. 'But I really shall have to refer to our records if you want details.' He shouted: 'Bring in the Cleeve file, Sue!'

A minute or two passed then the girl with the high-rise breasts teetered in and dropped a pocket file on her boss's desk; she went out again without a word spoken.

Harris riffled through the contents of the file and came up with a few pages of typescript clipped together. 'Here we are! The subject was male, Caucasian; name of Shirley—Jack Philip Shirley. Our client said the man had been released from Parkhurst in October 1960 after serving five-and-a-half years of an eight-year sentence for

335

burglary. At that time Shirley was twenty-nine years old. . .six-foot-one in height, and weighed approximately two hundred pounds. We received our instructions last March. . .'

'What were you expected to do?'

'To find out what had happened to him in the last twenty-odd years.'

'And what did you find?'

Harris showed his yellowing teeth. 'I hope you'll remember this when the occasion arises, Mr Wycliffe. . . .We had no trouble in picking him up after Parkhurst. He was an electrician by trade and he got a job with a firm near Southampton docks. Eighteen months later he was still there but then he was caught flogging material from the firm's store and sacked. They didn't prosecute and Shirley just faded out. We didn't pick up any trace of him again until a fortnight ago. I'd even asked Mr Cleeve if he wanted us to go on with it because these enquiries cost money—'

'What happened a fortnight ago?'

Harris turned the pages of the report. 'You can see for yourself. We had a report—largely by chance—that Shirley was dead. Not long after he left Southampton he was working for a fly-by-night firm in Brixton and it seems he contracted pneumonia and was taken to hospital where he died within forty-eight hours—a weak ticker. Here's a copy of the death certificate, dated August 15th 1962.'

'You reported this to Cleeve?'

'On the 15th of this month I sent him a copy of this.'

'Have you any idea why Cleeve was interested in this man?'

A grimace. 'We don't investigate our clients, Mr Wycliffe; we shouldn't keep 'em long if we did.'

'I would like a copy of that report; the department will pay reasonable clerical charges.'

'Really?' Harris was ironical. 'But I wouldn't like to milk the Law. I'll get Sue to run off a copy, it will stop her brooding on her boobs for ten minutes. As you go out, tell her where to send it.'

Wycliffe was beginning to like Harris and they parted with mutual regard.

He joined the Saturday-morning shoppers. One could still catch the atmosphere of a country market-town with the farmers and their wives coming in from the villages for a morning's shopping and a meal out. He promised himself a decent lunch later.

In March, probably at the time he received his second playing-card warning, Cleeve had instructed this security firm to investigate Jack Philip Shirley, released in October 1960 after serving five-and-a-half years. That meant that Shirley had been tried and sentenced early in 1955—the key year as Wycliffe saw it.

He made for the Central nick and received V.I.P. treatment. He drafted a telex to C.R.O.—"Urgent and Immediate. Details of offence for which Jack Philip Shirley received eight years in 1955." He directed that the reply should be sent to his headquarters. Criminal Records would have to dig in their card indexes for Shirley's offence ante-dated Big Brother's computer.

D.S. Mitchell arrived; he was responsible for trying to fill in the detail of Larkin/Cleeve's stay in Exeter. Mitchell was young, hard, and ambitious; a career cop with a very clear idea of where he thought he was going. Mr Polly would have recognized him instantly as a fully paid-up member of the Shoveacious Cult. At the moment he was bright-eyed and bushy-tailed.

'I've got something on the Mellor Street flats, sir.'

Perhaps Wycliffe looked vague, for Mitchell went on: 'Where Larkin shared a flat with the real Cleeve on the same floor as the Wynn woman when she lived there as a girl. . .'

Wycliffe re-orientated. 'Well?'

'There's an old man, living in a home out at Heavitree, who occupied the flat below the two men.'

'Good! You've talked to him?'

'This morning, sir. He's quite with it—I mean he's mentally alert.'

Wycliffe had a feeling that Mitchell might have been reluctant to say the same of him.

'He remembers Larkin and Cleeve and he says Larkin gave up the flat immediately after Cleeve's death which wasn't long after the Wynns went. As he put it, "It was all-change on that floor."'

'Anything else?'

'Yes. He says that about six months after Larkin went, the police

337

came enquiring about him; they questioned everybody in the building, but he had no idea what it was all about.'

'You'd better see if you can find anything in our records.'

'I'll get right on to it, sir.'

When Mitchell had gone Wycliffe leafed through the telephone directory in search of Prouts. There were more of the clan than he had supposed, but only one Gervaise C. and his address was given as Bankside, St Germans. He wanted to see where Prout called home and it turned out to be not a great way from the Watch House; both were on the Cornish side of the river. He could drive over that evening or leave it until he was on his way back to Roseland in the morning.

Before leaving Exeter he ate fillet of sole with cream and onion sauce and drank a single glass of lager, sharing a table with an aged clergyman who must have slipped from between the pages of Trollope. He lectured Wycliffe on the relative merits of Bath, Portland and Caen stone for building churches. All this within sight of the great west front of the cathedral.

Afterwards, feeling philosophical, he walked to the car park, collected his car, and drove back to headquarters.

Saturday afternoon: the big, ugly building, a honeycomb of glass and concrete, was almost deserted and his footsteps echoed in the empty corridors. His own department was reduced to one detective sergeant and two constables.

He spoke to Mr Oldroyd, his chief, on the telephone, then drafted a statement for the press. Saturday afternoon was a good time to issue a press release as nobody would expect him to lay on a briefing until Monday morning. The statement confirmed that the murdered man had been threatened for some months before he was killed. It went on to say that the man known to the public as Peter Stride, and in private, as David Cleeve, was in fact, John Larkin. All this was as neatly wrapped up as a potato in its jacket and Wycliffe hoped that it would take the media a while to work out the implications.

There was a reply to his telex, succinct, but heartwarming in its promise: "Jack Philip Shirley sentenced eight years Bristol assize 13th May 1955 for his part in burglary of Shotton House, Yeovil, Somerset 4th September 1954. Indicate further details."

338

Wycliffe was pleased, and it was the dates which pleased him; they checked with those on the first and third of the playing cards sent to Cleeve; which must mean something. But Shirley was dead and had been for 20 years when the cards were sent. He certainly needed details but he preferred to get them from a less impersonal source than Criminal Records.

He telephoned Jim Clarke, his opposite number in the Somerset police and a companion of various official jaunts and jamborees.

'Yes, I know about the case, Charles, but it was before my time here. The papers called it The Shotton House Shooting—'

'Shooting?'

'Yes, a police constable was shot and killed by a man resisting arrest after a burglary. As far as I remember there were four men involved but only two were caught—one of them got the chop.'

Murder! And murder of a police officer, a crime which at that time was almost certain to incur a death sentence.

Clarke was saying: 'Officially I suppose the case is still open. What's this all about, Charles?'

Wycliffe explained and Clarke offered to turn up the files.

'I'd rather talk to someone who worked on the case; is there anyone still around?'

Clarke laughed. 'I'll say! Joe Enderby; it was Joe's hour of glory as a chief D.I. He's retired now, of course—living with his daughter near Chard.'

'Do you think he would talk to one of my chaps or to me?'

'Joe would talk to a brass monkey about that case if he thought the creature was listening. I'll give you his number. . .'

But ex-Chief Detective Inspector Joe Enderby was at a cricket match and Wycliffe arranged to ring him later in the evening.

Scales arrived and for a couple of hours they discussed administrative matters and cases on hand, while in the real world outside the flow of traffic into the city, with people returning from the countryside and beaches, reached its peak. It was seven o'clock when he and Scales parted company in an almost empty car park. He could have driven straight back to Roseland but he had told Nora he would be home for a meal. He decided to take a look at Prout's house, then go home as arranged.

Bankside was not the name of Prout's house, as he had thought, but of a road, lined with detached houses on one side; houses in the upper bracket, worth £80,000 to £100,000 out of anybody's piggy bank. They overlooked the river but the tide was out, leaving an expanse of mud which gave off a rank smell of decay. Trees were obviously encouraged, gardens were immaculate, and those houses which had names avoided the worst excesses—no Dunroamins or Beuna Vistas, and certainly no Teddimars or Patruths. The cars in the driveways were Rovers, B.M.W.s, Audis and Jaguars. In one of the gardens a military-looking gentleman was shaving his hedge with an electric clipper.

'Gervaise Prout? Let me see. . .' He squinted into the evening sun. 'Two, three—four houses along, the one with an *Amanagowa* cherry sticking up like a blasted maypole in the middle of his lawn—quite absurd!'

No car in the drive and the grass around the *Amanagowa* in need of a trim; Wycliffe rang the doorbell. A short delay, then the door was opened by a plump little woman in a floral dress reminiscent of a seed packet. She looked very slightly dishevelled, as though disturbed during a nap.

He introduced himself. 'Is Dr Prout at home?'

A rich brogue and an obvious desire to please. 'I'm afraid not, sir. He's away at present, but I'm his housekeeper. Do come inside, sir, perhaps I can help. . .'

With plausible mendacity Wycliffe said, 'I thought I might catch him at home; I know he's working on a dig down west but it seemed likely that he might come home at the weekend.'

He was shown into a large room, nominally a drawing-room, with lounge chairs; actually a library where bookshelves were interspersed with display cases containing reconstituted pots, querns, spindle whorls, and tools and ornaments of bone, ceramic and metal. . . . Above the cases and shelves the walls were hung with framed photographs of archaeological occasions.

'Like a museum, isn't it? That's what I say to him; more like a museum than a sitting-room.' The housekeeper had obvious pride in her charge. Wycliffe looked in vain for a desk or table. 'Is this where he works?'

'Oh, no! His study is next door—here, I'll show you.'

She opened a communicating door into an adjoining room which looked out on a patio and the back garden. A large, square table, more shelves but this time they were loaded down with the proceedings and transactions of learned societies. Above the mantelpiece there was a portrait in oils of a young girl, a compelling portrait conveying an impression of fragility, so vulnerable that one could scarcely imagine the subject cooking a meal, catching a bus, playing a game, or doing anything other than being her lovely self. But her eyes were strange—oddly blank.

'Isn't she beautiful?' The housekeeper, aware of his interest. 'She must have been his sweetheart when he was young—I suppose she could have been his wife. He never mentions her but there's a photograph of her on his dressing table.' She added, speaking in a lower voice: 'Some tragedy, I reckon. You've only got to look at her to see she wasn't the sort to make old bones.'

Wycliffe changed the subject. 'I should have thought Dr Prout would have been home fairly often, seeing his dig isn't all that far away.'

She shook her head. 'He came up last Wednesday for a meeting at the university, and he spent the night here on the way back—the first time I'd seen him for nearly a fortnight and then it wasn't for long. He was late home from the meeting and not in the best of tempers because he had trouble with his car. He'd left it in the garage down the road and he was afraid it might not be ready for him in the morning.'

'And was it?'

'Oh, yes. I told him it would be; Mr Trewin looks after his regulars.'

As she spoke she was constantly tidying this or straightening that, her hands were never still. 'I suppose you wanted to talk to him about those terrible murders?'

'Yes, I did, but I shall be down there tomorrow, so it's of no importance. I'll talk to him then.'

'He'll be so upset. If I got it right, this Mr Cleeve, apart from being a friend, was paying for the work down there.' She turned to him, shrewdly confiding: 'There's no money in archaeology, you know, sir. If the doctor wasn't well off he couldn't carry on. He's a director of a company—Fecundex—you've probably seen their adverts on the television.'

She came with him to the gate, after failing to persuade him to stay for a cup of tea.

At the corner, there was a garage on what was virtually an island site. 'Bankside Garage: Petrol and Repairs.' Wycliffe slowed down, hesitated, then pulled in on to the forecourt. Thirty years of experience had made him cautious. A dark, youngish man came out of the cave-like interior of the repair shop, wiping his hands on a rag.

'Mr Trewin?'

'He's not here. Can I help?'

Wycliffe produced his warrant card. 'A routine enquiry to eliminate one of your customers from a hit-and-run case.' A euphemism rather than a lie.

'Fire away.'

'Dr Gervaise Prout—his car is a dark-green Granada saloon?'

'You must know that it is.'

'Were you here on Wednesday evening?'

'I've been on every evening this week.'

'On Wednesday evening did Dr Prout bring his car in for attention and leave it with you?'

'He did; the engine was missing—a bit of trouble with the electrics. I told him I'd see to it right away. He said he wanted to drive down west in the early morning and would I leave the car ready on the forecourt where he could pick it up before we opened.'

'You did that?'

'Yes, but Bert—that's Mr Trewin, told me he didn't pick her up until well on in the morning, then he was in a tearing hurry.'

'Thanks, that's all I wanted to know. It eliminates Dr Prout from our enquiry.'

So much for that.

He drove through a tortuous maze of lanes to the Watch House. Nora had a cold meal ready for him—sliced ham with potato salad.

'If you wanted something hot you should've said when you was coming.'

'This is fine.'

'There's beer and a bottle of white wine in the fridge if you want it.'

After the meal he put through a call to ex-Detective Inspector Enderby. A woman answered the telephone. 'I'll get father, it will take a minute or two because he's not as spry as he used to be—arthritis, you know.'

'I'm sorry.'

A few words of introduction and explanation then Enderby was launched.

'Yes, there were four of 'em involved—Jonathan Welsh, Jack Shirley, John Larkin, and Roger John Cross—all in their early twenties. . . .At that time Shotton House was in the hands of the Wallis family and the old man collected boxes.'

'Boxes?'

'Snuff boxes, bonbonnières, patch boxes, rouge boxes—you name it, little things in silver and gold and porcelain; easy to carry, easy to fence—made for it. Lovely! Worth a bit, too.

'We'd had three or four of these robberies with the same M.O. in less than six months and nobody to put 'em down to. You couldn't use the motorway alibi in those days because there was no motorway.'

'How did the shooting come about?'

'It was as the four were leaving the house; one of our patrol cars came up the drive and they were spotted—'

'There was nobody in the house?'

'The family was on holiday abroad and the married couple who had charge of the place were in Wellington overnight for their son's wedding. Somebody who knew the house should have been empty, saw a light in one of the rooms and phoned the nick.'

'Go on.'

'Well the plan was for the four of them to split up as soon as they left the house and, according to Shirley, that's what they did. Welsh had a different tale; he said that when they saw the patrol car, Shirley and Cross bolted, but he and Larkin stayed together. They hared off through the shrubbery in the direction of the boundary fence and the road. It was then that they ran into our young copper using his initiative.'

Enderby was shaken by a spasm of coughing. 'Sorry about that! It's these damned cigarettes—they'll be the death of me yet. Anyway, Welsh admitted threatening the P.C. with a pistol but he said he had no intention to shoot.'

'Did he admit that it was his pistol which killed the man?'

'He didn't have any choice because we were able to show that the bullets taken from the body had been fired from a gun of the same calibre and type as one purchased illegally by Welsh a fortnight earlier.'

'Wasn't the gun ever found?'

'Never.'

'Go on.'

'Welsh claimed that he merely threatened the P.C. to frighten him off but that Larkin grabbed the gun from his hand, slipped the safety catch, and fired three times at point-blank range. He said Larkin had panicked and would have gone on firing if the gun hadn't jammed.'

'It doesn't sound very likely.'

'No, and it didn't impress the judge or the jury. In his summing up the judge said, "You may think, members of the jury, that a man who carries a loaded weapon while perpetrating a crime, intends to use that weapon if the occasion arises." Anyway, Welsh got what was coming to him. Killing a copper in those days was a sure way to the big drop.'

'Did the others know that Welsh was armed?'

'Shirley swore that he didn't and he didn't think the others did either. I was inclined to believe him—Welsh was a wild man—a vicious streak there.

'As you know, it was six months later when we got two of them and, to be honest, we wouldn't have got them if Shirley hadn't tried to flog a couple of snuff boxes. He fingered Welsh but he'd lost touch with the others and didn't know where they were. We eventually traced Larkin to Exeter but the bird had flown long before. . .That was it—until now.'

'Presumably Welsh had a family?'

'Oh, yes. Very respectable people; his father owned a business in Newton—fertilizers and horticultural supplies—that kind of thing.

Of course it was a great tragedy for them. There was a sister too; it seems she doted on her brother and I remember reading a long time after that she had committed suicide.'

'What was Shirley like?'

'Not very bright—that was my impression anyway, though he was supposed to have been a wizard with alarm systems. He learnt his trade as an electrician in a factory that made the things so I suppose he knew something about them. I don't know what happened to him when he came out of jail but it wouldn't surprise me if he got back in soon after.'

'I suppose there was a hue and cry after the other pair—Larkin and Cross?'

'You're telling me! More hours and overtime than I care to remember, and all for nothing. There was a rumour that Cross had tried his luck abroad and ended up as a mercenary in darkest Africa but I've no idea if it was true.'

'Presumably you had some background?'

'Yes, but they were both loners to some extent. Larkin had been brought up as an only child by his mother; they lived in Crewkerne and she made a small income painting and selling pictures. When Larkin left school he got a job on the local paper; mother died, the boy had to do his National Service and that's where he met the others. . .'

'And Cross?'

'Something of the same story except that mother was a former member of the *Ballets Russes*—Ukrainian by birth, and married to a British businessman who died young and left her fairly comfortably off. The boy went to Oxford and read languages, then he had to do his National Service and, like I said, that was where the four of them got together.'

Wycliffe's thanks were sincere; the kind of information Enderby had given him wasn't the sort one finds in the files.

'When I'm your way we'll have a jar together.'

Enderby said, 'No bother! It's nice to be taken down and dusted now and then.'

Early to bed.

✱

345

On most fine Sunday mornings at some time between eight and nine he would be walking along the foreshore to St Juliot, the village nearest the Watch House, to collect his newspapers. But this Sunday, by half-past seven, he was already well on the way back to Roseland. The roads were quiet, hardly any traffic down the county and only a sprinkling of cars and caravans the other way. The bulk of the weekly emmet migration and counter-migration takes place on Saturdays, much of it under cover of darkness.

Wycliffe took stock. On the whole he was pleased with his weekend's work. He had identified the criminal act, 28 years ago, which seemed to be the source of Cleeve's fears and the motive for his murder. Four men: Jonathan Welsh, Jack Shirley, Roger John Cross and John Larkin—the Four Jacks? Was that too fanciful? Whether it was or not, three of them were dead. Welsh had been executed, Shirley had died a natural death, and Larkin/Cleeve had been murdered. That left Cross. . . .It occurred to Wycliffe that Cleeve had not, apparently, made any enquiry about Cross. Did this mean that he knew where Cross was or what had happened to him?

Progress. But was he any nearer finding out who had first threatened, then murdered Cleeve? Both he and Cross had escaped the law; they had that much in common. . .His thoughts chased each other in circles but he was beginning to feel optimistic. He even sang in a cracked voice:

'There'll be blue birds over the white cliffs of Dover. . .' and on the few open stretches of road his speedometer clocked an almost unprecedented 70.

'I'm high,' he told himself, 'it must be Nora's egg and bacon.'

He turned off the spine road which links the granite moors through the county and travelled south-westwards into china-clay country. A glimpse of sunlit sea as he approached St Austell entranced him and even the grim moonscape of the china-clay workings failed to depress. By half-past eight he was back in Roseland and entering the village, past the villas which bordered the creek. The pines and palms and a limpid quality of the light created a Mediterranean air, then he rounded a bend and the whole waterfront of the village was before him. It really was a toy-town

346

village, the little houses painted in pastel colours, self-consciously neat, most of them with their tubs of flowers outside. There were few people about, only the boatmen getting their craft ready for the day, carrying cans of fuel and waterproof cushions across the quay and down iron ladders to their moored boats.

Wycliffe parked his car and let himself into the cottage. Helen had just got up and was making coffee.

A welcoming kiss and, 'Shall I get you some breakfast?'

'I've had the full treatment from Nora—bacon, egg and tomato—"A man needs a good breakfast inside him," Nora said.'

'I'll bear it in mind but what about a cup of coffee for now?'

He telephoned the Incident Room to say that he was back; and Division with instructions to send another telex to C.R.O.—the full treatment on Welsh and Shirley.

Helen said, 'Any chance of meeting for lunch?'

He was tempted but decided against. 'No, I can't promise anything.'

A few minutes later he was turning off the waterfront up Zion Steps. The shops were closed. He wondered how Geoffrey Tull would be spending his Sunday. With his brother-in-law's money on the family horizon the future must look brighter. And Laura Wynn?

In The Vegetarian benches were stacked on the tables and a woman was on her knees washing the floor. As he approached the photographer's Borlase came out of his shop followed by the hideous yellow dog on a lead. The photographer was in his Sunday suit of mottled grey. He saw Wycliffe, pretended not to have done, and turned up the Steps, then he changed his mind and faced about with a nervous smile.

'Ah, Mr Wycliffe! I wasn't expecting to see you, they told me you were away.'

'Did you want to see me?'

Borlase looked paler, more pasty than ever; his eyes were bloodshot and his manner was timid. 'Only to tell you about the arrangements for Celia's funeral. I've got the coroner's certificate and I—we have arranged the funeral for two o'clock tomorrow. Celia is being taken into our chapel in the morning and we shall gather there for a short service at two o'clock before proceeding to the cemetery.'

'I shall try to be there.'

He walked along Chapel Street to the Incident Room and felt that he had been a long time away. D.C. Shaw was duty officer and D.S. Lane was sitting at her table; both were reading Sunday newspapers so crime did not press on the Lord's day.

'I thought you might want a word, sir.'

'I do.' He gave her an account of his progress. 'What news of Kitson?'

'He hasn't done anything exciting; he seems to have a regular routine—'

'Does he know that he's being watched?'

'It seems not. Weekes and Trembath have divided the daylight hours between them and they say he's never given the slightest sign. If he does know he must be playing some sort of game.'

'That wouldn't surprise me.'

Lucy referred to her reports. 'On Saturday morning he was up at half-past seven when he let the cat out, then there was music, apparently from a record player. Trembath, who has an ear, says it was Schumann. At a little before nine Kitson came out of the cottage leaving the door wide open and went off carrying a shopping bag. An hour and a half later he was back with a load of groceries and whatever.'

'And after lunch?'

'After lunch he was typing for a while then he had a visit from Mrs Cleeve who went in without knocking. She had her dog with her and the dog settled by the front door, very much at home. Mrs Cleeve stayed until four and after she'd gone, more typing, then music for the rest of the evening and bed at about half-past ten.'

'No other visitors?'

'No, sir.'

Wycliffe was restless, unsure of his next move. He ambled about the drab hall, stooping now and then to retrieve screwed-up bits of paper which had missed the waste bins, fiddling with the carousel, staring out of the window at the drama of life in Chapel Street. From time to time he checked the wall clock against his watch.

Finally, at twenty minutes to eleven, he came to a stop by Lucy Lane's table.

'I'm going to talk to Kitson; he's on the telephone so you can reach me there if you want me.'

'Good luck!'

For some reason he felt cheered.

Chapter Eight

Sunday July 24th

THE SINGLE BELL was clanging out its summons to loyal members of the establishment, while dark-suited men waited at the chapel door to welcome the non-conforming elect. Exactly one week earlier Wycliffe had been calling on Sergeant Pearce and was taken to The Buckingham Arms for a drink. At that time Celia Dawe would have been in one of the other bars and David Cleeve was probably pottering about in his library-study afflicted by that Sunday-morning lassitude which is the fate of unbelievers. Now they were both dead, but nothing seemed to have changed, the village went about its business and its pleasures and the sun still shone. Wycliffe recalled that someone had said, 'Living is like making a hole in water.'

He was walking up the now familiar hill; the prolonged drought was taking its toll, the hedges were dustier, the grass browner and the last of the foxgloves had lost their petals. He passed the gates to Roscrowgy. Somewhere across the river they were harvesting— unthinkable on the Sabbath when he was a boy. At first sight Henry's Field seemed deserted but as he turned off the road he saw a couple of the students, towels over their shoulders, strolling from tents to wash-ups. He crossed the field, passed the caravan, and glimpsed Prout's white head bent over some task with the spectacled Wrighton at his side. Neither of them looked up. He reached the burned-out hut, turned down the lane through the wood, and approached the clearing. D.C. Trembath emerged from the trees like Uncas, the last of the Mohicans.

'He's working, sir; every now and then the typewriter clatters away for a bit, then it's quiet again.'

350

Trembath had been seconded from division; a mountain of a man but light on his feet, and with the gentle features and manner which often go with great bulk.

'Have you seen him today?'

'Only when he put the cat out just after seven.'

Wycliffe said, 'I want you to come in with me.'

He opened the creaky gate and together they walked up the path to the front door. Kitson was at the table with the typewriter in front of him. In the middle of the table the cat was fast asleep.

Kitson looked up in mild surprise to see Trembath blocking the doorway. 'Ah! The spy has come in from the cold.'

Wycliffe said, 'Detective Constable Trembath.'

'Won't you both sit down? Bring up a chair from the corner there. . . .Mr Trembath, make yourself comfortable if you can.'

Wycliffe said, 'One or two points. . .'

'I thought you people kept that for when you've been interrogating some poor devil for days on end—"One or two points. . ."'

Kitson's manner was light, bantering, but Wycliffe sensed that he was keyed-up, braced for a climax, and this would be the more understandable if he knew that he had been under observation for 36 hours.

In a conversational tone Wycliffe said, 'Jonathan Welsh, Jack Shirley, John Larkin, Roger John Cross.' A lengthy pause, then: 'All four were involved in a burglary at Shotton House near Yeovil on September 4th 1954.'

Wycliffe had settled as comfortably as he could on his hard chair and was filling his pipe. 'Do you mind?'

'No! Smoke by all means—you too, Mr Trembath. I've noticed that during your vigil you favoured cigarettes; so do I, though Cleeve used to call them coffin nails.'

Poor Trembath looked like a naughty boy.

Wycliffe went on, 'In trying to avoid arrest, Jonathan Welsh shot and killed a policeman. Six months later he and Shirley were arrested. Welsh was hanged for murder and Shirley was sentenced to eight years for burglary. . .' Wycliffe's speech and actions were deliberate and slow, as though he was setting the tempo for a protracted session. He added, 'But I think you know all this.'

Kitson turned briefly to face Wycliffe. 'Why should I know anything of these people?'

Wycliffe said: 'Cleeve must have known them; he employed a private inquiry agent to find out all there was to be known about Shirley, and you were very well acquainted with Larkin.'

'Indeed?'

'Of course, you prefer to speak of him as Cleeve and I find it difficult not to but, as we both know, Cleeve was the name he adopted when he was wanted by the police after the Shotton House killing.'

Kitson tapped ash from his home-made cigarette. Trembath stared at a threadbare rug on which there was no trace of pattern remaining. A little clock wedged between books on a shelf became obtrusively audible in the silence.

Kitson said, 'Is this going on for much longer? If so I would like to do something about my lunch.'

Wycliffe shook his head. 'I shouldn't worry, Mr Kitson; if the only inconvenience one suffers from all this is a late lunch then it will be nothing to complain of.

'Returning to these four young men; they must have had romantic notions of crime. The Four Jacks—I wonder why they picked on jacks? The knaves in the pack, I suppose?'

The sun was shining through the little square panes of glass, directly on to the faded spines of rows of books. Another very hot day but small windows and thick walls kept the room pleasantly cool.

'I wonder which of the four was the Jack of Diamonds? The five playing cards sent to Cleeve were Jacks of Diamonds.' Wycliffe was speaking very quietly as though half to himself. 'Roger John Cross is the only one of the four not accounted for; the other three are dead.'

Trembath shifted his position and the strut-back Windsor creaked in protest.

With a sudden briskness of manner Wycliffe said: 'Do you have a birth certificate, Mr Kitson?'

'Not in my possession.'

352

'But you could get one?'

'I suppose so, if necessary.'

Wycliffe reverted to his former casual, rather sleepy manner. 'I wonder what it would tell us? That your name isn't Kitson but Cross? Of course, birth certificates are not to be relied upon; look at your friend Cleeve; I've no doubt he had a birth certificate—don't you have to in order to get married?'

Kitson was silent for a long time then he said, very quietly: 'All right, having got so far you are sure to find proof if you look for it.'

'You are Roger John Cross?'

'Yes.' He said it with a sigh which might have been of relief.

A plane flew low over the cottage, shattering the silence; the cat leapt off the table and padded about the floor bemused. Kitson lifted the creature on to his lap and made soothing sounds. Then, without any prompting, he began to talk:

'It was bound to come to this when David was murdered and perhaps I wouldn't have wanted it otherwise. . . . We met, the four of us, by chance or fate or whatever you like to call it—four beds in a row in a barrack room when we were National Service rookies. For some reason we formed a natural group—at least it seemed natural in the circumstances. Shirley could scrounge anything anywhere; Welsh could talk his way round the recording angel, while Larkin and I were as green as grass and scared of the whole business—the cretinous NCOs, the military bull, and the stark reality of dossing down with twenty others in the same room. We were more than glad to latch on to a couple who seemed to know their way about. I'm not sure what we contributed but there were no complaints.' One side of Kitson's face twitched in a smile.

Aware of legal thin ice, Wycliffe warned him that he was under no obligation either to answer questions or talk about events which might incriminate him.

He responded with a laugh. 'What have I got to lose?'

Outside the long grass, the nettles, the docks and the brambles got on with the business of take-over in silence.

'The Korean war was going strong and, after training, we were drafted with the British contingent and largely owing to Welsh's wire-pulling we kept together.'

Kitson paused and began the lengthy process of rolling one of his cigarettes. He spoke, concentrating on the manipulations involved. 'Fifteen months out there strengthened the bonds between us, whatever they were. We became known as The Four Jacks— inseparable and slightly crazy.'

'Was that when you adopted the playing cards as symbols?'

'No, not then, it was just that we happened to have—all four of us—names that might be reasonably shortened to Jack.'

Wycliffe reminded himself that he was engaged in a police investigation; the atmosphere was more conducive to quiet nostalgic recollection.

'When we finally got back to this country, Welsh said that we mustn't just separate and lose sight of each other so, at his suggestion, we agreed to meet every three months. As I said, Welsh was a persuasive talker, but I don't suppose any of us thought it would last long. Our first get-together was on a Saturday early in September '52, and it came as a surprise to three of us. We met at a pub we had frequented during training but after a drink or two we went to an hotel where Welsh had laid on a little dinner—very civilized. There were place cards, each one a jack from a deck of playing cards with our names on them—that was how the playing-card business started. Typical Welsh, by the way, he had a strong element of fantasy in his make-up.'

'Who was which of the four jacks?'

'Shirley was the spade, Larkin the club, Welsh the diamond, and I was the heart.' A twisted grin. 'Don't ask me on what grounds the allocation was made. Anyway, in addition we were each given a little lapel badge in the shape of our suit with a "J" in the middle.'

'These quarterly meetings continued?'

'They became a ritual.'

'Did you communicate with each other in between?'

'No, at each meeting we fixed up the next. It was Welsh's idea that they should be our only contact and as we settled back into civilian life and moved around we didn't even know each other's addresses.'

'What sort of man was Welsh?'

Kitson took time to consider his answer. 'Blond, with almost

354

feminine good looks; slight of build but hard as they come.'

'I was thinking of his character.'

'I know, but that's more difficult. Have you read *Medicus*?'

'Yes.'

Kitson re-lit his cigarette. 'I've always thought that Aldo in *Medicus* was based on Welsh.'

'Wasn't he the chap who in some way or other mutilated every girl he slept with?'

'Yes, but at other times he was a pleasant, entertaining fellow, generous, affectionate, even sentimental. That was Welsh; I'm not saying that he mutilated girls but he certainly had a cruel streak which didn't show most of the time.'

It was odd, this concentration on Welsh, the man of the four who had been dead for 28 years; yet Wycliffe felt convinced that he was the key. Even the warning cards sent to Cleeve had been Jacks of Diamonds.

'Did you know anything of his family?'

'Only that they were in some sort of business. They must have been well off because Welsh was always in funds and he was sometimes absurdly generous—embarrassingly so. As to the family, I remember some mention of a sister—Barbara, I think she was called.'

'What about the burglaries?'

Kitson continued stroking the cat for a while without speaking then he said: 'If you mean how did they start, it was a casual conversation at one of our get-togethers—at least I thought it was casual at the time. When we met again we seemed to go on talking from where we'd left off; there was a lot of nonsense about a modern Raffles but I didn't think anyone took it seriously. By the second or third meeting after it was first mentioned, we were actually planning a robbery—just for an experiment. That was the way things went when you were with Welsh—he was a remarkable chap. He would float an idea, let it hang around for a bit, start a discussion leading to argument, then say, "Why not put it to the test? Just for the hell of it. . . ."'

'The idea was to pick a smallish country house where the owners were away or just out for the evening, take only small, easily portable objects of moderate value, then separate—no get-away car or any of that nonsense; each to find his own way home with his share of the loot, to meet later at an agreed rendezvous. Welsh knew something that I didn't at the time—Shirley had worked in a factory where they made alarm systems.

'Well it worked and, inevitably, we had to repeat the experiment. Welsh did all the planning; he selected the houses, decided on the timing and the kind of thing we should take. He seemed to know these houses from the inside and I suspect they were the houses of friends of his family.'

'What happened on the night of the killing? Did you know that Welsh was carrying a gun?'

Kitson paused long enought to collect his thoughts. 'No, I didn't know. As to what happened, we came out of the house and immediately saw a police car in the drive with two uniformed men getting out. We scattered and I saw no one after that but I did hear three shots which seemed to come from the other side of the drive.'

'Do you think it likely that Welsh and Larkin kept together?'

'According to what Larkin—strange to call him that now—told me, they did not, and I believed him.'

'When did you first meet Larkin again after the Shotton House affair?'

'It happened just as I told you, when we were both working in the museum. By that time, of course, he was calling himself Cleeve and I was Kitson. We stuck to our new names quite firmly, even when we were alone together.'

'What happened to you in the meantime?'

The cat was clawing at the tablecloth and Kitson lifted her down to the floor and straightened the cloth. 'A great deal, but nothing relevant to your case.'

'Your injuries?'

'Yes, but don't get any wrong ideas about them.' A grim smile. 'I spent some time abroad and this was the work of an unfriendly gentleman I met.'

'Did you kill Cleeve?'

Wycliffe's manner was relaxed, conversational, as though they were having an academic discussion rather than pursuing a police inquiry. 'There is the point that if you didn't kill him, who else could have had sufficient knowledge to do it in the way it was done—cards and all?'

Kitson turned to face him and his manner was grave. 'I did not kill him—why in God's name should I? As to who might have done it, don't you think I've racked my brains over that?'

'With any result?'

'None. When David received those cards I thought it was leading up to a blackmail attempt, and I said so. I could just about see Shirley in that role, but we know now that Shirley was dead and, in any case, the cards led not to blackmail but to murder.'

'What did Cleeve himself think?'

Kitson made a helpless gesture. 'I really never knew what he was thinking about anything, I sometimes wonder if he knew himself. He lived so much in that strange fantasy world of his books that he half believed in the reality of situations he had created. He pretended to believe that he was a guilty man—deserving of punishment—that was the image he presented.'

'And it was false?'

A frown. 'I'm not saying that it was false, but it was exaggerated.'

Wycliffe stood up. 'I shall leave D.C. Trembath to keep you under surveillance until the Somerset police take over responsibility.'

'What happens then?'

'I don't know; you may have to face a charge of burglary.'

'And?'

Wycliffe turned away and when it seemed that he would not answer, he said: 'After twenty-eight years?'

As a small boy Wycliffe had played Snakes and Ladders with his sister. On their board an awesome snake writhed across from within a few squares of *Home* to somewhere quite near *Start*. He could still recall what it felt like to land on that repulsive head and have to slither down all the way under his sister's watchful eye. He felt much the same now, oppressed by a sense of anticlimax. The playing-card nonsense had been unscrambled and that should have been the end of the case. But why would Cross want to kill Larkin or Kitson kill Cleeve? For his wife? Wycliffe had already decided that that kite

357

wouldn't fly. He doubted if they were having a real affair and to imagine Kitson setting up that elaborate charade with the cards—for what? It would only point back to him in any case.

Lunchtime. Nora's breakfast at six-thirty was only a memory. He hesitated between a pub meal and The Vegetarian, but pub food on a Sunday was often below its best and he wanted something light. He was glad to find The Vegetarian still with several empty tables, then he saw Dr Hodge, but not before Dr Hodge had seen him.

'Come and join me!' Hodge was having soup with a crusty roll. 'My wife has gone to St Ives to see her mother; I'm on call. This soup is good if you like celery. What's the matter with you? You're taking all this too seriously—you look wisht about the gills, as the Cornish say. . . .So our late lamented genius was hiding under yet another name—hiding from something pretty nasty I should say, reading between the lines.'

'Is there something in the papers?'

'Radio—I haven't seen a paper today, too busy. I heard it on the car radio.'

The waitress came.

'I'll have the same as Dr Hodge.' He was in a strange mood, weak and suggestible.

Hodge said, 'Now there's a rumour going round that Mrs C wasn't Caesar's wife after all. It's a wicked world, but surely a woman like her wouldn't fancy poor old Kitson?'

There were a few enterprising reporters outside the Incident Room but he got away after promising a Monday-morning briefing. Inside, most of the tables were occupied, the ponderous routine of the case churned on—most of it precautionary, in case things turned sour, then everybody could say: 'No avenue unexplored! No stone unturned!' Nobody with egg on his face. Well, he didn't make the rules of the game, thank God.

He sat at his desk and looked across at Lucy Lane feeling mildly guilty. The girl seemed to be there whether she was officially "on" or "off" and he wasn't bringing her into the conduct of the case as he would have done with her predecessors. He called her over and they talked for half an hour.

'So where do we go from here?'

She didn't answer at once, then she said, 'Do you think we know all we should about the Welsh family? I mean, if they really believed in the young man's innocence and in Cleeve's or Larkin's guilt, then there would be a powerful motive, even after this lapse of time.'

He was impressed because it was the conclusion he had reached himself. 'But it's not only a question of motive; there must be someone here and now—'

'There's a Miss Byrne wants to speak to you, sir; she won't say what it's about.' Dixon, the duty officer, in a low voice.

Wycliffe glanced across the room to the duty desk. Carrie Byrne, the housekeeper-cousin from Roscrowgy, looking anything but dowdy in a plain emerald-green frock. 'I'll talk to her.'

It was only as he got close to her that he saw her face was blotchy and the skin round her eyes was creased with tiredness. The woman was on the point of breakdown.

'You want to speak to me, Miss Byrne?'

'In private.' The words seemed to be jerked out of her and she looked round the room with apprehension.

'Of course!' He led the way between the tables to a little room at the back which was probably a store-cupboard when the place was a school. Now it had a little table and two bentwood chairs. Light came from a small window high up; like a cell.

She sat, holding her handbag with both hands. 'I haven't been able to sleep since that night. . .I feel so ashamed. . . .'

Wycliffe, sitting opposite her, said nothing, but tried to look kindly and attentive.

'Patricia has always been good to me—more like a sister than a cousin, and I've everything to thank her for.'

'What do you want to tell me?'

'It's about the night David. . .'

'Wednesday night.'

'Yes, he had a telephone call saying something had happened to Roger.'

'Roger Kitson?'

'Yes. That was why he went out and if he hadn't gone he

359

wouldn't have been killed.' She suppressed a sob which became a snort; she took out a handkerchief and held it to her nose and mouth.

Light dawned on Wycliffe.

'You were with Mr Cleeve at the time?'

She nodded, helplessly, like a child.

'You were upstairs in his part of the house?'

'We were in bed.' Words came in a rush now. 'I wasn't really being disloyal to Patricia; I mean, if it hadn't been me it would have been one of the others and he had to go out for them. David couldn't do without women. . .'

'Is there a telephone in his bedroom?'

'No, it rang in the library but the door between was open.'

'You could hear what he said?'

She nodded again.

'Tell me.'

She wiped her nose and her eyes. 'He sounded irritable; he said: "Oh? What do you want at this time of night? . . .Of course I'm alone!" Then his voice changed and he was obviously worried. I can't remember his exact words but they were something like: "Is he hurt? . . .Don't be a fool, you must know. . . .No, don't do that, I'll be right over. . .tell him I'm on my way." I heard him drop the phone then he must have picked it up again because I could hear him dialling, but he couldn't have got through because he didn't speak to anybody. He came back into the bedroom and dressed very quickly.'

'Did he say anything?'

She hesitated. 'He just said, "It's about Roger. You'd better get back to your room." He went into the library again, I suppose to fetch something, then he was gone.'

It left a pathetic picture; Carrie gathering together her clothes with the shreds of her modesty and stealing back to her room.

'Did you get the impression that he was speaking to Kitson?'

'No, I didn't; I thought he was speaking about Roger to someone else.' Her lower lip trembled. 'I should have told you this before but I couldn't bear. . .'

'Never mind, you've told us now. I'm going to hand you over to

360

Miss Lane and she will write out what you have said and ask you to sign it. We shan't use it unless it is absolutely necessary.'

He left the two women together in the glorified cupboard which had to serve as an interview room. The unassuming, unaspiring Carrie Byrne had solved one problem which had troubled him—how Cleeve had been lured out of his house late at night and induced to cross Henry's Field in the darkness. Now he knew how, but by whom?

He went back to his table. It was very hot and the atmosphere was somnolent. He was thinking about Welsh, the young man with whom it had all started. Jonathan Welsh, Jack of Diamonds; blond with almost feminine good looks, slight of build, but hard, a great talker, affectionate, sentimental, but with a cruel streak; sometimes absurdly generous, a strong element of fantasy—Kitson's assessment. Enderby had said '. . .a real wild man—a vicious streak'.

Contradictory, mutually incompatible elements provide the mix for every one of us but this recipe must have added up to more than ordinary instability and on a July morning 28 years ago that young man had been led out from his cell to the scaffold.

'Welsh is dead!' Wycliffe muttered to himself.

Dixon came over from the duty desk. 'Somerset police are sending a detective sergeant and a constable to interview Kitson, sir.'

'Do they want to take him back with them?'

'No, sir. Their instructions are to take his statement, then all the papers will be sent to the D.P.P. for an opinion.'

Which probably meant that Kitson and the police would be let off the hook.

He had thought about Welsh, now he was thinking about the crime, the crime of the Four Jacks. Four young men had set out to commit a particular type of crime—robbing country houses. It was a good recipe; there was something in it for everybody—profit, risk, and for the squeamish it was all down to insurance. Shirley was dim and probably went along with the others because one way of avoiding slog was as good as another. Larkin and Cross probably needed the element of adventure, even of romance. If it wasn't robbing the rich to pay the poor it was the next best thing. And the playing-card Jacks were a symbol of their camaraderie; they even had badges.

All this planned and organized by Welsh who had thought up the scheme and skilfully sold it to the other three. . . .And Welsh was the wild man.

Did it really add up? Wycliffe wasn't sure.

It was Sunday and he had been on the go since six-thirty. Suddenly he was very tired. 'I'm going home.'

The trippers were returning after a day in the sun. On the waterfront there was a general movement towards the car park; at the quay one ferry was loading and another waited for the berth. He had no idea how Helen had spent the day and he felt guilty.

She was waiting for him. 'I've had a lazy day. This morning I went to church at St Just; I had lunch in the wine bar and this afternoon I took a book and lay on the grass below the castle. I think I slept most of the time.'

'Do you want to go out for a meal?'

'If you like, but I've got a couple of veal cutlets in the fridge. . .'

'Suits me.'

They drank sherry in the kitchen while the meal was prepared. Afterwards they sat in the living-room with the window open to the waterfront. Helen was browsing through the Sunday supplements, Wycliffe was drifting between sleeping and waking, slumped in his chair. 'Do you think we know enough about the Welsh family?' Lucy Lane's question; the answer was an emphatic 'No!' It occurred to him that the Welshes had run their business in Newton and it was there that his former sergeant—Kersey—had been transferred as C.I.D. inspector. He got up from his chair.

'What are you going to do?'

'I'm going to ring Kersey.'

It took a little while speaking of this and that then they got to business. 'Do you know anything of a family called Welsh who run some sort of horticultural business in Newton?'

'Afraid not, sir. There's no horticultural firm trading under that name.'

Wycliffe explained what he was after. 'The son was executed in '55; I think there was a daughter who later committed suicide. I want to know what happened to the family after '55 and to their firm. . . .Phone me at the Incident Room sometime tomorrow afternoon, you should have something by then.'

When he replaced the phone Helen said, 'Are they all right?'

'What?'

'The Kerseys—how are they getting on?'

'Oh, fine. . .fine!'

'Is Joan still having trouble with her back?'

'I forgot to ask.'

'Oh, Charles!'

Chapter Nine

THE PROMISED PRESS briefing was held at sub-division, partly because there were better facilities, partly to keep the reporters out of the village. He had to drive to King Harry, cross the river by the chain-ferry, then drive up the hill past Trelissick to the Truro road. As a way to work there was much to recommend it, especially on a morning when the air was as fresh and sweet as on the first day of creation. Georgian Lemon Street was a pleasant sight too, but the nick, though newish, was much like any other when one was inside.

He gave a succinct account (he hoped) of the case so far; a digression on the Four Jacks, and a brief résumé of the Shotton House affair. Hard luck on the Cleeve family but there was no way around that. A young man was involved in several burglaries, in the last one a policeman was shot and killed; one of the young man's accomplices was hung for murder, but he adopted a false identity and wrote himself into fame and fortune. Then, nearly 30 years later, after a series of melodramatic warnings, he was killed by a poisoned dart and his body cremated. . . . Plenty of column-inches there; not only for the proverbial nine days but for a re-hash at each stage of the legal grind if it ever came to that.

A little monkey-face reporter whom Wycliffe knew of old, said, 'It's like The Ten Little Nigger Boys, Mr Wycliffe, except that there are only four. One was executed, one died a natural death, one was murdered and then there was one—what happened to him?'

'The police are in touch with the fourth man.'

'Is he in custody?'

'No, we have no case against him and the Shotton House burglary is the concern of another force.'

'May we know the fourth man's name?'

'The Jack of Hearts.'

Guffaws. They were in a good humour, with more than enough to be going on with.

When they had gone the D.I. was waiting for him. 'There's a package from C.R.O. and another from the Somerset police—I was going to send them on by messenger but—'

In the D.I.'s office he unpacked his parcels and laid out their contents. He spent an hour working through the material and ended up with three mug-shots of Welsh, a copy of his official record, and a series of notes taken from statements made at the time. He had also constructed a little table which pleased him:

Dates on the playing cards	*Events which they recorded*
Saturday September 4th	The Shotton House killing
Tuesday March 8th	Arrest of Welsh and Shirley
Friday May 13th	Trial verdicts
Thursday June 16th	Rejection of Welsh's appeal
Monday July 18th	Welsh executed
(The card symbolically torn across)	

A riddle finally solved.

A uniformed copper brought coffee on a tray, a whole pot with a cup and saucer instead of a mug; rich tea biscuits—luxury.

Wycliffe studied the photographs while he nibbled his biscuits. Despite the white-sheet background and the front lighting the man came through. There was certainly something immature as well as feminine about the features, and his mouth had that curious delicacy which one associates with cruelty. But it was the eyes which compelled Wycliffe's attention; they were empty of expression, looking out with a disturbing blankness at the camera and the world. Wycliffe was reminded of young, blond, brainwashed Nazis in their field-grey uniforms with swastikas on their arms. Perhaps that was why this man's face seemed familiar. . . .

Then he remembered the girl in the painting.

It was not an experience comparable with Saul's on the Damascus road, not even with that of Archimedes in his bath, but from that moment Wycliffe knew that he was at last pointed in the right direction.

Enderby had said that the Welsh family ran some sort of horticultural business in Newton, way back in 1955; Prout's housekeeper had told him with pride that her employer was a director of Fecundex—a firm in the same line of business. Coincidence? Perhaps, but add to that the fact that Welsh had a sister and that his mug-shots, despite the unsubtle techniques of H.M. prison photographer, vividly recalled the painting of the girl which hung in Prout's study. . . .

He picked up the telephone and spoke to the switchboard operator: 'I want to know if Fecundex Limited are listed in the Exeter district directory—I'll hold on . . .'

It took only a moment. 'They're listed as Fecundex Horticultural Products—'

'And the address?'

'Tanner's Lane, Newton, sir.'

That seemed to clinch it, but there would be news from Kersey later.

Another telephone call, this time to the Incident Room; he spoke to Lucy Lane: 'I want a couple of D.C.s to keep an eye on Prout—as discreetly as possible but he mustn't be allowed to give us the slip.'

As he approached the village on his way back he turned off the road and up the drive to Roscrowgy. He parked in front of the house and caught sight of Patricia dead-heading a rhododendron bush not far off. He was mildly shocked. Would Helen go on with her gardening routine if he were lying dead? Why not? He had to admit that she probably would; the sensible thing to do. . . . He walked over.

'I wonder if you will spare me a few minutes?'

She dropped a couple of browning heads into a plastic sack. Her features were drawn and she looked tired, but she seemed pleased rather than otherwise to see him.

'I was just thinking that I'd earned a cold drink and I'm sure you could do with one. Let me take you to the courtyard then I'll see about something long and iced.'

They sat on the white metal chairs in the shade of an umbrella maple. The drinks turned out to be lager in tall glasses, misted over. Very refreshing.

He said: 'You may have heard from Kitson how the case has developed?'

'Yes; Roger telephoned.' She was silent for a while, sipping her drink, then she said: 'It is an humiliating experience to discover that for twenty years one has been . . .' She hesitated for a word then went on: 'one has been totally ineffective.'

'Ineffective?'

Her face was turned away from him but her voice betrayed her emotion. 'When I married David I saw it as my job to make it easier for him to do the work I so much admired. Yet in twenty years I never succeeded in winning his confidence sufficiently to help him in the one way which might have meant something.'

Wycliffe said, 'I think you are very hard on yourself.'

'That is kind.' She turned to him, suddenly brisk. 'Forgive me! I am being morbid. What did you want to ask me?'

'About the dig in Henry's Field: I wonder if you know how it came about that Gervaise Prout undertook the work?'

She was clearly surprised and diverted by the question. 'You mean how it all started?'

'Did the initiative come from your husband?'

'No, David was interested in the remains and he sometimes spoke of the possibility of a dig and Christie was keen, but it was a letter from Gervaise which set it going.'

'They knew each other?'

'No, the letter came out of the blue. It simply said that the site was an interesting one and might be important for Iron-Age studies in the south-west. He wondered if David would consider the possibility of a dig if funds could be raised.'

'What happened?'

She placed her empty glass with Wycliffe's on a tray. 'I think David made some enquiries about Prout's academic standing then he invited him down. He was impressed by Prout's enthusiasm and not only agreed to the dig but offered to finance it.' She smiled. 'Something must have impressed him.'

'Didn't it strike you as odd that, avoiding all forms of publicity as he did, he should invite a stranger down and be willing to co-operate in a venture like that?'

She nodded. 'I suppose it did, but I was very pleased; it came at a time when he was beginning to . . . to loosen up, to go out more and to be more responsive to contacts. I see now that he was beginning to feel more secure.'

It was an idyllic spot; the sunshine and shade, the patterns of shadows, the fragrance of flowers and the sound of water trickling into the pool. . . . Wycliffe thought that it might be hard not to feel secure in these surroundings.

'What was your husband's opinion of Dr Prout?'

Such a direct question jarred on her sense of propriety but she responded. 'I think he was amused by him—by his single-mindedness, but also a little irritated. He said once that Gervaise was like an iceberg, only one-seventh above water. Although David was so secretive himself he couldn't stand that characteristic in others.'

'And you—what do you think of Dr Prout?'

A frown and a moment to consider. 'He is an agreeable man with enthusiasm for his subject which he can communicate to others.'

'But?'

She laughed despite herself. 'There are no buts—or only a little one. I have to confess that at first I was irritated by his curiosity. I was a victim, so was Christie.'

'About what was he curious?'

'About us as a family. At one point I wondered if he was trying to steal a march on David's would-be biographers. When he found that we had nothing to tell he stopped asking questions.' She smiled. 'It was only a small thing, mildly irritating.'

Wycliffe got up. 'Thank you for the drink and for being patient with my questions. Do you mind if I go through the tunnel to the dig and leave my car where it is?'

'Please do whatever is convenient.'

She walked with him back to the spot where she had broken off her work and he continued through the tunnel and through the wicket gate into Henry's Field. As he crossed the field he saw that Prout's caravan had been shifted to a position near the marquee and the site of the wooden hut. Nearby a man was working on the telephone pole which carried the wires to Kitson's cottage. Wycliffe went over and found Prout, standing in the shade of his van, watching the man at work.

'I'm having our communications restored, Mr Wycliffe.' Prout being rather self-consciously jovial. 'The phone was previously in the wooden hut and as they are not very willing to connect it to a marquee I'm having it in the van.'

'I suppose you need the telephone?'

A quick glance. 'Without it one feels cut off on these digs, and the students like to be able to ring home. I had to go into the village this morning to phone my housekeeper; one doesn't like to disturb Patricia at this time.'

'I expect your housekeeper told you that I called on her on Saturday?'

A frown. 'Yes, she did. I suppose one must get used to having one's every statement checked in these circumstances.'

'I'm afraid so.'

Wycliffe was no longer watching the telephone engineer, but Prout. 'Odd that Kitson's line should have been cut on the night of the fire, don't you think? His wire came nowhere near the hut.'

'These things happen.' Prout met his gaze, blue eyes unflinching.

With a casual parting word Wycliffe made his way across the site. After a month of almost unbroken sunshine the students were as brown as Indians. Christie, wearing shorts and a bra, her auburn hair caught in a pony-tail, was trowelling away soil from a trench, occasionally dropping sherds of pottery into a plastic bowl. She looked up as Wycliffe's shadow fell across the trench.

He said something fatuous: 'Everything under control?'

She smiled. 'Yes, I think so, thanks.'

He returned to his car and drove back to Chapel Street and the Incident Room. A few minutes with Lucy Lane, then it was lunchtime. He went down the Steps. How long was it since he first set eyes on Zion Steps? Nine days; yet the Steps had taken their place in his daily routine. Now the episode was almost over; in a day or two all that had happened in those nine days would be condensed into just another case-file and the people he had met would either be forgotten or they would be remembered as witnesses who would wait their turn to enter the box at any trial there might be . . .

At any trial there might be . . . a trial in which the innocent would suffer more than the guilty.

Borlase was in his favourite position, just behind the glass door of his shop, looking out. Laura Wynn had customers, he could see her standing behind the counter, serenely detached, while they examined her wares. Farther down, Geoffrey Tull was on his doorstep, talking to a pin-stripe suit with a briefcase. In The Vegetarian all the tables seemed to be occupied.

Wycliffe would have found it hard to say what was in his mind. Was he conning the field? Hardly, because he was no longer in doubt of the outcome. Scarcely aware of any intention he ended up at The Buckingham Arms. Business was good but he was immediately signalled from behind the bar. Polmear's heavy features were flushed and covered with little beads of sweat.

'If this weather goes on I shall just melt away and trickle down the nearest drain.'

'Leaving a fortune behind.'

Polmear grinned. 'You should be here for the other nine months of the year.' He called a waitress. 'Here, Judy, lay-up for Mr Wycliffe in the cubby.'

'Are you going to the funeral this afternoon?'

'Of course! She worked here, didn't she? And she was damned good at her job. I miss her. Life isn't all about bed, Mr Wycliffe—only mostly.'

Wycliffe meditated on this observation while he ate a very tasty quiche with a green salad and drank a carafe of Liebfraumilch.

The graveyard was on the slope above the village; the air was filled with the resinous scent of pines. The mourners gathered at the graveside and they could look down on the houses, descending in steps to the creek. Wycliffe was surprised by their number, most of whom were unknown to him. Borlase was much in evidence in a black suit which must have survived many funerals and was now turning green with age. His sisters had not come. Polmear had squeezed himself into a grey suit which was too small for him and

370

sported a black tie. Wycliffe spotted Dr Hodge and, next to him, Andrew Cleeve, wrapped about with a dark raincoat several inches too short, probably a relic of his schooldays and looking ludicrous in the sunshine.

The words of the burial service, rendered with all the elocutory skill of an auctioneer in a cattle market, still came through as solemn and moving. Celia Dawe's coffin was lowered into the grave and the party was over. People moved away, murmuring platitudes. Wycliffe lingered and so did Andrew Cleeve. The boy looked across at him, tentative, anxious.

Wycliffe walked over to join him. 'A lot of people.'

'Yes, but not many bothered with her when she was alive.'

They walked down the steep slope together. Andrew slipped off his coat and rolled it under his arm. As they reached the gate he said: 'There's something I have to tell you. . . . Mother agrees that I should.'

Wycliffe waited.

'We were talking about what you said to mother this morning when Christie mentioned something I hadn't heard before—that Gervaise Prout was in Exeter on Wednesday and that he didn't come back until Thursday lunchtime.'

'He went to the University for a symposium. Didn't you know?'

'No, I didn't, but his car was in its usual place on Wednesday night. He keeps it in the lane to Roger Kitson's cottage, just off the road. When I was coming back from Truro and saw the fire I got out of the car and ran down the lane far enough to see where it was before haring off home to raise the alarm. Prout's car was there then but I thought nothing of it. Of course when I got home I found that one of your chaps had already called the brigade.'

Wycliffe walked back to the Incident Room, feeling lucky; he had not dared to hope for such direct evidence. Andrew's evidence would clinch a possibility which had been in his mind since he had seen the relatively isolated garage where Prout's car was supposed to have spent the night on the forecourt. An hour's trip either way, the job done, and back before anyone was about. Very cool.

Prout had called Cleeve on the telephone from the wooden hut and Wycliffe thought he could make a good guess at providing the other half of the conversation overheard by Carrie Byrne:

'This is Gervaise.'

'Oh? What do you want at this time of night?' Irritated.

'Are you alone?'

'Of course I'm alone.'

'I'm speaking from the wooden hut; Kitson is here, there's something very wrong with him—'

'Is he hurt?' Anxious.

'I don't know, he—'

'Don't be a fool, man, you *must* know—'

'No, I don't; he was talking wildly and he kept asking for someone called Larkin. Now he's gone quiet and I can't rouse him. Do you think I should call a doctor?'

'No, don't do that, I'll be right over. . . . Tell him I'm on my way.'

That or something like it would have lured Cleeve out of his house into the open. Even so he had tried to check. Carrie Byrne had heard him dial a number to which there was no reply—no reply because Kitson's telephone had been cut beforehand. And Cleeve had gone back into the library—to fetch his pistol?

In the Incident Room Potter was duty officer.

'Anything from Mr Kersey?'

'No, sir.'

But Kersey came through a few minutes later.

Wycliffe said, 'I think I know something of what you've got for me—that the Welsh family business is now Fecundex Horticultural Products.'

'That's right. They changed their name way back in '56 after all the notoriety over the murder case. I've just been talking to the managing director—a chap called Bannister. I know him slightly, we use the same local, and he's been with the firm since the flood.'

'Is the family still involved?'

'There's none of 'em left. They had only the one son, and a daughter, the daughter was a couple of years older and she married—guess who?'

'Gervaise Prout?'

'Ah, you knew. Anyway, he was a research student without twopence to his name but it seems to have been a real love match and Papa Welsh approved. He even persuaded Prout to come into the firm.'

'Did it work?'

'Very well, apparently. Prout was soon in charge of sales and he also showed a flair for gadgetry. He patented several bits and pieces for crop spraying, for greenhouse control systems and that sort of thing. His patents made a nice fat profit for the firm.

'The Shotton House affair came three years after Prout had married into the family and it was the beginning of the end of the Welshes. The parents were devastated, and the sister devoted herself first to proving her brother's innocence then, when that failed, she went all out for a reprieve. It seems she spent her time chasing lawyers, gathering what she imagined to be fresh evidence, and God knows what else. She took a room near the prison and visited her brother as often as the authorities allowed—right up to the last.

'Of course, she didn't stand a chance, it was an open and shut case, and it broke her. Eighteen months after the execution she was put in a mental home and spent a year there, then she was sent home, supposed to be cured. Within a fortnight of coming home she went out into the garden, soaked her clothes in paraffin and set herself alight. . . . Poor old Prout found her while there was still life in her body.'

Wycliffe said: 'And afterwards?'

'Prout stayed with the firm and in 1962 Papa Welsh died; his wife had died three years before. In his will the old man left all his personal estate and a two-thirds' interest in the firm to Prout—the other third went to Bannister.'

'Was that when Prout felt the call back to archaeology?'

'No, it seems he kept up his interest all through but it wasn't until the 'seventies that he began to spend most of his time away from the factory; now he's only there two or three days a month.'

'Did Bannister query your interest in all this?'

'No, he'd read about Cleeve's involvement in the Shotton House business and he seemed to think it natural that we should come asking questions about the Welshes—God knows why.'

'Do you think he'll pass on news of your visit to Prout?'

'I shall be surprised if he doesn't. Is that bad?'

'It doesn't matter at all. In fact, there's something else I want you to see him about, and you can make this official. We need to know whether his firm manufactures or stocks any compounds containing nicotine. If so, we want to know the nature of the preparation, its nicotine content and its availability to anyone with access to the factory. We shall also want a sample for analysis.'

Wycliffe remembered Joan Kersey's back just in time.

'Oh, she's found an osteopath who seems to have a winning way with backs—at least I hope that's what it is.'

Wycliffe's feelings were oddly ambivalent. The three Wise Monkeys must be satisfied at last: Motive, Means, and Opportunity, but if it hadn't been for the luckless Celia Dawe . . .

One more gap: he spoke to John Scales on the telephone. 'I want you to send someone to Prout's house at St German's with a warrant. There's a housekeeper. We want to know whether Prout has a workshop—any sort of D.I.Y. set-up: once upon a time he patented gadgets for horticultural equipment. . . . If there is such a place, put seals on it until we can arrange a proper examination by Forensic.'

Four o'clock and the weather seemed even hotter. Wycliffe's shirt stuck to his back and he was conscious of damp patches under his arms; he was tempted to go back to the cottage for a shower and a change of clothes but decided against; he was inventing ways of putting off the inevitable. Perambulating around the room he came to a stop by Lucy Lane's table. 'I'm going up to the site and I want you to come with me.'

She brought his car to the door; they drove up the hill past the entrance to Roscrowgy, and turned down the lane to the dig. They parked behind Prout's Granada, left the car, and walked down the dry rutted track as far as the burned-out hut.

Henry's Field seemed deserted, the caravan, the tents and the marquee were still there but there were no students to be seen, only the hairy, bespectacled Wrighton, a pathetic figure trailing a plastic sack and stooping now and then to pick up a sweet paper or cigarette packet left by litter-bugs. D.C. Curnow emerged from behind the marquee. 'He's in the caravan, sir; been there since just after one.'

Wycliffe approached Wrighton: 'All on your own?'

The young man looked at Wycliffe through his big round lenses. 'It was too hot to work out of doors so Dr Prout gave them the afternoon off and they've all gone swimming. Dr Prout is in his caravan and doesn't want to be disturbed.' Wrighton seemed to feel excluded from both camps.

Wycliffe knocked on the door of the caravan; no response, so he knocked again. Wrighton had stopped work to watch. Still no answer.

'You wait outside for the moment.' To Lucy Lane.

He turned the handle, opened the door, and found himself in the kitchen section. To his left he was vaguely aware of the sleeping compartment but to his right there was a more roomy area resembling the saloon of a yacht: a table, bench seats, shelves and cupboards, all built in. Prout was sitting at the table and open in front of him was a bulky ring-file of the kind used by students.

He raised his eyes from the file in the manner of one who suffers an unwelcome though anticipated intrusion. 'Ah, you've come.'

Prout had changed, he looked older, but more than that it was as though a mask had been discarded and it seemed to Wycliffe that he was seeing the real man for the first time. Gone the defensive bonhomie; gone, too, the high-pitched voice which had seemed always to tremble on the edge of a nervous little laugh. The face of the man at the table was grave, introspective, and closed.

Speaking very slowly, Prout said: 'There is no point in prolonging this; I am very tired. Of course I realized from the start how it might end and I have no doubt that your case against me is a strong one. I shall make no attempt to defend myself in law.' He paused, resting a slender hand on the open pages of his file. 'For the rest, my justification is here. Nothing of this is mine, it is my wife's work, a record of her fight to establish her brother's innocence and of her efforts to secure a reprieve.'

The door of the caravan had remained open and Wycliffe could

375

see Lucy Lane waiting only a few feet away. He should have yielded to protocol and called her in but he wanted to gauge the temper of the situation first.

Prout had gone back to his file; he was turning the pages with deliberation, almost with reverence, as a monk might turn the pages of a holy book. Wycliffe waited. Only when he had reached the end of the file did Prout look up:

'See what she wrote on the last page.'

The page was blank except for three words, written in a schoolgirlish hand: "I failed him." Melodramatic but, in the context, moving.

Prout's voice became harsh. 'It destroyed our life together and in the end it destroyed her. She spent a year in a nursing-home under treatment . . . They said she was cured but within weeks of her coming back to me . . .'

A long pause, then he went on, 'I made him suffer—though not as much as I would have wished.' He closed the file. 'I've no regrets.'

'And the girl? What about Celia Dawe?'

Prout passed a hand across his face. 'That girl . . .' He shook his head. 'Isn't it always the innocent who suffer most?'

'You believe in your brother-in-law's innocence?'

For the first time Prout showed signs of anger, his pale features flushed. 'Would I have done what I have done otherwise?'

'You could have been wrong, you may still be wrong.'

A faint smile. 'Oh, no! I can't deny moments of weakness—of doubt, but now, thank God, I'm sure.' He turned in his seat to open a little cupboard. 'This is my proof.' He laid an automatic pistol on the table. 'Your experts will tell you that this is the pistol which killed that young policeman at Shotton House, twenty-eight years ago—the crime for which my wife's brother was hanged. It is of the same calibre and make. I took it from Larkin's body on Wednesday night and you will find his prints on it as well as my own.'

Wycliffe reached across for the gun and Prout made no attempt to stop him, then Wycliffe signalled to Lucy Lane to join him. Prout glanced up as she entered but made no comment.

'Gervaise Adam Prout, I am taking you into custody in connection with the murder of John Larkin, alias David Cleeve.

You are not obliged to say anything but anything you do say may be taken down in writing and used in evidence.'

Tuesday July 26th
In the Incident Room Wycliffe was turning the pages of the ring-file. On the first page was a single word: "Jonathan". The file was a detailed record of everything Welsh's sister had done, over a period of four months, to save her brother. It included correspondence with lawyers, Welsh's own letters from prison, correspondence with Members of Parliament, with the Home Office, and even a petition to the Queen. There were detailed accounts of visits and interviews; of rebuffs and, more rarely, of encouragements. There was nothing of sentiment or bitterness in this stark record which spoke for itself, and Wycliffe was moved. Only in two places did emotion break through: a photograph of four young men in battledress was labelled with their names: John Cross, Jack Shirley, John Larkin and Jonathan Welsh. The figure of Larkin was ringed about in pencil so heavily that the point of the pencil had cut into the print; the other instance came at the end where the girl had written, "I failed him."

On an adjoining table the contents of Prout's pockets were laid out: a ring of keys, a few coins, a handkerchief, a notebook and pencil, and a wallet of tooled leather. The wallet contained a few pounds in notes, a couple of credit cards, and four photographs—one protected by a polythene envelope. This was the girl in the painting, his wife. The other three had been "taken off" and enlarged from a group—Shirley, Cross and Larkin; the prints were faded and creased.

Had Prout arrived at Roscrowgy in all innocence and found his quarry by chance? Or had he tracked the man down and made a plausible approach? That was what the photographs seemed to suggest. At any rate, within eight months of his first visit, on the precise anniversary of the Shotton House killing, Cleeve had received the first of the five playing cards.

The atmosphere in the Incident Room was lethargic, deflated; the process of winding down had started. In a day or two they would be moving out and their precious files would be transferred to headquarters, there to provide the ingredients on which lawyers would go to work. The mass of paper would continue to grow and the personalities and events of the case concerned would be slowly digested into a legal soup.

Wycliffe, brooding, shifted irritably in his chair and muttered: 'Adolescent games!'

'Sir?' Lucy Lane at the next table, preoccupied with filing reports.

'Adolescent games and attitudes. That's what this case has been about—people who have never grown up.'

'I'm sorry; I don't understand.'

'I'm not surprised. But didn't all this start with four young men in the throes of a retarded adolescence? They dressed up their crimes in romantic trappings—all the nonsense of reunions, and badges, and calling themselves by the names of cards—like kids playing cops and robbers, or star wars. . . . Then we have the ineffable Prout, married to and deeply in love with a beautiful though fundamentally unbalanced young woman. When she was overwhelmed by the terrible consequences of her brother's wildness and killed herself, he turned real tragedy into melodrama with his absurd vendetta; working out his fantasy at the cost of two more lives—one of them certainly innocent.' He spread his hands in a gesture of helplessness. 'Don't you agree that such people corrupt themselves through a sort of juvenile naïvety?' Then he broke off, slightly embarrassed. 'End of sermon!'

'You believe that the Welsh boy was guilty?'

'He was convicted and sentenced after what seemed to be a fair trial.'

She persisted with diffidence. 'But?'

A vague gesture. 'I've talked to Cleeve and read his books; you've made a study of his work: what impressed you most about the man who wrote them?'

She smiled. 'Write your answer using one side of the paper only; do not write in the margins. . . . I suppose it was his obsession with evil and with our apparent helplessness to control or contain it.'

Wycliffe nodded. 'Perhaps he was one of the Four Jacks who finally grew up and realized his responsibilities.'

'For responsibilities, read guilt.'

'Perhaps.'

The mills continued to grind. Kersey reported that Fecundex held a small stock of an outmoded pesticide containing 40 per cent nicotine; a sample had been sent for analysis. Scales telephoned to say that a garden shed in Prout's back yard was fitted up with the usual home-handyman's equipment and it had been sealed pending the arrival of the man from Forensic.

The message from Ballistics did not arrive until late afternoon. Wycliffe spoke briefly on the telephone then turned to Lucy Lane. 'It seems the gun Prout handed to us is the one purchased illegally by Welsh a fortnight before the Shotton House killing. They are carrying out further tests but they've no real doubt that it fired the bullets which killed the policeman.'

It was the last day of his official holiday and the Wycliffes decided they would have one more excursion to look back on. They would drive to Pendower, walk along the coast to Portloe, and return to the car by way of Veryan.

'Have we got the map?'

'It's in the car.'

'The binoculars?'

'They're on the window seat.'

'We're ready then . . .'

Instinctively they both turned to look at the telephone, but it did not ring.

THE END

WYCLIFFE
AND THE QUIET VIRGIN

Mulfra is a tiny hamlet in Penwith, known for its chamber tomb or 'quoit'. I have taken the liberty of using the name for a village on the coast road between Zennor and Morvah, a village which only exists in the pages of this book.

W. J. B.

Chapter One

MARSDEN OPENED HIS eyes; the plaster between the rafters was greyish white, the rafters themselves cobalt blue, painted by Emma; spiders' webs in the corners. The light from the little window was grey and cold, the air damp; even the sheets felt clammy. He could hear Emma downstairs in the kitchen, running water, the only place in the house where there was water and that came from an overhead tank, pumped from a well.

Marsden scratched himself.

Twenty-five minutes to nine by the alarm clock on the little cast-iron mantelpiece which was also cobalt blue. Marsden raised himself on his elbow so that he could see out of the window. Fine rain out of a leaden sky.

'Bloody hell!'

The front door slammed, then the car door; the starter of Emma's M-registered Mini whined a couple of times, seemed to give up, then in its last gasp, set the little engine puttering. An uncertain cough or two, a spluttering in the exhaust, and Emma was away.

Marsden got out of bed; a large man, fleshy without being fat, powerful; built like a gorilla. A mop of black hair, and a generous moustache; good features, eyes wide apart, and a broad, high forehead. He thought he looked like Balzac and cultivated the resemblance. The locals said that he had Romany blood and that pleased him too. He was forty-six.

He stood by the window, stooping to clear the sloping roof. Down the narrow valley mist blotted out the sea. Brown smoke came from the Lemarques' chimney, the only house he could see, perched some way up the opposite hill, white against the sludge-green heather. A mail van picked a cautious way along the old mine track which led there. He pulled on a paint-stained dressing-gown, fished his slippers from under the bed with his toes, and wriggled his feet into them without stooping. He slouched across the room to the landing, the floorboards creaked under his weight and the jars and bottles on Emma's dressing-table clinked together. He negotiated the narrow, twisted stairs down to the living-room.

A large, square table covered with a plastic cloth and on it, a battered blue enamelled coffee pot and a mug inscribed 'Hugh' (from the days when Emma still believed that he could be domesticated). There was a note in Emma's writing propped against the milk jug: 'I've shut that blasted cat out because he messed in the kitchen again. If it's still there when I come home this evening you'll be doing the cooking, not me.'

'Bitch!' Mechanical, without venom.

Marsden opened the front door; the cat, a complacent tabby, was asleep in the shelter of the porch. Marsden picked him up, made soothing noises, and carried him indoors. He poured milk into a saucer and put it on the floor. 'There, Percy, old boy! She's gone now.' The cat lapped up the milk, purring away like a Rolls Royce.

Marsden felt the coffee pot then went to the kitchen to warm it on the stove. While he was in the kitchen he splashed cold water over his face and groped for the towel. The flow from the tap was a mere trickle. 'The bloody tank's empty again!'

With his mug full of black coffee he came back through the living-room and into his studio, followed by the cat. The studio was a lean-to built on to the end of the house in times past, as stabling for mules. With his own hands he had removed the roof and replaced it with corrugated perspex which gave a diffused north light when it was not covered with moss and gull shit.

He ferreted about, looking for matches, and when he found them he lit the paraffin stove. There was an electric heater but he used that only when he had a model. A canvas stood on one of the two easels: a landscape, blocked in. Although Marsden was best known for his landscapes and marines he was a studio painter. 'None of that muffler and hot-water bottle crap for me; I find my *plein air* in the studio next to the oil-stove; "Emotion recollected in tranquility"—in comfort anyway.' He reached for a brush from the pot, changed his mind and drank his coffee instead, in two or three great gulps. Then he lit a cigarette. Marsden was coming to life, the skin round his eyes seemed less taut and his mouth had lost its sour taste. He moved to the second easel where there was another canvas, this one covered by a cloth; he removed the cloth and stood looking at the painting: Portrait of a Young Girl. She wore a flowered wrap which had slipped to expose one breast, and she regarded herself in a large mirror with an ornately carved frame; her expression intent, frowning. Red-gold hair reached to her shoulders, her cheeks were lightly flushed. Marsden had caught the fine delicacy of the girl's brows, of her lashes, of her lips but mostly he had captured her total self-absorption.

He stood back. 'Marsden, my boy, you're a painter!'

The mirror and the padded seat were still set up in one corner of the studio.

He had told Emma nothing of the sittings which had taken place while she was at work and his studio was sacrosanct, but yesterday he had shown her the painting. He could have written the script in advance:

'That's the Lemarque girl.'

'Full marks for observation.'

'She's jail-bait in any language. How did you manage it? At that age they want more than sweeties. Really, Hugh, you must be out of your mind!'

'I painted the girl, I didn't screw her.'

'Even if I believed you it wouldn't make any difference; she's quite capable of saying that you did.'

'If it came to that I'd prefer her mother; there's a dark little mystery package that needs working on! Unfortunately, now that her husband's out of clink, there's a sitting tenant.'

385

'You're vile!'

His palette for the painting, covered with cling-film, stood on a table by the easel. He couldn't make up his mind whether or not he had finished with it. He replaced the cloth and started to sing in a croaking baritone: 'The rich get richer and the poor get children'.

The cat, couchant by the oil-stove, tucked in his paws and prepared for sleep.

Marsden said: 'I wonder what she would do if somebody locked her in without a loo,' and chuckled at the thought. 'I tell you what, Percy, I'll make you a cat-flap. I know I've said it before but this time I really will!'

The letter-box in the front door rattled and he went back to the living-room.

A small shower of mail on the mat. Marsden gathered it up and shuffled through the envelopes with a certain urgency, then he seemed to relax: Christmas cards for Emma, a couple of circulars, an electricity bill, a letter from a West End gallery: '. . . We regret that we cannot offer you a one-man show in the coming year but if you will consider joining with—' Marsden screwed up the letter and aimed it at the fireplace. 'No, sir! Not with that bloody ponce. We haven't got quite there yet.'

The final envelope was also for Emma. He recognized brother Tim's prissy italic script and he knew those letters by heart as Emma always left them lying about. There would be the usual news of successful-accountant brother Tim, of his pasty-faced wife, and of their two brats—with snapshots thrown in to highlight the attractions of conjugal felicity. Then the brotherly advice: variations on a theme—'I've heard from mum and dad again. Really, Em, I can't understand why you throw yourself away on that man. Apart from being an absolute scoundrel, he's nearly old enough to be your father . . .'

'I am old enough to be her bloody father,' Marsden had said. 'I started early.' He propped Emma's mail on the mantelpiece, against a vase in the form of a fish standing on its tail.

'He's right though, Marsden, you scum! Give the gentleman his sister back.'

The time had come to allow her family to entice Emma away. She was taking over and, in any case, life had grown too complicated.

He opened the front door to stand in his little porch, looking up at the sky. Fine rain still drizzled out of low cloud. '*Gloom!* Damp, grey, dreary, bloodless gloom!' Eight hours between sunrise and sunset, the twenty-third of December, two days to Christmas, the very nadir of the year.

Jane Lemarque was in her living-room; a smoky fire burned in the grate, the room was furnished with unmatched and incongruous pieces which looked what they were, random discards from a more affluent home. She stood by the window, looking out on a familiar scene; mist hid the sea and inland she could just distinguish the grey rectangular bulk of the church tower. This, and the hill opposite, scarred by old mine-workings and capped by a great cairn of boulders, set the limits of her world for days at a time.

Jane had dark hair and deep blue eyes, an oval face, rather pale; and an expression of madonna-like serenity. Only people who knew her well (and few did) realized that though she might seem passive she was anything but serene. Even now as she stood gazing out of the window her lips moved and she murmured a barely articulate form of words, half prayer, half incantation: 'Please God make it all come right . . . Oh, Lord, don't let it happen . . . Dear Lord I promise . . . Don't let Francine . . . Don't let Alain . . .'

She looked across at the painter's cottage, crouched at the foot of the hill, last of the struggling outliers of the village. Marsden, in his dressing-gown, was standing in his porch, staring up at the sky. The sight of the man increased her disquiet. Recently she had tried to avoid coming face to face with him but sometimes on her way to or from the village they would meet. He was always polite but he looked at her in such an intimate and knowing way that she felt vulnerable, naked, so that her flesh trembled and her face burned.

387

Now he was taking an interest in Francine, encouraging and helping her with her painting; he had given her colours and brushes which she believed were expensive to buy. 'Please don't let . . .'

Her attention was distracted from the painter by a figure in an anorak trudging along the narrow road which led from the cove, past the painter's cottage and on to the village. Paul Bateman, youngest of the Bishop clan. The Bishops, Penzance lawyers for generations, lived at Mynhager House down by the cove. Paul was seventeen and for the past six months he had pursued Francine with earnest solicitude. Either he was on his way to the village or he was coming to see her now and she was still in bed. Jane watched the boy. He had reached the painter's cottage and he would continue along the road or he would turn off down a steep footpath to the bridge over the stream. Jane watched him. 'Please God he doesn't come here . . . Please God . . .' But God wasn't listening, the boy turned down the footpath to the bridge.

Agitated, Jane went to the bottom of the stairs and called to her daughter. She could hear the radio playing, the eternal Radio One.

'Francine!' She called twice before she was answered by a voice that sounded petulant rather than sleepy.

'What is it?'

'Paul is on his way here.'

Silence.

'It's nearly half-past nine, don't you think it's time you got up?' Pleading.

'Tell him I'm sick.'

'I can't tell him a deliberate lie.'

'Why not? You want to stop me seeing him.'

'I didn't say that, Francine! I said it wouldn't be a good idea to let your friendship with Paul grow into something more. That doesn't mean—'

'I wish you'd make up your mind what you do mean.' But the radio was switched off. 'All right, I'm coming down.'

Jane felt tears of misery and frustration smarting in her eyes. She returned to the window. Paul was climbing the flight of steps which led up to the front door. She opened the door before he knocked but did not invite him in. The boy stood there, long and lean, droplets of moisture dripping from his hair and running down his face.

'I wondered if Francine would come with me to St Ives this afternoon. John Falls is putting on an exhibition of those crazy models of his. He thinks he might sell one or two as Christmas presents and I said I would come.'

'I can't. I've got the play at the church this evening.' Francine had come downstairs silently; she was wearing a track suit, her hair uncombed about her shoulders.

'I know, but we shall go in the car and be back long before then.' Paul had just passed his driving test.

'I've got to finish learning my lines.'

Jane said, 'So Paul has wasted his trip over here. Why didn't you phone, Paul?'

The boy looked embarrassed. 'I didn't mind the walk.' He lingered. 'If Francine can't come this afternoon perhaps I could pick you both up this evening and take you to the church—unless Mr Lemarque is going . . .'

Jane felt trapped, she didn't dare refuse. 'That is kind of you, Paul. I don't think he will be going.'

'Half-past seven, then . . . Will that do? Earlier if you want.'

'Half-past seven will be all right,' Francine said.

Paul smiled uncertainly and took himself off.

Jane looked sorrowfully at her daughter. 'Really, Francine!'

'What have I done now?'

At Mynhager House, down by the cove, Virginia Bishop was perched on a tall step-ladder in a corner of the big drawing-room, pinning up the last of the Christmas decorations. Elaborate though faded paper-chains festooned from the central chandelier and there was a Christmas tree, draped with tinsel and hung with shiny balls and coloured lights. Seen from this unfamiliar angle the room seemed more shabby than ever; the colours of wallpaper, upholstery, carpet and curtains had merged to the same drab fawn; the gilt-framed oil paintings might have been hanging in a saleroom and the sprigs of holly tucked behind their frames seemed absurdly incongruous. Even the grand piano, Carrie's pride and joy, had a bluish bloom on its polished lid.

Virginia looked down at her sister, kneeling on the floor, putting away unwanted decorations for another year, putting them back into a box which had held them for a lifetime. Virginia thought: Caroline is putting on weight, and slacks do nothing for her figure. At least I've kept slim. Of course, she drinks too much. There was a time when people used to take us for twins. They couldn't now.

She came down the steps and brushed her hands together. 'That cornice is thick with dust.'

'You say that every year, Vee.'

Virginia stood by the window. 'This damned mist, you can't see a thing.'

'What do you expect in December? If it's not fog it's wind.' Caroline got to her feet and stooped to massage her knees. 'Well, that's done for another year, thank God! Why do we bother? Christmas! I feel worn out already and it hasn't even started.'

'We've got Ernest's friend, Wycliffe, coming this afternoon.'

'I can do without reminding. I wish Ernest wouldn't invite people here to stay. Poor old Ada is getting beyond it and the extra work falls on us.'

'Mother used to cope with a houseful.'

'Mother was a marvel but don't let's start getting all sentimental or I shall howl. I need a drink.'

'Where's Paul?'

'I'm not sure but I think he's gone to see Francine.'

'He's been seeing a lot of her recently.'

'Yes, I'd rather he wasn't.'

'Why?'

'For one thing I think she's got all the makings of a little whore.'

'And?'

'Isn't that enough?'

'Yes, but I don't think it's true. I think we see the worst side

390

of Francine. Jenny Eggerton is her form mistress and she was saying Francine's main trouble is that she keeps herself too much to herself. She holds everybody at arm's length—other girls, staff, and boys. Incidentally, Jenny was at a rehearsal for the vicar's nativity play and she was really impressed by Francine's performance as the Virgin.'

'I don't doubt she puts on a good act but she would need to in that role.'

'She's got a wonderful voice for a girl of her age.'

'I know, but that doesn't stop me wishing she would keep away from Paul. Not that what I think will make any difference; I'm only his mother.' Caroline moved towards the door. 'I'm going to fetch that drink; are you sure you won't have something?'

'All right, a small sherry, just to celebrate.'

Virginia was left alone. Thirty-five, a spinster, a teacher of biology in a comprehensive school; at nineteen it would have seemed a fate worse than death, now she thought there were compensations. The mist had thinned and through the mullioned window she could see the lichen-covered balustrade at the end of the terrace and the grey sea beyond. To her left she glimpsed the hump of Gurnard's Head only to lose it again almost at once. Mynhager House, built on the rock platform of an ancient landslip, facing four-square to the Atlantic and backing on a steep boulder-strewn slope.

'Here we are, then!' Caroline with a whisky and a dry sherry on a tray.

They sat on one of the massive settees.

Virginia said: 'Are you meeting Gerald off the train this evening?'

'No, he's driving down, thank goodness!'

'How long is he down for?'

Caroline sipped her whisky. 'I've no idea. The House reassembles on the seventh or eighth but with luck he should have gone back before then. There's a cabinet reshuffle in the wind and they're all running round in circles with their little pink tongues hanging out. It seems Sir James is almost certain to be kicked upstairs to the Lords and if that happens,

Stafford will step into his shoes and Stafford has more than hinted to Gerald that he would be very much in the running as his P.P.S.'

'Gerald will end up in the cabinet himself one of these days.'

Caroline pouted. 'If he doesn't it won't be for the want of keeping in with the right people.'

'You're hard on that husband of yours.'

'You think so?'

'You won't even live in his constituency.'

'I told him when we were married "This is my home".'

'He wasn't an M.P. then.'

'That's his affair.' Caroline rolled the whisky tumbler between her plump hands. 'Incidentally, I shall be out this afternoon.'

'Isn't your car in dock? Of course you can borrow mine if you want it.'

'Thanks all the same, but I can walk where I'm going.' Caroline said this with a certain smugness.

Virginia looked at her sister, perplexed at first, then accusing: 'You're going to see Marsden!'

'How did you guess?'

Virginia was shocked; she got up and crossed to the window. 'Really, Carrie! You told me that was all over . . . It's like going to a brothel.'

'Why not? Women's lib and all that. But perhaps you'd prefer it if he came here?' Caroline yawned. 'There's no point in turning pi on me, Vee. For Christ's sake try living in the real world for once!'

'With your son here and your husband coming home tonight . . . I just don't know what to say!'

'Then don't say anything, dear. I need a man now and then, a real man, it's as simple as that. Sleeping with Gerald is like bedding down with a wet fish—and that's all I've got to look forward to for the next week at least. I don't know how you manage and I don't ask; perhaps we're different.'

'My God, I hope so! It's obscene!'

Caroline sounded bored. 'Don't be so damned self-righteous, Vee!'

Two o'clock. Joseph Bishop's glasses had slipped to the end of his nose and his eyes were closed; a long, thin hand rested on the open book in his lap. At seventy-four Joseph remained physically active and mentally alert but in the hour after lunch he was often overtaken by drowsiness which he resented and did his best to combat. He usually took his exercise in the mornings, walking on the cliffs or over the moor, and in the afternoons he read, though now his reading was increasingly restricted to books he had read before. When he drowsed he seemed to be half remembering, half dreaming of the days when his father was alive and Mynhager House was still part of the cultural gilt on the Cornish gingerbread.

There were photographs on the walls: D.H. Lawrence with Frieda, Middleton Murry with Katherine Mansfield, Maynard Keynes, Lytton Strachey, Duncan Grant, the Woolfs—all taken on the balcony outside the very room where he now sat. Virginia Woolf's genuine original lighthouse, setting aside all Hebridean substitutes, was just a few miles up the coast. And cheek-by-jowl with the photographs were paintings given to his father or to him by notables of the St Ives and Newlyn schools. There was a single portrait, the head and shoulders of a young woman with auburn hair coiled on the top of her head like a coronet. The frame carried a little plaque: Ursula 1929.

A knock at the door. Joseph roused himself, adjusted his glasses and closed the book on his finger. 'Come in!'

His son, Ernest.

The old man said, 'You're home early!'

'Charlie Wycliffe is arriving this afternoon and I thought I'd better be here to welcome him.'

At forty-five Ernest had only to look at his father to see what he would himself become in another thirty years—if he lived that long. The Bishop line must have accumulated a hoard of dominant genes; their men were tall, thin, and long-

393

boned, with a tendency to early baldness. And so far, through several generations, they had shown a marked aptitude for survival in a changing world.

'Do you mind if I help myself to a sherry?' Ernest went to a little cupboard and lifted out a tray with a bottle of Tio Pepe and glasses. 'Will you join me, father?'

'I've just had my lunch. Have you got something on your mind?'

Ernest poured himself a glass of sherry. 'I had a visitor in the office this morning. Who do you think?'

His father made an irritable movement. 'I've never been any good at guessing games, Ernest. Get on with it!'

'Lemarque.'

He had the satisfaction of seeing the old man surprised. 'Lemarque? What did he want?'

'He came about the cottage.'

'They're moving out.'

'On the contrary. He gave me a cheque to cover the rent for the two years during which, as he put it, "I was detained elsewhere". Of course I said there was no need but he insisted.'

'And?'

'He said he wanted to continue the tenancy for at least a year and he suggested an agreement. He said he would understand if we wanted to raise the rent and that he would pay what was reasonable.'

Joseph stroked his silky moustache. 'Extraordinary! What's behind it? Why didn't he come here?'

'I suppose he wasn't too sure of his welcome and he wanted to keep it business-like.'

'I haven't seen him since he came out, how does he look?'

'I don't think he's suffered unduly from the slings and arrows but he's drinking; he's got that look. Apart from anything else it was just before one when he came to see me and he was smelling of whisky then.'

The old man shook his head. 'I don't understand what he's up to. What did you say to him?'

'That they are more than welcome to stay on in the cottage

394

for as long as it suits them but that we would prefer not to enter into any formal agreement.'

'All you could say. This scheme he's supposed to be involved with, do you know anything about it?'

'Only that it's in some way connected with Rosemergy Minerals.'

'That's Tim Trewhella; you should talk to Tim.'

'I have, and I'm no wiser.'

Joseph sighed. 'Curiouser and curiouser! Have you mentioned this to Caroline?'

'Not yet.'

'Then don't. Have a quiet word with Gerald when he comes; we don't want any upset over Christmas.'

Ernest drained his glass. 'I'm wondering if this is in some way to do with Gerald.'

'Why should it be?'

'At the time, Lemarque said he had enough evidence to take Gerald to jail with him.'

A dry laugh. 'Just talk! You've always had a tendency to believe what people say, Ernest. Fatal in our profession. But even if Lemarque was speaking the truth he's missed the boat. He's left it too late.'

'Too late to put Gerry in jail, perhaps, but not too late to throw a spanner in his political works, or at least to threaten to.'

'Blackmail?' The old man dismissed the idea. 'You're dramatizing the situation! All the same I'd be interested to know what Rosemergy Minerals can do for Lemarque and even more in what they think he can do for them.'

Ernest said: 'I don't like the idea of him settling here. Whatever we say in the interests of the family, you and I know that Lemarque is a very clever rogue though not quite clever enough. Gerald was mixed up in his shady business and he was lucky to get out of it without a major scandal. All I'm saying is that I hope we're not going to get the scandal now.'

Joseph brushed the notion aside. 'You worry too much, Ernest! Relax!'

Ernest stood up, still holding his empty glass, 'I'll take this

395

down. Don't forget we've got Wycliffe with us for dinner this evening.'

'I'm not yet totally senile, Ernest. As a matter of fact, I'm looking forward to meeting the man. What's he like? Will he get on with Carrie and Vee?'

'If he doesn't it won't be his fault.'

A broad grin. 'You'll have to keep Gerald out of his hair.'

'I think Charles can take care of himself.'

Joseph, now thoroughly roused from his lethargy, said: 'Good! I feel I'm going to have a nice Christmas. Tell Ada I intend to be hungry tonight.'

Chapter Two

'TURN LEFT HERE unless you're going through St Ives.'
Wycliffe muttered the words. It was what Helen would have
said had she been with him. But Helen was far away in
Kenya, staying with their newly married son who had a job
there. In a year or two they would be grandparents. Salutary
thought! As a couple they were post-reproductive, being
gently but surely edged aside by the main stream of existence.
Perhaps the slippered pantaloon bit was still some way off but
one saw it coming. He found wry consolation in the thought
that he must be in Shakespeare's fifth stage: 'the justice, In
fair round belly with good capon lined . . . full of wise saws and
modern instances.' Not so wide of the mark for he was on his
way to spend Christmas with Ernest Bishop, a lawyer with a
practice in Penzance.

Wycliffe did not even know him very well; they had met in
the courts and on various committees. During a three-day
conference Bishop had stayed with the Wycliffes, now he was
repaying the hospitality debt. Quiet, reserved, with a wicked
wit, his comments on the law and its practitioners were
trenchant and amusing. He had a curious hobby which was
characteristic of him: he collected and studied flies.

But Wycliffe was not at all keen on the prospect. Ernest was
a bachelor and the house was run by his two sisters, one of
whom was married to Gerald Bateman, M.P., so that the
position of Ernest's guest might be uncomfortably peripheral.

Three o'clock and raining out of a sombre sky; hardly any
traffic, but when another car did pass, the bow waves sprayed
both vehicles. Dipped headlights and the screen-wipers
rocking. He climbed the slope outflanking Trencrom Hill

and came out at last on the coast road. Another three or four miles.

The sea on his right, the granite moorland on his left, a bleak landscape where the men of Bronze built strange megaliths for their dead and the men of Iron had seemed content to live in their thatched huts and cultivate their little fields. The dimly shining strip of road rose and fell like a miniature switchback, complicated by meanders originally plotted by medieval cattle. An early nineteenth-century traveller got it about right: 'the moorstone or granite lies dispersed in detached blocks, many of them huge enough for another Stonehenge. Scarcely a shrub appears to diversify the prospect; and the only living beings that inhabit the mountainous parts are goats . . .' Wycliffe saw no goats.

Suddenly he was there; houses on both sides of the road—the village of Mulfra, a mining village when there were mines. The houses, mostly small, were strung out along the coast road and clustered round the church; black soil, granite walls, and slate roofs covered with grey lichen. The church tower, four-square, no nonsense, and forty feet high, to remind hardened hearts of the all-seeing eye. Some of the villagers had tried to ameliorate this stark severity with gaily painted front doors and bits of scrolled ironwork but they would have had more success with paper chains in a morgue.

Ernest's letter had said that he must turn down by the pub. He spotted a narrow gap between pub and cottage and a blue and white wall sign which read: 'To Mulfra Headland and Cove.' The pub was The Tributers and Wycliffe prided himself (a foreigner) on knowing that tributers were 'free' miners working under contract for the adventurers. Cornishmen avoided being wage slaves whenever they could.

A few more cottages and the road degenerated to a dirt track between low granite walls. Another cottage, standing alone, and the track became even rougher with a rising boulder-strewn slope on one side and a shallow reedy valley on the other. A sudden twist in the track and he had arrived. Mynhager House was perched on a ledge above the sea, stark against a darkening sky, but there were lights in several of the windows.

He pulled into a paved courtyard, muttering to himself: 'I'm not looking forward to this.'

A door from the house opened and Ernest Bishop in a shabby waterproof and a cap came across to him. 'Charles! So very pleasant to see you again! No use apologizing for the weather, it's what we expect here at this time of the year.'

Ernest insisted on carrying his suitcase and led him through a short passage into the front hall. He dropped the suitcase and pulled a grubby white handkerchief from the pocket of his raincoat to wipe his glasses. With the handkerchief came a little shower of glass specimen tubes. Ernest picked them up, smiling, 'For my flies. I'm never without them.'

Wycliffe was introduced to a dark haired woman in her late thirties. 'My sister, Mrs Bateman.' Ernest smiled. 'Caroline to you, I think.'

Caroline was running to fat and she had that pouting, slightly sullen expression of the spoiled self-indulgent woman. Her greeting was polite but without warmth. 'I expect you would like to go to your room and freshen up . . . I hope you will be comfortable.'

He was given a front bedroom overlooking the sea and the cove. A huge Victorian wardrobe, a dressing table, a chest of drawers, a monumental brass bedstead and a couple of armchairs, still left plenty of room on the well-worn Wilton.

Caroline said, 'There's only a shared bathroom, through that door.' She laughed. 'As long as you secure yourself from the other side you'll be all right. If there's anything you want don't hesitate to say.'

At the door she turned back. 'Oh, do come down to the dining-room when you're ready. Make yourself at home. This evening we shall have our meal early because some of the family go to the Song Play at the church, a thing the vicar does every Christmas. I know it sounds awful but they do it quite well and you might even enjoy it.'

So far so good!

He put his hand on a massive old-fashioned radiator which looked as though it had been built for the Albert Hall. It was hot. There was a washbasin and two rough turkish towels on a heated towel rail. Things could have been a lot worse. He walked over to the window; almost dark. He could see a paved terrace below the window, then a steep slope of forty or fifty feet to the sea. It was calm and the gentle surge of the dark water could be detected only in the changing pattern of reflections from its surface. To his left he could just make out the cove which seemed to be choked with leg-trapping boulders.

Half-an-hour later he went downstairs, hair combed, hands clean, and washed behind the ears. Ernest was hovering in the hall, a nervous host.

'There you are, Charles! Come into the drawing-room, you must be longing for a cup of tea.'

In the large, time-worn drawing-room Caroline was standing by the fire talking to her husband who was seated in one of the armchairs and Wycliffe had the impression that their conversation had not been amicable. Gerald Bateman M.P., known to everyone for his TV appearances, always ready with concise, dogmatic pronouncements on any issue from genetic engineering to the decline of flax growing on St Helena: 'My dear Robin (or Brian, or John), I fully appreciate the complexity of the problem but . . .' His real hobby horse was Law and Order: the Supremacy of the Law, Individual Responsibility, Justice, and Punishment.

In the corridors of power they called him The Sheriff, but behind the political facade there was a thin-lipped intelligence which had enabled him to keep head and shoulders well above water through the recession.

Ernest said: 'You've already met Caroline; this is her husband. No introduction necessary, I'm sure.'

Bateman sprang to his feet with instant charm: 'My dear Mr Wycliffe! This is a real pleasure. I'm quite sure we shall have some interesting talks while you are here; interesting and instructive for me at any rate.'

Ernest said: 'Gerald is anxious to brief himself for a debate on the crime statistics when the House reassembles. Remember, Charles, you do not have to say anything but whatever you do say may be taken down and used in his speech.'

Bateman smiled. 'Ernest must have his little joke; it is a family idiosyncracy.'

Bateman was forty-six, tall, with a youthful figure, and good looking in the clean-limbed, manly virtues fashion: dark hair well cut, carefully trimmed guards' moustache, and perfectly shaved.

Ernest turned to his sister: 'See if you can hurry up Virginia with the tea, dear.'

A tall, elderly woman made an entrance. No question that she was a Bishop: big boned, spare, with angular features and deep-set eyes. She wore a mauve satin frock, badly creased, an orange silk scarf loosely knotted, and her grey hair had a wispy wildness. The White Queen straight out of Alice.

Ernest hastened to introduce her. 'Mrs Burnett-Price, my Aunt Stella: Chief Superintendent Wycliffe.'

The old lady acknowledged the introduction with gravity then went on: 'I'm so glad you are here though it surprises me that they should send a chief superintendent to deal with a few instances of pilfering. However, as my husband used to say: "The army has its own way of doing things" and I suppose it is the same with the police.' She laughed, still a musical sound; she must have been a charmer in her day.

An imploring look from Ernest. Wycliffe merely nodded and looked amiable. Ernest conducted his aunt to a straight backed chair near the fire.

Tea arrived on a trolley, with Virginia, a younger, slimmer version of her sister.

'Two more members of the family still to meet,' Ernest said. 'Father, who doesn't put in an appearance until we sit down to our evening meal, and my nephew Paul of whom the same can usually be said.'

Tea and little rock cakes which had spent too long in the oven. Ernest said: 'I don't know if Caroline mentioned the vicar's play which is on this evening . . . I usually go, so do Virginia and Paul. I wondered if you might be interested?'

Wycliffe protested that he was looking forward to it.

In what promised to be a stilted conversation with Caroline he happened to mention the piano, by far the most elegant piece of furniture in the room, and she warmed to him at once.

'It's a Steinway, and it's mine; father indulged me terribly when I showed some talent for music. It wasn't literature, which would have pleased him more, but it was something to have a daughter who would make a name for herself in music. Of course, I never did. All the same, it's my one claim to any sort of culture.' She laughed. 'Pictures, sculpture, literature, and even gourmet eating, leave me cold, but music . . . Music to me is like sex; with the advantage that it lasts longer and they tell me you can still enjoy it in old age.'

Wycliffe realized that he had been received into that circle of acquaintances with whom Caroline found it amusing to flirt.

Bateman, left out, stood alone looking patient, like a well-mannered Doberman waiting to be noticed and patted. Obviously the distinguished politician cut little ice at Mynhager.

When Caroline was called to the kitchen she was replaced by Virginia; the Bishops were not neglecting their guest. He was briefed on the family and the house. 'The house was built by my great great grandfather. The Bishops have always been slightly crazy. They made money out of tin and banking, and building Mynhager was their bizarre way of proving that they had it. Then my grandfather imported culture; he was a Cambridge Apostle and this place became a sort of Cornish outpost for the Bloomsbury Set.'

Virginia talked with animation and from time to time she glanced up at him with a disarming grin as though apologizing for her chatter. 'I even owe my name to Virginia Woolf of blessed memory who delighted grandfather by sending him pre-publication copies of her novels.'

Unexpectedly Aunt Stella weighed in from her chair by the fire: 'My husband used to call them "a pack of left-wing intellectuals, ready to bite the hands that fed them." He couldn't bear to stay in the house when any of them were here. And that included poor Arnold Forster who was such a nice man and, although he was a socialist, really quite civilized. He wrote a book about gardening in this part of the world and he lived at Eagle's Nest, just up the coast from here.'

Virginia said, as though in total explanation: 'Uncle George was in the army.'

'Your uncle was a major general, my dear,' Aunt Stella amended.

They had their meal at six and Wycliffe met Joseph, head of the family, and young Paul, for the first time. The old man was an earlier edition of Ernest: tall, spare, amiable, and with a caustic wit. By the same token the seventeen-year-old Paul was every inch another Bishop. Wycliffe wondered how Bateman came to terms with the fact that his paternal contribution had been so effectively swamped.

During the meal Joseph, in a relaxed mood, told stories of village feuds in the Cornwall of sixty years ago and wound up: 'I tell you, Wycliffe, they were a sombre lot around here and they still are. Wesley spread a veneer of religion over 'em but he didn't change the nature of the beast.'

Afterwards, Ernest said, 'Virginia and Paul are going to pick up Jane Lemarque and her daughter, Francine. The Lemarques live in a little house on the other side of the valley, and Francine is playing the Virgin in tonight's play.'

So Wycliffe went with Ernest in his ancient, 3-litre Rover which the family called 'The Hearse'. Ernest drove through the darkness and the mist with the caution appropriate to an acrobat balancing a pretty girl in a wheelbarrow on the high wire.

'I must apologize, Charles, for not warning you about Aunt Stella. Since George died she's been a bit queer in the head. She hides things, forgets where she's put them, then imagines they've been stolen. But it isn't all genuine. She's not above putting on an act for the fun of it, as she did this evening.' Ernest laughed: 'You may have gathered that some of the family have a peculiar sense of humour.'

403

They reached the church well before eight when the play was due to begin; the bells were ringing a peal. The leafless sycamores in the churchyard made weird shapes and shadows and there was a misty halo around the lamp over the church porch. People were arriving in a thin but steady stream. Virginia and Paul were already in their seats with another woman, an attractive brunette. As they filed into the same pew, Ernest murmured introductions: 'Mrs Jane Lemarque, Mr Wycliffe . . . Francine, Jane's daughter, is the star this evening.'

The dark woman smiled, the closed smile of a nun.

Wycliffe found himself between Ernest and his sister. A large man with a mass of curly black hair came in and sat a couple of seats in front of them.

Ernest said: 'That chap who's just come in—the big fellow who looks like a gypsy, that's Marsden, our local painter—I wonder why he's here; I wouldn't have said this was his sort of thing, would you, Vee?'

'I've no idea!'

Wycliffe thought she had snubbed her brother and wondered why.

The bells stopped ringing, the hushed conversations died away, the organ played a melancholy little tune of single notes, like a pipe; the lights dimmed and went out. For a long moment the church was in total darkness then a light in the form of a star came on over the chancel. A large suspended backdrop hid the altar and was illuminated from behind by slowly changing coloured lights: green to blue, to mauve to violet . . . There was no-one to be seen, but a girl's voice sang, sweet and true and unaccompanied:

'I cannot rest beloved, fear steals away my sleep;
   Why should a humble maiden have such a trust to keep?
Did I but dream of the Angel, did I but think him there?
   How can I hope that my body the infant Christ will bear?'

A baritone voice answered:

'Be not afraid, sweet Mary; queen among women, blest;
  God and His Holy Angels shall set your fears at rest.
High in the heaven above us the natal star doth shine,
  Token that God in His mercy will grant the gift divine.'

Came the inevitable duet. A trite little song, simply and
honestly sung, but in the old parish church with no
performers in view, and no set, only the empty chancel and
the discreetly changing hues of the backdrop, the audience
was caught and held.

Darkness once more, then the star.

Mary, seen now, in a simple blue dress with her baby on
her lap. She had red-gold hair, like the Renaissance
madonnas, coiled loosely on the top of her head. As she bent
over the child it caught the light and there was the suggestion
of a halo. She sang a plaintive cradle song and an invisible
choir brought the glad news to the shepherds. 'Glory to God
in the highest and on earth peace, good will toward men.'

The shepherds, first seen as shadows on the backdrop
growing in size, came into view singing lustily like Disney's
dwarfs. The clowns of the piece, three folk-lore rustics, they
became silent and subdued in the presence of the girl with her
baby. Shyly, they handed her their tributes—three posies of
wild flowers, and gravely she took them, one at a time, and
said: 'White flowers for Innocence . . . red for Majesty . . .'
And after a long pause, and in a low voice, 'and purple for
Death.'

In that moment Wycliffe felt that he had glimpsed the
forgotten magic of Christmas.

Solemn organ music heralded the approach of the kings as
their shadows grew larger. They introduced themselves with
courtly manners and in elegant language spoke of the star
they had seen in the east. They foretold the greatness of the
child and presented their gifts.

Mary received them, saying: 'From Melchior, Gold for
Royalty . . . From Caspar, Frankincense for Divinity . . .'
And in a low voice which seemed to falter: 'From Balthazar,
Myrrh for Death.'

She thanked them and the kings departed. Joseph had his dream in which he was warned by an angel of Herod's intent and the play ended with the Holy Family setting out on the flight into Egypt. Mary sang her final song which was a prayer for their safety.

Wycliffe was moved and deeply impressed, in particular by the girl. She had seemed quite unaware of her audience. With scarcely any movement and with an expression of grave wonder, she had allowed the action to take place about her but leaving no-one in any doubt that she was the still centre and focus of it all.

It had lasted an hour and when the vicar gave his benediction the audience sat on for a while as though reluctant to come back into the real world. Wycliffe turned to congratulate Jane on her daughter's performance but she had already left the pew.

Paul said: 'Mrs Lemarque has gone to the vestry to help Francine. If you will excuse me . . .'

Ernest laughed. 'Poor lad! After tonight he'll be in deeper than ever. Anyway, there are refreshments in the church room; if we go along we shall be able to meet the vicar and his cast. What about it?'

'I'd like to meet that girl,' Wycliffe said.

Ernest was pleased. 'Better than all the tinsel and shiny balls, don't you think? A little magic now and then for thy soul's sake.' He sighed. 'Francine is a very talented girl, but difficult.'

Outside the rain had stopped, it was very dark and still and the air was fresh with the tang of salt.

The church hall was a converted barn, clean but spartan; dedicated women stood behind trestle tables selling tea, coffee, and sausage rolls in aid of the church restoration fund. Within a remarkably short space of time seventy or eighty people were clustered in groups, each with a cup and saucer in one hand and a sausage roll in the other. The vicar, at the centre of the largest group, towered head and shoulders above them, lean, blond and saintly.

'He's not liked by everyone,' Virginia said. 'For one thing

he's a bachelor and that doesn't suit, then he's too "high" for some: confession, incense, and all that sort of thing, but he's a clever man, and a kind one.'

'Ah, Miss Bishop!' The vicar ploughed through to speak to Virginia. 'Mrs Lemarque asked me to pass on her apology. Francine is being difficult again. It seems that as soon as our play ended she changed back into her ordinary clothes and walked out.'

'Walked out? But where has she gone?'

'Home, presumably. Her mother is very upset and insisted on going home herself. I begged her to wait, then Paul wanted to drive her home but she wouldn't hear of it.' The vicar smiled. 'I think there will be some straight talking in the Lemarque household tonight. A pity!'

'But what was the matter with Francine?'

The vicar raised his hands. 'What is ever the matter with Francine? I suppose we must allow for temperament but really I think she should have stayed. Everyone wants to congratulate her, we have two reporters here, and I know that the Women's Guild have a very nice present for her.'

Somebody said: 'Was she holding a real baby? Once I thought I heard it whimper.'

The vicar smiled. 'No, not a real baby; that was Francine's black doll. It seems to be her mascot.'

'A black doll?'

'Why not? Apart from any other consideration they tell us that our Lord probably had a dusky skin.'

Wycliffe was introduced to the vicar and he met the rest of the cast, all a little flustered by success: Joseph, a local farmer's son; the shepherds, members of an amateur pop group; the three kings, the choir . . .

As the church clock was striking ten Wycliffe and Ernest were walking back to the car and in The Tributers they were singing Good King Wenceslas with variations.

The drawing-room at Mynhager looked as festive as it was ever likely to. A good fire burned in the large open grate which Ernest called 'The Miners' Friend', though tonight it was burning logs.

Joseph had stayed up later than usual in deference to their guest and everyone was drinking. Joseph nursed a glass of port which he frequently replenished. Wycliffe, Gerald Bateman and Caroline drank whisky; Virginia, Paul and the elusive Ada drank white wine. Ernest had lime juice. It was the first time Wycliffe had seen Ada: a plump, energetic little woman of sixty-five with remarkably clear skin, and grey hair gathered into a bun on the top of her head.

Between sips of gin and tonic, Aunt Stella knitted. A long, scarf-like strip depended from her needles, overflowed her lap and reached for the floor. Wycliffe was reminded of Madame Defarge at the foot of the guillotine.

Caroline, watched by her husband, sprawled in one of the armchairs, showing a great deal of thigh; she had put away several whiskies and Wycliffe judged that she was drunk enough to cause a scene if Bateman attempted to interfere.

They talked about the 'festive season' and the inability of the English to celebrate; the Anglo Saxon's failure to overcome his inhibitions and let his hair down.

'Except in outbursts of drunken violence'—Virginia.

'Imagine Mardi Gras in Malvern'—Ernest.

Aunt Stella began: 'When George and I were in Madras . . .' But the memory, whatever it was, faded, and she lapsed into silence.

Paul said: 'At least we have Notting Hill.'

His father was derisive. 'The West Indians are responsible for that, it's their show. As far as Europeans are concerned it's only in those countries with a Catholic tradition that you get the true spirit of carnival.'

'Nonsense!' Joseph obviously welcomed a chance to challenge his son-in-law. 'Catholic, Protestant, Jew or Atheist, it makes no difference: celebration and self-denial or deprivation are two sides of the same coin. Ash Wednesday follows Shrove Tuesday; Easter Day follows Good Friday; there's no satisfaction—no joy, in the one without the other. Of course we can deceive ourselves. As a nation we've become

408

pathologically self indulgent but we pay the price in a joyless existence of boredom and frustration.'

The old man's eyes sparkled from the port he had drunk. 'Look at us now, preparing to celebrate the birth of our Lord; each one of us with a quiet determination to take aboard enough alcohol to enable us to endure the boredom until bedtime!' He turned to Wycliffe, 'Isn't that so?'

Wycliffe smiled. 'I'm certainly not bored.'

The old man laughed. 'No, I can believe that. For an observer of human nature a family like ours is better than a whole load of case-books.'

In an uncomfortable silence Paul said: 'I think I'll go to bed. Good night everybody.'

A chorus of good nights. A welcome signal for the party to break up.

Wycliffe climbed into the great bed and snuggled down under the blankets. A strange family! But aren't all families a bit odd seen from the inside?

He thought of Helen, living it up somewhere in the Kenyan highlands and wondered what the weather was like. Anyway she would be in bed; it would be three o'clock in the morning. Silently he wished her good night.

He lay there listening to the tide surging and chuckling between the boulders in the cove, then sucking back. As he listened the sounds seemed to get louder. He tried to imagine what it would be like in a Force 10 nor' westerly when those boulders must grind together like the mills of God.

'White flowers for innocence . . .' The words came back to him and with them a vivid mind-picture of the girl. There was something about her . . . How old was she? Seventeen? Eighteen, perhaps?—not more . . . Lemarque; they must be of French extraction . . . No mention of a father . . . He hoped there would be a chance to meet her . . .

'. . . and purple for death.' How absurd! He could not get the girl or the play out of his mind.

He fell asleep still thinking of Francine.

Chapter Three

CHRISTMAS EVE MORNING. Wycliffe went out on to the terrace and stood, arms resting on the balustrade. Further along a herring gull perched on one leg, motionless. The weather was sunny and still. He was missing his after-breakfast pipe; a fortnight of abstinence had convinced him that this was the time of day when resistance was at its lowest ebb. Virginia came out of the house and the gull launched itself into the air with an angry squawk.

'Good morning! Lovely day!'

She wore a fluffy woollen jumper and a matching skirt. Wycliffe thought she looked young, fresh, and wholesome; sorting through his stock of adjectives he might have conceded pretty. She joined him, arms resting on the balustrade.

'Wonderfully mild for the time of year, isn't it?'

She was dark, with freckles which stopped short of her eyes and reminded him that this was the first time he had seen her without her glasses. They stood, looking down into the water, so clear they could see the yellow sandy bottom with a school of small fish darting and wheeling above it like a flock of starlings in the air.

'Is the sand uncovered at low tide?'

'No, thank goodness! If it was we should be over-run with trippers in the season.'

A fishing boat rounded Gurnard's Head and cruised parallel with the shore.

'Half-decked St Ives gig.' Virginia said, showing off. 'That'll be the *Jennifer*, Bert Gundry's boat; he takes us out now and then.'

410

A figure at the tiller raised a hand in salute and she waved back.

'Fishing, another dying industry in these parts.' She pointed across to the ruins of a mine stack and engine house jutting up like a broken tooth from one of the smaller promontories. 'Tin, copper and fish, the three-legged Cornish stool. The first two have dropped off and the third is suffering from Common Market disease; so we sit back and watch our county being destroyed by tourism.'

Wycliffe chuckled. 'A sombre diagnosis.'

'A plain statement of fact.'

'Isn't that Ernest over there?' Wycliffe pointed across the inlet to a rocky beach strewn with kelp washed up by the tide. A crouching man in a khaki waterproof seemed totally absorbed in turning over the weed.

'He's looking for flies.'

'At this time of year?'

Virginia laughed. 'I don't know much about the group but I think quite a few species are about in winter, especially in a mild spell like this. In any case there are larvae which live between the tide lines.'

Wycliffe said: 'Interesting, don't you think? the things people choose to do as opposed to the things they have to do to get a living.'

'Yes. But the lucky ones make a livelihood out of their interest. Ernest became a lawyer because it was expected of him, but he's a good naturalist and might have made a good biologist. Did you choose to be a policeman?'

'I'm afraid I did.'

'Why? Not because you enjoy ordering people about; you obviously don't.'

Even his wife had never asked him such a direct question and he was embarrassed, but he had raised the subject. 'When I was young I didn't quite know why, but as I've got older I've realized that I have a horror of disorder; the prospect of anarchy appals me and I suppose I feel I'm helping to stave it off.'

411

She looked at him in surprise. 'You see anarchy as an immediate threat?'

'Sometimes I feel that we live in a house of cards and the thought gives me nightmares.'

At that moment Paul came out of the house and, with a brief apology to Wycliffe, approached his aunt. He looked worried.

'I tried to ring Francine, but she isn't there and her mother says it seems she didn't come home last night.'

Virginia was incisive. 'Seems? Doesn't she know?'

'Apparently Mr Lemarque was in bed when Mrs Lemarque got home from the church and she thought Francine must have gone to bed too. It wasn't until half-an-hour ago, when they called Francine and she didn't answer, that they realized she wasn't in her room. Her bed hadn't been slept in.'

'Haven't they any idea where she might be?'

'Mrs Lemarque thinks she's gone to stay with a school friend; she says she's done it before.'

'Without a word to her parents?'

'I think so, yes.'

'Are they making enquiries among her friends?'

Helplessness and frustration got the better of the boy. 'I don't know what they're doing. Nothing, I expect!'

Virginia took pity on her nephew. 'Would you like me to look in and try to be helpful?'

'Would you, Vee?' Aunt and nephew were clearly on good terms.

'Tell your mother that Mr Wycliffe and I are going for a walk but I shall be back in plenty of time to help with the lunch.'

'I don't suppose I can do anything?'

She grinned up at him. 'No, you just stay here and worry.'

She watched the boy return to the house. 'Poor lad! He's in a bad way.'

Wycliffe said: 'You can't want me with you.'

'Why not? I'd like you to meet the Lemarques. I'll get a coat and you could probably do with one.'

As they walked along the track away from Mynhager she pointed out the Lemarques' cottage on the other side of the valley.

'It belongs to us and originally we let it to Alain only as a weekend place. At that time he and Gerald were partners in a London company with a chain of antique shops and picture galleries, doing very well; then things went badly wrong. Alain was a good business man but it seems he didn't know when he was beaten. Gerald got out, but Lemarque dug himself in deeper and deeper until he finished up in jail for fraud. He came out a few weeks ago.'

'Are they French?'

'Alain's father came over with De Gaulle and stayed. Jane is English and Francine was born in Richmond where they lived when they had money. They lost everything and now the cottage is the only home they have.'

'Hard on the wife and child.'

'It is, very.'

'How old is Francine?'

'Just sixteen; she had a birthday last month.'

'Sixteen! Surely her parents should be taking this more seriously?'

'Yes, you would think so but Jane may be right. Francine is a talented girl but difficult. Like a lot of young people these days she's got a keen sense of justice and if she thought she had a real grievance I wouldn't put it past her to walk out like this.' She laughed. 'Young Paul will have his problems if their friendship ever comes to anything but I don't think it will. Francine gives him very little encouragement.'

Wycliffe was intrigued by Virginia's uninhibited but amiable gossip. There is an appealing innocence about the virgin schoolgirl turned virgin teacher.

They were approaching another cottage, standing alone, just a yard or two back from the dirt road. Music came from inside: old style jazz played very loud.

'That's Marsden's place, the painter; you saw him in church last night.'

'Does he live alone?'

'With a succession of different women; the present one's been there several months, longer than most; usually they come and go in a matter of weeks. He's our scapegoat for scandal; very convenient, I suppose, but we could well do without him. There's been talk recently of Francine going to the cottage when the woman is away at work.' Virginia made a little gesture of distaste. 'I doubt if there's any more substance in that than there is in most of the gossip round here. You know what villages are. All the same it's very unpleasant.'

The sunshine heightened colours in the landscape, the drab green of heather and gorse, the red-brown splashes of dead bracken, and the grey-white boulders. But out to sea black clouds were creeping up the sky.

'Of course, a lot of Francine's trouble is that she reacts against her mother.'

'Why against her mother?'

Virginia considered. 'Jane is a difficult woman to live with; she seems to carry about her an aura of sadness, as though she were in perpetual mourning for somebody or something.'

'Is this because of her husband going to jail?'

'No. She's been like that for years. Odd, really, she used to be such a cheerful girl when we first knew her. She's never been the same since Francine was born.'

They turned off down the steep slope which led to the footbridge and because it was narrow they had to walk in single file.

On the other side she went on: 'It's hard to explain. Jane is the most passive of women if passive is the right word but if I had to live with her I'd probably end up by doing something dramatic and stupid like Francine, just to provoke a response.'

So Francine was barely sixteen, he had thought her older.

The Lemarques' cottage, weathered and grey, seemed to have grown out of the hillside, a larger version of the granite boulders which littered the slope. Parked at the bottom of the steps which led up to the front door was a small grey van, several years old, with patches of red paint on the grey to cope with rust.

'Poor Alain used to drive a Jaguar,' Virginia said. 'A new one every couple of years.'

Jane Lemarque must have seen them from the window for as they reached the other side of the footbridge the front door opened and she was standing at the top of the steps. Dark hair and blue eyes, a pale oval face with high cheek bones. Beauty without artifice, perhaps without awarenesss.

'Compliments of the season, Jane!' Virginia could hardly wish her a merry Christmas. 'Paul told us about Francine and as we were out for a walk I thought we might look in and see if we could be of any help.'

'You're a stranger, Vee! Do come in.'

The words were welcoming but the voice was flat and indifferent; the beautiful face was not exactly vacant but unresponsive.

They were shown into the living-room, characterless and uncared for. A coal fire burned half-heartedly in the grate. No Christmas decorations, no tree; the only sign of Christmas, a number of cards arranged on the mantelpiece. In the adjoining kitchen something simmering on the stove gave off little jets of steam and an unappetising smell.

'I'll call Alain.' She called him, standing at the bottom of the stairs, 'Virginia is here, Alain. With a friend.'

Alain came down the stairs; a small man, very dark, swarthy. At first sight Wycliffe thought that he must have seen the man before, then he realized that he was recognizing a type, a genus. Lemarque had the sad, deeply furrowed yet mobile face of a clown. His manner was uneasy, a man not at home in his own house.

'Hullo, Vee!' Sheepish.

Wycliffe was introduced. At close quarters he noticed a slight reddening around the mouth and nose. A whisky flush? If so it had been acquired in a few weeks.

'You haven't come about my daughter?' Suspicious.

It struck Wycliffe as odd that this strange little man could claim Francine as his daughter. He said: 'No, I happened to be staying at Mynhager and we were out for a walk.'

Virginia, insensitive to the pitfalls of social contact between an ex-con and an officer of the C.I.D., ploughed in: 'But Mr Wycliffe could be very helpful if you decided to call in the police.'

Lemarque looked at his wife. 'Jane says she's done this before, while I've been away.'

Jane said nothing now. She sat bolt upright and quite still, her gaze fixed on the fireplace. Her hands were clasped so tightly together in her lap that her arms seemed to tremble. Safety valve screwed right down.

But she was beautiful. Watching her, Wycliffe had unchaste thoughts, though it might be like sleeping with a sphinx. Probably only Lemarque had had the chance to find out. But agile little men, simian types, are often proud of their sexual prowess. Would Lemarque have been content with a frigid wife? Anyhow the hazards of sexual selection and the genetic lottery had produced Francine. Irrelevant thoughts of a chief superintendent.

Virginia was saying: 'Why does she do it—go off without a word?'

Jane said: 'To punish me.' The words seemed to escape almost against her will.

'To punish you, Jane? Surely not!' Virginia.

Lemarque glanced quickly at Wycliffe and away again.

Silence.

Virginia tried to bridge the gap with words. 'I'm sure Francine is quite safe but, if you don't hear today, think how worried you'll be; and all that time lost!'

Wycliffe felt that the tension had little to do with the missing girl. They were like actors playing a part while preoccupied with their real lives. There was no rapport between man and wife or between them and their drab surroundings. More than once Wycliffe saw the woman's lips moving as though in prayer.

The room was a collection of odds and ends; nothing chosen or valued or cared for. The little window looked out across the valley and from where Wycliffe sat there was no sky to be seen, only the dun coloured and barren hillside opposite. A dismal, lonely prospect. What did the woman do all day when her husband was away? No books, magazines or newspapers; no sewing or knitting; not even a television set or a radio.

The silence seemed to challenge someone to break it; even Virginia was subdued. Lemarque said: 'What do you think, Jane?'

'It's up to you.'

They seemed to exist in a limbo of inaction and yet under almost insupportable tension. Lemarque turned to Wycliffe. 'What do we have to do?'

'Nothing at the moment. I'll arrange for someone to come and talk to you about Francine, and the routine enquires will go ahead.'

With any other parents he would have felt the need to reassure them: 'The police are quite good at this sort of thing; it happens more often than you think so don't worry too much . . .'

He could have telephoned from the cottage; the telephone was there in the living room but he preferred to wait until he was back at Mynhager. One reason was that he did not want to appear too directly involved.

Jane seemed greatly relieved to see them go; she even came out on to the steps and wished them a happy Christmas.

It was a relief to be once more out in the sunshine. As they were crossing the bridge Wycliffe said: 'An extraordinary couple! It's hard to imagine what life must be like in that . . . that vacuum. And the girl . . . Is Jane Lemarque frightened of something?'

Virginia said: 'She certainly seems worse than she was. I'm really glad you came, they wouldn't have done anything otherwise. What do you think about Francine?'

'What can one think? I very much doubt if she's staying with a school friend. Can you imagine any parent collecting a young girl, late in the evening, without previous contact with her parents?'

'You think something has happened to her?'

'That's what we've got to find out, but her parents know more than they've told us. Do you teach Francine?'

'No, she goes to a different school.'

Unconsciously he was adopting his professional role. He was disturbed.

Back at Mynhager he telephoned Chief Inspector Clarke of Divisional C.I.D. When the conversation was over Clarke put down the telephone, crushed out his half-smoked cigarette and cursed. 'Right on his bloody doorstep, and over Christmas. That's all we needed!'

He picked up the telephone again and called Detective Inspector Wills. 'I've just had the chief super on the line, Jim. He's spending Christmas in Mulfra village with Bishop, the lawyer. Some kid, a girl of sixteen, has gone missing right under his nose. Here are the details, such as they are . . . Ready?' He passed on the information he had. 'It's your patch, Jim, so watch your step. You're to send somebody to talk to the parents pronto, and the governor must be kept informed . . . Didn't Curtis work under him on some case? . . . The undertaker, that's it! Then Curtis is the man for this job. Not that it will amount to much. The kid will be back with mamma, wet and weepy by tonight. But if there's any cock-up, for God's sake let me know and put your head on the block, ready. And a very merry Christmas to you and yours!'

So the file which was not yet a file ended up on the desk of Detective Sergeant Curtis.

'That damned girl is going to spoil your Christmas, Wycliffe. Don't let her! She's only trying to make some impression on her mother. Not that I blame her for that. Lemarque spent years trying to do the same thing and look where it landed him!' The old man chuckled. 'Jane is like Everest, an enduring provocation simply by being there.' He turned to his son-in-law, 'Isn't that so, Gerald?'

They were at lunch and Gerald Bateman was trying to retrieve a small pat of butter from the table cloth without being noticed. He snapped: 'I'm quite sure Jane had nothing whatever to do with Lemarque's troubles.'

Caroline said: 'It wouldn't surprise me if she had gone off with some man, and I mean, man.'

Paul was staring at his plate without eating.

Aunt Stella, appetite unimpaired by age, consumed cheese and biscuits with the concentration and delicacy of a chimpanzee grooming for lice. She broke a water biscuit into four and placed a modicum of cheese on each section. 'If she's gone away then at least she is showing more discretion than most of them do these days.'

There was a noticeable silence then Ernest said with quiet emphasis: 'We are talking about Francine, aunt—Jane's daughter.'

Stella looked surprised. 'Francine? But she's only a child! It's hardly—'

'Francine is sixteen, aunt.'

Stella took into her mouth a portion of biscuit and cheese, patted her lips with a napkin and said: 'Isn't that what I was saying? These days they behave at sixteen as we wouldn't have dared to do at twenty-five!'

After the meal Wycliffe said to Ernest: 'I hope you don't mind; I've asked my people to keep me informed here.'

'My dear chap! You're doing us a favour.'

Wycliffe felt drowsy; the unaccustomed combination of whisky before, and white wine during lunch, was having its effect. He went into the drawing-room where there was a fire in the grate and the presents were laid out like votive offerings round the Christmas tree ready for distribution that night. The room was empty. He settled in one of the easy chairs with a magazine and was slightly embarrassed to wake up and find Ada standing over him.

'Sergeant Curtis wants to see you; I've put him in the dining-room.'

It was half-past three and almost dark. In the gloomy panelled dining-room Ada had switched on the dusty chandelier with its crystal drops.

Wycliffe knew Curtis of old and was pleased to renew the acquaintance. Curtis had the build of a heavyweight wrestler, with a great moon-like face in which eyes, nose and mouth were grouped together like palm trees in a desert oasis. A man of few words, he supplemented speech with gesture which sometimes reached the level of mime. He took a notebook from his pocket and placed it on the table but Wycliffe knew that he would not refer to it.

'I talked to madame; monsieur was out.' The huge hands seemed to pluck little manikins from the air and present them for inspection. 'They've no idea where or why the girl might have gone. Extraordinary! The woman seems to know nothing about her own daughter, about her school, her teachers or her friends . . .'

Curtis stared at the ceiling. 'I tried to find out what could have made the girl go off. Something must have. Had there been a row? "We don't have rows" madame informed me.' Curtis looked wide-eyed. 'Funny family in that case! Of course I suppose it's possible the girl was abducted but that hardly seems likely to me.

'I asked about friends visiting the house, letters . . . Friends don't visit, madame told me, but Francine does have letters occasionally. Big deal! Who from? Where from? . . . The silly woman doesn't have a clue. "We don't spy on our daughter."' Curtis heaved a profound sigh, 'Neither did we on ours but we made damn sure we had some idea of what she was up to. I looked at the cards on the mantelpiece—most of 'em were for Francine, all signed with pet names. Unisex. Madame could only tell me about one which came from the Bateman boy and you'll know about him, sir.'

'Did you ask about relatives that she might have gone to?'

'It seems that Lemarque has no relatives in this country that he is in contact with.'

'And Jane?'

'She has a sister in Bristol and an aunt in Oxford; they keep in touch more or less, but she says Francine scarcely knows them.'

'Did you see the girl's room?'

'No problem. When I asked, Madame said: "Upstairs; the door in front of you". Liberty Hall! Didn't tell me much though.' Curtis sketched a box in the air. 'Poky little room; the usual posters of pop stars on the walls; the usual collection of teenage clobber in the wardrobe and drawers—all looking as though it had been thrown out by Oxfam. When I was young, girls wanted to look pretty. I asked madame if she had taken any clothes with her other than what she wore. Madame, (would you believe?) wasn't sure. All she was sure of was that the girl had taken her doll.'

'Her doll?'

'A black-faced doll she's had since she was an infant. She always slept with it in her bed. Our Gwen had a teddy bear which she put on her pillow every night right up to the time she got married. Afterwards too, for all I know.'

'Go on.'

Curtis recovered his narrative: 'About her bedroom: there were a few books, all school issue except one on adolescent sex. (I suppose that could be school issue too, these days). A few tubes of paint, some brushes, and a blank sketch-pad. No pictures of hers or anybody else's. I had the impression she was thumbing her nose at me and at any other snoopers that happened along: "Make something out of this, Buster!"'

Curtis grinned. 'I couldn't and didn't.'

'Did you ask about what money she might have had?'

'I did, sir, but not to much purpose. It seems she had a job as a waitress in St Ives during the last summer holidays but what she earned or what she did with it her mother has no idea. Otherwise mother gave her money as she wanted it for some specific thing.'

'So what is your general impression?'

Curtis closed the notebook to which he had not once referred. 'A planned flit with a deliberate touch of the old melodrama. The day before Christmas Eve, and after playing the star role in the vicar's play, Bingo! the lady vanishes.' A deep sigh. 'Is that how you see it, sir?'

Wycliffe wasn't sure. Curtis's diagnosis seemed reasonable; a gesture of defiance, an expression of frustration, an assertion of independence. Take it out of that.

'You've got a photograph?'

421

Curtis looked sour. 'Two years out of date.'

'What else have you put in hand?'

'I've got a couple of chaps trying to make contact with her teachers and, through them, with her school friends. The chances are she talked to somebody. A teenage girl who doesn't tell at least some of it to her best friend would be a very rare bird. Of course, she may be just that.' Curtis shook his great head. 'Having Christmas round the corner doesn't make it easier. I found that in the village; characters who would be glad to talk their heads off normally have something better to do.'

'Did you get anything?'

'Not much. Of course you never know what the Cornish think, only what they say, and that's often the family or the village line. In this case they're saying that Francine is no better than she ought to be and that her mother and father are not liked.' Curtis lowered his voice. 'I'm afraid that's true of the Bishops too.'

'Nothing specific on the girl?'

'Just two things. The other members of the cast who were in the vestry when the play ended say she came in, went behind the curtain, changed into her outdoor clothes and left without a word to anybody.'

'And the other thing?'

'A little old woman, living alone . . .' Curtis's hands somehow conveyed five-feet nothing of skin and bone. 'A real tartar with a tongue like a serpent's tooth. After telling me that a chap called Marsden, a painter, is having it off with half the female population of the district including the girl, she said she saw him talking to Francine last night after the play. They were just beyond the church.'

Marsden: Virginia had mentioned the gossip. Wycliffe said: 'It may not mean much but if he was the last person to be seen with her we'd better talk to him.'

He went into the drawing-room to leave word that he was going out but there was no one there. In the end he found Caroline in the kitchen. She was topping a trifle with little blobs of whipped cream and there was a strong smell of brandy. Ernest was with her, licking his fingers like a guilty schoolboy.

'I'm afraid I have to go out in connection with the Francine business.' He felt like a schoolboy himself, asking permission to leave the room, but Caroline was cheerfully indifferent.

'It's every man for himself until we eat at seven. Don't be late then.'

Wycliffe had to admit to a more than professional interest in this painter who looked like a gypsy, had a reputation as a seducer, and listened to jazz blasted out in megabels.

Curtis was waiting in his car. It was quite dark now with a thin rain which smelled and tasted of the sea. Still no wind. They drove along the track, Curtis hunched over the wheel of his little Fiesta like some giant animal brooding its young. There was light in the painter's window and as soon as the engine cut they could hear the inevitable jazz. Not for the first time, Curtis surprised Wycliffe.

'Benny Goodman's "One o'clock jump"; that takes me back!'

They knocked, then banged on the door until the music was shut off. Heavy footsteps, then the door opened and there was Marsden; monumental against the light, like a Graham Sutherland portrait in 3-D. They introduced themselves.

'You'd better come in.'

The room was spartan. Apart from the record-player in one corner it was little different from how it must have been a century earlier when a Cornish mining family lived there. A floor of blue slate slabs with mats; a large deal table now littered with dirty dishes; and a couple of Windsor armchairs, one on each side of the fire. In one, a tabby cat was asleep, in the other there was an open book, and on the floor by the chair, a bottle of wine and a glass.

Marsden placed two kitchen chairs for his visitors. 'What's this about, then? I suppose I should apologize for the mess but it's the servants' night out. You know how it is with the lower classes these days.'

He spoke in a guttural voice and the words seemed to surface with some difficulty from a great depth.

423

Wycliffe said: 'I suppose you know that Francine Lemarque is missing?'

Marsden's expression froze. 'Missing? How long since?'

It was Curtis who said: 'Since last night.'

Marsden turned to Curtis. A confrontation between heavyweights; they were summing each other up. Wycliffe was amused, but though the two men had something in common, they were very different. Curtis was shrewd and subtle but essentially gentle, whereas in Marsden one sensed a potentiality for violence.

Marsden's attention came back to Wycliffe. 'You must think this is serious; a chief super on the job already.'

'Not necessarily. I happen to be involved because I'm staying with the Bishops over Christmas.'

Marsden grinned. 'Ah, the Bishops! God bless their little grey souls.' He took a cigarette pack from his pocket and lit one. Despite his bulk there was no clumsiness; he was as delicate and precise in his movements as a fastidious girl. 'I spoke to Fran after the church do last night. But the village K.G.B. will have told you that; it's probably why you're here.'

'Did she say why she didn't stay for the vicar's little party?'

'She said she couldn't face the vicar's sausage rolls.'

'How did you come to be talking to her?'

'Well, I saw her standing on the pavement like she was waiting for somebody. I told her I'd enjoyed the play and we chatted for a minute or two. I thought she was probably waiting for the Bateman boy to take her home the long way round. I believe that sort of thing is still done.'

Curtis said: 'Was she carrying anything?'

Marsden looked at Curtis with a speculative gaze. 'Ah! The monkey as well as the organ grinder. Yes, she was; a little hold-all. "What did she have in it?" you say. And I say: "I do not know. I did not ask."'

Wycliffe said: 'I believe Francine sometimes comes here to your cottage.'

'True!'

'You are on friendly terms with her?'

'I am. She's a very intelligent girl, bored to the eyeballs most of the time by the people she has to cope with. Me too, when I was a boy.'

'She comes here regularly?'

'She does, but I don't screw her if that's what you're asking.'

'Was the young woman who lives with you here last night?'

'No, the young woman who lives with me was not here last night; she went home to mother for Christmas.'

Curtis asked: 'Is she coming back?'

'I never ask women if they're coming back; it makes 'em think they're important. But she left her clobber here so I suppose she will.'

With an irritable movement Marsden threw the remains of his cigarette into the fire and got to his feet. 'I'll show you something. Come with me.'

He crossed the room, led them through a curtained doorway in the end wall, and switched on a strip-light which flickered into life. A large, bare room with a sloping roof on which the rain was pattering.

'My studio.'

It was very cold.

A couple of easels, a trolley painting-table, canvases stacked against the walls, a random assemblage of possible props, and the all-pervading smell of oil paint.

'Over here!'

Another strip-light. 'These things are supposed to give a north light, so that I can paint at night. No good! They're all wrong in the bloody yellows. Still, they're the best you can buy.

'Now look at this.' He lifted a cloth from a canvas on the second easel. 'There's our Fran for you. Stand back! You're not looking for the sodding signature.'

Wycliffe stood back and was impressed. A study in blues and greys and greens and purples with just a flush of pink in the flesh tones. The girl wore a flowered wrap, one breast exposed, and she looked at herself in a mirror.

Marsden said: 'She's not seeing herself; she's catching a

glimpse of the promised land and she's not sure that she's going to like it. She's on the threshold. In another week, another month, perhaps a little longer, she'll have crossed over, she'll be a woman, then nobody will ever see that look again. But there it is on canvas; caught like a butterfly pinned out in a box. For good!' Marsden sighed. 'To do that you have to be a painter, and a bloody good one!'

Curtis said: 'It's a nice picture.'

Marsden turned to Wycliffe. 'Now you've seen that, do you think I screwed her—or, for that matter, that anybody else did? I could have; she's ready for it, and I'd have been a damn sight better for her than some sweaty youth, all elbows and acne who doesn't know what he's about. But I didn't.'

He continued to look at his picture. 'She'd hold that pose, with rests, for two hours without moving a muscle, and do you know what she'd say at the end of it?'

'I've no idea.'

'She'd say: "That's eight quid you owe me."'

'You paid her?'

'Of course I paid her; well above the going rate. She wouldn't have sat for me otherwise. She's not stupid.'

'How many times did she sit for you?'

'God knows! Seven or eight; you'll have to ask my secretary.'

He shepherded them back to the living-room, sat in his chair, and lit another cigarette. 'Now we know where we stand I've made up my mind to pass on one or two things I gathered from Fran.' He looked at Wycliffe. 'Of course, you know about papa Lemarque?'

'What about him?'

'That he's been in jug and only recently come out.'

'Go on.'

'It seems that Francine was very much looking forward to him coming home. You know how girls can get a fix on father; well, I won't say it went as far as that but, after the best part of two years living with mother, I think she was counting on it all coming right when dad came back. It hasn't.'

'What was wrong, living with mother?'

Marsden pouted his thick lips. 'I'm not her confessor. She talks sometimes while I'm working and mostly I don't even answer, let alone ask questions, so I've no more than an impression.'

'And that is?'

'You've met the lady?'

'Mrs Lemarque? Briefly.'

'Then you can't fail to have noticed the Mona Lisa façade; the beautiful constipated nun look. One's natural reaction to that is: "Get behind it, mate, and you'll be all right." But what if there's no getting behind it? I know the score with her sort, it goes on and on until she gets clobbered and some poor bastard is carried away screaming: "There's nothing there! It was only a bloody record!"'

'Is that an expert assessment of why Francine has gone away?'

Marsden laughed. 'It's what you like to make it, mate. Now, if you don't mind, I was listening to some music and getting pissed ready for Christmas.'

'Benny Goodman,' Curtis said.

Marsden gave him a sour look. 'Who's a clever boy, then? I'll tell you something: when you pass this cottage you're just as likely to hear Bach or boogie-woogie.'

Outside, Curtis said: 'That gorilla isn't altogether stupid; I'll give him that.'

Wycliffe grumbled, 'Everybody seems anxious to talk about the mother rather than the girl. But it looks as though you were right. A planned get-away and she probably isn't short of money. It seems that somebody was due to pick her up in a car, so before we enlist the media with the "Have you seen?" bit we ought to really get down to finding who it was. There must have been quite a few people about, collecting their cars after the play. Only a fraction of the audience stayed for the sausage rolls but, according to the vicar, people came from all over this part of the county so you need to rope in other sections and get more men on the job. I'll speak to Division.'

Curtis said: 'I'll run you back to Mynhager, sir.'

'No need; I'll walk. I can do with the fresh air.'

'It's dark and it's damp, sir.'

'I'll survive.'

When Curtis drove off in the direction of the village the intensity of the darkness took Wycliffe by surprise. He set out with the fine rain in his face, picking his way with care, but soon the vague outlines of the landscape materialized out of the night and he walked with more confidence. The only light he could see came from across the valley, a dimly glowing orange rectangle, the window of the Lemarques' living room. It happened that as he watched, their front door opened, illuminating a second rectangle; a figure appeared briefly in the light then the door closed again. Someone had come out of the house, someone with a torch; he could see the wavering pin-point of light as, whoever it was, descended the steps.

A few minutes later he rounded the bend which brought him in sight of the lights of Mynhager. Suddenly the sea sounded much louder and at intervals the low cloud was lit by diffused flashes from the lighthouse down the coast.

The meal over, they moved into the drawing-room. The wind had risen and despite the thick walls and heavy velvet curtains they could hear the waves breaking over the rocks and surging into the cove.

Joseph said: 'It's going to blow tonight.'

Time for party games.

Wycliffe sat in one of the big armchairs and his gaze ranged over the assembled Bishops and their distaff branch, the Batemans. He was bored and he amused himself by trying to sum them up. Joseph, head of the clan, naturally domineering, presumed on the privileges of old-age to be caustic and sometimes cruel. A widower. Presumably the young woman in the only portrait amongst the pictures had been his wife. Ernest, over-dutiful son, suffered like his prototype in the parable. No fatted calf for Ernest. And the sisters? Virginia: unmarried, but still eligible if she got a move on: intelligent, good to look at, though spoiled at the moment by a too fussy hair-do and spectacles with shiny rims that were too large for

428

her. Prim, in her royal-blue Jaeger frock, and probably in her panties, too. A hint of suppressed tension? Perhaps.

He wished that he could smoke but pride forbade it. Helen had said: 'Give it up in the New Year; you'll never hold out over Christmas.'

Then Caroline: plump but by no means cosy; her trouble was drink; more accurately, drink was the symptom of her trouble. Twenty-four hours at Mynhager was enough to convince anybody that her relationship with Gerald was not based on connubial felicity. Caroline, blatantly sexy, had opted to be separated from her husband for most of the year. There must be a story there. Wycliffe ruefully decided that he had missed his role in life; he should have been a housewife, peering through lace curtains. Are there any left?

Bateman was the odd man out. He lounged elegantly in one of the big chairs, smoking a cigarette, and staring at the ceiling but very far from being relaxed. No one could fail to be aware of his isolation, even from his son. It occurred to Wycliffe that Gerald had not yet subjected him to the threatened interrogation and he wondered why. They had scarcely exchanged half-a-dozen words.

Virginia, anxious to promote the party spirit, asked: 'What shall we play?'

Paul said: 'Let's play Who am I?' The boy looked very pale but he was behaving normally; keeping a stiff upper lip.

Who am I? turned out to be a version of Twenty Questions in which one of them assumed the identity of a famous personage, living or dead, and the others had to discover that identity in not more than twenty questions.

Ernest, the first victim, was unmasked as Oscar Wilde by the sixteenth question. Virginia followed, and beat the field as Lady Astor.

Aunt Stella said: 'I knew Nancy Astor; we were invited to Cliveden several times. I always felt sorry for poor Waldorf, he was such a kindly man and Nancy was a dragon!'

Then it was Gerald's turn.

Joseph had been taking a lively part in the questioning; now he said: 'I'm enjoying this! Psychological striptease!

Who would have thought poor old Ernest had tendencies or that Vee's frustrations were political? Your turn now, Gerry, and you'd better watch your step, you're treading on eggs! What about Churchill, or Ramsey Mac? Or go the whole hog with Talleyrand, he turned his coat so often that nobody knew for certain whose side he was on.'

Some years earlier Gerald had crossed the floor of the House and kept his seat.

Virginia and Ernest ignored their father but Gerald became very tense. In a manner far from his usual self-assured benevolence he said: 'I thought this was a game; but if you intend to use it as an occasion to work off some of your mischievous witticisms I am sure that you will manage just as well without me!' With that, Gerald got up and walked out, closing the door carefully behind him.

Joseph had cut too deep and he felt foolish. In the silence he said: 'What's the matter with him?'

Caroline muttered: 'Stupid bastard!'

Very slowly the party recovered its equanimity and its momentum. At ten o'clock Wycliffe was called to the telephone.

Curtis reporting: 'Some progress, sir. A witness says she saw the girl who took the part of the Virgin, getting into a car near the church at about nine-fifteen. She couldn't say what make the car was and she couldn't see its colour because the light was poor, but she thought it could have been red. She thought it looked a bit like a sports car, but old. She couldn't see who was driving.'

'Anything else?'

'Yes, and it ties up. One of my chaps unearthed the girl's form teacher. She says that at least twice in the last few days of term Francine didn't catch the school bus home; she was picked up by somebody in a red car. She only saw the car from a distance and couldn't see who was driving, but she had heard that Francine's father was back home and assumed that he was calling for her but didn't like to come too near the school.'

'You may have a good lead there.'

Back in the drawing-room they were passing round refreshments, little morsels on sticks and balanced on biscuits. Surely Christmas must be the feast of Gluttony. Then more games, more drinks. At a little before midnight Gerald came back and resumed his seat as though nothing had happened. Glasses were filled with Joseph's '55 port then, with the radio switched on, they waited for the time signal. At midnight precisely they drank a toast 'To Christmas, friends and family!'

Even then Joseph had the last word: ' "And God bless us all! said Tiny Tim." '

Came the presents; distributed by Paul, the youngest member of the party; the great business of unwrapping, the floor littered with pretty Christmas paper; the cries of surprise and delight; the somewhat effusive expressions of gratitude; and the moments of secret misgiving when one wonders whether one's own contributions have matched the general level, appearing neither ostentatious nor mean.

And finally, at about one o'clock, up the stairs to bed. By this time the gale was blowing in mighty gusts so that the old house shuddered. A single gust might last for fifteen or twenty seconds, followed by an abrupt and uneasy calm, an interval while the wind seemed to gather force for its next assault. Occasionally the electric lights flickered and Wycliffe wondered what it must have been like when the only lighting came from candles and oil lamps.

In his bedroom Wycliffe drew back the curtains but dared not open the windows. The roar of the sea and wind merged in a fury and it was impossible to decide whether the water streaming down the window panes came from rain or from spray. Through the watery curtain he looked down on the seething whiteness of breakers racing into the cove. He listened, and thought he could hear the great boulders grinding together, underscoring the rest of the wild orchestration.

In 120 years the house must have come through worse.

He thought about the Bishops. They had been pleasant

enough, almost embarrassingly attentive, thoughtful and generous with their presents. Leaving aside the old man's mischievous wit, their hospitality could hardly be faulted. But he felt uncomfortable; there was an atmosphere: they all seemed edgy and preoccupied. They were going ahead with the business of entertaining him and with the rituals of Christmas but he had the impression that their thoughts were on something quite different.

Francine Lemarque?

Perhaps. It was natural that they should be concerned about the girl but there seemed to be more to it than that.

His thinking was muzzy; he had had rather too much to drink. He prepared for bed and got between the sheets.

Despite the pandemonium outside he could hear a woman's voice in the next room: Caroline, quarrelling with her husband. A happy Christmas.

He switched off the bedside lamp and snuggled down, thinking vaguely of Helen and tropical nights.

Chapter Four

HE SLEPT WELL considering the violence of the storm. Now and then, when rain or spray lashed against the windows with malevolent force he would mutter sleepily to himself, but he had gone to bed slightly tipsy, enough to feel superior to the elements.

He was up by eight-thirty; the worst seemed to be over though the wind blew at storm force and from time to time squalls of drenching rain swept in from the sea. The sky was a low canopy of driven clouds and the sea was lashed to foam for as far as the eye could see. The terrace was drenched by every wave and spume slid down the window panes.

Breakfast was a scratch affair, with Virginia and Ada in the kitchen handing out coffee and toast to anyone who turned up. Ernest was there, eating toast with so much butter on it that his moustache dripped and made Wycliffe feel slightly embarrassed. Joseph, Gerald, and Paul did not appear but to Wycliffe's astonishment, Caroline was in the drawing-room playing Rachmaninov with tremendous zest in the fortissimo passages. The morning after? A release from frustration? Or a celebration of victory? Strange woman!

Ernest said: 'Carrie is good, don't you think? She was at the Royal College and she did a year in Paris. She could have made a career but she said she'd been away from home long enough, so that was that. A real Cornish girl, our Carrie!'

Wycliffe asked: 'Have you heard from the Lemarques this morning?'

'No, I haven't. I'll telephone presently if the lines aren't down.'

A few minutes later Curtis came through. 'Not too early for

you, I hope, sir? A happy Christmas! I'm speaking from home, as you can probably hear.'

Thumps, squeals and shrieks in the background from Curtis's grandchildren.

'Anything fresh?'

'We've traced the red car, sir, a 1975 Triumph belonging to a young layabout called Pellowe—Timothy Pellowe. His father is a builder in a small way in St Buryan.'

'How young is young?'

'Oh, he's not exactly a boy, he's nineteen, rising twenty. The perpetual student type who never studies anything. He got chucked out of university last July for failing his exams and he's been bumming around ever since, coming home to mum and dad when times are hard but taking off into the wide blue yonder when it suits him. Like now. This time he's been home since early December.'

'Anything known?'

'No, he hasn't got form but, from what I hear, he's not the sort I'd want a daughter of mine running off with.'

'His parents haven't any idea where he might be?'

'Not a clue; nor has anybody else we've talked to so far. All he said was that he'd probably be back in a few days.'

'Of course you must do this through Division, but I want all you've got on the couple and the car put on the telex. At the same time they might try to find somebody in the TV and radio newsrooms who stays awake over Christmas and see if we can get a mention.'

Ernest could not get through to the Lemarques. 'Their line is dead; it's usually like this after a blow; a toss-up who gets cut off and who doesn't. I'll take a walk over there directly.'

Wycliffe said: 'I thought of going over myself.' He contrived without being offensive to convey the message that he wanted to go alone.

'Oh! In that case . . .' After a pause Ernest went on: 'This young fellow she's gone off with; they must have planned it.'

'Of course.'

'Then wouldn't you have expected her to leave a note of some sort?'

'Perhaps she did.' Wycliffe went on quickly: 'I don't know if you would care to give Paul the latest news—such as it is.'

Perversity decided him to walk, despite the weather. He put on his heavy waterproof and a matching peaked cap which, according to Helen, made him look like Our Man in Berlin. It was not actually raining but mist and spray mingled in the rampageous air and he was driven along the dirt road by the force of the wind. He reached the painter's cottage where there was no sign of life. Marsden was probably sleeping it off. He turned down the footpath to the bridge, but the bridge, a ramshackle affair at best, had collapsed and been swept away by the stream, now a miniature torrent of brown water. He would have to walk to the village and down the old mine track on the other side.

He was out of humour with himself, low on Christmas spirit, and disgruntled with his job. Why was he getting into this anyway? A missing girl, a juvenile who had run away with a boy three or four years older. Teenagers went missing every day; and every day a few more took to glue sniffing; smoking pot; swallowing, sniffing or injecting themselves with daydreams which turned into nightmares. And the police were all but helpless. Every day young people (older ones too) robbed or mugged or raped or murdered, and many chief constables would be over the moon if their detection rate came within shouting distance of 50 per cent. Add to this strikes, violence on the picket lines, violence at football matches, violence at demonstrations for and against almost everything.

He was Canute, striving to halt the tide; Quixote, tilting at windmills; better still, that Greek chap, Sisyphus, condemned through all eternity to roll a stone up-hill so that it could roll down again.

Sensible people raised the drawbridge, kept their fingers crossed, and learned Russian. But here he was, getting wet to bring to the Lemarques news of their daughter's stupidity. Curtis could and would have done all that was needed. The truth was that he felt uneasy. During the night he had recalled an incident that had occurred on his way back from

435

the painter's cottage in the dark. The orange rectangle of the Lemarques' window, the opening and closing of their door, and the erratic movements of a flashlight held in someone's hand. It was absurd, but that trivial sequence of events had acquired a dramatic significance in his mind.

In the village street a little boy was pedalling furiously around on a brand new 'Chopper' bicycle, oblivious of the weather, imagining himself on a Yamaha or a Honda. Outside two or three of the houses cars were unloading guests laden with parcels; there were Christmas trees with lights in several windows and through some he could see the flickering glow of a television set. The Tributers was not yet open but there were a few cars parked by the church and he could hear the sound of the organ.

He had trouble finding the alley which led to the mine track but came upon it at last between the Mechanics' Institute (1853), and a terrace of cottages. In places it was rough going with puddles of peaty water which could only be avoided by taking to the heather, and now the wind was in his face. Head down, he fought against it and reached the cottage at last. There was no van parked at the bottom of the steps and he was wondering if they had gone out when he saw that the front door was open. From that moment he had no doubt that his instinct had been right.

He climbed the steps. The door was wide open and the drab carpet and mats in the little passage were sodden with blown rain. A flimsy plant-stand had been overturned, perhaps by the wind, so that plant and pot had parted company and there was soil strewn over the floor.

He was picking his way through to the living-room when he heard a sound and he called out: 'Is anyone there?'

Heavy footsteps, and Marsden appeared in the doorway of the living-room. He looked at Wycliffe in a bemused, uncomprehending way and for a moment Wycliffe thought he was drunk. He was wearing slacks that were wet below the knees and a roll-neck pullover stained with paint and grime; his black curls had been flattened by the rain and there were droplets of moisture caught in his moustache.

436

Wycliffe said: 'What are you doing here?'

The painter supported himself against the doorpost and spoke as though he were short of breath. 'I saw from my place that the door was open when I got up this morning . . . Half-an-hour later it was still open and I wondered if there was something wrong. Lemarque's van wasn't there and I thought they might have gone off and not shut the door properly . . . The bridge was down so I had to walk round.' He gestured weakly. 'There seemed to be nobody here and it was obvious the door had been open for a long time. I couldn't understand it so I came in to look round . . . Of course, I found her.'

'Francine?' Wycliffe's voice was sharp.

'Not Francine, Jane. She's up in the bedroom, and she's dead.'

'Stay where you are!'

Wycliffe went up the stairs. At the top was a landing with three doors opening off. The room in front of him was Francine's, he could see the single bed and the pop-star posters on the wall. Another door opened into a tiny bathroom with a loo. He turned to the third door; it was almost closed and he pushed it open. There were yellow curtains drawn over the tiny window and a pale, jaundiced light reached into the room from the grey world outside. It was a moment before his eyes became adjusted to the gloom. A double bed took up most of the space and the bed was made up though untidily, as if someone had been lying across it.

Then he saw her, on the floor, her body was wedged between the bed and the dressing-table. She was wearing the drab woollen two-piece he had seen her in the day before. He bent over her. In order to do so he had to sprawl across the bed. She was lying on her side but her head was twisted so that he could see her face. The pale, serene features had been grossly mutilated by a bullet leaving her skull; a bullet which must have made its entry through the back of the head or the neck. He reached down and tried to raise her hand. Jane Lemarque was dead and she had been dead for several hours.

He got to his feet and looked at his watch. Ten thirty-five.

437

'At ten thirty-five on the morning of December 25th I entered the larger of the two bedrooms and found the deceased lying on the floor between the bed and dressing table. She appeared to be fully clothed. She was in such a position that I was able to see the injury to the upper part of her face which I took to be the wound of exit of a bullet fired from behind. I satisfied myself that life was extinct . . .'

Accustomed to such scenes, his reactions were professional, but he had never become hardened. He was still deeply shocked by violent death; by the senseless destruction of a web of consciousness which reached back to the womb.

Marsden mustn't be left downstairs alone. What the hell had he been doing in the living-room anyway? And he was not wearing a coat or mackintosh, only a pullover and slacks . . . But Jane Lemarque had been dead for many hours.

Downstairs, Marsden was still standing in the doorway of the living-room as though dazed.

'You saw her?'

He couldn't keep the man standing there, he was liable to fall down but if he let him go back into the living-room the scene-of-crime chaps would go berserk.

'You can sit on the stairs.'

Marsden lowered his bulk on to the second stair and sat with his hands on his knees. His pullover was quite dry.

'Where's your coat?'

Marsden pointed to the living room. 'In there.' He passed a hand over his forehead. 'Christ! I hardly know what I'm doing. I went in there to telephone but the bloody wires had been cut . . . I was going to call your lot and I thought the quickest way would be to twist the ends together.' He held out his right hand and opened it. He had been gripping a small penknife with an open blade which had cut into the flesh and brought blood.

'I was stripping the wires when you came.'

'And your coat?'

He shifted irritably. 'I slipped the bloody thing off because it was in the way. Why keep on about it?'

It sounded feasible.

438

'You stay where you are.'

Wycliffe went into the living-room and to the telephone. The wires had been cut near the instrument and the ends were bared. Marsden's coat—stained and worn suede with lambswool facings—lay in a heap on the floor.

He twisted the wires together as best he could and it worked. He made the routine calls. To Division: Locate Detective Sergeant Curtis; send a patrol car, a couple of uniformed men, and a police surgeon; notify the coroner. Then he spoke to his own office. That Christmas morning the duty strength at C.I.D. headquarters was a detective sergeant and two constables, all three engaged in the perilous cut and thrust of gin-rummy. Along with a lot of other people they were about to have their simple pleasures brutally cut short.

Wycliffe's deputy, Chief Inspector John Scales, was located at the home of a friend and from now on the wheels would begin to turn. The pathologist would be notified, a mobile incident post would be sent to Mulfra and preparations put in hand to get a team on the road. The leader of the team: Detective Inspector Kersey. In the interests of promotion Kersey had served his time in the wilderness, now he was returning to the fold and no one was more pleased than Wycliffe.

He rejoined Marsden.

Marsden had a cigarette going and he had recovered something of his usual poise. 'So that's how it's done.'

Wycliffe said: 'You will be required to make a statement later but I am going to ask you a few questions.'

'Ask away.'

'Yesterday morning I saw an old grey Escort van parked outside here. Is it theirs?'

'I suppose so; it turned up shortly after he came out of jail.'

'You knew Lemarque before he went to prison?'

Marsden looked around for somewhere to dispose of the butt-end of his cigarette then pitched it through the open doorway. 'I knew him by sight and to pass the time of day. They came down quite often and stayed at the cottage for a weekend; longer, sometimes. He had money and a Jag then.' Marsden grinned in something like his old style. 'But no

439

particular interest in impoverished genius, women, or booze, so our paths didn't cross.'

'While Lemarque was in jail, did his wife associate with other men?'

'How the hell should I know?'

'You were recommended to me as an expert on such matters.'

A short laugh. 'I'm flattered. But I'm no expert where that lady is concerned. She strikes me as the sort who needs a man about as much as I need a hole in the head but you never can tell; impressions can be deceptive.' He broke off. 'Christ! It's hard to remember that she's up there, poor little cow! Was that a shot-gun wound?'

'No. What time did you get up this morning?'

Marsden passed a hand over his hair and looked at it foolishly when he realized that it was wet. 'I shall catch my death over this, I've got a weak chest. My mother used to say, "Keep your head, your feet and your bum dry and you'll be all right." It must've been about nine.'

'And the van was already gone?'

'Yes.'

'When did you last see Lemarque?'

The painter grimaced. 'I haven't a clue.'

'His van?'

'You'll think I spend my time looking out of the bloody window like the old bags in the village, but it happens I did see the van yesterday afternoon, at about half-two, perhaps earlier, being driven along the track towards the village. I suppose Lemarque was driving. I don't think Jane can—could.' He hesitated. 'You think he killed her?'

Wycliffe said, 'Do you? Or do you have good reason to know that he didn't?'

The painter shook his head. 'My God! This should teach me not to play the good Samaritan. In future, Marsden, you'll keep your head down, and your eyes shut. I don't know whether Lemarque killed his wife but it wouldn't surprise me; not that I know anything about Lemarque but some women are born victims and she was one.'

On the face of it the shooting had taken place sometime the previous evening or early in the night. It had the marks of a domestic crime; no evidence of burglary (was there anything to take?), apparently no sexual overtones; and no husband available for comment. Unless he had a cast-iron alibi it looked as though the case would be as good as over when Lemarque was brought in. And that shouldn't be difficult.

It would be simple to put Lemarque and his van on the telex. As an ex-con Lemarque would be on record and details of the van should be available through Vehicle Registration. But he needed to get Marsden off his hands first. He didn't want an audience.

The sound of a car grinding along the track. Wycliffe went to the door. Two coppers in a patrol car, their meditations on the Nativity in some quiet lay-by rudely interrupted. Curtis came hard on their heels. Wycliffe put him in the picture.

Curtis's button-eyes looked at Wycliffe with concern. 'Do you think this has anything to do with the girl?'

'How do I know? But it makes it all the more important to find her.' He gave Curtis detailed instructions to put Lemarque and his van on the telex, then he called Marsden over. 'Mr Marsden will go with you to make his statement.'

Marsden gave him a sour look. 'And when will Mr Marsden get back to feed his cat and perform other necessary domestic chores?'

'That depends on Mr Marsden.'

'I suppose I can take my coat?'

'Not for the moment; anyway, there's central heating in the nick.'

As Curtis was leaving with Marsden, two uniformed men arrived in a Panda car with a detective sergeant from Division.

It would be the better part of two hours before the pathologist or the headquarters circus could arrive so he left the detective sergeant in charge and got one of the patrolmen to drive him back to Mynhager. The car jolted over the bumpy track and splashed through the pools while the uniformed driver sat beside him, stiff and silent as though stuffed. It was raining hard again; the village street streamed with water, gleaming darkly, and was utterly deserted. There were cars outside The Tributers, the bar was brightly lit, and they caught a snatch of song as they passed. Turning off down the road to Mynhager they met the full force of the wind with the rain driving straight off the sea.

'Are you due off at two?'

'With a bit of luck, sir, I'll be able to spend some time with the kids.'

'Have a good day, what's left of it.'

Wycliffe was thinking of Francine's disappearance and of her mother's murder. A connection? He believed in coincidence as he believed in Santa Claus but coincidences do happen. Arthur Koestler wrote a book about them. A girl goes missing on the night before Christmas Eve, and on Christmas morning her mother is found, shot dead. And her father? Wycliffe was relieved that Francine had been seen getting into the red car, otherwise the prospect might have seemed even more sinister.

But his immediate problem was with the Bishops. The Bishops, the Batemans and the Lemarques had been closely associated for years and the Lemarques had been almost members of the family. Not any more. After Bateman pulled out of the partnership and Lemarque got the bit between his teeth to end up in jail, the situation had changed.

Policemen are fated to be an embarrassment to their friends and to themselves. Accept a lift in a friend's car and he thinks you are checking his tax disc, his speed and his braking. Jane Lemarque had been murdered and now questions would be asked, some of them relevant, others not. But the people questioned would feel disturbed and possibly threatened, and the Bishops and Batemans were bound to be in the forefront. Even if it turned out that Lemarque had killed his wife, the police would need to know why, and they would look to Mynhager for at least part of the answer.

Ergo: it was impossible for him to continue as a guest in the house.

*

442

Ernest, his glasses pushed up on to his forehead, was sitting at a table looking down a binocular microscope at a minute insect impaled on a pin. On the table was a shallow, cork-lined drawer with its glass cover lying beside it. In the drawer, other flies, similarly impaled, were lined up like guardsmen, each with a tiny cardboard label. A cabinet under the window held at least a score of such drawers.

'I hope I'm not disturbing you.'

Ernest swivelled his chair away from the table. 'My dear Charles! I'm merely filling in time until lunch looking at a few flies I took yesterday.'

His 'den' was a little room sandwiched between dining-room and drawing-room. The window, covered with a grubby net curtain, looked out on the courtyard at the back of the house.

'Any news of Francine?'

'Not of Francine but I'm afraid there's very bad news of the Lemarques.'

'Indeed?' A look of concern.

'Jane has been shot; when I saw her earlier this morning she had been dead for several hours at least.'

Ernest's features expressed total incredulity. 'Shot? You mean she's killed herself?'

Wycliffe shook his head. 'It wasn't suicide, it was murder.'

'And Alain?' The question seemed to be forced from him.

'Lemarque and his van are missing.'

'Oh God!' He got up from his chair and went to the window. 'Are you suggesting that he killed his wife—murdered her?'

'All I can say is that Jane Lemarque has been murdered and that her husband is missing. You know them better than I do. Is it credible that he murdered her? Is he a violent man? Do you know of any motive he may have had or thought he had?'

An electric clock on the wall above the table flicked the seconds away. Ernest had his back to the room; he was wearing a woolly cardigan which hung limply from his thin shoulders and his whole body seemed to droop. He looked like

443

an old man. At last he turned away from the window. 'Alain is not a violent man, Charles, quite the contrary, and I'm sure that he was fond of Jane.' But he spoke without conviction. 'I don't know what to say. Is this anything to do with Francine running away?'

'I've no idea.'

Ernest said: 'I suppose you will be taking charge of the investigation? You don't need me to tell you that you are welcome to stay on here.'

'I'm very grateful but it wouldn't do at all. You must see that.'

Ernest looked at him in pained surprise. 'Surely, this isn't going to affect us—our relationship, I mean?'

'I'm afraid it's bound to do until the case is over. I have to go back to being a policeman. You're a lawyer, you know the score. How can I possibly conduct an investigation while remaining on intimate terms with a family so closely connected with the dead woman?'

Ernest slumped into his chair and swivelled listlessly to and fro. 'No, I suppose you are right, but I have to admit that it's a blow . . . What a Christmas Day this has turned out to be!'

Wycliffe was aware of the curious museum-like smell of the room, a blend of cork, naphthalene, old books, and preserving spirit. He had the odd notion that it was Ernest's main concern to arrest the passage of time, to hold on to the moment and preserve the status quo . . .

'So you are leaving us . . . You'll stay to lunch—you won't just walk out?' It was a plea.

'Of course I'll stay; and thank you.'

'Good! Just give me a few minutes to break the news to the others.'

In the dining-room everyone was subdued and Wycliffe felt like a leper though they seemed anxious to make it clear that his position was understood. Only Joseph and Aunt Stella were seated, Paul wasn't there, and the others stood about going through the motions of helping themselves to bits of chicken, slices of ham, and a variety of salads, all laid out on the table.

Virginia said: 'It's hardly credible! In less than forty-eight hours, the whole family . . . Just gone!'

Caroline picked at the chicken with her fork. 'I can't believe that Alain killed her. Jane was difficult, God knows, but she was the only one for him. I doubt if he ever looked at another woman.'

Joseph was helping himself from a bottle of hock. 'If I'd been married to Jane I can imagine a situation in which I might have strangled her, but shooting, that's another thing altogether. You have to have a gun, you have to load it, aim it, and pull the trigger. Premeditation.' The old man shook his head. 'But who else is there?'

Aunt Stella had seemed unaware of or indifferent to what had happened and what was being said; she had a plate of food and she was working through it. Then, abruptly, with perfect enunciation, she recited:

> ' "Lizzie Borden with an axe,
> Hit her father forty whacks.
> When she saw what she had done,
> She hit her mother forty-one." '

A shocked silence, but the old lady was in no way subdued. She looked round at the family. 'What's the matter? All I'm saying is I would be more willing to believe it of the girl than of her father. We all know that Alain Lemarque is a rogue but nothing will convince me that he is a murderer.'

Virginia was outraged. 'But that's monstrous, Aunt Stella! A terrible thing to say!'

Caroline turned on her sister. 'You've always defended Francine but there's something in what Aunt Stella says. I don't know whether Francine could or would have done it but I don't forget what she was like when she was here. Don't you remember when she smashed her mother's gold watch just because she was stopped from going on some trip? How old was she then . . . five? . . . six? No tears, no show of temper

445

but straight up the stairs to her mother's dressing table. And that's not the only—'

'Stop it, Carrie!' Ernest's voice raised in real anger. 'There may be some excuse for Aunt Stella but there is none for the rest of us. We are turning a tragedy affecting our friends into poisonous gossip!'

Wycliffe noted the effect of this outburst on the others. Bateman nodded agreement. Old Joseph looked at his son with a faint smile on his lips. Caroline's expression was one of unbelief like a cat who has been bitten by a mouse. Stella remained unperturbed.

Lunch was over at last and Wycliffe went upstairs to do his packing. There was a knock on his bedroom door and Gerald Bateman came in, a diffident and confiding Bateman.

'I hope I'm not intruding but I felt that I must speak to you before you cease to be a guest and become a policeman.' A thin smile. 'You can imagine how I feel. I've known Alain and Jane for twenty years. Alain and I not only worked together but we shared a good deal of our social life both here and in London. The differences I had with Alain which ended our partnership and led eventually to his trouble with the law in no way diminished my affection and respect for them both. We continued friends.'

'Have you seen anything of him since you've been home this time?'

'I called there; it was my first chance following his release.'

'How did you find him?'

The great man considered. 'I found him changed but what could one expect?'

'Depressed?'

'Not depressed, subdued.' He lowered his voice. 'As a matter of fact he was sounding me out about putting up capital for a scheme he had in mind. He wasn't ready to discuss it in any detail but I gathered that it was local and concerned with tourism. More than that he was not prepared to say at this stage.'

'Were you able to give him any encouragement?'

'Yes, I was, and not only out of a desire to help an old

446

friend. Alain is a first rate businessman and, with certain safeguards, I would be fully prepared to back a scheme he believed to be sound. Of course, a partnership would hardly be practicable in the new circumstances but I think he has it in mind that I should provide the capital and he would run the business for a share in the profits.'

Wycliffe stooped to fasten his suitcase. Politicians are by nature devious and he was wondering about the real purpose of Bateman's confidences. However, he rarely tried to meet guile with subtlety. The suitcase secured, he straightened up, put on his ruminating-cow look, and asked: 'Why are you telling me all this?'

By the same token Bateman was far too old a hand to be disconcerted. 'Because I want you to know that whatever precipitated this tragedy it was not, I think, a feeling of hopelessness about the future.'

Wycliffe thought, he wants me to believe that Lemarque murdered his wife and he may well be right. He said: 'Paul wasn't at lunch; if he's around I would like a word with him before I leave.'

No doubt Bateman had survived many more devastating snubs and he took this one in his stride. 'There is just one other matter: I hope you won't be influenced by the talk during lunch. I'm afraid my wife is in the habit of making outrageous remarks, just to shock. The family take no notice, but to a stranger . . .' A bleak smile. 'As for Aunt Stella's nonsense! . . .'

Wycliffe said: 'I expect I shall hear a great deal of nonsense during the next few days.'

Bateman nodded. 'You reassure me. If you want Paul you will almost certainly find him in his workshop. It's his refuge in time of trouble. The old wash-house, I'll show you.'

They had to go through the kitchen where Ada was washing dishes, then through an empty cavernous room with whitewashed walls and a slate floor.

'Here we are!' Bateman pushed open another door and they were in a businesslike workshop. There was a carpenter's bench, woodworking tools neatly arranged in racks, and the

447

delectable blended smells of resin and sawdust. Paul was there, bending over what looked like a bench-end, supported on trestles.

'Paul is carving new ends for some of the pews in the church . . . I'll leave you to it.' Bateman, being discreet.

Paul straightened. He was holding a gouge and he was engaged in carving a new bench-end which had already been shaped. The motif was a herring gull, about to touch down on the water. It was simple and incisive, fitting the rectangular space. There were three more ends lying against one of the walls, carved with a crab, a lobster, and a St Ives gig.

'I came here because I couldn't think of anything else to do.' He stood, taller than Wycliffe, pale faced, diffident and slightly embarrassed. 'It's only a hobby for the holidays.'

'But they will be used, surely?'

'Well, yes. The Vicar thinks the Victorian bench ends are dull; there are only two survivors of the original sixteenth-century ones and he feels that we could liven some of the rest up a bit. Uncle Ernest said he would pay for the wood and the fitting if I carved them.' He paused awkwardly. 'I don't suppose there's any news of Francine?'

'I'm sorry, no. I came here because I thought you might help me. I'm trying to find out what things were like in the Lemarque household before and after Mr Lemarque came out of prison . . . You realize, Paul, that the time has gone for any kind of reticence.'

The boy nodded. 'I see that, but there's very little I can tell you. Francine never talks much about her home. I don't think she got on very well with her mother and sometimes she seemed quite rude to her, but I think Mrs Lemarque used to exasperate Francine by always being . . .'

'Being what?'

'I don't know; sort of miserable, I suppose, and resigned to being miserable. I think that is what upset Francine.'

'What was Francine's attitude to her father?'

'She seemed to look forward to him coming home.'

'And was she disappointed?'

He hesitated. 'I think she was.'

'Have you any idea why?'

He looked worried. 'It's very difficult to say, but Mr Lemarque had changed; I could see that. He was very quiet and he seemed depressed. He didn't have a lot to say before, but he used to be cheerful, he would tease people, especially Francine, and they used to laugh together.'

'Have there been quarrels since he came home?'

'I don't know; I only know that Francine was even more unhappy. Just a couple of days before she went away she said: "There's one thing you learn from parents—never get married." '

Wycliffe said: 'You are obviously very fond of Francine and you will not want to betray her confidences but in the new circumstances you must realize that you can help best by being completely frank. Has Francine said anything to you recently which, with hindsight, might throw any light on what has happened?'

Paul stood, testing the edge of the gouge with his thumb, 'I can't think of anything. I mean, she doesn't confide in me much . . . The only thing she said recently which I didn't understand was something about me knowing more about her . . .'

'What exactly did she say?'

'It was something like: "When you know more about me you won't want me".'

'There's more, isn't there?'

He coloured. 'I said that I wanted to spend my life getting to know her and she laughed. She said that it wouldn't take that long; that I might find out more than I wanted to know very soon.'

Why did Wycliffe at that moment feel that Paul would follow in his uncle's footsteps? A confirmed bachelor, never taking a firm grip, making the best of a life divided between his work and his hobbies: the legal practice, Mynhager, wood carving, the aunts . . .

Wycliffe said: 'Thanks; you've straightened out my ideas a bit. I'll let you know as soon as we hear any news of Francine.'

Paul turned to put the gouge he was holding back in the

rack so that Wycliffe could not see his face. 'Did my father. . .?'

'Yes?'

He shook his head. 'Sorry! It doesn't matter.'

'You missed lunch. See if Ada has any food left in the kitchen.'

The boy smiled. 'I might do that.'

Wycliffe's case was in the hall; someone had brought it down. Ernest and Virginia came out to see him off. Ernest said: 'I hope you'll come again, bring Helen, and stay longer.'

Ernest walked with him to the car. 'Carrie's tongue runs away with her. She really doesn't mean what she says. Alain, Jane and Francine were like members of the family and what has happened is a tragedy for all of us.'

Chapter Five

HE DROVE BACK to the Lemarques' cottage. Still raining, and in an hour or so the gloom would merge with the dusk. In the village, at the turn-off to the mine track, a uniformed copper was poised to direct new arrivals and divert the inquisitive. When he saw Wycliffe's indicators flash he raised a minatory hand and came to the car window.

'Do you have business down there, sir?' Water dribbled off his flower-pot helmet as he stooped to speak.

'Chief Superintendent Wycliffe.'

'Sorry, sir! I didn't recognize you. You know where it is?'

'I don't think I shall miss it. Has anybody arrived?'

'The police surgeon has been and gone, sir; a headquarters party is there, and Dr Franks, the pathologist, went down a couple of minutes ago.'

So far none of the locals seemed to have realized that anything was happening, but that would change; with more police activity than the village had seen since D.H. Lawrence and Frieda were chased out as suspected German spies during the First War.

Lined up along the track beyond the cottage were two police cars, a police Range Rover, and a lethal-looking James Bond vehicle which could only belong to Dr Franks, the pathologist.

Franks himself was standing just inside the front door of the cottage, spick and span in herring-bone tweed with a striped shirt and a club tie.

'Hullo, Charles! Is this your idea of Christmas? Apparently the lady most concerned in all this is upstairs and Fox is up there with the photographer taking pictures while she's in situ, so to speak. Fox is a keen lad; he doesn't want me prodding her about until they've finished. What's it all about?'

'A shooting.'

'I know that, but why was she shot? A domestic tiff?'

'I've no idea.' Although they had worked together for years, Franks still irritated Wycliffe by his frivolous attitude in the face of death, with the effect that Wycliffe became morose and taciturn.

'I hear that you are staying down here.'

Wycliffe pointed across the valley. 'With the Bishops; he's a lawyer, you may know him.'

Franks grimaced. 'I do. Christmas with him must be as exciting as a Jewish funeral. And this place—fine in summer but now! You're a masochist, Charles! I hear Helen is in Kenya. Nights of tropical splendour and all that. Well, I suppose that's how you want it.'

'Ready for you, doctor.' Sergeant Fox, in charge of the scene-of-crime investigation and successor to the misanthropic Smith, now retired. This was Fox's first murder case since joining the squad. Seeing Wycliffe, he came downstairs and Franks went up. Fox was twenty-eight, thin with sandy coloured hair and freckles; he had a prominent nose and a receding chin but contrived to look intelligent despite everything.

'I didn't know you were here, sir.' Fox was preoccupied, watching Franks as he climbed the stairs; he said wistfully: 'I wish Dr Franks would wear the correct gear.' Fox, himself, looked like a one-man decontamination squad. The idea was to minimise 'exchange' at the scene of crime, to ensure that traces left by the criminal were neither confused nor destroyed by the investigator. Wycliffe remembered a pathologist who scattered cigar ash over the scene of crime as a priest sprinkles holy water.

He was depressed by changes, they made him feel old; like the reading glasses, tucked neatly in their case in his right-hand jacket pocket. He would bring them out only when absolutely necessary, and put them on with the surreptitious air of a man who is forced to zip up his flies in public.

The doldrums: a period after the discovery of a major crime during which resources are mobilized and the preliminary technical data are established. No point in rushing around in ever diminishing circles while this is going on.

Dr Franks came down the stairs. 'She's on the bed now, Charles. Move her when you like.'

'The van is on the way. What have you got for me?'

'Not much. She was shot with a large calibre bullet which your chaps will dig out of the walls or the woodwork. It must have played merry hell inside her head and neck. She's been dead between sixteen and twenty hours so she was shot between four and eight yesterday. No sign of other injuries that I can see; no indications of assault, sexual or otherwise, apart from the shooting. If there's any more to tell you, after I've had a chance to take a real look, I'll be in touch later today. Who's attending?'

'Inspector Trevena from Division is coming with the van.'

Franks stood at the top of the steps. It was quite dark now, every light in the little cottage was switched on and a weak orange glow reached out into the pit-like darkness of the valley. It had stopped raining but the air was full of moisture and tangy with salt. The gale had blown itself out but the continuous muffled roar of the sea seemed sometimes very close, sometimes distant.

He held out his hand. 'I'll be off then. What a way to spend Christmas!'

A moment or two later, the roar of his car engine, two great shafts of light cleaving the valley, a skidding of tyres, and he was away.

Not robbery, not a sex crime; just a housewife shot with a heavy calibre gun. Probably she had been threatened downstairs and, terrified, she had retreated up the stairs with some idea of protecting herself, only to be ruthlessly cornered and shot. Like an execution.

By her husband? Caroline Bateman hadn't thought so. 'She was the only one for him. I doubt if he ever looked at another woman.' And Wycliffe suspected that Caroline

453

understood these things. But a passionate quarrel, perhaps over Francine running away? A quarrel which suddenly flared into uncontrollable violence? Joseph had pointed out the snags there. 'You have to have the gun . . . load it, aim it, and pull the trigger.' It becomes in some degree a premeditated act. But what other possibilities were there? Francine? There were cases on record of young girls murdering their parents, but he couldn't take the possibility seriously here. Anyway, what had happened to Lemarque? There remained the ubiquitous outsider . . .

His instinct was to wander around the little house, soaking up the atmosphere, getting the feel of how it had been lived in, but if he did this before the scene-of-crime boys had finished he would be unpopular with Fox. Criminal investigation, like other social studies, was struggling to qualify as a science, to join the other sacred cows and become a private stamping ground for experts. Wycliffe sympathized to some extent with the ineffable Poirot and his little grey cells. 'It is the psychology, *mon ami!*' In particular he agreed with the Belgian that a clue two-foot long is in no way inferior to one that must be sought under a microscope.

He growled like an irritated grizzly, giving vent to a vague and disquieting awareness that he was becoming increasingly out of step with the way things were going in his profession. He climbed the stairs. Fox, as though activated by a spring, came out from the main bedroom. 'You wanted me, sir?'

'No.'

'We've got the bullet and cartridge-case. It's a nine-millimetre.' Good dog, waiting to be patted.

A cold look. 'You know what to do, I suppose?' Wycliffe, like Talleyrand, distrusted enthusiasm: Above all, gentlemen, not the slightest zeal.

He followed Fox into the bedroom. The room looked as though it had been got ready for the removal men; the bed was dismantled, the bedding neatly folded; drawers were removed and the furniture pulled as far as possible away from the walls.

'Found anything?'

Fox pointed to the dressing table. Laid out on the top were a number of documents and papers beside an old-fashioned cash box with a brass handle. 'The papers were in the box and the box was in one of the drawers, locked.'

Wycliffe looked through the haul: passports for the family, none of the stamps less than three years old; birth certificates, marriage lines; a couple of policies, one for the van; a few bank statements, and an envelope boldly marked with a date: 15.4.79.

Fox said: 'One of the other drawers is stuffed full of letters but I haven't had a chance to go through them yet.'

Wycliffe was intrigued by the dated envelope but all it held was a press cutting:

Professional Men's Annual Dinner.
Nearly a hundred members of the West Cornwall Association of Professional Men, with their guests, attended their annual dinner at The Royal Hotel on Easter Saturday. Mr Ernest Bishop, retiring chairman, presided, and the guest speaker was Mr Gerald Bateman M.P.. The theme of Mr Bateman's address was the need to maintain high standards of integrity and independence in the face of growing domination of the professions by central and local government . . .

And three bags full! Why had Lemarque kept this cutting along with things which he obviously regarded as important?

Wycliffe said: 'I'll take this and give you a receipt.'

He left Fox to his work and crossed the landing to Francine's room. He stood in the small space between bed and chest of drawers, looking about him. Francine's school books were on two shelves above the chest of drawers. In addition to her textbooks there was a pile of exercise books, neatly arranged: Mathematics, English, Chemistry, French, Biology, History . . . Wycliffe flicked through some of them. The handwriting was more sophisticated than he would have expected from a girl of her age; the marks were average, the comments often acid. On the chest itself there was a swing mirror, a sketch pad and a box of watercolours, along with a few cosmetic jars and bottles. He tried the drawers, the top left-hand one, the only one fitted with a lock, was quite empty. The other top drawer held a jumble of underclothes and a box of cheap jewellery—beads, bracelets, rings and earrings. The other drawers were given over to clothes.

The empty drawer was where she had kept those things without which the little room became anonymous. Her letters, cards, snapshots, sketches, and all the other trifles she had thought worth keeping. She had taken them with her—or she had destroyed them.

Jane Lemarque had been murdered and her husband was missing, yet Wycliffe's thoughts still centred on their runaway daughter. He could not rid himself of the memory of the girl in the blue dress who, in that little grey church, had evoked the Madonna; remote, mysterious, and deeply moving in her sad presentiment: '. . . and purple for death.' Twenty minutes later she had been picked up by the youth in the red car.

'Francine is a very talented girl but she can be difficult . . . if she thought she had a real grievance . . . Young Paul will have his problems if their friendship ever comes to anything.' Virginia.

'It wouldn't surprise me if she had gone off with some man, and I mean, man.' Caroline.

Then there was the story of Francine and her mother's watch.

The Lizzie Borden fantasy was bizarre but he felt in his bones that the runaway girl held the key to her mother's murder.

He returned his attention to the rest of the room. No desk, no table, not even a chair. Probably she had done her homework sitting up in bed, scribbling away with a ballpoint while pop music kept the silence at bay. Her radio was on the floor within reach of her hand. The bed was a divan with a narrow gap underneath to accommodate the castors. He knelt down, felt underneath, and came out with a little paper-covered notebook and a ball-point. One up on Curtis!

But no real score. Most of the pages had been torn from the notebook and the remaining five or six had been used for notes on biology. There were headings: Eye Colour, Hair Colour, Skin Pigmentation, Blood . . . with brief notes under each and, in one case, a diagram.

Heredity. Wycliffe had only vague notions on the subject, derived from elementary lessons at school on the breeding prospects of peas and little red-eyed flies. He put the notebook back where he had found it.

Curtis was right, the girl had made sure that nobody would learn much from her room. In fact, he could get no feeling anywhere in the house that it had been really lived in, only that people had camped out there.

A voice at the bottom of the stairs said: 'Mr Wycliffe! Mr Kersey is here, sir.'

The return of the prodigal. Warmth on both sides.

'Good to be back, sir! Like old times.' The difference being that Kersey was now an inspector instead of a sergeant. 'The van is parked by the church and D.C. Dixon is duty officer, so we are in business.'

Now they had a base linked in to the police communication network as well as the public telephone service.

The two men had always worked well together though physically and temperamentally they were very different. Wycliffe, spare, thin featured, thin lipped, and sandy haired, nick-named The Monk. Kersey, stocky of build, full of face, very dark, with features which looked as though they had been roughly moulded out of plasticene and carelessly stuck on. By the same token, Wycliffe was taciturn and inclined to be prudish in speech and attitude, while Kersey often thought aloud and was not averse to what he called basic English. Together, they drove back to the village.

At Mynhager the family would be sitting down to their Christmas meal: turkey with all the trimmings, pudding with clotted cream, (cholesterol by the spoonful), plenty of wine; crackers to pull, and flushed faces afterwards. In the village people were beginning to take an interest in what was going on. Although it was quite dark people were standing in their doorways, others had the curtains drawn back in their front-rooms. Not that there was much to see.

The van was parked near the wall of the churchyard and opposite the village's two shops, now closed for the holiday. Inside the van the radio crackled in staccato outbursts: 'Alpha one-four to Alpha Victor. I am attending an R.T.A. at . . .' 'Alpha Victor to Alpha three. A householder at Nance Cottage, Sancreed, reports an intruder in her garden . . .'

A disturbance by youths on motorcycles in a car-park, a Ford Escort saloon apparently abandoned . . . The bread and butter of police work.

D.C. Dixon had a mug of tea at his elbow, already somebody was pecking away at a typewriter in the next cubicle, the van was an old model and had the authentic smell of a nick. The blinds were down and there was an atmosphere of stuffy cosiness; some wag had suspended a sprig of mistletoe from one of the roof struts. Home from home.

Dixon had news: 'Message from D.S. Curtis, sir. He's on his way here with Timothy Pellowe. He said you would understand.'

So Pellowe and his red car had, presumably, been picked up on their doorstep. And Francine?

While they were waiting Wycliffe put Kersey in the picture.

Timothy Pellowe was lean and lank and pale, a weed grown in poor soil and a bad light. At nineteen he retained an adolescent spottiness, and the inability to cope with his legs and arms. He sprawled over a chair and on to the small table which separated him from Wycliffe. They were in the interview cubicle of the van; Kersey sat by the door, just out of the boy's line of sight.

'I was staying with a friend in Exeter; we had a party last night and it was lunch time before I was up. Then, on the news, I heard about Mrs Lemarque. They said the police wanted to contact her husband and daughter; then they said the police wanted to interview the driver of a red Triumph and they gave my number . . .' His voice faltered. 'It was as if they thought . . .' Words failed him.

'You were asked to go to the nearest police station; why didn't you?'

The muscles round his right eye twitched in a nervous tic. 'I was scared; I mean, once the police get hold of you . . .' He realized that he was not being diplomatic and dried up.

'So what did you do?'

'I drove home and told father; he said I should talk to Mr Curtis and explain to him.'

'Now Mr Curtis has brought you here, so you can explain to me. Where is Francine?'

The pale blue eyes sought Wycliffe's in pathetic appeal. 'I don't know—honest to God I don't. I—'

'When did you last see her?'

'The night before last when I dropped her off outside Exeter railway station; she said she was catching a train and that the lift would save her a good chunk of the fare.'

'What time was it?'

He frowned: 'I picked her up just down the road here at a bit before half-nine, so it must've been about half-eleven when I dropped her.' His manner became petulant, as with a child coming near to tears. 'Like I said, I just gave her a lift . . . I haven't done anything!'

'Obviously you picked her up by arrangement; when was the arrangement made?'

'She rang me up that morning. She knew I was going to Exeter for Christmas and that I was driving up that evening. She asked me to pick her up in the village between a quarter and half after nine. It just meant going a bit later than I intended to; no bother.'

Pellowe turned his uneasy gaze on Kersey who looked about as reassuring as a lion working up an appetite for his next Christian.

Wycliffe persisted: 'Did she say why she wanted the lift—where she was going?'

'She said she was going to spend Christmas with relatives,

that was all. Fran never says much, I mean, she never really tells you anything.'

'Did you know that her parents had no idea that she was going away?'

'Of course I didn't! How could I? She said she was going to stay with relatives.'

'How did you meet her?'

'At a disco in St Ives. She goes there most Friday nights and she would let me take her home.' Naive in his humility.

'And after school? You picked her up from school sometimes?'

Pellowe nodded. 'A couple of times.'

Kersey said: 'Did you have it off with her?'

The boy jumped. 'By God! She's not that sort!'

'No? What sort is she, then?'

He hesitated. 'It's hard to say. I mean, I don't think any other girl could get away with it.'

'With what?'

He searched for words. 'Well, you have to make all the running; she never sort of meets you half-way, but she can still take her pick.'

'And she picked you?'

The boy was not stupid; he saw the point. 'Yes, well, I never try anything on, I mean nothing much. I know she won't stand for it.' He grinned for the first time. 'Only last week a bloke got a bit randy with her; she poured a whole glass of iced coke down his jeans and said: "Better if chilled before serving".'

'According to you she doesn't say a lot, but you must have been with her for a couple of hours in the car on your way to Exeter. What did you talk about?'

He shook his head. 'We didn't. When I tried she just said, "Oh, shut up, Timmy! I'm trying to think." Of course it isn't always like that; she can be very sort of friendly and nice.'

More questions, but no more revealing answers. In the end Wycliffe left him with a D.C. to make his statement.

Kersey said: 'A made-to-measure Wet!'

Wycliffe was thoughtful. 'I wonder if she's with her father.'

'It's a possibility.'

The investigation was getting off the ground. Four men, working in pairs, had started house-to-house enquiries. Wycliffe had small hope of picking up any direct leads and the questions were largely camouflage for gossip which he hoped might be a worthwhile harvest.

Sergeant Fox and his team were still at the cottage. End of a day. Christmas Day.

Chapter Six

WYCLIFFE OPENED HIS eyes and wondered where he was.
Light from a street lamp filtered through orange curtains
drawn over a small square window. There was a sloping
ceiling with beams exposed. Then he remembered: he was
staying at The Tributers, and Kersey was in the next room.
The rest of the headquarters people were at a boarding house
in St Ives. He switched on the bedside lamp to look at his
watch: five minutes past seven. Boxing Day. A funny
Christmas!

He listened; the silence seemed absolute, then he began to
hear the ticking of the grandfather clock at the bottom of the
stairs. He felt relaxed. An accommodating landlady had
taken them in on Christmas night and fed them on cold
turkey with a salad. She had promised them breakfast at
eight, earlier than they could reasonably expect over the
holiday.

'Think nothing of it, my lovers! If you can find out who
'twas that put a bullet in that poor soul's head then you'll be
doing us all a big favour. I can't say I exactly liked the little
woman, nor him neither, but I wouldn' wish that on my worst
enemy, an' tha's a fact!'

The Tributers had been in the hands of the Tregidgo
(second g, soft) family since the early 1800s and Phyllis was
first cousin as well as wife to the present owner. 'We've always
tried to keep it in close family, sort of,' she said. ' 'Tis the best
way.'

At ten minutes to eight he joined Kersey in the dining-
room. Kersey looked like the morning after; dark people are
rarely at their best in the morning. 'She asked me if we

wanted the full treatment and I said we did.' A delicious smell of frying bacon came from the kitchen next door. 'I don't know about you but I'm not allowed to have it at home; Joan says she wants me to live long enough to draw my pension and that means two rounds of wholemeal toast with margarine scrape, or a bowl of some bloody cereal with bran in it, and black coffee. Sometimes I wonder if it's worth it.'

Phyllis came in with heaped plates: bacon, egg, sausage and tomato. 'Now then! Get that inside of you an' you'll feel better. 'Tis a mucky ol' morning.' Phyllis, at fifty, was plump, clear skinned and rosy cheeked, low in polyunsaturates, high in cholesterol.

On the radio, the weather forecast: 'The mild weather over south-west England will continue. Winds will be light and variable and in the extreme south-west mist and fog now affecting coasts and hills will persist for most of the day.'

As the light strengthened they could see that the dining-room looked out on a small patch of garden but the boundary hedge remained insubstantial as a shadow. At intervals the foghorn on Pendeen Watch moaned piteously.

They listened to the eight o'clock News which, in deference to Christmas, tried to mitigate its intrinsic gloom. At the end there was a brief item on the Cornish murder, followed by: 'The police are anxious to contact the husband and daughter of the murdered woman, Alain and Francine Lemarque. Anyone with information which may help to trace them should telephone 0736 212121 or contact their nearest police station.'

At half-past nine, someone did. Wycliffe and Kersey were in the Incident Van. D.C. Potter was duty officer, a man not made to fit into cubicles so that he had difficulty in accommodating himself between desk and partition. He had a bottled gas heater going which made the air steamy instead of merely moist.

In the next cubicle Wycliffe and Kersey heard him take the call.

'Yes, Miss . . . That is correct. Can I have your name, please? . . . No, it isn't essential . . . Yes, I'll put you through

463

to the officer in charge.' Potter being diplomatic for once.

Wycliffe picked up his telephone and switched on the desk amplifier. The girl's voice was harsh and brittle; her manner aggressive. Wycliffe imagined her, thin, angular, mousey coloured hair, pinched nose, tiny mouth.

'Are you the man in charge?'

'Chief Superintendent Wycliffe.'

'They said on the radio you want to know where Francine Lemarque is. She's at Flat 4, 14, Burbage Street, Camden.'

'Thank you. Is she with her father?'

'I don't know anything about her father; I'm telling you about her. You got the address? 14, Burbage Street, Flat 4.' And she put the phone down.

Potter stood in the doorway. 'That was a pay-phone call, sir.'

Wycliffe said to Kersey. 'More than a bit of spite behind that but it didn't sound like a hoax. We'll check with the Met and get them to make contact. We want her here but if she doesn't want to come it will be difficult; I doubt if we have grounds for compulsion so it will have to be persuasion.'

'She must know about her mother.'

'I shall be surprised if she doesn't but that must be the Met's initial approach, to break the news. Boxing Day: no trains and no coaches. Potter! Find out if there is an afternoon or evening flight from Heathrow to St Mawgan, or even Plymouth. If there is, and the Met can get her on it . . .'

Kersey said, 'We'd better warn them in case her father is with her, we don't want him to slip through our fingers.'

Wycliffe agreed, but casually.

Across the square from the church there were two shops, and one of them, Mulfra General Stores, was open, a phenomenon unknown in most places on Boxing Day. A constant trickle of customers kept the doorbell jangling. Kersey stood up. 'I want to slip over to the shop.' He had sufficient tact not to mention cigarettes.

Kersey's attempts to kick the habit were regular and only briefly sustained; this was an interregnum but he was resolved to try again in the New Year. Wycliffe watched him cross the

464

square. No doubt the shop also sold pipe tobacco. He sucked the end of his ball-point and reflected that human existence was a long sad story of self-denial. Then he saw Marsden making for the shop, carrying a shopping bag, and ploughing along like an old Thames barge under full sail.

Kersey returned with a question: 'Did you see the chap who came into the shop after me?'

'A big fellow with dark curly hair?'

'Yes.'

'That's Marsden, the painter who found the body. His statement came in this morning. What about him?'

'I've seen him before somewhere.'

'He's not the sort you'd be likely to forget.'

Kersey brooded. 'It was a good while ago and he didn't have the trim on his upper lip, but I'm damned if I can remember when it was or in what connection.'

'You think you've come across him professionally?'

'I'm sure of it.'

'Then you'd better try to remember.'

'It's no good forcing it.' Kersey was thoughtful. 'What's he like, apart from his looks?'

'I think he could cut up rough if provoked. He's fond of women, very much in the plural. For what it's worth I'd say he's a good painter. He plays jazz music very loud . . . Oh, yes, and he's got a cat called Percy.' Kersey looked at his chief, puzzled. Even after years of working together there were still quirks of character which he could never understand. 'They took his prints yesterday for elimination purposes so if you have any suspicion we can check with C.R.O.'

On Wycliffe's table little heaps of typescript had begun to grow and in yet another cubicle a D.C. was going full-hammer to maintain the supply. Wycliffe put on his spectacles. Franks had dictated a memo over the telephone, his preliminary report. No revelations. Jane Lemarque had died of 'injuries to her head and neck inflicted by a heavy calibre bullet which had entered in the region of the axis vertebra and pursued a complex course through the skull to exit anteriorly through the face, destroying a large area

465

around the bridge of the nose, and affecting the eyes and the orbits on both sides. The trajectory suggests that the deceased might have been in a crouching position at the time the shot was fired. This would be consistent with her position when the body was found, between the bed and the dressing table.'

Regarding the time of death, Franks showed his usual caution: 'Death probably occurred at some time between four in the afternoon and eight in the evening of the 24th.'

'The poor woman was cornered and trying to shield herself by squeezing under the bed,' Wycliffe said. 'It looks more and more like cold-blooded murder.'

Kersey agreed. 'But cut out passion and you have to look for a rational motive.'

Wycliffe doodled on a scrap pad. 'We've got to know more about what went on in that house before and after Lemarque came out of jail.'

'The girl should be a help there.'

The girl—Francine, the Virgin in the blue gown. Once more Wycliffe recalled the deep impression she had made on him with her air of total detachment. Marsden, in his painting, had interpreted it as self absorption. Perhaps he was right. Anyway, what did it matter? Irritably, he pushed his doodle aside—a thing of triangles and squares. 'I think that we shall get from the girl only what she chooses to tell us, but I'm hoping for another angle from the chaps on house-to-house. The woman can't have lived in complete isolation while her husband was in jail; there must be someone who can claim to know her.'

Kersey was turning over a slim bundle of questionnaires already completed in house-to-house enquiries. 'There's not a lot here. The locals seem generally anti-Lemarque but on no specific grounds. I get the impression that outsiders are simply unwelcome and if you happen to be one you have to keep running to stay where you are.' He flipped through the pages. 'There is something though: Two people say they saw Lemarque's van being driven through the village on Saturday afternoon—Christmas Eve. It was travelling in the direction of Pendeen. One of them says Lemarque was driving.'

'At least that ties up with what Marsden told us.' Wycliffe sounded bored.

Kersey took the hint and stood up. 'I'll get on to the Met and ask them to check that address. We should have something from them during the morning.'

'One more thing: we need to know something about Lemarque. I want H.Q. to go to work on the story of the Lemarque/Bateman partnership. What were they up to? What went wrong? And what precisely landed Lemarque in jail? Anything which helps to put the man in focus.'

'I'll pass the word.'

Left alone, Wycliffe tried to take stock. Of the Lemarque family, Jane Lemarque had been murdered, and her husband and daughter were missing. He now had a line on the girl but none on her father. Passports for all three had been found in a drawer of the dressing table and among a few letters in a sideboard drawer downstairs, there was an address for Jane's sister in Bristol. She was being contacted through her local police. Fox had reported that most of the clothes in the main bedroom wardrobe belonged to Lemarque: three good suits, a couple of raincoats, and an overcoat, as well as a good range of casual clothes; relics of past prosperity. Impossible to say what he might have taken with him, but Fox's guess was, very little. Not, apparently, a planned exit.

Wycliffe was staring out of the window of his cubicle. A few yards away in a bay-window of one of the larger houses, a little old man in a tartan dressing gown was seated in some sort of wheel chair and he seemed to be returning Wycliffe's stare but his old eyes were probably too weak to focus at the distance. Behind him the light caught the shiny balls on a Christmas tree.

The scene-of-crime people had now finished at the cottage; some material had gone to the forensic laboratories for the boffins to brood over, including the fatal bullet and a nine millimetre cartridge case, but the fingerprint and photographic evidence was at headquarters for processing. No joy yet, and forensic eggs are sometimes addled before they have the chance to hatch.

Which left the house-to-house enquiries, and they had produced little so far. But he had not yet tackled the most promising of the houses.

He could hear Kersey's voice in the next cubicle, talking to somebody at the Met. Time to stir himself. *Courage mon brave!* He said to Potter: 'I shall be at Mynhager.'

He got into his car and drove past the pub along the track to Mynhager and the sea. Mist enveloped the moors and rolled down the slopes, dissolving and condensing by turns, so that the near landscape was at one moment clearly seen and at the next, entirely hidden. He felt blinkered, and lowered the car window in the hope of better vision. Although there was no breath of wind a sea swell, aftermath of the storm, continued to break along the shore with a booming sound which reverberated up the valley, through the fog.

He parked in the courtyard of Mynhager and went round the house to the front door. The terrace was drenched in spray from the last tide. Caroline answered his ring.

She seemed surprised and pleased to see him. 'Charles!' She looked behind her into the hall and lowered her voice. 'Come in.' Her manner was almost conspiratorial. 'In here! Ernest has gone out.' She led him into Ernest's little office and closed the door. 'I wanted to talk to you, Charles, but I didn't want to be seen going to your caravan thing by the church. Do sit down.'

Caroline in slacks and a woolly jumper. A different and diffident Caroline, uneasy, perhaps in search of reassurance. She looked pale, her eyes were puffy with tiredness and she had been drinking. 'I'm worried, Charles. I suppose I can talk to you? I mean, if what I tell you isn't directly relevant to . . . to Jane's death, it won't go any further, will it?'

'If it really isn't relevant, no.'

She was sitting in Ernest's swivel chair, swinging from side to side like a nervous child. 'Hugh Marsden was taken to the police station to make a statement, because he found her. At least I suppose that was the reason. You see, I can't find out

468

anything; I mean, Hugh isn't on the phone, and as things are I daren't go there . . .' She paused, apparently in the hope of getting some encouragement, but Wycliffe merely looked at her, benevolently non-committal, and she went on: 'You must have guessed if you haven't already been told, that Gerald and I are not the ideal married couple. We keep going for Paul's sake and for appearances generally.' Another pause, then: 'He's my cousin, you know—mother's twin sister's child. He used to spend a lot of time here when mother was alive. I don't know why I married him—he was handy, I suppose.'

'Why are you telling me this?'

She wriggled in her chair, easing her slacks round her thighs like a man. 'Because I've been having an affair with Marsden off and on for the past two years.'

'So?'

'My God! You don't make it easy! I'm trying to tell you that I know Hugh Marsden very well; he confides in me; we are good friends, quite apart from the other thing.' She was staring out of the window though there was nothing to see but the grubby net curtain and the mist beyond. 'There are no strings; I don't care a damn about his reputation.'

'You mean that your relationship with him is different—special.'

She turned on him angrily then decided against aggression. 'All right, damn you!—yes. As a matter of fact he's getting rid of the girl who lives with him; she's never been much more than a housekeeper anyway.'

Wycliffe wondered where all this was leading but he asked no questions.

She came out with it abruptly: 'Is Hugh under suspicion?'

'He wasn't detained after making his statement.'

She made a derogatory gesture. 'That's a big help!' She hesitated, then went on: 'Of course I know he's had other women, everybody knows it; what they don't know is that one of those women was Jane Lemarque—just the once, while Alain was in jail.'

'So?'

A look of intense exasperation. 'Jane, being the fool she is—was, might have told Alain when he came out.'

Wycliffe was beginning to see light through the fog. 'Presumably Marsden told you.'

'Only because I made him tell me about his other women.'

'Are you suggesting that the incident between Jane Lemarque and Marsden gave her husband a motive for murdering her?'

She looked at him quickly and away again. 'I don't know about that. I've told you this because I'm pretty sure Hugh won't. You mightn't think so but he has scruples about things and they could land him in trouble.'

'I see. You think that when we find Lemarque all this could come out anyway.'

No answer. He imagined that as far as Caroline was concerned their *tête à tête* was now over but she had more to say: 'There's something else. I shouldn't have said what I did about Francine yesterday. About her going off with a man and the idea that she might . . . Well, what Aunt Stella said was obvious nonsense and I shouldn't have encouraged her.'

'You've seen her portrait?'

She had been staring out of the window and she turned on him, ready to spit fire, but once more she changed her mind and managed a sheepish grin instead. 'You're a clever bastard in some ways. I suppose when it comes down to it I'm like any other woman where a man is concerned, I can cope with competition from my own age group but if it comes to teenagers . . .'

Wycliffe said: 'In this case I don't think it has.'

She looked at him, surprised. 'No? Well, thanks for that anyway.' She got up. 'I suppose you came to see Ernest but, as I told you, he's out. He should be back in time for lunch.'

Wycliffe remained seated. 'I came to talk to your husband.'

She seemed surprised. 'Gerald? Gerald has gone to lunch with one of his party cronies in Penzance. God knows when he'll be back. Late this afternoon, probably.'

'Is Paul about?'

'Paul? He's gone out walking with his uncle.' She saw

Wycliffe glance out of the window at the fog. 'I know; they're both mad.'

'Perhaps you will tell Paul that we have some news of Francine. An anonymous telephone caller said that she was staying at an address in Camden. That was all; but we are arranging for someone to go to that address and, if she is there, they will try to persuade her to come home.'

A mocking grin; something of the old Caroline. 'My, my! There is, after all, someone in this house who's managed to kindle a spark. Anyway, I'll tell him!'

Wycliffe got up to go. 'Just two more questions: How long has Marsden lived down here?'

'About four years, perhaps a bit more.'

'Have you any idea where he came from?'

'Why don't you ask him?' Aggressive.

'Perhaps I will. I wonder if I am allowed to ask if he rents or owns the cottage?'

She relented. 'Sorry! People have it in for Hugh just because he doesn't fit into any of their mean little pigeon holes. Before he came here he lived in London—Bayswater, I think. The cottage belongs to us. Believe it or not there is a Bishop Estates Limited in which we all have shares. It's some sort of tax wangle, I think. When my great great grandfather built the place he bought the whole valley and the farms on both sides.'

'Thank you.'

'You said there were two questions.'

'So I did! I wonder if you remember whether the Lemarques were down here for Easter '79?'

She frowned. 'I can't remember '79 especially but they never missed being here for Easter. Why?'

'Just routine.'

Poor Caroline! A real home-loving Cornish girl but unable to do without sex and preferably sex without a husband cluttering up the place.

As she was seeing him off in the hall, Joseph came down the stairs. 'Wycliffe!' The old man descended the remaining three or four steps. 'No news of Lemarque?'

471

'Not so far.'

'And Francine?'

'It seems she's staying at a flat in Camden; we've had an anonymous call and we're following it up.'

Joseph laughed. 'She'll give you a run for your money, that one! She's one of the new breed, Wycliffe. The future, if there is one, belongs to the women. Do you realize that? They're flexing their muscles, testing their strength; come the sexual revolution, Francine and her kind will be the brains behind it. Have you heard the latest R.C. joke? At the next Vatican conference bishops will bring their wives. At the one after that the Pope will bring her husband. Thank God I shall be dead by then! Anyway, don't let me detain you; I'm off for my walk.'

'Not in this fog, father!'

Joseph looked at his daughter. 'Your time is not yet, my child. A man can still make some decisions for himself.'

Chapter Seven

WITHOUT MUCH CONVICTION Wycliffe supposed that he must be making progress. Seemingly unrelated events were falling into an intelligible pattern and what more could he ask? Lemarque, having been home for a matter of weeks, learns from his wife that she has been to bed with the painter. Surely more than enough to raise the tension in the Lemarque household. Francine, caught in the middle, decides to get out, presumably until the worst is over. Then, on Christmas Eve night, with matters made worse by Francine running away, Lemarque, in a blazing row, loses all control and shoots his wife. Exit Lemarque.

Tidy. Tidy and simple. Most homicides turn out that way when you are lucky enough to pick up the right lead. Now they were on the track of the girl and the next step was to find Lemarque and charge him.

In his mind's eye Wycliffe saw the little man: the solemn features of a clown, the long-limbed, agile frame of a monkey. He recalled Lemarque sitting in the dismal living room of the cottage, trying to play second fiddle to his wife who refused to play at all. A killer? Well, there must be a great deal more to him than appeared that morning. He had helped to build a very successful business and he had shown sufficient resolution to stay with it against the odds. Foolish, perhaps, but neither stupid nor weak.

He parked his car by the police van and went in. The clock over Potter's table showed twenty minutes to twelve. The lights were on in the van, fighting the gloom of the morning.

Potter said: 'A nice mug of coffee? Keep the fog out.'

But Wycliffe was irritable. 'You missed your calling,

473

Potter: a white coat and a coffee bar in Cornwall Street. Is Mr Kersey in?'

'Next door, sir.'

Kersey was waiting for him. 'The Met really got their skates on. I had their report a few minutes ago. The Burbage Street flat is occupied by three girls and a boy, students at the Poly. Oh, to be eighteen again! In my day you had to make do with the shop doorway furthest from the street lamp. But I'll bet they've got that poor stupe doing the cooking and the washing-up. Anyway, two of the girls went home to mummy for the Christmas hols, leaving a cosy *ménage à deux* until Francine turned up. Unexpected, according to Cuthbert. Believe it or not, that's his name. It seems she had a school-kid thing going with him when they both lived in Richmond, ring-a-roses in the park, and they've kept in touch. He's a couple of years older, of course, and is a bit coy about it now. One gathers his flat mate wasn't enthusiastic about Francine's arrival but they let her stay.'

'How did she explain, turning up there like that?'

'The universal password: getting away from the family.'

'At some stage they must have heard about the shooting.'

'Not until this morning. It seems that the young miss who phoned us got up early. That means any time up to eleven, and she heard our bit on the radio. Instead of telling the others she went out to a public box and phoned us. When she got back she woke her boy friend and they decided to confront Francine.'

'Well?'

'They couldn't. The bird had flown.'

'When?'

'They reckon she must have gone during the night or early morning. She had a radio in her room and she probably heard the news before they did.'

'So we are back to square one.'

'Except that we know she isn't with papa.'

'Wasn't with papa, you mean.' Wycliffe was not pleased; he had counted on making contact with the girl, even if it had to be at second-hand.

Kersey said: 'She may be trying to get home but with no public transport she's likely to have problems.'

'Anything else?'

'The Bristol aunt telephoned—Jane Lemarque's sister, a Mrs Devlin; she's on her way down by car. Sounds prosperous and capable.'

'I'm glad somebody is.'

Kersey said: 'It's still Christmas. What about a drink before lunch? Phyllis told me she serves a genuine home-brew in the bar. They get it from a brother in Helston or some place.'

'Nobody cares a damn! It's Christmas. No newspapers, no trains, no buses, no mail; the television squeezing out strawberry mousse with whipped cream topping. This week has been cancelled; the whole country is in a coma.'

Kersey grinned, mellowed by the Tregidgo home-brew: 'Scrooge!'

But Wycliffe was not to be diverted. 'At any other time Lemarque's van would have been spotted and we should be getting reports of him having been seen anywhere and everywhere between the Isle of Mull and Oxford Street.'

'Don't tell me you miss our friends of the press?'

'Perverted as it may be, I do.'

It was half-past two, they were back in the Incident Van; Dixon had replaced Potter on the desk. There was a tap at the door and D.C. Curnow came in, one of the house-to-house team. A young giant, he had to stoop to clear the lintel.

'I've just come from 6, Wesley Terrace, sir, a Mrs Evadne Penrose, a widow. She says she was a close friend of the dead woman and that they were in touch on Christmas Eve, the day of the murder.'

'And she's just remembered it?'

'No, sir. She spent Christmas with her mother in Padstow and didn't hear about the murder until she got back this morning.'

'Well?'

'She won't talk to me; it has to be "the officer in charge" and she won't come here, though God knows why not.'

'What's she like?'

An amused grin. 'Very forthright and she talks a lot about astrology.'

'Kinky?'

'I wouldn't say kinky, sir, eccentric.' D.C. Curnow had a nice feeling for words. 'I think she's probably reliable.'

Wesley Terrace was a row of sizeable cottages near the Mechanic's Institute and number six was double-fronted. The front door was provided with a cast-iron knocker in the shape of a lion's head. Wycliffe knocked and the door was answered by a small, thin woman with sharp features and frizzy, greying hair cut short.

'Mrs Penrose?'

'Evadne Penrose. You must be the chief superintendent.' Almost an accusation.

Wycliffe was shown into an over-furnished little room which reminded him of the parlour of the farmhouse in which he had been born. There was a three-piece suite, an upright piano, a chiffonier, a fireplace with brass fire-irons, and framed coloured prints on the walls.

'I'm sorry to get you here but when I have something to say I believe in saying it to the man in charge but I didn't fancy going along to that hut on wheels in the square.' Her brown eyes darted fierce glances, like a firecracker giving off sparks, and her bony little paw gripped like a pincers. 'Do sit down.'

'You knew Mrs Lemarque?'

A vigorous nod. 'I was Jane's friend, perhaps her only friend. After that terrible business with Alain going to prison I could see that she needed someone. Apart from anything else there was the dramatic change in their circumstances. She lost everything! Of course, the people round here are terribly clannish; they've no room for outsiders, and they tolerate me only because my husband was one of them . . . You don't mind if I smoke?' She brought out a cigarette pack from the pocket of her woollen frock, lit one and inhaled like a deprived addict.

476

Wycliffe made a bid for the initiative. 'We need to know more about Mrs Lemarque, about the family and their connections. As a friend, you may be able to help if you are ready to be quite frank.'

She had perched herself on the arm of the settee. 'But that's why I've asked you to come here, so that I can be frank! That's why I'm talking to you instead of to your young men who are making the rounds like Kleeneeze salesmen.'

Wycliffe tried again. 'You became friendly with Jane Lemarque after her husband went to prison?'

'I knew her long before that; they were down here quite a lot, either staying with the Bishops or at their cottage, but it was only after the calamity that I really got to know Jane. I made a point of it, because I could see that she was a woman at the end of her tether, and when I see something that needs doing, I do it.' A pause for this to sink in. 'I'm a Sagittarian, you know. Poor Jane was a Piscean; emotionally dependent, incapable of any decisive action. I spotted her at once, I wonder if you've noticed that Pisceans can sometimes be recognized by their slightly protruding eyes and vacant expressions?

'No wonder there was stress in their marriage. Alain is an Arien.' Evadne looked around for an ashtray.

Wycliffe said: 'So the Lemarque marriage was not a success?'

Evadne snorted irritably. 'My dear man! I've just told you it was a disaster! They were incompatibles. Alain is vigorous, aggressive, demanding, while Jane was merely passive. I can assure you that Ariens expect more from a woman than passivity; I was married to one. Aries is the sign of the Ram.'

Wycliffe felt a pang of sorrow for the late Mr Penrose who, Arien or not, must have lived out his married life under a constant threat of being eaten.

'I understand that Lemarque was fond of his wife.'

'In the same way as you might be fond of a cat. All is well as long as the cat purrs, rubs round your legs, and jumps on to your lap. Alain's fondness demanded continuous recognition, a constant response, but Pisceans are incapable of any sort of constancy or, indeed, of any deep emotion. And when they

477

find themselves in double harness with an Arien. . .' She left the prospect to his imagination.

'The point is that after Alain came out of prison they found it even more difficult to live together.' She lowered her voice. 'Neither of them was the sort to clear the air with a row, so they each suffered in their own way and in silence.' Through the haze of tobacco smoke she fixed Wycliffe with an unblinking stare, and spoke slowly, emphasizing her words: 'Jane was afraid that Alain would commit suicide. I told her there was no risk of that with an Arien but she was convinced that she had let him down so badly that he would kill himself. Apparently he had a gun.'

'He had a gun?' Wycliffe did his best not to seem unduly interested.

'So she said; it seems he got it when they were living in Richmond and had all sorts of valuable antiques and pictures in the house.'

'You were in touch with Jane on the day she died?'

'Indeed I was. She telephoned; she often did when she was depressed and alone.'

'At what time did you speak to her?'

'At half-past four.'

'You are sure of that?'

'Quite sure. I was on the point of leaving to spend Christmas with my mother and sister when the phone rang. I said to myself: "Half-past four! I'm late already!" Of course it was Jane. The usual thing: she was depressed and she was sure that Alain was going to kill himself and that if he did it would be her fault. She said that he had gone out soon after lunch and that she was alone when the policeman came about Francine. She'd just been to the drawer of the dressing table where he kept his gun, the drawer was locked but she found a key that fitted, and there was no gun there; it had gone.' Evadne sighed. 'I didn't think Alain was likely to kill himself so I didn't take it very seriously. Of course, I wish I had now. But I did ask her how long it was since she had last seen the gun and she couldn't remember. When it came to the point, she wasn't even sure if she'd seen it since they left Richmond.'

For the first time she looked at Wycliffe with a certain diffidence. 'I suppose he shot her? I don't think that possibility had ever occurred to her, or to me . . .'

Wycliffe went off at a tangent: 'I suppose it was the strain between her parents that induced Francine to go away?'

'Of course! Why else would she walk out like that? I admit that she's a difficult girl and sometimes I've felt like giving her a good slap but she's had a hard time in many ways and, of course, she's a Scorpio. You know what that means.'

Wycliffe didn't and didn't want to. He got up from his chair. 'You've been very helpful, Mrs Penrose. I'll send someone along to take your formal statement.'

She came with him to the door and watched while he walked along the street towards the van.

Kersey said: 'Any joy, sir?'

'Lemarque had a gun, at least he had when he was living in Richmond, and Jane Lemarque was speaking to our widow on the telephone at four-thirty on Christmas Eve afternoon.'

'Is the woman sure?'

'There is nothing of which Evadne Penrose is not sure including, as far as I could tell, that Lemarque shot his wife because she didn't purr when she was stroked. But to be fair, I think she's probably reliable in matters of fact.'

A girl's voice in the next cubicle, talking to Dixon. A tap on the door and Dixon came in. 'Francine Lemarque, sir.'

She stood in the doorway. She wore jeans and an anorak, both darkened by rain and obviously soaked through. Her dripping hair hung round her shoulders in rat's tails and her face was wet. She looked pale and very tired.

For a long moment Wycliffe just stared at her; he found it hard to accept that this was the girl he had last seen as the Virgin in the blue gown.

'Are you the man in charge?'

'Chief Superintendent Wycliffe.' Absurdly, he felt uncomfortable under the girl's steady gaze.

'I remember you were staying with the Bishops.' She spoke as though recalling something which had happened a long time ago.

479

Wycliffe, recovering his poise, said: 'How did you get here? You were in London last night.'

'I hitched. I was lucky; I did it in two hops as far as Truro. Last night I heard on the radio what had happened to my mother. They said on the radio that she was shot; is that true?'

'I'm afraid so.'

'And you think he did it?'

'We don't know who did it; we are trying to find out. Naturally we want to speak to your father but so far we haven't been able to find him.'

He was puzzled by her manner; she was certainly distressed, but her strongest emotion was incredulity. 'Don't you think you should get into some dry clothes? We can talk afterwards.'

She ignored him. 'Whoever did it must have had a gun.'

'Some time ago your mother told Mrs Penrose that your father had a gun which he got when you lived in Richmond.'

A momentary hesitation. 'Yes he did, a revolver. I remember him showing me how it worked and explaining how dangerous it was. He was always afraid of being burgled in those days. Are you saying that my mother was shot with that gun?'

'You said it was a revolver?'

'Yes, it had a cylinder thing where you put the bullets. I asked you if you thought my mother was shot with that gun?'

'She wasn't shot with a revolver.'

'Well, then!'

Wycliffe saw trouble ahead. In the Children and Young Persons' Act, 1969, a child is defined as someone under the age of fourteen; a young person is someone over the age of fourteen but under eighteen. So here was a young person. He was vague about the provisons of the Act affecting young persons in need of care but his heart sank at the thought of becoming the meat in the sandwich between Francine and some dragon of a social worker. Then he remembered and thanked God for the Bristol aunt.

'Your aunt is on her way down from Bristol; she should be here shortly.'

'Aunt Alice. I hardly know her.'

'When she comes we can make some arrangements: where you will stay and who will look after you. At the moment we don't know where your father is.'

'Why can't I stay at the house and look after myself?'

'That isn't possible, certainly not while the police investigation lasts.'

He had not said one word of sympathy nor offered any consolation. He felt as though he had been justifying himself. Absurd!

She stood for a moment as though making up her mind then she said: 'All right! But if I can't stay at the house I need to collect some things from my room.'

'I'll take you down there.'

He picked up her holdall and took her out to the car. She got in, fastened her seat belt and sat there perfectly composed.

The old mine track to the cottage was even more rutted and pot-holed than the one to Mynhager and the mists were going to outlive the day. It must have been a desperately sad and depressing homecoming, but she gave no sign.

Have you had anything to eat?'

'I had a snack in Truro.'

'This must have been a very great shock to you.'

'Yes.'

He could think of nothing more to say.

He parked the car and they climbed the steps to the front door. He fumbled with the key in the lock and she said: 'Give it to me; there's a knack.' Then, inside: 'I want to collect a few things from my room.'

He almost told her to go ahead but thought better of it. He did not want her in her parents' room. 'I'll come up with you.'

He followed her up the stairs on to the landing. 'Why don't you go into the bathroom and dry yourself?'

'Where shall I be staying?'

'At The Tributers I suppose, until your aunt comes at least.'

She went into the bathroom, taking her bag with her, and ten minutes later, came out with her hair in a frizzy mass, wearing a dry pair of jeans and a woolly top. She spent some

481

time in front of the little swing mirror in her bedroom, brushing her hair until it looked like a TV shampoo advertisement.

Although Wycliffe was watching her from the landing, she behaved exactly as though he wasn't there and he began to wonder why he was. It had been one of those spot decisions which, if they turn out to be justified, are credited to a good copper's instinct.

She was going through her drawers, putting selected items into a travelling case which she brought from the landing cupboard. Finally she snapped the catches shut and straightened up. 'All right.'

He was on the landing and she was in the doorway with her hand on the electric light switch when she suddenly darted back into the room, stooped by the bed, and picked up the little red notebook he had found there. She looked at him with a hint of uncertainty in her manner.

'I might need this; something to write on.'

It was not; for the few pages which remained had already been used. Her uncertainty and the need she had felt to explain were so out of character that he reacted: 'Let me have it, please.'

She held out the little book without hesitation, he took it and slipped it into his pocket. 'You won't mind if I hold on to it for a day or two?'

She looked at him briefly, then turned away.

Alice Devlin was a year or two older than her sister but more animated, more responsive, and Wycliffe liked her on sight. Fortune had dealt with her more kindly. A sporty Sierra, current year; a suede coat, and underneath, a simple frock of some luscious Liberty fabric, definitely not by D.I.Y. out of Pattern Book.

'I knew nothing about it until the police came, I suppose we hadn't been listening to the news over Christmas. It was a shock.' She was clearly upset, grieved, but by no means prostrated. 'Jane and I had gone our separate ways but we had kept loosely in touch; you know the sort of thing:

birthday and Christmas cards with the occasional note.'

Her attitude to Francine was warm and sympathetic without being cloying or intrusive. 'You're living through a nightmare, my dear, but it will pass. Try to feel that you are not alone. I don't want to press you but you can come back with me and stay until things are sorted out—or as long as you want. Philip and I would like that.'

They took rooms at The Tributers and Phyllis laid on an early meal. Wycliffe sat in on the meal without taking part and through it all Francine remained quietly aloof. Had she been persuaded out of the eternal jeans? At any rate she wore her woolly jumper with a tartan skirt. Her hair, dry now and shining in the light, was caught back with a clasp. She still looked very tired; her eyes dark, her face pale, her features a trifle pinched. When their meal was over Wycliffe said, 'Now we have to talk.'

Francine's response was immediate; she turned to her aunt. 'I want to talk to him alone.'

'Of course! That's natural.' Understanding woman.

In the Incident Van Wycliffe said: 'Before we start, why don't you ring Paul?'

'Paul? What for?'

'He's been worried about you.'

She hesitated, then: 'All right, if you like.'

Wycliffe said to Dixon: 'Get Paul Bateman on the telephone for me, please.'

When the boy was on the line Wycliffe handed over to Francine.

'Is that Paul?. . . It's me—Francine. . .' He could hear the boy's elated response but Francine remained casually matter-of-fact. '. . . No, I'm with the police in their van thing . . . Yes, in the village . . . No, I shouldn't think so . . . I'm all right. My aunt is down . . . I can't talk any more now.' And she put down the telephone.

She and Wycliffe faced each other across the table in the little interview cubicle. Kersey sat by the door. It would have been politic to have a W.P.C. sitting in on the interview but the girl had committed no offence; on the contrary.

'You ran away—why?' Wycliffe manner was sympathetic, not accusing.

'I didn't run away, I left home.'

'For good?'

'That depended.'

'On what?'

'On whether I could get a job and on what happened at home.'

'Getting a job was bound to take time; how did you intend to live meanwhile?'

'I had money. I've been working in the holidays and saving for a long time.'

'With the idea of leaving home?'

'Perhaps.'

'Why did you make up your mind to go?'

She smoothed her hair away from her eyes with a slow movement of her hand but said nothing.

'Weren't you happy at home?'

'Happy? No, I wasn't.'

'Were your parents unkind to you?'

'No.' She sounded mildly impatient. 'I can't explain; you wouldn't understand. It was like being smothered in cotton wool.'

'Over protective?'

'I told you you wouldn't understand.'

'And things got worse when your father came home?'

'Yes.'

'You blame your mother?'

'I don't blame anybody; mother had to make herself suffer.'

'I don't understand.'

'There's no reason why you should!' With tired indifference.

'As a policeman, I'm afraid there is. Why was the situation worse when your father came home?'

The atmosphere in the little cubicle was claustrophobic. An electric lamp in the low ceiling gave a yellow light which shone on the girl's hair and was reflected dimly off the scuffed and worn plastic surfaces of the walls and fittings. Outside it

484

was quite dark and a blind was drawn over the tiny window. The three of them seemed as isolated as if they had been in a space capsule; the only sound came from sporadic chatter on the radio in the adjoining cubicle.

Kersey said: 'You don't seem to realize, Francine, that we are trying to find out who killed your mother and why.'

She turned to face Kersey then back to Wycliffe. 'When there was just the two of us mother was always explaining how she had failed as a wife or failed me. If it wasn't that, it was how everyone despised her for being such a failure.' She had been looking down at the table top, now she raised her eyes to meet Wycliffe's. 'I think she really believed what she said but she didn't do anything about it. It was so hopeless!' Her voice softened and he thought that she might weep but the moment passed. 'And that Penrose woman with her nonsense about the stars didn't help. "My dear Jane, you are a Piscean! You can't change that!" ' For an instant the indomitable Evadne was in the room with them.

Wycliffe persisted: 'But how did your father coming home make things worse?'

'Does it matter?'

'I think you should tell us.'

With a small helpless gesture, still with her eyes on Wycliffe, she said: 'While he was in prison mother let the painter come to the cottage.'

'What do you mean, she let him come to the cottage?'

'All right! She let him go to bed with her.'

'More than once?'

'Not as far as I know.' Indifferent.

'And your father found out?'

'She told him.'

'What happened?'

'Nothing happened.'

'Didn't your father become angry?'

'He was never angry, and that made mother worse. She wanted to be punished.'

Not a trace of emotion; she spoke of her mother, her father, and even of herself, as though none of them had any more

485

significance than the characters in a novel. Once more Wycliffe was aware of the stillness which seemed to envelop this girl like an aura; never once did she fidget, and all her movements were deliberate and controlled. He reminded himself that she was just sixteen, a schoolgirl; he had seen her room with its posters of pop stars, and her school books; in six months time she should be taking her O-levels. She had lost her mother, and her father was missing in suspicious circumstances, yet she fended off any attempt at sympathy or understanding as a boxer parries a blow.

'Did you know about your mother and Marsden when you sat for your portrait with him?'

'She told me.' After a pause: 'Mother had to tell everything. When she couldn't get me to listen she would go and confess to the vicar.'

'The Marsden business didn't upset you?'

She looked at him blankly. 'What difference did it make?'

Was she truly indifferent? Or was she maintaining a profound reserve, refusing to allow him any insight into her mind or her emotions?

He tried another approach. 'You must have planned to go away at least a day or two before you left. Why didn't you leave a note?'

'I did.'

'Both your father and your mother said there was no note.'

'Perhaps they didn't want you to see what was in it.'

'Did you say in the note where you were going?'

'No.'

'What did you say? The kind of things you've told me now?'

'More or less.'

'Have you any idea where your father might be? With a relative, or a friend?'

'I've no idea.'

'Who do you think killed your mother?' Gently.

'I don't know. I've sometimes thought that she might take her own life; are you sure that she didn't?'

Wycliffe changed the subject. 'Your father had some idea

of going back into business; do you know anything about that?'

'I've heard them talking; something about a tourist park on some waste ground where there used to be mine workings. He was expecting somebody to put up money for it.'

'Did your parents have many outside contacts? I mean, did people visit them, ring them up, or did they go out a lot?'

She shook her head. 'Only the Penrose woman came to our house and sometimes mother would ring her up.'

'And your father?'

'Nobody came to see him but he went out a lot with the van.'

'Did he get phone calls?'

'I think he made his phone calls when I wasn't there.'

'What makes you think so?'

'Because sometimes when I came in he would be on the phone to someone and he would ring off as soon as he could.'

'You realize that anything you can tell us may help to solve the mystery of your mother's death and your father's disappearance. Is there anything you can tell us that you overheard on the phone?'

'No, I didn't take much notice.'

'Did you gather what his phone conversations were about?'

'Oh, about money and business.'

'Were they friendly conversations?'

'Just ordinary. One day last week he seemed to be annoyed. He was almost shouting until he saw me.'

'What was he saying?'

She frowned. 'It didn't make much sense. Something like: "Five years ago we were all in the same boat—or perhaps I should say the same car. Not any more! I no longer belong to the club." Then he turned round and saw me and I realized that I had put him off.'

What more could he ask? He walked back with her to The Tributers. The misty rain had stopped and the weather seemed to be clearing; stars twinkled through rifts in the clouds.

'Good night, Francine.'

487

'Good night.' Casual.

He was moved by her isolation. Rarely in the thousands of interviews he had conducted had he learned so little of the personality of the other party. Business men, lawyers, even the Mr Bigs of the crime world, all gave something of themselves away, but not this girl of sixteen. Although she had answered his questions, at no time had he been allowed a glimpse of her private world; he still had no idea of what she thought or felt, no clue to suggest what she might do. Talking to her was like playing chess with a computer, yet everything about her pointed to an intense emotional life behind the façade.

Kersey said: 'It adds up to Alain Lemarque. When a man murders his wife we look for the instant of passion but Lemarque wasn't that kind of man. The girl says he never got angry; what she means is he didn't show it. In other words, he's the type who's capable of nursing a sense of outrage, coming to a decision and carrying it out. Now we know he had a gun.'

'A revolver according to Francine.'

'Surely she was mistaken!'

'From her description, that seems unlikely. What did you make of her?'

Kersey, although he looked like Red Riding Hood's surrogate grandmother, had two lovely daughters and could be considered something of an authority. 'My guess would be that she's putting up a smoke screen, but why?'

Wycliffe had no answer for that. 'According to Evadne Penrose, Jane Lemarque thought her husband intended to kill himself and Francine seemed to believe that her mother might commit suicide. A suicide pact isn't out of the question, I suppose, though there's every sign that the woman was trying to escape being shot. We just don't know what's happened to Lemarque, whether he's alive or dead.'

They were having their evening meal, waited on by a village girl called Lorna; dark, freckled, and pretty. In the bar next door things were warming up, with the occasional shout and outbursts of laughter, punctuating the general level of chatter. They had spoken quietly with an eye on Lorna's comings and goings but she must have heard something. 'I saw Mr Lemarque's van out to Mennear Bal Saturday afternoon.'

Kersey said: 'That was Christmas Eve.'

'Right first time.'

'The day his wife was shot. You haven't said anything about this before; why not?'

'Well, I wasn't asked, was I? They came and talked to mum and dad but nobody said a word to me. In any case, as I heard it, she was shot in the evening in her own home, and this was in the afternoon between three and four.'

'Where is Mennear Bal?'

'Just a bit down the coast; it's where there used to be mine workings; now 'tis no more 'n a lot of old ruins and heaps of spoil. There's plenty of tracks though and his old van was going slow along the one out near the cliff. My Aunt Flo lives near the workings and she says she seen him down there once before since he was let out of prison. There's a rumour that he's after renting the ground from the mine company though like my dad says, God knows what he thinks he'll do with it.'

'Did you see Lemarque?'

'I didn't see anybody, just the van; I was a good way off. I recognized it because it's the only one around like that.'

'And this was definitely at three o'clock?'

She pouted. 'I can't say to the minute but I was home by half-past so it must have been close. I had to walk home and when I got there mother was just leaving to catch the half-past three bus.'

When they were dawdling over their coffee, Wycliffe said: 'It ties up nicely; Marsden saw Lemarque's van being driven towards the village at about three or a bit earlier; it was seen passing through the village in the direction of Pendeen; now we have it among the mine dumps where, apparently, he hoped to build his tourist park. Curtis arrived at the cottage at about 2.45 and Lemarque had already gone. It ties up, without meaning a damn thing as far as we are concerned because, like the girl said, Jane Lemarque wasn't shot at

Mennear Bal but in her own home, at some time between four and eight.'

'It looks as though he drove home, shot his wife, then took off.'

Wycliffe was thoughtful. 'Perhaps I saw him leaving.' He told Kersey what he had seen on his way back to Mynhager from the painter's cottage. 'But I don't believe it.'

Lorna came back into the dining-room: 'You're wanted on the telephone.'

He took the call, standing in the passage between the cloakroom and the bar. It was Helen, calling from Kenya.

'I rang Mynhager and spoke to Ernest. He told me you were on a case and gave me another number . . .'

He explained, but contending with the racket from the bar probably meant that his explanation lacked lucidity.

'Anyway, there's nothing wrong with you?' Helen getting down to the things that mattered.

'No, I'm fine. And you?'

'It's nearly midnight here and we've been sitting out of doors with iced drinks; me in a sleeveless dress. Wish you were here . . .'

'Me too.'

'If I bring home all I've bought, our place is going to look like the Museum of Mankind . . . Well dear, I mustn't run up their bill. Dave and Elsa send their love. Look after yourself, darling. Night . . .'

'I will; and you . . . Night.'

It took him a minute or two to bring himself back.

Chapter Eight

JANE LEMARQUE WAS shot 'with a nine-millimetre automatic, using a parabellum cartridge with a Neonite propellant. The markings on the bullet and the cartridge case strongly suggest that it was fired from a Walther P-38.' A dribble of technical jargon from the ballistics expert. Useful, if they had found a gun or the person who had used one. There was also a sheaf of scene-of-crime photographs with a report from Fox, necessary documentation when and if it came to preparing a case; not much use now. He had reported on prints found at the cottage: family only, except for Marsden's prints on the telephone and those of 'one of the investigating officers'. Fox had tact as well as zeal.

But it hardly looked as though the boffins would make a great contribution to the case.

Wycliffe and Kersey were in the Incident Van and the village had a different, more cheerful aspect this morning, a fine morning after yesterday's gloom: blue skies, sunshine, and not a breath of wind. An interlude between fronts, the weathermen said. Both the village shops were open today and the second one turned out to be a butcher's.

Already a green bus had lumbered into the square, lingered for a minute or two, then moved off without picking up a single passenger. But, like Noah's olive leaf, it was a token from an awakening world outside. Kersey collected a selection of newspapers but the Cornish murder rated only a few lines on an inside page of one of them.

The Chief Constable telephoned: Bertram Oldroyd, a good policeman and a sensitive man, keenly aware of the need to strike a balance between protection and repression.

He had a horror of political manipulation. As he grew older in the professional tooth he devoted more of his time to public relations and left the general administration of the force to his departmental heads. He fended off interfering politicians and reserved his most scathing rebukes for those of his staff who lost their footing on the tightrope between Left and Right, Black and White, Pro and Anti.

'Nasty business, Charles! A domestic, I gather.'

'Probably.'

'The girl is safe and sound so that's something. I believe this chap Lemarque was in partnership with Bateman at one time. Any complications from that direction?'

'He seems content to be a spectator at the moment.'

'Good! But you'll need to watch him; he can be a pest.'

'I thought he was on our side.' Wycliffe being naughty.

But Oldroyd only laughed. 'Well, you know what they say: Who needs enemies while we've got friends like him? What about the media?'

'Sleeping off Christmas.'

'Let's hope it stays that way. Heard from Helen?'

'She telephoned last night. David and Elsa are doing her proud.'

'We had a card from her a couple of days before Christmas; give her our love when you're next in touch. But you should be out there, Charles! You take too much on your own shoulders instead of delegating. We're a team—remember?' The big chief chuckled. 'Wasn't it Kant's dove who thought he might fly better in a vacuum?'

The only Chief Constable in captivity to read philosophy.

Kersey was looking out of the window. 'You spoke too soon; we've got visitors: Ella with a cameraman in tow.'

Ella Bunt: freelance crime reporter, thirty-five, a redhead and a militant feminist. ('We're not equal, we're better! I've proved it in bed and out.') Ella owed her husky voice to cigarettes and her complexion to whisky but she rarely missed out on a story and few editors could afford to ignore her. Wycliffe knew her of old and between them there was a love-hate relationship.

Kersey met her at the door. 'No pets! Leave him outside, Ella.'

The cameraman said: 'I'll be about.'

Ella sat opposite Wycliffe. 'Had a good Christmas with your lawyer friend? You won't mind if I smoke?'

'Make yourself at home, Ella.'

She blew smoke across the table. 'Awkward for you; finding yourself a house guest with the principal suspects, but I gather you moved out. Sensible! Warm in here.' She stood up and slipped off a fleece-lined leather jacket which smelt of goat. 'It looks dicey for The Sheriff. I wouldn't be surprised if this started a whole lot of rumours. And him all set for office. I've been doing my homework on the Lemarque/Bateman set-up. It's a wonder he survived that and kept his seat; he may not be so lucky this time. Of course he must have friends. Lemarque probably felt he'd been left holding the shitty end and maybe he was intending to get his own back.'

Wycliffe said: 'Don't let me spoil things for you, Ella, but it was Mrs Lemarque who was shot.'

'I know. Odd that. Something went wrong somewhere. So you've found the girl; what does she have to say?'

'Very little.'

'Can I talk to her?'

'It's not up to me; her aunt is down.'

'Where's her papa?'

'I was hoping you might help me to find him. I expect you've had the hand-outs about him and his van.'

'And that's all you've got on him?'

'Scout's honour.'

'No reported sightings?'

'Not one.'

'There you are then! It would make more sense than killing her, don't you think?'

'I try not to. Look, Ella, if you haven't got any questions I can answer, why not let us get on with it in our own bumbling fashion?'

'I want background.'

Wycliffe made a broad gesture. 'It's all out there. Take what you want.'

'Very funny! How about a couple of shots inside the Lemarque house?'

'Not a chance, but you can take all you want outside.'

'Thank you for nothing. What about the gun?'

'A .38 automatic.'

'Have you found it?'

'No.' Wycliffe stood up. 'You want the human interest angle, Ella. Go and talk to Evadne Penrose, 6, Wesley Terrace, but don't say I sent you. Friend of the dead woman, astrologer extraordinaire, and probably glad of somebody to talk to.'

'Are you fobbing me off?'

'I wouldn't dare.'

She got up and struggled into her jacket. 'I hope not. Anyway, I'll be around for a bit.'

When she had gone Wycliffe said: 'Ella's nobody's fool but she and Evadne deserve each other, don't you think?'

Among other memoranda that morning there was one from C.R.O. in response to Kersey's enquiry about Marsden. Their reply was succinct: 'This subject has no criminal record.'

Kersey stared at the memo. 'I know I've come across that great baboon somewhere, in a nick and on the wrong side of the counter, but I'm damned if I can remember—' He broke off in a triumphant *eureka* moment of recall: 'I've got it! I was a wooden top in Paddington on a six month stint as part of an exchange programme; finding out about the other half. Marsden was nicked by the art forgery boys. I wasn't on the case but a mate of mine in C.I.D. was roped in to help with the leg work and it opened his eyes to what goes on in the art racket.'

'Did it come to court?'

'I can't remember; I may not have heard because it was towards the end of my time. He can't have been convicted otherwise he'd have form.'

Wycliffe was putting on his overcoat. 'Follow it up. I'm going prospecting.'

'Around Mennear Bal; I thought you might.'

Wycliffe drove out of the village in the direction of Pendeen. Beyond the Mechanics' Institute the cottages petered out, and the road ran between dry-stone hedges with an occasional dwarf hawthorn, sculptured like a fox's brush by the salt winds. After half-a-mile the hedge on the right gave way to an open space with a few cottages and ramshackle bungalows scattered at random among patches of rough grass. Several tracks led off in the general direction of the sea. He pulled off the road and got out. Three or four old bangers were dotted about, parked or dumped, and a stocky young man with curly black hair was working on one of them. He did not look up though Wycliffe came to stand within a couple of feet of him. The genuine Cornish article, unadulterated by foreign genes. He and his kind were already established in the county when the upstart Celts arrived and ever since they've been plagued by strangers.

'Good morning! Is this Mennear Bal?'

'Used to be.' Still without looking up.

'Which of these tracks leads to the cliff?'

'They all do.'

'Can I drive out there?'

'Tha's up to you; whether yer bothered about yer suspension.'

Wycliffe was and decided to walk; he chose the first of the tracks he came to. The ground was flat (an elevated plain of marine denudation, geologists said) and dotted with ruined buildings, heaps of rubble, and the occasional inhabited cottage. Between St Ives and Cape Cornwall copper and tin mines were once strung out along the coast like beads on a string, now only one is working; the others are in ruins, or have disappeared altogether or, like the quoits, graves, standing stones, and courtyard houses of prehistory, are being preserved because of their archaeological interest.

Mennear Bal was a ruin, rather a collection of ruins; a chimney stack or two, crumbling engine houses, roofless sheds, and intimations of what once had been a maze of arsenic flues. In the sunshine and the silence it was hard to

495

imagine scores of bal maidens and buddle boys thronging the site, smashing ore, feeding the stamps, and doing homage to their employer for fivepence a day. Even harder to imagine bands of happy campers paying their dues to Bateman and Lemarque. Wycliffe had heard the expression, 'cheerful as a knacked bal', now he knew what it meant.

But a quarter-of-a-mile ahead the sea sparkled under the sun, an enduring backdrop. Wycliffe's track joined others and eventually he was walking along a broad path, parallel with the sea; on his left the grass curved smoothly and swiftly away to the cliff edge and a drop of more feet than he cared to think about. At a short distance off-shore a St Ives boat was cruising, perhaps her first chance to put out following the storm and the fog. Far out a container ship forged her way up-channel.

The track, made up of coarse mineral waste from the spoil heaps, was peppered with pot-holes and there were broad puddles, but scarcely any mud. He had hoped to find traces of Lemarque's van but he was disappointed. The man had probably stopped somewhere along the track to brood like Moses on the promised land; though, again like Moses, he would have needed all his entrepreneurial optimism to see milk and honey in the prospect. Which did not mean that he would be in a mood to go home and shoot his wife.

Wycliffe continued walking until he was leaving the mineworkings behind. At this point, just before the track narrowed to a footpath, he noticed furrows in the grass bordering the track on the sea side, and the furrows were of a kind that might have been made by the wheels of a car or van. The slope to the cliff edge was steep, too steep and slippery for a man to risk climbing down, and the furrows were cut into the mounded grass where it met the path; he could distinguish three of them clearly with the hint of a fourth. Once over that mound nothing could have stopped any vehicle hurtling down.

As he examined the surface of the track he could see that the ballast had been disturbed by a swirling movement of the kind made by skidding back wheels. He worked back along the way he had come for about two hundred yards, examining the ground carefully as he went, and found what he had missed before: two wheel-ruts where the back wheels of the vehicle had dug in as a consequence of rapid acceleration. The story seemed to tell itself. Someone in a vehicle which was either stationary or moving very slowly, suddenly accelerated, steered for the end of the track where it narrowed, swerved off down the grassy slope and over the cliff.

An accident? An improbable one.

Was it Lemarque's van which had left those tell-tale signs? More than likely. It would explain why the van had not been spotted, or Lemarque either. But he had to bear in mind the possibility that one of the inhabitants of Mennear Bal had finally tired of his vintage jalopy and hoisted it over the cliff. The authorities might frown on such practices but there was a maverick strain in these people who shared their ancestry with Bishop Trelawny.

He looked around for any position where he might get a view of the cliff face but there was none, then he spotted a place where the grassy slope to the cliff edge looked less steep and less slippery, where the grass grew in hummocks which offered some sort of foothold. He stepped gingerly off the track, wedging his foot against one of the hummocks; it felt precarious and immediately the edge seemed much nearer and the sea a very long way down. He decided to sacrifice dignity to relative stability and got down on all fours. Working backwards, groping with his feet, and clutching at the mounds of grass with his hands, he moved crabwise down the slope feeling like a fly on the wall.

'Police Chief Killed in Fall from Cliff: Foul Play Not Excluded', nor idiocy neither. He was as near the edge as he dared go; now he had to wriggle round so that he could look over. The grass was short near the edge where soil was almost non-existant and his knees suffered painful encounters with protruding rocks, but he managed it. He peered over the edge and received a dizzy impression of dark blue water and a lacy edge of foam; he was never at ease when his feet were

497

higher than his head but he collected his wits and realized that the cliff was not sheer to the sea. Half-way down, perhaps eighty feet or so, there was a substantial abutment, presumably the result of a landslip, and lodged on this broad ledge was a vehicle of some sort. It was lying on its side and all he could see of it was a front wheel and part of the bonnet in profile. He felt sure that it was Lemarque's Escort van but he could not be certain.

He crawled back with less difficulty than he had experienced getting down but when he stood once more on the old track he was trembling; his trousers were covered in greenish slime and his right hand was bleeding from a graze. He tidied himself as best he could and found his way through the maze of tracks to where he had left his car.

They studied the map, identified the tiny inlet where Lemarque's car might be, and agreed on a map reference. Wycliffe arranged for the cliff track to be sealed off and for a scene-of-crime team under Fox to make a meticulous search of the whole stretch. Prospects were poor after the storm on Christmas Eve but it had to be done.

Then a telephone call to the Naval Air Station and an accommodating Lieutenant Commander. Yes, they had an Air Sea Rescue helicopter in the neighbourhood on a training flight; no problem to have a look-see. Call you back. That simple.

Kersey said: 'If Lemarque is at the bottom of that cliff he must have shot his wife before he went joy-riding among the mine dumps.'

'If he shot his wife, what you say seems reasonable.'

Outside a car engine cut, a door slammed, and they heard Alice Devlin's voice talking to Potter. She came in, crisp and fresh and smelling expensive.

'I hope I've done the right thing; I've allowed myself to be persuaded or bulldozed. That young lady knows her own mind and I had little option. I've left her with the Bishops.' She slipped off a suede shoulder bag and put it on the table.

'Do sit down. This is Detective Inspector Kersey. I don't

suppose you want to risk police coffee? . . . I don't blame you.'

'She asked me to take her there. I suppose it was only natural she should want to see them and they her, the two families were very close before Alain got into trouble. But I must admit I was surprised when they asked her to stay at Mynhager and she agreed—just like that; no argument, no discussion. Of course I don't know her very well but it seemed out of character. I think they were a bit surprised too.'

'Who did you see?'

'Ernest, is it? And his two sisters; the old man, and a lad called Paul. Early on we were joined by Gerald Bateman M.P.' She smiled. 'I hadn't realized we were moving in the corridors of power; the name didn't click at first.'

'Did she give you any idea why she is so anxious to stay with the Bishops?'

'Only that she knew them well and that she had spent a good deal of time in the house. She feels closer to them than to me, so I suppose it's all right for the time being.'

She sat back in her chair. 'No news of Alain?'

'I'm afraid not. I assume you are doing the necessary to put other members of the family on your side in the picture, but we are concerned about the Lemarques. We've no contact. I don't suppose you can help?'

She shook her head. 'All I know is that Alain's father came over with the Free French during the war.'

Wycliffe tested the water. 'I suppose you realize that one possibility is that your sister was killed by her husband?'

'Of course I've thought of that.'

'You think it credible?'

A lengthy pause. 'I simply don't know. I've seen Alain three or four times and then only briefly. He struck me as being very fond of Jane and perhaps over anxious to please her.'

'I don't want to put any pressure on Francine but I suspect she could tell us more than she has.'

Pursed lips. 'You could be right but if she's keeping anything from you, she hasn't confided in me. I've been kept very much in my place as a visiting aunt of slender acquaintance. Not that I blame her, poor child.'

499

She picked up her bag. 'I suppose it might be useful if I was around for a day or two?'

'I'm sure it would be.'

'Good! Apart from anything else, Francine may need a shoulder to weep on, though I doubt it.'

They talked briefly of the inquest, of the need for a disposal certificate and of the funeral which must come sometime.

Sensible woman!

On cue, as the Sierra was driven off, the Lieutenant Commander called: 'I think we've located your motor; the chaps have just radioed in. Something the worse for wear I gather. Ford Escort van, grey; registration number: Oscar Foxtrot Quebec One Three Four Papa. Snap?'

'Snap.'

'They couldn't get close enough to read the engine number. Sorry!' Funny man. 'No sign of any occupant; one door missing, the other hanging, three wheels adrift and the bodywork suffering from multiple contusions.'

'Any ideas on accessibility?'

'I enquired. Our chaps say the vehicle is caught on a sort of abutment, a land slip, about eighty feet above the tide line. They reckon the base of the cliff is uncovered at low water but it sounds as though you'll need a lift if you want to recover.'

'Any chance of your people taking it on?'

'Why not? It would be a useful exercise. I'd have to get clearance but I think that could be arranged if your lot are prepared to pay the piper.'

'Just one more thing: we want the driver of the van. He may or may not have gone over with it but we have to start looking.'

'Did all this happen before or after the force 10 on Saturday?'

'Shortly before. I wondered if you could manage a low-level sweep or two while your chaps are in the air?'

'Can do, but I don't hold out much hope of finding anything. The van didn't go all the way, but he probably did and it's unlikely that he's still in one piece.'

'Thanks. I'm notifying Coastguard and I'll keep in touch.'

Kersey said: 'I agree that we want the van and having the fly-boys lift it is probably the best way. But we want Lemarque more. If we don't find him the case folds.'

Wycliffe glanced at his watch: 'Eleven-fifteen. Just over five hours of something like daylight. If the tide is right and there's a boat available we could take a look.'

'That "we"—is it the royal, the editorial, or does it just mean you and me?'

'In this instance it means you.'

'I was afraid of that. Marine exploration is not my thing.'

'It broadens the mind.'

'And empties the stomach.'

'If Lemarque did go overboard with the van, the longer the delay the less chance we have of finding him in identifiable pieces if at all. Get on to Coastguard and see if you can arrange for the inshore lifeboat. Take one of our chaps along who's grasped the rudiments of being able to stand upright on a slippery rock. I don't want any mountaineering; if it comes to that we'll bring in the professionals. And don't be defeatist; it's like a millpond out there.'

'Until you're on it.'

Kersey reached for the telephone.

'Do it next door.'

Alone, Wycliffe pared his nails, brooded, and tried to order his thoughts. Whether they admitted it or not, all concerned seemed to assume that Lemarque had killed his wife. And it was a reasonable assumption, given support by the finding of the van. Lemarque had taken his van to Mennear Bal and committed suicide by driving over the cliff. A believable reaction to a crime of passion. Remorse, promptly followed by a dramatic and final expiation. But Wycliffe had already questioned the passion, and all but settled for premeditation. So, a different sequel: After shooting his wife, Lemarque had ditched the van at Mennear Bal to create the impression that he had killed himself, and was now on the run.

But there were flaws, possibly fatal to both notions: Franks believed that Jane Lemarque had died between four and eight, and it now seemed that the dead woman had been talking to the ineffable Evadne at four-thirty.

A fat boy sitting on the low wall of the churchyard was watching him solemnly and intently through the window. Wycliffe winked at him and immediately felt guilty when he saw the shocked look on the lad's face. One more recruit to the ranks of disillusioned youth.

Where was he? A third alternative—was there such a thing? Anyway, a third possibility: Lemarque had ditched his van before killing his wife. Improbable but not impossible. It would mean that he had really planned the killing in cold blood.

At least he had clarified his own thoughts. The thing now was to recover the van and find Lemarque, alive or dead.

By dint of persuasion, warnings, even threats, he obtained authority from the mandarins in Accounts to employ an R.N.A.S. helicopter for the recovery of Lemarque's van.

'Is it absolutely essential to the chain of evidence? Is there no other way in which recovery could be effected? By boat, for example? Have you considered recovery by sea? Surely there is a well known climbing school and cliff rescue centre in that neighbourhood—couldn't they do what is necessary? You do realize that helicopters are fiendishly expensive to hire? I mean even more expensive than fixed-wing aircraft.'

'I suppose a fixed-wing aircraft might scoop the thing up at a hundred and twenty knots provided it didn't hit the cliff face.'

'You are being facetious, Chief Superintendent. I am only trying to do my job.'

'Aren't we all?'

Probably the Lieutenant Commander would have complementary difficulties with his administration, but at last the financial and logistical problems would be solved and arrangements made. Too late for that day.

Wycliffe arranged for the house-to-house to be extended to the cottages at Mennear Bal. Others might have heard or seen as much or more than the girl at The Tributers.

He had a snack lunch alone in the bar. Ella Bunt was

there, sharing a table with Marsden. They seemed to be getting on well together.

As Wycliffe passed their table on his way out, Ella looked up. 'Thanks for the tip; you did me proud. I'll remember it.'

Thanks from a reporter must sound ominous in the ears of any policeman. Wycliffe wondered what she had cooked up with Evadne Penrose and the painter.

It was not Kersey with his inshore lifeboat who found Lemarque but a St Ives boatman, catching up on the wind and fog. Lemarque's body, drifting just below the surface of the water, nuzzled his bows, slid silently along the port side and would have cleared his stern had he not seen it, cut his engine and grabbed it with a boathook. He secured a rope round the legs and towed it back because it was difficult to get aboard without assistance. In any case he didn't fancy the job.

Arrived in harbour, he telephoned the police, and Sergeant Curtis came down to inspect his catch. Curtis recognized Lemarque, the proportions rather than the features, and reported to Wycliffe.

'The left side of his neck and the right side of his face are badly damaged, sir. The fish have been busy but there's more to it than that. He was shot, or he shot himself.'

Wycliffe left the duty officer to make the routine notifications and drove to St Ives.

St Ives: 'a pretty good town and grown rich by the fishing trade'—Daniel Defoe, a one-man K.G.B., reporting to Speaker Harley in 1702. Now it has grown richer, not on fish but on tourists and the reputations of dead painters. But, despite its prosperity, for seven or eight months of the twelve its streets are empty and many of its shops, cafés and restaurants are closed. Wycliffe arrived in the after-glow of sunset, the town in shadow, the bay lambent and still. A few figures on the quay, motionless in silhouette, standing near a little mound of plastic sheeting.

Curtis was there. 'This is Jack Martin; he brought him in. Found him floating in the lee of Clodgy Point.'

A short stout man in a sailor's cap and a duffle coat held out a firm plump hand.

The plastic sheet was lifted. Lemarque wore an anorak, zipped to the neck, brownish trousers, no shoes. The shoes belonging to Lemarque at the cottage were all non lace-ups, so it was likely that those he had been wearing had fallen off. His socks had been nibbled at in several places revealing sometimes pallid skin, sometimes abraded flesh. But Wycliffe's attention focused on the face and neck. No doubt that Lemarque had shot himself or been shot; a bullet had entered the neck just below the jaw-bone and made its exit high up the face on the other side. The wound of entry had been enlarged and made more ragged after death, presumably by the fish. It would be up to the pathologist and the ballistics experts to decide, but there seemed no obvious reason why the original bullet wound could not have been self-inflicted.

He was wearing a wrist watch, and the metal bracelet had cut into the swollen flesh. The glass of the watch, badly cracked, must have let in water but the hands were undamaged and showed twelve minutes past three. There was a day/date inset but Wycliffe could not read the display; the experts would have no difficulty.

'All right, you can cover him up.'

The police surgeon arrived, a man of few words, he made a cursory examination and left. A van brought the plastic shell in which the body would be conveyed to the mortuary, there to await the arrival of Dr Franks for the post mortem. Wycliffe spent a few minutes with Curtis in the local station then drove up the long steep hill out of the town on his way back to Mulfra.

It was almost dark but far out the sea gleamed in the last remnants of the day, and the sky was faintly flushed with red; the promise of a fine tomorrow.

So Lemarque was dead; shot through the neck and head, as his wife had been. Suicide or murder? The positions of the wounds of entry and exit were consistent with either. Lemarque could have driven his van over the grassy hump which bordered the cliff track and in those seconds while it was hurtling to the cliff edge, he could have shot himself. It was not especially uncommon for determined suicides to do a belt-and-braces job: shooting themselves in the instant of jumping off a bridge; taking poison, then drowning themselves. There was even a case on record of a man who hanged himself and cut his throat.

The van had landed on a projecting platform of rock well down the cliff face and the shock of impact would almost certainly have burst open the doors so that a man in the driving seat might well have been thrown clear and continued on down to the water. Memo: check on tides. Was Lemarque left-handed?

But now came the crunch: was it likely that Lemarque had carefully planned and executed his wife's murder, then committed suicide? More than that, if the time by Lemarque's watch was an indication of the time of his death then there was no way in which he could have been his wife's killer.

Adding it all up, Wycliffe was being forced to face the possibility of a double murder and if that was the case he was literally without a clue where to begin, they were up the creek without a paddle.

When he arrived back at the van Kersey was plaintive. 'Have you ever been out in one of those inflatables? It's like putting to sea on a couple of salami sausages; the damn thing keeps bobbing up and down like a cork. Under the cliff you catch the swell going in and bouncing back. My stomach feels like an overworked yo-yo. And all for nothing! Some other guy a mile or two up the coast beats us to it.'

Joseph had spent most of the day in his room, a good deal of it looking out of the window. He had watched an Air Sea Rescue helicopter fluttering up and down, following the configuration of the coastline, at or below cliff-top height. Then, later, the inshore lifeboat had taken over, nosing into the coves and inlets, lost to sight for long periods but always emerging to round the next promontory. It was not a novel routine, it happened in the tourist season when a too confident swimmer or some idiot on an air-bed got swept out to sea, and something similar occurred in the winter when they were searching for drums of toxic chemicals washed overboard from a freighter, or for bodies from a wrecked ship. But today's activity had worried Joseph because he could not get it out of his head that they were looking for Lemarque.

Now it was dark and the search had either ended or been postponed.

He could not focus the reason for his unease. Jane Lemarque had been murdered, apparently by her husband; a tragedy in any circumstances but the more stark because it concerned people one knew, people with whom there had been intimacy and friendship. But Joseph had never been a sentimentalist and now he had reached an age when, like any sensible man, he had cultivated a nodding acquaintance with death and the habit of distancing himself from grief.

His disquiet stemmed from an illogical conviction that the tragedy was not yet played out, that it would move nearer home. He looked round at his books, at his photographs and paintings, at the room which sustained him in his old age and for the first time felt insecure. Absurdly, he associated this foreboding with the arrival of the girl. That morning she had moved in . . .

He got up from his chair and in a single irritable movement swept the curtains over the window so that the wooden rings rattled together. 'God! I'm going soft in the head!'

A tap at the door and Ernest came in. 'Are you all right?' Concerned.

The old man snapped at him. 'Of course I'm all right! Why shouldn't I be?'

Ernest, not reassured, knew better than to argue. 'Wycliffe has been on the phone.'

'They've found Lemarque.'

'How on earth do you know?'

'Dead?'

'Yes.'

'Drowned?'

'Shot, but Wycliffe didn't give details. All I know is that his van was found half-way down the cliff at Mennear Bal and his body was picked up floating in the sea. He wanted to know if Lemarque was left-handed.'

'He wasn't, was he?'

'No. I suppose they're thinking of suicide, presumably after killing Jane.'

The old man made an irritable movement. 'All nice and tidy! So it's as good as over; soon everybody can pack up and go home.'

Ernest's astonishment was obvious. 'I don't understand.'

'You wouldn't! Has anybody told the girl?'

'Vee is with her now.'

'Yes, well, we shall see.'

Caroline came into the room from the kitchen, Virginia from the hall. The family, apart from the two sisters, was already seated round the table which was set with nine places.

Joseph sat at the head of the table, waiting.

Somebody said: 'Is she coming down, Vee?'

'I think so; she wants to change first.'

Joseph thought: Vee's pleasure in life consists in persuading people to do what they don't want to. The born schoolteacher.

The high, gloomy room, panelled by its nineteenth-century architect, was dimly lit by electric bracket lamps in the form of fake candles. Family portraits by indifferent Victorian and Edwardian painters were flattered by the poor lighting.

Paul was staring at his empty plate and fiddling with his soup spoon. 'She won't let me talk to her.'

'You must give her time, Paul.'

Too easily hurt. Paul had the Bishop looks, something of the Bishop temperament, but not the Bishop hide.

Joseph's feelings of unease increased, he sensed that they were moving towards a crisis. A premonition? He did not believe in such things. Or did he? At seventy-five he realized that all his life he had adopted postures to defend himself against a corroding sense of insecurity. These postures had fathered his beliefs. Was this true of others? Of Bateman, for instance? If it was, did he know it?

507

All Joseph knew at this moment was that he was listening to meaningless verbal exchanges between members of his family while underneath . . .

Virginia took her place beside Paul; something more than auntly affection there. She was explaining: 'When I went to her door I could hear her voice and I thought someone must be with her but she was alone. She was sitting in the dark by the window with the curtains drawn back. I said: "I thought you were talking to someone", and she said: "I was, I was talking to Blackie."'

Joseph was impelled to question. 'Blackie?'

'The black-faced doll she's had since she was a baby.'

Caroline amended: 'I gave her that doll on her third birthday.'

Stella reached for a bread roll and started to crumble it on her side plate. Joseph thought: Stella can't wait for her food. At least I haven't become greedy in my old age. Not for food, anyway. Stella was saying something: 'I used to talk to my dolls when George was away. I had thirty of them from every part of India.'

Bateman made his contribution: 'She's had a terrible shock, poor girl. How is she taking it, Vee?'

'I really don't know. She seemed strange rather than grieved but you can't . . .' She broke off as Francine entered the room.

Joseph drew in his breath. Francine wore a blue dress that was almost a gown; her red-gold hair was gathered into a coil on the top of her head displaying her long youthful neck. Beautiful! Necks and ankles are the erogenous zones for a young woman. The eighteenth century understood this: display the neck, titillate with the ankles. Women have lost the art of titillation.

Joseph felt compelled to pay homage. 'I'm very glad you've come down, my dear.'

'Thank you, daddy Jo.' It was the name she had called him from the time she had learned to talk. God alone knew why.

Caroline said: 'I'll tell Ada we're ready.' She came back a minute or two later, with Ada carrying a large tureen of soup.

When it had been served, they settled down to their meal. No one could think of anything to say and as the silence lengthened so the tension seemed to rise. Several times Ernest cleared his throat as though to speak but changed his mind.

Joseph thought: He's on edge. He keeps looking at the girl. Covert glances, as though he's anxious not to be seen to look at her. If I didn't know him I'd think it was lust. What's the matter with him? There is a streak of weakness, a flaw, which makes him unpredictable. Even as a child . . .

Then there was Gerald, nephew and son-in-law, yet Joseph had always found it difficult to think of him as one of the family. He sat bolt upright, staring straight ahead, going through the motions of drinking the soup like an automaton. He was good at it, never spilling a drop. Joseph thought: He knows; his politician's antennae are signalling trouble ahead.

Caroline was uneasy too. She was of coarser stuff than her sister but more perceptive. Vee lived on the surface of things, responsive to every wind that blew, but Carrie was aware of the undertow of life, which was probably why she needed to drink. Neither of the girls had turned out like their mother.

Joseph felt a warmth behind the eyes, remembering his wife. Ursula. Her name still had the power to move him. He was trying to recall how she had looked when they first met. Ursula at seventeen . . . 1927; talkies and the slow fox-trot; Rex Whistler at the Tate, Aldous Huxley, Evelyn Waugh, Virginia Woolf . . .

His gaze rested once more on Francine and he was startled. Why had he never realized it before? Or was he imagining it now? He had never seen the girl with her hair up until tonight . . .

Vee was helping Ada to serve the main course. Spare ribs of beef in a marinade: one of his favourite dishes but his appetite had gone. He was watching Francine. She had small helpings but she ate with prim and delicate efficiency. Apart from Stella she seemed to be the only one untroubled by the silence.

After the meal they went into the drawing-room for coffee. Conversation, which began around the percolator, continued when they sat down; the spell of silence had been broken. They talked about the weather; the mild spell, the prospect of January frosts and, inevitably, someone quoted: 'As the days begin to lengthen, the cold begins to strengthen.'

Francine sat in one of the smaller armchairs and Virginia squatted on the floor at her side. Virginia was a great floor squatter. Joseph could see her lips moving almost continuously, provoking only occasional responses from the girl then, abruptly, during a lull in other conversation, Francine's voice became clearly audible to all: 'The man they found this afternoon was not my father!' Her voice was taut and brittle. She got to her feet, looked about her uncertainly, then hurried from the room. Virginia went after her and Paul, very pale, followed them.

Bateman said: 'Poor child!'

Caroline looked round at the others. 'Do you think I should go up?' And when no one answered decided to stay where she was.

Ernest sat in his chair, staring with absorbed attention at his empty coffee cup.

Stella went on with her knitting as though nothing had happened and the ultimate platitude was left to Ada: 'She'll be better after a good cry.'

Chapter Nine

WEDNESDAY MORNING; Christmas Day plus three. A second fine day in a row, an achievement for late December. When it happens a Cornishman begins to wonder if something has gone wrong with the Divine Order. Wycliffe and Kersey arrived at the Incident Van at half-past eight after breakfasting with Alice Devlin. Alice had decided to stay on until after the joint funeral of her sister and brother-in-law. 'But I must slip up to Bristol for one or two nights to deal with things. My husband is in Brussels.'

The newspapers were on Wycliffe's table and Ella Bunt had made the front page of one of the tabloids under an 'exclusive' tag.

Former Partner of Law and Order M.P. Missing.

Alain Lemarque, recently released from prison after serving a sentence for fraud, is wanted for questioning in connection with the murder of his wife, Jane, at their Cornish cottage on Christmas Eve.

Gerald Bateman M.P., known to his colleagues as 'The Sheriff', and tipped for office in the forthcoming government re-shuffle, was a partner in the Lemarque enterprises before they ran into trouble; trouble which culminated in Lemarque being sentenced to two years for fraud. Mr Bateman, when he is not at Westminster or in his constituency, lives across the valley from the Lemarques with his in-laws, the Bishop family who, for generations, have been lawyers in the neighbouring town of Penzance.

By coincidence, the head of the area C.I.D. Chief Superintendent Charles Wycliffe, now in charge of the inquiry, was staying with the Bishops at the time of the tragedy. It is understood that he has since removed himself to the local inn . . .

Wycliffe muttered: 'It could have been worse I suppose.'
At nine o'clock Dr Franks telephoned his preliminary report on the autopsy.
'Obviously the man was shot not drowned but his body must have got into the sea very shortly after death . . . He was shot through the left side of his neck with an upward inclination of the weapon and the bullet emerged higher up on the other side. A repeat performance of his wife's killing except that the gun was probably held close to the skin if not actually touching. . . . Difficult to be quite sure about that because the wound of entry was enlarged through being nibbled by fish. On the evidence of the body alone ¹ I'd say it could have been either suicide or murder.'
'He wasn't left-handed.'
'Ah! I was coming to that, but it doesn't make much difference. If he was steering the van to the edge of the cliff when he fired he would have had his right hand on the wheel. If he didn't steer the van Sod's Law would see to it that the thing tipped over and stuck half-way down the slope without reaching the edge. Very frustrating for a chap all set to make a dramatic exit. And you must know that it isn't difficult to fire a gun with your left hand if you don't have to aim it.'
Wycliffe was watching Kersey light a cigarette. Automatically he reached into his right-hand jacket pocket where for twenty-five years he had kept his pipe; it was no longer there. Frustration, and an empty feeling akin to hunger. He muttered angrily to himself: 'I'm like an infant deprived of its dummy!' Absurdly, his manner towards Franks became noticeably sharper: 'The real question is whether Lemarque was in the van when the shot was fired. For all we know it was pushed empty over the cliff.'
Franks was amused. 'Fascinating! The idea of this bloke pushing his van over the cliff, then taking a running jump

after it, shooting himself on the way. A bit whimsical, don't you think?'

A rueful laugh. 'Go to hell! What I'm really saying is that the evidence of his watch makes it less likely that he killed himself. Why should he if he hadn't killed his wife?'

'Search me! Motive is not my problem, Charles. I can tell you though that if he was shot in the van, whether he did it himself or not, I'd expect a fair old mess of spattered blood and soft tissue. At least you'll be able to check on that when they hoist the van aboard. And one more thing you can chew over in the silent watches: when we were undressing him we came across plant fragments caught between his anorak and his shirt. They included two dried up, papery little bladder-like objects. My assistant, who knows about such things, says they are the calyces of the sea campion. It seems these often survive on the flower stalk through the winter; and the sea campion, according to her, is found on the grassy slopes of cliffs. So it looks as though our friend might have had a roll in the grass before finally taking off. How's that for service beyond the call of duty?'

Wycliffe had to admit that Franks had given him more than he could reasonably expect in a preliminary report. And on balance it seemed to strengthen the case for believing that Lemarque had been murdered. A double murder.

With any luck they would have the wrecked van available for examination later in the morning. The weather was calm, the sea placid, visibility excellent. Ideal flying weather, and there might not be another such day for weeks. The van would be lifted by the helicopter on to a truck parked on the cliff-top, then taken to a police garage for forensic examination.

Detailed arrangements had been made and it was all systems go.

Kersey said: 'This case, like Topsy, jes growed! From a silly girl going a.w.o.l. to a couple of homicides.'

'And we've next to nothing to go on. I want you to get in touch with Rosemergy Minerals and find out the state of play between them and Lemarque over the Mennear Bal site, also how far Bateman is known to be involved.'

Kersey had been turning over the latest reports.

'Anything new?'

'What there is comes from Mennear Bal. Two more sightings of the grey Escort van being driven in the direction of the cliff at around three o'clock on Christmas Eve. More interesting: there's a statement from a man out walking his dog. . .' Kersey seached for the page. 'Alamein Montgomery Choak, aged forty-two; he would be with a name like that, poor bastard! He was walking along the track at the cliff edge when he came across the van, parked unattended. He actually passed it.'

'Interesting! What time was that?'

'He says about half-past three.'

'Say, an hour before Jane Lemarque telephoned Evadne Penrose. Was Lemarque alive or dead at that time?'

Kersey put the report back in its file. 'Good question. If we go by his watch he was already dead.'

Wycliffe got up from his seat. 'I shall be at Mynhager for the next hour or so.'

'Anything particular in mind?'

'Just a fishing expedition.'

Outside in the sunshine he decided to walk to Mynhager. It was part of the folk-lore of headquarters that the chief never drove if he could walk because walking was quicker. The truth was that he disliked being driven, and when he drove he rarely clocked much over 50. Anyway it was a nice day, almost like summer, though tomorrow or the day after could bring a tempest or a frost. At the moment women stood in their doorways, and little knots of people were gossiping outside the shops and on the sunny side of the street.

Wycliffe turned down by the pub, preoccupied. If there had in fact been a double murder, why had anyone wanted to kill Lemarque and his wife? Bateman and the Bishops had been on more or less intimate terms with them for nearly twenty years so Mynhager was the obvious place to start. But there was more to it than that.

An ancient Mini passed him and came to a stop a little way ahead, by the painter's cottage. A blonde young woman got out, came round to the back, opened the boot and lifted out a large travelling case, obviously empty. Marsden's woman friend come to collect her belongings? She slammed the boot shut and went into the cottage. As he drew level Wycliffe could see the two of them through the window of the living-room.

He plodded on along the track until he rounded the bend and came in sight of Mynhager. Even in the sunshine the house stood out starkly against the sky. He went round to the front and rang the bell. To his surprise it was answered by Francine. She looked strained, hollow-eyed and pale, but her manner was not unwelcoming. She even managed a smile.

'You'd better come into the drawing-room; I don't know who you want to see . . .'

Sunshine flooded through the big window so that the fire in the grate was dimmed by its brilliance but the room itself appeared more tatty than ever, the holly looked sad, the paper chains, pathetic.

She picked up a large photograph album from one of the settees. 'Shall I tell them you're here?'

'Family photographs?'

'I was looking at them.'

'Do you mind if I look?'

He sat on the settee, took the book from her hands, and turned the pages while she stood over him. He had the impression that she was not displeased.

The usual family snapshots, mainly of groups of people either posed formally on the terrace or snapped casually on picnics or boating trips. None of them was recent.

'Most of them were taken before I was born.'

He stopped at a lively group taken in a sandy cove. It was dated 1967. She said: 'Mamma Bishop took most of these. I used to call her that; she died when I was five.' The men, Joseph among them, wore trunks or shorts, the girls, bikinis.

'That's my mother, a year before I was born.' Even in the snapshot the girl stood out as a quite exceptional beauty; she was laughing and seemed to be putting up token resistance to an attempt by a boisterous Bateman to place a garland of seaweed round her neck. All the others wore crowns and garlands of seaweed while Ernest had contrived a kilt for himself and stood in regal pose holding a paddle in place of a trident. Lemarque crouched frog-like on the sand beside a slimmer, almost lithe Caroline, who was adding something to his crown. Virginia watched her sister with obvious disapproval.

In later snapshots Francine was there, first as a baby in the arms of one or the other, later as a toddler, then as a trim, self-possessed little girl.

Wycliffe was puzzled, not by the snapshots but by Francine's satisfaction in his interest. It was as though she was saying: 'I want you to see how things were.'

Then the door opened and Bateman came in. His astonishment was obvious. 'Charles! I had no idea you were here. I've been wondering if we might be in touch. Of course I heard from Ernest . . .'

Francine said: 'If you want to talk I'll go somewhere else.' She went out, taking the album with her.

Bateman went on: 'I was greatly tempted to ring you but I knew you wouldn't wish to be pestered until you were ready.'

What was it about this man which made Wycliffe bristle? Paleface speak with forked tongue but what politician does not? Nearer the truth, he had a barely conscious prejudice against those who swim where others sink; against chronic survivors. Totally irrational! Where would we be without them? But Wycliffe's sympathies were with the dinosaurs.

'Francine should have told me you were here but the poor child has had such a terrible shock.'

Bateman was casually elegant in corduroy slacks, checked Viyella shirt, cashmere cardigan, and custom-made house shoes. His broad dark moustache bristled in a perfect symmetry of graded lengths, and he was meticulously shaved. 'May I offer you something, Charles?'

'Thank you, no. It seems that Francine is taking an interest in times past.'

'Oh, the album . . . It belonged to my mother-in-law who never failed to record every family occasion. I don't know how Francine got hold of it.' Bateman dismissed the irrelevance and went on smoothly: 'I suppose we all knew in our hearts that this was the outcome to be expected but it still comes as a great shock.'

Wycliffe looked blank. 'What outcome? I don't understand.'

Bateman sat in an armchair, entirely relaxed. 'I merely meant that for a man like Alain there could be no other way. He must have been devastated by what he had done in a moment of madness.'

'You are assuming that he committed suicide after killing his wife?'

'What other explanation can there be?'

'We've reason to think that Lemarque predeceased his wife.'

Bateman's expression was one of total incredulity. 'Forgive me, but there must be some mistake! Who, other than Alain, could possibly have murdered Jane? Who had a motive? And why, if Jane was not dead at the time, did Alain kill himself? I can understand that a man facing the rebuilding of his life in middle age might feel intensely depressed but I have already told you that he was absorbed in a new venture which, knowing him, would certainly have restored his zest for life.'

Unconsciously Bateman was adopting his House of Commons tactics: beginning with an assertion and embroidering it with rhetorical questions.

By contrast, Wycliffe sounded casual. 'It's more than likely that Lemarque did not commit suicide.'

'I don't understand.'

'It's probable that he too was murdered.'

Bateman's hazel eyes studied Wycliffe intently for several seconds before he said: 'I find that quite incredible!'

At that moment there was a roar overhead and a helicopter appeared from over the house, flying low and following the line of the coast. At a distance of about half-a-mile it hovered, lost more height and vanished, hidden by the intervening headlands.

Both men were gazing out of the window. The sea stretched to the horizon, filling the framed picture except for a succession of headlands sheering away to the south-west. They could hear the pulsing of the helicopter's rotor blades but could not see it.

Wycliffe said: 'They're going to pick up Lemarque's van, what's left of it.'

He sensed a tremor of disquiet affecting them both. Was it that the tragedy seemed suddenly more real? But for Wycliffe at least the moment soon passed. Policemen, like doctors, deal in cases not tragedies.

He said: 'If this is a case of double murder, and I feel sure that it is, then we have to look outside the Lemarque family for a motive and for the killer. So far we know almost nothing about them, while you and the Bishops have known them since before their marriage; naturally, we come to you for information.'

Bateman sat, finger tips matched; he spoke with careful deliberation: 'I can't believe that you are right but I will co-operate in any way I can and I'm sure the same goes for the rest of the family.'

Wycliffe's poker face would not have shamed Andrei Gromyko. 'For the moment I have only two or three questions: the first is probably the most important. From your knowledge of the Lemarques can you think of anyone with a grudge against them—against either or both?'

'No, I cannot.'

'I would like you to keep that question in mind; give yourself time to think about it. I suggest that you go back over the past few years which saw the break-up of your partnership and Lemarque's conviction for fraud. Later I may have to ask you for an account of your relations with Lemarque over those years and of his other contacts so far as they are known to you.'

'And your second question?' Bateman's cordiality had vanished.

'I need to know if Lemarque had any relatives in this country and whether he was in touch with them.'

'There, I'm afraid, I can't help you. Alain was always reticent about his family. To the best of my knowledge he

518

came over here with his parents as a very young child, at the time of Dunkirk.'

'My next question is a simple matter of fact: when did you last see Lemarque or his wife?'

'I saw them both briefly on Christmas Eve.'

'At what time?'

Bateman was accustomed to being interrogated by TV interviewers about his politics, not by policemen about his private life; his distaste was obvious and his answer curt. 'At about two o'clock or perhaps a little later.'

'After your lunch here.'

'Certainly! You were our guest if you recollect.' Acid. 'I went for a walk and it occurred to me that it would be a friendly gesture to call on the Lemarques and try to cheer them up. At the same time I hoped to hear something more of the type of investment Alain had in mind.'

'And did you?'

'No. I had chosen a bad moment; how bad I've since realized. I could see that they were both under considerable strain and though they were perfectly civil it was obvious that I was anything but welcome at that particular time. Of course, as soon as I could decently extricate myself, I left. I wasn't in the house above five minutes.'

'Had you offered or been persuaded to back Lemarque's project with a large sum of money?'

Bateman looked startled. 'Certainly not! I didn't even know what he had in mind. All I did was to indicate a sympathetic interest.'

'What did you do when you left the cottage?'

A long slow look. 'I continued my walk.'

'Where did you go?'

This was too much for Bateman. 'Really! This begins to look like an interrogation.'

Wycliffe was coldly objective. 'I am asking you questions which seem proper in the circumstances but you don't have to answer them at this stage. As far as I know you were the last person to see Jane Lemarque alive apart from her husband and her killer. For that reason your evidence is important

519

and you will be asked to make a written statement later.'

Bateman realized that he had made a tactical error, and acknowledged it with a thin smile. 'You are quite right. One has to get used to the idea of being a suspect but it is not something which comes easily.'

Wycliffe declined the bait. 'So where did you go?'

'I walked as far as Busullow and back through Morvah. I need plenty of exercise as I spend too much time at a desk.'

'Did you meet anyone?'

This was bloody-mindedness, but Bateman was not going to make the same mistake twice; he answered mildly: 'I suppose I must have done, especially walking back along the road but I don't remember anyone in particular.'

It was a reasonable answer.

Wycliffe had been watching Bateman, trying to sum him up, not because he had any real suspicion of the man but because he found the Bateman phenomenon interesting. A perceptive doctor, merely by looking at his patient, may spot the constitutional weakness which could mean future trouble in one or other of the organ systems of the body. Wycliffe tried to do something similar in his professional encounters though he was looking for moral weakness, for the heel of Achilles which made them vulnerable. In Bateman's case he thought he had found it. Bateman was a strong man but a vain one and his vanity laid him open on all fronts. He had to succeed or learn to despise the object of his failures.

Wycliffe wondered how he had come to terms with his marriage and his situation in the Bishop household.

'Just one more point.' Wycliffe drew from his pocket the envelope containing the newscutting, found amongst Lemarque's papers.

Bateman took it, read it, and handed it back. 'I don't understand. Where did you find that?'

Bateman had done his best to sound casual but Wycliffe was in no doubt that he was disturbed. 'You remember the occasion?'

'Of course I remember it. As you see I was guest speaker at the dinner.'

'Was Lemarque there?'

'As a guest, yes. Ernest invited him. The Lemarques were staying with us and it was an evening out for Alain.'

'Not for Jane?'

Bateman laughed. 'I'm afraid not; it was a stag party occasion. But why the interest?'

'These things crop up.'

Abruptly, the sound of the helicopter rotors, a muffled beat, increased in volume and the helicopter appeared, hovering clear of the headlands. Suspended from it by an invisible cord was a box-like contraption which could only have been the wreck of Lemarque's van. The helicopter moved a small distance inland, hovered, and again lost height. The transfer of its load to the waiting truck took place out of their sight, hidden by intervening higher ground. The truck would take the wreckage to the vehicle department at headquarters where Fox would examine it with an expert from Forensic.

Wycliffe got to his feet. He had learned something from Bateman, enough to be going on with. There would be time for more questions when he had more ammunition. 'Well, thank you for your co-operation; I'll arrange for someone to take your statement. Now, is your father-in-law at home?'

Bateman seemed surprised but made no comment. 'I think so. I'll take you to his room if you like.'

But in the hall they were waylaid by Aunt Stella who seemed to be doing sentry-go at the foot of the stairs. Aunt Stella in a blue silk blouse and a red skirt with the inevitable orange scarf.

'Ah, there you are, Mr Wycliffe! I've been waiting for you, but we can talk better in my room . . .'

Bateman shrugged and made his escape.

Aunt Stella had one of the bedrooms as a sitting-room. It was like a cave; the windows were draped with heavily patterned net; the decor, from the Bukhara carpet to the flock wallpaper and the upholstery of the Edwardian suite, was predominantly red. There were wall-cabinets chock full of bric-a-brac: ivory and ebony elephants of all sizes, multilimbed Shivas in brass and bronze, various Buddhas cheek by jowl with Hindu gods and goddesses. Two massive radiators maintained a hothouse temperature.

'Do sit down, Chief Superintendent.' Stella's manner was confiding, even conspiratorial. 'Coffee to begin with I think.'

A coffee percolator on the hearth emitted jets of steam accompanied by vulgar noises and there was a tray with cups, a bowl of sugar, and a jug of cream on a low table near the window.

'As you can see, I have my own rooms.' She pointed to a door which broke the line of wall cabinets. 'My bedroom and bathroom are through there.'

The little red light on the percolator glowed, and its flatulence subsided. 'Ah, there we are! Black or white?. . . An oatmeal biscuit, Chief Superintendent?'

She had style, Wycliffe could imagine her, the pukka memsahib, presiding at tea parties, entertaining Indian bigwigs and high ranking civil servants to dinner. Always serene, always amusing and ready with that morsel of gossip, delicately spiced, which would titillate without vulgarity.

The preliminaries over, Aunt Stella said: 'I suppose keeping a gun without a permit is a serious offence?' She went on without waiting for an answer: 'They've probably told you that I'm weak in the head and that my memory is not what it was; that may be true, but I'm not bonkers, you understand.'

She looked at him, her little grey eyes alert for his reaction but he gave no sign. He sat in his chair, bolt upright, looking blank but not bored; his listening role. Over the years he had found that most people will talk more freely to a neutral listener, one who gives little indication of being either for or against, believing or unconvinced.

'They say I hide things then accuse people of having taken them; I assure you that I don't hide things—or not very often. I put them away and forget where I put them . . .' A girlish laugh. 'Of course I sometimes say things just to shock them—silly things, I suppose, but even at my age one has to get some fun out of life. Now and then I'm quite wicked and I embarrass them in front of their friends, then they have to explain that I'm not quite right in the head.' She chuckled. 'But Ernest is so stuffy, worse than his father! And the two girls irritate me with their patronizing attitudes. I suppose it comes of having lived such sheltered lives.'

He felt sure that she was preparing the way for an admission which she regarded as more serious than possession of an unregistered firearm.

The room was so hot that he could feel the little beads of sweat forming on his forehead.

'About your gun, Mrs Burnett-Price . . .'

'I don't have a gun, Chief Superintendent! I was thinking of my husband's. He was a major general, you know. As an officer he had a service revolver but I am speaking of a rather special pistol which was given him by a maharajah. The butt was inlaid with silver and it carried an inscription: "Given in friendship to Major General George Burnett-Price, C.B.E., M.C., September 1947." George was very proud of it.'

'Where is it now?' Wycliffe's manner was such that he could have been a doctor enquiring about a patient's symptoms rather than a policeman conducting a case.

She patted her hair in a vain attempt to control the wispy escapes. 'I don't know: it's gone.'

'When did you last see it?'

She looked at him, frowning. 'Months ago, it could be a year. I'd forgotten all about it.'

'What reminded you?'

'Why, the Lemarques, what else? Both of them were shot were they not?' Her voice faltered and suddenly all trace of her rather coy silliness vanished, leaving her a sad and very worried old woman. She smoothed her skirt then clasped her bony misshapen hands in her lap. 'It was late last night; I was sitting here brooding on the Lemarques when it occurred to me that if they had been shot . . .' She hesitated and stopped speaking as though she wished to rephrase what she was about to say; then she went on: 'I thought I ought to see if George's pistol was in its proper place, in the cupboard where I kept it.'

'Why connect your husband's pistol with what happened to Jane and Alain Lemarque?'

She was silent for a time. Somewhere in the house somebody was using a vacuum cleaner while outside the window gulls were screeching. When she spoke her manner was petulant.

'Do you think this is Chicago, Chief Superintendent? How many guns would you expect to find in Mulfra?' Whatever the shortcomings of her memory, she was shrewd.

'Go on.'

'Well, I looked for the gun and it wasn't there.'

Wycliffe said: 'Just now you spoke of your husband's service revolver, but you called the gun given him by the maharajah, a pistol—do you know the difference between a pistol and a revolver?'

She was contemptuous. 'I wasn't married to an army officer for nearly fifty years without learning something about firearms. In fact, when we were in India I did a certain amount of target shooting myself.'

'Show me where the gun was kept.'

She went to one of the cupboards below the glass-fronted display cases and brought out a sandalwood box. He saw a look of astonishment on her old face as she lifted the box but she said nothing. She placed it on a low table and raised the lid.

Inside were gun-cleaning materials and a chamois leather pouch in the shape of a holster. The butt of an automatic pistol, inlaid with silver, protruded from the pouch.

The old lady looked at the contents of the box in bewilderment, then at him. 'I don't understand! It wasn't there last night.' She repeated with emphasis: 'It really was not there!'

She put out her hand to pick up the pistol.

'Don't touch it!' He went on: 'So you are quite sure the gun was not in its place last night?'

She nodded. 'I wish to God I wasn't.'

'Can you tell me what sort of gun this is?'

She went back to her chair and sat down, obviously

distressed. In a tired voice she said: 'It's a Walther P-38. German—that was the one thing which disappointed George. Of course they are wonderful pistols but he hadn't got over the war . . .'

Wycliffe murmured: 'Jane Lemarque was killed with a .38 automatic, almost certainly a Walther.'

She said nothing but he saw her hands tighten on the arms of her chair.

He spoke gently: 'I shall have to take this away with me for tests—box and all. Were there any cartridges?'

She made a feeble gesture with her hand. 'That little cardboard box in with the gun: there were a few single cartridges in that. I don't know how many . . . or how many are left.' She went on as though speaking to herself: 'To think that someone took the pistol . . . and put it back. They must have put it back in the night . . . they must have!'

'Who knew that you had this gun?'

'Who knew? Why, everybody must have known about it when it was presented to George—all the family, I mean.'

'But that was thirty-seven years ago. Most of the people in this house now were either very young or they had not been born.'

This brought her up short. 'I hadn't thought of that. One forgets how time passes . . .'

'When did you come to Mynhager to live?'

'Three years ago; after poor George died. Before that we lived in Dorset.'

'Did you speak to anyone about the gun then or have you mentioned it since?'

She shook her head. 'I don't think so. I can't remember.' She was becoming agitated. 'I just don't know!'

He was sorry for her. 'I know this is very distressing for you but I want you to say nothing about it to anyone for the time being. Will you agree to that?'

'If you say so.'

'I'll give you a receipt for the box and its contents.' He wrote out a receipt and handed it to her. 'Just one question: Who, in your opinion, could have come into your room during the night or this morning to put the gun back?'

She looked at him, frowning. 'Anyone! Anyone at all. I close my bedroom door at night so I wouldn't have heard anyone in this room.'

'And this morning?'

'This morning?' She looked troubled and a certain vagueness returned to her manner. He mustn't push her too far.

But she went on: 'This morning I got up at seven as I usually do and my breakfast was brought to me here at eight-thirty. I was here until just before you arrived.'

He left, carrying the sandalwood box in a Marks and Spencer bag she had given him. In the hall he encountered Bateman who was obviously intrigued by the bag but did not refer to it.

'Did you speak to my father-in-law?'

'No. I'm afraid that wasn't possible; I spent some time with Mrs Burnett-Price.'

A suave smile.

Bateman saw him off.

His thoughts were sombre. Two guns, one a revolver belonging to Lemarque, the other, an automatic, belonging to Stella Burnett-Price but accessible to the whole household at Mynhager.

It now seemed that the Lemarques had both been murdered by the same hand and that he was in possession of the weapon. Jane Lemarque had died at some time after four-thirty on Christmas Eve, her husband probably earlier, at about three o'clock.

Wycliffe's thoughts went back to that day. In the morning he had been at the Lemarques' cottage with Virginia; he had lunched with the family at Mynhager and afterwards, feeling drowsy from too much drink, he had dozed in an armchair in the drawing-room until Curtis arrived. He recalled that he had joined Curtis in the dining-room at half-past three, by which time Lemarque must have been already dead . . .

Had he seen any of the others after lunch? Caroline and Ernest in the kitchen; she was making a brandy trifle and he

526

was dipping his fingers in the cream . . . Then he and Curtis had gone to see Marsden. He was back at Mynhager in good time for dinner at seven . . . He had gone to his room and by that time Jane Lemarque was almost certainly dead.

Was it possible that he had sat at table that evening with a double murderer?

He was walking back along the track to the village; the Mini was still parked outside Marsden's cottage but now the back was packed, almost to the roof, with cardboard boxes and bulging polythene bags. As he reached the cottage the young woman he had seen before came out of the front door carrying yet another bag. She looked at him with a hint of aggression. A handsome blonde, in peevish mood.

'Is Mr Marsden at home?'

'No.'

'I am Chief Superintendent Wycliffe.'

'I know. If you want him you'll find him at The Tributers.' She bundled her latest bag in on top of the rest and slammed the car door. As she turned away she seemed surprised to find him still standing there.

'Perhaps you will give me a few minutes of your time.'

She was about to refuse but thought better of it. 'All right, but you'd better come inside.'

In the living room he was not asked to sit down. The fire in the grate had gone out and Marsden's cat was sleeping in the fender. The table was littered with an even greater accumulation of dirty dishes and empty tins. The girl stood by the table, hands thrust deep into the pockets of her bush jacket, waiting.

'You are Miss . . .'

'Call me Emma.'

He realized that this was not a concession, rather a refusal to tell him her surname. 'Your name, please?'

'Emma Gregory.'

'You've lived here for how long?'

'Nearly a year.'

'And now you are moving out.'

'As you see.' Her jaw set in a hard line.

'You know that Mr and Mrs Lemarque are both dead?'

'I knew about Mrs Lemarque; he told me about the husband this morning.'

'You mean that Mr Marsden told you?'

'Yes.'

'Since you have lived here have either of the Lemarques called on Mr Marsden?'

'I work in St Ives; I've no idea what happens when I'm away, but I've never seen her here.'

'What about Mr Lemarque?'

'He's only been out of jail a few weeks but in that time he's called twice in the evenings—that is to say when I've been here.'

'Did he stay long?'

An impatient movement. 'I wasn't watching the clock. About an hour each time, I suppose. They went into the studio to talk, presumably because they didn't want me to hear what was said.'

'Perhaps they were discussing pictures.'

'Perhaps.'

'Did they seem friendly to each other?'

'Not especially.'

'What does that mean?'

'That they didn't seem particularly friendly.'

Wycliffe snapped: 'Don't play games, Miss Gregory! In what way did they seem unfriendly?'

She had flushed at his change of tone. She was not as hard as she pretended. 'Well, Hugh didn't seem pleased to see him and when they were in the studio I heard Hugh's voice raised several times. Of course it doesn't take much to make him shout.'

'On Lemarque's first visit did Marsden seem surprised to see him?'

'That wasn't my impression.' She glanced at her watch. 'If there's nothing more I've got a lot to do.'

'I won't keep you but I would like your address in case we need to get in touch.'

She hesitated, realized that it was pointless to refuse and

said: 'Emma Gregory, 14, Seaview Road, Penzance. But I hope you won't want me, my parents have had more than enough to put up with as it is.'

He continued on his way back to the village. Clouds which had been building over the hills were spreading seawards, obscuring the sun, and as he reached the van the first drops of rain began to fall. It was one o'clock and Kersey was waiting.

Wycliffe put his carrier bag on the table.

'Been shopping, sir?'

'I want this properly packed and sent by special messenger for ballistic tests.'

Kersey was made to feel that his humour was ill-timed but he wasn't easily repressed. 'Is one allowed to enquire where it came from?'

Wycliffe brought him up to date then he put through a call to a friend in Ballistics asking for most urgent treatment.

'One more thing before we eat.' Once more Wycliffe produced his envelope with the newscutting. 'I want someone to go through the Incident Records for anything of note occurring in this area on the 15th and 16th of April 1979.'

'I'll see to it, sir.'

They walked across to The Tributers with the rain gathering purpose, and went up to their rooms to wash.

'See you in the bar later.'

Wycliffe was the first down; he had to pass the open door of the kitchen to reach the bar. Phyllis was in the kitchen, wearing a white apron, cutting up meat on a floury board. There were several little heaps on the board.

'Do you like pasties—real Cornish pasties, I mean?'

'What? Yes, I think so . . .'

She laughed. 'Bless the man! He's miles away. Pasties—that's what you'll get this evening unless you say different now.'

'Yes, pasties—very nice.'

In the bar less than half the tables were occupied but Marsden was there reading a newspaper, a glass of ale, an empty soup bowl and a spread of crumbs in front of him. He acknowledged Wycliffe with a lift of the hand.

Lorna was behind the bar, archly familiar: 'So what can we do for you today?'

'A half of home-brew.'

'Nothing to eat?'

'I'll wait for Mr Kersey.'

He took his drink to a table by the window. It was raining hard now, vertical silvery cords blotted out the view and the gloom inside made it difficult to see across the bar. Lorna switched on the lights. 'Let the dog see the rabbit.'

Kersey arrived and they ordered bowls of soup and bread rolls with garlic butter.

Kersey spoke in a low voice: 'I had a bit of news this morning about our friend. My mate called. He's station officer now. He remembered the case but he's been digging around for details. Of course it was four years ago.'

Wycliffe was staring across at the painter who seemed absorbed in his newspaper. Kersey wasn't sure whether to go on or not. In the end he said: 'He can't hear us.'

Wycliffe seemed indifferent.

'Marsden was charged with selling a painting of his own, executed in the style of and purporting to be the work of another—in English, flogging a fake. They could have brought half-a-dozen similar charges but the one they chose referred to an alleged Gauguin. He sold it through a go-between to a seemingly reputable dealer. The case didn't hold up in court because the jury couldn't make up their minds at what stage the picture was provided with its forged documentation or who added a spidery little "P Gauguin" in one corner of the picture.'

Kersey waited but Wycliffe went on with his meal.

'Don't you want to know the name of this reputable dealer?'

Wycliffe muttered something.

'Lemarque Galleries Limited; a subsidiary of Lemarque Holdings.'

Wycliffe emptied his soup bowl and patted his lips with a paper napkin. 'You may be right. Lemarque's organization may have had dealings on the shady side of the street and it's possible that Marsden worked for him. The fact that the two of them have been in contact since Lemarque came out of jail seems to support the idea and we should know more when we get a report on the Lemarque/Bateman partnership. But we are looking for a motive for the murder of Lemarque and his wife by someone who had access to the pistol kept in Stella Burnett-Price's room. That limits the range of motives as it limits the number of suspects.'

'But it leaves Bateman in with a chance.'

Wycliffe got to his feet. 'If you've finished your meal let's go.'

Kersey said: 'What meal?'

Chapter Ten

AS THEY LEFT Marsden once more raised his hand in casual salutation.

Wycliffe was worried—afraid, yet he could think of no particular reason for fear. The killer had done his work (her work?) so all that remained for him to do was to 'identify and apprehend' as they used to say in the days when quite ordinary people spoke English. And if he was right about the pistol he had only to look among that small circle which formed the household at Mynhager. The process would be painful but the outcome certain.

They crossed the square to the van in drenching rain which was coming down faster than the drains could carry it away. As they were hanging up their waterproofs Kersey said: 'Something wrong?'

'The girl. I'd feel happier if we could get her away from Mynhager.'

Wycliffe went into the cubicle he had adopted as his temporary office and slid himself on to the bench between table and wall.

'How did you get on with Rosemergy Minerals?'

Kersey stood in the doorway. 'I've got an appointment in Penzance at 2.30 with a chap called Trewhella, their estate manager.' He glanced at his watch. 'I'd better get started.'

Wycliffe was left to brood on his in-tray. Away from headquarters he missed the guiding hand and steely resolve of his personal assistant, Diane. Diane, the immaculate, would never have permitted such an accumulation. The mound consisted of reports and memoranda, each one with an attached tag on which he was expected to indicate how the item should be dealt with.

He picked up the first document, glanced through it, and slipped it to the bottom of the pile; the next he initialled for filing, and the next. The fourth item was the little page-depleted notebook which he had found under Francine's bed and stopped her from taking away. Why? Now his action seemed insensitive and officious. But there had been something odd about the way she had darted back into the room at the last moment, something self-consciously deceitful in her manner which seemed out of character. At the same time he was prepared to believe that retrieving the notebook had been her main purpose in going upstairs.

He turned over a few pages. Francine's writing had character, a mature hand, bold and decisive. But her style was cryptic. He was reminded of his rough notebook at school where barely comprehensible statements were interspersed with doodles and unflattering sketches of the teacher. No sketches here.

'Blue eyed people homozygous for recessive but more to it than that: Modifiers. Possible for blue-eyed parents to have brown-eyed child but only a 1:50 chance.' The figures were ringed.

'Dark hair dominant to blond but dark haired parents can have redheads or auburn haired offspring.'

There was a page on blood grouping on the ABO system with two heavily underlined sentences: 'Not possible for parents both lacking agglutinogen B to have a child of group B or AB.' And: 'For a mother of group A to have a child AB the father would have to be group B or AB.'

The last page was blank except for the query: 'Body form?'

The telephone rang. 'Records for you, sir.'

A list of incidents in the area on 15/16 April 1979, covering the night of the professional men's dinner in Penzance. The clerk gabbled through them. A routine lot: a couple of break-ins; a spate of minor R.T.A.s; vandalism on the promenade at Penzance, youths tearing up flower beds . . . The only major incident, a hit-and-run with a young girl killed and her body left in the ditch. This, at some time after midnight in, of all places, a country lane between Badger's Cross and New Mill.

'Was the driver traced?'

'No, sir. The file remains open. There was strong suspicion but insufficient evidence.'

Wycliffe vaguely recalled the case through reports. 'Send the file on to me here.'

He spread an Ordnance map on his table and identified the lane in which the girl had been killed then he called in D.C. Curnow. 'I believe you come from these parts?'

'Born and brought up in Penzance, sir.'

'You know this lane?'

'Very well. It runs past the site of the iron-age village at Chysauster.'

'You wouldn't go that way if you were driving from Penzance here, I imagine?'

'Certainly I wouldn't, sir. You can see it puts a good distance on the trip and the road is poor—no more than a country lane.'

'Is it much used?'

'There's a fair amount of traffic in the summer with visitors to the site but otherwise, next to nothing.'

Well, he would give the file an airing. Curnow returned to his cubby-hole and a minute or two later there was another telephone call. Pigeons returning to roost, bread which had been cast upon the waters . . . This time, Sergeant Fox with a preliminary report on the recovered van:

'I've been over the vehicle with Alan Taylor from Forensic. Of course, there's all the detailed work still to be done but we've got identifiable prints. In the driving compartment Lemarque's dabs are all over the place; with two or three of hers in the passenger seat area. No strangers in the front of the van. The same applies to the exterior bodywork, but in the load compartment, apart from Lemarque's we found three sets all from male subjects; two belonging to the same man and fairly old, the third recent and fresh.

'We've collected dust and other detritus samples and Taylor is taking them back for examination.'

'Any sign of blood or other body tissue?'

'None, sir. Of course the door on the driver's side was not recovered but Taylor thinks it virtually impossible that the man could have shot himself while in the driving seat, causing the wound of exit described, without contamination of the interior.'

So Lemarque had not shot himself in the act of driving over the cliff; neither had he shot himself nor been shot in the van. Was it conceivable that he had pushed his van over, then shot himself as he jumped? Fantasy! Lemarque had been murdered as his wife had been murdered.

He drew geometrical designs on his scratch pad but his thoughts were far from forming any rational sequence. He sometimes said that he was incapable of real thought because his mind was preoccupied with recollected pictures, with snatches of conversation, and incidents of dubious relevance, which presented themselves with compelling clarity but in random sequence. He would play with his recollections, fitting them together, discarding and rearranging, until he made a credible pattern. 'Like a child playing with bricks,' he told himself. Did they still play with bricks? Or with computer graphics?

Francine with the shepherds' posies . . . 'and purple for death'.

The Lemarques' living-room where the two of them played out their mysterious charade for his benefit and for Virginia's. Why had they suppressed the note which Francine said she had written?

Jane Lemarque wedged between dressing table and bed with half her face blown away.

Alain Lemarque, his little simian body distended, lying on the quay in a puddle of seawater which had drained from his clothing.

'She's never been the same since Francine was born . . .'

'Why does she do it—go off like that?' . . . 'To punish me.'

'She's only trying to make an impression on her mother . . .

535

Lemarque spent years trying to do the same thing and look where it landed him . . .'

'She let him go to bed with her.'

'Mother has to tell everything.'

And mother had told Evadne Penrose: '. . . he must have taken the gun!'

Of another gun Aunt Stella had said: 'It wasn't there last night . . . They must have put it back . . .'

So many fragments of memory. They crowded in, taking possession of his mind and seeming to jockey for position. Now there was this damned notebook.

'Not possible for parents both lacking agglutinogen B. . .'

He brought his fist down on the table and probably woke D.S. Shaw in the next cubicle. He picked up the telephone. 'Try to get Dr Franks on the line.'

For once Franks was in his room at the hospital. 'Not another body for me, Charles?'

'I suppose you did blood grouping tests on the Lemarques?'

'As a matter of routine. I don't put the results in my preliminary report unless they seem relevant. If you hold on I'll look them up.'

Franks didn't keep him long. 'Jane Lemarque was Group A Rhesus positive, and her husband, also Rhesus positive, was Group O.'

'So they could not have had an AB child?'

'You know the answer to that as well as I do, Charles.'

So Francine was not Alain Lemarque's daughter. Not difficult to believe, but hardly a motive for double murder, though it might explain a good deal about Francine.

Four-thirty, and already it was dark. The lights were on in the van and he pulled down the blind. Deprived of his pipe, he played with matches from a box Kersey had left behind. By slotting the ends with his penknife he contrived a creature which suggested a cross between a donkey and a kangaroo and when Kersey arrived back from his appointment in Penzance he found his chief putting the finishing touches to this chimera.

'Make another and we could race 'em.'

Kersey inserted himself into the bench seat and Wycliffe brought him up to date but he was unimpressed.

'So the girl was conceived on the wrong side of the duvet. Who was her real father? One of the Mynhager lot? If so, sexual limitations being what they are, there aren't many candidates. There's Ernest, Bateman, and the old man. But really, sir, who is likely to worry unduly about it after nearly seventeen years?'

Wycliffe said: 'The girl, perhaps.' But he agreed with Kersey. 'Anyway, how did you get on in Penzance?'

'Tim Trewhella, their estate manager, is a decent chap. He was helpful once he'd grasped the situation. It seems Lemarque approached him about a month ago with a scheme for leasing and developing the Mennear Bal site. He'd worked it out, presumably during his long idle hours in the nick. The idea was to clear the site to within 200 metres of the cliff and lay it out for chalets and touring caravans with a swimming pool, restaurant, shop and the rest.

'Trewhella asked about capital and Lemarque said he had one backer for £50,000 and, once the scheme was launched, he had no doubt he could raise the rest.'

'Was the backer's name mentioned?'

'Apparently not.'

'What about planning?'

'Lemarque reckoned that the authorities would play along because the scheme would reclaim an industrial wasteland in an area of great natural beauty.'

Wycliffe, a conservationist, said: 'Of the two, I'd prefer the mine dumps. Sounds like a pipe dream to me.'

'Me too. Trewhella said businessmen are liable to these flights of fancy and that reality only moves in with the accountants.'

Wycliffe adjusted the hind-legs of his creature so that it stood properly. 'You think it likely that Bateman committed himself to put £50,000 into that?'

'Perhaps Lemarque was in a position to squeeze; in which case we have a man with a motive.'

'For a double murder? Anyway we shan't get much further

along those lines until we hear from John Scales what he's been able to find out about the Lemarque/Bateman partnership.' He picked up the telephone and asked to be put through to D.C.I. Scales at police headquarters.

'Is that you, John? . . . About the Lemarque/Bateman partnership . . . It's the information I want, John, not bits of paper to stick in a file . . .'

Kersey thought: Temper! He's missing his pipe.

Wycliffe wedged the phone against his neck while he went through the still clumsy ritual of putting on his spectacles, then he began to scribble notes. It was five minutes before he put down the phone and turned back to Kersey.

'Lemarque was a bigger rogue than we've taken him for. The Bishops gave the impression that he was a victim of circumstance but according to this he was operating several profitable rackets in the art trade: fencing choice items of stolen property, arranging illicit export deals, and handling fakes . . . He had a high powered organization with two or three recognized experts on his pay-roll. The Met, using a softly-softly approach, were building up a nice dossier when there was a leak, somebody pressed the self-destruct button and the organization just melted away. At the finish the Met boys were left with red faces and Lemarque on a comparatively minor charge.'

'What about Bateman?'

'According to this he was responsible for the antiques side of the business—a separate company which seems to have been more or less above board. Bateman's main source of embarrassment came from an alleged statement by Lemarque, quoted in a coat-trailing Sunday paper, to the effect that if he went to jail he could take Bateman with him. There was a libel action against the paper, settled out of court, but there were awkward questions and for a time it looked bleak for Bateman politically, then it all blew over.'

'So where do we go from here?'

'We talk to Marsden. If he can't do anything else he may be able to throw a bit more light on the Bateman/Lemarque set-up.'

'Now?'

'Why not?'

Outside, the rain had stopped and the air was clear and fresh. 'We'll walk.'

As they turned down the track by the pub they could hear the slow ripping sound of waves breaking along the shoreline. There was a light in Marsden's cottage and the music this time was neither jazz nor Bach but Tchaikovsky's *1812*, blasting hell out of the French and everyone else within range.

They had to bang on the door before Marsden heard them above the racket but their reception was not unfriendly. 'I suppose it's no use telling you I'm busy? You'd better come in.'

He switched off the record player and the instant silence assaulted the ears. With a certain reverence he slid the record back into its sleeve. 'Poor Peter Ilyich died from drinking water; a warning to us all.'

To Wycliffe's surprise the table had been cleared of dirty dishes and was now covered by a chenille cloth; the floor, too, looked reasonably free of debris. The painter read his thoughts: 'Yes, well, when you don't have a dog you have to do your own barking.'

A fire burned in the grate and Percy lay at full stretch on the hearth-rug.

Marsden looked at Kersey: 'What's this then, a new stooge?'

'Detective Inspector Kersey.'

Kersey said: 'We've met before.'

Marsden looked him over. 'The occasion escapes me.'

'Paddington Green nick 1980.'

'I was acquitted.'

Wycliffe lifted a bundle of newspapers off a chair and sat down. 'All the same, whether you signed them or not, whether you provided the authentication or not, you painted fakes for Lemarque Galleries.'

Marsden pushed a low stool in Kersey's direction and sat in his own armchair. 'Correction on two counts: I did not paint fakes; I painted pictures "in the style of" and I did not deal with Lemarque Galleries but, believe it or not, with The Stylov Gallery—Stylov—get it? You need to be six years old to really appreciate the subtlety of these guys. They had a shop in Kensington where they sold pictures in the style of almost any painter you fancied. Nothing illegal about it; all open and above board except for the mark-up they put on a poor bastard's blood and sweat. A couple of us did the grind and they collected.

'Say you wanted a picture in the style of that celebrated French Impressionist, Le Merde; if they hadn't got one in the racks, they would provide me with a suitable stretcher, I would refresh my memory of the gentleman's palette, style and technique and get cracking.

'It worked well enough until Lemarque Galleries bought out Stylov as a front to get hold of suitable canvases for "upgrading".' A throaty chuckle.

'And you expect us to believe that you didn't know what was going on?'

'All that matters to me is that the jury believed it.'

'Or had their doubts.'

'As you say, but their doubts were good enough for me. By the way, that was a damn fine Gauguin. The old rogue would have liked it and it would have taken me in if I hadn't painted it.'

Wycliffe said: 'But not, apparently, the experts.'

Marsden was contemptuous. 'Experts my arse! The clowns slipped up on the paperwork.'

Kersey lit a cigarette and threw the dead match in the direction of the fireplace. 'How come you end up down here within spitting distance of Lemarque and his former partner?'

Marsden picked up Kersey's match and put it in the fire. 'A gesture on the part of the old firm when the balloon was about to go up.'

'To encourage you to keep your mouth shut.'

'A reward for services rendered to art.'

'Not as a suitable base to start a spot of blackmail?'

Marsden coughed bronchially and spat in the fire. 'You'll find that horse won't run. Not my line.'

The room was utterly silent. Perhaps that was why Marsden felt the need from time to time to drench himself in sound. He settled back in his chair; a cigarette placed centrally between his lips seemed in imminent danger of setting his moustache alight.

Wycliffe said: 'These visits you've been receiving from Lemarque since he came out of prison: what was he after?'

Marsden looked mildly put out. 'Emma's been talking. Why are women so spiteful? Lemarque wanted to revive the Stylov caper; he's been scratching about looking for a new launch pad. He'd given himself twelve months. "In a year, one way or another, I'll be back up there—or I'll shoot myself." That sort of talk. I told him he'd have to manage without me. I've gone soft since I've been down here and I've got used to crowing on my own dung heap. What's more I've come to prefer genuine Marsdens to Stylov versions of museum fodder.'

'You told me that you had no contact with Lemarque.'

'A tiny fib in an ocean of truth.'

'In your position you can't afford such luxuries.'

Wycliffe tried another approach. 'Lemarque is supposed to have said that he could have taken Bateman to jail with him. What did you make of that?'

'A shot across the bows.'

'You mean he could have done it?'

A moment for consideration: 'I doubt it, but the threat would have made Bateman think twice about joining the hounds.'

'In your opinion, was Bateman involved in fraud?'

Marsden chuckled. 'My God! What a question! Let's say that in copper's terms he was probably in the clear.'

Some clarification; no enlightenment. They walked back to The Tributers and to Phyllis's pasties which spanned ten-inch dinner plates.

Afterwards Wycliffe said, 'Well, we're as fully briefed as we are ever likely to be. By the morning we should have official confirmation that it was the old lady's pistol which killed Jane

541

Lemarque and that gives us the necessary cover if anyone wants to get legalistic.'

'So?'

'So tomorrow we move in. Formal interviews and statements from every member of the household. I want you to do it with whatever assistance you need. Pick your own men. I shall hold a watching brief.'

'I'll fix it from the duty roster.' Kersey hesitated. 'I take it you want this done by the book—uniformed men outside?'

'By the book.'

Wycliffe walked across to the Incident Van where D.C. Curnow was duty officer until shut-down at ten o'clock.

Curnow, an earnest young man, put down an improving book. 'This arrived by messenger, sir.'

The file on the hit-and-run, a formidable bundle.

Wycliffe skimmed through it. A nineteen-year old girl was walking home after visiting a friend. Less than a mile separated their two houses. She was in one of the widest sections of the lane when, according to the pathologist, she was hit from behind by a vehicle travelling at a fair speed. In the off-season the lane was little used except by a few people who lived along it, and even during the day traffic was minimal.

Again, according to the pathologist, after the accident the girl's body had been dragged off the road into the ditch. The scene of the incident, worked over by experts, yielded nothing, mainly because of torrential rain later that night. The inquiry had been thorough: over 200 people questioned; publicans within a range of fifteen miles interviewed, and garage owners quizzed about damaged vehicles. Suspicion rested on a local character who at the time was under a ban for a drunken driving offence. But there was no real evidence and his alibi, though it offended police nostrils, could not be broken. The only possible material clue was a few fragments of glass recovered from the scene. According to the experts they were not from the fittings of any vehicle and probably had nothing to do with the incident.

Wycliffe put the documents back in the file. Almost

certainly an irrelevance. But why had Lemarque kept that press cutting?

Anyway, tomorrow they would move into Mynhager with all the ammunition they could hope to have in order to ask the right questions and be able to judge the answers. But tonight?

He was uneasy.

Curnow was ready to shut up shop for the night. With the rest of the headquarters team he was lodging in Penzance. Wycliffe signed the book and by the time he had reached the door of The Tributers the church clock was striking ten and the lights had gone out in the caravan.

He spent an hour with Kersey, working out the strategy for the morning.

Sleep would not come; he resigned himself and tried to resolve the confusion of his thoughts with one more review of the facts and their interpretation.

The Lemarques had been murdered and the sequence of events seemed clear. The killer made an appointment to meet Lemarque at the site of his proposed tourist park, ostensibly to discuss plans; in fact, to kill him. Lemarque was shot and his body pushed over the cliff. Later the van was driven erratically along the track and pushed over, to convey the impression of a suicidal act.

The van disposed of, the killer went to the cottage and in what must have been a horrifying scene, shot Jane Lemarque. He then left the cottage and Wycliffe believed that he had seen the light of the man's hand torch from the other side of the valley.

The crux of the problem was motive. Jane Lemarque was killed because she might have been able to point to her husband's killer; more than that, the strategy of the crime was to suggest that Lemarque had committed suicide after killing his wife. But why was Lemarque killed?

There was no evidence that Bateman was being blackmailed for his part in the Lemarque frauds; in fact there was no indication that he had been criminally involved. The

543

question of Francine's parentage provided no grounds for murder. There is no longer any blackmail in bastardy.

Wycliffe sat up in bed and pounded his pillow. The room was cold and the light from the street lamp coming through the curtains had a frosty brightness. Enough light to see the time by his travelling clock: a quarter past one. His thoughts had been going round in circles for two hours and he had indigestion. He had eaten Phyllis's pasty too greedily. He got out of bed, padded across to the washbasin, and drank half-a-glass of water from his tooth mug.

Back in bed, chilled, he still could not settle down. The pistol, the Walther P.38 with its inscribed silver plate, seemed to pin the crime down to Mynhager. Would he be in the absurd position of knowing the criminal without having discovered the motive? And what had happened to Lemarque's revolver?

Lemarque. From the day of his release he had set about promoting the new enterprises he had dreamed up in jail. 'In a year, one way or another, I'll be back up there, or I'll shoot myself!' All his activity seemed to be directed to this single end: his contacts with Rosemergy Minerals, with Bateman, with Marsden, his trips in the van and his surreptitious telephone calls sometimes cut short by the arrival of Francine.

Those telephone calls. What was it Francine had overheard him say? Something about five years ago and being in the same boat . . . 'Five years ago we were all three in the same boat, or should I say car? Not any more!' Something like that anyway.

Suddenly the words acquired a new and threatening significance. It was five years since the girl's death in a hit-and-run. 'All in the same boat, or should I say car?'

Wycliffe turned over violently, sweeping the bedclothes along with him. Was it possible . . . ?

Chapter Eleven

A CLEAR AND ALMOST windless morning. Hoar frost on the slopes.

'Just coffee and toast for me, Phyllis.'

'And me.'

A buttery laugh. 'Indigestion, I'll be bound! Didn't I say you had to work or walk down a pasty? Instead you spend your time sitting around, the pair of you. What you need after a pasty, apart from a bit of exercise, is a drink of tea—about an hour after, for preference, and with a bit of sugar in it. I don't hold with sugar in tea as a rule but after a pasty 'tis the best thing if you don't want to be going for the bicarbonate later.'

When they were alone Kersey said: 'Did I hear you go downstairs some time in the early morning?'

'I went for a drive.'

'Good God! Are you going to tell me about it?'

'Later, in the van.'

They were at the van well before nine but just in time to take a call from Forbes, the ballistics expert. Forbes was one of those fortunate people who are paid for work which they find totally absorbing. He functioned in a sound-proof basement and the succession of day and night meant as much to him as to a mole.

'I've only done the preliminary work on this one, Charles, but I can tell you that the bullet and cartridge case found at the scene of crime were from the Walther P.38 you sent me yesterday. The rifling and striation marks on the bullet, and the extraction marks and head scratches on the case correspond precisely with those on the test-fired specimens. No doubt at all. Incidentally the Walther wasn't properly

545

cleaned after firing and it hadn't been looked after before that. It's had very little use—probably fired less than half-a-dozen rounds since it was new in the mid-forties. The mechanism is stiff and the clown who used it was lucky it didn't jam.' Forbes felt about firearms as others feel about pets and children. 'Criminal to neglect such a nice mechanism!'

Wycliffe spent a few minutes looking over the newspapers. Ella Bunt's story had been taken up by the rest of Fleet Street to be re-run with variations and given extra punch by the discovery of Lemarque's body. The Cornish murders were news.

Kersey said: 'I'm more interested in your night driving. What made you go off in the small hours?'

Wycliffe explained.

Then the moment he had been waiting for and dreading. The evidence of the pistol made it certain that the killer of Jane Lemarque and, by extension, of her husband, was a member of the household at Mynhager.

He turned to Kersey. 'Are we ready?'

'All lined up, sir.'

Wycliffe, Kersey, D.S. Shaw, and a female clerk-typist, a blonde with a pretty little snub nose and a portable typewriter, went in Wycliffe's car. Two uniformed men followed in a Panda. At shortly after eleven o'clock they set out. Two cars one behind the other on a deserted track make a procession and so it must have seemed when they arrived in the courtyard at Mynhager. Even against the background of a glittering sea the house looked grim. Wycliffe had discovered that Mynhager could be translated from the Cornish as 'edge parlous'. It was apt; it had a sinister Arthurian ring.

One of the uniformed men remained in the courtyard; the other took up his post on the terrace. Anyone wishing to enter or leave the house would have to account for themselves. Kersey was aware of Wycliffe's intense distaste for what had to be done, and sympathised.

Ernest answered their ring. 'Ah, Charles! I suppose this is an official visit? You'd better come in.'

In the dim, cave-like hall the silence was punctuated by the majestic ticking of the grandfather clock. Wycliffe introduced his men. 'Inspector Kersey and Sergeant Shaw will be conducting the interviews . . . It would be helpful if they could have a room where they can be private and undisturbed.'

'The dining-room, perhaps . . .'

It would have been obvious to Ernest that something of the sort was bound to happen, he must have been expecting it. He escorted them to the dining-room. The heavy velvet curtains were almost meeting across the window allowing only a strip of light to enter. But it was warm; there were two of the Albert Hall type radiators.

'I hope this will suit you.'

Kersey said that it would, very well.

Ernest was pale and he looked as though he had lost a lot of sleep. His manner was dry, distant, and correct. They could hardly expect anything else.

Sergeant Shaw settled himself with his notebook and papers at one end of the long table. Unlike some of his colleagues, Shaw was always formally dressed and he might have been taken for the family solicitor on a business visit. The typist found a small table for her machine near the window.

Kersey said: 'I wonder if you can tell me, sir, whether any members of the household are out at the moment?'

Ernest went to the window and drew back the curtains so that light off the sea flooded into the room to combat its drabness. He said: 'I don't keep a register of comings and goings, Mr Kersey, but we are all here as far as I know.'

Shaw made an entry on one of his sheets of paper.

Kersey said: 'Thank you, sir. Could we start with Miss Bishop?'

Ernest looked surprised. Perhaps he had expected to head the list.

To Wycliffe the proceedings, although familiar enough in other settings, seemed unreal. Virginia arrived looking apprehensive. She took the seat Kersey offered, looking up at

547

Wycliffe as though in some hope that he might be taking over, but he joined Ernest in the hall.

'I would like to talk to your father if that is convenient.'

'I'll take you to him.'

Up the stairs and along the corridor, past the room where he had slept as a guest. Joseph's room was at the end of the passage. Ernest tapped on the door and opened it.

'A visitor for you, father.'

The old man was sitting by the window, a book on his lap. He dropped a half-smoked cheroot in the ashtray and got up. 'Ah, Wycliffe! Come in, my dear fellow, sit down . . .'

'Charles is here officially, father.'

'So? What difference does that make? He can still sit down, I suppose?'

'I'll leave you with father, Charles.'

As the door closed the old man said: 'He's never learned to be objective; always tripping over his own emotional bootlaces. So you're getting down to business and you've come to tell me about it.'

It was the first time Wycliffe had been in Joseph's room. The bow window opened up a tremendous panoramic sweep and the old man made an expansive gesture. 'This window faces due west, nothing between me and White Bay Newfoundland except, and thank God for it, the Gulf Stream.'

Wycliffe stayed on course: 'I had confirmation this morning that Jane Lemarque was shot with the pistol presented to your late brother-in-law Major General Burnett-Price. It seems likely that Alain Lemarque was shot with the same weapon but because of the circumstances we have no proof.'

Joseph picked up his cheroot which had gone out and threw it away. 'Go on.'

'Your sister looked for the pistol on Tuesday night and she was distressed to find that it was not in its usual place. Yesterday, Wednesday, she called me in to tell me it was missing but when she showed me where it was usually kept, there it was.'

The old man stroked his moustache with the back of his

hand. 'And your boffins were able to show that the gun had been recently fired?'

'More than that, they are able to prove that the bullet and cartridge case recovered at the scene of the crime came from that pistol.'

It was impossible to say how much of this was already known to him or guessed at but the old man had not batted an eyelid. 'So you concluded that someone in this house was responsible, certainly for the first crime.'

'I concluded that I had grounds for doing what is now being done.'

A shrewd glance. 'Of course! I wouldn't quarrel with that. You think you've established the means, that leaves opportunity and motive. I'm afraid I can't help you with either. I spent the whole of Christmas Eve afternoon here, conserving my energy for the festivities. I don't think I saw anyone—yes I did! At about four Ernest brought me my tea and biscuits; one of the women usually brings it but I gathered they were otherwise engaged.'

Wycliffe looked about him. It was obvious that the room and the man had grown together to such a point that separation would destroy them both. The paintings, the photographs, the books and the furniture were as much part of him as his memories, and together they constituted his life. Did he see them as threatened? If so, how far would he go in their defence?

'My wife, Ursula.'

Wycliffe happened at that moment to be looking at the only portrait in the room, a head-and-shoulders painting of a very beautiful young woman. Her light-auburn hair was coiled on top of her head; her attention seemed to be directed at something far away and one had the rather absurd impression that the painter had taken her unawares.

'She was nineteen when that was done. She had an identical twin sister, Gerald's mother. We are an inbred family.' The old man chuckled. 'Perhaps in danger of becoming incestuous.'

It was a fine performance. He was being offered a recipe for the investigation but whether with the intention of leading or misleading, it was impossible to say. He was not deceived by Joseph's apparent calm or by his almost bantering manner. The old man had suffered sleepless hours; the skin was drawn more tightly over the bones of his skull, his eyes seemed more deeply set and he was even paler than when Wycliffe had first seen him.

Joseph lit a fresh cheroot. 'I gather you've given up smoking. I shall soon be old fashioned in that respect as in most others. Ernest gave it up four or five years back—drinking too in his case, except for the occasional sherry, but at seventy-five I feel that self denial is likely to prove an unrewarding investment.'

A marble mantel-clock which looked like a graveyard ornament chimed prettily. A quarter to twelve. Joseph waited for the sounds to die away. 'I should imagine your principal difficulty will be motive. It's hard to see how anyone in this house would have gained through the deaths of Jane and Alain Lemarque.'

The pale grey eyes watched him with speculative detachment but Wycliffe, bland, attentive, almost deferential, gave nothing away.

'Alain and Jane looked upon this as a second home while my wife was alive; they, with our three and Gerald, were like brothers and sisters. As you know, Gerald had a business relationship with Lemarque which, for a number of years, strengthened the bond. Of course things went very wrong there. Alain's business methods ran foul of the law and he ended up in jail. Gerald had already broken with him but his political career was certainly not helped by the partnership. Even now it is a sensitive area.'

Joseph tapped the ash from his cheroot. 'Despite all that, it seems that Gerald was still prepared to put money into some scheme of Alain's. That shows how deeply they were attached. With Gerald's political prospects being what they are I think he was running a very considerable, perhaps a foolish risk of reviving old accusations and suspicions.'

Wycliffe thought: End of lesson. The old man had said his

say; he would not embroider. He had made up his mind about Wycliffe's intelligence, its scope and limitations, and calculated the dose he judged to be sufficient. If the family had to suffer there was an obvious sacrificial candidate.

Well! Two could play at that game. Wycliffe got to his feet. 'Thank you for talking to me, Mr Bishop. Inspector Kersey will be asking you certain questions and inviting you to make a formal statement later.'

It was not what the old man had expected and he was immediately uneasy. He glanced at the mantel-clock. 'I usually allow myself a glass of sherry at about this time; why not stay and join me?'

But Wycliffe excused himself and went downstairs.

The house was silent except for the muffled tapping of the typewriter. Yet the impression of calm was an illusion. They were all there, bottled up: Joseph and his three offspring, his grandson, and Bateman. Bateman who was in the family but not of it. And the pearl in the oyster—the Lemarque girl. Six days ago Wycliffe had arrived, wondering about his reception, now they were all watching him with apprehension. Not that the fact gave him any satisfaction.

He pushed open the door of the dining-room. Kersey was seated on one side of the big table with Caroline opposite him. So Virginia had had her turn. Shaw, at one end, was filling that most ancient role of scribe as, with slightly different materials, he might have done at the court of Sargon of Akkad, four millennia ago. Wycliffe wondered how long it would be before even low tech found its way into the legal labyrinth. By the window the typist was rattling out Virginia's statement which, later, she would be asked to sign.

Caroline glanced up as Wycliffe entered. She sat in one of the 'carvers' belonging to the dining suite, apparently relaxed, and somewhat slovenly in a woollen suit which seemed to cling in the wrong places.

'Did you see your husband shortly after lunch on Christmas Eve?'

'Yes, briefly, I was in the kitchen with my sister, washing up, when Gerald came in and said he was going for a walk. He had missed his morning walk and he likes to get in some exercise each day.'

'Do you happen to know at what time he returned from his walk?'

'No. The next time I saw him was between six and half-past when I went upstairs to put on a decent frock for the evening and he was in our bedroom changing into a suit.'

'You spent most of the afternoon in the kitchen?'

'Yes; getting ready for the evening.'

'Alone?'

'Most of the time. After we had finished washing up my sister went upstairs to do some cleaning but she came down again later.' Caroline glanced across at Wycliffe. 'The superintendent looked in at about half-past three to say that he was going out with Sergeant Curtis who had called to see him. My brother, Ernest, turned up shortly afterwards. We usually have a cup of tea around four. Ernest and I drank ours together in the kitchen then he took one up to father with a few biscuits . . .'

Wycliffe went over to the window and picked up the statement forms which had already been typed and were awaiting signature.

Virginia had said: 'Our housekeeper has the afternoons free and over Christmas there is a lot to do so my sister was working in the kitchen and I was upstairs doing some cleaning. I didn't come down again until nearly five, then I stayed with my sister in the kitchen getting things ready for the evening meal.'

Kersey was asking Caroline about the pistol.

'Of course I knew that my uncle had been presented with a pistol by the Maharajah of somewhere or other; it was part of the family lore, but it never occurred to me to wonder what had happened to it when he died and Aunt Stella moved in with us.'

'So you didn't know there was a pistol in the house?'

She made an impatient movement. 'I didn't know it or not know it; I simply never thought about it.'

Virginia had said: 'I knew the story about my uncle's pistol but I had no idea it was in the house.'

Kersey had finished with Caroline. 'Thank you Mrs Bateman.'

'Is that all?'

'For the present. We shall ask you to sign a statement later.'

She got up from her chair. Kersey looked after her as the door closed. 'She's a cool one. I wonder if she realizes how far she's helped to put her old man on the spot.'

Wycliffe was unsettled; he had an itch to be doing something but no clear idea what it should be. The interviews going on in the dining-room were an inquest into what had already happened; he was more concerned with what was likely to happen, what might be happening at this very moment. Where were the others? What was going on? What really troubled him was the possibility that the action might not be over.

If only he could smoke his pipe . . .

He left the dining-room and prowled about the hall like a suspicious dog sniffing out the corners. He found himself in the dark little passage behind the stairs which led to the kitchen. The kitchen door was ajar and he could hear voices. Ada was saying something in her sing-song brogue; then a man's voice. He pushed the door open.

Ada and Paul. Ada was at the sink, washing dishes, Paul was standing by her, listless, depressed. He must have come to her like that many times before, from infancy upwards. He looked around, startled, as Wycliffe came in; his eyes were red.

'Do you know where Francine is?'

The boy turned away. 'She's in her room, I think.' He was struggling to control his voice.

'Where is her room?'

Ada answered for him. 'Turn right at the top of the stairs and it's the last door on your left.'

'When did you begin to think that he might not be your natural father?'

553

She was sitting in a cane chair by the window of her room, looking out at the hillside swept by a curtain of rain. She wore jeans and a jumper of washed-out blue which suited her colouring. Her hair hung about her shoulders.

'At school last term we did a bit about human inheritance: blood groups, eye colour, hair colour, that sort of thing. I suppose that made me think. I brought home one of those do-it-yourself blood-group cards and tried it on mother just out of curiosity. That was while he was still in prison.'

'And?' Like any good interviewer he tried to confine his questions to prompting.

'Well, when he came home I asked him if he knew what his blood group was and he said that when we lived in Richmond he'd been a donor. He was group O. Of course I knew then.'

'Did you say anything?'

'To mother, not to him.'

'What did she say?'

'She admitted it. She'd had a thing with Paul's father.' A helpless gesture. 'You saw the photographs in the album. Of course that was why she's been so concerned about Paul and me. Poor mother! She needn't have worried.'

She spoke slowly, in a low monotonous voice without emphasis or inflexion but it was the first time he had heard her give expression to any sentiment or admit to any sympathy.

'You've told Paul?'

'Only last night.'

'He seems very upset.'

A slight movement of the shoulders. 'He'll get over it. It will suit him better to be a brother when he gets used to it.'

'And your true father; have you said anything to him?'

'This morning. I only told him that I knew. He wanted to talk about it but I wouldn't.'

'You'll have to, sooner or later.'

'Perhaps.'

They were silent for a time; the only sounds came from water gurgling in a downpipe outside the window. It was raining harder and although it was still short of one o'clock the light was so poor that the girl was hardly more than a silhouette against the greyness outside.

She was the first to speak. 'What happens if you find out who killed my mother but you can't prove it?'

'I don't think that is very likely.'

'But it can happen?'

'Sometimes we think we know the identity of a criminal but we are unable to prove it to the satisfaction of a jury.'

'What then?'

'Either there is no prosecution or the prosecution fails.'

'And the criminal goes free?'

'A suspect is not a criminal until he is found guilty of a crime.' Arid words but what else could he say? He was a policeman.

'I see.' After a pause she said: 'I suppose it depends on getting a good lawyer.'

He was concerned. 'I shouldn't think too much about it if I were you.'

She turned on him fiercely. 'You are talking about the man who killed my mother!'

He had never seen her so deeply moved and he was worried, but he hardly knew what to say. 'Your aunt will be back tomorrow.'

'I know.'

At shortly after one o'clock the interrogations were suspended and the police contingent went, in a body, to The Tributers. Afterwards Wycliffe and Kersey crossed over to the Incident Van where Fox was due with his photographs and a report on Lemarque's van.

One of the cubicles had been laid out with a display which could have been mistaken for a photographic exhibition and Fox was ready to expatiate but Wycliffe cut him short.

'At the moment we are only interested in the prints found inside the load compartment of the van.'

'Apart from Lemarque's, there were three sets, sir; two were several months old and probably belonged to the former

555

owner, but the third set, on the inside door-handle, was quite fresh.'

Fox pointed to a blow-up of part of a thumb and three fingers of a right hand and there were still larger versions of the individual digits.

'No problem about identification if we get hold of a comparison set, sir.'

Kersey said: 'The man out walking his dog went past the van, our chap hiding inside was scared and got careless—is that the idea?'

Wycliffe was dour. 'That is the idea; let's hope it's the right one.'

Chapter Twelve

IT WAS AFTER four o'clock and already almost dark when the interviews were resumed in the dining-room at Mynhager. Ada was first. Asked where she was on Christmas Eve afternoon, she said she had spent it in her room.

'What time did you leave your room?'

'I don't really know. Oh, yes I do, it must have been about four because I saw Ernest taking in Mr Joseph's tea.'

Bateman was next.

The cashmere cardigan had given place to a Harris tweed jacket. Looking slightly pale but otherwise as usual he sat opposite Kersey in the dining-room. Wycliffe watched and wondered whether they would achieve more than a fat file of statements.

'You gave an account of your movements on Christmas Eve to the chief superintendent.' Kersey turned to Shaw: 'Read it please.'

Sergeant Shaw referred to his papers. 'Mr Bateman said that he had visited the Lemarques at about 2.0 pm on Christmas Eve afternoon and stayed only five minutes. Afterwards he went for a walk which took him to the hamlet of Busullow; he then returned to the main road and came back through Morvah without meeting anyone who remained in his memory.'

Kersey said: 'Would you like to amend that in any way, sir?'

'No, that is what I did.'

'Can you say at what time you arrived back here?'

'Not exactly, but it would have been between half-past five and six.'

'So it was dark.'

'Oh, yes. Quite dark.'

'You know that Jane Lemarque was shot with a pistol which belonged to the late Major General Burnett-Price?'

'I have heard that, yes.'

'You knew about the pistol?'

'I knew that my uncle was given a pistol by a maharajah.'

'And that it was in the possession of your aunt?'

'I suppose I would have known that had I thought of it, but I didn't.'

Surprising the number of people who denied ever having thought about the pistol.

Bateman was gaining confidence; perhaps he was having an easier passage than he expected.

Kersey broached the possibility of blackmail but Bateman remained apparently unconcerned.

'You told Mr Wycliffe that you had not committed yourself to putting money into Lemarque's project. Is that correct?'

'Of course! How could I commit myself? I had no real idea what the project was.'

'Lemarque is supposed to have said that he could have taken you to jail with him; does that mean he was able to put pressure on you to support his scheme?'

A thin smile. 'To blackmail me, you mean. No, it does not. I've been the victim of gossip but I have never been vulnerable to blackmail by Lemarque or anyone else.'

Wycliffe was sitting at the end of the table furthest from the window, being as unobtrusive as possible but well aware that they were getting nowhere. Kersey, through no fault of his own, was fishing in dead water. What was needed was confrontation but a confrontation that achieves nothing is a self-inflicted wound. However, it was a risk he had to take. He got up quietly and went out. In the hall, he knocked on the door of Ernest's study and went in.

Ernest was sitting at his table, the binocular microscope had been moved to one side and in front of him was an open book, the text interspersed with drawings of the wings of flies. But he was not working.

'I hope I'm not disturbing you.' The banal courtesy was ironic in the circumstances.

'Not at all.' In a tired voice. 'Is it my turn for the black chair?'

Wycliffe seemed at a loss. He stood by the table looking vaguely about him. He picked up a glass jar which held a number of specimen tubes in which maggots were stored in spirit.

'Are these the little tubes you carry about with you?'

'Yes, I use them for bringing back adult specimens as well as for storing larvae, but I don't suppose you came here to talk about flies.' Ernest's manner was subdued, almost resigned.

Wycliffe put the jar down. 'You must drive into Penzance almost every day, which way do you go?'

'There isn't much choice. I go from here to Treen then across the county through New Mill; it's only six or seven miles.'

Wycliffe was looking over the bookcase, packed with literature on entomology, from massive Victorian volumes to paper covered transactions and proceedings of the societies. Not a legal tome in sight.

'I suppose it's further if you go by way of Chysauster?'

'Chysauster?' Ernest's voice had suddenly sharpened but immediately he resumed a conversational tone. 'Yes, it's further and not a very good road. Why do you ask?'

'Will you drive me to Penzance?'

Ernest closed the book in front of him with slow deliberation. 'If you wish. In the morning, perhaps?'

'Now.'

'If you say so.' Ernest displayed the absorbed concentration of a man picking his way through a minefield.

Wycliffe led the way out into the hall. He opened the door of the dining-room and spoke to Kersey. 'Mr Bishop is going to drive me to Penzance and I would like you and Mr Bateman to come with us.'

Bateman turned in his chair. 'May I ask the purpose of this excursion?'

'I want to clear up certain points which may have a bearing

559

on this investigation.' Deliberately meaningless and as pompous. Bateman, about to protest, thought better of it.

A few minutes later the four men, wearing raincoats, trooped out into the courtyard. It was quite dark except for the light from the house, and rain blew in from the sea. The watcher in the Panda car got out and approached Kersey.

Wycliffe said: 'Borrow his torch.'

Ernest reversed his car out of the old coach house and the three of them climbed in. Wycliffe insisted on Bateman travelling in front with Ernest.

At a sedate speed they covered the seven miles to Penzance almost in silence. Once Bateman said: 'This strikes me as some kind of charade! I hope it has some purpose.'

There was no response. As they reached the railway station on the outskirts of the town Ernest asked where he should take them.

'Drive along the waterfront and the promenade and stop by the Royal Hotel.'

There were few people about; Mounts Bay was a void, with the lights of Newlyn and Mousehole twinkling through the rain. Ernest drove the length of the promenade, negotiated the roundabout, and returned to pull up outside the Royal Hotel. When he cut the engine they could hear the waves breaking along the shore.

'Well, do we get out?' From Bateman.

'No, we go back by a different route.'

In a voice that was scarcely recognizable as his own, Ernest asked: 'What route is that?'

Wycliffe said: 'On Easter Saturday 1979 you both attended a dinner at this hotel. Lemarque was a guest. Do you remember the occasion?'

A barely audible affirmative from Ernest.

Bateman said: 'I told you I was the guest speaker.'

'You drove home together?'

'Naturally, but I can't see how it can have any possible connection with the crimes you are supposed to be investigating and I protest most strongly against this . . . this melodrama!'

'You are under no obligation to co-operate; perhaps you would prefer more formal questioning at the police station?'

'You are threatening me, Chief Superintendent.'

'No sir. I am offering you an alternative. So the three of you drove home together. In this car?'

'Yes.'

'Mr Bishop, were you driving on that occasion?'

A police prowl car cruised along the promenade, slowed suspiciously as it drew level with them, then continued on its way.

Ernest said: 'I can't remember who was driving.'

'Mr Bateman?'

'To the best of my recollection, it was Lemarque.'

'And Lemarque is dead. At any rate you set out from here at about midnight. It was raining, as it is tonight. All I am asking is that we reconstruct your journey home. Shall we start?'

Ernest switched on the engine and they moved off, back along the promenade and the wharf, past the railway station, then they left the coast road and began the steady climb to the central moorland. As they were approaching the first fork Wycliffe said: 'Instead of turning off left, keep on this road.'

Ernest obeyed without comment but Bateman was truculent: 'You realize, I suppose, that we are now on our way to St Ives?'

The road climbed steeply between rows of cottages which soon gave place to hedges. Phantom streaks of rain gleamed in the headlights and the screen wipers beat with the regularity of a metronome. Wycliffe tried to convince himself that he was not organizing a fiasco. The greenish light from the dashboard lit up the faces of the two men in front, obliquely and in profile. Kersey sat, hunched in his corner, so still that he could have been asleep.

'Turn left at Badger's Cross and that will bring us back eventually to the road home.'

'Which we need not have left as far as I can see.' Bateman again.

At Badger's Cross Ernest turned off into a lane which ran

between high hedges; it was undulating and sinuous. From time to time the headlights picked out a farm gate, or a stile, and once or twice they saw the lights of a house. Wycliffe had in his mind an accurate picture of the area for, apart from studying the map, he had driven along the road in the small hours of the morning.

'On the night of your dinner, at about midnight, a girl was walking home along this road. She had been visiting a friend in the house now coming up on our right and she lived about a mile further on. She was nineteen, home on vacation from a teacher training college.'

Ernest was driving even more slowly now; the old Rover revved away, mostly in second gear and the hedges crept by with majestic slowness.

A road sign, caught and held in the headlights, read: 'Chysauster: Ancient Village'. The remnants of a cluster of iron-age huts lay two or three fields away, up on their right; a bleak place.

'The girl was killed in a hit-and-run and the police were convinced they were looking for a drunken driver but they never found him; torrential rain later that night had washed away any clues there might have been.

'The girl's father searched the road between the two houses but failed to find her and called in the police. By that time it was raining heavily and they were working under difficulties but they found her at last, dead. She had been dragged off the road into a ditch. It was then half-past three in the morning.'

Wycliffe was talking into a wall of silence. Once Bateman turned abruptly in his seat as though to say something but he did not speak.

The headlights shone on a house straight ahead which seemed to block the way. Ernest negotiated a ninety degree turn at a snail's pace then stalled the engine as he tried to accelerate. 'I'm not going on with this!' But there was more of despair than defiance in his voice.

'Will you drive, Mr Bateman?'

'Certainly not!'

'Then Mr Kersey . . .'

Without a word Kersey got out and went round the car to take Ernest's place at the wheel. Ernest climbed into the back with Wycliffe. 'I'm sorry . . .'

Wycliffe said to Kersey: 'About a quarter-of-a-mile; I'll tell you when to stop.'

Kersey restarted the engine and they cruised down a gentle slope, past another little house with outbuildings.

'At the bottom.'

Kersey pulled off the road on to a patch of rough grass and brought the car to a halt. When he cut the engine the silence was complete.

'The pathologist reported that the girl had suffered a compound fracture of the left femur along with other less serious injuries, none of them likely to prove fatal in ordinary circumstances. The compound fracture was complicated by her being moved off the road into the ditch but the immediate cause of death was loss of blood. She bled to death and, according to the pathologist, it would have taken about three hours.'

The windows were beginning to steam up and Wycliffe wound down the one on his side, letting in the moist night air and the fresh but slightly acrid smell of the moor.

'This is the place where it happened. The girl lived in a little house at the top of the next slope. You can see the light.'

Although the evening was not cold Wycliffe shivered. Suddenly in a harsh voice he said: 'Get out and see for yourselves where she died!'

They trooped out like tourists on their way to inspect some curiosity *en route*. They crossed the road, Kersey played his torch on the ground and lit up the ditch which was overhung by gorse and brambles.

Wycliffe's voice came, dry and unrelenting. 'She was walking on the right hand side of the road. There was plenty of room for any vehicle to pass.'

They stood there, a disconsolate group with the quiet rain sifting out of the darkness.

'All they found here was a few fragments of broken

glass—very thin glass, perhaps a broken specimen tube. It meant nothing to the police at the time.'

Bateman had been silent for a while, now in a more conciliatory tone, he said: 'Of course we knew of this tragedy, Mr Wycliffe, everyone did in this part of the county at least, but I cannot see—'

'Shut up!' Wycliffe's voice, vicious with suppressed anger, silenced the politician as if a switch had been thrown. They stood there a little longer in the moist darkness then, wearily, Wycliffe said: 'Let's get back.'

Kersey took the wheel and they drove up the slope, past the house where the girl had lived, then down the other side to join their road back just beyond New Mill. Another fifteen minutes and they were pulling into the courtyard at Mynhager. Not a word had been spoken on the way.

Caroline was in the hall where a uniformed constable tried hard to be invisible. She tackled her husband: 'What the hell is happening?'

Bateman snapped: 'I've no idea!'

'Those cretins in there wouldn't tell me anything.'

Wycliffe ignored her and turned to the two men. 'I want to talk to you in the dining-room, one at a time; you first, Mr Bishop. Mr Bateman will remain with the constable.'

In the dining-room Ernest occupied the chair. Shaw was in his place at the end of the big table and the typist had moved away from the window into a better light. Wycliffe did not sit down but stood near Ernest's chair. His voice was hard, his manner abrasive.

'Jane Lemarque was shot with a pistol taken from your aunt's room and returned there without her knowledge. So the killer is a member of this household; one of the family.'

Ernest said nothing; he sat, his soft white hands clasped tightly together, on the table in front of him.

'Lemarque was also shot but we have no evidence concerning the weapon though I think defence counsel would have difficulty in separating the two crimes.'

Ernest removed his spectacles and began to polish them.

'The problem was motive; neither Bateman's possible

involvement in the Lemarque frauds nor the question of Francine's parentage, both hinted at by your father, seemed to stand up. It was only in following up the curious matter of Lemarque's press cutting, reporting your dinner, that I came upon the hit-and-run affair and finally linked the two. Three professional men on their way home after a night out. The driver was so drunk that he missed his way on a familiar road, and a girl was knocked down, injured, and pushed into a ditch to die.'

There was a long silence. Wycliffe was oppressed by the contemptible shabbiness he had uncovered, by a spectacle of self-interest carried to the length of murder so that three lives were sacrificed to secure the personal ambition of a politician and the comfortable humdrum existence of a small-town lawyer.

Ernest broke the silence at last; in a low voice he said: 'We thought she was dead. Lemarque was quite positive.' He coughed, then spoke more strongly. 'He said he was absolutely certain and he was the only one who touched her. Otherwise . . .'

Wycliffe drew a deep breath like a sigh, then in a voice that was almost coaxing he said: 'Lemarque was not driving that night, was he?'

There was an interval. Shaw and the typist, roused out of their professional apathy, were hanging on Ernest's words. 'I was.'

Wycliffe turned to Shaw. 'Ask Mr Bateman to join us please.'

Ernest sat motionless, staring straight in front of him, his features devoid of any expression.

Bateman came in, alert, suspicious, metaphorically sniffing the air. Wycliffe pointed to a chair next to Ernest. 'Please sit down,' and went on at once: 'We now know that Mr Bishop was driving his car when the accident involving the girl occurred.'

Bateman looked at Ernest, then at Wycliffe, hoping for a lead but found none. 'Is this some kind of trap?'

'Ask Mr Bishop.'

In a flat voice Ernest said: 'I told him. I've lived with this for five years and, God knows, that is long enough.'

It was impossible to interpret Bateman's expression but he must have been struggling desperately to adjust and adapt, finally he seemed to resign himself: 'Then we shall have to pay for our folly. All I can say is that if I had suspected for a moment that the girl was not dead I would have summoned assistance whatever the consequences. As it was, I allowed myself to be persuaded. Believing that nothing could be done for her I admit that I did consider the possible consequences of making a report. Ernest's whole career and way of life would have been irreparably damaged and, though I was only a passenger in the car, I should have suffered politically. My decision was highly improper but, in the circumstances, I think understandable.'

A worthy extempore performance.

Wycliffe was staring intently at Bateman. His face gave nothing away but under his gaze Bateman became increasingly restless. He began to tap on the table with the fingers of his right hand, a tension reflex which had often irritated his colleagues in the House.

'I can well understand: a country-town lawyer and an ambitious politician. I doubt if even clergymen are so vulnerable.' Wycliffe was scathing. 'After you had failed to call assistance at the time of the accident and even more so when it became known that the girl had not died until three hours after she had been dragged into a ditch, you both knew without a shadow of a doubt that the truth would ruin you. As a businessman and an entrepreneur Lemarque might have scraped by, but a lawyer, and a politician with a taste for office . . .' He spoke directly to Bateman: 'You must have realized too that the business was so unsavoury that even those people who will sometimes provide a niche for a discredited politician would have found you untouchable.'

Bateman's fingers were working overtime, tapping out a monotonous rhythm. 'Will you tell me where all this is leading?'

'To the point that you were wide open to blackmail and

566

Lemarque was quick to take advantage of the fact when he came out of jail. "Five years ago", he said, "we were all three of us in the same boat or should I say car? Not any more! I no longer belong to the club." You remember Lemarque on the telephone? I can see that you do. From that point onwards your political career was going to be expensive. No doubt Ernest's turn would come but you were to be first in line.'

Ernest sat quite motionless, staring down at the table top.

'But Lemarque had underestimated you and that mistake cost him and his wife their lives.'

'You weren't your brother-in-law, he would have bought his peace of mind. Or tried to.'

Bateman had come to a decision. 'I have nothing more to say. I am in your hands for the moment, but I warn you that I shall exercise all my rights under the law.'

'What you say is noted. The constable in the hall will go with you to your room and you will point out to him the clothing you were wearing on Christmas Eve afternoon. This will be checked and sent for forensic examination. Later you will be escorted to the Divisional police station where your fingerprints will be taken for comparison with prints found inside Lemarque's van. You will be given the opportunity to make statements in respect of the hit-and-run accident and the unlawful killings of Alain and Jane Lemarque.'

To his surprise Bateman raised no objection; he would make no more difficulties and answer no more questions until he was in the hands of his lawyer. Wycliffe signed to Kersey who escorted him into the hall.

Wycliffe was left in the dining-room with Ernest, Sergeant Shaw, and the young typist. They heard voices, footsteps on the stairs, then nothing.

Ernest had scarcely moved, he sat staring at his hands, clasped together on the table top. In a tired voice he asked: 'What happens to me?'

'You will be taken to the police station and given the opportunity of making a statement in connection with the hit-and-run accident. You will be asked further questions in connection with the deaths of Lemarque and his wife.'

The minutes dragged by, the silence broken only by the sporadic rattle of the typewriter. Wycliffe wondered what was happening to the others. Were they gathered together, speculating on the turn things had taken or were they each hiding in their separate cells? And of the future: what would happen to Francine? Would she go back with her aunt to a new and different world? Wycliffe felt sure she would not; far more likely that she would join the Mynhager menage where life would go on much as before free of intrusions by the alien Bateman.

In rapid succession three shots echoed through the old house as through a cavern. Wycliffe made for the door, crossed the hall, and bounded up the stairs. On the first landing Kersey was bending over Bateman who lay in a great pool of blood; the uniformed constable was standing by, dazed, still holding a plastic bag full of clothing.

In a voice scarcely recognizable, Kersey said: 'Dead! Shot through the neck and chest. I saw her standing on the landing when they went up to his room but the gun was hidden . . . Then, as they came back along the corridor to the top of the stairs, she fired . . .'

Wycliffe heard Shaw preventing the family from coming up; mercifully it seemed that they were all downstairs. Francine was standing just a few feet from the dead man, the gun still in her hand, held limply at her side.

'Give it to me.'

She did so without a word.

Wycliffe was in the Incident Van; rain drummed on the roof. Potter was at the duty desk; it was almost midnight. A car drew up outside, a door slammed and a minute or so later Kersey came in.

'Well?'

'I've handed her over. A W.P.C. is looking after her and she seems perfectly calm. She insisted on taking her black doll with her.'

For a long time the two men sat opposite each other in silence. Wycliffe was the first to speak.

'I feel responsible. It never occurred to me that she had taken Lemarque's gun with her when she left home, yet from her point of view it was an obvious precaution.'

'On the principle of keeping matches away from children.'

'Yes, you could put it like that. She cross questioned me about what would happen if we couldn't prove our case and I still didn't see . . .'

Kersey said: 'She wasn't prepared to leave anything to chance.'

THE END